THE UNIVERSITY OF VIRGINIA EDITION OF
THE WORKS OF STEPHEN CRANE

VOLUME II

THE RED BADGE OF COURAGE

An engraving of the *Repulse of Jackson's Men at Hazel Grove, by Artillery under General Pleasonton* from *Century Magazine*, XXXII, no. 5 (Sept., 1886), 756. The engraving illustrated an article, one of a series of eyewitness accounts called *Battles and Leaders of the Civil War*, that Crane used in his researches for *The Red Badge*.

STEPHEN CRANE

THE RED BADGE OF COURAGE

An Episode of
the American Civil War

EDITED BY
FREDSON BOWERS
LINDEN KENT PROFESSOR OF ENGLISH AT
THE UNIVERSITY OF VIRGINIA

WITH AN INTRODUCTION BY
J. C. LEVENSON
EDGAR ALLAN POE PROFESSOR OF ENGLISH AT
THE UNIVERSITY OF VIRGINIA

THE UNIVERSITY PRESS OF VIRGINIA

CHARLOTTESVILLE

CENTER FOR EDITIONS OF
AMERICAN AUTHORS

AN APPROVED TEXT

MODERN LANGUAGE
ASSOCIATION OF AMERICA

®

Editorial expenses for this volume have been
met in part by grants from the National
Endowment for the Humanities administered
through the Center for Editions of American
Authors of the Modern Language Association.

First published 1975

The University Press of Virginia

ISBN: 0–8139–0514–1
Library of Congress Catalog Card Number: 68–8536
Printed in the United States of America

To
Clifton Waller Barrett

FOREWORD

THIS volume presents Crane's most famous work, *The Red Badge of Courage*, in a critical text. The copy-text for the present edition is the holograph manuscript in the Clifton Waller Barrett Collection of the University of Virginia Library. The editor is indebted to Mr. Barrett and to the University of Virginia Librarian for permission to base his text on this manuscript and to Alfred A. Knopf, Inc., which holds the Crane copyrights on unpublished material. The manuscript provides Crane's own system of punctuation, spelling, capitalization, paragraphing, and word-division. It contains the text for several passages omitted from the first edition by a typist's error, and in addition it offers the evidence by which a large number of transmissional errors in the lost typescript and in the typesetting of the first edition may be restored to their authoritative form. The analysis of the two major revisions that Crane gave the manuscript, fully recorded in the apparatus, reveals much of interest about the growth and perfection of this masterpiece, as do the fragments of the antecedent draft manuscript that are reprinted here as well. For the first time the transmission of the text from manuscript to book form, including the newspaper serialization, has been analyzed and dated in something approaching a reliable manner. This analysis has also brought order for the first time into the irregular treatment in manuscript and first edition of the dialect speech due to two changes in intention during the revisions, the final system being only partially imposed in the annotation of the typescript hurriedly performed in New Orleans.

The introduction by Professor Levenson analyzes the sources and the growth of the novel against the background of Crane's literary development. The editor's "The Text: History and Analysis" details the physical forms of the texts, their authority and transmission, and examines specific problems concerned with the establishment of the text in its present critical form. The general principles on which the editing has been based are stated in "The Text of the Virginia Edition" prefixed to Volume I, BOWERY TALES (1969). The apparatus is intended to make this volume self-sufficient in its records of all of the textual documents that survive, including every change made during the inscription and the course of two major revisions of the manuscript. However, close study of the text of the manuscript and of the preserved pages of its antecedent draft may be somewhat simplified by reference to *The Red Badge of Courage: A Facsimile Edition of the Manuscript*, edited by Fredson Bowers, with an introduction and apparatus (Washington, D.C.: Bruccoli Clark Book, NCR/Microcard Editions, 1973), where the records of alteration and revision are keyed directly to the photographs of the manuscript pages and the introduction is more detailed in its analysis of the physical form and the inscription of the manuscript.

The expenses of the preparation of this volume with its introductions and apparatus have been subsidized by a grant from the National Endowment for the Humanities administered through the Modern Language Association of America and its Center for Editions of American Authors, but with generous support, as well, from the University of Virginia.

The editor is much in debt for assistance and various courtesies to Professor Robert Stallman of the University of Connecticut, Professors Matthew J. Bruccoli and Joseph Katz of the University of South Carolina, and his colleague Professor Levenson of the University of Virginia. Professor Don L. Cook of Indiana University, who examined this volume for the seal of the Center for Editions of American Authors, made various useful suggestions. Mr. Kenneth A. Lohf, Librarian of Rare Books and Manuscripts of the Columbia University Libraries, has been of unfailing and particular assistance. The editor is grateful to the Special Collections of the Columbia University Libraries, the Houghton Library of Harvard University, and the Henry W. and Albert A. Berg Collection of the New York Public Library, the Astor, Lenox and Tilden Foundations, for permission to transcribe the leaves in their possession of the discarded original Chapter XII. The constant assistance of the custodians of the Barrett Collection at the University of Virginia has been invaluable. Miss Joan Crane kindly checked the bibliographical descriptions and furnished the color designations. The editor is grateful to Miss Carolinda Hales, Mrs. Thomas Armstrong, Mr. John O'Connor, Mrs. Alan Buster, Miss Judith Nelson, and especially to Mrs. Malcolm Craig, all of whom have assisted at various stages in the collation of texts, the checking of the apparatus, and the reading of proofs. The editor's deepest obligation is reserved for Miss Gillian G. M. Kyles, however, who has been in complete charge of all of the organization of textual research and proofreading and who, with the assistance of Mrs. Craig, made a definitive description and analysis of the manuscript alterations before lamination dulled some of the important evidence of line and intensity of inks. In these days of relatively rapid editorial publication no single scholar can hope to assume the burden of the repeated checking for accuracy of collation, transcription, and notation enforced by the standards for the CEAA editions, all of which Miss Kyles has organized and personally supervised as well as taking an important part herself in the actual operations.

A considerable amount of the editor's research for the introduction and of the actual editing of the text was performed during a period of leisure afforded by the start of a John Simon Guggenheim Memorial Foundation Fellowship in February 1972 and during a Visiting Fellowship at All Souls College, Oxford, during Trinity Term 1972, for both of which the editor is more than ritualistically grateful.

The editor's personal debt to Mr. Clifton Waller Barrett and his magnificent collection at the University of Virginia remains constant and can be expressed only by the dedication of this edition to him.

F. B.

Charlottesville, Virginia
August 12, 1974

CONTENTS

INTRODUCTION

A T TWENTY-ONE Stephen Crane was modest, but he hoped he had something to be modest about. Reticence, which came naturally to him, was also a part he played. In keeping his name off his first novel, he was not simply acting shy or timid. He hoped the more to surprise the world: "You see, I was going to wait until all the world was pyrotechnic about Johnston Smith's 'Maggie' and then I was going to flop down like a trapeze performer from the wire and, coming forward with all the modest grace of a consumptive nun, say, I am he, friends!" [1] The fireworks did not go off for *Maggie*, but with his next work *The Red Badge of Courage* he hit a popular success which was dazzling in his own time and which has not begun to dim. The novel even survives adoption in the schools, where duress cannot extinguish the liveliness of the writing. Indeed, widespread familiarity adds to the almost mythic resonance of the tale: whoever remembers how the book spoke to him at fourteen is likely to find that his questions twenty or thirty years later, while they may be more sophisticated, are not categorically different from those of the naïve reader. For individual readers and for the general audience it has commanded since it came out in 1895, *The Red Badge* has had durable interest. The brilliance of the prose has been evident long enough not to seem merely pyrotechnic, and so too with the portentous, elusive, yet somehow allegorical suggestiveness of the storytelling. The book did not come casually from the hand of an inspired boy. It had lasting power because behind it was the slow and purposive development of a mature artist and the most sustained painstaking effort of his life. Crane was young and he liked fireworks, but he was deadly serious.

[1] Thomas Beer, *Stephen Crane, a Study in American Letters* (New York: Knopf, 1923), p. 90.

Crane's greatest reticence, perhaps, was in the handling of ideas. He rarely spoke in abstract terms or offered theoretical statements of what he aimed for in his work. Yet he had ideas sufficiently powerful and clear that can be derived from his practice and confirmed by his few laconic utterances on general aims and theories. By the time he began *The Red Badge of Courage* he had arrived at a style which expressed his personal vision. The splendid opening of the novel, which goes far to define both style and vision, sets the historical problem of how Crane came to write the book he did. The novel begins:

The cold passed reluctantly from the earth and the retiring fogs revealed an army stretched out on the hills, resting. As the landscape changed from brown to green the army awakened and began to tremble with eagerness at the noise of rumors. It cast its eyes upon the roads which were growing from long troughs of liquid mud to proper thoroughfares. A river, amber-tinted in the shadow of its banks, purled at the army's feet and at night when the stream had become of a sorrowful blackness one could see, across, the red eye-like gleam of hostile camp-fires set in the low brows of distant hills.

In the first sentence the disarmingly obvious unconventionality of *reluctantly* calls attention to a key word which not only personifies the cold, but by its unexpected force brings to life other more conventional terms. The animating effect extends to the *retiring* fogs, and though it slackens somewhat with a picturesque *stretched* and *resting* army, yet in the next sentence the army wakes as a man. The personified army trembles with eagerness and casts its eyes down roads, while at night, across the river, its counterpart can be seen in "the red eye-like gleam of hostile camp-fires set in the low brows of distant hills." There is enough straightforward statement and conventional rhetoric so that the first paragraph can be taken as realism slightly embellished, but the overall effect is subtle: the reader enters an animistic scene in which red eyes gleam beneath the low brows of hills and the whole world of consciousness is alive and active and menacing.

An interesting critical witness to this point is Hamlin Garland, who in April, 1894, read *The Red Badge* in manuscript and twenty years later recollected: "The first sentence fairly took me captive. It described a vast army in camp on one side of a river confronting with its thousands of eyes a similar monster on the opposite bank." Garland's false recollection depended on phrasing which became explicit only in the second chapter, after young Henry Fleming's anxiety had a chance to grow, when "from across the river the red eyes were still peering" and "shadows . . . moved like monsters" and armies were seen as "huge crawling reptiles." Garland checked his copy of the book, and misled by his spotting some other cuts, he decided that Crane had got rid of "the prodigious opening sentence which so impressed me on that memorable day." Given the early leveling off of his own literary rise, Garland had developed a need to condescend to the youthful novelist he had once befriended. He simply could not believe in the subtlety with which Crane prepared a scene that could serve for both objective narration and subjective vision. Yet his own insistent slip discloses a latent power in the opening sentence that is even more prodigious than the "vivid pictures of battle" he knew he admired.[2] The young novelist could work his reader from plain facts and almost commonplace figures of speech to a heightened awareness of what war feels like when it penetrates the depths of a mind.

The beginning of *The Red Badge* is not summed up by the opening paragraph which sets the outward and the inner scene. The reader who has been absorbed, and unwittingly self-absorbed, in observing the landscape is abruptly moved to a vantage of ironic detachment. In the next paragraph, instead of seeing self-projected monsters, he is invited to note the veritable

---

[2] "Stephen Crane As I Knew Him," *Yale Review*, iii, n.s. (April, 1914), 498, 505. Garland's false memory, which supplies such unusual psychological testimony, misled him into thinking that " 'The Red Badge' in its printed form did not in my judgment have the quality that was in the manuscript which came to me in the boy's pocket" (p. 505). John Berryman guessed that the mistake was a displacement from other Crane stories or "just a syncopation of the novel's actual, beautiful opening paragraph" (*Stephen Crane* [New York: William Sloane, 1950], p. 76). R. W. Stallman takes Garland at face value and conjectures that he read some other manuscript than the surviving one in the Clifton Waller Barrett Collection at the University of Virginia (*Stephen Crane, a Biography* [New York: George Braziller, 1968], p. 576). But this first completed version of *The Red Badge*, which is the basic authority from which the revised final text derives, is precisely the manuscript which Garland read. Fredson Bowers has demonstrated this by identifying Garland's handwritten comment and notations on the manuscript (*The Red Badge of Courage: A Facsimile Edition of the Manuscript*, 2 vols. [Washington, D.C.: Bruccoli Clark Book, NCR/Microcard Editions, 1973], I, 8–9).

commonness of human action and the self-importance with
which men ordinarily see and feel: "Once, a certain tall soldier
developed virtues and went resolutely to wash a shirt." The ironic
paragraph which follows, like the initial animistic one, has a
vividness that tends to primary colors. When the tall soldier
hears a rumor of military action, he comes "flying back from a
brook waving his garment, banner-like" and adopts "the important air of a herald in red and gold." The two paragraphs also
share a generality which, despite the difference of rhetorical
mode, consistently supports an allegorical effect. The more Crane
changes, the more he seems to stick to the same single purpose
of rendering how embattled man conducts himself under the
condition of changefulness.

What Crane was doing becomes clearer if he is set beside
Ernest Hemingway, with whom he is linked by a general like-
ness and a degree of influence, for the differences between them
are illuminating. Both the animistic scene and the vignette of the
shirt-washing, banner-waving soldier stand in contrast to the
opening of *A Farewell to Arms*, in which the narrator tries to put
in order his impressions of the world by severely restricting himself to what he sees. Hemingway animates nothing; he registers
the objects of vision as if his seeing were impersonal. His paint-
erly—indeed, Cézanne-like—eye apprehends the dry, white river-
bed, the swift narrow channels of blue, the trunks of trees, and
the dust raised by marching soldiers, and then the same landscape in autumn. When he observes the small Italian king in the
back of the small gray motorcar, he expresses irony by the same
visual means as his deep commitment to find order in the landscape. Keeping oneself a passive register makes it possible to record, with the dignified outrage of understatement, the coming
of winter rain and cholera "and in the end only seven thousand
died of it in the army." [3] Hemingway's austere discipline of seeing and stating reflects his artistic commitment to take the measure of war and the way in our time that mortality thrusts its
terrors close to us. Crane's plasticity as he moves from one rhetorical mode to another indicates no less commitment perhaps,
but it conveys also the hopeful malleability of youth. The element of play comes into his discourse as discipline into Heming-

[3] New York: Scribner's, 1929, p. 4.

way's. If wounds and losses and unexplained horrors do not seem to touch Henry Fleming quite so bone-deep as they do Hemingway's heroes, that is one reason why. Another reason is that the Hemingway hero, confronting a world of disorder, tries to learn to live in it and maybe thus pragmatically to learn what it is all about; he is comparatively an intellectual hero who aims to master a skill and thereby win, perhaps, an ultimate knowledge. Henry Fleming finds out how to live in a world of disorder, but he does so through a series of discoveries that he has not willed and through a personal maturation that he has not particularly aimed at. If he seems thus a diminished literary figure, fitter for a comic action than a tragic, Crane made him so on purpose. What he must learn is how not to be a hero. Insofar as he schools his will, it is to settle for life without brass or bombast. What he becomes is not a hero but a man. In his world a man does not live by stoic resoluteness alone. In it there is room for comic irony and comic affirmation and a future rich with possibility. It is a young man's world in which changes and new starts are to be met with as well as stark finalities. Whereas Hemingway began *A Farewell to Arms* when he was twenty-eight and a seasoned artist, Crane began *The Red Badge of Courage* when he was twenty-one and just attaining his majority as a writer.

Crane's resources at twenty-one were varied, and his literary use of them accounts for the elements of style which he was to fuse in *The Red Badge*. The animistic imagination that brought alive dusky hills and red campfires had asserted itself in his first sustained effort in fiction, the "little grotesque tales of the woods," as he described them, "which I wrote when I was clever." [4] The Sullivan County tales he thus referred to emanated from one of the geographic and psychic centers of his boyhood. When Stephen was six, his father, the Reverend Jonathan Townley Crane, was called to be minister of the Drew Methodist Church of Port Jervis, New York. There the boy enjoyed a Tom Sawyer-ish small-town life and happy access to wooded backcountry where the fishing and hunting and camping seemed to get better every year. Eventually his brother William, who practiced law very

[4] To Copeland and Day, New York, [June, 1895], *Stephen Crane: Letters*, ed. R. W. Stallman and Lillian Gilkes (New York University Press, 1960), p. 59.

successfully in Port Jervis, became a charter purchaser of Hart-wood, a 6,000-acre forest tract with clubhouse and summer cot-tages in nearby Sullivan County; so Stephen, long after his father died, had not only his boy's town to come home to, but also his boy's woods, and come back he did. He returned to his fishing haunts every summer that he could, and when his war novel proved a success, he even bought a five-hundred-dollar share in Hartwood. Just as no town is more than relatively safe, no first-growth woods is more than relatively tame. Nevertheless, the forest adventures of Stephen Crane which gave rise to the Sulli-van County tales can be thought of as domesticated seasonal recreation. As he himself remarked, the modern black bear of his time survived precisely by not being a fighter. Wilderness ferocity tended to be a matter of the past or of fiction. If some-one were to encounter ferocity in the Sullivan County woods, it would depend very much on what he brought there himself in the way of culture and imagination. Crane's "little man," as he calls the protagonist of his tales, brings a lot. Unlike so many other little men of modern literature, who may be diminished by society, machinery, or the violence of the age, he seems little mainly because he exaggerates the drama of his every situation and then, when the facts eventually show forth in their ordinary proportions, he is made small by the puncture of his delusions. The delusions characteristically occur with the fall of night, when fear is released in the vague dark of the imagination. In one such story the little man, having climbed to the point of ex-haustion and come to a mountain lake where "a leaping pickerel off on the water created a silver circle that was lost in black shadows," thinks he sees eyes in the mountain. Indeed he goes on to get the notion that the mountain is approaching him men-acingly, he jumps to his feet and throws stones at his supposed enemy, he scrambles hysterically to the summit at last, and once there he swaggers and thrusts his hands "scornfully in his pock-ets." Against the lurid subjective drama stands the ambiguous final sentence which conveys at once his sense of victory and the narrator's assurance that in objective terms nothing has hap-pened: "The mountain under his feet was motionless." [5]

[5] "The Mesmeric Mountain," TALES, SKETCHES, AND REPORTS, *Works*, VIII (1973), 268–271.

Crane's yarns of outdoor life do not supply much lore of hunting, fishing, or woodsmanship, but they supply an enduring
theme of his work. As James Colvert has powerfully argued, the
little man in the "Sullivan County Sketches" is a prototype of the
Crane characters who demonstrate vainglory by fabricating "a
private world of swollen heroic illusions." [6] But finding his theme
did not bring the young writer instant mastery, and he was right
to use a somewhat deprecatory tone about his tales of the woods.
The little man is not a Nick Adams, and notwithstanding the
vividness of his responses, he has scarcely any deeply felt inter-
action with the country where he hunts and fishes. He makes no
lasting discoveries about the outer world or his inner self. The
author convinces us that both an outer world and an inner self
exist in these stories, but their relations are ephemeral. In "The
Octopush," a drunken guide rows the little man and his friends
to the stumps in the woodland pond from which they are to fish.
Then, absorbed in his private revels, the guide refuses to pick
them up at the day's end. Isolated in the encroaching night mist,
the little man beholds a world transformed: "The pond became
a grave-yard. The grey tree-trunks and dark logs turned to monu-
ments and crypts. Fire-flies were wisp-lights dancing over graves,
and then, taking regular shapes, appeared like brass nails in
crude caskets." [7] But the guide has become drunk enough so that
his stump is transformed also; it turns into an octopus with the
coiled roots as tentacles, and his fright galvanizes him into
jumping into his boat again and picking up his charges. The
drunkard's "octopush" makes light of the little man's fantasy
and releases him from his isolation and fear. The strength of the
story is in a touch like the coming of the fireflies as nature lends
reinforcement to the illusions of man. The weakness of the story
is in the clever ending which easily sets aside the question of
what constitutes experience and whether or how the emotional
life really counts.

Even though the "Sullivan County Sketches" tend to repeat the

[6] "Structure and Theme in Stephen Crane's Fiction," *Modern Fiction Studies*,
v (Autumn, 1959), 202. See also Colvert's "Stephen Crane's Magic Mountain" in
Stephen Crane: A Collection of Critical Essays, ed. Maurice Bassan (Englewood
Cliffs, N.J.: Prentice-Hall, 1967), pp. 95–105, and Colvert's Introduction, TALES
OF WAR, *Works*, VI (1970), especially pp. xvii–xxiii.
[7] *Works*, VIII, 233.

same theorem without moving on, it was no small thing for Crane to show how emotion can transform the perceiver's consciousness of a world which itself objectively changes hardly at all. Other devices to which he would come back in *The Red Badge* have their beginnings in these early tales. The characters are mostly unnamed, for instance, and the vivid colors of Crane's distinctive prose are splashed around. But namelessness claims more attention than it justifies; it is a twist of storytelling that provokes some curiosity and adds a certain spooky vagueness, but does little else. Just as no meaning accrues from the characters' not bearing names, no discernible individuation results from their having been modeled on particular people.[8] Similarly the use of a high palette takes on little significance. There is for the Crane reader who turns to these tales a pleasurable recognition of the "crimson beams" of sunset light and the "crimson oaths" of the fisherman stranded on a stump.[9] Such occasional flashes intensify the rhetorical effect of the particular passages, but they do not occur with the frequency and proximity which can imbue the visible with the imaginary red and make the language a medium for presenting the outer and the inner worlds as not easily separable. Crane had read about Goethe's affective theory of color, he lived among young painters, he had heard of impres-

---

[8] Melvin Schoberlin, in the Introduction to his pioneering edition of *The Sullivan County Sketches of Stephen Crane* (Syracuse University Press, 1949), identifies the little man as Louis E. Carr, Jr., the pudgy man as Frederic M. Lawrence, the tall man as Louis C. Senger, Jr., and the quiet man as Stephen Crane. He also points out that only the little man and the pudgy man are explicitly referred to in the action, even though the others of the four friends and fellow outdoorsmen are often implicitly present (p. 18). The little man, whose mental life is most fully presented, seems for that reason all the more surely to be a projection of Crane himself.

Given Crane's stinginess in inventing names for characters, it is worth noting that the little man is referred to in direct discourse as Billie. Billie is also the one named character in "The Open Boat"—the oiler who drowns at the end. Another name which occurs in these early Sullivan County stories is that of Jim Crocker, a man who dies in a forest cabin. Jim and Jimmie are recurrent names in Crane, and if one New York machine politician's name is in some sense interchangeable with another's, then Jim Crocker's [Croker's] name is virtually reused for Jim Conklin, the tall soldier who dies in *The Red Badge*. In this case the recurrence not only suggests persistent musing and thus a degree of unconscious projection, but also helps to rebut any notion that Jim Conklin's name is the result of conscious symbolic contrivance. On Crane's recurrent use of names, see Berryman, *Crane*, p. 154, and J. C. Levenson, Introduction, TALES OF WHILOMVILLE, *Works*, VII, xxii–xxiii and xliv–xlvii.

[9] *Works*, VIII, 257, 232.

sionism; in short, conscious experiment and unconscious obsession with color were plausible enough in the future author of *The Red Badge*. But the young writer of the Sullivan County tales, whose metaphoric gift could contrive "great lurid oaths which blazed against the sky," had not yet made the hues of emotion into a medium of expression.[10] In the novel, by contrast, the resting army awakens as the landscape changes from brown to green, and the day completes its cycle with the amber-tinted river turning to a sorrowful blackness before the red, eyelike gleam of hostile campfires is to be seen. The subtle figuration that makes the scene massive, monstrous, and alive is of a different order from the witty coloring of the earlier work.

Crane himself thought the Sullivan County tales were well left behind him. When he was deep into the writing of *The Red Badge*, he spoke his satisfaction at having "renounced the clever school in literature" and given up his "clever, Rudyard-Kipling style." What he thus referred to is unclear. He almost certainly meant to include overreaching for color effects, for the Kipling of *The Light That Failed* (1891), with its artist-hero, laid on color lavishly at times. Kipling's sun, as a "wrathful red disc," a "savage red disc," and finally as "a blood-red wafer," gives ample precedent for the red sun of *The Red Badge* which is "pasted in the sky like a fierce wafer." [11] Yet Kipling's is not a colorful style as Crane's was to be, and Kipling's ironic jauntiness, founded on social rather than visual perspective, was not the same as the young American's, either. When Crane abandoned his "clever, Rudyard-Kipling style," moreover, he did not give up color or irony, though he would be using them more subtly thereafter.

[10] *Works*, VIII, 233. Frank Noxon, a classmate at Syracuse University, testifies to Crane's interest in Goethe's theory of colors (Noxon to Max J. Hertzberg, Washington, Dec. 7, 1926, *Letters*, p. 336). Robert L. Hough, in "Crane and Goethe: A Forgotten Relationship," *Nineteenth Century Fiction*, XVII (Sept., 1962), 135–148, explores the high correlation of *Goethe's Theory of Colors* (*Farbenlehre*, 1810; tr. Charles Eastlake, 1840) and Crane's own use of primary colors for particular classes of effect in his early writing. Hough makes the point that Crane probably encountered the book as a student and was putting affective ideas of color to use before he was well aware of painting.

[11] To Lily Brandon Munroe, New York, [late winter or early spring, 1894], *Letters*, pp. 31–32; *The Light That Failed* (London & New York: Macmillan, 1891), pp. 14, 33, 66. See also Scott C. Osborn, "Stephen Crane's Imagery: 'Pasted like a Wafer,'" *American Literature*, XXIII (Nov., 1951), 362, and James B. Colvert, "The Origins of Stephen Crane's Literary Creed," *University of Texas Studies in English*, XXXIV (1955), 179–188.

What he mostly gave up was being *clever*; that is the word that recurs in the 1895 letter which refers to the Sullivan County tales "which I wrote when I was clever," and warns that "I can make no more." [12] He had outgrown the Kipling manner of story-making which focused on anecdotal complication and nicely turned endings. The rejection of cleverness, as he described it, was the beginning of his realistic faith:

It seemed to me that there must be something more in life than to sit and cudgel one's brains for clever and witty expedients. So I developed all alone a little creed of art which I thought was a good one. Later I discovered that my creed was identical with the one of Howells and Garland and in this way I became involved in the beautiful war between those who say that art is man's substitute for nature and we are the most successful in art when we approach the nearest to nature and truth, and those who say—well, I don't know what they say. [13]

Crane's conversion to realism took place in 1891 and 1892, and the scene was the New Jersey coast which was his second boy-hood home. He had known the Methodist summer colony at Ocean Grove since earliest childhood when his father had first taken the family there. Adjacent to it on the north was Asbury Park, more crowded, commercial, and crass, but still mostly a quiet and proper place for Bishop Asbury's flock. The widowed Mary Helen Crane moved her family there when Stephen was eleven. A little to the south was Avon-by-the-Sea, a resort which made good its bard-inspired name by sponsoring cultural events. In contrast to Port Jervis, the old river town with half-tame wilderness beyond, the New Jersey shore was metropolitan, a seasonal place of refuge and recreation for New Yorkers and to some extent for Philadelphians. Crane's brother Townley was the New York *Tribune* agent for resort news from the area, and with sometimes as much as a page to fill with news notes of vacationers and vacationing, he had more than one man could do. In fact he helped support the family by providing reportorial opportunities for his mother, his brother Wilbur, and in time for young Stephen. In the summer of 1891, just after he had fin-

[12] *Letters,* p. 59.
[13] *Letters,* pp. 31–32.

ished his first and only year of college, Stephen covered the lecture on Howells which Hamlin Garland gave. Garland conveyed Howells' belief in "truthful treatment of material" and something more, for as Garland interpreted the leading proponent of realism in America, he put emphasis on truthfulness as requiring that "the novelist be true to himself and to things as he sees them." [14] Garland was impressed with the nineteen-year-old reporter who wrote of him so clearly, and he and Crane got better acquainted, playing catch together and conversing on American literature and its prospects. In the summer of 1892, when Garland came back and evidently renewed the acquaintance, Crane was a good deal more seasoned. [15] During the intervening year, he had committed himself to being a writer. His mother had died in December, 1891, and though he took his brother Edmund as guardian and often stayed with Edmund's family in Lake View, New Jersey, he had a first taste of what it was to be a free lance in New York. Some of his early, straightforward sketches of Sullivan County came out in the winter and spring, but his grotesque tales did not begin to appear in the *Tribune* until July, 1892, when his distinctive reportage also began to come out regularly. Crane's later recollection, though not quite definite, strongly implied that first he wrote his clever tales and then he developed his realistic bent. But the interwoven and often simultaneous publication dates of the two kinds of writing suggests that both his earlier and his later, more deeply thought out conceptions of writing were coming to fruition at the same time. That the mind should run along two rather different lines at once would fit his emerging sense of unpredictable multiple consciousness. While his Sullivan County fiction projected an imagination which could make every bush a bear, his Asbury Park dispatches spoke for a cool perception that simply did not see things as convention dic-

[14] "Howells Discussed at Avon-by-the-Sea," *New York Tribune*, Aug. 18, 1891, p. 5; *Works*, VIII, 507–508.

[15] Donald Pizer, "The Crane-Garland Relationship," *Huntington Library Quarterly*, XXIV (Nov., 1960), 77–78, infers the renewal of acquaintance in 1892, and although the renewal would have been brief, it makes a plausible link between the first meeting of 1891 and Garland's cordial responsiveness and hospitality to Crane in New York in March, 1893, when he introduced him to Howells and especially in the crucial period from December, 1893, to April, 1894, when Crane began to visit Garland often, shared with him his first poems, and then let him read *The Red Badge* in manuscript.

tated: "The average summer guest here is a rather portly man, with a good watch-chain and a business suit of clothes, a wife and about three children. He stands in his two shoes with American self-reliance and, playing casually with his watch-chain, looks at the world with a clear eye." [16] He also caught types who were less frequently to be seen against the background of lace parasols and white flannel trousers, the patriotic marchers of the Junior Order of United American Mechanics: "The procession was composed of men, bronzed, slope-shouldered, uncouth and begrimed with dust. Their clothes fitted them illy, for the most part, and they had no ideas of marching. They merely plodded along, not seeming quite to understand, stolid, unconcerned and, in a certain sense, dignified—a pace and a bearing emblematic of their lives." [17] The young reporter who could write thus was on his way to becoming the novelist who saw soldiers as so many men in blue clothes and who guessed that the virtue of shirt-washing might feed a soldier's complacence in much the same way as the more heralded military virtues.

As it happened, his excellent reportage sped the young Crane toward becoming a fully committed novelist, for the politically sensitive *Tribune* (its publisher Whitelaw Reid was Republican candidate for vice-president) found that patriotic workingmen did not understand unconventional writing and so denounced it as hostile. Crane's relations with the *Tribune* were quickly and permanently severed. So he experienced at a popular literary level (as Howells and Garland had at a more high-flown one) the bitter resistance to literary nonconformity that gave rise to the so-called wars of realism. He was ready now to give himself to a project in which he was bringing together his two different kinds of writing. Supposedly he began a story like *Maggie* in the spring of 1891 when he was a student at Syracuse, and the effort bespoke a boyish daring that was twofold: he defied conventionality by writing about a New York streetwalker, and he ignored the difficulty of his knowing so little of the slum life from which his streetwalker came. After his mother's death in Decem-

---

[16] "On the Boardwalk," *New York Tribune*, Aug. 14, 1892; *Works*, VIII, 515–519.

[17] "On the New Jersey Coast," *New York Tribune*, Aug. 21, 1892; *Works*, VIII, 521–522.

ber, 1891, his sense of being cut free from convention was stronger and, after his first months as a New Yorker, so was his knowledge of the city. In early 1892, according to Thomas Beer's questionable dating, he showed a manuscript version of *Maggie* to a friend and remarked, "I wrote it in two days before Christmas." [18] But Crane's own report of sustained effort puts a believable emphasis on the work which went on after the productive summer of 1892 and which lasted past his November 1 birthday. His report clarifies the history both of his first novel and of his second: "At 20 I began *Maggie* & finished it when I was somewhat beyond 21. Later in the same year I began *The R. B. of Courage* and finished it some months after my 22nd birthday." [19] He must have thought he had done with his first book when he applied for copyright in January, 1893, but he was still working at it in February when he named the characters and gave Maggie's name to the novel itself. The naming took place at the suggestion of brother William. So did the application for copyright: "I had not even that much sense," Stephen said. When half a year of intensive work had carried Stephen from having no outlet in the press to the discovery that he could not get a publisher for his novel either, he might have faltered. But William helped again: he took title to Stephen's share of their mother's house in Asbury Park and in return provided the thousand dollars which enabled the young novelist to have the book printed himself.[20]

[18] Beer, *Crane*, p. 81.

[19] To the Editor of *The Critic*, Hartwood, N.Y., Feb. 15, 1896, *Letters*, p. 117. See also *Letters*, p. 95, cited in note 36 below.

[20] Beer cites both Wallis McHarg and William Crane as witnesses to the existence of a manuscript in which the characters were unnamed (*Crane*, pp. 80–81). Ames W. Williams and Vincent Starrett, in *Stephen Crane: A Bibliography* (Glendale, Calif.: J. Valentine, 1948), give the copyright application received at the Library of Congress on January 19, 1893, as having a title page that read:

> A Girl of the Streets,
> A Story of New York,
> –by–
> Stephen Crane.

They date the naming of characters and of the book as February, 1893 (pp. 13–14). Although Beer has William Crane lending Stephen one thousand dollars in November, 1892, to pay for the printing of *Maggie*, Thomas A. Gullason's research into Crane family finances suggests a better date—and a plausible explanation of the hardheaded older brother's apparent generosity. Gullason notes that Stephen sold William his one-seventh share in their mother's house in January, 1893, as did brother Wilbur at about the same time. He also reports from examining a copy of the deed that Mrs. Crane had paid $7,000 for the

Crane then waited for the world to become pyrotechnic about *Maggie*. If he took satisfaction in Brentano's stocking the book, his hopes were to be sunk when he heard that their total sale was two. He was more successful at giving the book away. He gave copies to Garland and, at Garland's suggestion, to William Dean Howells, and the praise and friendship he had from them were the highest triumph of esteem he could conceive. What Howells admired was Crane's absolutely honest representation of "the semi-savage poor, whose types he had studied in that book," his rendering of "the lurid depths which he gave proof of knowing better than anyone else." Howells was one day to contrast this accuracy of *Maggie* with *The Red Badge* and what he called its "whirl of wild guesses at the fact from the ground of insufficient witness." [21] Crane's accuracy in the first novel comes through vividly in the opening scene, in which the little boys of Rum Alley battle the howling urchins from Devil's Row, and in other fine street scenes throughout the book. But the accuracy of his creative eye is far more vital than the accuracy with which he transcribed. What Howells was to praise as "perhaps the best tough dialect which has yet found its way into print," today has the resonance of local-color quaintness. The seducer's first sweet words to Maggie are "Say, Mag, I'm stuck on yer shape. It's outa sight." The way people talk is less convincing than Crane's guess as to the way Maggie sees the show Pete takes her to, "an entertainment of many hues and many melodies where she was afraid she might appear small and mouse-colored." [22] More important, Crane was learning to modulate from straight narrative or objective description to a disclosure of what sympathetic imagination

---

house in June, 1883 ("Last Will and Testament of Mrs. Mary Helen Peck Crane," *American Literature*, xl [May, 1968], 232–234). Considering the development of Asbury Park in the intervening decade, one may be sure that the property had not depreciated. William's shrewd business sense was evidently not available to his younger brother when Stephen proceeded to get skinned by the printer: "The bill for printing eleven hundred copies was $869 and Appleton's tell me that the printer must have made about $700 out of me. . . . A firm of religious and medical printers did me the dirt. You may take this as proffered evidence of my imbecility" (Beer, *Crane*, pp. 90–91).

[21] Howells to Cora Crane, Annisquam, Mass., July 29, 1900, *Letters*, p. 306; Howells, "Frank Norris," in *North American Review*, clxxv (Dec., 1902), reprinted in *Stephen Crane's Career*, ed. Thomas A. Gullason (New York University Press, 1972), pp. 92–93.

[22] Howells, "Life and Letters," *Harper's Weekly*, xxxix (1895), 533; *Maggie: A Girl of the Streets* (1893 ed.), pp. 49, 54.

sees that cannot be verified by witnesses. From the boys' fight of the opening scene he moves out to watchers in nearby windows and then to the river's edge and beyond: "Some laborers, unloading a scow at a dock at the river, paused for a moment and regarded the fight. The engineer of a passive tugboat hung lazily to a railing and watched. Over on the Island, a worm of yellow convicts came from the shadow of a grey ominous building and crawled slowly along the river's bank." So, too, in narrating Maggie's final descent to the river, he momentarily leaves off his somber detachment to tell what "the blackness of the final block" was like for her: "The shutters of the tall buildings were closed like grim lips. The structures seemed to have eyes that looked over her, beyond her, at other things." [23] While Crane's study of the urban poor need not be scanted, in his rendering of the fight or the approach to death he drew on more than simple observation. Yet observation there had to be—Howells was right about that. If it were not for idle tugboats and prison islands or looming warehouses along dark streets, Crane's detachment and his sympathy would count as inconsistencies of style. Because inner imagination functioned in the same world as objective action, the author's shifts of perspective have a coherence that makes both detachment and sympathy credible.

By the time he was twenty-one, then, Crane had developed a fine prose instrument for storytelling. The difference between witty expedients and a unified style came about, in his own sense of the matter, because he found a coherent purpose around which his virtuoso talents organized themselves. Instead of being satisfied with cleverness, even of a high order, he determined that he would try for nothing less than truth. Of course there never was a time when he had not, like most people, felt himself committed to truth as a moral and intellectual value, but the idea of applying the term to storytelling only gradually took hold of him. For Crane it was an event much like a conversion, and he held it to be crucial to the making of *The Red Badge*. His ingenuous "veneration and gratitude," [24] as he expressed it to Howells, bears witness to a real debt, but Howells' coolness to the war novel indicates that the faith struck him as somewhat changed

---

[23] *Maggie*, pp. 5, 148.
[24] From Crane's inscription in Howells' copy of the book, *Letters*, p. 62.

in the new believer. If Crane did not notice the discrepancy, Howells did. In preaching the value of representation, Howells meant writers to be faithful to what they could see and hear around them. In *Criticism and Fiction* (1891), he had argued that "there is no greatness, no beauty, which does not come from truth to your own knowledge of things." [25] When Garland spread the doctrine, as I have suggested, there was a slightly different emphasis: "Impressionism, in its deeper sense, means the statement of one's own individual perception of life and nature, guided by devotion to truth." [26] The same idea was to be carried one step further by Crane: "I understand that a man is born into the world with his own pair of eyes, and he is not at all responsible for his vision—he is merely responsible for his quality of personal honesty. To keep close to this personal honesty is my supreme ambition." [27] Crane had come to the discovery that things are as they are known. Men cannot come to terms with things as they are unless they learn to deal with things as they are felt.

In writing *Maggie*, Crane discovered that he had to explore not only the world a man inhabits but the inner life which conditions his vision of that world. He had become a psychological novelist committed to dealing with the knower as well as the known. In large part without the aid of abstractions, he had arrived at the crucial idea that life consists of "the adjustment of inner to outer relations." This formulation out of Herbert Spencer, William James declared, is one of the fertile ideas of nineteenth-century thought because "it takes into account the fact that minds inhabit environments which act on them and on which they in turn react." [28] Crane's first problem in turning his hand to a war novel

[25] New York: Harper and Brothers, 1891, p. 145.

[26] *Crumbling Idols* (Chicago and Cambridge: Stone and Kimball, 1894), p. 50. The essays in *Crumbling Idols* cover the same topics under the same heads as Garland's lectures at Avon-by-the-Sea in 1891, when he was working out his own ideas in response to Howells. Garland recalled lecturing on "The Local Novel" (title of Chapter VI of *Crumbling Idols*) when he was becoming acquainted with Crane. He also lectured on "Logical Prophecy: The Future of Poetry and Fiction"; the chapter from which the quoted sentence on Impressionism comes is called "Literary Prophecy." For the syllabus of Garland's course at Avon-by-the-Sea, see Jean Holloway, *Hamlin Garland, a Biography* (Austin: University of Texas Press, 1960), pp. 55–56.

[27] To John Northern Hilliard, n.p., [Jan., 1896], *Letters*, p. 110.

[28] William James, *The Principles of Psychology* (New York: Henry Holt & Co., 1890), I, 6.

was to understand the environment which soldiers inhabit, and in the effort to answer the question What is war? he put more energy into research than at any other time of his life. Where research was possible, he pursued it without a trace of the naïve and doctrinaire realist belief that only his own eyewitness experience could serve the literary artist. But he early arrived at a second question for which research provided little help. Given the fact of war, how to account for a middling character who behaves according to the patterns of common life rather than those of heroic literature? Specifically, he set himself the task of understanding a young man who could fight and run and fight again, eventually to become the seasoned soldier who merits being called a veteran. In a story called "The Veteran," a curious sequel to *The Red Badge* which Crane wrote in 1896, he made the problem clear. In this tale old Henry Fleming, a Sullivan County farmer, shocks his hero-worshiping grandson and his other listeners by telling how he got scared in his first battle and ran: "That was at Chancellorsville. Of course, afterward I got kind of used to it. A man does." [29] Despite the freely admitted act of cowardice, the story makes clear that old Fleming can still perform acts of courage and perhaps even, if we were sure of the meaning of the term, of heroism. There is no need to suppose that such a storytelling veteran first gave Crane the boy-listener the germ of his plot, but it is necessary to recognize that Crane saw his fiction as coming out this way in the end. If courage really matters, how is one to fathom a character who can change and change again, who falls badly short of his own ideals and yet may be capable of living up to them another time?

Crane hardly knew what he was getting into at first. As a poor young writer in New York, he may have undertaken the story with a casualness that is curiously like the legendary beginning of Fenimore Cooper's literary career. According to Thomas Beer:

One afternoon he was idle in the rooms of William Dallgren, watching Dallgren sketch Acton Davies when Davies tossed him Emile Zola's "La Débâcle," in a translation. Davies was a round

[29] *Works*, VI, 83.

youth who doted on Zola and when Crane slung the book aside he was annoyed.

"I suppose you could have done it better?"

"Certainly," said Crane.[30]

The plausible time of this occasion, if indeed it occurred, would be the fall of 1892 when Crane was first living regularly among artist-friends in New York. But the Beer story of Crane's almost instantaneous rejection of the Zola novel cannot account for his knowing what it was about sufficiently well to claim that he could surpass it. Given the known paucity of Crane's reading, it would be too much to suppose that he had already read a current best-seller or would soon read, in order to emulate, it. James Colvert makes a suggestion more in character with Crane when he points out that as early as July 10, 1892, the day when Crane's "The Broken-Down Van" appeared in the New York *Tribune,* there was a review of *La Débâcle* in the same paper. The *Tribune* reviewer noted:

Since no one is more painstaking than M. Zola in collecting and verifying the facts employed in his books, it is fair to assume that the representations in *La Débâcle* are trustworthy and not exaggerated. That they agree in the main with the historical chronicles is self-evident, the one distinction between him and contemporary French historians being that he makes no effort to soften anything, but aims at presenting the truth of the terrible events which he describes, as he has been able to ascertain it. It is the war with Germany which he treats here; not, of course, in detail, but upon large lines, marked by well-chosen pictures of particular episodes, intended to emphasize the chief causes of disaster. . . . In making his witnesses private soldiers or non-commissioned officers, he has clearly taken a leap from Tolstoy's *Peace and War.* . . . The plan is indeed a good one, his purpose being to show what the experiences and sufferings of the rank-and-file really were. . . . The scene opens in a camp of raw troops near Mulhausen. The men are still full of the blind confidence which was expressed in the popular cry, "To the Rhine!" Yet nobody knew the plans of the generals, and they did not appear very clear about them themselves. Then came rumors of encounters, victories, defeats. Next came a confused series of marches, first in advance, then in retreat. From day to day

[30] Beer, *Crane,* pp. 97–98.

the soldiers became more bewildered and irritated. . . . The heavy marching began to demoralize the young troops.[31]

As Colvert points out, the reviewer was setting forth the "aims, method, and point of view" of *The Red Badge*, and yet the reviewer's phrase—"not, of course, in detail, but upon large lines" —suggests why Crane should later have flung the book aside so quickly. Although Zola's novel opened, as Crane's would, with an army resting in twilight beside a river, the description lacks a particular register. If Crane ventured only a few pages into the opening chapter, he would have read that "the whole black, motionless camp seemed to be annihilated beneath the oppressive weight of that dense, evil night, heavy with something fearful which was as yet without a name." [32] The words described such a world as his Union soldiers were to share, but Crane knew ways to be less general than Zola and less remote.

The veracities as well as the uncertainties of the Beer anecdote throw light on the origins of *The Red Badge of Courage*.[33] The young Crane had more than a glimmer of his own powers even though he had not yet fully assayed them. He moved freely among unproven artists and aspiring illustrators, journalists, and medical students, young men with serious intentions, high spirits, and little money. They were Bohemians for a time, and Crane's name for them, "Indians," correctly suggests that a child's-play epithet described their wildness as a stronger term for outsiderness would not.[34] When the Indians foregathered for

[31] *New York Tribune*, July 10, 1892, p. 14, reprinted in James B. Colvert, *"The Red Badge of Courage* and a Review of Zola's *La Débâcle," Modern Language Notes*, LXXI (1956), 98–100.

[32] *The Downfall*, tr. Ernest A. Vizetelly (1892; later ed., London: Chatto and Windus, 1902), p. 18.

[33] The anecdote has at least one other source. Ripley Hitchcock, Crane's editor at Appleton, wrote in his Preface to the 1900 reprinting of *The Red Badge*: "nor is it possible to verify the tale that its origin was the challenge of an artist friend uttered in response to Mr. Crane's criticism of a battle story which he had just read" (p. vi). Since Hitchcock's professional relation with Crane did not lead to close personal friendship, there is no reason to believe that he could have been the one to supply Beer with the names of Dallgren and Davies.

[34] Since R. W. Stallman has suggested in his Introduction to *Sullivan County Tales* that Crane's term derives from his description of the poor last Mohican of Sullivan County and implies something close to beggary and utter demoralization, it is worth noting that the term is not only a playful one in Crane's usage, but also in the repeated usage of C. K. Linson, who offers the fullest personal memoir of Crane's Bohemian days in New York in *My Stephen Crane*, ed. Edwin H. Cady (Syracuse University Press, 1958).

His friend C. K. Linson got at the paradox of slow thought and fast writing more specifically: "The writing of *The Red Badge*, he [Crane] told Hamlin Garland, was as unaccountable to him as the writing of the later 'Lines.' He wrote it throughout with the unhesitating speed of one who did not have to contrive incident or think it through at all; it was simply the labor of writing. But he had really lived for months with his Henry Fleming, a shadowy accompaniment of his every move. . . . I know that his writing was as effortless as the flowing of a stream." [39]

Before the effortless flow, Linson had witnessed Crane's initial effort and to some extent, the frustrated retreat which followed. Linson had the habit of picking up old *Century* magazines when he found them in secondhand bookstores, for a young artist could find in them a wealth of examples from the hands of the country's most distinguished illustrators. R. W. Gilder's *Century* was a stronghold of literary realism too. During the mid-1880s Gilder had three novels going simultaneously in serial form, James's *The Bostonians*, Howells' *The Rise of Silas Lapham*, and Mark Twain's *Adventures of Huckleberry Finn*, and at the same time he was continuing the monumental series of articles called *Battles and Leaders of the Civil War*. Crane frequented Linson's studio in the early months of 1893 and went through the magazines avidly. Among all the military chronicles by generals and field-grade officers, there was one series by Warren Lee Goss called "Recollections of a Private." In the very first of Goss's articles, he moves his narrative quickly from the sensations of enlisting and marching off from home to the infantry panic and flight at Bull Run. The second begins with an anecdote on getting laundry done under military conditions, and it moves on to tell of the power of rumor in an army that waits and pointlessly marches and waits again. In the third, when he gets to baptism of fire and the sensation of fear, Goss offers the account of "a comrade in Hooker's division." [40] He describes moving

[39] *My Stephen Crane*, pp. 44–45.
[40] *Century*, xxix (March, 1885), 774–776. Daniel Aaron points to similar effects to be derived from George F. Williams, "Lights and Shadows of Army Life," *Century*, xxviii (Oct., 1884), 803–819; he develops his view of Crane as an antiofficial writer about war, both in *The Red Badge* and in later work, in *The Unwritten War* (New York: Knopf, 1973), chap. 14.

the soldiers became more bewildered and irritated. . . . The heavy marching began to demoralize the young troops.[31]

As Colvert points out, the reviewer was setting forth the "aims, method, and point of view" of *The Red Badge*, and yet the reviewer's phrase—"not, of course, in detail, but upon large lines" —suggests why Crane should later have flung the book aside so quickly. Although Zola's novel opened, as Crane's would, with an army resting in twilight beside a river, the description lacks a particular register. If Crane ventured only a few pages into the opening chapter, he would have read that "the whole black, motionless camp seemed to be annihilated beneath the oppressive weight of that dense, evil night, heavy with something fearful which was as yet without a name." [32] The words described such a world as his Union soldiers were to share, but Crane knew ways to be less general than Zola and less remote.

The veracities as well as the uncertainties of the Beer anecdote throw light on the origins of *The Red Badge of Courage*.[33] The young Crane had more than a glimmer of his own powers even though he had not yet fully assayed them. He moved freely among unproven artists and aspiring illustrators, journalists, and medical students, young men with serious intentions, high spirits, and little money. They were Bohemians for a time, and Crane's name for them, "Indians," correctly suggests that a child's-play epithet described their wildness as a stronger term for outsiderness would not.[34] When the Indians foregathered for

[31] *New York Tribune,* July 10, 1892, p. 14, reprinted in James B. Colvert, *"The Red Badge of Courage* and a Review of Zola's *La Débâcle,"* *Modern Language Notes,* LXXI (1956), 98–100.

[32] *The Downfall,* tr. Ernest A. Vizetelly (1892; later ed., London: Chatto and Windus, 1902), p. 18.

[33] The anecdote has at least one other source. Ripley Hitchcock, Crane's editor at Appleton, wrote in his Preface to the 1900 reprinting of *The Red Badge*: "nor is it possible to verify the tale that its origin was the challenge of an artist friend uttered in response to Mr. Crane's criticism of a battle story which he had just read" (p. vi). Since Hitchcock's professional relation with Crane did not lead to close personal friendship, there is no reason to believe that he could have been the one to supply Beer with the names of Dallgren and Davies.

[34] Since R. W. Stallman has suggested in his Introduction to *Sullivan County Tales* that Crane's term derives from his description of the poor last Mohican of Sullivan County and implies something close to beggary and utter demoralization, it is worth noting that the term is not only a playful one in Crane's usage, but also in the repeated usage of C. K. Linson, who offers the fullest personal memoir of Crane's Bohemian days in New York in *My Stephen Crane,* ed. Edwin H. Cady (Syracuse University Press, 1958).

poker or for a powwow with music, tobacco, and free-flowing drink, they were taking a holiday from high seriousness rather than trying to make a lasting escape from responsibility. Along with his gift for partying, Crane had the gift of sitting on the floor and writing away undisturbed at whatever work then engrossed him. If the casual dismissal of Zola betokened an amazing readiness, in a writer, to do without books, his lightly undertaken commitment to do a war piece got him into more sustained research than any other book he was ever to write. One old Port Jervis friend, Louis Senger, unsmilingly saw Crane's "Pendennis Club" as merely an Avenue A boardinghouse "where he lived with a crowd of irresponsibles," but Senger at the same time bore witness that Crane did not and could not stray for long from his artistic commitment:

One day he told me he was going to write a war story and later he showed me some chapters of the *Red Badge*. "I deliberately started in to do a pot-boiler," he told me then, "something that would take the boarding-school element—you know the kind. Well, I got interested in the thing in spite of myself, and I couldn't, I couldn't. I *had* to do it my own way." This was the first and only time I ever knew Crane's courage to falter in the least, and this was after five years of it, and he was writing then on the paper the meat came home in.[35]

Senger had his inaccuracies: Crane did not write *The Red Badge* —or, so far as we know, anything else—on butcher paper, and the ordeal of poverty did not last five years. But he was close to the mark in suggesting that the trial of courage in the tale had something to do with a similar trial in the author.

The vagueness of timing in this account gives a clue as to how the writing of *The Red Badge* came to be a personal test. Crane's own accounts are as vague as Senger's. In one of his recollections he reported: "After completing Maggie I wrote mainly for the *New York Press* and for the *Arena* magazine. The latter part of my twenty-first year I began *The Red Badge of Courage* and completed it early in my twenty-second year." [36] But after completing *Maggie* in January or February, 1893 (he turned twenty-one on November 1, 1892), he had no newspaper jobs that have yet

[35] Louis C. Senger to Hamlin Garland, Port Jervis, N.Y., Oct. 9, 1900, *Letters*, p. 319.
[36] To John Northern Hilliard, Hartwood, N. Y., Jan. 2, [1896], *Letters*, p. 95.

Directly he was working.

He sped toward the rear.

He stopped, horror stricken.

He could hear the tattered man
bleating.

Illustrations for *The Red Badge* from *New York Press*, Dec. 9, 1894.

It crushed upon the youth's head.   "Yeh've been grazed by a ball."

"Charge! Charge!"   Wrenched the flag from the dead man.

Illustrations for *The Red Badge* from *New York Press*, Dec. 9, 1894.

been traced. Except for three terribly slight pieces, "Why Did the Young Clerk Swear?", "At Clancy's Wake," and "Some Hints for Playmakers," he went over a year without breaking into the newspapers or magazines at all. (Hamlin Garland's favorable review of *Maggie* in the June, 1893, issue of *Arena* explains his gilded memory of that magazine.) He wrote a few minor sketches of New York life and, if C. K. Linson's memory for dates was correct, he wrote one fine story, "The Pace of Youth," during the late winter or early spring of 1893. (Since he did not publish it till 1895, the date may be off by a year.) The lapsed time between novels became still vaguer in Crane's other dating of his war novel, already cited: "At 20 I began *Maggie* & finished it when I was somewhat beyond 21. Later in the same year I began *The R. B. of Courage* and finished it some months after my 22nd birthday." [37] The *later* in this version covers his first attempt to write a war story and his backing away from it for several months thereafter, and the lapse of time contradicts in some degree the impression he gave that the writing came easily. Thus Willa Cather, in reporting her 1895 talks with Crane in Lincoln, Nebraska, gives in the two halves of a single paragraph the paradoxical contraries of easy writing that came hard:

I mentioned "The Red Badge of Courage," which was written in nine days, and he replied that, though the writing took very little time, he had been unconsciously working the detail of the story out through most of his boyhood. His ancestors had been soldiers, and he had been imagining war stories ever since he was out of knickerbockers, and in writing his first war story he had simply gone over his imaginary campaigns and selected his favorite imaginary experiences. [*Thus far* Miss Cather *makes it sound easy, but then———.*] He declared that his imagination was hide bound; it was there, but it pulled hard. After he got a notion for a story, months passed before he could get any sort of personal contract with it, or feel any potency to handle it. "The detail of a thing has to filter through my blood, and then it comes out like a native product, but it takes forever," he remarked. I distinctly remember the illustration, for it rather took hold of me. [38]

[37] To the Editor of *The Critic, Hartwood,* N.Y., Feb. 15, 1896, *Letters,* p. 117.
[38] "When I Knew Stephen Crane," by Henry Nicklemann (pseud.), in *The Library,* 1 (Pittsburgh, June 23, 1900), 17–18; reprinted in Maurice Bassan, ed., *Critical Essays,* p. 16.

His friend C. K. Linson got at the paradox of slow thought and fast writing more specifically: "The writing of *The Red Badge*, he [Crane] told Hamlin Garland, was as unaccountable to him as the writing of the later 'Lines.' He wrote it throughout with the unhesitating speed of one who did not have to contrive incident or think it through at all; it was simply the labor of writing. But he had really lived for months with his Henry Fleming, a shadowy accompaniment of his every move. . . . I know that his writing was as effortless as the flowing of a stream." [39]

Before the effortless flow, Linson had witnessed Crane's initial effort and to some extent, the frustrated retreat which followed. Linson had the habit of picking up old *Century* magazines when he found them in secondhand bookstores, for a young artist could find in them a wealth of examples from the hands of the country's most distinguished illustrators. R. W. Gilder's *Century* was a stronghold of literary realism too. During the mid-1880s Gilder had three novels going simultaneously in serial form, James's *The Bostonians*, Howells' *The Rise of Silas Lapham*, and Mark Twain's *Adventures of Huckleberry Finn*, and at the same time he was continuing the monumental series of articles called *Battles and Leaders of the Civil War*. Crane frequented Linson's studio in the early months of 1893 and went through the magazines avidly. Among all the military chronicles by generals and field-grade officers, there was one series by Warren Lee Goss called "Recollections of a Private." In the very first of Goss's articles, he moves his narrative quickly from the sensations of enlisting and marching off from home to the infantry panic and flight at Bull Run. The second begins with an anecdote on getting laundry done under military conditions, and it moves on to tell of the power of rumor in an army that waits and pointlessly marches and waits again. In the third, when he gets to baptism of fire and the sensation of fear, Goss offers the account of "a comrade in Hooker's division." [40] He describes moving

[39] *My Stephen Crane*, pp. 44–45.
[40] *Century*, xxix (March, 1885), 774–776. Daniel Aaron points to similar effects to be derived from George F. Williams, "Lights and Shadows of Army Life," *Century*, xxviii (Oct., 1884), 803–819; he develops his view of Crane as an antiofficial writer about war, both in *The Red Badge* and in later work, in *The Unwritten War* (New York: Knopf, 1973), chap. 14.

through the tangle of woods after the engagement and putting his hand on the shoulder of a silent marksman only to discover that the man is dead; but after indulging himself in an exclamation point only, he proceeds to explain how a man may be shot through the brain so suddenly as to preserve in death his look of watchfulness. As much as the generals with their ponderous but precise official accounts, the one contributor who supplied the young writer with useful details merited Crane's impatient protest: "I wonder that *some* of these fellows don't tell how they *felt* in those scraps! They spout eternally of what they *did*, but they are as emotionless as rocks!" [41]

The emotionless prose of the officers was equaled by *Century's* exemplary private, who wrote with such considered detachment. When Goss portrayed military psychology, he did so from the outside: "In a camp of soldiers, rumor, with her thousand tongues, is always speaking. The rank and file and under-officers of the line are not taken into the confidence of their superiors. Hence the private soldier is usually in ignorance as to his destination. What he lacks in information is usually made up in surmise and conjecture; every hint is caught at and worked out in possible and impossible combinations. He plans and fights imaginary battles." [42] Goss's failure to render the changing rumors and imaginary battles as they were felt could not have been lost on anyone who looked at the facing page of the magazine and read of Huck Finn's responses to the bloody last battle of imaginary Grangerfords and Shepherdsons. After the "Kill them, kill them!" of the Shepherdsons, Buck Grangerford's friend Huck is made "so sick I most fell out of the tree." Hearing guns go off and seeing the little gangs of armed men twice gallop by, tugging the bodies from the river and covering their faces, striking through the woods and not finding Jim at first, puts Huck through fear and grief and fear again in rapid succession, but after he makes good his escape to Jim and the raft, the emotions of feuding are themselves quickly left behind: "Other places do seem so cramped up and smothery, but a raft don't. You feel mighty free and easy and comfortable on a raft." [43] The juxtaposition of Mark Twain and Warren Lee Goss, of experience in all its flux as felt

[41] *My Stephen Crane*, p. 37.   [42] xxix (Dec., 1884), 279.
[43] xxix (Dec., 1884), 278.

by an imaginary character like Huck Finn and events imper-
sonally recorded by the private soldier who was actually there,
sets the crucial problem Crane had to deal with in writing *The
Red Badge*. Somehow the inner drama of consciousness and the
objective action of violent conflict had to be brought together.

Crane's fundamental premise about experience, and about
writing which would be true to experience, was that character
and incident were inseparable. If he were to write about fear, he
must present it not simply as an inner feeling, but as an emotion
with practical consequences; his protagonist would not only
think like a man afraid, he would under some particular circumstances throw down his arms and run. When he set to work, however, he found that the protagonist was more easily imagined
than the circumstances. He had to sustain his inner logic further
than he had ever tried before, but with the Sullivan County tales
and *Maggie* behind him, he knew the direction he wanted to take.
This side of his task seemed, in the recollection of Willis Johnson, to go well. Speaking of the spring of 1893, Johnson remembered Crane as "greatly engaged with 'The Red Badge of
Courage'; not so much on paper as in his own mind. He spoke
frequently of its hero as 'growing.' 'He's getting to be quite a character now,' he said one day; just as a fond parent would say 'My
Johnny is getting to be quite a big boy.' The character was as
clear and vital to him, in his mind, as a living person could have
been." [44] On the other hand, devising the web of incident within
which the growing character would act and react proved hard,
despite the effort Crane was willing to put into it. Having read
all he could in Linson's old magazines, he went on to the full
four-volume collection of *Battles and Leaders* which *Century* had
later put out. In borrowing the volumes from an old family
friend, he committed himself to strenuous research—he did not
believe that firsthand experience was the writer's single indis-
pensable source of material. When he returned the books on
April 2, 1893, he could not say that they had served his purpose.
"Thank you very much for letting me keep these so long," he
wrote. "I have spent ten nights writing a story of the war on my
own responsibility but I am not sure that my facts are real and

[44] "The Launching of Stephen Crane," *Literary Digest*, IV (April, 1926), 289.

the books won't tell me what I want to know so I must do it all over again, I guess." [45] Since there is no trace of that abortive war story among Crane's papers, his words can be taken to mean that he discarded it altogether.

Having to start over was not so casual a matter as Crane made it sound. His money was beginning to run out, and the more seriously he took his war story, the less time and energy he had for writing anything else for which he might be paid. He knew he was committing himself to a task that almost certainly involved hardship. His easy tone expressed a resolve that was well beyond the faltering stage which Louis Senger noted. Almost at the moment when he indicated his decision this way, he received the kind of encouragement which confirmed that the heavy stakes were worth it. William Dean Howells sent word at last that he had read *Maggie*, that he found it admirable and would like to meet the author. When they met, he let the younger man know how much he respected not only his skill but his "literary conscience." [46] Such praise from the country's foremost novelist and critic naturally elated Crane, and it certainly heartened him for his renewed effort even though there might be nothing to show for a while. During the rest of the spring, he evidently wrote no more of his war story. His living arrangements were being disrupted; his "Pendennis Club" on Avenue A turned into just another boardinghouse as the landlady moved her establishment downtown and left behind the medical students who were her paying customers and his not-so-wild Indian cronies. Before long, Crane was living mostly in Lake View, although his downtown friends, mostly artists and illustrators, saw to it that even when broke he had a place to stay in New York. C. K. Linson, who left Crane the key to his studio in June (though Crane never did find it that summer), thought he wrote *The Red Badge* at his brother Edmund's in Lake View that summer. But Linson's conjecture only means that Crane had not yet begun writing; Linson did not see him again till December.[47] In the spring Linson knew

---

[45] To Mrs. Olive Brett Armstrong, Beer, *Crane*, p. 98.

[46] The meeting occurred after Crane's letter of March 28, 1893 (*Letters*, p. 16), prompted Howells to read the book, and the gist of the talk is given in Howells' letter to Crane, New York, April 8, 1893 (*Letters*, p. 18).

[47] *My Stephen Crane*, pp. 38–40.

that his *Century* magazines were being well used, but he did not know that a novel was being planned.

In the interval between the ten-nights' tale which he discarded and the actual setting down of *The Red Badge* on paper, Crane's talk, as reported by a variety of witnesses, makes clear his concentration on that project. What writing he got done in that period was in its way relevant to the project, also. His Tommy sketches portray a little boy from the tenements who steals, or rather, takes without the least sense of guilt, whether it be another child's bright red fire engine or a gleaming lemon from a fruit-vendor's stand.[48] The middle-class child with the fire engine knows the meaning of "mine," but not the slum child. Tommy, with his preconventionalized consciousness, responds directly to appearances and in doing so provides a model for how the mind may work in conditions of free psychic flow, outside the rational patterns of received culture. Guiltless stealing, like reflexive panic under conditions of physical conflict, suggested the ironic failure of commonplace moralism to cover some not so exceptional cases. What might seem disarming in the story of a child or be explained away in a story of the slums could turn out to be, when adapted to the case of a representative young American under arms, a dangerous insight. The prevailing moral assumptions applied only in a limited area of experience, and while those who lived securely within that area might regard childhood or even tenement poverty as a passing phase, war was another question altogether.

What Crane read is harder to establish than what he was writing during this interim period. He evidently came back to *Battles and Leaders*, and in the fall when he moved into the studio of friends in the old Art Students League building on East 23rd Street, he brought Linson's *Century* magazines with him. R. G. Vosburgh, one of the original occupants of that studio, recalled how Crane read and reread them and concluded, "All of his knowledge of the war and of the country depicted in 'The Red

---

[48] Linson (*My Stephen Crane*, p. 39) tells of taking "An Ominous Baby" and "A Great Mistake" with him when he left for the Ramapo Hills in June, 1893; Crane hoped he would prepare illustrations for them during the summer. For the stories, see *Works*, VIII, 47–52.

Badge of Courage' was gathered from those articles and from
the study of maps of that region." [49] Vosburgh was too quick in
his judgment, for he observed Crane at a stage when he was using the *Century* articles as workbooks. The articles could indeed
supply details of terrain, deployment, and chronology, but by
Crane's own testimony they could not give him what he needed
to know if his facts were to become real in the life of a character.
On the other hand, given his conscientious study of *Battles and
Leaders*, presumably he would not ignore any help he could get.
He may have got some of the details of a soldier's initiation, for
example, from a fictionalized war memoir by Wilbur F. Hinman,
called *Corporal Si Klegg and His "Pard."* The book, published in
1887 and going into a second edition in 1890, sold some 26,000
copies. Hinman wrote, he said, of ordinary soldiers who had
"their prototypes in every regiment." Many of his details of every-
day military life have their parallels in Goss's "Recollections of a
Private," but some details he shares with Crane and not Goss:
the encounter with a special comrade, the questioning of one's
own courage, the baptism of fire, and the seasoning of recruit
into veteran. He salted his narrative with colloquial speech, and
in his own style he came closer to flexible, idiomatic prose than
Goss, even though compared to Crane he expressed typicality in
a limp, generalized way. H. T. Webster, who first noted the like-
nesses of Hinman and Crane, also was the first to observe that
parallel passages illustrate their difference too:

[Hinman:] In their minds [the new troops'] there was an odium
connected with the idea of seeking cover. It was too much like showing the white feather. But in the fullness of time they all got over
this foolish notion.
[Crane:] Some wished to fight like duellists, believing it to be correct
to stand erect and be, from their feet to their fore-heads, a mark.
They said they scorned the devices of the cautious. But the others
scoffed in reply and pointed to the veterans on the flanks who were
digging at the ground like terriers.[50]

[49] "The Darkest Hour in the Life of Stephen Crane," *The Book-Lover*, II, no.
8 (Summer, 1901), 338.
[50] *Corporal Si Klegg and His "Pard"* (Cleveland: Williams, 1887), p. 409;
The Red Badge, Va. 26.5–10. These and other parallel passages are cited by
H. T. Webster, "Wilbur F. Hinman's *Corporal Si Klegg* and Stephen Crane's
The Red Badge of Courage," *American Literature*, XI (Nov., 1939), 285–293.

The "idea of seeking cover" cannot match the energetic and visible "digging at the ground like terriers," but the plainspoken Hinman at least made clear how raw and veteran troops behaved. Hinman, instead of arguing the physiological probabilities, told how things felt in the most literal sense. When Si Klegg is grazed by a bullet, he feels a rap on his head such that he asks his pard whether he has bumped him with his gun. Crane, by turning the paradox upside down, had the means of giving Henry Fleming the inglorious wound which, passed off as the real thing, let him rejoin his unit without shame. Hinman, focusing on the experience of a particular soldier, provided authentic materials that Crane would not have spurned.

The most important book that lies behind *The Red Badge* is Tolstoy's *Sebastopol*, which came into Crane's hands early and impressed him profoundly. It provided him a norm for realism in an account of war. Because it pointed the way in which he would go beyond the conventions of American realism, it reminds us that in the 1890s, as before and since, a fresh access to major European writing has helped young Americans to become strongly original. It even helped bring together the generations of American realists, for Howells, overwhelmed by his reading of Tolstoy in the mid-1880s, had become the first major critic in the English-speaking world to declare the Russian's central importance. Howells continued his ardent advocacy during the next decade and more as the reading public came to share his judgment. Nor did he conduct his advocacy in his critical writings only, as if it were only a matter of literary opinion. When young Theodore Dreiser met him, Howells urged the case so strongly that Dreiser, reporting the interview, concluded by quoting a Howells essay on Tolstoy: "I can never again see life in the way I saw it before I knew him. Tolstoy awakens in his reader the will to be a man; not effectively, not spectacularly, but simply, really. He leads you back to the only true ideal, away from the false standard of the gentleman, to the man who sought not to be distinguished from other men, but identified with them." Whether, five years earlier, Howells conveyed the same message to Crane in their first meeting, no one can know. There is a strong probability that he did so through the written word at least, and though the evidence is complex and takes the story back yet another five years, it gives an idea of Tolstoy's pervasive influence and his particular importance for Crane.[51]

Writing about the summer of 1888, when Crane was seventeen years old, Thomas Beer reported: "And a Canadian lady, nameless in the record, gave him a paper bound copy of Count Tolstoy's 'Sevastopol.' " In 1888, as the recognition of Tolstoy was quickening, three translations of *Sebastopol* had come out within two years. The paperback edition to which Beer refers, the translation of Laura E. Kendall, came out in the "Seaside Library" and was evidently intended for circulation in places like Asbury Park. Mrs. Kendall translated painstakingly from the Russian—her title-page refers to Count "Lyof" Tolstoy—but she labored so hard at the task that she partly lost command of her native tongue. Her Russian-English dictionary style makes it difficult to get to Tolstoy, difficult enough so that quite possibly Crane would have tossed the book aside as he later did *La Débâcle*. He would not, however, have put down the fine translation from the French of Frank D. Millet, an American war correspondent whose clean idiomatic prose can hold the reader at every page. The Millet version, published in regular cloth binding by Harper's, lacks the supporting testimony of Beer that Crane had read it, but strong circumstantial evidence forces it into consideration. It had an introduction by Howells in which he praised Tolstoy for getting closer to human nature than any other writer. Howells praised the Russian's fidelity to "the life common to all men," and he singled out "Peace and War"—a locution also adopted by Crane for Tolstoy's novel—for its "great assertion of the sufficiency of common men in all crises, and the insufficiency of heroes." Howells' words seem to echo in the statement Crane later made when, speaking as the author of *The Red Badge*, he identified his own ideals with those of the Russian master: "I decided that the nearer a writer gets to life the greater he becomes as an artist, and most of my prose writings have

[51] Ellen Moers, *Two Dreisers* (New York: Viking, 1969), pp. 43–56, gives the most penetrating account of Tolstoy's impact on American culture in this period, citing Dreiser's interview with Howells and his use of the Howells passage in his subsequent article. She calls particular attention to the fact that the 1898 interview occurred as Dreiser was coming to his momentous decision to become a novelist.

been toward the goal partially described by that misunderstood and abused word, realism. Tolstoi is the writer I admire most of all." Even more they help explain Crane's words in the copy of *The Red Badge* which he gave to the older novelist: "To W. D. Howells this small and belated book as a token of the veneration and gratitude of Stephen Crane for many things he has learned of the common man and, above all, for a certain re-adjustment of his point of view victoriously concluded some time in 1892." At any rate the Tolstoy Crane admired was decidedly the author of *Sebastopol*. According to Beer, Crane as a nineteen-year-old college student was ready to declare Tolstoy the "world's foremost writer," and yet he apparently did not read *Kreutzer Sonata*, *War and Peace*, or *Anna Karenina* until well after finishing *The Red Badge*, and when he did read them, he expressed reservations about each of these works and tempered his enthusiasm accordingly. The judgment which he first made as a naïve boy, the mature writer confirmed with an assurance based on how the book stood up for him.[52]

What surely appealed to Crane was the way Tolstoy proved in his Crimean sketches how near a writer can get to life. Writing from the bastions of the besieged city, the young Russian officer, as he was then, proved sensitive to the whole multifarious world about him. In what he wrote, the action is at all points palpable; events register themselves on the senses without the mediation of received idea or hackneyed phrase. Some of the incidents, as

[52] Beer, *Crane*, p. 54. Of the translations available to Crane, that of Isabel F. Hapgood (New York: Crowell, 1888) does not seem to be in question. The Kendall translation (New York: George Munro, 1888) came out in a paperbound pocket edition, no. 1108 of the Seaside Library, and cost twenty cents. The Millet translation with Howells' introduction (New York: Harper and Brothers, 1887) would have cost Crane only seventy-five cents. It is also quite possible that when Howells met Crane in the spring of 1893, he might have given the young novelist a copy in reciprocation of Crane's earlier gift of *Maggie*. In any case Crane would have been interested in an edition introduced by the American novelist whom he most admired. Evidence for such hypotheses is worth seeking because of the intrinsic likelihood that the better written version would have influenced Crane. The Howells praise (*Sebastopol*, pp. 5–12) is echoed in Crane's letter to an editor of *Leslie's Weekly* (n.p., n.d.) about November, 1895 (*Letters*, p. 78). Crane's inscription in his gift copy for Howells of *The Red Badge* he backdated to August 17, 1895, more than a week before he received title-page proof, much less an advance copy (*Letters*, p. 62). The college boy's statement on Tolstoy, since Beer had little information on Crane's semester at Lafayette, may have come from one of his cronies at Syracuse and would in that case date from the spring of 1891. See Beer, *Crane*, p. 55.

Lars Åhnebrink first noted, may have been used by Crane: the overdramatic bestowal of letters to be sent home in case of death, the fraternizing of enemy troops during a lull, Vladimir Koseltzoff's inner struggle with cowardice. But incidents which have no parallel in *The Red Badge* seem equally close in feeling. The first of the book's three sketches, "Sebastopol in December, 1854," spans a fictive day from the first tinge of dawn till the dark of evening when, in the doomed city, "a regimental band is playing an old waltz, which sounds far over the water, and to which the cannonade of the bastions forms a strange and striking accompaniment." Everything is seen, heard, felt—the quietly courageous amputees and the newly wounded, screaming curses; the methodical surgeons at their work and the officer who calmly rolls a cigarette as shells go off around him; the archaic general who tells his troops, "Children, we will die, but we will not surrender Sebastopol," and the soldiers who reply, "We will die, hurrah!" [53]

Realism like this could be dangerous. Tolstoy, who began his book as a resolute patriot, ended with pictures of butchery and disarray that put him at odds with Tsarist censorship. But the danger did not lie merely with obvious content. The book was more powerful than censors could guess. Tolstoy himself believed so strongly in the importance of his convictions to his writing that he gave hardly more than a clue. But he lived up to the claim of having no hero but Truth, and in doing so he

[53] *The Beginnings of Naturalism in American Fiction* (Uppsala and Cambridge: Lundequistska Bokhandeln and Harvard University Press, 1950), pp. 347–350; *Sebastopol*, Millet translation, pp. 43–44. The last paragraph of "December, 1854" in the Kendall and Millet versions is a fair sample of their difference:

Kendall	Millet
The day is waning; the sun, which will soon disappear below the horizon, is shining through the gray clouds that surround it, and illumining with its crimson rays the ripples of the emerald sea, covered with boats and ships, and the white houses of the town. On the boulevard a band is playing a familiar waltz, to which the cannonade from the bastions forms a strange and weird accompaniment (p. 23).	Day closes; the sun, disappearing at the horizon, shines through the gray clouds which surround it, and lights up with purple rays the rippling sea with its green reflections, covered with ships and boats, the white houses of the city, and the population stirring there. On the boulevard a regimental band is playing an old waltz, which sounds far over the water, and to which the cannonade of the bastions forms a strange and striking accompaniment (pp. 43–44).

made a book which was unique in its being without a hero. Heroic acts were possible and men might sometimes be heroic, but the consistent pursuit of great purpose, such as traditionally defines heroism, is allowed to none of the characters. Nor is there, to put it somewhat differently, the consistent expression of great principles. The young Tolstoy had not yet framed the conception of history which in *War and Peace* delimits the powers of man or the vision of nature which transcends history. The world of *Sebastopol* far exceeds the comprehension of any character in the work, and the author gives no sign of knowing more than his characters. Committed to writing nothing but the truth, Tolstoy not only dissociated himself from the official point of view, but even took the youthful risk—*Sebastopol* is the early effort of a writer in his twenties—that he might subvert beliefs more fundamental than political allegiances. In fact, presenting the world as he did, he was undermining the rationalist assumption that man could in some degree understand and control his own destiny. Coherent meanings, in that world, seemed to occur only as parts happened momentarily to fit together. When Tolstoy juxtaposed waltzes and cannonades, oratory and anguish, the offense to ideologues and patriots should not conceal the greater threat to commonsense notions of how the world ought to work.

A brief digression may make it clearer how Tolstoy could help Crane move beyond the conventions of the older American realists. In contrast to *Sebastopol*, the *Personal Memoirs of U. S. Grant*, the finest realistic narrative to come directly from the Civil War experience, offered no offense to ideologues, patriots, or serious literary critics.[54] It was Howells' kind of book, as *The Red Badge* never was. For one thing, it began in history: Grant's clear, strong recognition of the political and social causes of the war makes it into a special phase of human history rather than a world that is simply given, behind which one can perceive no other way that things might be. Moreover, it had a clear, strong plot. From the moment of Grant's mustering volunteers at Galena, there is a consistent rising action. Grant grapples at first with bureaucratic tangles and undisciplined troops more than with the anarchic forces of actual conflict. But the scale of com-

---

[54] 2 vols., New York: Charles L. Webster & Co., 1885.

mand gradually expands—from the Twenty-first Illinois Volunteers to the Department of the Tennessee to the armies of the West to the post of the general-in-chief of the Union armies. The military objectives become more difficult as well as more complex, yet Grant is able to impose his will and intelligence on events. The lucid imperturbable writing speaks for the same qualities in the man of action, and the book as a whole invites us to see the world as one in which heroic intelligence can master chaotic circumstance. There are no heroics, but Grant, for all his modesty, makes us see that a general can be a hero as judged not by archaic, but by widely held, current values. The book, which began in a couple of articles for the *Battles and Leaders* series, and which, heroically brought to completion by the dying Grant, became a best-seller, could not have escaped Crane's notice. No book should have appealed to him more, considering his pride in the military exploits of his Revolutionary ancestors, his having from early childhood played games of tactics and not just of fighting, his rise as a schoolboy cadet to the rank of captain, and his youthful hopes of going to West Point. But nothing in the record suggests that he responded in any way at all to a book which was everything that *The Red Badge* was not.

When commonly held values do not organize a literary work, other values come into play. In *Sebastopol* the controlling purposes of characters do not shape the action, but their collective authority as registers of experience brings out the objective ironies that are centers of meaning within the larger and seemingly incomprehensible world. As the fragmentary clarifications fall into a pattern, they suggest an implicit plot of discovery in which the young narrator arrives at his first decisive encounter with death. Tolstoy's last sketch ends with the deaths of two brothers. The older Koseltzoff thinks it is nonsense when he hears of the French assault, he feels pain for barely a moment when two bullets pierce his chest, and he reacts with little more than mechanical surprise when the doctor who examines him gives way to the priest. The priest offers comfort not so much by his prayer for the dying or his cross as by his falsehood to the effect that the Russian lines are holding. Mikhail Semenovitch, weeping with joy at the priest's lie, turns his last thought to his brother and wishes, "God grant him the same happiness!" Elsewhere in the battle the younger brother Vladimir (affectionately, Volodia) has had his taste of panic, but when he sees his orderly acting like a despicable coward, he feels his own courage flow back as if by a reflex. But it turns out that in the pinch the orderly fights and saves himself and, when he looks for his beloved lieutenant, sees no such man but only "a shapeless thing, clothed in a gray overcoat," lying "face to earth." [55] With these two episodes to which the whole narrative of *Sebastopol* has led, Tolstoy for all practical purposes defined the kinds of irony that were to be characteristic of Crane's writing about war: in the story of the older brother there is the ironic distance between delusion and fact, and in the story of the younger there is the ironic distance between character and event. Perhaps even more important than the lessons in irony is Tolstoy's ultimate nihilistic report on what war felt like. He let his narrative end in defeat, death, dispersal—the opposites of will, understanding, organized personal force such as might define not only heroism but life itself. For a realistic writer who wanted his reader to apprehend experience beyond the familiar, this was the last degree of otherness, beyond which there was nowhere to go. For Crane it was to be a theme to return to again and again throughout his career.

Tolstoy helped free Crane of the anxiety—literary influence often works thus—of working all alone with new materials and not knowing whether his facts were real. He provided Crane with suggestions of incident, technique, theme, and he stood as an exemplar that certain literary ideas were viable. On the other hand, a writer's debt to another, to be worth serious notice, assumes that the debtor does much more than repeat the other's work. Once rid of the burden of having to do everything over again for himself, Crane proved that he could do things which Tolstoy could not—specifically in the rendering of psychology. His radical breakthrough came from his premise that mental life primarily consists in witnessing the vivid immediate presences within one's own mind, that is, in the flux of consciousness. So far as consciousness is concerned, self-projected images have equal status with sense data. The practical demands of life re-

[55] *Sebastopol*, Millet translation, pp. 232, 235.

quire that we sort out the two kinds of impressions, and the sorting goes on all the time since, as prior impressions may be falling into place, new images constantly stream into consciousness. The sorting out, moreover, is a natural function of living and not a ratiocinative process. For example, when Tolstoy's Volodia wonders whether he will panic and run, he engages in interior debate on the extent to which the resolved will can match the power of physical fear. When Crane's Henry Fleming first wonders about his courage, it is ironically clear that despite his pondering, he could not "mathematically prove to himself that he would not run from a battle." He must regard himself as "an unknown quantity" and settle the matter by "experiment." Although he would like to "remain close upon his guard lest those qualities of which he knew nothing should everlastingly disgrace him," even he does not think that his resolved will can make much difference. At the outset the argument of the book is thus set as an exercise in empirical psychology. When Fleming comes back to the problem, he sees that "the only way to prove himself was to go into the blaze and then figuratively to watch his legs to discover their merits and faults. He reluctantly admitted that he could not sit still and, with a mental slate and pencil, derive an answer." His theoretical doctrine is sound, but in reverting to his problem over and over again, he illustrates the process by which he germinates panic within himself. His reasoning is a compulsive and in that sense irrational act comparable to his gift for seeing monstrous images, the conscious manifestation of an underlying process, morbid in this case, which can be known only as it manifests itself in this way. The difference between *Sebastopol* and *The Red Badge*, while partly to be explained by the literary shift from an omniscient narrator to a restricted point of view, involved a radically new idea of the individual consciousness which Crane was trying to render.

After the setback he reported at the beginning of April 1893, Crane may have taken as much as six months to read, reflect, plan, and let his novel grow. He spent much of the late spring and summer at his brother Edmund's, where he was remembered for teaching the young people of Lake View to play football (that college sport was just beginning to spread into popular culture) rather than for his industry at the writing table. Besides, the easygoing Edmund, though he might be Stephen's choice as the ideal guardian, had only rudimentary notions of what writers tried to do and never did strike his younger brother as someone on whom to try out his work in hand. In New York, on the other hand, it was his time of direst poverty and most unsettled living until in the fall he moved in as coproprietor with three artist friends of a studio in the old Art Students League building on East 23rd Street. "He could contribute nothing to its maintenance," R. G. Vosburgh would later recall, "but he added very little to the expense, and the others were glad to have him. For seven or eight months, from one autumn until the following summer, the four men lived together. It was during that time that 'The Red Badge of Courage' was written." Vosburgh's account is interesting for what it leaves out as well as for what it puts in. There is no mention of notes, plans, or prior draft from which Crane worked. He seems to have written straight off almost without correction. Confident as he was that he could sustain the story he had conceived, he nonetheless kept Linson's *Century* magazines at hand so that he could be sure of the matrix of objective detail within which his story took place. And he tried things out as he went along, using his friends to help him decide how the psychological narrative stood up. Vosburgh wrote:

The articles in the *Century* then were full of interest and fascination for Crane, and when he moved to the studio on Twenty-third street he borrowed the magazines and took them with him to read and study. All of his knowledge of the war and of the country depicted in "The Red Badge of Courage" was gathered from those articles and from the study of maps of that region.

He always worked at night, generally beginning after 12 o'clock and working until 4 or 5 o'clock in the morning, then going to bed and sleeping the greater part of the day. . . .

Crane spent his afternoons and evenings studying the war and discussing his stories. Every incident and phase of character in "The Red Badge of Courage" was discussed and argued fully and completely before being incorporated into the story. In this he worked differently from the way in which his short stories were written.

At the time of beginning "The Red Badge of Courage" he was writing sketches of East Side children, some of which have been published since; he could not sell them when they were written. These sketches were quite brief, and most of them were written in one night without previous discussion. After writing a story he would put it away for two or three weeks, and work on something else until his mind was thoroughly clear for a fresh consideration of it. When the story was taken out for revision it would be turned over to his friends for criticism, and Crane would argue with them about the objections they would make. He often accepted suggestions for changes, but it always seemed as though these changes were those he had already decided upon himself before they were mentioned by others. This was also characteristic of the discussions of "The Red Badge of Courage." He convinced himself; others might help him, but he arrived at his own conclusions.[56]

Another artist of the 23rd Street group set down his recollection of Crane in 1893 considerably later, but with similar persuasive detail:

He was at that time writing "The Red Badge of Courage." I remember one time when he was lying in a hammock of his saying "That is great!" It shocked me for the moment. I thought how conceited he is. But when he read me the passage, I realized at once how wonderfully real it was, and said that the writer had that advantage over us painters in that he could make his men talk, walk and think. Where as a painter can only depict a man in one position at a time. He seemed very pleased with this compliment. . . . He was absolutely indifferent to comfort or discomfort. I can remember so well how when he came down from the country he would come in and put his little hand bag down in the middle of the Studio floor, sit down on a little sketching stool, pull out his pad, pen, and a bottle of ink, and begin to write with only a few words of greetings. I do not remember that he ever erased or changed anything. His writing was clean and round with a ring around his periods. He wrote

[56] Edith Crane to Thomas Beer, Port Jervis, N.Y., Nov. 19, 1922, Barrett Collection, University of Virginia Library, on Crane at Lake View. Crane to Willis Brooks Hawkins, Hartwood, Nov. 19, [1895], on Crane's view of Edmund as a critical reader: "He is an awful stuff in literature" (*Letters*, p. 76). My construction of the case contradicts Beer, *Crane*, p. 102, who seems to have put together Linson's conjecture about Crane's writing *The Red Badge* at Lake View and Vosburgh's report of reading aloud at the studio; Beer indulged in such improvisation with some frequency. Vosburgh, "Darkest Hour," p. 338.

slowly. It amazed me how he could keep the story in mind while he was slowly forming the letters.[57]

Crane's sociable friends proved to be as necessary to him as *Battles and Leaders*; as he used the *Century* articles to check the reasonableness of his topography and order of battle, he used them to check the reasonableness of his psychology. Measuring their response to what he wrote, he worked closer to his audience than writers of fiction usually can. Vosburgh, who was to make a distinguished place for himself as an art critic, was probably the most acute of his listeners, but not even he could claim to be more than an experimental control so far as psychology was concerned. However, it was control and not expertise that Crane needed. The originality of his approach lay in his radical sense of what he wanted to do—to "see war from within," [58]—and his friends had but to accept that premise as given in order to tell him what he wanted to know. His originality did not lie with a sustained theoretical development that might require of his listeners close reasoning and professional knowledge. A more sophisticated audience might have had trouble with the book, for a shift in premise like Crane's made possible a number of new systems of explanation. The Henry Fleming who sees serpentine armies and bivouac dragons illustrates an epiphenomenalism that has as little to do with things as they are as the heroic-chivalric legends that have evidently affected him. He expects that under stress of battle his personality will be savingly transformed, and on the occasion of his first skirmish he is twice transformed. First he is caught up in the crowd psychology which makes him "not a man but a member" and gives

---

[57] David Ericson to Ames W. Williams, Provincetown, Mass., Nov. 4, 1942, *Letters*, pp. 341–342. Vosburgh shared the impression that Crane never erased or changed anything: "His manuscripts were always scrupulously neat and clean, written in ink on legal cap paper without erasures and without interlineations. In revising his work he would rewrite a whole sheet when a correction was necessary rather than make an erasure, if only to change one word" ("Darkest Hour," p. 339). Crane did try to keep his manuscripts neat, and there were relatively few deletions (by lining out) and interlineations in a freshly completed manuscript. The basic neatness of the manuscript for *The Red Badge* meant that it could sustain three serious revisions by Crane, in addition to alterations made during the inscription, and still be legible in high degree.

[58] Ripley Hitchcock, quoting Crane in the Preface to the 1900 edition of *The Red Badge of Courage*, p. vii.

him his first delusive notion of what the sense of brotherhood may be. Then to the accompaniment of such symptoms as blistering sweat, burning eyeballs, roaring ears, he becomes a raging beast, man reduced to his primitive essence. Afterwards he wakes from his "battle-sleep" and thinks he has passed his test of courage. At the next onset of battle and battle fever, the effect is different. The man next to him is hit, screams, and runs, and like an automaton, he too throws down his gun and flees. There are many ways in which the conscious personality can disintegrate, especially for an imaginative young man whose eye more than half creates the world he sees. The various psychic patterns which Crane implicitly set up, like the various systems of imagery and suggestion which he changefully evoked, express the multiplicity of a world which simply does not present itself to us as tradition teaches or reason hopes, namely, in a form that can be immediately recognized and unequivocally interpreted. In this he was not acting waywardly: he wrote just as the science of psychology, focusing on the phenomena of consciousness as the primary source for understanding the roots of behavior, had begun to proliferate. But just as with his exuberant rhetorical inventiveness, his theoretical inventiveness depended on his having an entirely plausible narrative which could support more than one interpretation. The question of whether he could pass this test was one which he put to daily trial.

Crane's most interesting psychological suggestions occur in the chapter which follows Fleming's panic and flight. What he feels at first is outward-directed shame, fear of the disgrace that will be his if his fellow soldiers find out he has run. This becomes even worse when he learns that the army has held while he was fleeing, for he knows that he cannot say he ran like everyone who had any sense. Had there only been a general rout, saving himself might have won approval as the kind of prudence that saves an army. On the contrary he can only expect derision. Along with resentment of his fellows and evasion of their censure, he now acts, however, from a related motive that seems to have its source deep within—the desire to "bury himself" in obscurity. He heads into the depths of the woods, "seeking dark and intricate places" where the crack of rifles and the rumble of death can no more be heard. "Going from obscurity into promises of a greater obscurity," he finally reaches an innermost sanctum, a "chapel" made by arching boughs, and softly pushing the green doors aside, he starts to pass through into the dimness. Suddenly at this point the regressive fantasy comes to a halt: in the inmost forest, seated against a tree, is the gruesome decaying body of a soldier. To this he has been led, whether reacting to the supposed demands of all who see him or to an inner wish for a place of respite, secure, soft, and maternal. Whichever psychology applies, he is caught within the boundaries of his own mind. The one thing that can break his morbid self-engrossment is the shock of encountering actual death. When this occurs, he recoils.

Henry Fleming's revulsion from the gruesome corpse in the forest turns the direction of his flight and starts him back toward the battle. He traverses a sector that seems to belong to the dead, and then gets to the edge of a road where he can see the stream of the maimed and dying. When he was withdrawing from life, he came upon death. When he returns to life, he comes upon the dying, men who curse, groan, laugh, sing, or grit their teeth in silence. One, a talkative tattered man, even tries to make friends, to welcome him back, as it were, into society. But when he asks in his chatty way, "Where yeh hit, ol' boy?" the younger man has no answer, and despite the "brotherly tone" in which the question is put, he turns away to lose himself in the crowd. Fleming is still a runaway, not to be changed by any single climactic turn but, if at all, by starts and stops. He learns by repetition, habituation. So, in the next two chapters (ix and x), he twice more encounters death on the closest terms. First he falls in with the spectral soldier who turns out to be his old friend, the washer of shirts and herald of rumor, Jim Conklin. Evidently badly hit and walking slowly and stiffly "like one who goes to choose a grave," Jim welcomes him as a comrade who will guard him from falling beneath the wheels of the artillery wagons. For Fleming it is a supreme moment of loyalty and of woe felt for another, but he can help only for a brief space. Jim, led out of the path of an approaching battery, breaks free to go his own way into the fields as if to a purposed destination. Then with his face composed in "a curious and profound dignity" and his legs buckling in "a sort of hideous horn-pipe," he topples to earth. The tattered man, having casually rejoined Henry and watched the grotesque but moving death scene with him, leads him away. He is able to draw Henry from his brooding grief partly because he too is seriously wounded and makes a call on the sense of comradeship. But in his rambling conversation he expresses his concern for Fleming by asking once again where he has been hurt. "Oh, don't bother me," is the reply. Exasperation turns into hatred, and in response to the tattered man's half-delirious solicitude, Fleming abruptly leaves him. Deserting one comrade so soon after having done his best to stick by another, he hardly seems to exemplify any kind of progress, but involvement with the dying is different from that first encounter which was only with the dead.

Loyalty and disloyalty, though they make little difference to the practical outcome of inevitable death, somehow matter to Fleming. More is now at stake in his conduct than delusions of glory and self-engrossment. He does not cease to be the youth he was, but in his involvement with other people in their ultimate need, another quality begins to show. His capacity for shame, questionable at the beginning of these two episodes, seems at the end of the second to fasten at least momentarily on conduct rather than on how things look. At the beginning of Chapter IX, when he has left the tattered soldier for the first time and joined the procession of the wounded, shame for him means public disgrace at least as much as inward reproach. His first thought tends to be concern for his image in the eyes of other people: "Because of the tattered soldier's question, he now felt that his shame could be viewed. He was continually casting sidelong glances to see if the men were contemplating the letters of guilt he felt burned into his brow." At such a moment he can fatuously envy the wounded: "He conceived persons with torn bodies to be peculiarly happy. He wished that he, too, had a wound, a red badge of courage." (Crane's manuscript shows that he had in mind Fleming's childishness as well as his other-directedness, for there the wish is for a "little" red badge of courage.) After the death of Jim Conklin, whose side "looked as if it had been chewed by wolves," the envy of torn bodies seems even more patently absurd. Yet, when he has deserted the tattered soldier, Fleming wishes himself not wounded but dead. The "society that probes pitilessly at secrets" is still on his mind, and the softness of the grass or the forest floor where the dead lie, also on his mind, suggests that he still can think longingly of easeful death. Even so, the wish seems to be tied to the event. Having climbed the fence and started away, Fleming can still hear the confused pleas of the dying tattered man, who identifies him with a hometown friend even as, correctly, Jim Conklin did:

> Once, he faced about angrily. "What?"
> "Look—a—here, now, Tom Jamison—now—it ain't——"
> The youth went on. Turning at a distance he saw the tattered man wandering about helplessly in the fields.
> He now thought that he wished he was dead. He believed that he envied those men whose bodies lay strewn over the grass of the fields and on the fallen leaves of the forest.

In the last chapter of *The Red Badge* it turns out that his desertion of the tattered soldier is the "sin" which Henry Fleming must learn to live with and put at a distance, and the whole series of episodes leading up to the desertion allows him to say that he has "been to touch the great death and found that, after all, it was but the great death." These are the touchstones of his coming to manhood, and the narrative to this point warrants that they should be. In the second half of the novel, neatly complementary to the first, Fleming will go through a series of episodes in which he is the aggressor rather than the runaway, exploring rage rather than fear and learning in quite another sense how a man lives on close terms with death. In the second half, also, he attains a sense of comradeship based neither on the false fraternal sensations of mass behavior nor on terrible awareness of loss and betrayal: the friendship that develops between Fleming and Wilson is based on the shared experience of real events. The two halves hold together in that the test of maturity is for Fleming, having once run, to come back and fight another day. To get to his second half, however, Crane needed to invent a plausible and, if he could, a significant sequence of incidents that would bring the straggler back to his regiment.

The success he eventually had in finishing the novel as he wanted conceals the difficulty he struggled with in the actual writing.

One reason for the difficulty, probably, was that he did not have his end precisely in view. He seems to have written with neither a detailed plan nor a scenario: no such working papers exist for *The Red Badge* or for any other of his novels except for the start of a plan and some deathbed notes for his unfinished novel, *The O'Ruddy*. With the *The Red Badge* he seems to have gone from draft to draft, writing ninety-some pages of a first draft before starting from the beginning on what became the final manuscript. He put plenty of effort into revision, but he did not plan. In his most circumstantial account of how he wrote his novels, he told a story which fits well with his discovery of how seriously challenging a subject he had taken up, his silent period of letting it germinate, and his testing the narrative among his studio friends as he went along. The interviewer for *The Illustrated American* reported:

> His method, he told me, is to get away by himself and think over things. "Then comes a longing for you don't know what; sorrow, too, and heart-hunger." He mixes it all up. Then he begins to write. The first chapter is immaterial; but, once written, it determines the rest of the book. He grinds it out, chapter by chapter, never knowing the end, but forcing himself to follow "that fearful logical conclusion;" writing what his knowledge of human nature tells him would be the inescapable outcome of those characters placed in those circumstances.[59]

Inescapable logic posed problems for Crane in two different ways. As for the narrative bridge he needed, he could at least be certain that there was a thematic coherence between the half of his novel that began in fear and ended with death, desertion, and despair, and the half that might begin in rage and end with Fleming's attaining a degree of control. He had a second plot, however, which seemed to get out of hand as he reached the climax of his novel. The plot was a plot of ideas, and it turned

[59] Herbert P. Williams, "Mr. Crane as a Literary Artist," *The Illustrated American*, xx (July 18, 1896), 126.

out that Crane, who could logically render the irrational surface of consciousness so well, had no such talent for dramatizing the intellectual progress of his central character. He got deeper into doing so than he intended. Eventually, in a victory of critical intelligence over instinct, he decided that his talent lay with understatement and he drastically cut and subordinated his second plot. But knowing that received ideas as well as unschooled emotions made the complications of Fleming's story, he did not present him as a creature of sensations only. Part of his aim was, to use once more the formulation of his final chapter, to tell how Fleming outgrew "the brass and bombast of his earlier gospels."

Brass and bombast meant in the first instance the dream of heroism that would account for so many excesses of emotion and behavior. In the opening chapter the words took on meaning in sensible terms: there was the frantic enthusiast who clanged the church bell "to tell the twisted news of a great battle," and then, when "the voice of the people" had done its work and Fleming enlisted, there was the "blue and brass" of his new appearance which he thought might flutter a schoolgirl's heart. The earlier gospels that he would have to relinquish would thus be the Homeric and chivalric tales from which he derived his grand illusions. Such definitions apply well enough to the whole novel to support the Q.E.D. of the ending. But in the course of the telling, Crane let the meanings shift and become more inclusive, as he fell into doing because he kept so close to the mind of his character. He let Fleming, despite the inadequacy of "mental slate and pencil," continually reflect on events, and before he was through, he had set up the stream of ideas as an expressive medium that vied with the stream of images. After his first skirmish, Fleming comments to himself: "It was surprising that nature had gone tranquilly on with her golden processes in the midst of so much devilment." The sentence cuts at once to the heart of Crane's metaphysics, which like his psychology depended on a simple, radical—and tenable—insight. Crane believed that, despite man's readiness to project ideas of order—and even attitudes toward himself—upon external nature, the universe is only a neutral backdrop to human activity. In asserting that nature could not provide sanctions for human value systems, he was in 1893 in an avant-garde of the tough-minded. William James's most eloquent statements of the argument were not yet set to paper, though others besides James could have cited the earlier American empiricist Chauncey Wright, who had long since described the natural universe as a background to human action that went on like the weather, doing and undoing.[60] Not that Crane knew the work of either philosopher; had he done so he might have handled his subject better. As matters stood, he was reduced to showing how, reacting to his own changeable situation, a man might regard nature in various ways. He showed how Fleming's ideas shifted with the *inner* weather, but he had no means, as he had with the irreducible finalities of the battle narrative, for conveying whether those ideas should be taken as valid. No doubt he would have liked to establish his irony on firmer ground and indicate subtly whether ideas were right or wrong, but he would not have denied that Fleming's philosophical divagations were, in the current jargon, ego trips. He would have liked the term, for he saw Fleming's adolescent reflections as consistently egotistical. The language in which Fleming frames his ideas expresses self-pity and self-congratulation in varying mixtures. It stands as the primary example of bombast in the novel as Crane was writing it.

Because Crane cut the key meditative passages out of the book, it is necessary to go to the surviving fragments of draft and manuscript, for only there can one see what the story was that forced itself into the narrative and eventually required of the novelist some of his hardest artistic decisions. First of all, they concern man and the universe rather than man and society. Fleming gives but one fleeting thought to the possibility that he was duped into his enlistment by a "merciless government." The book is as devoid of historical thought as it is of chronological or geographical location; though it flouts received ideas of patriotism or heroics, it does not call institutions into question. One reason lies in Fleming's (and Crane's) proclivity to jump at once to larger questions: "He rebelled against the

[60] Cited in William James, *The Will to Believe* (New York and London: Longmans, Green & Co., 1897), p. 52.

source of things, according to his law that the most powerful
should recieve the most blame." [61] Secondly, the cut passages fill
out the gamut of possible reactions which Fleming intellectual-
izes. In Chapter VII as it stands, the young man as he gets into
the quiet of the woods personifies Nature as benign and maternal,
"with a deep aversion to tragedy." When he casually tosses a
pinecone at a squirrel and makes it run, he notes the squirrel's
not "baring his furry belly to the missile" as earlier he might
have noted that veterans do not expose themselves like duelists;
seeing the squirrel's prudence in running away, he takes it as a
sign that "nature was of his mind" and "reinforced his argument
with proofs." After the encounter with the decaying corpse in the
forest chapel, Crane did not originally leave the chapter with
Fleming's illusions simply deflated. Instead of ending with the
soft wind and sad silence that belonged to the landscape as well
as the character, he went on:

Again Fleming was in despair. Nature no longer condoled with
him. There was nothing, then, after all, in that demonstration she
gave—the frightened squirrel fleeing aloft from the missile.
He thought as he remembered the small animal capturing the fish
and the greedy ants feeding upon the flesh of the dead soldier, that
there was given another law which far-over-topped it—all life existing upon death, eating ravenously, stuffing itself with the hopes of
the dead.
And nature's processes were obliged to hurry [MS 65.20–30]

Because we have the cancelled passage at the bottom of the
manuscript page but not the discarded next page on which the
chapter once continued, we see only the beginning of a meditation on death as the ultimate law. But Crane, having made his
point with the chapel scene, was hardly strengthening his case.
The problem seems to reverse itself when hindsight is available,

[61] Draft, p. 75.4–6. Crane scarcely changed the meaning when he made the
sentence a little more stylish and the irony a little more subtle in his complete
manuscript: "He rebelled against the source of things, according to a law, perchance, that the most powerful shall recieve the most blame." Here, and
throughout, my study depends on the research, analysis, exposition, and apparatus of Fredson Bowers' *Facsimile Edition of the Manuscript*, cited above
(n. 2). His definitive treatment of textual problems makes it possible to see in
detail how the story grew under Crane's hand in the course of more than a
year.

and one asks not why he cut the passage but why he put it in.

The key word seems to be *despair*, especially since the next such deleted passage occurs in Chapter x, just after Fleming's betrayal of the tattered soldier and his momentary horrified wish that he were dead. There is one more turn to Fleming's immediate reaction to the event as he considers the tattered man's questions to be knife thrusts that foreshadow society's probing to come, from which he will not be able to escape. There the chapter now ends. But in Crane's original version, both draft and manuscript, Fleming's "old rebellious feelings" return and are directed "against the source of things"—"War, he said bitterly to the sky, was a make-shift created because ordinary processes could not furnish deaths enough." He goes on, we know from the draft, to accuse nature of inventing glory in order to seduce men to fight: "From his pinnacle of wisdom, he regarded the armies as large collection of dupes. Nature's dupes, who were killing each other to carry out some great scheme of life." He works himself into a rage, turning his "tupenny fury upon the high, tranquil sky," but the emotion is crossed with bitter self-congratulation that "among all men, he should be the only one sufficiently wise to understand these things." When purposeful action is balked, cosmic feelings come welling to the surface of consciousness, and from the depths of self-contempt, Fleming raises himself to a pinnacle of illusory wisdom.

When Fleming's consciousness is once again in touch with outward events, as it is immediately thereafter in Chapter xi, Crane had him repeat the same wild emotional swings. When he sees disorganized, fear-swept troops retreating, he takes comfort in supposing that their disorder vindicates his own flight. Yet when he sees an advancing column, he can so envy them as once more to wish himself a hero, even a dead hero. The surge of that old emotion lets him briefly feel "sublime," but as soon as he thinks of the difficulties of rejoining his unit, his "fire" begins to wane. Back then from heroic illusion through bafflement to self-hate. Because he can think of no answer to the questions which the world will surely ask, he is thrust back into confusion. The only salve for "the sore badge of his dishonor" would be a general defeat of the army, which would mean for him a vindication. But then he recognizes how murderous his wishes are and—"Again he thought that he wished he was dead." As a last hope it occurs to him that he might invent "a fine tale which he could take back to his regiment and with it turn the expected shafts of derision." But he cannot invent, he can only think of the barbs that will hit home. In whatever direction his mind casts, action is blocked.

At this point in the novel Crane brilliantly resolved the impasse in his plot, but in the writing he first took time—in his original Chapter XII—to let the impasse itself have ample expression. In a way the discarded chapter represented a false lead for him: instead of seeing the war from the inside, he was seeing his character from the inside. Feelings without an immediate context of fact raised the same doubts as facts without human response to them. But the chapter is nevertheless of great interest. If, as is probable, the impasse in Fleming's career was matched by an impasse Crane had reached in the composition of his novel, then the chapter is a unique document of the author's imaginative effort to find his way out. He groped his way through patterns of thematic development that in the following chapter he would handle as narrative incidents. At the very least the chapter stands as Crane's experiment with a kind of psychological system quite different from the others he suggested in the course of the novel, one for which he did not have a language, but which has to be taken seriously. The possibility is remote that he knew anything of Schopenhauer or of Nietzsche, but if he was inventing his own crude version of a birth of tragedy, he was also providing fresh evidence that the philosophers offer perfected models of the way others think. Crane depicted the illusion of the secure personality, clear-sighted, standing alone and able to hold out in its identity; in Schopenhauer's figure, it is like a small ship that successfully resists being engulfed by storm. In the midst of almost overwhelming turmoil, such a one sees underlying order and confidently maintains its own individuality. Counter to this is the psychology of the self which, thwarted in its worldly aims, sees the apparent order of things as false and, yearning for the collapse of formal limits and inauthentic order, wants to return to a primordial unity. In this scheme the personality lacks a sense of purposeful integration; feeling beset and pulled in all directions, it wants the relief of being restored to wholeness, absorbed into a totality that embraces all things. The two schemes underscore the connection of personality and culture, for whether they be called by Nietzsche's terms Apollonian and Dionysian or not, the psychological models correspond to basic cultural configurations.

Crane seems spontaneously to have developed this model in his draft. When the original Chapter XII picks up Fleming's stream of thought shortly after he has found himself totally blocked, he has made the jump to an illusory security:

It was always clear to Fleming that he was entirely different from other men, that he had been cast in a unique mold. Also, he regarded his sufferings as peculiar and unprecedented. No man had ever achieved such misery. There was a melancholy grandeur in the isolation of his experiences. He saw that he was a speck raising his [tiny *deleted*] minute arms against all possible forces and fates which were swelling down upon him like storms. He could derive some consolation from viewing [his *deleted*] the sublimity of the odds.

But, as he went on, he began to feel that, after all, [his rebellion, nature perhaps had not concentrated herself against him, or, at least, that *deleted*] nature would not blame him for his rebellion. He still distinctly felt that he was arrayed against the universe but he began to believe that there was no malice agitating [his *deleted*] the vast breasts of his space-filling foes. [He w *deleted*] It was merely law. [MS(d) 84.1–19; Va. 177.10–23]

Crane made it clear that the sense of uniqueness, by which Fleming asserted his individuality, was a matter of spiritual pride: "His egotism made him feel [safe *deleted*] secure for a time from the iron hands." The grand law which Fleming sees is that all things "fight or flee . . . resist or hide" according to how strong or wise they may be, and on this basis he feels justified in resisting the forces of exposure that pursue him. Presumably the irony is also intended whereby, following this higher law, Fleming hopes he may be saved from the iron hands of the merely "inevitable." One reason for thinking so is that in the paragraph before the inevitable seems to lose its inevitability, Fleming has allowed himself "a small grunt of satisfaction as he saw with what brilliancy he had reasoned it all out." Secure in such reasoning, he passes judgment on his own flight: "It was not a fault; it was a law." The whole meditative excursus which leads to this climax can be seen as a curious sublimation of the wish for general military defeat, which Fleming thought would be his moral vindication. Having ruled out that wish, he has built instead "a vindicating structure of great principles."

The second phase of this meditative chapter begins with the collapse of the vindicating structure. In Fleming's view "it was the calm toes of tradition that kicked it all down about his ears." Because men blindly stick to what the dead past has told them to believe, they will not accept his new wisdom. The enlightened calm of the reasoner gives way to vatic utterance as Fleming feels himself "the growing prophet of a world-reconstruction." Instead of explaining things as they are in the external world, he now speaks from "far down in the pure depths of his being," from "the gloom of his misery." With a quick swing from despair to self-intoxication, he is sure that all men will adhere to his new gospel. Instead of on a pinnacle of wisdom, he now sees himself "a sun-lit figure upon a peak" (at least he is gesturing, not preaching), and instead of his supposed wisdom being undercut by illogicality, his heart-wrung truth is undercut by bombast. But such bombast reaches its nadir only after he recognizes that his dream of freeing all men from false tradition, like his vindicating structure of reason, must collapse. When he recognizes that "he would be beating his fists against the brass of accepted things," he gives way to abuse and railing. When most carried away, however, he still remains egotistical: "To him there was something terrible and awesome in these words spoken from his heart to his heart. He was very tragic." Thus far the draft fragment, but of the surviving leaves from the discarded chapter in the later manuscript, a couple carry us further into Crane's original version—Fleming has reached a stage in which the suffering of the unheeded prophet passes beyond tragic bombast to pure incoherence. He possibly recalls that he was seeking a salve for "the sore badge of his dishonor," for he reuses the word and thus reminds readers of what has caused his perplexities: "For himself, however, he saw no salve, no reconciling opportunities. He was entangled in errors." He rages against "circumstances," bemoans his "martyrdom," fumbles in his "mangled intellect"(!) to find the ultimate cause, which is of course nature. In a perfect expression of disintegrated personality, he wishes his collapse upon the world: "He desired to revenge himself upon the universe. Feeling in his body all spears of pain, he would have capsized, if possible, the world and made chaos." But the trouble is that he has expressed suffering without in any way advancing the plot.

The treatment of tragic passion and moral confusion in this way was simply not Crane's style—quite literally not his style, as a couple of touches in the later manuscript suggest. Revising and embellishing as he rewrote, Crane began the chapter with the original opening sentence, but after stating Fleming's conviction that "his mind had been cast in a unique mold," he went on to elaborate not only the idea but also the image. The more he developed the image, the more he made the passage sound like authentic Crane: "Minds, he said, were not [all *deleted*] made all with one stamp and colored green. . . . The laws of the [wrong *deleted*] world were wrong because through the vain spectacles of their makers, he appeared, with all men, as of [the *deleted*] a common size and of a green color." This witty reference to dollar-bill conformity reminds us of the outside world and of the darts and barbs of public derision which had once been Henry Fleming's great fear, but such wit deflects attention from the boy's introverted thrashing around and from his inability to focus on anything outside himself. Similarly, intellectual agonies do not mix with humor, as another manuscript passage (for which we do not have the draft version) indicates. When the would-be prophet sees that he may not convert the human race, his mind, for a moment like the runaway soldier's, turns to other people: "He saw himself chasing a thought-phantom across the sky before the assembled eyes of mankind. He could say to them that it was an angel whose possession was existence perfected; they would declare it to be a greased pig." It is a literary if not a psychic impossibility that Henry Fleming, after chasing a greased pig on one page, should shake the foundations of the universe on the next.

Although it was not his style, the writing of this chapter gave a peculiarly direct expression of his method. The comment he made on his method of novel-writing suggests that the author represented his balked and floundering character with the help of firsthand knowledge: " 'Then comes a longing for you don't know what; sorrow, too, and heart-hunger.' He mixes it all up. Then he begins to write." The mixed-up quality of the original Chapter XII, which is to say the relative lack of conscious control, invites one to take with less qualification than otherwise Garland's remark that Crane's "mind was more largely subconscious in its workings than that of any man of my acquaintance." [62] But it was the craftsmanly and not the personal subconscious that he was talking about. No doubt there are personal disclosures here: where Fleming rails against the world, Crane can be said to hint a certain resentment of his own. The reference to minds stamped of a size and colored green suggests that money is not his measure, especially when put with Fleming's later comment on those who learned to reconcile themselves with the world and "accept the [cla deleted] stone idols and the greased pigs, when they contemplated the opportunities for plunder." Considering how poor Crane was while he worked on *The Red Badge*—poor enough to go without meals and once, at least, to have gone without shoes—the wonder is that the hints are so slight. More consciously but still not quite in control, he carried his analysis of youthful emotion back to childhood images. When Fleming decides that he will stand out against the "inevitable," he determines "to kick and scratch and bite like a child in the hands of a parent," and the Oedipal pattern of his revolt is emphasized by the superficially bowdlerized revision in the manuscript, "as a stripling in the hands of a murderer." In the manuscript there are more such primal images of the revolt against authority. When Fleming would, if possible, bring chaos back again, his next following thought is of impotence: "Much cruelty lay in the fact that he was [without power *deleted*] a babe." Since he cannot fight, he thinks of hiding:

---

[62] *Roadside Meetings* (New York: Macmillan, 1930), p. 206, quoting at length his own memorial article of 1900, "Stephen Crane: A Soldier of Fortune," *Saturday Evening Post*, CLXXIII (July 28, 1900), 16–17, reprinted in *The Book-Lover*, II (Autumn, 1900), 6–9.

Admitting that he was powerless and at the will of law, he yet planned to escape; menaced by fatality he schemed to avoid it. He thought of various places in the world where he imagined that he would be safe. He remembered [once *deleted*] hiding once in an empty flour-barrel that [had *deleted*] sat in his mother's pantry. His playmates, hunting the [p *deleted*] bandit-chief, had thundered on the barrel with their fierce sticks but he had lain snug and unde- tected. They had searched the house. He now created in thought a secure spot where an all-powerful eye would fail to percieve him; where an all-powerful stick would fail to bruise his life. [MS 102.17– 20; Va. 142.26–35]

This flight of imagination, despite its clinical refinement of de- tail, was wasted effort for Crane since he had already handled the theme of regression far more successfully in the episode of the forest chapel. But not all his efforts in this chapter repeated what had gone before. Of the trial imaginings that carried him forward to the turning point of his main plot, perhaps the most interesting occurred when Fleming concentrated "the hate of his despair" upon nature. For once the fear of shameful exposure, vague and confused, is transformed explicitly into the fear of death, comparatively a healthy emotion in itself and reasonably connected with his experience of nature: "He again saw [the grim *deleted*] her grim [He *deleted*] dogs upon his trail. They were unswerving, merciless and would overtake him at the ap- pointed time. His mind pictured the death of Jim Conklin and in the scene he saw the shadows of his fate." [63] The clue to what he wanted next to do in his narrative was far more explicit than anything else which Crane's groping imagination had touched on. It pointed him away from inner drama and toward conscious- ness fastened to realities, and it may have suggested the incident by which he could pull together the most important motifs of this chapter and keep it from being simply a wasted experiment.

As Crane wrote the next chapter, all the pieces fell into place. The column whose advance Fleming had admired as heroic

---

[63] Across that last sentence, just after the word "scene," Crane put a large question mark (Manuscript, p. 101.32).

comes sweeping back in disarray. As in a fairy story, his wish for a general rout has come true even though he retracted it. Having struggled in his own mind against "forces and fates [th *deleted*] which were swelling down upon him like storms" and against other imaginary "space-filling foes," he now faces, in the words of the draft, an objective foe "coming storm-wise to flood the army." He is still the would-be hero, with an "impulse to make a rallying speech, to sing a battle-hymn," but in this situation his bombast fails him. Instead he inarticulately repeats the words "Why—why—," the same words that had been his inarticulate answer to the tattered man's sensitive probing. When no one will stop to answer him, he clutches the arm of a running soldier, and the frantic runaway, unable to break free, smashes him across the head with his rifle. The spurting blood gives Fleming his wished-for red badge, but it is not merely a badge. The heavy blow tests his will to live. His dreams are now acted out. Struggling with his pain, he is "like a man wrestling with a creature of the air"—only this is no phantom. Half unconscious, he has to try to raise himself from the ground in order not to be trampled. At last he succeeds, twisting himself to his hands and knees and then "like a babe trying to walk" to his feet. Lurching forward with head down and eyes on the ground, he "fought an intense fight with his body. His dulled senses wished him to swoon and he opposed them stubbornly, his mind picturing unknown dangers and mutilations if he fell upon the field. He went forward, Conklin-fashion. He thought of secluded spots where he could fall and be unmolested. To reach [them, *deleted*] one, he strove against the tide of his pain."

With Fleming's arrival at his Conklin-like struggle against death, the pattern is complete. The incident occurs on the last page of the surviving draft, though Crane probably wrote on to the end of the chapter. In rounding off the chapter, Crane had Fleming meet up with a cheerful soldier, talkative and friendly, whose questions help him to identify Fleming's regiment—no answers beyond the first inarticulate "Uh" are presented—and whose chatter supports the injured youth, that is, becomes the total content of his awareness, until he is in sight of his proper campfire. The cheerful soldier leaves without Fleming ever looking up and seeing his face. He appears mysteriously and goes mysteriously. There is a fairy-tale quality to his role, and indeed to Fleming he seemed "to possess a wand of a magic kind. He threaded the mazes of the tangled forest with a strange fortune." He is indeed a wish fulfillment, but the fulfillment is plausible, given the wish. Crane's great task in the narrative was to render events, internal as much as external, which could lead logically to the framing of the wish. Before Fleming could rejoin his unit, Crane had to find out, as it were, whether his character wanted to die more than he wanted to live, and once the image of Jim Conklin came to mind, the question could define itself.

From the groping of the original twelfth chapter, what remained in the eventual twelfth chapter (originally Chapter XIII), included two interesting vestiges. One was a reference back to discarded material. Caught in the swirl of the rout, Fleming "forgot he was engaged in combating the universe. He threw aside his mental pamphlets on the philosophy of the retreated and rules for the guidance of the damned." (In the manuscript Crane made the restoration to an objective world even clearer by adding: "He lost concern for himself.") Again, when Fleming is barely able to lurch and shuffle forward, he engages in interior argument once more, but this time it is specifically on the question of giving up or pressing on to safety: "He often tried to dismiss the question but his body persisted in rebellion and his senses nagged at him like pampered babies." The imagery of authority and rebellion, of adulthood and childishness, has been reversed. Instead of feeling inchoate rebelliousness and regressive longings, which could have made him want to yield to the physical blow and its effect, he fights to live. That means fighting against the forces of confusion, finding the irreducible purpose which, even in an imperfectly organized world, cannot be dispensed with.

In the original Chapter XIII Crane did much more than untangle the snarled materials of Chapter XII. Fleming had wished for a rout and the wish came true, he had wished for a wound and the wish came true, he had wished for a way to rejoin his unit and the wish came true. Events plausible in themselves connected with wishes plausible in themselves, and yet there is something fortuitous in the connection of wishes and fulfillments. Discrete incidents do not fall into a causal relation as that is traditionally conceived. So Fleming's wish to be a hero turns out in the event to be much different—and much less impressive —than anything he had dreamed. He consciously intends to stop the fleeing troops by his eloquence and he ends in fiasco. On the other hand, he does physically stop a soldier. By commonsense moral criteria he deserves no credit for willing what is evidently an accident: an impulse from the flux of inner impulses happens to connect by physiological reflex with a passerby who is part of the outward flux of events. Perhaps the impulse which causes the physical act is linked with the prior wish, but it cannot be demonstrated. When the discrete pieces are put together, they comprise a moral act which should not be undervalued. But should the actor feel anything but a distrust of his merits? The will is not enough to enact the event without the intervention of chance, a term which refers equally to Crane's dynamic psychology and his empiricist sense of the nature of things. In this respect the intervention of chance is comparable to the necessary intervention of grace in a theological view; in secular terms, it teaches the distrust of egotism. This scheme was Crane's great invention for putting together his psychological insights with his moral concerns. He would use it again to the same purpose in some of his best stories: "A Mystery of Heroism" and "Three White Mice" and "The Monster" recapitulate the situation in which an act can be measured only by figuratively watching the legs, not by examining the conscious will. The old-fashioned moral slate and pencil won't do. The experiment announced in the opening chapter of the novel came thus to its logical climax.

Crane had worked out a remarkably original narrative scheme for conveying his vision of the world and man, but he did not count on his readers to grasp his subtleties. "Trust their imaginations?" he was one day to be quoted; "Why, they haven't got any!" [64] No one can miss the fact that Fleming had one other wish fulfilled, the wish that he could invent a tale to take back such as would enable him to escape derision and public shame. The wound he sustained, whatever its possible moral or psychological significance, was not the badge of courage in any military sense. His making it so was a falsehood, and when he got back to his unit he would at the first opportunity turn it into a positive

[64] Williams, "Mr. Crane as a Literary Artist," p. 126.

lie. Readers who want to discern in Fleming a moral redemption must settle for something considerably less. Psychological subtlety is not necessary to a recognition that his merits are less than saving. In Crane's novel the radical imperfection of man was as fundamental as the unpredictable disorder of the world which men experience.

Crane, according to the strongest probability, finished his thirteenth chapter, and instead of going on with the one draft we know, he returned at once to the opening chapter and began the writing of what was to become the basic manuscript of his novel. Since the first page of the draft does not survive, it is the manuscript which lets us know that the novel at this stage of composition was titled *Private Fleming, His Various Battles*. The manuscript, insofar as it involved some revision of the draft, confirmed Crane's essential purpose of sharpening detail as much as he could. Sometimes he added a touch to the objective scene: when Jim Conklin heraldlike brings the rumor of impending battle, a Negro teamster who has been dancing for a crowd of soldiers finds himself suddenly without an audience. Sometimes he added a touch of figurative language, as when Fleming conceives his uniqueness as not being minted and dyed like everyone else's. There were more revisions than usual in the floundering Chapter XII, where he even tried to patch up the anomaly whereby Fleming might obey natural law and thus defy the inevitable: for "it was not his duty to bow to the inevitable" he now wrote that "it was not his duty to bow to the approaching death. Nature did not expect submission." Many of the changes were inconsequential tinkering: at first he copied the draft and compared Jim Conklin, solemnly lurching toward death, to "a priest of some mad religion," but then he toned it down to "a devotee of a mad religion." But retrospective questions about how Crane revised the draft as he went along give way to questions of another sort when the end of the original Chapter XIII is reached. Conceivably there was an earlier draft that Crane could follow for the second half of his novel, but no trace of such a draft exists. The possibility exists that Crane, having taken time away from his novel to work on other things and perhaps to enjoy the Christmas holidays of 1893, resumed by starting a new inscription and thus getting back the momentum of the narrative. But the simplest explanation is that, having resolved the most difficult crux in the telling of his story, he could see his way clear to the end and confidently begin a polished and, he hoped, a final version.

Crane could be confident of writing the rest of his novel straight through because the narrative problems were less demanding. The downward slope toward despair and the disintegration of personality had been so complex that he improvised several psychological schemes to go with Fleming's various grim encounters with the world and himself. For the other side of Fleming's personality, the aggressiveness that would make him act heroically in the eyes of the world, he could use a simpler scheme. Indeed he was so pleased with the possible simplification that he often made it sound as if all his psychological explorations could be summed up as having learned the emotions of *The Red Badge* on the football field. The repeated assertion, if not taken at face value, at least serves to warn the reader that he was practicing an empirical psychology rather than working out doctrinaire notions, usually classified as "Naturalistic," concerning heredity or environment, instinct or culture. He willingly conceded that any or all such causes of behavior might have affected his own thinking, but he emphasized the fact of truthful psychological representation as against the genetic causes of particular conduct. Speaking of *The Red Badge* as a "psychological portrayal of fear," he wrote "I know what the psychologists say, that a fellow can't comprehend a condition that he has never experienced, and I argued that many times with the Professor. Of course, I have never been in a battle, but I believe that I got my sense of the rage of conflict on the football field, or else fighting is a hereditary instinct, and I wrote intuitively; for the Cranes were a family of fighters in the old days, and in the Revolution every member did his duty." The testimony that Crane had given the problem serious thought since his college days makes it clear that more than intuition was involved, but not all of Crane's football references were so serious. He stuck to his great working insight that the psychology of children gives a model of adult sensations without the obscuring overlay of cultural habit, and he told Hamlin Garland, in what Garland recognized as a self-derisive remark, that he owed all his knowledge of war to football: "The psychology is the same. The opposite team is an enemy tribe!" [65] It is impossible to decide whether Crane referred to the American myths of "wild Indians" or to the children's games that gave them popular forms. Probably both, for Crane acted on the belief that popular culture and children's play could disclose truths to the discerning.

Crane tried to move in the direction of simplifying his narrative, and football helped him with a vocabulary of figurative reference. Fleming in an attack fixes his eye on the military objective, a clump of trees in enemy hands, and runs toward it "as toward a goal." Racing to get to the woods before being picked off, "he ducked his head low like a foot-ball player." But Crane's world was too various for him ever to confine himself to one kind of imagery. In Fleming's battle career, coming after his career as a runaway, imagery is ferociously changed. Chickens turn into hell-roosters, and the kitten turns into a wildcat. The essence of the fight seen from within is unchanged, however, from Crane's first treatment of it as rage, frenzy, madness. Nothing less would satisfy the conditions of war, even though there are important degrees of war-madness. In the first of three engagements in which Fleming now takes part, only the thought of the fight, out of all "the chaos of his brain," is in his consciousness; so intent is he in his hate that he goes on firing unaware that the engagement is over. In the second engagement, he is past the stage of blind hate, so that he seems to see everything in minute detail: "Each blade of the green grass was bold and clear." Sensing things so sharply, "his mind took mechanical but firm impressions, so that, afterward, everything was pictured and explained to him, save why he himself was there." Once the given is accepted, men and masses are much alike: "These intent regiments apparently were oblivious of all larger purposes of war and were slugging each other as if at a matched game." In the third engagement, Fleming can see what must be done and renew the charge on command, but the key words "mad," "frenzy," "hatred" recur. If his vision is clear, it enables him now

[65] To John Northern Hilliard, [Oxted, Surrey, 1897], *Letters*, p. 158; *Roadside Meetings*, p. 196.

to see at close quarters how the enemy flag bearer, staggering grotesquely as Jim Conklin had done, as he himself had done, falls and, dying, turns his face to the ground. The tableau is like the end of *Sebastopol,* but the effect is not. Fleming, who has seen "the despair of the lost" in the man's eyes, continues nonetheless to see things sharply to the last detail: "There was much blood upon the grass-blades." Practice disciplines the soldier's vision.

Egotism too is a persistent theme. There is room for modification of character in this respect, and Wilson, the loud young soldier, seems an ideal example of change. When Fleming returns to camp, he finds that his comrade is no longer "continually regarding the proportions of his personal prowess." Transformed by his first experience of battle, Wilson evidently has "climbed a peak of wisdom from which he could perceive himself as a very wee thing." Originally, in a cancelled passage at the end of this chapter (xiv), Crane had Fleming think his way to the realization that he is not unique and that his old pretensions are ridiculous. But no such simple transformation finally does occur for Fleming. Instead, he resorts once more to self-delusion in order to restore his moral strength. Because Wilson in fear of death had left him with a packet of letters, Wilson's weakness made him feel strong. Because he had "performed his mistakes in the dark," he can ignore them himself and assume the right to sound "pompous and veteran-like." When the "air of courage" breeds courage, he regards his conduct in the first engagement after his return as heroic: "Regarding it, he saw that it was fine, wild and, in some ways, easy. He had been a tremendous figure, no doubt. By this struggle, he had over-come obstacles which he had admitted to be mountains. They had fallen like paper peaks and he was now what he called a hero. And he had not been aware of the process. He had slept and, awakening, found himself a knight." Fleming's mountains are mesmeric, and his illusory conquest of them gives him no shift of view. Awake he dreams his chivalric dreams, and when such consciousness fades, it is because he has become absorbed in the intentness of killing.

But something does happen to his ego. Before the second engagement he and Wilson, going to fetch water, overhear the divisional commander talking with an officer of his staff. Their regiment, the 304th, though spoken of scornfully as mule drivers, can best be spared to anticipate the expected enemy charge. The general soberly observes, "I don't believe many of your mule-drivers will get back," and the soldiers hurry back to their unit. They are scared, but though they pass word that they are about to charge, they keep the scary last sentence to themselves. In fact the general's words have had an unpredictable effect on Fleming: "New eyes were given to him. And the most startling thing was to learn suddenly that he was very insignificant." The perspective of modesty, when it occurs, seems inexplicable, and it is ironically similar to the fury of the fight, a "temporary but sublime absence of selfishness." But the irony is itself undercut in the moment of heroism. When Wilson and Fleming together seize the flag from their dying color sergeant, they are rivals of a special kind: "The youth and his friend had a small scuffle over the flag. 'Give it t' me.' 'No—let me keep it.' Each felt satisfied with the other's possession of it but each felt bound to declare by an offer to carry the emblem, his willingness to further risk himself. The youth roughly pushed his friend away."

Even after the third engagement, there is plenty of egotism left in Fleming. At the end of the novel as he reflects upon his deeds, those which he had performed before his comrades' eyes march in memory "in wide purple and gold." He prefers to gild the self that he has presented to the world, and only the unbidden memory of the tattered man casts a shadow on his meditation. When he musters the force to put his sin at a distance, he does not merely free himself for undisturbed complacence. He sees things in a way that makes him now despise "the brass and bombast of his earlier gospels." Even so, residual egotism makes the ending ambiguous. When Crane explained the source of Fleming's hard-won assurance, he wrote, "He had been to touch the great death and found that, after all, it was but the great death." But in the manuscript as first inscribed, he continued the sentence with the phrase, "and was for others." The phrase proved more ambiguous than he wanted. Fleming had to learn to live with the deaths of other people as close in friendship as Jim Conklin, as close in physical proximity as the enemy flag bearer, as close in moral obligation as the tattered soldier. But his strength did not exist in youthful and invidious exultation over his own survival, as the phrase also implied. From his various battles and his various kinds of witness he learned that death could also be for him, and he also came to see that the possibility was not so momentous that he could not learn to live with it.

The musing on events in the last chapter is not the same as philosophizing, though there was also some of that which Crane would later want to cut. The comments which tie off the several themes of the book are reflections on actual events which Fleming can summon to mind with a good deal of accuracy. Neither absorbed in looking inward nor blinded by war madness, he sees. He will make new mistakes and to some extent repeat old ones. Some of the old fatuity seems to be there as he turns from war thoughts to soft thoughts of peace. But if Crane stubbornly insisted that the basic human material remains the same, he also made it clear that Fleming had entered a new psychological phase. Recollection in tranquillity teaches him something about the nature of perception, as he notes on an earlier occasion. After the second engagement—that is, after he has had a glimpse of his insignificance—he has time to look back at the scene of the charge:

> The youth, in this contemplation, was smitten with a large astonishment. He discovered that the distances, as compared with the brilliant measurings of his mind, were trivial and ridiculous. The stolid trees, where much had taken place, seemed incredibly near. The time, too, now that he reflected, he saw to have been short. He wondered at the number of emotions and events that had been crowded into such little spaces. Elfin thoughts must have exaggerated and enlarged everything, he said. [MS 167.17–25; Va. 117.14–22]

When feeling is intense, the trivial is made great, short distances are lengthened, time is expanded. This is the reason why Crane would, rather too deprecatingly, refer to *The Red Badge* as "a mere episode in life, an amplification." [66] At a distance

---

[66] To an editor of *Leslie's Weekly*, n.p., [ca. Nov., 1895], *Letters*, p. 79. In the letter to Hilliard just cited, he used almost the same words: "a mere episode, or rather an amplification" (*Letters*, p. 159).

Fleming's change might seem as simple and decisive as Wilson's. Close to, it is easy to see how the exaggerations of the senses can easily modulate from illusion to gross delusion. The effects which Crane mostly wrote of as changing visual perspectives are of a kind with his psychology, in which the ego may amplify its importance and distort perception accordingly. Both are connected with the sense of time he conveyed in his narrative. The whole novel covers the events of two days, one day's downward action toward despair, the next day's rage gradually brought under harness.

This changeable sense of time accounts for an ambiguity in the last paragraphs of the novel. When Fleming "trudged from the place of blood and wrath," Crane could have been describing the end of the battle or the end of the war. He had used such foreshortening at the end of *Maggie* where, as Matthew Bruccoli has put it, there are "two time-schemes: a literal account of one night; and symbolic compression of Maggie's remaining nights." [67] But Crane was being ambiguous about more than the passage of time. In his first inscription, he took literally the sentence which followed that about touching the great death—"He was a man."—and two paragraphs later, when the army slogs through the mud dispiritedly, we see not the youth but the man —"Yet the man smiled, for he saw that the world was a world for him, though many discovered it to be made of oaths and walking-sticks." With such a conclusion Fleming attains at once manhood and the ability to perceive an objective world. In that world ambiguities disappear; whatever is not verifiable fact is stylish rhetoric which declares the author's and the character's confidence that fact and glistening appearance can be easily distinguished. When Crane revised the manuscript, he corrected himself, remembering that the man who smiled upon reality and could tell it from oaths and walking sticks was still "the youth." And he added a short passage which stretched the time, generalized the experience, and seemed to set Fleming on his way into another world of wishful fantasizing on received ideas: "He had rid himself of the red sickness of battle. The sultry nightmare was in the past. He had been an animal blistered and sweating in the heat and pain of war. He turned now with a

[67] "Maggie's Last Night," *Stephen Crane Newsletter*, II, no. I (Fall, 1967), 10.

lover's thirst, to images of tranquil skies, fresh meadows, cool brooks; an existence of soft and eternal peace." In the changeable world of Crane's fiction, maturation is relative and unstable, and just about as sure as inevitable death is the rule of life by which imperfect man, whatever he does, has to do it again. For readers who want Fleming transformed by his two days' seasoning, his dream of soft and eternal peace seems to undercut everything. For Crane it was only a sign that the mind is as various as the changeable world to which it instinctively turns for moral reinforcement. Finally, between the last revision of the manuscript and the actual going to press, he added yet another sentence: "Over the river a golden ray of sun came through the hosts of leaden rain clouds." The loaded diction suggests how Henry Fleming may have viewed the scene, but this last sentence, set off in a separate paragraph, is not his alone. It is also a report of the changeable weather which is nature's backdrop to the thoughts and deeds that men take to be significant. The sun shines and the clouds glower equally on the dispirited and the hopeful. In the last sentence of the novel as in the first, Crane fused objective narrative and subjective vision.

The subtle and important changes which Crane made in his ending remind us that when he brought the story to its final scene, he had by no means finished his novel. He thought he had, to be sure, since he had all along worried whether his facts were real and put his greatest effort into working out the sequence of incidents and the responses of characters. Having done so much to make his plot come right, he thought he had done all, and he brought his manuscript to the typist. In fact he was about to start a series of revisions which would make his first typescript obsolete before he even got it back. His first revision was precipitated by his hearing that Hamlin Garland was shortly to leave New York.[68] He wanted to show Garland the novel before he went. Although he could not pay for the typing he had laid on, he did get back the first half of his manuscript, leaving the rest, and the typescript, with the typist as security. On this handwritten manuscript he began making revisions which would

[68] The chronology of the handling of the manuscript by Garland and later by McClure and Bacheller is discussed on pp. lxxxiii–lxxxix below.

leave his plot intact in its precise detail and yet essentially change the book. He set about systematically removing the names of Fleming and Wilson and Jim Conklin. In doing so he was acting on one of his earliest artistic decisions, now seen in a new light. Even when he had been studying *Battles and Leaders* every afternoon and writing every evening, he seems never to have thought of naming a battle with a specific locality and date. As to that decision, he later explained that "it was essential that I should make my battle a type and name no names." [69] With characters too he now found that he could best attain general effects by first making sure that his particulars were exactly right. With characters more complicated than the tattered soldier or the cheerful soldier, it may have been useful that he started with names, but it was not easy to change. He did not hit at once on the epithets he was to use instead, *the youth, the loud soldier,* and *the tall soldier.* For a while Conklin, agitated by the rumor of battle, was *the excited soldier*; and Wilson was to be *the loud young soldier* until Crane decided that youth should be the explicit characteristic only of Henry Fleming. But after thirty-eight pages of cutting out names, he thought his principle of revision so clear that he could give the manuscript to Garland without taking more time for pen-and-ink correction.

On Garland's suggestion, he soon added a second principle, radically to cut the use of dialect. Crane took advice from the older writer, as he did from his artist friends, when his own reasoning led him that way. Naturally he tended to agree with the man who had introduced him to literary ideas, and in taking the novel to him, he implied at least a little deference to experience and authority. When he had held his breath and then heard Garland praise the book not simply with the greatest enthusiasm, but with the most serious critical respect, he was even more open to advice. Even so, he did not delete all the passages which his friend X'd out. To a large degree, but not entirely, he followed the counsel summed up in Garland's marginal note: "Don't use this form where it is accented." [70] In his general revision, starting back at page 1, he not only cut names from the narrative (leaving them in direct discourse as verisimilitude required), but also

[69] To John Phillips, Hartwood, Dec. 30, [1895], *Letters*, p. 84.
[70] Manuscript, p. 15.

began restoring the speech of the main characters pretty much to standard usage. He soon recognized, however, that in specifically deleting three characters' names, he had misled Garland and perhaps himself. For a chapter or so his book did seem to be about three characters, as if it were a realistic filiation from *The Three Musketeers* and Kipling's *Soldiers Three*, but he still meant it to be about "Private Fleming, His various battles." The name did not matter but the individual focus did, and so Crane concentrated on purifying the dialect of "the youth" only. On the other hand, he rewrote several chapter endings where less of the troops' homely dialogue served better than more to give the local flavor he wanted. With their casual speech as a kind of realistic verbal background, he could vary his usual high style without losing the predominant cadence and texture of his prose.

Taken together, the preliminary changes before Garland read the manuscript and the overall revision thereafter made Henry Fleming more than ever the center of the book. In the substitution of epithets for names, he came out with the designation which was most typifying and yet he scarcely lost individuality thereby. The taking away of names began with Jim Conklin in the second paragraph of the novel. After the preliminary revision Garland saw him there as "a certain soldier." In the general revision Crane changed that to "a certain tall soldier." Besides giving the epithet some specific content, he caught a biblical cadence that was stylish perhaps, but also portentous. If the epithet is finally somewhat hollow, the reason is that Jim Conklin has less character than Wilson or Fleming; his initial virtue of shirt-washing and vice of excitability have little to do with his main function in the story, which is to die. Wilson, more significantly, is the loud soldier until he is quieted by experience, and then he becomes simply a friend. Fleming, however, is consistently the youth, as Crane saw at the end when he restored the epithet even after Fleming had evidently become a man. Thinking over what might have been a simple question of verbal consistency, Crane penetrated to consistency of character: he had "the youth" not only learn to see the world as it is, but also irrepressibly envision a better one. In rendering his speech, Crane again was more original than he may have realized. Historically the use of standard speech and dialect in the same work has indicated high and low characters, so that in normalizing the speech of *Private* *Fleming* he was invoking deeply rooted conventions concerning class in literature as if on purpose to discard them. Instead of class sanction, individual interest accounts for the youth's emerging from the group of soldiers even as he remains in discourse with them. With respect to both his name and his speech, the youth loses merely adventitious marks of identity. In his individuality, in all his felt involvement with events, he stands forth clearer than before.

With the overall revision that he made in the spring of 1894, Crane once more reached a point where he could think that he had finished his novel. This time he brought his revised manuscript to a publisher, S. S. McClure, and while he may have hoped for an instant response like Garland's, he got instead a runaround that lasted almost six months. After that he brought his manuscript, now rather worn, to Irving Bacheller, who did react just as quickly and positively as Crane could have wished. Bacheller took the novel for his newspaper syndicate even though it was longer than newspapers would use. So Crane found himself preparing copy for a typist once more and making a final revision of his manuscript. McClure's delay may have given him time to conceive of the title he wanted and, beyond that, to become detached enough from his novel so that he could undertake his most difficult cuts, and Bacheller's need for a shorter text may have precipitated the actual cutting. But circumstance alone can hardly explain this last phase of revision, in which Crane purposefully followed through on what he had already done.

Although Garland was to remember Crane's manuscript as being untitled, he seems to have been the victim of his own imaginative sympathy in this as in his memory of the opening sentence of the novel with its thousands of eyes. Perhaps Crane told him, in explaining the deletion of proper names, that he meant to discard a working title that put Private Fleming's name into the most prominent spot in the book. However, it is by no means certain that Crane deleted the original title even when, after Garland's reading, he made his most extensive overall revision. The obvious inference is that he did not yet have a new title to put in its stead, and the inference is supported by

Crane's not mentioning the new title in his correspondence before he inscribed it on his manuscript in the fall.[71] Garland was constructively right. Not until some six months after he had read the manuscript did Crane finally write at the top of page 1: "The Red Badge of Courage. An Episode of the American Civil War. By Stephen Crane."

The heaviest work of Crane's last manuscript revision was his deleting meditative passages at the end of Chapters VII, X, and XIV and the whole of his original Chapter XII. Neither Garland nor, so far as we know, any of Crane's friends ever cast doubt on these passages. Yet they were as wrong as the new emblematic title was right for showing how to generalize in a world of particulars such as Crane presented. The emblem could substitute for Private Fleming's name because it is rooted in his particular experience, both inner and outer. But the meditative passages in which his inner struggles express themselves in grand conceptions of the universe do not, like the new title, have a necessary grounding in situations faced by Private Fleming of the 304th New York Infantry. Yet Crane might never have parted with passages in which he had spent so much of himself if he had not since the early months of 1894 been writing poems which conveyed, far better than his extended indirect discourse monologues, the ironic posturings of man as he sets himself against the arrayed forces of the universe. The succinctness of "I saw a man pursuing the horizon" was far more effective than the protracted metaphysical agonies of Henry Fleming, and Crane knew it. So he made his cuts. But he never entirely conceded that Fleming made philosophizing seem a mental colic which has to be outgrown. He took seriously his ironic perception of *homo cogitans* and loved *The Red Badge* less for its leaving out such matter. Claiming to be fonder of his book of poems *The*

[71] *Roadside Meetings*, p. 196, again confirming his original 1900 piece, "Stephen Crane: A Soldier of Fortune." "Stephen Crane As I Knew Him" (1914, cited above, n. 2), which introduces Garland's recall of the opening sentence, does not repeat his impression that there was no title. His section on Crane in "Roadside Meetings of a Literary Nomad," *The Bookman*, LXX (Jan., 1930), 523–528, is virtually the same as the book version.

As for there being no reference to *The Red Badge* by its proper title before October, 1894, evidence turned up hereafter may well require modification of that statement, but the one anomaly in currently available evidence is only apparent. The letter to John Henry Dick which mentions "the Red Badge" is misdated in *Letters*, p. 30; see p. lxxxviii below and n. 81.

Black Riders, he one day explained: "The reason, perhaps, is that it was a more ambitious effort. My aim was to comprehend in it the thoughts I have had about life in general, while 'The Red Badge' is a mere episode in life, an amplification." [72] At that moment he did not recognize that the allegorical force of the novel comes from its not being about life in general, but in the crucial moment of artistic decision he had known better.

Knowing better had not, of course, been the matter of a moment or of one decision. From his first worry about getting his facts to come real through his last revision of the manuscript and beyond, he had sustained a single purpose. He was determined to show that it took someone's vital response to give meaning to facts and that it took involvement with actual events to give meaning to one's inner life. Simple transcription of outward realities like homely dialogue or of inner thoughts about life in general were equally irrelevant and had to be cut out. On the other hand, ideas when they were rooted in particulars were the great means of clarifying life. This was the point of his substituting for the specificity of *Private Fleming, His Various Battles* the abstract terms of *The Red Badge of Courage: An Episode of the American Civil War*. The new subtitle, though it sounds flat and unassertive, takes the variability of Private Fleming's world to a metaphysical conclusion: events which count for much in a man's life may from another view be mere episodes, implying nothing about a larger scheme of things, and it would be vanity to claim more. As for the new title itself, without Private Fleming's name it still refers to his individual case. Also, even though it is abstract, it has a specificity of its own. It has to be understood both literally and ironically in relation to the details of the book. Its meaning, thus established, did not exist in the book only. The further Crane penetrated into what war might

[72] I saw a man pursuing the horizon;
Round and round they sped.
I was disturbed at this;
I accosted the man.
"It is futile," I said,
"You can never——"

"You lie," he cried,
And ran on.

To an editor of *Leslie's Weekly* (ca. Nov., 1895), *Letters*, p. 79.

feel like, the more he found that its terms served better than any others he knew to convey his moral psychology. Courage and cowardice were good common words for the strength to live and the possible collapse of will. So, describing "An Experiment in Misery," a Bowery tale he wrote in early 1894 as he was finishing *The Red Badge*, he said that he "tried to make plain that the root of Bowery life is a sort of cowardice. Perhaps I mean a lack of ambition or to willingly be knocked flat and accept the licking." One working definition of courage was in a sentence of the cancelled Chapter XII: "He would be saved according to the importance of his strength." [73] But Crane thought that simple assurance of strength was as egotistical and foolish as pride in one's weakness. In the inward war with which he was concerned, egotism set the ultimate condition of the test. In his own youthful experience he was to find that he could endure derision and want easier than success and acclaim, and when he found success more bewildering than hardship, he pledged himself to "make a sincere, desperate, lonely battle to remain true to my conception of my life": "When I speak of a battle I do not mean want, and those similar spectres. I mean myself and the inherent indolence and cowardice which is the lot of all men. I mean, also, applause." [74] The language of battle came naturally when the author of *The Red Badge* described his own encounters with challenges, real and spectral, unpredictably presenting themselves in the flux of experience.

In his final manuscript revision Crane inscribed his title on the top of page 1. The evidence beyond that consists of little more than his bridging page numbers and chapter numbers to cover his cutting of the meditative passages. Thereafter he had a chance to make numerous small corrections in the typescript, and either then or in proof, he added the final sentence which took the last word from the youth's dream of eternal peace and gave it instead to the changing weather which is equally the backdrop of muttering and confidence. But in these last stages he was finishing off a work which largely belonged to his past. Between the first time he thought he had finished *The Red Badge*, when he showed the manuscript to Garland in April 1894,

[73] To Catherine Harris, n.p., [1896], *Letters*, p. 133; MS 99.10–11.
[74] To Nellie Crouse, Hartwood, [Jan. 26, 1896], *Letters*, p. 105.

and its publication on September 27, 1895, he completed, sold, and saw through publication his first book of verse, wrote another New York novel, *George's Mother*, visited the West and Mexico, and plunged into writing sketches and stories at a remarkable rate. Still, his response to success when it came, his resolve to fight the battle with the self, showed how deeply *The Red Badge* had become a part of himself. In the various tests he was still to encounter, natural, social, and psychological, he had some reverses, but on the whole he came through with great distinction. Living as intensely as he did, he compressed an entire career into a span of years which by other measures might encompass a mere episode. At twenty-eight, the age when Hemingway wrote his war novel, Stephen Crane was dead.

Although Crane's artist friends must not be underestimated for the help they offered just by listening and talking, the external history of *The Red Badge of Courage* begins with his taking the manuscript to Garland. In the early months of 1894 (Garland thought March), Crane began calling on the older writer, who lived in a Harlem apartment with his actor brother, for conversation and for some badly needed meals. He also had some of his earliest poems to show—"lines," as he called them—and Garland's critical approval helped keep him writing verse. Evidently Crane stopped coming for a while, for Garland wrote on April 17: "I'd like to know how things are going with you." He also warned that he would be leaving for the West on April 25. Crane answered the next day with a report on himself, including the success of his first publicly read poems and the speed with which his short stories were now coming; he said nothing about a novel.[75] Shortly he turned up for lunch with a bulging pocket. In Garland's account:

"What have you there," I demanded, "more lines?"
"No, it is a tale," he said with that queer, self-derisive smile which was often on his lips at this time.
"Let me see it," I said, knowing well that he had brought it for that purpose.

[75] Garland to Crane, [New York], April 17, 1894, Crane to Garland, New York, [April 18, 1894], *Letters*, p. 35, with conjectural date of editors of *Letters* corrected.

He handed it over to me with seeming reluctance, and while he went out to watch my brother getting lunch I took my first glance at the manuscript of "The Red Badge of Courage," which had, however, no name at this time. The first sentence fairly took me captive. . . .

At the table, while he applied himself with single-hearted joy to my brother's steak, I brooded over his case, and looking across at him, sallow, yellow-fingered, small, and ugly, I was unable to relate him in the slightest degree to the marvelous manuscript which he had placed in my hands. True, his talk was vivid, but it was disjointed and quaint rather than copious or composed.

Upon returning to my little study I said to him very seriously, "Crane, I daren't tell you how much I value this thing—at least not now. But wait! Here's only part of the manuscript. Where's the rest of it?"

Again he grinned, sourly, with a characteristic droop of his head. "In hock."

"To whom?"

"Typewriter."

"How much do you owe him or her?"

"Fifteen dollars."

Plainly this was no joking matter to him, but my brother and I were much amused by his tragic tone. At last I said, "I'll loan you the fifteen dollars if you'll bring me the remainder of the manuscript to-morrow."

"I'll do it," he said as if he were joining me in some heroic enterprise, and away he went in high spirits.

He was as good as his word, and when I had read the entire story I set to work to let my editorial friends know of this youngster.[76]

Besides Garland's mistakes about the title and the opening sentence, he set his story a year earlier than it occurred, he made it sound as if he lent the money on the spot, and he misremembered the nature of his help with publishers. Fifteen dollars was a big enough sum so that the Garland brothers did not have it on hand, but on April 22 he wrote to compliment Crane on "An Experiment in Misery," published that day in the Sunday *Press*, and to say, "If you'll come to the stage door tomorrow night and ask for my brother he will hand you $15. . . . [¶] Don't trouble yourself about the borrowing, we all have to do that some-

[76] *Roadside Meetings*, pp. 196–197.

times. You'll be able to pay it back soon and more too. You're
going to get on your feet mighty soon." Garland, besides being
generous and tactful, gave practical help that should have
turned out better than it did. He evidently sent Crane to S. S.
McClure, even though his introducing Crane to him earlier had
not led to anything. He seems to have hedged the risk by giving
Crane an undated letter to Richard Watson Gilder, also. "Dear
Gilder," he wrote, "I want you to read a *great* M. S. of Stephen
Crane's making. I think him an astonishing fellow. And have
advised him to bring the M. S. to you." Although he could not
have got the second half of the manuscript before April 23 and
he left town on the twenty-fifth, he was seeing to it that he could
serve his friend in absentia. On the Gilder letter is Crane's penciled note: "This is not the MS spoken of. This is a different
one." If Crane used his insurance letter in that way, presumably
Garland had written in the same tone to McClure and Crane had
reason to be hopeful when he left the manuscript with him. Certainly Crane reported his hopes to his friend and sponsor, who
wrote from Chicago on May 8: "What is the state of things? Did
McClures finally take that war story for serial rights? Write me
all the news." On May 9 Crane sent Garland a chatty letter with
all the news, but it did not contain a word about *The Red Badge*
except for the catchall promise: "When anything happens I'll
keep you informed." [77]

One reason Crane sounded sanguine (and it would explain
Garland's not putting a date on his letter, too) was that time had
to be allowed after Garland's reading the manuscript for Crane
to make his painstaking overall revision. After that, he was concerned with putting together his book of poems. In August he
wrote Copeland and Day a letter of inquiry about the latter book,
studiedly casual and with a turn of phrase which suggests that
he might have sent the same letter to McClure about *The Red
Badge*: "Dear Sirs:—I would like to hear from you concerning

---

[77] Garland to Crane, [New York], April 22, 1894. Garland to Gilder, n.p., n.d.,
Letters, pp. 36, 16. Garland's reference to a manuscript, not a book, in his letter
to Gilder rules out *Maggie* as the reference, since Garland saw that only in book
form; besides, it was *The Red Badge* that stirred him from sincere praise to
superlatives. On several grounds, then, the identification and dating of Beer and
of Stallman and Gilkes are invalid. Garland to Crane, Chicago, May 8, 1894,
Crane to Garland, [New York], May 9, 1894, *Letters*, pp. 36–37.

my poetry. I wish to have my out-bring all under way by early fall and I have not heard from you in some time. I am in the dark in regard to your intentions." If he hoped for a coordinated "out-bring," he was to be disappointed. But the response from Copeland and Day about *The Black Riders* kept him busy till the end of October when he sent in copy of his title poem and began what was to be a long wait till publication. During his work on the poetry he developed an editorial toughness and a way of thinking about his book as a whole. In September he wrote the publisher in strong terms: "It seems to me that you cut all the ethical sense out of the book. All the anarchy, perhaps. It is the anarchy which I particularly insist upon. . . . There are some which I believe unworthy of print. These I herewith enclose. As for the others, I cannot give them up—in the book." [78]

With such talk he strengthened himself to wrest his manuscript from the dilatory McClure. This he did some time in October, 1894. His involvement with McClure, about which he was sanguine in May, ended in bitterness. McClure made himself known for hard business practice, though Crane would have to learn the lesson several times in the next few years. On this occasion he held and held a manuscript which he did not want to buy, yet thought he might want to use at a later time. In effect he took an option without paying for it. This was perhaps his most notorious cruelty in his publishing career. His keeping the manuscript almost six months (Crane in his bitterness later stretched it to eight) gave Crane the fallow period which, coinciding with intensive work on *The Black Riders,* helped him see that he should cut the philosophical thrashing-about of Henry Fleming from the novel. But Crane at the time did not count mixed blessings; he knew only that he was angry. Even when he had good news to report, he let Garland know how ill used he had been: "I have just crawled out of the fifty-third ditch into which I have been cast and I now feel that I can write you a letter that wont make you ill. McClure was a Beast about the war-novel and that has been the thing that put me in one of the ditches. He kept it for six months until I was near mad. Oh yes, he was go-

[78] To Copeland and Day, Pike Co., Pennsylvania, [Aug., 1894], and [Hartwood?], Sept. 9, 1894, *Letters*, pp. 39–40.

ing to use it, but—Finally I took it to Bacheller's. They use it in January in a shortened form." [79]

Whether the "shortened form" referred to Crane's own cuts or to Bacheller's plan to syndicate a version of the novel abridged for newspaper readers to a little more than one-third its length cannot be settled for sure. He could have done his cutting before or after Bacheller read the manuscript and accepted it. So too with his deciding on a title: his reporting to Garland about having sold his "war-novel" opens the possibility that Bacheller as well as McClure saw "Private Fleming, | His various battles," but Bacheller himself nowhere hints that he ever knew the book except by its proper title. At any rate things now moved fast. Bacheller, who had just started his newspaper syndicate and needed talented writers to supply him with salable material, knew something of Crane from New York newspaper acquaintances, so that when the young man came to his office and introduced himself, he was well received. In Bacheller's account:

He brought with him a bundle of manuscript. He spoke of it modestly. There was in his words no touch of the hopeful enthusiasm with which I presume he had once regarded it. No doubt it had come back to him from the "satraps" of the great magazines. They had chilled his ardor, if he ever had any, over the immortal thing he had accomplished. This is about what he said:

"Mr. Howells and Hamlin Garland have read this stuff and they think it's good. I wish you'd read it and whether you wish to use the story or not, I'd be glad to have your frank opinion of it."

The manuscript was a bit soiled from much handling. It had not been typed. It was in the clearly legible and rather handsome script

[79] To Garland, New York, Nov. 15, [1894], *Letters*, p. 41. The October date for his taking the manuscript from McClure to Bacheller is roughly established by the contract form which the Bacheller Syndicate printed and sent out as its official announcement of being open for business. Its advertising material listed Crane as one of the firm's authors but did not yet list his (abridged) novel as "on hand" for the October 29 start of syndicate service to subscribing newspapers. Before printing such a contract in October, 1894, Bacheller presumably had read *The Red Badge* and come to an understanding with Crane. The exaggeration of the months McClure held the manuscript came in a letter to an editor of *Leslie's Weekly*, written more than a year after the fact: "A rather interesting fact about the story is that it lay for eight months in a New York magazine office waiting to receive attention. I called on the editor time and again and couldn't find out whether he intended to publish it or not, so at last I took it away" (*Letters*, p. 79).

of the author. I took it home with me that evening. My wife and I
spent more than half the night reading it aloud to each other. We
got far along in the story, thrilled by its power and vividness. In the
morning I sent for Crane and made an arrangement with him to use
about fifty thousand of his magic words as a serial. I had no place
for a story of that length, but I decided to take the chance of putting
it out in instalments far beyond the length of those permitted by my
contracts. It was an experiment based on the hope that my judgment would swing my editors into line. They agreed with me.

So it happened that the vital part of *The Red Badge of Courage*
first went out to the public.[80]

Bacheller's acceptance had an immediate effect on the young
man's morale. Crane wrote to Holmes Bassett: "I have just sold
another book and my friends think it is pretty good and that
some publisher ought to bring it out when it has been shown as
a serial. It is a war-story and the syndicate people think that
several papers could use it." So the conditions in which Crane
made his final revision of the manuscript and prepared it for
typing were tranquil. As late as November 15, when he expected
January publication, he conveyed no sense of rush. But Bacheller
asked to have a typescript to cut up for his abridgment almost
at once. When the call for copy came, Crane had, as usual, no
money with which to pay and sent an S.O.S. to his friend John
Henry Dick: "DEAR DICON: Beg, borrow or steal fifteen dollars.
——like the *Red Badge* and want to make a contract for it. It's
in pawn at the typewriter's for fifteen." The reference to a contract was not quite accurate perhaps, but Bacheller, who was not
in a position to be lavish with money, had presumably agreed to
pay cash on delivery of typescript or even on publication day.
The fact that Bacheller had read a unique manuscript and
needed clean copy to which he could apply the scissors would
explain the stipulation. The letter to Dick was the first occasion
when Crane referred to his novel by its name. By anyone's standards matters moved quickly from this point to the first publication in the Philadelphia *Press* December 3–8, 1894. Shortly
thereafter Bacheller took Crane to Philadelphia to meet Talcott
Williams, editor of the *Press*. "Word flew from cellar to roof,"
Bacheller recollected, "that the great Stephen Crane was in the

[80] *Coming up the Road* (Indianapolis: Bobbs-Merrill, 1928), pp. 277–278.

office. Editors, reporters, compositors, proof-readers crowded around him shaking his hand. It was a revelation of the commanding power of genius." [81]

After such encouragement Crane was ready to try for book publication. The same naïveté that had him bring his novel to newspaper syndicates led him to bring short stories to D. Appleton. Evidently both the handwritten and the typed copies of *The Red Badge* were beyond his reach, perhaps at one of his brothers' houses, when he made up his mind to call. In any case it was his newspaper success that he regarded as the best ground for putting himself forward. Ripley Hitchcock, his editor at Appleton's, tells what happened:

It was in December, 1894, that Mr. Crane came to the editorial office of D. Appleton and Company, bringing two short stories as examples of the work which he was then doing for the newspapers. The impression made by the stories was so strong that Mr. Crane was asked if he had a story long enough for publication in book form. He replied hesitatingly that he had written one rather long story, which was appearing in a Philadelphia newspaper, and "some of the boys in the office seemed to like it." He was asked to send the story at once, and presently there appeared a package of newspaper cuttings containing The Red Badge of Courage, which was promptly accepted for publication. [82]

Promptness once again turned out to be a relative term. On December 18 Crane sent the clippings and a letter to Hitchcock: "This is the war story in it's syndicate form—that is to say, much smaller and to my mind much worse than its original form." Hitchcock saw enough to ask for the complete manuscript, perhaps even making a tentative commitment. But he did not proceed to the next step until Crane had left for the West and Mexico as a feature writer for Bacheller. On January 30, 1895, Crane wrote him from St. Louis: "Any news of the war story will be grateful to me. If you had not read the story, I would wish you

[81] To Holmes Bassett, n.p., n.d. (misdated in Beer, *Crane*, p. 107, and *Letters*), *Letters*, p. 29; to John Henry Dick, n.p., n.d., *Bookman*, xxxv (May, 1912), 235 (conjectural reference and dating corrected from *Letters*, p. 30); *Coming Up the Road*, pp. 278–279.
[82] Preface, 1900 edition, pp. v–vi.

to hear the Philadelphia Press staff speak of it. When I was there some days ago, I was amazed to hear the way in which they talked of it." At just the point of his trip when Crane was feeling lowest—and most broke—a letter from Hitchcock reached him in Lincoln, Nebraska, making a firm offer to publish. Crane replied unhesitatingly: "I would be glad to have Appleton and Co publish the story on those terms. I am going from here to New Orleans. The Mss could be corrected by me there in short order. I shall have to reflect upon the title." [83] The terms and other details of negotiation can be supplied from other documents. The agreement, as ratified in an official contract which Crane signed when he returned to New York in June, was not a good one financially for Crane: no payment specified for time of contract, manuscript delivery, or publication; annual instead of semi-annual accountings, with February (the time of informal agreement) as the month for payment; a minimal royalty of ten per cent, with no provision for step increases to go with larger sales or for sharing proceeds of foreign sales; no payment at all to be made until the cost of manufacture and publication be met.[84] The schedule was clarified when Crane wrote from New Orleans on February 20 that the manuscript could be sent to him in care of Marrion Baker of the *Times-Democrat*. He wrote apologetically, "I know it is a most inconvenient arrangement but as I am extremely anxious to have you bring out the book, I am hoping that the obstacles of the situation will not too much vex you." Hitchcock sent the manuscript by express on February 25, so that if Crane held to his schedule and left New Orleans on March 2, he had only three or four days in which to make corrections in the Appleton typed copy. However, it was not until March 8 that he wrote Hitchcock from Galveston: "I sent the Ms from New Orleans. I made a great number of small corrections. As to the name I am unable to see what to do with it unless the word "Red" is cut out perhaps. That would shorten it." Crane was back in the United States in May and in New York in June, when evidently he saw proofs at about the time he signed the formal contract with Appleton. Copyright was applied for on

[83] To Hitchcock, New York, Dec. 18, 1894, St. Louis, [Jan. 30, 1895], Lincoln, [Feb. 12?, 1895], *Letters*, pp. 46, 49, 51.
[84] *Stephen Crane Newsletter*, II, no. 4 (Summer, 1968), 6–9.

September 27, 1895, and the book came out in October. William Heinemann bought the British rights for £35 and brought the book out in London at the end of November.[85] While Appleton, through Ripley Hitchcock, invited Crane's apologies for being away on newspaper work when they were ready to publish, Heinemann, through his partner Sydney S. Pawling, sent a different message. On December 4, 1895, Pawling wrote to the novelist he had never met:

My dear Sir,

My partner M[r] Heinemann has gone to Paris on business and so I have the pleasure of writing to you. We would like very cordially to express our appreciation of your book "The Red Badge of Courage" which we have purchased for England from Mess[rs] Appleton & C[o] of New York. We think so highly of your work—of its actuality—virility & literary distinction that we have been very pleased to take special pains to place it prominently before the British public. I have sent about one hundred gratis copies to the leading literary men of this country, & have personally seen some of the principal London reviewers. I have called M[r] Sheldon's attention to some of the excellent reviews obtained already—M[r] Sheldon represents Mess[rs] Appleton over here. I hope in the January number of our review "The New Review" to have a special article by the Hon George Wyndham MP on the book. M[r] Wyndham is now secretary to M[r] A. J. Balfour the Leader of our House of Commons, & served as a soldier in Her Majesty's Guards: he has also done very excellent literary work. I think there is no doubt the book will obtain the success it so eminently deserves, & I have thus early made an opportunity to write to you to say how pleased we are to be identified with your work. I hope we shall in the future have the privilege of publishing your books in this country, and if there is any way in which we can be of service to you over here, I beg that you will not hesitate to let us know.[86]

Crane received no money for the British edition (though two years later when Pawling learned this, he saw that an honora-

[85] To Hitchcock, New Orleans, Feb. 20, 1895, Galveston, March 8, 1895, *Letters*, p. 53; D. Appleton & Co. to William Heinemann, [New York], Oct. 23, 1895; receipt for £35 for British and Colonial rights (except Canada), *Stephen Crane Newsletter*, II, no. 4 (Summer, 1968), 9 n.

[86] London, Dec. 4, 1895, ALS, Columbia University Libraries. Crane thought enough of the letter to copy it in his own hand (Dartmouth College Library).

rium of £30 went to Crane at once). Obviously he received much more, a belief in his attainment that helped assure success for his work. Wyndham's "A Remarkable Book" proved to be a remarkable essay, still one of the best critical comments on the novel. It helped set the terms in which *The Red Badge* could be intelligently valued, and it helped swell the applause which in one mood Crane saw as a test of character. After what he had known of hardship, he was afraid of being made giddy by success, but he found a good middle tone when he spoke of the British reviews, Wyndham's in particular, as his "one pride— may it be forgiven me." In the United States there were good reviews too, "an enormous raft" of them, and Appleton and Company wrote Crane "quite a contented letter about the sale of the book." Crane soon found himself asked by editors for information, ideas, and reminiscence. When he obliged in the latter line, he thought of *The Red Badge* as "an effort born of pain —despair, almost," and yet he could feel nostalgic for "the uncertain, happy-go-lucky newspaper writing days" when he "used to dream continually of success." [87] But the responses were too various and extreme to let him be reminiscent for very long. General A. C. McClurg, owner of the Chicago literary magazine *The Dial*, heartily attacked Henry Fleming for being "without a spark of patriotic feeling, or even of soldierly ambition" and Stephen Crane for writing a work of "diseased imagination." On the other hand, one of the book's nearly anonymous critics, Colonel John L. Burleigh, declared to a man who happened to know the author, "I was with Crane at Antietam." [88] The author himself, more susceptible to barbs and derision than to comic effects, found that the best way to hold to his conception of himself was to get on with his work.

J. C. L.

[87] To Hilliard, to Willis Brooks Hawkins, Hartwood, Nov. 1, 1895, to an editor of *Leslie's Weekly*, *Letters*, pp. 158, 66, 78–79. It was to Hawkins that he sent the original manuscript of *The Red Badge* from Hartwood, Jan. 27, 1896 (*Letters*, p. 107).

[88] McClurg, "The Red Badge of Hysteria," in *The Dial*, xx, no. 236 (April 16, 1896), 227; Burleigh quoted in R. W. Stallman, *A Biography*, p. 181.

THE RED BADGE OF COURAGE

CHAPTER I

THE cold passed reluctantly from the earth and the retiring fogs revealed an army stretched out on the hills, resting. As the landscape changed from brown to green the army awakened and began to tremble with eagerness at the noise of rumors. It cast its eyes upon the roads which were growing from long troughs of liquid mud to proper thoroughfares. A river, amber-tinted in the shadow of its banks, purled at the army's feet and at night when the stream had become of a sorrowful blackness one could see, across, the red eye-like gleam of hostile camp-fires set in the low brows of distant hills.

Once, a certain tall soldier developed virtues and went resolutely to wash a shirt. He came flying back from a brook waving his garment, banner-like. He was swelled with a tale he had heard from a reliable friend who had heard it from a truthful cavalryman who had heard it from his trust-worthy brother, one of the orderlies at division head-quarters. He adopted the important air of a herald in red and gold.

"We're goin' t' move t'morrah—sure," he said pompously to a group in the company street. "We're goin' 'way up th' river, cut across, an' come around in behint 'em."

To his attentive audience he drew a loud and elaborate plan of a very brilliant campaign. When he had finished, the blue-clothed men scattered into small arguing groups between the rows of squat brown huts. A negro teamster who had been dancing upon a cracker-box with the hilarious encouragement of two-score soldiers, was deserted. He sat mournfully down. Smoke drifted lazily from a multitude of quaint chimneys.

"It's a lie—that's all it is. A thunderin' lie," said another private loudly. His smooth face was flushed and his hands were thrust sulkily into his trousers' pockets. He took the matter as an affront to him. "I don't believe th' derned ol' army's ever goin' t' move. We're sot. I've got ready t' move eight times in th' last two weeks an' we ain't moved yit."

The tall soldier felt called upon to defend the truth of a rumor he himself had introduced. He and the loud one came near to fighting over it.

A corporal began to swear before the assemblage. He had just put a costly board-floor in his house, he said. During the early spring he had refrained from adding extensively to the comfort of his environment because he had felt that the army might start on the march at any moment. Of late, however, he had been impressed that they were in a sort of eternal camp.

Many of the men engaged in a spirited debate. One out-lined in a peculiarly lucid manner all the plans of the commanding general. He was opposed by men who advocated that there were other plans of campaign. They clamored at each other, numbers making futile bids for the popular attention. Meanwhile, the soldier who had fetched the rumor bustled about with much importance. He was continually assailed by questions.

"What's up, Jim?"

"Th' army's goin' t' move."

"Ah, what yeh talkin' about? How yeh know it is?"

"Well, yeh kin b'lieve me er not—jest as yeh like. I don't care a hang."

There was much food for thought in the manner in which he replied. He came near to convincing them by disdaining to produce proofs. They grew much excited over it.

There was a youthful private who listened with eager ears to the words of the tall soldier and to the varied comments of his comrades. After receiving a fill of discussions concerning marches and attacks, he went to his hut and crawled through an intricate hole that served it as a door. He wished to be alone with some new thoughts that had lately come to him.

He lay down on a wide bunk that stretched across the end of the room. In the other end, cracker-boxes were made to serve as furniture. They were grouped about the fire-place. A picture from an illustrated weekly was upon the log wall and three rifles were paralleled on pegs. Equipments hung on handy projections and some tin dishes lay upon a small pile of fire-wood. A folded tent was serving as a roof. The sun-light, without, beating upon it, made it glow a light yellow shade. A small window shot an oblique square of whiter light upon the cluttered floor. The smoke from the fire at times neglected the clay-chimney and wreathed into the room. And, too, this flimsy chimney of clay and sticks made endless threats to set a-blaze the whole establishment.

The youth was in a little trance of astonishment. So they were at last going to fight. On the morrow perhaps there would be a battle and he would be in it. For a time, he was obliged to labor to make himself believe. He could not accept with assurance an omen that he was about to mingle in one of those great affairs of the earth.

He had of course dreamed of battles all of his life—of vague and bloody conflicts that had thrilled him with their sweep and fire. In visions, he had seen himself in many struggles. He had imagined peoples secure in the shadow of his eagle-eyed prowess. But awake he had regarded battles as crimson blotches on the pages of the past. He had put them as things of the bygone with his thought-images of heavy crowns and high castles. There was a portion of the world's history which he had regarded as the time of wars, but it, he thought, had been long gone over the horizon and had disappeared forever.

From his home his youthful eyes had looked upon the war in his own country with distrust. It must be some sort of a play affair. He had long despaired of witnessing a Greek-like struggle. Such would be no more, he had said. Men were better, or more timid. Secular and religious education had effaced the throat-grappling instinct, or else firm finance held in check the passions.

He had burned several times to enlist. Tales of great movements shook the land. They might not be distinctly Homeric, but there seemed to be much glory in them. He had read of marches, sieges, conflicts, and he had longed to see it all. His busy mind had drawn for him large pictures, extravagant in color, lurid with breathless deeds.

But his mother had discouraged him. She had affected to look with some contempt upon the quality of his war-ardor and patriotism. She could calmly seat herself and with no apparent difficulty give him many hundreds of reasons why he was of vastly more importance on the farm than on the field of battle. She had had certain ways of expression that told that her statements on the subject came from a deep conviction. Besides, on her side, was his belief that her ethical motive in the argument was impregnable.

At last, however, he had made firm rebellion against this yellow light thrown upon the color of his ambitions. The newspapers, the gossip of the village, his own picturings, had aroused him to an uncheckable degree. They were in truth fighting finely down there. Almost every day, the newspapers printed accounts of a decisive victory.

One night, as he lay in bed, the winds had carried to him the clangoring of the church-bell as some enthusiast jerked the rope frantically to tell the twisted news of a great battle. This voice of the people, rejoicing in the night, had made him shiver in a prolonged ecstasy of excitement. Later, he had gone down to his mother's room and had spoken thus: "Ma, I'm going to enlist."

"Henry, don't you be a fool," his mother had replied. She had then covered her face with the quilt. There was an end to the matter for that night.

Nevertheless, the next morning, he had gone to a town that was near his mother's farm and had enlisted in a company that was forming there. When he had returned home, his mother was milking the brindle-cow. Four others stood waiting.

"Ma, I've enlisted," he had said to her diffidently.

There was a short silence. "The Lord's will be done, Henry," she had finally replied and had then continued to milk the brindle-cow.

When he had stood in the door-way with his soldier's clothes on his back and with the light of excitement and expectancy in his eyes almost defeating the glow of regret for the home bonds, he had seen two tears leaving their trails on his mother's scarred cheeks.

Still, she had disappointed him by saying nothing whatever about returning with his shield or on it. He had privately primed himself for a beautiful scene. He had prepared certain sentences which he thought could be used with touching effect. But her words destroyed his plans. She had doggedly peeled potatoes and addressed him as follows: "You watch out, Henry, an' take good care of yerself in this here fighting business—you watch out an' take good care of yerself. Don't go a-thinkin' you can lick the hull rebel army at the start, because yeh can't. Yer jest one little feller amongst a hull lot of others and yeh've got to keep quiet an' do what they tell yeh. I know how you are, Henry.

"I've knet yeh eight pair of socks, Henry, and I've put in all yer best shirts, because I want my boy to be jest as warm and comf'able as anybody in the army. Whenever they git holes in 'em, I want yeh to send 'em right-away back to me, so's I kin dern 'em.

"An' allus be careful an' choose yer comp'ny. There's lots of bad men in the army, Henry. The army makes 'em wild and they like nothing better than the job of leading off a young feller like you—as ain't never been away from home much and has allus had a mother—and a-learning 'im to drink and swear. Keep clear of them folks, Henry. I don't want yeh to ever do anything, Henry, that yeh would be 'shamed to let me know about. Jest think as if I was a-watchin' yeh. If yeh keep that in yer mind allus, I guess yeh'll come out about right.

"Yeh must allus remember yer father, too, child, an' remember he never drunk a drop of licker in his life and seldom swore a cross oath.

"I don't know what else to tell yeh, Henry, excepting that yeh must never do no shirking, child, on my account. If so be a time comes when yeh have to be kilt or do a mean thing, why, Henry, don't think of anything 'cept what's right, because there's many a woman has to bear up 'ginst sech things these times and the Lord'll take care of us all.

"Don't fergit about the socks and the shirts, child, and I've put a cup of blackberry jam with yer bundle because I know yeh like it above all things. Good-bye, Henry. Watch out and be a good boy."

He had of course been impatient under the ordeal of this speech. It had not been quite what he expected and he had borne it with an air of irritation. He departed feeling vague relief.

Still, when he had looked back from the gate, he had seen his mother kneeling among the potato-parings. Her brown face, upraised, was stained with tears and her spare form was quivering. He bowed his head and went on, feeling suddenly ashamed of his purposes.

From his home, he had gone to the seminary to bid adieu to many schoolmates. They had thronged about him with wonder and admiration. He had felt the gulf now between them and had swelled with calm pride. He and some of his fellows who had donned blue were quite over-whelmed with privileges for all of one afternoon and it had been a very delicious thing. They had strutted.

A certain light-haired girl had made vivacious fun at his martial-spirit but there was another and darker girl whom he had gazed at steadfastly and he thought she grew demure and sad at sight of his blue and brass. As he had walked down the path between the rows of oaks, he had turned his head and detected her at a window watching his departure. As he perceived her, she had immediately begun to stare up through the high tree branches at the sky. He had seen a good deal of flurry and haste in her movement as she changed her attitude. He often thought of it.

On the way to Washington, his spirit had soared. The regiment was fed and caressed at station after station until the youth had believed that he must be a hero. There was a lavish expenditure of bread and cold meats, coffee, and pickles and cheese. As he basked in the smiles of the girls and was patted and complimented by the old men, he had felt growing within him the strength to do mighty deeds of arms.

After complicated journeyings with many pauses, there had come months of monotonous life in a camp. He had had the belief that real war was a series of death-struggles with small time in between for sleep and meals but since his regiment had come to the field, the army had done little but sit still and try to keep warm.

He was brought then gradually back to his old ideas. Greek-like struggles would be no more. Men were better, or more timid. Secular and religious education had effaced the throat-grappling instinct or else firm finance held in check the passions.

He had grown to regard himself merely as a part of a vast blue demonstration. His province was to look out, as far as he could, for his personal comfort. For recreation, he could twiddle his thumbs and speculate on the thoughts which must agitate the minds of the generals. Also, he was drilled and drilled and reviewed, and drilled and drilled and reviewed.

The only foes he had seen were some pickets along the river bank. They were a sun-tanned, philosophical lot who sometimes shot reflectively at the blue pickets. When reproached for this, afterwards, they usually expressed sorrow and swore by their gods that the guns had exploded without their permission. The youth on guard duty one night, conversed across the stream with one of them. He was a slightly ragged man who spat skilfully between his shoes and possessed a great fund of bland and infantile assurance. The youth liked him personally.

"Yank," the other had informed him, "yer a right dum good feller." This sentiment, floating to him upon the still air, had made him temporarily regret war.

Various veterans had told him tales. Some talked of grey, bewhiskered hordes who were advancing with relentless curses and chewing tobacco with unspeakable valor; tremendous bodies of fierce soldiery who were sweeping along like the Huns. Others spoke of tattered and eternally-hungry men who fired despondent powder. "They'll charge through hell's-fire an' brimstone t' git a holt on a haversack, an' sech stomachs ain't a-lastin' long," he was told. From the stories, the youth imagined the red, live bones sticking out through slits in the faded uniforms.

Still, he could not put a whole faith in veterans' tales, for recruits were their prey. They talked much of smoke, fire and blood but he could not tell how much might be lies. They persistently yelled "Fresh fish," at him and were in no wise to be trusted.

However, he perceived now that it did not greatly matter what kind of soldiers he was going to fight, so long as they fought, which fact no one disputed. There was a more serious problem. He lay in his bunk pondering upon it. He tried to mathematically prove to himself that he would not run from a battle.

Previously, he had never felt obliged to wrestle too seriously with this question. In his life, he had taken certain things for granted, never challenging his belief in ultimate success and bothering little about means and roads. But here he was confronted with a thing of moment. It had suddenly appeared to him that perhaps in a battle he might run. He was forced to admit that as far as war was concerned he knew nothing of himself.

A sufficient time before, he would have allowed the problem to kick its heels at the outer portals of his mind but, now, he felt compelled to give serious attention to it.

A little panic-fear grew in his mind. As his imagination went forward to a fight, he saw hideous possibilities. He contemplated the lurking menaces of the future and failed in an effort to see himself standing stoutly in the midst of them. He re-called his visions of broken-bladed glory but, in the shadow of the impending tumult, he suspected them to be impossible pictures.

He sprang from the bunk and began to pace nervously to and fro. "Good Lord, what's the matter with me," he said aloud.

He felt that in this crisis his laws of life were useless. Whatever he had learned of himself was here of no avail. He was an unknown quantity. He saw that he would again be obliged to experiment as he had in early youth. He must accumulate information of himself and, meanwhile, he resolved to remain close upon his guard lest those qualities of which he knew nothing should everlastingly disgrace him. "Good Lord," he repeated in dismay.

After a time, the tall soldier slid dexterously through the hole. The loud private followed. They were wrangling.

"That's all right," said the tall soldier as he entered. He waved his hand expressively. "Yeh kin b'lieve me er not—jest as yeh like. All yeh got t' do is t' sit down an' wait as quiet as yeh kin. Then pretty soon yeh'll find out I was right."

His comrade grunted stubbornly. For a moment he seemed to be searching for a formidable reply. Finally he said: "Well, yeh don't know everythin' in th' world, do yeh?"

"Didn't say I knew everythin' in th' world," retorted the other sharply. He began to stow various articles snugly into his knapsack.

The youth, pausing in his nervous walk, looked down at the busy figure. "Going to be a battle, sure, is there, Jim?" he asked.

"Of course there is," replied the tall soldier. "Of course there is. Yeh jest wait 'til t'morrah an' yeh'll see one of th' bigges' battles ever was. Yeh jest wait."

"Thunder," said the youth.

"Oh, yeh'll see fightin' this time, m' boy, what'll be reg'lar out-an'-out fightin'," added the tall soldier with the air of a man who is about to exhibit a battle for the benefit of his friends.

"Huh," said the loud one from a corner.

"Well," remarked the youth, "like as not this story'll turn out just like them others did."

"Not much it won't," replied the tall soldier, exasperated. "Not much it won't. Didn't th' cavalry all start this mornin'?" He glared about him. No one denied his statement. "Th' cavalry started this mornin'," he continued. "They say there ain't hardly any cavalry left in camp. They're goin' t' Richmond or some place while we fight all th' Johnnies. It's some dodge like that. Th' reg'ment's got orders, too. A feller what seen 'em go t' head-quarters told me a little while ago. An' they're raisin' blazes all over camp—anybody kin see that."

"Shucks," said the loud one.

The youth remained silent for a time. At last he spoke to the tall soldier. "Jim!"

"What?"

"How do you think the regiment'll do?"

"Oh, they'll fight all right, I guess, after they onct git inteh it," said the other with cold judgment. He made a fine use of the third person. "There's been heaps 'a fun poked at 'em b'cause they're new, 'a course, an' all that, but they'll fight all right, I guess."

"Think any of the boys'll run?" persisted the youth.

"Oh, there may be a few of 'em run but there's them kind in every reg'ment, 'specially when they first goes under fire," said the other in a tolerant way. " 'A course, it might happen that th' hull kit-an'-boodle might start an' run, if some big fightin' come first-off, an' then ag'in, they might stay an' fight like fun. But yeh can't bet on nothin'. 'A course they ain't never been under fire yit an' it ain't likely they'll lick th' hull rebel army all-t'-onct th' first time, but I think they'll fight better than some, if worser than others. That's th' way I figger. They call th' reg'ment, 'Fresh fish,' an' everythin', but th' boys come 'a good stock an' most 'a 'em'll fight like sin after-they-onct-git-shootin',," he added with a mighty emphasis on the four last words.

"Oh, you think you know——" began the loud soldier with scorn.

The other turned savagely upon him. They had a rapid altercation, in which they fastened upon each other various strange epithets.

The youth at last interrupted them. "Did you ever think you might run yourself, Jim?" he asked. On concluding the sentence he laughed as if he had meant to aim a joke. The loud soldier also giggled.

The tall private waved his hand. "Well," said he profoundly, "I've thought it might git too hot fer Jim Conklin in some 'a them scrimmages an' if a hull lot 'a boys started an' run, why, I s'pose I'd start an' run. An' if I onct started t' run, I'd run like th' devil an' no mistake. But if everybody was a-standin' an' a-fightin', why, I'd stand an' fight. B'jiminy, I would. I'll bet on it."

"Huh," said the loud one.

The youth of this tale felt gratitude for these words of his comrade. He had feared that all of the untried men possessed a great and correct confidence. He now was, in a measure, reassured.

CHAPTER II

THE next morning, the youth discovered that his tall comrade had been the fast-flying messenger of a mistake. There was much scoffing at the latter by those who had yesterday been firm adherents of his views, and there was, even, a little sneering by men who had never believed the rumor. The tall one fought with a man from Chatfield Corners and beat him severely.

The youth felt however that his problem was in no wise lifted from him. There was, on the contrary, an irritating prolongation. The tale had created in him a great concern for himself. Now, with the new-born question in his mind he was compelled to sink back into his old place as part of a blue demonstration.

For days, he made ceaseless calculations, but they were all wondrously unsatisfactory. He found that he could establish nothing. He finally concluded that the only way to prove himself was to go into the blaze and then figuratively to watch his legs to discover their merits and faults. He reluctantly admitted that he could not sit still and, with a mental slate and pencil, derive an answer. To gain it, he must have blaze, blood and danger, even as a chemist requires this, that and the other. So, he fretted for an opportunity.

Meanwhile, he continually tried to measure himself by his comrades. The tall soldier, for one, gave him some assurance. This man's serene unconcern dealt him a measure of confidence for he had known him since childhood and from his intimate knowledge he did not see how he could be capable of anything that was beyond him, the youth. Still, he thought that his comrade might be mistaken about himself. Or, on the other hand, he might be a man heretofore doomed to peace and obscurity but, in reality, made to shine in war.

The youth would have liked to have discovered another who

suspected himself. A sympathetic comparison of mental notes would have been a joy to him.

He occasionally tried to fathom a comrade with seductive sentences. He looked about to find men in the proper moods. All attempts failed to bring forth any statement which looked, in any way, like a confession to those doubts which he privately acknowledged in himself. He was afraid to make an open declaration of his concern because he dreaded to place some unscrupulous confidant upon the high plane of the unconfessed from which elevation he could be derided.

In regard to his companions, his mind wavered between two opinions, according to his mood. Sometimes, he inclined to believing them all heroes. In fact he usually admitted, in secret, the superior developement of the higher qualities in others. He could conceive of men going very insignificantly about the world, bearing a load of courage unseen, and although he had known many of his comrades through boy-hood, he began to fear that his judgment of them had been blind. Then, in other moments, he flouted these theories and assured himself that his fellows were all privately wondering and quaking.

His emotions made him feel strange in the presence of men who talked excitedly of a prospective battle as of a drama they were about to witness, with nothing but eagerness and curiosity apparent in their faces. It was often that he suspected them to be liars.

He did not pass such thoughts without severe condemnation of himself. He dinned reproaches, at times. He was convicted by himself of many shameful crimes against the gods of tradition.

In his great anxiety, his heart was continually clamoring at what he considered to be the intolerable slowness of the generals. They seemed content to perch tranquilly on the riverbank and leave him bowed down by the weight of a great problem. He wanted it settled forthwith. He could not long bear such a load, he said. Sometimes, his anger at the commanders reached an acute stage and he grumbled about the camp like a veteran.

One morning, however, he found himself in the ranks of his prepared regiment. The men were whispering speculations and recounting the old rumors. In the gloom before the break of the day, their uniforms glowed a deep purple hue. From across the river the red eyes were still peering. In the eastern sky, there was a yellow patch like a rug laid for the feet of the coming sun. And against it, black and pattern-like, loomed the gigantic figure of the colonel on a gigantic horse.

From off in the darkness, came the trampling of feet. The youth could occasionally see dark shadows that moved like monsters. The regiment stood at rest for what seemed a long time. The youth grew impatient. It was unendurable, the way these affairs were managed. He wondered how long they were to be kept waiting.

As he looked all about him and pondered upon the mystic gloom, he began to believe that at any moment the ominous distance might be a-flare and the rolling crashes of an engagement come to his ears. Staring, once, at the red eyes across the river, he conceived them to be growing larger, as the orbs of a row of dragons, advancing. He turned toward the colonel and saw him lift his gigantic arm and calmly stroke his moustache.

At last, he heard from along the road at the foot of the hill the clatter of a horse's galloping hoofs. It must be the coming of orders. He bended forward scarce breathing. The exciting clickety-click as it grew louder and louder seemed to be beating upon his soul. Presently, a horseman with jangling equipment, drew rein before the colonel of the regiment. The two held a short, sharp-worded conversation. The men in the foremost ranks craned their necks.

As the horseman wheeled his animal and galloped away, he turned to shout over his shoulder. "Don't forget that box of cigars." The colonel mumbled in reply. The youth wondered what a box of cigars had to do with war.

A moment later the regiment went swinging off into the darkness. It was now like one of those moving monsters wending with many feet. The air was heavy and cold with dew. A mass of wet grass, marched upon, rustled like silk.

There was an occasional flash and glimmer of steel from the backs of all these huge crawling reptiles. From the road, came creakings and grumblings as some surly guns were dragged away.

The men stumbled along still muttering speculations. There was a subdued debate. Once, a man fell down and as he reached for his rifle, a comrade, unseeing, trod upon his hand. He of the injured fingers swore bitterly and aloud. A low, tittering laugh went among his fellows.

Presently, they passed into a road-way and marched forward with easy strides. A dark regiment moved before them, and, from behind, also, came the tinkle of equipments on the bodies of marching men.

The rushing yellow of the developing day went on behind their backs. When the sun-rays at last struck full and mellowingly upon the earth, the youth saw that the landscape was streaked with two long, thin, black columns which disappeared on the brow of a hill in front and rearward vanished in a wood. They were like two serpents crawling from the cavern of the night.

The river was not in view. The tall soldier burst into praises of what he thought to be his powers of perception. "I told yeh so, didn't I?"

"Huh," said the loud soldier.

Some of the tall one's companions cried with emphasis that they too had evolved the same thing and they congratulated themselves upon it. But there were others who said that the tall one's plan was not the true one at all. They persisted with other theories. There was a vigorous discussion.

The youth took no part in them. As he walked along in careless line, he was engaged with his own eternal debate. He could not hinder himself from dwelling upon it. He was despondent and sullen and threw shifting glances about him. He looked ahead often, expecting to hear from the advance the rattle of firing.

But the long serpents crawled slowly from hill to hill without bluster of smoke. A dun-colored cloud of dust floated away to the right. The sky over-head was of a fairy blue.

The youth studied the faces of his companions, ever on the watch to detect kindred emotions. He suffered disappointment. Some ardor of the air which was causing the veteran commands to move with glee, almost with song, had infected the new regiment. The men began to speak of victory as of a thing they knew. Also, the tall soldier received his vindication. They were certainly going to come around in behind the enemy. They expressed commiseration for that part of the army which had been left upon the river-bank, felicitating themselves upon being a part of a blasting host.

The youth, considering himself as separated from the others, was saddened by the blithe and merry speeches that went from rank to rank. The company wags all made their best endeavors. The regiment tramped to the tune of laughter.

The loud soldier often convulsed whole files by his biting sarcasms aimed at the tall one.

And it was not long before all the men seemed to forget their mission. Whole brigades grinned in unison and regiments laughed.

A rather fat soldier attempted to pilfer a horse from a dooryard. He planned to load his knapsack upon it. He was escaping with his prize when a young girl rushed from the house and grabbed the animal's mane. There followed a wrangle. The young girl, with pink cheeks and shining eyes, stood like a dauntless statue.

The observant regiment, standing at rest in the road-way, whooped at once and entered whole-souled upon the side of the maiden. The men became so engrossed in this affair that they entirely ceased to remember their own large war. They jeered the piratical private and called attention to various defects in his personal appearance. And they were wildly enthusiastic in support of the young girl.

To her from some distance came bold advice. "Hit him with a stick."

There were crows and cat-calls showered upon him when he retreated without the horse. The regiment rejoiced at his downfall. Loud and vociferous congratulations were showered upon the maiden who stood panting and regarding the troops with defiance.

At night-fall, the column broke into regimental pieces and the fragments went into the fields to camp. Tents sprang up like strange plants. Camp-fires, like red, peculiar blossoms, dotted the night.

The youth kept from intercourse with his companions as

much as circumstances would allow him. In the evening, he wandered a few paces into the gloom. From this little distance, the many fires with the black forms of men passing to and fro before the crimson rays made weird and satanic effects.

He lay down in the grass. The blades pressed tenderly against his cheek. The moon had been lighted and was hung in a tree-top. The liquid stillness of the night, enveloping him, made him feel vast pity for himself. There was a caress in the soft winds. And the whole mood of the darkness, he thought, was one of sympathy for himself in his distress.

He wished without reserve that he was at home again, making the endless rounds, from the house to the barn, from the barn to the fields, from the fields to the barn, from the barn to the house. He remembered he had often cursed the brindle-cow and her mates, and had sometimes flung milking-stools. But from his present point of view, there was a halo of happiness about each of their heads and he would have sacrificed all the brass buttons on the continent to have been enabled to return to them. He told himself that he was not formed for a soldier. And he mused seriously upon the radical differences between himself and those men who were dodging, imp-like, around the fires.

As he mused thus, he heard the rustle of grass and, upon turning his head, discovered the loud soldier. He called out. "Oh, Wilson."

The latter approached and looked down. "Why, hello, Henry, is it you? What yeh doin' here?"

"Oh—thinking," said the youth.

The other sat down and carefully lighted his pipe. "Yeh're gittin' blue, m' boy. Yeh're lookin' thunderin' peek-ed. What th' dickens is wrong with yeh?"

"Oh—nothing," said the youth.

The loud soldier launched then into the subject of the antic-ipated fight. "Oh, we've got 'em, now." As he spoke his boyish face was wreathed in a gleeful smile and his voice had an exultant ring. "We've got 'em, now. At last by th' eternal thunders, we'll lick 'em good.

"If th' truth was known," he added more soberly, "*they've* licked *us* about every clip up t' now, but this time—this time, we'll lick 'em good."

"I thought you was objecting to this march a little while ago," said the youth coldly.

"Oh, it wasn't that," explained the other. "I don't mind marchin' if there's goin' t' be fightin' at th' end of it. What I hate is this gittin' moved here an' moved there with no good comin' of it, as far as I kin see, exceptin' sore feet an' damn' short rations."

"Well, Jim Conklin says we'll get a-plenty of fighting this time."

"He's right fer once, I guess, 'though I can't see how it come. This time we're in fer a big battle an' we've got th' best end of it certain-sure. Gee-rod, how we will thump 'em."

He arose and began to pace to and fro excitedly. The thrill of his enthusiasm made him walk with an elastic step. He was sprightly, vigorous, fiery in his belief in success. He looked into the future with clear, proud eye. And he swore with the air of an old soldier.

The youth watched him for a moment in silence. When he finally spoke, his voice was as bitter as dregs. "Oh, you're going to do great things, I suppose."

The loud soldier blew a thoughtful cloud of smoke from his pipe. "Oh, I don't know," he remarked with dignity. "I don't know. I s'pose I'll do as well as th' rest. I'm goin' t' try like thunder." He evidently complimented himself upon the modesty of this statement.

"How do you know you won't run when the time comes?" asked the youth.

"Run?" said the loud one. "Run? Of course not." He laughed.

"Well," continued the youth, "lots of good-a-'nough men have thought they was going to do great things before the fight but when the time come, they skedaddled."

"Oh, that's all true, I s'pose," replied the other; "but I'm not goin' t' skedaddle. Th' man that bets on my runnin', will lose his money, that's all." He nodded confidently.

"Oh, shucks," said the youth. "You ain't the bravest man in the world, are you?"

"No, I ain't," exclaimed the loud soldier indignantly. "An' I didn't say I was th' bravest man in th' world, neither. I said I was goin' t' do my share of fightin'—that's what I said. An' I am, too. Who are yeh, anyhow? Yeh talk as if yeh thought yeh was Napolyon Bonypart." He glared at the youth for a moment and then strode away.

The youth called in a savage voice after his comrade. "Well, you needn't get mad about it." But the other continued on his way and made no reply.

He felt alone in space when his injured comrade had disappeared. His failure to discover any mite of resemblance in their view-points made him more miserable than before. No one seemed to be wrestling with such a terrific personal problem. He was a mental out-cast.

He went slowly to his tent and stretched himself on a blanket by the side of the snoring tall soldier. In the darkness, he saw visions of a thousand-tongued fear that would babble at his back and cause him to flee while others were going coolly about their country's business. He admitted that he would not be able to cope with this monster. He felt that every nerve in his body would be an ear to hear the voices, while other men could remain stolid and deaf.

And as he sweated with the pain of these thoughts, he could hear low, serene sentences. "I'll bid five." "Make it six." "Seven." "Seven goes."

He stared at the red, shivering reflection of a fire on the white wall of his tent until exhausted and ill from the monotony of his suffering he fell asleep.

CHAPTER III

WHEN another night came, the columns changed to purple streaks, filed across two pontoon bridges. A glaring fire wine-tinted the waters of the river. Its rays, shining upon the moving masses of troops, brought forth here and there sudden gleams of silver or gold. Upon the other shore, a dark and mysterious range of hills was curved against the sky. The insect-voices of the night sang solemnly.

After this crossing, the youth assured himself that at any moment they might be suddenly and fearfully assaulted from the caves of the lowering woods. He kept his eyes watchfully upon the darkness.

But his regiment went unmolested to a camping-place and its soldiers slept the brave sleep of wearied men. In the morning they were routed out with early energy and hustled along a narrow road that led deep into the forest.

It was during this rapid march that the regiment lost many of the marks of a new command.

The men had begun to count the miles upon their fingers. And they grew tired. "Sore feet an' damned short rations, that's all," said the loud soldier. There was perspiration and grumbling. After a time, they began to shed their knapsacks. Some tossed them unconcernedly down; others hid them carefully, asserting their plans to return for them at some convenient time. Men extricated themselves from thick shirts. Presently, few carried anything but their necessary clothing, blankets, haversacks, canteens, and arms and ammunition. "Yeh kin now eat, drink, sleep an' shoot," said the tall soldier to the youth. "That's all yeh need. What d' yeh want t' do—carry a hotel?"

There was sudden change from the ponderous infantry of theory to the light and speedy infantry of practice. The regiment, relieved of a burden, received a new impetus. But there was much loss of valuable knapsacks and, on the whole, very good shirts.

But the regiment was not yet veteran-like in appearance. Veteran regiments in this army were likely to be very small aggregations of men. Once, when the command had first come to the field, some perambulating veterans, noting the length of their column, had accosted them thus: "Hey, fellers, what brigade is that?" And when the men had replied that they formed a regiment and not a brigade, the older soldiers had laughed and said: "Oh, Gawd!"

Also, there was too great a similarity in the hats. The hats of a regiment should properly represent the history of head-gear for a period of years.

And, moreover, there were no letters of faded gold speaking from the colors. They were new and beautiful, and the color-bearer habitually oiled the pole.

Presently, the army again sat down to think. The odor of the peaceful pines was in the men's nostrils. The sound of monotonous axe-blows rang through the forest and the insects, nodding upon their perches, crooned like old women. The youth returned to his theory of a blue demonstration.

One grey dawn, however, he was kicked in the leg by the tall soldier and then before he was entirely awake, he found himself running down a wood-road in the midst of men who were panting from the first effects of speed. His canteen banged rhythmically upon his thigh and his haversack bobbed softly. His musket bounced a trifle from his shoulder at each stride and made his cap feel uncertain upon his head.

He could hear the men whisper jerky sentences. "Say—what's all this—about?" "What th' thunder—we—skedaddlin' this way fer?" "Billie—keep off m' feet. Yeh run—like a cow." And the loud soldier's shrill voice could be heard: "What th' devil they in sech a hurry fer?"

The youth thought the damp fog of early morning moved from the rush of a great body of troops. From the distance, came a sudden spatter of firing.

He was bewildered. As he ran with his comrades, he strenuously tried to think but all he knew was that if he fell down, those coming behind would tread upon him. All his faculties seemed to be needed to guide him over and past obstructions. He felt carried along by a mob.

The sun spread disclosing rays and, one by one, regiments burst into view like armed men just born of the earth. The youth perceived that the time had come. He was about to be measured. For a moment he felt in the face of his great trial, like a babe. And the flesh over his heart seemed very thin. He seized time to look about him calculatingly.

But he instantly saw that it would be impossible for him to escape from the regiment. It enclosed him. And there were iron laws of tradition and law on four sides. He was in a moving box.

As he perceived this fact, it occurred to him that he had never wished to come to the war. He had not enlisted of his free will. He had been dragged by the merciless government. And now they were taking him out to be slaughtered!

The regiment slid down a bank and wallowed across a little stream. The mournful current moved slowly on and from the water, shaded black, some white bubble-eyes looked at the men.

As they climbed the hill on the further side artillery began to boom. Here the youth forgot many things as he felt a sudden impulse of curiosity. He scrambled up the bank with a speed that could not be exceeded by a blood-thirsty man.

He expected a battle-scene.

There were some little fields girted and squeezed by a forest. Spread over the grass and in among the tree-trunks, he could see knots and waving lines of skirmishers who were running hither and thither and firing at the landscape. A dark battle-line lay upon a sun-struck clearing that gleamed orange-color. A flag fluttered.

Other regiments floundered up the bank. The brigade was formed in line of battle and, after a pause, started slowly through the woods in the rear of the receding skirmishers who were continually melting into the scene to appear again further on. They were always busy as bees, deeply absorbed in their little combats.

The youth tried to observe everything. He did not use care to avoid trees and branches, and his forgotten feet were constantly knocking against stones or getting entangled in briars. He was aware that these battalions, with their commotions, were woven red and startling into the gentle fabric of softened greens and browns. It looked to be a wrong place for a battle-field.

The skirmishers in advance fascinated him. Their shots into thickets and at distant and prominent trees spoke to him of tragedies, hidden, mysterious, solemn.

Once, the line encountered the body of a dead soldier. He lay upon his back staring at the sky. He was dressed in an awkward suit of yellowish brown. The youth could see that the soles of his shoes had been worn to the thinness of writing-paper and from a great rent in one, the dead foot projected piteously. And it was as if fate had betrayed the soldier. In death, it exposed to his enemies that poverty which in life he had perhaps concealed from his friends.

The ranks opened covertly to avoid the corpse. The invulnerable dead man forced a way for himself. The youth looked keenly at the ashen face. The wind raised the tawny beard. It moved as if a hand were stroking it. He vaguely desired to walk around and around the body and stare; the impulse of the living to try to read in dead eyes the answer to the Question.

During this march, the ardor which the youth had acquired when out of view of the field rapidly faded to nothing. His curiosity was quite easily satisfied. If an intense scene had caught him with its wild swing as he came to the top of the bank he might have gone roaring on. This advance upon nature was too calm. He had opportunity to reflect. He had time in which to wonder about himself and to attempt to probe his sensations.

Absurd ideas took hold upon him. He thought that he did not relish the landscape. It threatened him. A coldness swept over his back and it is true that his trousers felt to him that they were no fit for his legs at all.

A house, standing placidly in distant fields, had to him an ominous look. The shadows of the woods were formidable. He was certain that in this vista there lurked fierce-eyed hosts. The swift thought came to him that the generals did not know what they were about. It was all a trap. Suddenly those close forests would bristle with rifle-barrels. Iron-like brigades would appear in the rear. They were all going to be sacrificed. The generals were stupids. The enemy would presently swallow the whole command. He glared about him, expecting to see the stealthy approach of his death.

He thought that he must break from the ranks and harangue his comrades. They must not all be killed like pigs. And he was sure it would come to pass unless they were informed of these dangers. The generals were idiots to send them marching into a regular pen. There was but one pair of eyes in the corps. He would step forth and make a speech. Shrill and passionate words came to his lips.

The line, broken into moving fragments by the ground, went calmly on through fields and woods. The youth looked at the men nearest him and saw, for the most part, expressions of deep interest as if they were investigating something that had fascinated them. One or two stepped with over-valiant airs as if they were already plunged into war. Others walked as upon thin ice. The greater part of the untested men appeared quiet and absorbed. They were going to look at war, the red animal, war, the blood-swollen god. And they were deeply engrossed in this march.

As he looked, the youth gripped his out-cry at his throat. He saw that even if the men were tottering with fear, they would laugh at his warning. They would jeer him and if practicable pelt him with missiles. Admitting that he might be wrong, a frenzied declamation of the kind would turn him into a worm.

He assumed, then, the demeanor of one who knows that he is doomed, alone, to unwritten responsibilities. He lagged, with tragic glances at the sky.

He was surprised, presently, by the young lieutenant of his company who began heartily to beat him with a sword, calling out in a loud and insolent voice. "Come, young man, get up into ranks there. No skulking'll do here." He mended his pace with suitable haste. And he hated the lieutenant, who had no appreciation of fine minds. He was a mere brute.

After a time, the brigade was halted in the cathedral-light of a forest. The busy skirmishers were still popping. Through the aisles of the wood could be seen the floating smoke from their rifles. Sometimes it went up in little balls, white and compact.

During this halt, many men in the regiment began erecting

tiny hills in front of them. They used stones, sticks, earth and anything they thought might turn a bullet. Some built comparatively large ones while others seemed content with little ones.

This procedure caused a discussion among the men. Some wished to fight like duellists, believing it to be correct to stand erect and be, from their feet to their fore-heads, a mark. They said they scorned the devices of the cautious. But the others scoffed in reply and pointed to the veterans on the flanks who were digging at the ground like terriers. In a short time, there was quite a barricade along the regimental front. Directly however they were ordered to withdraw from that place.

This astounded the youth. He forgot his stewing over the advance movement. "Well, then, what did they march us out here for?" he demanded of the tall soldier. The latter with calm faith began a heavy explanation although he had been compelled to leave a little protection of stones and dirt to which he had devoted much care and skill.

When the regiment was aligned in another position, each man's regard for his safety caused another line of small intrenchments. They ate their noon meal behind a third one. They were moved from this one also. They were marched from place to place with apparent aimlessness.

The youth had been taught that a man became another thing in a battle. He saw his salvation in such a change. Hence this waiting was an ordeal to him. He was in a fever of impatience. He considered that there was denoted a lack of purpose on the part of the generals. He began to complain to the tall soldier. "I can't stand this much longer," he cried. "I don't see what good it does to make us wear out our legs for nothing." He wished to return to camp, knowing that this affair was a blue demonstration; or, else, to go into a battle and discover that he had been a fool in his doubts and was in truth a man of traditional courage. The strain of present circumstances he felt to be intolerable.

The philosophical tall soldier measured a sandwich of cracker and pork and swallowed it in a nonchalant manner. "Oh, I s'pose we must go reconnoiterin' around th' kentry jest t' keep 'em from gittin' too clost, or t' develope 'em, or somethin'."

"Huh," said the loud soldier.

"Well," cried the youth, still fidgeting, "I'd rather do anything 'most than go tramping 'round the country all day doing no good to nobody and just tiring ourselves out."

"So would I," said the loud soldier. "It ain't right. I tell yeh if anybody with any sense was a-runnin' this army, it——"

"Oh, shut up," roared the tall private. "Yeh little fool. Yeh little damn'-cuss. Yeh ain't had that there coat an' them pants on fer six months yit an' yit yeh talk as if——"

"Well, I wanta do some fightin' anyway," interrupted the other; "I didn't come here t' walk. I could a' walked t' home, 'round an' 'round th' barn, if I jest wanted t' walk."

The tall one, red-faced, swallowed another sandwich as if taking poison in despair.

But, gradually, as he chewed, his face became again quiet and contented. He could not rage in fierce argument in the presence of such sandwiches. During his meals, he always wore an air of blissful contemplation of the food he had swallowed. His spirit seemed then to be communing with the viands.

He accepted new environment and circumstance with great coolness, eating from his haversack at every opportunity. On the march he went along with the stride of a hunter, objecting to neither gait nor distance. And he had not raised his voice when he had been ordered away from three little protective piles of earth and stone, each of which had been an engineering feat worthy of being made sacred to the name of his grandmother.

In the afternoon, the regiment went out over the same ground it had taken in the morning. The landscape then ceased to threaten the youth. He had been close to it and become familiar with it.

When, however, they began to pass into a new region, his old fears of stupidity and incompetence re-assailed him but this time he doggedly let them babble. He was occupied with his problem and in his desperation he concluded that the stupidity did not greatly matter.

Once he thought he had concluded that it would be better to get killed directly and end his troubles. Regarding death thus out of the corner of his eye, he conceived it to be nothing but rest and he was filled with a momentary astonishment that he should have made an extraordinary commotion over the mere matter of getting killed. He would die; he would go to some place where he would be understood. It was useless to expect appreciation of his profound and fine senses from such men as the lieutenant. He must look to the grave for comprehension.

The skirmish-fire increased to a long clattering sound. With it was mingled faraway cheering. A battery spoke.

Directly, the youth could see the skirmishers running. They were pursued by the sound of musketry fire. After a time, the hot dangerous flashes of the rifles were visible. Smoke-clouds went slowly and insolently across the fields, like observant phantoms. The din became crescendo like the roar of an oncoming train.

A brigade ahead of them and on the right went into action with a rending roar. It was as if it had exploded. And, thereafter, it lay stretched in the distance behind a long grey wall that one was obliged to look twice at to make sure that it was smoke.

The youth, forgetting his neat plan of getting killed, gazed spell-bound. His eyes grew wide and busy with the action of the scene. His mouth was a little ways open.

Of a sudden, he felt a heavy and sad hand laid upon his shoulder. Awakening from his trance of observation, he turned and beheld the loud soldier.

"It's m' first an' last battle, ol' boy," said the latter, with intense gloom. He was quite pale and his girlish lip was trembling.

"Eh?" murmured the youth in great astonishment.

"It's m' first an' last battle, ol' boy," continued the loud soldier. "Somethin' tells me——"

"What?"

"I'm a gone coon this first time an'—an' I w-want yeh t' take these here things—t'—my—folks." He ended in a quavering sob of pity for himself. He handed the youth a little packet done up in a yellow envelope.

"Why, what the devil——" began the youth again.

But the other gave him a glance as from the depths of a tomb, and raised his limp hand in a prophetic manner and turned away.

CHAPTER IV

THE brigade was halted in the fringe of a grove. The men crouched among the trees and pointed their restless guns out at the fields. They tried to look beyond the smoke.

Out of this haze they could see running men. Some shouted information, and gestured, as they hurried.

The men of the new regiment watched and listened eagerly while their tongues ran on in gossip of the battle. They mouthed rumors that had flown like birds out of the unknown.

"They say Perry has been driven in with big loss."

"Yes, Carrott went t' th' hospital. He said he was sick. That smart lieutenant is commanding 'G' Company. Th' boys say they won't be under Carrott no more if they all have t' desert. They allus knew he was a——"

"Hannises' batt'ry is took."

"It ain't either. I saw Hannises' batt'ry off on th' left not more'n fifteen minutes ago."

"Well——"

"Th' general, he ses he is goin' t' take th' hull command of th' 304th when we go inteh action an' then he ses we'll do sech fightin' as never another one reg'ment done."

"They say we're catchin' it over on th' left. They say th' enemy driv' our line inteh a devil of a swamp an' took Hannises' batt'ry."

"No sech thing. Hannises' batt'ry was 'long here 'bout a minute ago."

"That young Hasbrouck, he makes a good off'cer. He ain't afraid 'a nothin'."

"I met one of th' 148th Maine boys an' he ses his brigade fit th' hull rebel army fer four hours over on th' turnpike-road an' killed about five thousand of 'em. He ses one more sech fight as that an' th' war'll be over."

"Bill wasn't scared either. No, sir. It wasn't that. Bill ain't a-gittin' scared easy. He was jest mad, that's what he was. When that feller trod on his hand, he up an' sed that he was willin' t' give his hand t' his country but he be dumbed if he was goin' t' have every dumb bushwhacker in th' kentry walkin' 'round on it. So he went t' th' hospital disregardless of th' fight. Three fingers was crunched. Th' dern doctor wanted t' amputate'm an' Bill, he raised a heluva row, I hear. He's a funny feller."

The din in front swelled to a tremendous chorus. The youth and his fellows were frozen to silence. They could see a flag that tossed in the smoke angrily. Near it were the blurred and agitated forms of troops. There came a turbulent stream of men across the fields. A battery changing position at a frantic gallop scattered the stragglers right and left.

A shell screaming like a storm-banshee went over the huddled heads of the reserves. It landed in the grove and, exploding redly, flung the brown earth. There was a little shower of pine-needles.

Bullets began to whistle among the branches and nip at the trees. Twigs and leaves came sailing down. It was as if a thousand axes, wee and invisible, were being wielded. Many of the men were constantly dodging and ducking their heads.

The lieutenant of the youth's company was shot in the hand. He began to swear so wondrously that a nervous laugh went along the regimental line. The officer's profanity sounded conventional. It relieved the tightened senses of the new men. It was as if he had hit his fingers with a tack-hammer at home.

He held the wounded member carefully away from his side so that the blood would not drip upon his trousers.

The captain of the company, tucking his sword under his arm, produced a handkerchief and began to bind with it the lieutenant's wound. And they disputed as to how the binding should be done.

The battle-flag in the distance jerked about madly. It seemed to be struggling to free itself from an agony. The billowing smoke was filled with horizontal flashes.

Men, running swiftly, emerged from it. They grew in numbers until it was seen that the whole command was fleeing. The flag suddenly sank down as if dying. Its motion as it fell was a gesture of despair.

Wild yells came from behind the walls of smoke. A sketch in

grey and red dissolved into a mob-like body of men who galloped like wild-horses.

The veteran regiments on the right and left of the 304th immediately began to jeer. With the passionate song of the bullets and the banshee shrieks of shells were mingled loud cat-calls and bits of facetious advice concerning places of safety.

But the new regiment was breathless with horror. "Gawd, Saunders's got crushed," whispered the man at the youth's elbow. They shrank back and crouched as if compelled to await a flood.

The youth shot a swift glance along the blue ranks of the regiment. The profiles were motionless, carven. And afterward he remembered that the color sergeant was standing with his legs apart as if he expected to be pushed to the ground.

The bellowing throng went whirling around the flank. Here and there were officers carried along on the stream like exasperated chips. They were striking about them with their swords and, with their left fists, punching every head they could reach. They cursed like highwaymen.

A mounted officer displayed the furious anger of a spoiled child. He raged with his head, his arms and his legs.

Another, the commander of the brigade, was galloping about bawling. His hat was gone and his clothes were awry. He resembled a man who has come from bed to go to a fire. The hoofs of his horse often threatened the heads of the running men, but they scampered with singular fortune. In this rush they were apparently all deaf and blind. They heeded not the largest and longest of the oaths that were thrown at them from all directions.

Frequently over this tumult could be heard the grim jokes of the critical veterans, but the retreating men apparently were not even conscious of the presence of an audience.

The battle reflection that shone for an instant in the faces on the mad current made the youth feel that forceful hands from heaven would not have been able to have held him in place if he could have got intelligent control of his legs.

There was an appalling imprint upon these faces. The struggle in the smoke had pictured an exaggeration of itself on the bleached cheeks and in the eyes wild with one desire.

The sight of this stampede exerted a flood-like force that

seemed able to drag sticks and stones and men from the ground. They of the reserves had to hold on. They grew pale and firm, and red and quaking.

The youth achieved one little thought in the midst of this chaos. The composite monster which had caused the other troops to flee had not then appeared. He resolved to get a view of it and then, he thought he might very likely run better than the best of them.

CHAPTER V

THERE were moments of waiting. The youth thought of the village street at home before the arrival of the circus-parade on a day in the spring. He remembered how he had stood, a small thrillful boy, prepared to follow the dingy lady upon the white horse or the band in its faded chariot. He saw the yellow road, the lines of expectant people, and the sober houses. He particularly remembered an old fellow who used to sit upon a cracker-box in front of the store and feign to despise such exhibitions. A thousand details of color and form surged in his mind. The old fellow upon the cracker-box appeared in middle prominence.

Some one cried: "Here they come!"

There was rustling and muttering among the men. They displayed a feverish desire to have every possible cartridge ready to their hands. The boxes were pulled around into various positions and adjusted with great care. It was as if seven hundred new bonnets were being tried on.

The tall soldier having prepared his rifle, produced a red handkerchief of some kind. He was engaged in knotting it about his throat, with exquisite attention to its position, when the cry was repeated up and down the line in a muffled roar of sound. "Here they come! Here they come!" Gun-locks clicked.

Across the smoke-infested fields came a brown swarm of running men who were giving shrill yells. They came on stooping and swinging their rifles at all angles. A flag tilted forward sped near the front.

As he caught sight of them, the youth was momentarily startled by a thought that perhaps his gun was not loaded. He stood trying to rally his faltering intellect so that he might recollect the moment when he had loaded. But he could not.

A hatless general pulled his dripping horse to a stand near

the colonel of the 304th. He shook his fist in the other's face. "You've got to hold 'em back," he shouted savagely. "You've got to hold 'em back."

In his agitation, the colonel began to stammer. "A-all r-right, general, all right, by Gawd. We-we'll do our—we-we'll d-d-do—do our best, general." The general made a passionate gesture and galloped away. The colonel, perchance to relieve his feelings, began to scold like a wet parrot. The youth turning swiftly to make sure that the rear was unmolested, saw the commander regarding his men in a highly resentful manner as if he regretted, above everything, his association with them.

The man at the youth's elbow was mumbling as if to himself: "Oh, we're in for it, now. Oh, we're in for it now."

The captain of the company had been pacing excitedly to and fro in the rear. He coaxed in school-mistress fashion as to a congregation of boys with primers. His talk was an endless repetition. "Reserve your fire, boys—don't shoot 'til I tell you—save your fire—wait 'til they get close up—don't be damned fools——"

Perspiration streamed down the youth's face which was soiled like that of a weeping urchin. He frequently with a nervous movement wiped his eyes with his coat-sleeve. His mouth was still a little ways open.

He got the one glance at the foe-swarming field in front of him and instantly ceased to debate the question of his piece being loaded. Before he was ready to begin, before he had announced to himself that he was about to fight, he threw the obedient, well-balanced rifle into position and fired a first wild shot. Directly, he was working at his weapon like an automatic affair.

He suddenly lost concern for himself and forgot to look at a menacing fate. He became not a man but a member. He felt that something of which he was a part—a regiment, an army, a cause, or a country—was in a crisis. He was welded into a common personality which was dominated by a single desire. For moments, he could not flee no more than a little finger can commit a revolution from a hand.

If he had thought the regiment about to be annihilated perhaps he could have amputated himself from it. But its noise gave him assurance. The regiment was like a fire-work that, once ignited, proceeds superior to circumstances until its blazing vitality fades. It wheezed and banged with a mighty power. He pictured the ground before it as strewn with the discomfited.

There was a consciousness always of the presence of his comrades about him. He felt the subtle battle-brotherhood more potent even than the cause for which they were fighting. It was a mysterious fraternity, born of the smoke and danger of death.

He was at a task. He was like a carpenter who has made many boxes, making still another box, only there was furious haste in his movements. He, in his thoughts, was careering off in other places, even as the carpenter who as he works, whistles and thinks of his friend or his enemy, his home or a saloon. And these jolted dreams were never perfect to him afterward but remained a mass of blurred shapes.

Presently he began to feel the effects of the war-atmosphere —a blistering sweat, a sensation that his eye-balls were about to crack like hot stones. A burning roar filled his ears.

Following this came a red rage. He developed the acute exasperation of a pestered animal, a well-meaning cow worried by dogs. He had a mad feeling against his rifle which could only be used against one life at a time. He wished to rush forward and strangle with his fingers. He craved a power that would enable him to make a world-sweeping gesture and brush all back. His impotency appeared to him and made his rage into that of a driven beast.

Buried in the smoke of many rifles, his anger was directed not so much against the men whom he knew were rushing toward him, as against the swirling battle-phantoms who were choking him, stuffing their smoke-robes down his parched throat. He fought frantically for respite for his senses, for air, as a babe, being smothered, attacks the deadly blankets.

There was a blare of heated rage, mingled with a certain expression of intentness on all faces. Many of the men were making low-toned noises with their mouths and these subdued cheers, snarls, imprecations, prayers, made a wild, barbaric song that went as an under-current of sound, strange and chant-like, with the resounding chords of the war-march. The man at the youth's elbow was babbling. In it there was something soft and tender, like the monologue of a babe. The tall soldier was swearing in a loud voice. From his lips came a black procession of curious oaths. Of a sudden another broke out in a querulous way like a man who has mislaid his hat. "Well, why don't they support us? Why don't they send supports? Do they think——"

The youth in his battle-sleep, heard this as one who dozes, hears.

There was a singular absence of heroic poses. The men bending and surging in their haste and rage were in every impossible attitude. The steel ram-rods clanked and clanged with incessant din as the men pounded them furiously into the hot rifle-barrels. The flaps of the cartridge-boxes were all unfastened, and bobbed idiotically with each movement. The rifles, once loaded, were jerked to the shoulder and fired without apparent aim into the smoke or at one of the blurred and shifting forms which upon the field before the regiment had been growing larger and larger like puppets under a magician's hand.

The officers, at their intervals, rearward, neglected to stand in picturesque attitudes. They were bobbing to and fro, roaring directions and encouragements. The dimensions of their howls were extraordinary. They expended their lungs with prodigal wills. And often they nearly stood upon their heads in their anxiety to observe the enemy on the other side of the tumbling smoke.

The lieutenant of the youth's company had encountered a soldier who had fled, screaming, at the first volley of his comrades. Behind the lines, these two were acting a little isolated scene. The man was blubbering and staring with sheep-like eyes at the lieutenant who had seized him by the collar and was pummeling him. He drove him back into the ranks with many blows. The soldier went mechanically, dully, with his animal-like eyes upon the officer. Perhaps there was to him a divinity expressed in the voice of the other, stern, hard, with no reflection of fear in it. He tried to re-load his gun but his shaking hands prevented. The lieutenant was obliged to assist him.

The men dropped here and there like bundles. The captain of the youth's company had been killed in an early part of the action. His body lay stretched out in the position of a tired man, resting, but upon his face there was an astonished and sorrowful look as if he thought some friend had done him an ill turn. The babbling man was grazed by a shot that made the blood stream widely down his face. He clapped both hands to his head. "Oh," he said and ran. Another grunted suddenly as if he had been struck by a club in the stomach. He sat down and gazed ruefully. In his eyes there was mute, indefinite reproach. Further up the line a man, standing behind a tree, had had his knee-joint splintered by a ball. Immediately, he had dropped his rifle and gripped the tree with both arms. And there he remained, clinging desperately, and crying for assistance that he might withdraw his hold upon the tree.

At last, an exultant yell went along the quivering line. The firing dwindled from an uproar to a last vindictive popping. As the smoke slowly eddied away, the youth saw that the charge had been repulsed. The enemy were scattered into reluctant groups. He saw a man climb to the top of the fence, straddle the rail and fire a parting shot. The waves had receded, leaving bits of dark debris upon the ground.

Some in the regiment began to whoop frenziedly. Many were silent. Apparently, they were trying to contemplate themselves.

After the fever had left his veins, the youth thought that at last he was going to suffocate. He became aware of the foul atmosphere in which he had been struggling. He was grimy and dripping like a laborer in a foundry. He grasped his canteen and took a long swallow of the warmed water.

A sentence with variations went up and down the line. "Well, we've helt 'em back. We've helt 'em back—derned if we haven't." The men said it blissfully, leering at each other with dirty smiles.

The youth turned to look behind him and off to the right and off to the left. He experienced the joy of a man who at last finds leisure in which to look about him.

Under foot, there were a few ghastly forms, motionless. They lay twisted in fantastic contortions. Arms were bended and heads were turned in incredible ways. It seemed that the dead men must have fallen from some great height to get into such positions. They looked to be dumped out upon the ground from the sky.

From a position in the rear of the grove a battery was throwing shells over it. The flash of the guns startled the youth at first. He thought they were aimed directly at him. Through the trees, he watched the black figures of the gunners as they worked swiftly and intently. Their labor seemed a complicated thing. He wondered how they could remember its formula in the midst of confusion.

The guns squatted in a row like savage chiefs. They argued with abrupt violence. It was a grim pow-wow. Their busy servants ran hither and thither.

A small procession of wounded men were going drearily toward the rear. It was a flow of blood from the torn body of the brigade.

To the right and to the left were the dark lines of other troops. Far in front, he thought he could see lighter masses protruding in points from the forest. They were suggestive of unnumbered thousands.

Once he saw a tiny battery go dashing along the line of the horizon. The tiny riders were beating the tiny horses.

From a sloping hill came the sound of cheerings and clashes. Smoke welled slowly through the leaves.

Batteries were speaking with thunderous oratorical effort. Here and there were flags, the red in the stripes dominating. They splashed bits of warm color upon the dark lines of troops.

The youth felt the old thrill at the sight of the emblems. They were like beautiful birds strangely undaunted in a storm.

As he listened to the din from the hill side, to a deep, pulsating thunder that came from afar to the left, and to the lesser clamors which came from many directions, it occurred to him that they were fighting too, over there and over there and over there. Heretofore, he had supposed that all the battle was directly under his nose.

As he gazed around him, the youth felt a flash of astonishment at the blue, pure sky and the sun-gleamings on the trees and fields. It was surprising that nature had gone tranquilly on with her golden processes in the midst of so much devilment.

CHAPTER VI

THE youth awakened slowly. He came gradually back to a position from which he could regard himself. For moments, he had been scrutinizing his person in a dazed way as if he had never before seen himself. Then he picked up his cap from the ground. He wriggled in his jacket to make a more comfortable fit and, kneeling, re-laced his shoe. He thoughtfully mopped his reeking features.

So it was all over at last. The supreme trial had been passed. The red, formidable difficulties of war had been vanquished.

He went into an ecstasy of self-satisfaction. He had the most delightful sensations of his life. Standing as if apart from himself, he viewed the last scene. He perceived that the man who had fought thus was magnificent.

He felt that he was a fine fellow. He saw himself even with those ideals which he had considered as far beyond him. He smiled in deep gratification.

Upon his fellows, he beamed tenderness and good-will. "Gee, ain't it hot, hey?" he said affably to a man who was polishing his streaming face with his coat-sleeve.

"You bet," said the other, grinning sociably. "I never seen sech dumb hotness." He sprawled out luxuriously on the ground. "Gee, yes! An' I hope we don't have no more fightin' 'til—'til a week from Monday."

There were some hand-shakings and deep speeches with men whose features only were familiar but with whom the youth now felt the bonds of tied hearts. He helped a cursing comrade to bind up a wound of the shin.

But, of a sudden, cries of amazement broke out along the ranks of the new regiment. "Here they come ag'in! Here they come ag'in!" The man who had sprawled upon the ground, started up and said: "Gosh!"

The youth turned quick eyes upon the field. He discerned forms begin to swell in masses out of a distant wood. He again saw the tilted flag, speeding forward.

The shells, which had ceased to trouble the regiment for a time, came swirling again and exploded in the grass or among the leaves of the trees. They looked to be strange war-flowers bursting into fierce bloom.

The men groaned. The lustre faded from their eyes. Their smudged countenances now expressed a profound dejection. They moved their stiffened bodies slowly and watched in sullen mood the frantic approach of the enemy. The slaves toiling in the temple of this god began to feel rebellion at his harsh tasks.

They fretted and complained each to each. "Oh, say, this is too much of a good thing. Why can't somebody send us supports."

"We ain't never goin' t' stand this second bangin'. I didn't come here t' fight th' hull damn' rebel army."

There was one who raised a doleful cry. "I wish Bill Smithers had trod on my hand insteader me treddin' on his'n." The sore joints of the regiment creaked as it painfully floundered into position to repulse.

The youth stared. Surely, he thought, this impossible thing was not about to happen. He waited as if he expected the enemy to suddenly stop, apologize and retire, bowing. It was all a mistake.

But the firing began somewhere on the regimental line and ripped along in both directions. The level sheets of flame developed great clouds of smoke that tumbled and tossed in the mild wind near the ground for a moment and then rolled through the ranks as through a grate. The clouds were tinged an earth-like yellow in the sun-rays and, in the shadow, were a sorry blue. The flag was sometimes eaten and lost in this mass of vapor but more often it projected, sun-touched, resplendent.

Into the youth's eyes there came a look that one can see in the orbs of a jaded horse. His back was quivering with nervous weakness and the muscles of his arms felt numb and bloodless. His hands, too, seemed large and awkward as if he was wearing invisible mittens. And there was a great uncertainty about his knee-joints.

The words that comrades had uttered previous to the firing

began to appear to him. "Oh, say, this is too much of a good thing." "What do they take us fer—why don't they send supports." "I didn't come here t' fight th' hull damn' rebel army."

He began to exaggerate the endurance, the skill, and the valor of those who were coming. Himself reeling from exhaustion, he was astonished beyond measure at such persistency. They must be machines of steel. It was very gloomy, struggling against such affairs, wound up, perhaps, to fight until sun-down.

He slowly lifted his rifle and catching a glimpse of the thick-spread field he blazed at a cantering cluster. He stopped then and began to peer as best he could through the smoke. He caught changing views of the ground covered with men who were all running like pursued imps, and yelling.

To the youth, it was an onslaught of redoubtable dragons. He became like the man who lost his legs at the approach of the red and green monster. He waited in a sort of a horrified, listening attitude. He seemed to shut his eyes and wait to be gobbled.

A man near him who up to this time had been working feverishly at his rifle, suddenly dropped it and ran with howls. A lad whose face had borne an expression of exalted courage, the majesty of he who dares give his life, was, at an instant, smitten abject. He blanched like one who has come to the edge of a cliff at midnight and is suddenly made aware. There was a revelation. He too threw down his gun and fled. There was no shame in his face. He ran like a rabbit.

Others began to scamper away through the smoke. The youth turned his head, shaken from his trance by this movement as if the regiment was leaving him behind. He saw the few fleeting forms.

He yelled then with fright and swung about. For a moment, in the great clamor, he was like a proverbial chicken. He lost the direction of safety. Destruction threatened him from all points.

Directly he began to speed toward the rear in great leaps. His rifle and cap were gone. His unbuttoned coat bulged in the wind. The flap of his cartridge-box bobbed wildly and his canteen, by its slender cord, swung out behind. On his face was all the horror of those things which he imagined.

The lieutenant sprang forward, bawling. The youth saw his

features, wrathfully red, and saw him make a dab with his sword. His one thought of the incident was that the lieutenant was a peculiar creature, to feel interested in such matters upon this occasion.

He ran like a blind man. Two or three times he fell down. Once he knocked his shoulder so heavily against a tree that he went headlong.

Since he had turned his back upon the fight, his fears had been wondrously magnified. Death about to thrust him between the shoulder-blades was far more dreadful than death about to smite him between the eyes. When he thought of it later, he conceived the impression that it is better to view the appalling than to be merely within hearing. The noises of the battle were like stones; he believed himself liable to be crushed.

As he ran on, he mingled with others. He dimly saw men on his right and on his left, and he heard footsteps behind him. He thought that all the regiment was fleeing, pursued by these ominous crashes.

In his flight, the sound of these following footsteps gave him his one meagre relief. He felt vaguely that death must make a first choice of the men who were nearest; the initial morsels for the dragons would be, then, those who were following him. So he displayed the zeal of an insane sprinter in his purpose to keep them in the rear. There was a race.

As he, leading, went across a little field, he found himself in a region of shells. They hurtled over his head with long wild screams. As he heard them, he imagined them to have rows of cruel teeth that grinned at him. Once, one lit before him and the livid lightning of the explosion effectually barred his way in his chosen direction. He grovelled on the ground and then springing up went careering off through some bushes.

He experienced a thrill of amazement when he came within view of a battery in action. The men there seemed to be in conventional moods, altogether unaware of the impending annihilation. The battery was disputing with a distant antagonist and the gunners were wrapped in admiration of their shooting. They were continually bending in coaxing postures over the guns. They seemed to be patting them on the back and encouraging them with words. The guns stolid and undaunted, spoke with dogged valor.

The precise gunners were coolly enthusiastic. They lifted their eyes every chance to the smoke-wreathed hillock from whence the hostile battery addressed them. The youth pitied them as he ran. Methodical idiots! Machine-like fools! The refined joy of planting shells in the midst of the other battery's formation would appear a little thing when the infantry came swooping out of the woods.

The face of a youthful rider who was jerking his frantic horse with an abandon of temper he might display in a placid barnyard was impressed deep upon his mind. He knew that he looked upon a man who would presently be dead.

Too, he felt a pity for the guns, standing, six good comrades, in a bold row.

He saw a brigade going to the relief of its pestered fellows. He scrambled upon a wee hill and watched it sweeping finely, keeping formation in difficult places. The blue of the line was crusted with steel-color and the brilliant flags projected. Officers were shouting.

This sight, also, filled him with wonder. The brigade was hurrying briskly to be gulped into the infernal mouth of the war-god. What manner of men were they, anyhow. Ah, it was some wondrous breed. Or else they didn't comprehend—the fools.

A furious order caused commotion in the artillery. An officer on a bounding horse made maniacal motions with his arms. The teams went swinging up from the rear, the guns were whirled about, and the battery scampered away. The cannon with their noses poked slantingly at the ground grunted and grumbled like stout men, brave but with objections to hurry.

The youth went on, moderating his pace since he had left the place of noises.

Later, he came upon a general of division seated upon a horse that pricked its ears in an interested way at the battle. There was a great gleaming of yellow and patent-leather about the saddle and bridle. The quiet man, astride, looked mouse-colored upon such a splendid charger.

A jingling staff was galloping hither and thither. Sometimes the general was surrounded by horsemen and at other times he was quite alone. He looked to be much harassed. He had the appearance of a business man whose market is swinging up and down.

The youth went slinking around this spot. He went as near as he dared, trying to over-hear words. Perhaps the general, unable to comprehend chaos, might call upon him for information. And he could tell him. He knew all concerning it. Of a surety, the force was in a fix and any fool could see that if they did not retreat while they had opportunity—why——

He felt that he would like to thrash the general, or, at least, approach and tell him in plain words exactly what he thought him to be. It was criminal to stay calmly in one spot and make no effort to stay destruction. He loitered in a fever of eagerness for the division-commander to apply to him.

As he warily moved about, he heard the general call out irritably. "Tompkins, go over an' see Taylor an' tell him not t' be in such an all-fired hurry—tell him t' halt his brigade in th' edge of th' woods—tell him t' detach a reg'ment—say I think th' centre'll break if we don't help it out some—tell him t' hurry up."

A slim youth on a fine chesnut horse caught these swift words from the mouth of his superior. He made his horse bound into a gallop almost from a walk in his haste to go upon his mission. There was a cloud of dust.

A moment later, the youth saw the general bounce excitedly in his saddle.

"Yes—by heavens—they have!" The officer leaned forward. His face was a-flame with excitement. "Yes, by heavens, they've held 'em! They've held 'em!"

He began to blithely roar at his staff. "We'll wallop 'em now. We'll wallop 'em now. We've got 'em sure." He turned suddenly upon an aide. "Here—you—Jones—quick—ride after Tompkins —see Taylor—tell him t' go in—everlastingly—like blazes—anything."

As another officer sped his horse after the first messenger, the general beamed upon the earth like a sun. In his eyes was a desire to chant a paean. He kept repeating: "They've held 'em, by heavens."

His excitement made his horse plunge and he merrily kicked and swore at it. He held a little carnival of joy on horseback.

CHAPTER VII

THE youth cringed as if discovered at a crime. By heavens, they had won after all. The imbecile line had remained and become victors. He could hear cheering.

He lifted himself upon his toes and looked in the direction of the fight. A yellow fog lay wallowing on the tree-tops. From beneath it came the clatter of musketry. Hoarse cries told of an advance.

He turned away, amazed and angry. He felt that he had been wronged.

He had fled, he told himself, because annihilation approached. He had done a good part in saving himself who was a little piece of the army. He had considered the time, he said, to be one in which it was the duty of every little piece to rescue itself if possible. Later, the officers could fit the little pieces together again and make a battle-front. If none of the little pieces were wise enough to save themselves from the flurry of death at such a time, why, then, where would be the army? It was all plain that he had proceeded according to very correct and commendable rules. His actions had been sagacious things. They had been full of strategy. They were the work of a master's legs.

Thoughts of his comrades came to him. The brittle blue line had withstood the blows and won. He grew bitter over it. It seemed that the blind ignorance and stupidity of those little pieces had betrayed him. He had been over-turned and crushed by their lack of sense in holding the position, when intelligent deliberation would have convinced them that it was impossible. He, the enlightened man who looks afar in the dark, had fled because of his superior perceptions and knowledge. He felt a great anger against his comrades. He knew it could be proven that they had been fools.

He wondered what they would remark when later he appeared in camp. His mind heard howls of derision. Their density would not enable them to understand his sharper point of view.

He began to pity himself acutely. He was ill-used. He was trodden beneath the feet of an iron injustice. He had proceeded with wisdom and from the most righteous motives under heaven's blue only to be frustrated by hateful circumstances.

A dull, animal-like rebellion against his fellows, war in the abstract, and fate, grew within him. He shambled along with bowed head, his brain in a tumult of agony and despair. When he looked loweringly up, quivering at each sound, his eyes had the expression of those of a criminal who thinks his guilt little and his punishment great and knows that he can find no words.

He went from the fields into a thick woods as if resolved to bury himself. He wished to get out of hearing of the crackling shots which were to him like voices.

The ground was cluttered with vines and bushes and the trees grew close and spread out like bouquets. He was obliged to force his way with much noise. The creepers, catching against his legs, cried out harshly as their sprays were torn from the barks of trees. The swishing saplings tried to make known his presence to the world. He could not conciliate the forest. As he made his way, it was always calling out protestations. When he separated embraces of trees and vines, the disturbed foliages waved their arms and turned their face-leaves toward him. He dreaded lest these noisy motions, and cries, should bring men to look at him. So, he went far, seeking dark and intricate places.

After a time, the sound of musketry grew faint and the cannon boomed in the distance. The sun, suddenly apparent, blazed among the trees. The insects were making rhythmical noises. They seemed to be grinding their teeth in unison. A wood-pecker stuck his impudent head around the side of a tree. A bird flew on light-hearted wing.

Off, was the rumble of death. It seemed now that nature had no ears.

This landscape gave him assurance. A fair field, holding life. It was the religion of peace. It would die if its timid eyes were compelled to see blood. He conceived nature to be a woman with a deep aversion to tragedy.

He threw a pine-cone at a jovial squirrel and he ran with

chattering fear. High in a tree-top, he stopped and, poking his head cautiously from behind a branch, looked down with an air of trepidation.

The youth felt triumphant at this exhibition. There was the law, he said. Nature had given him a sign. The squirrel immediately upon recognizing a danger, had taken to his legs, without ado. He did not stand stolidly, baring his furry belly to the missile, and die with an upward glance at the sympathetic heavens. On the contrary, he had fled as fast as his legs could carry him. And he was but an ordinary squirrel too; doubtless, no philosopher of his race.

The youth wended, feeling that nature was of his mind. She reinforced his arguments with proofs that lived where the sun shone.

Once he found himself almost into a swamp. He was obliged to walk upon bog-tufts and watch his feet to keep from the oily mire. Pausing at one time to look about him, he saw out at some black water, a small animal pounce in and emerge directly with a gleaming fish.

The youth went again into the deep thickets. The brushed branches made a noise that drowned the sounds of cannon. He walked on, going from obscurity into promises of a greater obscurity.

At length, he reached a place where the high, arching boughs made a chapel. He softly pushed the green doors aside and entered. Pine-needles were a gentle brown carpet. There was a religious half-light.

Near the threshold, he stopped horror-stricken at the sight of a thing.

He was being looked at by a dead man who was seated with his back against a column-like tree. The corpse was dressed in a uniform that once had been blue but was now faded to a melancholy shade of green. The eyes, staring at the youth, had changed to the dull hue to be seen on the side of a dead fish. The mouth was opened. Its red had changed to an appalling yellow. Over the grey skin of the face ran little ants. One was trundling some sort of a bundle along the upper lip.

The youth gave a shriek as he confronted the thing. He was, for moments, turned to stone before it. He remained staring into the liquid-looking eyes. The dead man and the living man exchanged a long look. Then, the youth cautiously put one hand behind him and brought it against a tree. Leaning upon this, he retreated, step by step, with his face still toward the thing. He feared that if he turned his back, the body might spring up and stealthily pursue him.

The branches, pushing against him, threatened to throw him over upon it. His unguided feet, too, caught aggravatingly in brambles. And, with it all, he received a subtle suggestion to touch the corpse. As he thought of his hand upon it, he shuddered profoundly.

At last, he burst the bonds which had fastened him to the spot and fled, unheeding the underbrush. He was pursued by a sight of the black ants swarming greedily upon the grey face and venturing horribly near to the eyes.

After a time, he paused and, breathless and panting, listened. He imagined some strange voice would come from the dead throat and squawk after him in horrible menaces.

The trees about the portal of the chapel moved sighingly in a soft wind. A sad silence was upon the little, guarding edifice.

CHAPTER VIII

THE trees began softly to sing a hymn of twilight. The sun sank until slanted bronze rays struck the forest. There was a lull in the noises of insects as if they had bowed their beaks and were making a devotional pause. There was silence save for the chanted chorus of the trees.

Then, upon this stillness, there suddenly broke a tremendous clangor of sounds. A crimson roar came from the distance.

The youth stopped. He was transfixed by this terrific medley of all noises. It was as if worlds were being rended. There was the ripping sound of musketry and the breaking crash of the artillery.

His mind flew in all directions. He conceived the two armies to be at each other panther-fashion. He listened for a time. Then he began to run in the direction of the battle. He saw that it was an ironical thing for him to be running thus toward that which he had been at such pains to avoid. But he said, in substance, to himself that if the earth and the moon were about to clash, many persons would doubtless plan to get upon roofs to witness the collision.

As he ran, he became aware that the forest had stopped its music, as if at last becoming capable of hearing the foreign sounds. The trees hushed and stood motionless. Everything seemed to be listening to the crackle and clatter and ear-shaking thunder. The chorus pealed over the still earth.

It suddenly occurred to the youth that the fight in which he had been, was, after all, but perfunctory popping. In the hearing of this present din, he was doubtful if he had seen real battle-scenes. This uproar explained a celestial battle; it was tumbling hordes a-struggle in the air.

Reflecting, he saw a sort of a humor in the point of view of himself and his fellows during the late encounter. They had taken themselves and the enemy very seriously and had imagined that they were deciding the war. Individuals must have supposed that they were cutting the letters of their names deep into everlasting tablets of brass or enshrining their reputations forever in the hearts of their countrymen, while, as to fact, the affair would appear in printed reports under a meek and immaterial title. But he saw that it was good, else, he said, in battle everyone would surely run save forlorn hopes and their ilk.

He went rapidly on. He wished to come to the edge of the forest that he might peer out.

As he hastened, there passed through his mind pictures of stupendous conflicts. His accumulated thought upon such subjects was used to form scenes. The noise was as the voice of an eloquent being, describing.

Sometimes, the brambles formed chains and tried to hold him back. Trees, confronting him, stretched out their arms and forbade him to pass. After its previous hostility, this new resistance of the forest filled him with a fine bitterness. It seemed that nature could not be quite ready to kill him.

But he obstinately took roundabout ways and presently he was where he could see long grey walls of vapor, where lay battle-lines. The voices of cannon shook him. The musketry sounded in long irregular surges that played havoc with his ears. He stood, regardant, for a moment. His eyes had an awe-struck expression. He gawked in the direction of the fight.

Presently, he proceeded again on his forward way. The battle was like the grinding of an immense and terrible machine to him. Its complexities and powers, its grim processes, fascinated him. He must go close and see it produce corpses.

He came to a fence and clambered over it. On the far side, the ground was littered with clothes and guns. A newspaper, folded up, lay in the dirt. A dead soldier was stretched with his face hidden in his arm. Further off, there was a group of four or five corpses, keeping mournful company. A hot sun had blazed upon the spot.

In this place, the youth felt that he was an invader. This forgotten part of the battle-ground was owned by the dead men, and he hurried, in the vague apprehension that one of the swollen forms would rise and tell him to begone.

He came finally to a road from which he could see, in the distance, dark and agitated bodies of troops, smoke-fringed. In the lane, was a blood-stained crowd streaming to the rear. The wounded men were cursing, groaning and wailing. In the air, always, was a mighty swell of sound that it seemed could sway the earth. With the courageous words of the artillery and the spiteful sentences of the musketry was mingled red cheers. And from this region of noises came the steady current of the maimed.

One of the wounded men had a shoeful of blood. He hopped like a school-boy in a game. He was laughing hysterically.

One was swearing that he had been shot in the arm, through the commanding general's mismanagement of the army. One was marching with an air imitative of some sublime drum-major. Upon his features was an unholy mixture of merriment and agony. As he marched he sang a bit of doggerel in a high and quavering voice.

> "Sing a song 'a vic'try,
> A pocketful 'a bullets,
> Five an' twenty dead men
> Baked in a—pie."

Parts of the procession limped and staggered to this tune.

Another had the grey seal of death already upon his face. His lips were curled in hard lines and his teeth were clenched. His hands were bloody from where he had pressed them upon his wound. He seemed to be awaiting the moment when he should pitch headlong. He stalked like the spectre of a soldier, his eyes burning with the power of a stare into the unknown.

There were some who proceeded sullenly, full of anger at their wounds and ready to turn upon anything as an obscure cause.

An officer was carried along by two privates. He was peevish. "Don't joggle so, Johnson, yeh fool," he cried. "Think m' leg is made of iron? If yeh can't carry me decent, put me down an' let some one else do it."

He bellowed at the tottering crowd who blocked the quick march of his bearers. "Say, make way there, can't yeh? Make way, dickens take it all."

They sulkily parted and went to the roadsides. As he was carried past, they made pert remarks to him. When he raged in reply and threatened them, they told him to be damned.

The shoulder of one of the tramping bearers knocked heavily against the spectral soldier who was staring into the unknown.

The youth joined this crowd and marched along with it. The torn bodies expressed the awful machinery in which the men had been entangled.

Orderlies and couriers occasionally broke through the throng in the road-way, scattering wounded men right and left, galloping on, followed by howls. The melancholy march was continually disturbed by the messengers and sometimes by bustling batteries that came swinging and thumping down upon them, the officers shouting orders to clear the way.

There was a tattered man, fouled with dust, blood and powder-stain from hair to shoes, who trudged quietly at the youth's side. He was listening with eagerness and much humility to the lurid descriptions of a bearded serjeant. His lean features wore an expression of awe and admiration. He was like a listener in a country-store to wondrous tales told among the sugar-barrels. He eyed the story-teller with unspeakable wonder. His mouth was a-gape in yokel fashion.

The serjeant, taking note of this, gave pause to his elaborate history while he administered a sardonic comment. "Be keerful, honey, you'll be a-ketchin' flies," he said.

The tattered man shrank back, abashed.

After a time, he began to sidle near to the youth and in a diffident way, try to make him a friend. His voice was gentle as a girl's voice and his eyes were pleading. The youth saw with surprise that the soldier had two wounds, one in the head, bound with a blood-soaked rag, and the other in the arm, making that member dangle like a broken bough.

After they had walked together for some time, the tattered man mustered sufficient courage to speak. "Was pretty good fight, wa'n't it?" he timidly said. The youth, deep in thought, glanced up at the bloody and grim figure with its lamb-like eyes. "What?"

"Was pretty good fight, wa'n't it?"

"Yes," said the youth shortly. He quickened his pace.

But the other hobbled industriously after him. There was an air of apology in his manner but he evidently thought that he needed only to talk for a time and the youth would perceive that he was a good fellow.

"Was pretty good fight, wa'n't it?" he began in a small voice. And then he achieved the fortitude to continue. "Dern me if I ever see fellers fight so. Laws, how they did fight. I knowed th' boys'd lick when they onct got square at it. Th' boys ain't had no fair chanct up t' now, but, this time, they showed what they was. I knowed it'd turn out this way. Yeh can't lick them boys. No, sir. They're fighters, they be."

He breathed a deep breath of humble admiration. He had looked at the youth for encouragement several times. He received none, but gradually he seemed to get absorbed in his subject.

"I was talkin' 'cross pickets with a boy from Georgie, onct, an' that boy, he ses: 'Your fellers'll all run like hell when they onct hearn a gun,' he ses. 'Mebbe they will,' I ses, 'but I don't b'lieve none of it,' I ses, 'an' b'jiminy,' I ses back t'um, 'mebbe your fellers'll all run like hell when they onct hearn a gun,' I ses. He larfed. Well, they didn't run t'-day, did they, hey? No, sir. They fit an' fit an' fit."

His homely face was suffused with a light of love for the army which was to him all things beautiful and powerful.

After a time, he turned to the youth. "Where yeh hit, ol' boy?" he asked in a brotherly tone.

The youth felt instant panic at this question although at first its full import was not borne in upon him.

"What?" he asked.

"Where yeh hit?" repeated the tattered man.

"Why," began the youth, "I—I—that is—why—I——"

He turned away suddenly and slid through the crowd. His brow was heavily flushed, and his fingers were picking nervously at one of his buttons. He bended his head and fastened his eyes studiously upon the button as if it were a little problem.

The tattered man looked after him in astonishment.

CHAPTER IX

THE youth fell back in the procession until the tattered soldier was not in sight. Then he started to walk on with others.

But he was amid wounds. The mob of men was bleeding. Because of the tattered soldier's question, he now felt that his shame could be viewed. He was continually casting sidelong glances to see if the men were contemplating the letters of guilt he felt burned into his brow.

At times, he regarded the wounded soldiers in an envious way. He conceived persons with torn bodies to be peculiarly happy. He wished that he, too, had a wound, a red badge of courage.

The spectral soldier was at his side like a stalking reproach. The man's eyes were still fixed in a stare into the unknown. His grey, appalling face had attracted attention in the crowd and men, slowing to his dreary pace, were walking with him. They were discussing his plight, questioning him and giving him advice. In a dogged way, he repelled them, signing to them to go on and leave him alone. The shadows of his face were deepening and his tight lips seemed holding in check the moan of great despair. There could be seen a certain stiffness in the movements of his body as if he were taking infinite care not to arouse the passions of his wounds. As he went on, he seemed always looking for a place, like one who goes to choose a grave.

Something in the gesture of the man as he waved the bloody and pitying soldiers away, made the youth start as if bitten. He yelled in horror. Tottering forward, he laid a quivering hand upon the man's arm. As the latter slowly turned his waxlike features toward him, the youth screamed.

"Gawd! Jim Conklin!"

The tall soldier made a little common-place smile. "Hello, Henry," he said.

The youth swayed on his legs and glared strangely. He stuttered and stammered. "Oh, Jim—oh, Jim—oh, Jim——"

The tall soldier held out his gory hand. There was a curious red and black combination of new blood and old blood upon it. "Where yeh been, Henry?" he asked. He continued in a monotonous voice. "I thought mebbe yeh got keeled over. There's been thunder t' pay t'-day. I was worryin' about it a good deal."

The youth still lamented. "Oh, Jim—oh, Jim—oh, Jim——"

"Yeh know," said the tall soldier, "I was out there." He made a careful gesture. "An', Lord, what a circus. An', b'jiminy, I got shot—I got shot. Yes, b'jiminy, I got shot." He reiterated this fact in a bewildered way as if he did not know how it came about.

The youth put forth anxious arms to assist him but the tall soldier went firmly on as if propelled. Since the youth's arrival as a guardian for his friend, the other wounded men had ceased to display much interest. They occupied themselves again in dragging their tragedies toward the rear.

Suddenly, as the two friends marched on, the tall soldier seemed to be over-come by a terror. His face turned to a semblance of grey paste. He clutched the youth's arm and looked all about him, as if dreading to be over-heard. Then he began to speak in a shaking whisper.

"I tell yeh what I'm 'fraid of, Henry—I'll tell yeh what I'm 'fraid of. I'm 'fraid I'll fall down—an' then yeh know—them damned artillery wagons—they like as not'll run over me. That's what I'm 'fraid of——"

The youth cried out to him hysterically. "I'll take care of you, Jim! I'll take care of you! I swear to Gawd I will."

"Sure—will yeh, Henry?" the tall soldier beseeched.

"Yes—yes—I tell you—I'll take care of you, Jim," protested the youth. He could not speak accurately because of the gulpings in his throat.

But the tall soldier continued to beg in a lowly way. He now hung babe-like to the youth's arm. His eyes rolled in the wildness of his terror. "I was allus a good friend t' yeh, wa'n't I, Henry? I've allus been pretty good feller, ain't I? An' it ain't much t' ask, is it? Jest t' pull me along outer th' road? I'd do it fer you, wouldn't I, Henry?"

He paused in piteous anxiety to await his friend's reply.

The youth had reached an anguish where the sobs scorched him. He strove to express his loyalty but he could only make fantastic gestures.

However, the tall soldier seemed suddenly to forget all those fears. He became again the grim, stalking spectre of a soldier. He went stonily forward. The youth wished his friend to lean upon him but the other always shook his head and strangely protested. "No—no—no—leave me be—leave me be——"

His look was fixed again upon the unknown. He moved with mysterious purpose. And all of the youth's offers he brushed aside. "No—no—leave me be—leave me be——"

The youth had to follow.

Presently, the latter heard a voice talking softly near his shoulder. Turning, he saw that it belonged to the tattered soldier. "Ye'd better take 'im outa th' road, pardner. There's a batt'ry comin' helitywhoop down th' road an' he'll git runned over. He's a goner anyhow in about five minutes—yeh kin see that. Ye'd better take 'im outa th' road. Where th' blazes does he git his stren'th from?"

"Lord knows," cried the youth. He was shaking his hands helplessly.

He ran forward, presently, and grasped the tall soldier by the arm. "Jim! Jim!" he coaxed, "come with me."

The tall soldier weakly tried to wrench himself free. "Huh?" he said vacantly. He stared at the youth for a moment. At last he spoke as if dimly comprehending. "Oh! Inteh th' fields? Oh!"

He started blindly through the grass.

The youth turned once to look at the lashing riders and jouncing guns of the battery. He was startled from this view by a shrill out-cry from the tattered man.

"Gawd! He's runnin'!"

Turning his head swiftly, the youth saw his friend running in a staggering and stumbling way toward a little clump of bushes. His heart seemed to wrench itself almost free from his body at this sight. He made a noise of pain. He and the tattered man began a pursuit. There was a singular race.

When he over-took the tall soldier, he began to plead with all the words he could find. "Jim—Jim—what are you doing—what makes you do this way—you'll hurt yourself."

The same purpose was in the tall soldier's face. He protested in a dulled way, keeping his eyes fastened on the mystic place of his intentions. "No—no—don't tech me—leave me be—leave me be——"

The youth, aghast and filled with wonder at the tall soldier, began quaveringly to question him. "Where you going, Jim? What you thinking about? Where you going? Tell me, won't you, Jim?"

The tall soldier faced about as upon relentless pursuers. In his eyes, there was a great appeal. "Leave me be, can't yeh? Leave me be fer a minnit."

The youth recoiled. "Why, Jim," he said, in a dazed way, "what's the matter with you?"

The tall soldier turned and, lurching dangerously, went on. The youth and the tattered soldier followed, sneaking as if whipped, feeling unable to face the stricken man if he should again confront them. They began to have thoughts of a solemn ceremony. There was something rite-like in these movements of the doomed soldier. And there was a resemblance in him to a devotee of a mad religion, blood-sucking, muscle-wrenching, bone-crushing. They were awed and afraid. They hung back lest he have at command a dreadful weapon.

At last, they saw him stop and stand motionless. Hastening up, they perceived that his face wore an expression telling that he had at last found the place for which he had struggled. His spare figure was erect; his bloody hands were quietly at his sides. He was waiting with patience for something that he had come to meet. He was at the rendezvous. They paused and stood, expectant.

There was a silence.

Finally, the chest of the doomed soldier began to heave with a strained motion. It increased in violence until it was as if an animal was within and was kicking and tumbling furiously to be free.

This spectacle of gradual strangulation made the youth writhe and once as his friend rolled his eyes, he saw something in them that made him sink wailing to the ground. He raised his voice in a last, supreme call.

"Jim—Jim—Jim——"

The tall soldier opened his lips and spoke. He made a gesture. "Leave me be—don't tech me—leave me be——"

There was another silence, while he waited.

Suddenly, his form stiffened and straightened. Then it was shaken by a prolonged ague. He stared into space. To the two watchers, there was a curious and profound dignity in the firm lines of his awful face.

He was invaded by a creeping strangeness that slowly enveloped him. For a moment, the tremor of his legs caused him to dance a sort of hideous horn-pipe. His arms beat wildly about his head in expression of imp-like enthusiasm.

His tall figure stretched itself to its full height. There was a slight rending sound. Then it began to swing forward, slow and straight, in the manner of a falling tree. A swift muscular contortion made the left shoulder strike the ground first.

The body seemed to bounce a little way from the earth. "Gawd," said the tattered soldier.

The youth had watched, spell-bound, this ceremony at the place of meeting. His face had been twisted into an expression of every agony he had imagined for his friend.

He now sprang to his feet and, going closer, gazed upon the paste-like face. The mouth was open and the teeth showed in a laugh.

As the flap of the blue jacket fell away from the body, he could see that the side looked as if it had been chewed by wolves.

The youth turned, with sudden, livid rage, toward the battle-field. He shook his fist. He seemed about to deliver a philippic.

"Hell——"

The red sun was pasted in the sky like a wafer.

CHAPTER X

THE tattered man stood musing.

"Well, he was reg'lar jim-dandy fer nerve, wa'n't he," said he finally in a little awe-struck voice. "A reg'lar jim-dandy." He thoughtfully poked one of the docile hands with his foot. "I wonner where he got 'is stren'th from? I never seen a man do like that before. It was a funny thing. Well, he was a reg'lar jim-dandy."

The youth desired to screech out his grief. He was stabbed. But his tongue lay dead in the tomb of his mouth. He threw himself again upon the ground and began to brood.

The tattered man stood musing.

"Look-a-here, pardner," he said, after a time. He regarded the corpse as he spoke. "He's up an' gone, ain't 'e, an' we might as well begin t' look out fer ol' number one. This here thing is all over. He's up an' gone, ain't 'e? An' he's all right here. Nobody won't bother 'im. An' I must say I ain't enjoyin' any great health m'self these days."

The youth, awakened by the tattered soldier's tone, looked quickly up. He saw that he was swinging uncertainly on his legs and that his face had turned to a shade of blue.

"Good Lord," he cried, "you ain't going to—not you, too."

The tattered man waved his hand. "Nary die," he said. "All I want is some pea-soup an' a good bed. Some pea-soup," he repeated dreamfully.

The youth arose from the ground. "I wonder where he came from. I left him over there." He pointed. "And now I find him here. And he was coming from over there, too." He indicated a new direction. They both turned toward the body as if to ask of it a question.

"Well," at length spoke the tattered man, "there ain't no use in our stayin' here an' tryin' t' ask him anything."

The youth nodded an assent, wearily. They both turned to gaze for a moment at the corpse.

The youth murmured something.

"Well, he was a jim-dandy, wa'n't 'e?" said the tattered man as if in response.

They turned their backs upon it and started away. For a time, they stole softly, treading with their toes. It remained laughing there in the grass.

"I'm commencin' t' feel pretty bad," said the tattered man, suddenly breaking one of his little silences. "I'm commencin' t' feel pretty damn' bad."

The youth groaned. "Oh, Lord!" He wondered if he was to be the tortured witness of another grim encounter.

But his companion waved his hand re-assuringly. "Oh, I'm not goin' t' die yit. There's too much dependin' on me fer me t' die yit. No, sir! Nary die! I *can't*! Ye'd oughta see th' swad 'a chil'ren I've got, an' all like that."

The youth glancing at his companion could see by the shadow of a smile that he was making some kind of fun.

As they plodded on, the tattered soldier continued to talk. "Besides, if I died, I wouldn't die th' way that feller did. That was th' funniest thing. I'd jest flop down, I would. I never seen a feller die th' way that feller did.

"Yeh know, Tom Jamison, he lives next door t' me up home. He's a nice feller, he is, an' we was allus good friends. Smart, too. Smart as a steel trap. Well, when we was a-fightin' this afternoon, all-of-a-sudden he begin t' rip up an' cuss an' beller at me. 'Yer shot, yeh blamed, infernal, tooty-tooty-tooty-too,' (he swear horrible) he ses t' me. I put up m' hand t' m' head an' when I looked at m' fingers, I seen, sure-'nough, I was shot. I give a holler an' begin t' run but b'fore I could git away, another one hit me in th' arm an' whirl' me clean 'round. I got dumb skeared when they was all a-shootin' b'hind me an' I run t' beat all, but I cotch it pretty bad. I've an idee I'd a' been fightin' yit, if t'wa'n't fer Tom Jamison."

Then he made a calm announcement. "There's two of 'em— little ones—but they're beginnin' t' have fun with me now. I don't b'lieve I kin walk much furder."

They went slowly on in silence. "Yeh look pretty peek-ed

yerself," said the tattered man at last. "I bet yeh've gota worser one than yeh think. Ye'd better take keer of yer hurt. It don't do t' let sech things go. It might be inside mostly, an' them plays thunder. Where is it located?" But he continued his harangue without waiting for a reply. "I see a feller git hit plum in th' head when my reg'ment was a-standin' at ease onct. An' everybody yelled out t' 'im: 'Hurt, John? Are yeh hurt much?' 'No,' ses he. He looked kinder surprised an' he went on tellin' 'em how he felt. He sed he didn't feel nothin'. But, by dad, th' first thing that feller knowed he was dead. Yes, he was. Dead—stone dead. So, yeh wanta watch out. Yeh might have some queer kind 'a hurt yerself. Yeh can't never tell. Where is your'n located?"

The youth had been wriggling since the introduction of this topic. He now gave a cry of exasperation and made a furious motion with his hand. "Oh, don't bother me," he said. He was enraged against the tattered man and could have strangled him. His companions seemed ever to play intolerable parts. They were ever up-raising the ghost of shame on the stick of their curiosity. He turned toward the tattered man as one at bay. "Now, don't bother me," he repeated with desperate menace.

"Well, Lord knows I don't wanta bother anybody," said the other. There was a little accent of despair in his voice as he replied. "Lord knows I've gota 'nough m' own t' 'tend to."

The youth, who had been holding a bitter debate with himself and casting glances of hate and contempt at the tattered man, here spoke in a hard voice. "Good-bye," he said.

The tattered man looked at him in gaping amazement. "Why —why, pardner, where yeh goin'," he asked unsteadily. The youth, looking at him, could see that he, too, like that other one, was beginning to act dumb and animal-like. His thoughts seemed to be floundering about in his head. "Now—now—look— a—here you Tom Jamison—now—I won't have this—this here won't do. Where—where yeh goin'?"

The youth pointed vaguely. "Over there," he replied.

"Well, now, look—a—here—now——" said the tattered man, rambling on in idiot-fashion. His head was hanging forward and his words were slurred. "This thing won't do, now, Tom Jamison. It won't do. I know yeh, yeh pig-headed devil. Yeh wanta go trompin' off with a bad hurt. It ain't right—now—Tom Jamison

—it ain't. Yeh wanta leave me take keer of yeh, Tom Jamison. It ain't—right—it ain't—fer yeh t' go—trompin' off—with a bad hurt—it ain't—ain't—ain't right—it ain't."

In reply, the youth climbed a fence and started away. He could hear the tattered man bleating plaintively.

Once, he faced about angrily. "What?"

"Look—a—here, now, Tom Jamison—now—it ain't——"

The youth went on. Turning at a distance he saw the tattered man wandering about helplessly in the fields.

He now thought that he wished he was dead. He believed that he envied those men whose bodies lay strewn over the grass of the fields and on the fallen leaves of the forest.

The simple questions of the tattered man had been knife-thrusts to him. They asserted a society that probes pitilessly at secrets until all is apparent. His late companion's chance persistency made him feel that he could not keep his crime concealed in his bosom. It was sure to be brought plain by one of those arrows which cloud the air and are constantly pricking, discovering, proclaiming those things which are willed to be forever hidden. He admitted that he could not defend himself against this agency. It was not within the power of vigilance.

CHAPTER XI

H E became aware that the furnace-roar of the battle was growing louder. Great brown clouds had floated to the still heights of air before him. The noise, too, was approaching. The woods filtered men and the fields became dotted.

As he rounded a hillock, he perceived that the road-way was now a crying mass of wagons, teams and men. From the heaving tangle issued exhortations, commands, imprecations. Fear was sweeping it all along. The cracking whips bit and horses plunged and tugged. The white-topped wagons strained and stumbled in their exertions like fat sheep.

The youth felt comforted in a measure by this sight. They were all retreating. Perhaps, then, he was not so bad after all. He seated himself and watched the terror-stricken wagons. They fled like soft, ungainly animals. All the roarers and lashers served to help him to magnify the dangers and horrors of the engagement that he might try to prove to himself that the thing with which men could charge him was in truth a symmetrical act. There was an amount of pleasure to him in watching the wild march of this vindication.

Presently, the calm head of a forward-going column of infantry appeared in the road. It came swiftly on. Avoiding the obstructions gave it the sinuous movement of a serpent. The men at the head butted mules with their musket-stocks. They prodded teamsters, indifferent to all howls. The men forced their way through parts of the dense mass by strength. The blunt head of the column pushed. The raving teamsters swore many strange oaths.

The commands to make way had the ring of a great importance in them. The men were going forward to the heart of the din. They were to confront the eager rush of the enemy. They felt the pride of their onward movement when the remainder of the army seemed trying to dribble down this road. They tumbled teams about with a fine feeling that it was no matter so long as their column got to the front in time. This importance made their faces grave and stern. And the backs of the officers were very rigid.

As the youth looked at them, the black weight of his woe returned to him. He felt that he was regarding a procession of chosen beings. The separation was as great to him as if they had marched with weapons of flame and banners of sun-light. He could never be like them. He could have wept in his longings.

He searched about in his mind for an adequate malediction for the indefinite cause, the thing upon which men turn the words of final blame. It—whatever it was—was responsible for him, he said. There lay the fault.

The haste of the column to reach the battle seemed to the forlorn young man to be something much finer than stout fighting. Heroes, he thought, could find excuses in that long seething lane. They could retire with perfect self-respect and make excuses to the stars.

He wondered what those men had eaten that they could be in such haste to force their way to grim chances of death. As he watched his envy grew until he thought that he wished to change lives with one of them. He would have liked to have used a tremendous force, he said, throw off himself and become a better. Swift pictures of himself, apart, yet in himself, came to him—a blue desperate figure leading lurid charges with one knee forward and a broken blade high—a blue, determined figure standing before a crimson and steel assault, getting calmly killed on a high place before the eyes of all. He thought of the magnificent pathos of his dead body.

These thoughts up-lifted him. He felt the quiver of war-desire. In his ears, he heard the ring of victory. He knew the frenzy of a rapid successful charge. The music of the trampling feet, the sharp voices, the clanking arms of the column near him made him soar on the red wings of war. For a few moments, he was sublime.

He thought that he was about to start for the front. Indeed, he saw a picture of himself, dust-stained, haggard, panting, flying to the front at the proper moment to seize and throttle the dark, leering witch of calamity.

Then the difficulties of the thing began to drag at him. He hesitated, balancing awkwardly on one foot.

He had no rifle; he could not fight with his hands, said he, resentfully, to his plan. Well, rifles could be had for the picking. They were extraordinarily profuse.

Also, he continued, it would be a miracle if he found his regiment. Well, he could fight with any regiment.

He started forward slowly. He stepped as if he expected to tread upon some explosive thing. Doubts and he were struggling.

He would truly be a worm if any of his comrades should see him returning thus, the marks of his flight upon him. There was a reply that the intent fighters did not care for what happened rearward saving that no hostile bayonets appeared there. In the battle-blur his face would, in a way, be hidden like the face of a cowled man.

But then, he said, that his tireless fate would bring forth, when the strife lulled for a moment, a man to ask of him an explanation. In imagination he felt the scrutiny of his companions as he painfully labored through some lies.

Eventually, his courage expended itself upon these objections. The debates drained him of his fire.

He was not cast-down by this defeat of his plan, for, upon studying the affair carefully, he could not but admit that the objections were very formidable.

Furthermore, various ailments had begun to cry out. In their presence, he could not persist in flying high with the wings of war; they rendered it almost impossible for him to see himself in a heroic light. He tumbled headlong.

He discovered that he had a scorching thirst. His face was so dry and grimy that he thought he could feel his skin crackle. Each bone of his body had an ache in it and seemingly threatened to break with each movement. His feet were like two sores. Also, his body was calling for food. It was more powerful than a direct hunger. There was a dull, weight-like feeling in his stomach and when he tried to walk, his head swayed and he tottered.

He could not see with distinctness. Small patches of green mist floated before his vision.

While he had been tossed by many emotions, he had not been aware of ailments. Now they beset him and made clamor. As he was at last compelled to pay attention to them, his capacity for self-hate was multiplied. In despair, he declared that he was not like those others. He now conceded it to be impossible that he should ever become a hero. He was a craven loon. Those pictures of glory were piteous things. He groaned from his heart and went staggering off.

A certain moth-like quality within him kept him in the vicinity of the battle. He had a great desire to see, and to get news. He wished to know who was winning.

He told himself that, despite his unprecedented suffering, he had never lost his greed for a victory, yet, he said, in a half-apologetic manner to his conscience, he could not but know that a defeat for the army this time might mean many favorable things for him. The blows of the enemy would splinter regiments into fragments. Thus, many men of courage, he considered, would be obliged to desert the colors and scurry like chickens. He would appear as one of them. They would be sullen brothers in distress and he could then easily believe he had not run any further or faster than they. And if he himself could believe in his virtuous perfection, he conceived that there would be small trouble in convincing all others.

He said, as if in excuse for this hope, that previously the army had encountered great defeats and in a few months had shaken off all blood and tradition of them, emerging as bright and valiant as a new one; thrusting out of sight the memory of disaster and appearing with the valor and confidence of unconquered legions. The shrilling voices of the people at home would pipe dismally for a time but various generals were usually compelled to listen to these ditties. He of course felt no compunctions for proposing a general as a sacrifice. He could not tell who the chosen for the barbs might be, so he could centre no direct sympathy upon him. The people were afar and he did not conceive public opinion to be accurate at long range. It was quite probable they would hit the wrong man who after he had recovered from his amazement would perhaps spend the rest of his days in writing replies to the songs of his alleged failure. It would be very unfortunate, no doubt, but in this case, a general was of no consequence to the youth.

In a defeat there would be a roundabout vindication of himself. He thought it would prove, in a manner, that he had fled early because of his superior powers of perception. A serious prophet, upon predicting a flood, should be the first man to climb a tree. This would demonstrate that he was indeed a seer.

A moral vindication was regarded by the youth as a very important thing. Without salve, he could not, he thought, wear the sore badge of his dishonor through life. With his heart continually assuring him that he was despicable, he could not exist without making it, through his actions, apparent to all men.

If the army had gone gloriously on, he would be lost. If the din meant that now his army's flags were tilted forward he was a condemned wretch. He would be compelled to doom himself to isolation. If the men were advancing, their indifferent feet were trampling upon his chances for a successful life.

As these thoughts went rapidly through his mind, he turned upon them and tried to thrust them away. He denounced himself as a villain. He said that he was the most unutterably selfish man in existence. His mind pictured the soldiers who would place their defiant bodies before the spear of the yelling battle-fiend and as he saw their dripping corpses on an imagined field, he said that he was their murderer.

Again he thought that he wished he was dead. He believed that he envied a corpse. Thinking of the slain, he achieved a great contempt for some of them as if they were guilty for thus becoming lifeless. They might have been killed by lucky chances, he said, before they had had opportunities to flee or before they had been really tested. Yet they would receive laurels from tradition. He cried out bitterly that their crowns were stolen and their robes of glorious memories were shams. However, he still said that it was a great pity he was not as they.

A defeat of the army had suggested itself to him as a means of escape from the consequences of his fall. He considered, now, however, that it was useless to think of such a possibility. His education had been that success for that mighty blue machine was certain; that it would make victories as a contrivance turns out buttons. He presently discarded all his speculations in the other direction. He returned to the creed of soldiers.

When he perceived again that it was not possible for the army to be defeated, he tried to bethink him of a fine tale which he could take back to his regiment and with it turn the expected shafts of derision.

But, as he mortally feared these shafts, it became impossible for him to invent a tale he felt he could trust. He experimented with many schemes but threw them aside one by one as flimsy. He was quick to see vulnerable places in them all.

Furthermore, he was much afraid that some arrow of scorn might lay him mentally low before he could raise his protecting tale.

He imagined the whole regiment saying: "Where's Henry Fleming? He run, didn't 'e? Oh, my!" He recalled various persons who would be quite sure to leave him no peace about it. They would doubtless question him with sneers and laugh at his stammering hesitation. In the next engagement they would try to keep watch of him to discover when he would run.

Wherever he went in camp, he would encounter insolent and lingeringly-cruel stares. As he imagined himself passing near a crowd of comrades, he could hear some one say: "There he goes!"

Then, as if the heads were moved by one muscle, all the faces were turned toward him with wide, derisive grins. He seemed to hear some one make a humorous remark in a low tone. At it, the others all crowed and cackled. He was a slang-phrase.

CHAPTER XII

THE column that had butted stoutly at the obstacles in the road-way was barely out of the youth's sight before he saw dark waves of men come sweeping out of the woods and down through the fields. He knew at once that the steel fibres had been washed from their hearts. They were bursting from their coats and their equipments as from entanglements. They charged down upon him like terrified buffaloes.

Behind them, blue smoke curled and clouded above the tree-tops and through the thickets he could sometimes see a distant pink glare. The voices of the cannon were clamoring in interminable chorus.

The youth was horror-stricken. He stared in agony and amazement. He forgot that he was engaged in combating the universe. He threw aside his mental pamphlets on the philosophy of the retreated and rules for the guidance of the damned.

The fight was lost. The dragons were coming with invincible strides. The army, helpless in the matted thickets, and blinded by the overhanging night, was going to be swallowed. War, the red animal, war, the blood-swollen god, would have bloated fill.

Within him, something bade to cry out. He had the impulse to make a rallying speech, to sing a battle-hymn, but he could only get his tongue to call into the air: "Why—why—what—what's the matter?"

Soon he was in the midst of them. They were leaping and scampering all about him. Their blanched faces shone in the dusk. They seemed, for the most part, to be very burly men. The youth turned from one to another of them as they galloped along. His incoherent questions were lost. They were heedless of his appeals. They did not seem to see him.

They sometimes gabbled insanely. One huge man was asking of the sky: "Say, where de plank-road? Where de plank-road?"

It was as if he had lost a child. He wept in his pain and dismay.

Presently, men were running hither and thither, in all ways. The artillery booming, forward, rearward, and on the flanks made jumble of ideas of direction. Landmarks had vanished into the gathered gloom. The youth began to imagine that he had gotten into the centre of the tremendous quarrel and he could perceive no way out of it. From the mouths of the fleeing men came a thousand wild questions but no one made answers.

The youth, after rushing about and throwing interrogations at the heedless bands of retreating infantry, finally clutched a man by the arm. They swung around face to face.

"Why—why——" stammered the youth struggling with his balking tongue.

The man screamed. "Letgo me! Letgo me!" His face was livid and his eyes were rolling uncontrolled. He was heaving and panting. He still grasped his rifle, perhaps having forgotten to release his hold upon it. He tugged frantically and the youth being compelled to lean forward was dragged several paces.

"Letgo me! Letgo me!"

"Why—why——" stuttered the youth.

"Well, then——" bawled the man in a lurid rage. He adroitly and fiercely swung his rifle. It crushed upon the youth's head. The man ran on.

The youth's fingers had turned to paste upon the other's arm. The energy was smitten from his muscles. He saw the flaming wings of lightning flash before his vision. There was a deafening rumble of thunder within his head.

Suddenly his legs seemed to die. He sank writhing to the ground. He tried to arise. In his efforts against the numbing pain he was like a man wrestling with a creature of the air.

There was a sinister struggle.

Sometimes, he would achieve a position half-erect, battle with the air for a moment, and then fall again, grabbing at the grass. His face was of a clammy pallor. Deep groans were wrenched from him.

At last, with a twisting movement, he got upon his hands and knees and from thence, like a babe trying to walk, to his feet. Pressing his hands to his temples, he went lurching over the grass.

He fought an intense battle with his body. His dulled senses wished him to swoon and he opposed them stubbornly, his mind portraying unknown dangers and mutilations if he should fall upon the field. He went, tall soldier-fashion. He imagined secluded spots where he could fall and be unmolested. To search for one, he strove against the tide of his pain.

Once, he put his hand to the top of his head and timidly touched the wound. The scratching pain of the contact made him draw a long breath through his clenched teeth. His fingers were dabbled with blood. He regarded them with a fixed stare.

Around him, he could hear the grumble of jolted cannon as the scurrying horses were lashed toward the front. Once, a young officer on a be-splashed charger nearly ran him down. He turned and watched the mass of guns, men and horses sweeping in a wide curve toward a gap in a fence. The officer was making excited motions with a gauntleted hand. The guns followed the teams with an air of unwillingness—of being dragged by the heels.

Some officers of the scattered infantry were cursing and railing like fish-wives. Their scolding voices could be heard above the din. Into the unspeakable jumble in the road-way, rode a squadron of cavalry. The faded yellow of their facings shone bravely. There was a mighty altercation.

The artillery were assembling as if for a conference.

The blue haze of evening was upon the fields. The lines of forest were long purple shadows. One cloud lay along the western sky partly smothering the red.

As the youth left the scene behind him, he heard the guns suddenly roar out. He imagined them shaking in black rage. They belched and howled like brass devils guarding a gate. The soft air was filled with the tremendous remonstrance. With it came the shattering peal of opposing infantry. Turning to look behind him, he could see sheets of orange light illumine the shadowy distance. There were subtle and sudden lightnings in the far air. At times, he thought he could see heaving masses of men.

He hurried on in the dusk. The day had faded until he could barely distinguish place for his feet. The purple darkness was filled with men who lectured and jabbered. Sometimes, he could see them gesticulating against the blue and sombre sky. There seemed to be a great ruck of men and munitions spread about in the forest and in the fields. The little narrow road-way now lay lifeless. There were over-turned wagons like sun-dried boulders. The bed of the former torrent was choked with the bodies of horses and splintered parts of war-machines.

It had come to pass that his wound pained him but little. He was afraid to move rapidly, however, for a dread of disturbing it. He held his head very still and took many precautions against stumbling. He was filled with anxiety and his face was pinched and drawn in anticipation of the pain of any sudden mistake of his feet in the gloom.

His thoughts, as he walked, fixed intently upon his hurt. There was a cool, liquid feeling about it and he imagined blood moving slowly down under his hair. His head seemed swollen to a size that made him think his neck to be inadequate.

The new silence of his wound made much worriment. The little, blistering voices of pain that had called out from his scalp, were, he thought, definite in their expression of danger. By them, he believed that he could measure his plight. But when they remained ominously silent, he became frightened and imagined terrible fingers that clutched into his brain.

Amidst it, he began to reflect upon various incidents and conditions of the past. He bethought him of certain meals his mother had cooked at home, in which those dishes of which he was particularly fond had occupied prominent positions. He saw the spread table. The pine walls of the kitchen were glowing in the warm light from the stove. Too, he remembered how he and his companions used to go from the school-house to the bank of a shaded pool. He saw his clothes in disorderly array upon the grass of the bank. He felt the swash of the fragrant water upon his body. The leaves of the over-hanging maple rustled with melody in the wind of youthful summer.

He was over-come presently by a dragging weariness. His head hung forward and his shoulders were stooped as if he were bearing a great bundle. His feet shuffled along the ground.

He held continuous arguments as to whether he should lie down and sleep at some near spot, or force himself on until he reached a certain haven. He often tried to dismiss the question but his body persisted in rebellion and his senses nagged at him like pampered babies.

At last, he heard a cheery voice near his shoulder. "Yeh seem t' be in a pretty bad way, boy?"

The youth did not look up but he assented with thick tongue. "Uh."

The owner of the cheery voice took him firmly by the arm. "Well," he said, with a round laugh, "I'm goin' your way. Th' hull gang is goin' your way. An' I guess I kin give yeh a lift." They began to walk like a drunken man and his friend.

As they went along, the man questioned the youth and assisted him with the replies like one manipulating the mind of a child. Sometimes he interjected anecdotes. "What reg'ment do yeh b'long teh? Eh? What's that? Th' 304th N' York? Why, what corps is that in? Oh, it is? Why, I thought they wasn't engaged t'-day—they're 'way over in th' centre. Oh, they was, eh? Well, pretty nearly everybody got their share 'a fightin' t'-day. By dad, I give myself up fer dead any number 'a times. There was shootin' here an' shootin' there, an' hollerin' here an' hollerin' there, in th' damn' darkness, until I couldn't tell t' save m' soul which side I was on. Sometimes I thought I was sure-'nough from Ohier an' other times I could 'a swore I was from th' bitter end of Florida. It was th' most mixed up dern thing I ever see. An' these here hull woods is a reg'lar mess. It'll be a miracle if we find our reg'ments t'-night. Pretty soon, though, we'll meet a-plenty of guards an' provost-guards an' one thing an' another. Ho, there they go with an off'cer, I guess. Look at his hand a-draggin'. He's got all th' war he wants, I bet. He won't be talkin' so big about his reputation an' all, when they go t' sawin' off his leg. Poor feller. My brother's got whiskers jest like that. How did yeh git 'way over here anyhow? Your reg'-ment is a long way from here, ain't it? Well, I guess we can find it. Yeh know, there was a boy killed in my comp'ny t'-day that I thought th' world an' all of. Jack was a nice feller. By ginger, it hurt like thunder t' see ol' Jack jest git knocked flat. We was a-standin' purty peaceable fer a spell, 'though there was men runnin' ev'ry way all 'round us, an' while we was a-standin' like that, 'long come a big fat feller. He began t' peck at Jack's elbow an' he ses: 'Say, where's th' road t' th' river?' An' Jack, he never paid no attention an' th' feller kept on a-peckin' at his elbow an' sayin': 'Say, where's th' road t' th' river?' Jack was a-lookin' ahead all th' time tryin' t' see th' Johnnies comin' through th' woods an' he never paid no attention t' this big fat feller fer a long time but at last he turned 'round an' he ses: 'Ah, go t' hell an' find th' road t' th' river.' An' jest then a shot slapped him bang on th' side th' head. He was a serjeant, too. Them was his last words. Thunder, I wish we was sure 'a findin' our reg'ments t'-night. It's goin' t' be long huntin'. But I guess we kin do it."

In the search which followed, the man of the cheery voice seemed, to the youth, to possess a wand of a magic kind. He threaded the mazes of the tangled forest with a strange fortune. In encounters with guards and patrols he displayed the keenness of a detective and the valor of a gamin. Obstacles fell before him and became of assistance. The youth with his chin still on his breast stood woodenly by while his companion beat ways and means out of sullen things.

The forest seemed a vast hive of men buzzing about in frantic circles but the cheery man conducted the youth without mistakes, until at last he began to chuckle with glee and self-satisfaction. "Ah, there yeh are! See that fire?"

The youth nodded stupidly.

"Well, there's where your reg'ment is. An', now, good-bye, ol' boy, good luck t' yeh."

A warm and strong hand clasped the youth's languid fingers for an instant, and then he heard a cheerful and audacious whistling, as the man strided away. As he who so be-friended him was thus passing out of his life, it suddenly occurred to the youth that he had not once seen his face.

CHAPTER XIII

THE youth went slowly toward the fire indicated by his departed friend. As he reeled, he bethought him of the welcome his comrades would give him. He had a conviction that he would soon feel in his sore heart the barbed missiles of ridicule. He had no strength to invent a tale; he would be a soft target.

He made vague plans to go off into the deeper darkness and hide, but they were all destroyed by the voices of exhaustion and pain from his body. His ailments, clamoring, forced him to seek the place of food and rest, at whatever cost.

He swung unsteadily toward the fire. He could see the forms of men throwing black shadows in the red light and as he went nearer, it became known to him in some way, that the ground was strewn with sleeping men.

Of a sudden, he confronted a black and monstrous figure. A rifle-barrel caught some glinting beams. "Halt—halt." He was dismayed for a moment but he presently thought that he recognized the nervous voice. As he stood tottering before the rifle-barrel, he called out: "Why, hello, Wilson, you—you here?"

The rifle was lowered to a position of caution and the loud soldier came slowly forward. He peered into the youth's face. "That you, Henry?"

"Yes, it's—it's me."

"Well, well, ol' boy," said the other, "by ginger, I'm glad t' see yeh. I give yeh up fer a goner. I thought yeh was dead sure-enough." There was husky emotion in his voice.

The youth found that now he could barely stand upon his feet. There was a sudden sinking of his forces. He thought he must hasten to produce his tale to protect him from the missiles already at the lips of his redoubtable comrade. So staggering before the loud soldier he began. "Yes, yes. I've—I've had an awful time. I've been all over. 'Way over on the right. Terrible fighting over there. I had an awful time. I got separated from the regiment. Over on the right, I got shot. In the head. I never saw such fighting. Awful time. I don't see how I could've got separated from the regiment. I got shot, too."

His friend had stepped forward quickly. "What? Got shot? Why didn't yeh say so first? Poor ol' boy, we must—hol' on a minnit; what am I doin'. I'll call Simpson."

Another figure at that moment loomed in the gloom. They could see that it was the corporal. "Who yeh talkin' to, Wilson?" he demanded. His voice was anger-toned. "Who yeh talkin' to? Yer th' derndest sentinel—why—hello, Henry, you here? Why, I thought you was dead four hours ago. Great Jerusalem, they keep turnin' up every ten minutes or so. We thought we'd lost forty-two men by straight count but if they keep on a-comin' this way, we'll git th' comp'ny all back by mornin' yit—where was yeh?"

"Over on the right. I got separated——" began the youth with considerable glibness.

But his friend had interrupted hastily. "Yes, an' he got shot in th' head an' he's in a fix an' we must see t' him right away." He rested his rifle in the hollow of his left arm and his right around the youth's shoulder.

"Gee, it must hurt like thunder," he said.

The youth leaned heavily upon his friend. "Yes, it hurts—hurts a good deal," he replied. There was a faltering in his voice.

"Oh," said the corporal. He linked his arm in the youth's and drew him forward. "Come on, Henry. I'll take keer 'a yeh."

As they went on together, the loud private called out after them. "Put 'im t' sleep in my blanket, Simpson. An'—hol' on a minnit—here's my canteen. It's full 'a coffee. Look at his head by th' fire an' see how it looks. Maybe it's a pretty bad un. When I git relieved in a couple 'a minnits, I'll be over an' see t' him."

The youth's senses were so deadened that his friend's voice sounded from afar and he could scarcely feel the pressure of the corporal's arm. He submitted passively to the latter's directing strength. His head was in the old manner hanging forward upon his breast. His knees wobbled.

The corporal led him into the glare of the fire. "Now, Henry," he said, "let's have look at yer ol' head."

The youth sat down obediently and the corporal, laying aside his rifle, began to fumble in the bushy hair of his comrade. He was obliged to turn the other's head so that the full flush of the fire-light would beam upon it. He puckered his mouth with a critical air. He drew back his lips and whistled through his teeth when his fingers came in contact with the splashed blood and the rare wound.

"Ah, here we are," he said. He awkwardly made further investigations. "Jest as I thought," he added, presently. "Yeh've been grazed by a ball. It's raised a queer lump jest as if some feller had lammed yeh on th' head with a club. It stopped a-bleedin' long time ago. Th' most about it is that in th' mornin', yeh'll feel that a number-ten hat wouldn't fit yeh. An' your head'll be all het up an' feel as dry as burnt pork. An' yeh may git a lot 'a other sicknesses, too, by mornin'. Yeh can't never tell. Still, I don't much think so. It's jest a damn' good belt on th' head an' nothin' more. Now, you jest sit here an' don't move, while I go rout out th' relief. Then I'll send Wilson t' take keer 'a yeh."

The corporal went away. The youth remained on the ground like a parcel. He stared with a vacant look into the fire.

After a time, he aroused, for some part, and the things about him began to take form. He saw that the ground in the deep shadows was cluttered with men, sprawling in every conceivable posture. Glancing narrowly into the more distant darkness, he caught occasional glimpses of visages that loomed pallid and ghostly, lit with a phosphorescent glow. These faces expressed in their lines the deep stupor of the tired soldiers. They made them appear like men drunk with wine. This bit of forest might have appeared to an ethereal wanderer as a scene of the result of some frightful debauch.

On the other side of the fire, the youth observed an officer asleep, seated bolt up-right with his back against a tree. There was something perilous in his position. Badgered by dreams, perhaps, he swayed with little bounces and starts like an old, toddy-stricken grandfather in a chimney corner. Dust and stains were upon his face. His lower jaw hung down as if lacking strength to assume its normal position. He was the picture of an exhausted soldier after a feast of war.

He had evidently gone to sleep with his sword in his arms. These two had slumbered in an embrace. But the weapon had been allowed, in time, to fall unheeded to the ground. The brass-mounted hilt lay in contact with some parts of the fire.

Within the gleam of rose and orange light from the burning sticks were other soldiers, snoring and heaving, or lying death-like in slumber. A few pairs of legs were stuck forth, rigid and straight. The shoes displayed the mud or dust of marches, and bits of rounded trousers, protruding from the blankets, showed rents and tears from hurried pitchings through the dense brambles.

The fire crackled musically. From it swelled light smoke. Over-head, the foliage moved softly. The leaves with their faces turned toward the blaze, were colored shifting hues of silver, often edged with red. Far off to the right, through a window in the forest could be seen a handful of stars lying, like glittering pebbles, on the black level of the night.

Occasionally, in this low-arched hall, a soldier would arouse and turn his body to a new position, the experience of his sleep having taught him of uneven and objectionable places upon the ground under him. Or, perhaps, he would lift himself to a sitting posture, blink at the fire for an unintelligent moment, throw a swift glance at his prostrate companion and then cuddle down again with a grunt of sleepy content.

The youth sat in a forlorn heap until his friend, the loud young soldier, came, swinging two canteens by their light strings. "Well, now, Henry, ol' boy," said the latter, "we'll have yeh fixed up in jest about a minnit."

He had the bustling ways of an amateur nurse. He fussed around the fire and stirred the sticks to brilliant exertions. He made his patient drink largely from the canteen that contained the coffee. It was to the youth a delicious draught. He tilted his head afar back and held the canteen long to his lips. The cool mixture went caressingly down his blistered throat. Having finished, he sighed with comfortable delight.

The loud young soldier watched his comrade with an air of satisfaction. He, later, produced an extensive handkerchief from his pocket. He folded it into a manner of bandage and soused water from the other canteen upon the middle of it. This crude arrangement he bound over the youth's head, tying the ends in a queer knot at the back of the neck.

"There," he said, moving off and surveying his deed, "yeh look like th' devil but I bet yeh feel better."

The youth contemplated his friend with grateful eyes. Upon his aching and swelling head, the cold cloth was like a tender woman's hand.

"Yeh don't holler ner say nothin'," remarked his friend, approvingly. "I know I'm a blacksmith at takin' keer 'a sick folks an' yeh never squeaked. Yer a good un, Henry. Most 'a men would a' been in th' hospital long ago. A shot in th' head ain't foolin' business."

The youth made no reply but began to fumble with the buttons of his jacket.

"Well, come, now," continued his friend, "come on. I must put yeh t' bed an' see that yeh git a good night's rest."

The other got carefully erect and the loud young soldier led him among the sleeping forms lying in groups and rows. Presently he stooped and picked up his blankets. He spread the rubber one upon the ground and placed the woolen one about the youth's shoulders.

"There now," he said, "lie down an' git some sleep."

The youth with his manner of dog-like obedience got carefully down like a crone stooping. He stretched out with a murmur of relief and comfort. The ground felt like the softest couch.

But of a sudden, he ejaculated. "Hold on a minute. Where you going to sleep?"

His friend waved his hand impatiently. "Right down there by yeh."

"Well, but hold on a minute," continued the youth. "What you going to sleep in? I've got your——"

The loud young soldier snarled. "Shet up an' go on t' sleep. Don't be makin' a damn' fool 'a yerself," he said, severely.

After this reproof, the youth said no more. An exquisite drowsiness had spread through him. The warm comfort of the blanket enveloped him and made a gentle languor. His head fell forward on his crooked arm and his weighted lids went softly down over his eyes. Hearing a splatter of musketry from the distance, he wondered indifferently if those men sometimes slept. He gave a long sigh, snuggled down into his blanket and in a moment, was like his comrades.

CHAPTER XIV

WHEN the youth awoke, it seemed to him that he had been asleep for a thousand years and he felt sure that he opened his eyes upon an unexpected world. Grey mists were slowly shifting before the first efforts of the sun-rays. An impending splendor could be seen in the eastern sky. An icy dew had chilled his face and immediately upon arousing he curled further down into his blanket. He stared, for a while, at the leaves over-head, moving in a heraldic wind of the day.

The distance was splintering and blaring with the noise of fighting. There was in the sound, an expression of a deadly persistency as if it had not begun and was not to cease.

About him, were the rows and groups of men that he had dimly seen the previous night. They were getting a last draught of sleep before the awakening. The gaunt, care-worn features and dusty figures were made plain by this quaint light at the dawning but it dressed the skin of the men in corpse-like hues and made the tangled limbs appear pulseless and dead. The youth started up with a little cry when his eyes first swept over this motionless mass of men, thick spread upon the ground, pallid and in strange postures. His disordered mind interpreted the hall of the forest as a charnel place. He believed for an instant that he was in the house of the dead and he did not dare to move lest these corpses start up, squalling and squawking. In a second, however, he achieved his proper mind. He swore a complicated oath at himself. He saw that this sombre picture was not a fact of the present, but a mere prophecy.

He heard then the noise of a fire crackling briskly in the cold air and turning his head, he saw his friend pottering busily about a small blaze. A few other figures moved in the fog and he heard the hard cracking of axe-blows.

Suddenly, there was a hollow rumble of drums. A distant

bugle sang faintly. Similar sounds, varying in strength, came from near and far over the forest. The bugles called to each other like brazen game-cocks. The near thunder of the regimental drums rolled.

The body of men in the woods rustled. There was a general up-lifting of heads. A murmuring of voices broke upon the air. In it there was much bass of grumbling oaths. Strange gods were addressed in condemnation of the early hours necessary to correct war. An officer's peremptory tenor rang out and quickened the stiffened movement of the men. The tangled limbs unravelled. The corpse-hued faces were hidden behind fists that twisted slowly in eye-sockets.

The youth sat up and gave vent to an enormous yawn. "Thunder," he remarked, petulantly. He rubbed his eyes and then putting up his hand felt carefully of the bandage over his wound. His friend, perceiving him to be awake, came from the fire. "Well, Henry, ol' man, how do yeh feel this mornin'," he demanded.

The youth yawned again. Then he puckered his mouth to a little pucker. His head in truth felt precisely like a melon and there was an unpleasant sensation at his stomach.

"Oh, Lord, I feel pretty bad," he said.

"Thunder," exclaimed the other, "I hoped ye'd feel all right this mornin'. Let's see th' bandage—I guess it's slipped." He began to tinker at the wound in rather a clumsy way until the youth exploded.

"Gosh-dern it," he said in sharp irritation, "you're the hangdest man I ever saw. You wear muffs on your hands. Why in good-thunderation can't you be more easy. I'd rather you'd stand off and throw guns at it. Now, go slow, and don't act as if you was nailing down carpet."

He glared with insolent command at his friend but the latter answered soothingly. "Well, well, come now, an' git some grub," he said. "Then, maybe, yeh'll feel better."

At the fire-side, the loud young soldier, watched over his comrade's wants with tenderness and care. He was very busy, marshalling the little, black vagabonds of tin-cups and pouring into them the steaming, iron-colored mixture from a small and sooty tin-pail. He had some fresh meat which he roasted hurriedly upon a stick. He sat down then and contemplated the youth's appetite with glee.

The youth took note of a remarkable change in his comrade since those days of camp-life upon the river-bank. He seemed no more to be continually regarding the proportions of his personal prowess. He was not furious at small words that pricked his conceits. He was, no more, a loud young soldier. There was about him now a fine reliance. He showed a quiet belief in his purposes and his abilities. And this inward confidence evidently enabled him to be indifferent to little words of other men aimed at him.

The youth reflected. He had been used to regarding his comrade as a blatant child with an audacity grown from his inexperience, thoughtless, head-strong, jealous, and filled with a tinsel courage. A swaggering babe accustomed to strut in his own door-yard. The youth wondered where had been born these new eyes; when his comrade had made the great discovery that there were many men who would refuse to be subjected by him. Apparently, the other had now climbed a peak of wisdom from which he could perceive himself as a very wee thing. And the youth saw that, ever after, it would be easier to live in his friend's neighborhood.

His comrade balanced his ebony coffee-cup on his knee. "Well, Henry," he said, "what d'yeh think th' chances are? D'yeh think we'll wallop 'em?"

The youth considered for a moment. "Day-before-yesterday," he finally replied with boldness, "you would've bet you'd lick the whole kit-and-boodle all by yourself."

His friend looked a trifle amazed. "Would I?" he asked. He pondered. "Well, perhaps, I would," he decided at last. He stared humbly at the fire.

The youth was quite disconcerted at this surprising reception of his remarks. "Oh, no, you wouldn't either," he said, hastily trying to retrace.

But the other made a deprecatory gesture. "Oh, yeh needn't mind, Henry," he said. "I believe I was a pretty big fool in those days." He spoke as after a lapse of years.

There was a little pause.

"All th' off'cers say we've got th' rebs in a pretty tight box," said the friend, clearing his throat in a common-place way. "They all seem t' think we've got 'em jest where we want 'em."

"I don't know about that," the youth replied. "What I saw over on the right makes me think it was the other way about. From where I was, it looked as if we was getting a good pounding yesterday."

"D'yeh think so?" enquired the friend. "I thought we handled 'em pretty rough yestirday."

"Not a bit," said the youth. "Why, lord, man, you didn't see nothing of the fight. Why——" Then a sudden thought came to him. "Oh! Jim Conklin's dead."

His friend started. "What? Is he? Jim Conklin?"

The youth spoke slowly. "Yes. He's dead. Shot in the side."

"Yeh don't say so. Jim Conklin? . . . . Poor cuss."

All about them were other small fires surrounded by men with their little black utensils. From one of these, near, came sudden sharp voices in a row. It appeared that two light-footed soldiers had been teasing a huge bearded man, causing him to spill coffee upon his blue knees. The man had gone into a rage and had sworn comprehensively. Stung by his language, his tormentors had immediately bristled at him with a great show of resenting unjust oaths. Possibly there was going to be a fight.

The friend arose and went over to them, making pacific motions with his arms. "Oh, here, now, boys, what's th' use?" he said. "We'll be at th' rebs in less'n an hour. What's th' good 'a fightin' 'mong ourselves."

One of the light-footed soldiers turned upon him red-faced and violent. "Yeh needn't come around here with yer preachin'. I s'pose yeh don't approve 'a fightin' since Charley Morgan licked yeh but I don't see what business this here is 'a yours or anybody else."

"Well, it ain't," said the friend mildly. "Still I hate t' see——"

There was a tangled argument.

"Well, he——" said the two, indicating their opponent with accusative fore-fingers.

The huge soldier was quite purple with rage. He pointed at the two soldiers with his great hand, extended claw-like. "Well— they——"

But during this argumentative time, the desire to deal blows seemed to pass, although they said much to each other. Finally the friend returned to his old seat. In a short while, the three antagonists could be seen together in an amiable bunch.

"Jimmie Rogers ses I'll have t' fight him after th' battle t'-day," announced the friend as he again seated himself. "He ses he don't allow no interferin' in his business. I hate t' see th' boys fightin' 'mong themselves."

The youth laughed. "You've changed a good bit. You ain't at all like you was. I remember when you and that Irish fellow——" He stopped and laughed again.

"No, I didn't used t' be that way," said his friend, thoughtfully. "That's true 'nough."

"Well, I didn't mean——" began the youth.

The friend made another deprecatory gesture. "Oh, yeh needn't mind, Henry."

There was another little pause.

"Th' reg'ment lost over half th' men yestirday," remarked the friend, eventually. "I thought 'a course they was all dead but, laws, they kep' a-comin' back last night until it seems, after all, we didn't lose but a few. They'd been scattered all over, wanderin' around in th' woods, fightin' with other reg'ments an' everything. Jest like you done."

"So?" said the youth.

CHAPTER XV

THE regiment was standing at order-arms at the side of a lane, waiting for the command to march when suddenly the youth remembered the little packet enwrapped in a faded yellow envelope which the loud young soldier with lugubrious words had entrusted to him. It made him start. He uttered an exclamation and turned toward his comrade.

"Wilson!"

"What?"

His friend, at his side in the ranks, was thoughtfully staring down the road. From some cause, his expression was at that moment, very meek. The youth, regarding him with sidelong glances, felt impelled to change his purpose. "Oh, nothing," he said.

His friend turned his head in some surprise. "Why, what was yeh goin' t' say."

"Oh, nothing," repeated the youth.

He resolved not to deal the little blow. It was sufficient that the fact made him glad. It was not necessary to knock his friend on the head with the misguided packet.

He had been possessed of much fear of his friend for he saw how easily questionings could make holes in his feelings. Lately, he had assured himself that the altered comrade would not tantalize him with a persistent curiosity but he felt certain that during the first period of leisure his friend would ask him to relate his adventures of the previous day.

He now rejoiced in the possession of a small weapon with which he could prostrate his comrade at the first signs of a cross-examination. He was master. It would now be he who could laugh and shoot the shafts of derision.

The friend had, in a weak hour, spoken with sobs of his own death. He had delivered a melancholy oration previous to his funeral and had, doubtless, in the packet of letters, presented various keep-sakes to relatives. But he had not died, and thus he had delivered himself into the hands of the youth.

The latter felt immensely superior to his friend but he inclined to condescension. He adopted toward him an air of patronizing good-humor.

His self-pride was now entirely restored. In the shade of its flourishing growth, he stood with braced and self-confident legs, and since nothing could now be discovered, he did not shrink from an encounter with the eyes of judges, and allowed no thoughts of his own to keep him from an attitude of manfulness. He had performed his mistakes in the dark, so he was still a man.

Indeed, when he remembered his fortunes of yesterday, and looked at them from a distance he began to see something fine there. He had license to be pompous and veteran-like.

His panting agonies of the past he put out of his sight.

In the present, he declared to himself that it was only the doomed and the damned who roared with sincerity at circumstance. Few, but they, ever did it. A man with a full stomach and the respect of his fellows had no business to scold about anything that he might think to be wrong in the ways of the universe, or, even with the ways of society. Let the unfortunates rail; the others may play marbles.

He did not give a great deal of thought to these battles that lay directly before him. It was not essential that he should plan his ways in regard to them. He had been taught that many obligations of a life were easily avoided. The lessons of yesterday had been that retribution was a laggard and blind. With these facts before him he did not deem it necessary that he should become feverish over the possibilities of the ensuing twenty-four hours. He could leave much to chance. Besides, a faith in himself had secretly blossomed. There was a little flower of confidence growing within him. He was now a man of experience. He had been out among the dragons, he said, and he assured himself that they were not so hideous as he had imagined them. Also, they were inaccurate; they did not sting with precision. A stout heart often defied; and, defying, escaped.

And, furthermore, how could they kill him who was the chosen of gods and doomed to greatness.

He remembered how some of the men had run from the battle. As he re-called their terror-struck faces he felt a scorn for them. They had surely been more fleet and more wild than was absolutely necessary. They were weak mortals. As for himself, he had fled with discretion and dignity.

He was aroused from this reverie by his friend who having hitched about nervously and blinked at the trees for a time, suddenly coughed in an introductory way, and spoke.

"Fleming!"

"What?"

The friend put his hand up to his mouth and coughed again. He fidgeted in his jacket.

"Well," he gulped, at last, "I guess yeh might as well give me back them letters." Dark, prickling blood had flushed into his cheeks and brow.

"All right, Wilson," said the youth. He loosened two buttons of his coat, thrust in his hand and brought forth the packet. As he extended it to his friend, the latter's face was turned from him.

He had been slow in the act of producing the packet because during it he had been trying to invent a remarkable comment upon the affair. He could conjure nothing of sufficient point. He was compelled to allow his friend to escape unmolested with his packet. And for this he took unto himself considerable credit. It was a generous thing.

His friend at his side, seemed suffering great shame. As he contemplated him, the youth felt his heart grow more strong and stout. He had never been compelled to blush in such manner for his acts; he was an individual of extraordinary virtues.

He reflected, with condescending pity: "Too bad! Too bad! The poor devil, it makes him feel tough!"

After this incident, and as he reviewed the battle-pictures he had seen, he felt quite competent to return home and make the hearts of the people glow with stories of war. He could see himself in a room of warm tints telling tales to listeners. He could exhibit laurels. They were insignificant; still, in a district where laurels were infrequent, they might shine.

He saw his gaping audience picturing him as the central figure in blazing scenes. And he imagined the consternation and the ejaculations of his mother and the young lady at the seminary as they drank his recitals. Their vague feminine formula for beloved ones doing brave deeds on the field of battle without risk of life, would be destroyed.

CHAPTER XVI

A SPLUTTERING of musketry was always to be heard. Later, the cannon had entered the dispute. In the fog-filled air, their voices made a thudding sound. The reverberations were continual. This part of the world led a strange, battleful existence.

The youth's regiment was marched to relieve a command that had lain long in some damp trenches. The men took positions behind a curving line of rifle-pits that had been turned up, like a large furrow, along the line of woods. Before them was a level stretch, peopled with short, deformed stumps. From the woods beyond, came the dull popping of the skirmishers and pickets, firing in the fog. From the right came the noise of a terrific fracas.

The men cuddled behind the small embankment and sat in easy attitudes awaiting their turn. Many had their backs to the firing. The youth's friend lay down, buried his face in his arms, and almost instantly, it seemed, he was in a deep sleep.

The youth leaned his breast against the brown dirt and peered over at the woods and up and down the line. Curtains of trees interfered with his ways of vision. He could see the low line of trenches but for a short distance. A few idle flags were perched on the dirt-hills. Behind them were rows of dark bodies with a few heads sticking curiously over the top.

Always the noise of skirmishers came from the woods on the front and left, and the din on the right had grown to frightful proportions. The guns were roaring without an instant's pause for breath. It seemed that the cannon had come from all parts and were engaged in a stupendous wrangle. It became impossible to make a sentence heard.

The youth wished to launch a joke—a quotation from news-papers. He desired to say: "All quiet on the Rappahannock," but the guns refused to permit even a comment upon their uproar. He never successfully concluded the sentence.

But at last, the guns stopped and among the men in the rifle-pits, rumors again flew, like birds, but they were now for the most part, black creatures who flapped their wings drearily near to the ground and refused to rise on any wings of hope. The men's faces grew doleful from the interpreting of omens. Tales of hesitation and uncertainty on the part of those high in place and responsibility, came to their ears. Stories of disaster were borne into their minds with many proofs. This din of musketry on the right, growing like a released genie of sound, expressed and emphasized the army's plight.

The men were disheartened and began to mutter. They made gestures expressive of the sentence: "Ah, what more can we do." And it could always be seen that they were bewildered by the alleged news and could not fully comprehend a defeat.

Before the grey mists had been totally obliterated by the sun-rays, the regiment was marching in a spread column that was retiring carefully through the woods. The disordered, hurrying lines of the enemy could sometimes be seen down through the groves and little fields. They were yelling, shrill and exultant.

At this sight, the youth forgot many personal matters and became greatly enraged. He exploded in loud sentence. "B'jiminy, we're generaled by a lot of lunkheads."

"More than one feller has said that t'-day," observed a man.

His friend, recently aroused, was still very drowsy. He looked behind him until his mind took in the meaning of the movement. Then he sighed. "Oh, well, I s'pose we got licked," he remarked, sadly.

The youth had a thought that it would not be handsome for him to freely condemn other men. He made an attempt to restrain himself but the words upon his tongue were too bitter. He presently began a long and intricate denunciation of the commander of the forces.

"Mebbe, it wa'n't all his fault—not all together. He did th' best he knowed. It's our luck t' git licked often," said his friend in a weary tone. He was trudging along with stooped shoulders and shifting eyes like a man who has been caned and kicked.

"Well, don't we fight like the devil? Don't we do all that men can?" demanded the youth loudly.

He was secretly dumb-founded at this sentiment when it came from his lips. For a moment his face lost its valor and he looked guiltily about him. But no one questioned his right to deal in such words, and, presently, he recovered his air of courage. He went on to repeat a statement he had heard going from group to group at the camp that morning. "The brigadier said he never saw a new regiment fight the way we fought yesterday, didn't he? And we didn't do better than many another regiment, did we? Well, then, you can't say it's the army's fault, can you?"

In his reply, the friend's voice was stern. "'A course not," he said. "No man dare say we don't fight like th' devil. No man will ever dare say it. Th' boys fight like hell-roosters. But still—still, we don't have no luck."

"Well, then, if we fight like the devil and don't ever whip, it must be the generals' fault," said the youth grandly and decisively. "And I don't see any sense in fighting and fighting and fighting, yet always losing through some derned old lunkhead of a general."

A sarcastic man who was tramping at the youth's side, then spoke lazily. "Mebbe yeh think yeh fit th' hull battle yestirday, Fleming," he remarked.

The speech pierced the youth. Inward, he was reduced to an abject pulp by these chance words. His legs quaked privately. He cast a frightened glance at the sarcastic man.

"Why, no," he hastened to say in a conciliatory voice, "I don't think I fought the whole battle yesterday."

But the other seemed innocent of any deeper meaning. Apparently, he had no information. It was merely his habit. "Oh," he replied in the same tone of calm derision.

The youth, nevertheless, felt a threat. His mind shrank from going near to the danger and, thereafter, he was silent. The significance of the sarcastic man's words took from him all loud moods that would make him appear prominent. He became suddenly a modest person.

There was low-toned talk among the troops. The officers were impatient and snappy, their countenances clouded with the tales of misfortune. The troops, sifting through the forest, were sullen. In the youth's company once, a man's laugh rang out. A dozen soldiers turned their faces quickly toward him and frowned with vague displeasure.

The noise of firing dogged their foot-steps. Sometimes, it seemed to be driven a little way but it always returned again with increased insolence. The men muttered and cursed, throwing black looks in its direction.

In a cleared space, the troops were at last halted. Regiments and brigades, broken and detached through their encounters with thickets, grew together again and lines were faced toward the pursuing bark of the enemy's infantry.

This noise, following like the yelpings of eager, metallic hounds, increased to a loud and joyous burst, and then, as the sun went serenely up the sky, throwing illuminating rays into the gloomy thickets, it broke forth into prolonged pealings. The woods began to crackle as if a-fire.

"Whoop-a-dadee," said a man, "here we are. Everybody fightin'. Blood an' destruction."

"I was willin' t' bet they'd attack as soon as th' sun got fairly up," savagely asserted the lieutenant who commanded the youth's company. He jerked without mercy at his little moustache. He strode to and fro with dark dignity in the rear of his men who were lying down behind whatever protection they had collected.

A battery had trundled into position in the rear and was thoughtfully shelling the distance. The regiment, unmolested as yet, awaited the moment when the grey shadows of the woods before them should be slashed by the lines of flame. There was much growling and swearing.

"Good Gawd," the youth grumbled, "we're always being chased around like rats. It makes me sick. Nobody seems to know where we go or why we go. We just get fired around from pillar to post and get licked here and get licked there and nobody knows what it's done for. It makes a man feel like a damn' kitten in a bag. Now, I'd like to know what the eternal thunders we was marched into these woods for, anyhow, unless it was to give the rebs a regular pot-shot at us. We came in here and got our legs all tangled up in these cussed briars and then we began to fight and the rebs had an easy time of it. Don't tell Me it's just luck. I know better. It's this derned old——"

The friend seemed jaded but he interrupted his comrade with a voice of calm confidence. "It'll turn out all right in th' end," he said.

"Oh, the devil it will. You always talk like a dog-hanged parson. Don't tell Me. I know——"

At this time, there was an interposition by the savage-minded lieutenant who was obliged to vent some of his inward dissatisfaction upon his men. "You boys shut right up. There's no need 'a your wastin' your breath in long-winded arguments about this an' that an' th' other. You've been jawin' like a lot 'a old hens. All you've got t' do is t' fight an' you'll get plenty 'a that t' do in about ten minutes. Less talkin' an' more fightin' is what's best fer you boys. I never saw sech gabbling jack-asses."

He paused, ready to pounce upon any man who might have the temerity to reply. No words being said, he resumed his dignified pacing.

"There's too much chin-music an' too little fightin' in this war, anyhow," he said to them, turning his head for a final remark.

The day had grown more white until the sun shed his full radiance upon the thronged forest. A sort of a gust of battle came sweeping toward that part of the line where lay the youth's regiment. The front shifted a trifle to meet it squarely. There was a wait. In this part of the field there passed slowly the intense moments that precede the tempest.

A single rifle flashed in a thicket before the regiment. In an instant, it was joined by many others. There was a mighty song of clashes and crashes that went sweeping through the woods. The guns in the rear, aroused and enraged by shells that had been thrown burr-like at them, suddenly involved themselves in a hideous altercation with another band of guns. The battle-roar settled to a rolling thunder which was a single, long explosion.

In the regiment, there was a peculiar kind of hesitation denoted in the attitudes of the men. They were worn, exhausted, having slept but little, and labored much. They rolled their eyes toward the advancing battle as they stood awaiting the shock. Some shrank and flinched. They stood as men tied to stakes.

CHAPTER XVII

THIS advance of the enemy had seemed to the youth like a ruthless hunting. He began to fume with rage and exasperation. He beat his foot upon the ground and scowled with hate at the swirling smoke that was approaching like a phantom flood. There was a maddening quality in this seeming resolution of the foe to give him no rest, to give him no time to sit down and think. Yesterday, he had fought and had fled rapidly. There had been many adventures. For to-day he felt that he had earned opportunities for contemplative repose. He could have enjoyed portraying to uninitiated listeners various scenes at which he had been a witness, or, ably discussing the processes of war with other proven men. Too, it was important that he should have time for physical recuperation. He was sore and stiff from his experiences. He had received his fill of all exertions and he wished to rest.

But those other men seemed never to grow weary; they were fighting with their old speed. He had a wild hate for the relentless foe. Yesterday, when he had imagined the universe to be against him, he had hated it, little gods and big gods; to-day he hated the army of the foe with the same great hatred. He was not going to be badgered of his life like a kitten chased by boys, he said. It was not well to drive men into final corners; at those moments, they could all develope teeth and claws.

He leaned, and spoke into his friend's ear. He menaced the woods with a gesture. "If they keep on chasing us, by Gawd, they'd better watch out. Can't stand *too* much."

The friend twisted his head and made a calm reply. "If they keep on a-chasin' us, they'll drive us all inteh th' river."

The youth cried out savagely at this statement. He crouched behind a little tree, with his eyes burning hatefully and his teeth set in a cur-like snarl. The awkward bandage was still about his head and, upon it, over his wound there was a spot of dry blood. His hair was wondrously towsled and some straggling, moving locks hung over the cloth of the bandage down toward his forehead. His jacket and shirt were open at the throat and exposed his young, bronzed neck. There could be seen spasmodic gulpings at his throat.

His fingers twined nervously about his rifle. He wished that it was an engine of annihilating power. He felt that he and his companions were being taunted and derided from sincere convictions that they were poor and puny. His knowledge of his inability to take vengeance for it made his rage into a dark and stormy spectre that possessed him and made him dream of abominable cruelties. The tormentors were flies sucking insolently at his blood and he thought that he would have given his life for a revenge of seeing their faces in pitiful plights.

The winds of battle had swept all about the regiment until the one rifle, instantly followed by others, flashed in its front. A moment later, the regiment roared forth its sudden and valiant retort. A dense wall of smoke settled slowly down. It was furiously slit and slashed by the knife-like fire from the rifles.

To the youth, the fighters resembled animals tossed for a death-struggle into a dark pit. There was a sensation that he and his fellows, at bay, were pushing back, always pushing fierce onslaughts of creatures who were slippery. Their beams of crimson seemed to get no purchase upon the bodies of their foes; the latter seemed to evade them with ease and come through, between, around and about, with unopposed skill.

When, in a dream, it occurred to the youth that his rifle was an impotent stick, he lost sense of everything but his hate, his desire to smash into pulp the glittering smile of victory which he could feel upon the faces of his enemies.

The blue, smoke-swallowed line curled and writhed like a snake, stepped upon. It swung its ends to and fro in an agony of fear and rage.

The youth was not conscious that he was erect upon his feet. He did not know the direction of the ground. Indeed, once he even lost the habit of balance and fell heavily. He was up again immediately. One thought went through the chaos of his brain at the time. He wondered if he had fallen because he had been shot. But the suspicion flew away at once. He did not think more of it.

He had taken up a first position behind the little tree with a direct determination to hold it against the world. He had not deemed it possible that his army could that day succeed and, from this, he felt the ability to fight harder. But the throng had surged in all ways until he lost directions and locations, save that he knew where lay the enemy.

The flames bit him and the hot smoke broiled his skin. His rifle-barrel grew so hot that, ordinarily, he could not have borne it upon his palms but he kept on stuffing cartridges into it and pounding them with his clanking, bending ram-rod. If he aimed at some changing form through the smoke, he pulled his trigger with a fierce grunt as if he were dealing a blow of the fist with all his strength.

When the enemy seemed falling back before him and his fellows, he went instantly forward, like a dog who seeing his foes lagging, turns and insists upon being pursued. And when he was compelled to retire again, he did it slowly, sullenly, taking steps of wrathful despair.

Once, he, in his intent hate, was almost alone and was firing when all those near him had ceased. He was so engrossed in his occupation that he was not aware of a lull.

He was re-called by a hoarse laugh and a sentence that came to his ears in a voice of contempt and amazement. "Yeh infernal fool, don't yeh know enough t' quit when there ain't anything t' shoot at? Good Gawd!"

He turned then and pausing with his rifle thrown half into position, looked at the blue line of his comrades. During this moment of leisure, they seemed all to be engaged in staring with astonishment at him. They had become spectators. Turning to the front again, he saw, under the lifted smoke, a deserted ground.

He looked, bewildered, for a moment. Then there appeared upon the glazed vacancy of his eyes, a diamond-point of intelligence. "Oh," he said, comprehending.

He returned to his comrades and threw himself upon the ground. He sprawled like a man who has been thrashed. His flesh seemed strangely on fire and the sounds of the battle continued in his ears. He groped blindly for his canteen.

The lieutenant was crowing. He seemed drunk with fighting. He called out to the youth. "By heavens, if I had ten thousand wild-cats like you, I could tear th' stomach outa this war in less'n a week." He puffed out his chest with large dignity as he said it.

Some of the men muttered and looked at the youth in awe-struck ways. It was plain that as he had gone on loading and firing and cursing without the proper intermission, they had found time to regard him. And they now looked upon him as a war-devil.

The friend came staggering to him. There was some fright and dismay in his voice. "Are yeh all right, Fleming? Do yeh feel all right? There ain't nothin' th' matter with yeh, Henry, is there?"

"No," said the youth with difficulty. His throat seemed full of knobs and burrs.

These incidents made the youth ponder. It was revealed to him that he had been a barbarian, a beast. He had fought like a pagan who defends his religion. Regarding it, he saw that it was fine, wild and, in some ways, easy. He had been a tremendous figure, no doubt. By this struggle, he had over-come obstacles which he had admitted to be mountains. They had fallen like paper peaks and he was now what he called a hero. And he had not been aware of the process. He had slept and, awakening, found himself a knight.

He lay and basked in the occasional stares of his comrades. Their faces were varied in degree of blackness from the burned powder. Some were utterly smudged. They were reeking with perspiration and their breaths came hard and wheezing. And from these soiled expanses they peered at him.

"Hot work! Hot work!" cried the lieutenant deliriously. He walked up and down, restless and eager. Sometimes, his voice could be heard in a wild, incomprehensible laugh.

When he had a particularly profound thought upon the science of war, he always unconsciously addressed himself to the youth.

There was some grim rejoicing by the men. "By thunder, I bet this army'll never see another new reg'ment like us."

"You bet!

> 'A dog, a woman, an' a walnut tree,
> Th' more yeh beat 'em, th' better they be.'

That's like us."

"Lost a piler men, they did. If an ol' woman swep' up th' woods, she'd git a dust-pan full."

"Yes, an' if she'll come around ag'in in 'bout an hour she'll git a pile more."

The forest still bore its burden of clamor. From off under the trees came the rolling clatter of the musketry. Each distant thicket seemed a strange porcupine with quills of flame. A cloud of dark smoke as from smouldering ruins went up toward the sun now bright and gay in the blue, enamelled sky.

CHAPTER XVIII

THE ragged line had respite for some minutes but during its pause, the struggle in the forest became magnified until the trees seemed to quiver from the firing and the ground to shake from the rushings of the men. The voices of the cannon were mingled in a long and interminable row. It seemed difficult to live in such an atmosphere. The chests of the men strained for a bit of freshness and their throats craved water.

There was one, shot through the body, who raised a cry of bitter lamentation when came this lull. Perhaps, he had been calling out during the fighting also but at that time no one had heard him. But now the men turned at the woful complaints of him upon the ground.

"Who is it? Who is it?"

"It's Jimmie Rogers. Jimmie Rogers."

When their eyes first encountered him there was a sudden halt as if they feared to go near. He was thrashing about in the grass, twisting his shuddering body into many strange postures. He was screaming loudly. This instant's hesitation seemed to fill him with a tremendous, fantastic contempt and he damned them in shrieked sentences.

The youth's friend had a geographical illusion concerning a stream and he obtained permission to go for some water. Immediately, canteens were showered upon him. "Fill mine, will yeh?" "Bring me some, too." "And me, too." He departed, ladened. The youth went with his friend, feeling a desire to throw his heated body into the stream and, soaking there, drink quarts.

They made a hurried search for the supposed stream but did not find it. "No water here," said the youth. They turned without delay and began to retrace their steps.

From their position as they again faced toward the place of the fighting, they could, of course, comprehend a greater amount of the battle than when their visions had been blurred by the hurlying smoke of the line. They could see dark stretches winding along the land and on one cleared space there was a row of guns making grey clouds which were filled with large flashes of orange-colored flame. Over some foliage they could see the roof of a house. One window, glowing a deep murderred, shone squarely through the leaves. From the edifice, a tall, leaning tower of smoke went far into the sky.

Looking over their own troops, they saw mixed masses slowly getting into regular form. The sun-light made twinkling points of the bright steel. To the rear, there was a glimpse of a distant road-way as it curved over a slope. It was crowded with retreating infantry. From all the interwoven forest arose the smoke and bluster of the battle. The air was always occupied by a blaring.

Near where they stood, shells were flip-flapping and hooting. Occasional bullets buzzed in the air and spanged into treetrunks. Wounded men and other stragglers were slinking through the woods.

Looking down an aisle of the grove, the youth and his companion saw a jangling general and his staff almost ride upon a wounded man who was crawling on his hands and knees. The general reined strongly at his charger's opened and foamy mouth and guided it with dexterous horsemanship past the man. The latter scrambled in wild and torturing haste. His strength evidently failed him as he reached a place of safety. One of his arms suddenly weakened, and he fell, sliding over upon his back. He lay stretched out, breathing gently.

A moment later, the small, creaking cavalcade was directly in front of the two soldiers. Another officer, riding with the skilful abandon of a cow-boy, galloped his horse to a position directly before the general. The two unnoticed foot-soldiers made a little show of going on but they lingered near in the desire to overhear the conversation. Perhaps, they thought, some great, inner historical things would be said.

The general, whom the boys knew as the commander of their division, looked at the other officer and spoke, coolly, as if he were criticising his clothes. "Th' enemy's formin' over there for another charge," he said. "It'll be directed against Whiterside, an' I fear they'll break through there unless we work like thunder t' stop them."

The other swore at his restive horse and then cleared his throat. He made a gesture toward his cap. "It'll be hell t' pay stoppin' them," he said, shortly.

"I presume so," remarked the general. Then he began to talk rapidly and in a lower tone. He frequently illustrated his words with a pointing finger. The two infantrymen could hear nothing until finally he asked: "What troops can you spare?"

The officer who rode like a cow-boy reflected for an instant. "Well," he said, "I had to order in th' 12th to help th' 76th an' I haven't really got any. But there's th' 304th. They fight like a lot 'a mule-drivers. I can spare them best of any."

The youth and his friend exchanged glances of astonishment.

The general spoke sharply. "Get 'em ready then. I'll watch developements from here an' send you word when t' start them. It'll happen in five minutes."

As the other officer tossed his fingers toward his cap and, wheeling his horse, started away, the general called out to him in a sober voice: "I don't believe many of your mule-drivers will get back."

The other shouted something in reply. He smiled.

With scared faces, the youth and his companion hurried back to the line.

These happenings had occupied an incredibly short time yet the youth felt that in them he had been made aged. New eyes were given to him. And the most startling thing was to learn suddenly that he was very insignificant. The officer spoke of the regiment as if he referred to a broom. Some part of the woods needed sweeping, perhaps, and he merely indicated a broom in a tone properly indifferent to its fate. It was war, no doubt, but it appeared strange.

As the two boys approached the line, the lieutenant perceived them and swelled with wrath. "Fleming—Wilson—how long does it take yeh t' git water, anyhow—where yeh been——"

But his oration ceased as he saw their eyes which were large with great tales. "We're going to charge—we're going to charge," cried the youth, hastening with his news.

"Charge?" said the lieutenant. "Charge? Well, b'Gawd! Now,

this is real fightin'." Over his soiled countenance there went a boastful smile. "Charge? Well, b'Gawd!"

A little group of soldiers surrounded the two youths. "Are we, sure-'nough? Well, I'll be derned. Charge? What fer? What at? Fleming, you're lyin'."

"I hope to die," said the youth, pitching his tones to the key of angry remonstrance. "Sure as shooting, I tell you."

And his friend spoke in reinforcement. "Not by a blame sight, he ain't lyin'. We heard 'em talkin'."

They caught sight of two mounted figures a short distance from them. One was the colonel of the regiment and the other was the officer who had received orders from the commander of the division. They were gesticulating at each other. The soldier pointing at them, interpreted the scene.

One soldier had a final objection: "How could yeh hear 'em talkin'," but the men, for a large part, nodded, admitting that previously the two friends had spoken truth.

They settled back into reposeful attitudes with airs of having accepted the matter. And they mused upon it, with a hundred varieties of expression. It was an engrossing thing to think about. Many tightened their belts carefully and hitched at their trousers.

A moment later, the officers began to bustle among the men, pushing them into a more compact mass and into a better alignment. They chased those that straggled and fumed at a few men who seemed to show by their attitudes, that they had decided to remain at that spot. They were like critical shepherds struggling with sheep.

Presently, the regiment seemed to draw itself up and heave a deep breath. None of the men's faces were mirrors of large thoughts. The soldiers were bended and stooped like sprinters before a signal. Many pairs of glinting eyes peered from the grimy faces toward the curtains of the deeper woods. They seemed to be engaged in deep calculations of time and distance.

They were surrounded by the noises of the monstrous altercation between the two armies. The world was fully interested in other matters. Apparently, the regiment had its small affair to itself.

The youth, turning, shot a quick, enquiring glance at his

friend. The latter returned to him the same manner of look. They were the only ones who possessed an inner knowledge. "Mule-drivers—hell t' pay—don't believe many will get back." It was an ironical secret. Still, they saw no hesitation in each other's faces and they nodded a mute and unprotesting assent when a shaggy man near them said in a meek voice: "We'll git swallered."

CHAPTER XIX

THE youth stared at the land in front of him. Its foliages now seemed to veil powers and horrors. He was unaware of the machinery of orders that started the charge, although from the corners of his eyes, he saw an officer, who looked like a boy a-horseback, come galloping, waving his hat. Suddenly, he felt a straining and heaving among the men. The line fell slowly forward like a toppling wall and with a convulsive gasp that was intended for a cheer, the regiment began its journey. The youth was pushed and jostled for a moment before he understood the movement at all but directly he lunged ahead and began to run.

He fixed his eye upon a distant and prominent clump of trees where he had concluded the enemy were to be met, and he ran toward it as toward a goal. He had believed, throughout, that it was a mere question of getting over an unpleasant matter as quickly as possible and he ran desperately as if pursued for a murder. His face was drawn hard and tight with the stress of his endeavor. His eyes were fixed in a lurid glare. And with his soiled and disordered dress, his red and inflamed features surmounted by the dingy rag with its spot of blood, his wildly swinging rifle and banging accoutrements, he looked to be an insane soldier.

As the regiment swung from its position out into a cleared space, the woods and thickets before it, awakened. Yellow flames leaped toward it from many directions. The forest made a tremendous objection.

The line lurched straight for a moment. Then the right wing swung forward; it in turn was surpassed by the left. Afterward the centre careered to the front until the regiment was a wedge-shaped mass but an instant later, the opposition of the bushes, trees and uneven places on the ground split the command and scattered it into detached clusters.

The youth, light-footed, was unconsciously in advance. His eyes still kept note of the clump of trees. From all places near it the clannish yell of the enemy could be heard. The little flames of rifles leaped from it. The song of the bullets was in the air and shells snarled among the tree-tops. One tumbled directly into the middle of a hurrying group and exploded in crimson fury. There was an instant's spectacle of a man, almost over it, throwing up his hands to shield his eyes.

Other men, punched by bullets, fell in grotesque agonies. The regiment left a coherent trail of bodies.

They had passed into a clearer atmosphere. There was an effect like a revelation in the new appearance of the landscape. Some men working madly at a battery were plain to them and the opposing infantry's lines were defined by the grey walls and fringes of smoke.

It seemed to the youth that he saw everything. Each blade of the green grass was bold and clear. He thought that he was aware of every change in the thin, transparent vapor that floated idly in sheets. The brown or grey trunks of the trees showed each roughness of their surfaces. And the men of the regiment, with their starting eyes and sweating faces, running madly, or falling, as if thrown headlong, to queer, heaped-up corpses, all were comprehended. His mind took mechanical but firm impressions, so that, afterward, everything was pictured and explained to him, save why he himself was there.

But there was a frenzy made from this furious rush. The men, pitching forward insanely, had burst into cheerings, mob-like and barbaric, but tuned in strange keys that can arouse the dullard and the stoic. It made a mad enthusiasm that, it seemed, would be incapable of checking itself before granite and brass. There was the delirium that encounters despair and death, and is heedless and blind to the odds. It is a temporary but sublime absence of selfishness. And because it was of this order was the reason, perhaps, why the youth wondered, afterward, what reasons he could have had for being there.

Presently the straining pace ate up the energies of the men.

As if by agreement, the leaders began to slacken their speed. The volleys directed against them had had a seeming wind-like effect. The regiment snorted and blew. Among some stolid trees it began to falter and hesitate. The men, staring intently, began to wait for some of the distant walls of smoke to move and disclose to them the scene. Since much of their strength and their breath had vanished, they returned to caution. They were become men again.

The youth had a vague belief that he had run miles and he thought, in a way, that he was now in some new and unknown land.

The moment the regiment ceased its advance, the protesting splutter of musketry became a steadied roar. Long and accurate fringes of smoke spread out. From the top of a small hill, came level belchings of yellow flame that caused an inhuman whistling in the air.

The men, halted, had opportunity to see some of their comrades dropping with moans and shrieks. A few lay under foot, still or wailing. And now for an instant the men stood, their rifles slack in their hands, and watched the regiment dwindle. They appeared dazed and stupid. This spectacle seemed to paralyze them, over-come them with a fatal fascination. They stared woodenly at the sights and, lowering their eyes, looked from face to face. It was a strange pause and a strange silence.

Then above the sounds of the outside commotion, arose the roar of the lieutenant. He strode suddenly forth, his infantile features black with rage.

"Come on, yeh fools," he bellowed. "Come on! Yeh can't stay here. Yeh must come on." He said more, but much of it could not be understood.

He started rapidly forward, with his head turned toward the men. "Come on," he was shouting. The men stared with blank and yokel-like eyes at him. He was obliged to halt and retrace his steps. He stood then with his back to the enemy and delivered gigantic curses into the faces of the men. His body vibrated from the weight and force of his imprecations. And he could string oaths with the facility of a maiden who strings beads.

The friend of the youth aroused. Lurching suddenly forward

and dropping to his knees, he fired an angry shot at the persistent woods. This action awakened the men. They huddled no more like sheep. They seemed suddenly to bethink them of their weapons and at once commenced firing. Belabored by their officers they began to move forward. The regiment involved like a cart involved in mud and muddle, started unevenly with many jolts and jerks. The men stopped, now, every few paces to fire and load, and in this manner moved slowly on from trees to trees.

The flaming opposition in their front grew with their advance until it seemed that all forward ways were barred by the thin leaping tongues and off to the right an ominous demonstration could sometimes be dimly discerned. The smoke, lately generated, was in confusing clouds that made it difficult for the regiment to proceed with intelligence. As he passed through each curling mass, the youth wondered what would confront him on the further side.

The command went painfully forward until an open space interposed between them and the lurid lines. Here, crouching and cowering behind some trees, the men clung with desperation as if threatened by a wave. They looked wild-eyed, and as if amazed, at this furious disturbance they had stirred. In the storm, there was an ironical expression of their importance. The faces of the men, too, showed a lack of a certain feeling of responsibility for being there. It was as if they had been driven. It was the dominant animal failing to remember in the supreme moments, the forceful causes of various superficial qualities. The whole affair seemed incomprehensible to many of them.

As they halted thus, the lieutenant again began to bellow profanely. Regardless of the vindictive threats of the bullets, he went about coaxing, berating and bedamning. His lips, that were habitually in a soft and child-like curve, were now writhed into unholy contortions. He swore by all possible deities.

Once, he grabbed the youth by the arm. "Come on, yeh lunkhead," he roared. "Come on. We'll all git killed if we stay here. We've on'y got t' go across that lot. An' then——" The remainder of his idea disappeared in a blue haze of curses.

The youth stretched forth his arm. " 'Cross there?" His mouth was puckered in doubt and awe.

"Cer'ly! Jest 'cross th' lot! We can't stay here," screamed the lieutenant. He poked his face close to the youth and waved his bandaged hand. "Come on!" Presently, he grappled with him as if for a wrestling bout. It was as if he planned to drag the youth by the ear on to the assault.

The private felt a sudden unspeakable indignation against his officer. He wrenched fiercely and shook him off.

"Come on yourself, then," he yelled. There was a bitter challenge in his voice.

They galloped together down the regimental front. The friend scrambled after them. In front of the colors, the three men began to bawl. "Come on! Come on!" They danced and gyrated like tortured savages.

The flag, obedient to these appeals, bended its glittering form and swept toward them. The men wavered in indecision for a moment and then with a long, wailful cry, the dilapidated regiment surged forward and began its new journey.

Over the field went the scurrying mass. It was a handful of men splattered into the faces of the enemy. Toward it instantly sprang the yellow tongues. A vast quantity of blue smoke hung before them. A mighty banging made ears valueless.

The youth ran like a madman to reach the woods before a bullet could discover him. He ducked his head low like a football player. In his haste, his eyes almost closed and the scene was a wild blur. Pulsating saliva stood at the corners of his mouth.

Within him, as he hurled himself forward, was born a love, a despairing fondness for this flag which was near him. It was a creation of beauty and invulnerability. It was a goddess, radiant, that bended its form with an imperious gesture to him. It was a woman, red and white, hating and loving, that called him with the voice of his hopes. Because no harm could come to it, he endowed it with power. He kept near as if it could be a saver of lives and an imploring cry went from his mind.

In the mad scramble, he was aware that the color-serjeant flinched suddenly as if struck by a bludgeon. He faltered and then became motionless, save for his quivering knees.

He made a spring and a clutch at the pole. At the same instant, his friend grabbed it from the other side. They jerked at it, stout and furious, but the color-serjeant was dead and the corpse would not relinquish its trust. For a moment, there was a grim encounter. The dead man, swinging with bended back, seemed to be obstinately tugging, in ludicrous and awful ways, for the possession of the flag.

It was past in an instant of time. They wrenched the flag furiously from the dead man, and, as they turned again, the corpse swayed forward with bowed head. One arm swung high and the curved hand fell with heavy protest on the friend's unheeding shoulder.

CHAPTER XX

WHEN the two youths turned with the flag, they saw that much of the regiment had crumbled away and the dejected remnant was coming slowly back. The men having hurled themselves in projectile-fashion, had presently expended their forces. They slowly retreated with their faces still toward the spluttering woods and their hot rifles still replying to the din. Several officers were giving orders, their voices keyed to screams.

"Where in hell yeh goin'?" the lieutenant was asking in a sarcastic howl. And a red-bearded officer, whose voice of triple brass could plainly be heard, was commanding: "Shoot into 'em! Shoot into 'em, Gawd damn their souls." There was a melee of speeches in which the men were ordered to do conflicting and impossible things.

The youth and his friend had a small scuffle over the flag. "Give it t' me." "No—let me keep it." Each felt satisfied with the other's possession of it but each felt bound to declare by an offer to carry the emblem, his willingness to further risk himself. The youth roughly pushed his friend away.

The regiment fell back to the stolid trees. There it halted for a moment to blaze at some dark forms that had begun to steal upon its track. Presently it resumed its march again, curving among the tree-trunks. By the time the depleted regiment had again reached the first open space, they were receiving a fast and merciless fire. There seemed to be mobs all about them.

The greater part of the men, discouraged, their spirits worn by the turmoil, acted as if stunned. They accepted the pelting of the bullets with bowed and weary heads. It was of no purpose to strive against walls. It was of no use to batter themselves against granite. And from this consciousness that they had attempted to conquer an unconquerable thing, there seemed to arise a feeling that they had been betrayed. They glowered with bent brows but dangerously upon some of the officers, more particularly upon the red-bearded one with the voice of triple brass.

However, the rear of the regiment was fringed with men who continued to shoot irritably at the advancing foes. They seemed resolved to make every trouble. The lieutenant was perhaps the last man in the disordered mass. His forgotten back was toward the enemy. He had been shot in the arm. It hung straight and rigid. Occasionally he would cease to remember it and be about to emphasize an oath with a sweeping gesture. The multiplied pain caused him to swear with incredible power.

The youth went along with slipping, uncertain feet. He kept watchful eyes rearward. A scowl of mortification and rage was upon his face. He had thought of a fine revenge upon the officer who had referred to him and his fellows as mule-drivers. But he saw that it could not come to pass. His dreams had collapsed when the mule-drivers, dwindling rapidly, had wavered and hesitated on the little clearing and then had recoiled. And now the retreat of the mule-drivers was a march of shame to him.

A dagger-pointed gaze from without his blackened face was held toward the enemy but his greater hatred was rivetted upon the man, who, not knowing him, had called him a mule-driver. When he knew that he and his comrades had failed to do anything in successful ways that might bring the little pangs of a kind of remorse upon the officer, the youth allowed the rage of the baffled to possess him. This cold officer upon a monument who dropped epithets unconcernedly down, would be finer as a dead man, he thought. So grievous did he think it that he could never possess the secret right to taunt truly in answer.

He had pictured red letters of curious revenge. "We *are* mule-drivers, are we?" And now he was compelled to throw them away.

He presently wrapped his heart in the cloak of his pride and kept the flag erect. He harangued his fellows, pushing against their chests with his free hand. To those he knew well, he made frantic appeals, beseeching them by name. Between him and the lieutenant, scolding and near to losing his mind with rage, there was felt a subtle fellowship and equality. They supported each other in all manner of hoarse, howling protests.

But the regiment was a machine run-down. The two men babbled at a forceless thing. The soldiers who had heart to go slowly were continually shaken in their resolves by a knowledge that comrades were slipping with speed back to the lines. It was difficult to think of reputation when others were thinking of skins. Wounded men were left, crying, on this black journey.

The smoke-fringes and flames blustered always. The youth peering once through a sudden rift in a cloud, saw a brown mass of troops interwoven and magnified until they appeared to be thousands. A fierce-hued flag flashed before his vision.

Immediately, as if the up-lifting of the smoke had been pre-arranged, the discovered troops burst into a rasping yell and a hundred flames jetted toward the retreating band. A rolling, grey cloud again interposed as the regiment doggedly replied. The youth had to depend again upon his misused ears which were trembling and buzzing from the melee of musketry and yells.

The way seemed eternal. In the clouded haze, men became panic-stricken with the thought that the regiment had lost its path and was proceeding in a perilous direction. Once, the men who headed the wild procession turned and came pushing back against their comrades screaming that they were being fired upon from points which they had considered to be toward their own lines. At this cry, a hysterical fear and dismay beset the troops. A soldier who heretofore had been ambitious to make the regiment into a wise little band that would proceed calmly amid the huge-appearing difficulties, suddenly sank down and buried his face in his arms with an air of bowing to a doom. From another, a shrill lamentation rang out filled with profane allusions to a general. Men ran hither and thither seeking with their eyes, roads of escape. With serene regularity as if controlled by a schedule, bullets buffed into men.

The youth walked stolidly into the midst of the mob and with his flag in his hands, took a stand as if he expected an attempt to push him to the ground. He unconsciously assumed the attitude of the color-bearer in the fight of the preceding day. He passed over his brow a hand that trembled. His breath did not come freely. He was choking during this small wait for the crisis.

His friend came to him. "Well, Henry, I guess this is good-bye-John."

"Oh, shut up, you damned fool," replied the youth and he would not look at the other.

The officers labored like politicians to beat the mass into a proper circle to face the menaces. The ground was uneven and torn. The men curled into depressions and fitted themselves snugly behind whatever would frustrate a bullet.

The youth noted with vague surprise that the lieutenant was standing mutely with his legs far apart and his sword held in the manner of a cane. The youth wondered what had happened to his vocal organs that he no more cursed.

There was something curious in this little intent pause of the lieutenant. He was like a babe which having wept its fill, raises its eyes and fixes upon a distant toy. He was engrossed in this contemplation, and the soft under-lip quivered from self-whispered words.

Some lazy and ignorant smoke curled slowly. The men, hiding from the bullets, waited anxiously for it to lift and disclose the plight of the regiment.

The silent ranks were suddenly thrilled by the eager voice of the lieutenant bawling out: "Here they come! Right onto us, b'Gawd." His further words were lost in a roar of wicked thunder from the men's rifles.

The youth's eyes had instantly turned in the direction indicated by the awakened and agitated lieutenant and he had seen the haze of treachery disclosing a body of soldiers of the enemy. They were so near that he could see their features. There was a recognition as he looked at the types of faces. He perceived with dim amazement that their uniforms were rather gay in effect, being light grey accented with a brilliant-hued facing. Too, the clothes seemed new.

These troops had apparently been going forward with caution, their rifles held in readiness, when the lieutenant had discovered them and their movement had been interrupted by the volley from the blue regiment. From the moment's glimpse, it was derived that they had been unaware of the proximity of their dark-suited foes, or, had mistaken the direction. Almost instantly, they were shut utterly from the youth's sight by the smoke from the energetic rifles of his companions. He strained his vision to learn the accomplishment of the volley but the smoke hung before him.

The two bodies of troops exchanged blows in the manner of a pair of boxers. The fast, angry firings went back and forth. The men in blue were intent with the despair of their circumstances and they seized upon the revenge to be had at close range. Their thunder swelled loud and valiant. Their curving front bristled with flashes and the place resounded with the clangor of their ram-rods. The youth ducked and dodged for a time and achieved a few unsatisfactory views of the enemy. There appeared to be many of them and they were replying swiftly. They seemed moving toward the blue regiment, step by step. He seated himself gloomily on the ground with his flag between his knees.

As he noted the vicious, wolf-like temper of his comrades, he had a sweet thought that if the enemy was about to swallow the regimental broom as a large prisoner, it could at least have the consolation of going down with bristles forward.

But the blows of the antagonist began to grow more weak. Fewer bullets ripped the air and finally when the men slackened to learn of the fight, they could see only dark, floating smoke. The regiment lay still and gazed. Presently, some chance whim came to the pestering blur and it began to coil heavily away. The men saw a ground vacant of fighters. It would have been an empty stage if it were not for a few corpses that lay thrown and twisted into fantastic shapes upon the sward.

At sight of this tableau, many of the men in blue sprang from behind their covers and made an ungainly dance of joy. Their eyes burned and a hoarse cheer of elation broke from their dry lips.

It had begun to seem to them that events were trying to prove that they were impotent. These little battles had evidently endeavored to demonstrate that the men could not fight well. When on the verge of submission to these opinions, the small duel had showed them that the proportions were not impossible, and by it they had revenged themselves upon their misgivings and upon the foe.

The impetus of enthusiasm was theirs again. They gazed about them with looks of uplifted pride, feeling new trust in the grim, always-confident weapons in their hands. And they were men.

CHAPTER XXI

P RESENTLY they knew that no firing threatened them. All ways seemed once more opened to them. The dusty blue lines of their friends were disclosed a short distance away. In the distance there were many colossal noises but in all this part of the field there was a sudden stillness.

They perceived that they were free. The depleted band drew a long breath of relief and gathered itself into a bunch to complete its trip.

In this last length of journey, the men began to show strange emotions. They hurried with nervous fear. Some who had been dark and unfaltering in the grimmest moments now could not conceal an anxiety that made them frantic. It was perhaps that they dreaded to be killed in insignificant ways after the times for proper military deaths had passed. Or, perhaps, they thought it would be too ironical to get killed at the portals of safety. With backward looks of perturbation, they hastened.

As they approached their own lines, there was some sarcasm exhibited on the part of a gaunt and bronzed regiment that lay resting in the shade of trees. Questions were wafted to them.

"Where th' hell yeh been?"

"What yeh comin' back fer?"

"Why didn't yeh stay there?"

"Was it warm out there, sonny?"

"Goin' home now, boys?"

One shouted in taunting mimicry. "Oh, mother, come quick an' look at th' sojers."

There was no reply from the bruised and battered regiment save that one man made broad-cast challenges to fist-fights and the red-bearded officer walked rather near and glared in great swashbuckler style at a tall captain in the other regiment. But the lieutenant suppressed the man who wished to fist-fight, and the tall captain, flushing at the little fanfare of the red-bearded one, was obliged to look intently at some trees.

The youth's tender flesh was deeply stung by these remarks. From under his creased brows, he glowered with hate at the mockers. He meditated upon a few revenges. Still, many in the regiment hung their heads in criminal fashion so that it came to pass that the men trudged with sudden heaviness as if they bore upon their bended shoulders the coffin of their honor. And the lieutenant recollecting himself began to mutter softly in black curses.

They turned, when they arrived at their old position, to regard the ground over which they had charged.

The youth, in this contemplation, was smitten with a large astonishment. He discovered that the distances, as compared with the brilliant measurings of his mind, were trivial and ridiculous. The stolid trees, where much had taken place, seemed incredibly near. The time, too, now that he reflected, he saw to have been short. He wondered at the number of emotions and events that had been crowded into such little spaces. Elfin thoughts must have exaggerated and enlarged everything, he said.

It seemed, then, that there was bitter justice in the speeches of the gaunt and bronzed veterans. He veiled a glance of disdain at his fellows who strewed the ground, choking with dust, red from perspiration, misty-eyed, dishevelled.

They were gulping at their canteens, fierce to wring every mite of water from them. And they polished at their swollen and watery features with coat-sleeves and bunches of grass.

However, to the youth there was a considerable joy in musing upon his performances during the charge. He had had very little time, previously, in which to appreciate himself, so that there was now much satisfaction in quietly thinking of his actions. He re-called bits of color that in the flurry, had stamped themselves unawares upon his engaged senses.

As the regiment lay heaving from its hot exertions, the officer who had named them as mule-drivers came galloping along the line. He had lost his cap. His towsled hair streamed wildly and his face was dark with vexation and wrath. His temper was displayed with more clearness by the way in which he managed his horse. He jerked and wrenched savagely at his bridle, stopping the hard-breathing animal with a furious pull near the colonel of the regiment. He immediately exploded in reproaches which came unbidden to the ears of the men. They were suddenly alert, being always curious about black words between officers.

"Oh, thunder, MacChesnay, what an awful bull you made of this thing," began the officer. He attempted low tones but his indignation caused certain of the men to learn the sense of his words. "What an awful mess you made. Good Lord, man, you stopped about a hundred feet this side of a very pretty success. If your men had gone a hundred feet further you would have made a great charge, but as it is—what a lot of mud-diggers you've got anyway."

The men, listening with bated breath, now turned their curious eyes upon the colonel. They had a ragamuffin interest in this affair.

The colonel was seen to straighten his form and put one hand forth in oratorical fashion. He wore an injured air; it was as if a deacon had been accused of stealing. The men were wiggling in an ecstasy of excitement.

But, of a sudden, the colonel's manner changed from that of a deacon to that of a Frenchman. He shrugged his shoulders. "Oh, well, general, we went as far as we could," he said calmly.

" 'As far as you could'? Did you, b'Gawd?" snorted the other. "Well, that wasn't very far, was it?" he added with a glance of cold contempt into the other's eyes. "Not very far, I think. You were intended to make a diversion in favor of Whiterside. How well you succeeded, your own ears can now tell you." He wheeled his horse and rode stiffly away.

The colonel, bidden to hear the jarring noises of an engagement in the woods to the left, broke out in vague damnations.

The lieutenant who had listened with an air of impotent rage to the interview spoke suddenly in firm and undaunted tones. "I don't care what a man is—whether he is a general, or what— if he says th' boys didn't put up a good fight out there, he's a damned fool."

"Lieutenant," began the colonel, severely, "this is my own affair and I'll trouble you——"

The lieutenant made an obedient gesture. "All right, colonel, all right," he said. He sat down with an air of being content with himself.

The news that the regiment had been reproached went along the line. For a time, the men were bewildered by it. "Good thunder," they ejaculated staring at the vanishing form of the general. They conceived it to be a huge mistake.

Presently, however, they began to believe that in truth their efforts had been called light. The youth could see this conviction weigh upon the entire regiment until the men were like cuffed and cursed animals but, withal, rebellious.

The friend, with a grievance in his eye, went to the youth. "I wonder what he does want," he said. "He must think we went out there an' played marbles. I never see sech a man."

The youth developed a tranquil philosophy for these moments of irritation. "Oh, well," he rejoined, "he probably didn't see nothing of it at all and got mad as blazes and concluded we were a lot of sheep, just because we didn't do what he wanted done. It's a pity old Grandpa Henderson got killed yesterday— he would have known that we did our best and fought good. It's just our awful luck, that's what."

"I should say so," replied the friend. He seemed to be deeply wounded at an injustice. "I should say we did have awful luck. There's no fun in fightin' fer people when everything yeh do— no matter what—ain't done right. I have a notion t' stay behind next time an' let 'em take their ol' charge an' go t' th' devil with it."

The youth spoke soothingly to his comrade. "Well, we both did good. I'd like to see the fool what'd say we both didn't do as good as we could."

"'A course, we did," declared the friend stoutly. "An' I'd break th' feller's neck if he was as big as a church. But we're all right, anyhow, fer I heared one feller say that we two fit th' best in th' reg'ment an' they had a great argyment 'bout it. Another feller, 'a course, he had t' up an' say it was a lie—he seen all what was goin' on an' he never seen us from th' beginnin' t' th' end. An' a lot more struck in an' ses it wasn't a lie—we did fight like thunder, an' they give us quite a send-off. But this is what I can't stand—these everlastin' ol' soldiers, titterin' an' laughin', an' then that general, he's crazy."

The youth exclaimed with sudden exasperation. "He's a lunk-head. He makes me mad. I wish he'd come along next time. We'd show him what——"

He ceased because several men had come hurrying up. Their faces expressed a bringing of great news.

"Oh, Flem, yeh jest oughta heard," cried one, eagerly.

"Heard what?" said the youth.

"Yeh jest oughta heard," repeated the other and he arranged himself to tell his tidings. The others made an excited circle. "Well, sir, th' colonel met your lieutenant right by us—it was damn'dest thing I ever heard—an' he ses, 'Ahem, ahem,' he ses, 'Mr. Hasbrouck,' he ses, 'by th' way, who was that lad what carried th' flag?' he ses. There, Flemin', what d' yeh think 'a that? 'Who was th' lad what carried th' flag?' he ses, an' th' lieutenant, he speaks up right away: 'That's Flemin', an' he's a jim-hickey,' he ses, right away. What? I say he did. 'A jim-hickey,' he ses—those'r his words. He did, too. I say, he did. If you kin tell this story better than I kin, go ahead an' tell it. Well, then, keep yer mouth shet. Th' lieutenant, he ses: 'He's a jim-hickey,' an' th' colonel, he ses: 'Ahem, ahem, he is indeed a very good man t' have, ahem. He kep' th' flag 'way t' th' front. I saw 'im. He's a good un,' ses th' colonel. 'You bet,' ses th' lieu-tenant, 'he an' a feller named Wilson was at th' head 'a th' charge, an' howlin' like Indians, all th' time,' he ses. 'Head 'a th' charge all th' time,' he ses. 'A feller named Wilson,' he ses. There, Wilson, m' boy, put that in a letter an' send it hum t' yer mother, hey? 'A feller named Wilson,' he ses. An' th' colonel, he ses: 'Were they, indeed? Ahem, ahem. My sakes,' he ses. 'At th' head 'a th' reg'ment?' he ses. 'They were,' ses th' lieu-tenant. 'My sakes,' ses th' colonel. He ses: 'Well, well, well,' he ses, 'those two babies?' 'They were!' ses th' lieutenant. 'Well, well,' ses th' colonel, 'they deserve t' be major-generals,' he ses. 'They deserve t' be major-generals.'"

The youth and his friend had said: "Huh!" "Yer lyin', Thompson." "Oh, go t' blazes." "He never sed it." "Oh, what a lie." "Huh." But despite these youthful scoffings and embarrassments, they knew that their faces were deeply flushing from thrills of pleasure. They exchanged a secret glance of joy and congratulation.

They speedily forgot many things. The past held no pictures of error and disappointment. They were very happy and their hearts swelled with grateful affection for the colonel and the lieutenant.

CHAPTER XXII

WHEN the woods again began to pour forth the dark-hued masses of the enemy, the youth felt serene self-confidence. He smiled briefly when he saw men dodge and duck at the long screechings of shells that were thrown in giant handfuls over them. He stood, erect and tranquil, watching the attack begin against a part of the line that made a blue curve along the side of an adjacent hill. His vision being unmolested by smoke from the rifles of his companions, he had opportunities to see parts of the hard fight. It was a relief to perceive at last from whence came some of these noises which had been roared into his ears.

Off a short way, he saw two regiments fighting a little separate battle with two other regiments. It was in a cleared space, wearing a set-apart look. They were blazing as if upon a wager, giving and taking tremendous blows. The firings were incredibly fierce and rapid. These intent regiments apparently were oblivious of all larger purposes of war and were slugging each other as if at a matched game.

In another direction, he saw a magnificent brigade going with the evident intention of driving the enemy from a wood. They passed in out of sight and presently there was a most awe-inspiring racket in the wood. The noise was unspeakable. Having stirred this prodigious uproar and, apparently, finding it too prodigious, the brigade, after a little time, came marching airily out again with its fine formation in no wise disturbed. There were no traces of speed in its movements. The brigade was jaunty and seemed to point a proud thumb at the yelling wood.

On a slope to the left, there was a long row of guns, gruff and maddened, denouncing the enemy who down through the woods were forming for another attack in the pitiless monotony of conflicts. The round, red discharges from the guns made a crimson flare and a high, thick smoke. Occasional glimpses could be caught of groups of the toiling artillerymen. In the rear of this row of guns stood a house, calm and white, amid bursting shells. A congregation of horses, tied to a long railing, were tugging frenziedly at their bridles. Men were running hither and thither.

The detached battle between the four regiments lasted for some time. There chanced to be no interference and they settled their dispute by themselves. They struck savagely and power-fully at each other for a period of minutes and then the lighter-hued regiments faltered and drew back, leaving the dark-blue lines, shouting. The youth could see the two flags shaking and laughing amid the smoke-remnants.

Presently, there was a stillness, pregnant with meaning. The blue lines shifted and changed a trifle and stared expectantly at the silent woods and fields before them. The hush was solemn and church-like, save for a distant battery that, evidently unable to remain quiet, sent a faint rolling thunder over the ground. It irritated, like the noises of unimpressed boys. The men imagined that it would prevent their perched ears from hearing the first words of the new battle.

Of a sudden, the guns on the slope roared out a message of warning. A spluttering sound had begun in the woods. It swelled with amazing speed to a profound clamor that involved the earth in noises. The splitting crashes swept along the lines until an interminable roar was developed. To those in the midst of it, it became a din fitted to the universe. It was the whirring and thumping of gigantic machinery, complications among the smaller stars. The youth's ears were filled cups. They were in-capable of hearing more.

On an incline over which a road wound, he saw wild and desperate rushes of men. It was perpetually backward and forward in riotous surges. These parts of the opposing armies were two long waves that pitched upon each other madly at dictated points. To and fro, they swelled. Sometimes, one side by its yells and cheers would proclaim decisive blows but, a moment later, the other side would be all yells and cheers. Once, the youth saw a spray of light forms go in hound-like leaps toward the waving blue lines. There was much howling and presently it went away with a vast mouthful of prisoners. Again, he saw a blue wave dash with such thunderous force against a grey obstruction that it seemed to clear the earth of it and leave nothing but trampled sod. And, always, in these swift and deadly rushes to and fro, the men screamed and yelled like maniacs.

Particular pieces of fence or secure positions behind collections of trees were wrangled over, as gold thrones or pearl bedsteads. There were desperate lunges at these chosen spots seemingly every instant and most of them were bandied like light toys between the contending forces. The youth could not tell from the battle-flags, flying like crimson foam in many directions, which color of cloth was winning.

His emaciated regiment bustled forth with undiminished fierceness when its time came. When assaulted again by bullets, the men burst out in a barbaric cry of rage and pain. They bended their heads in aims of intent hatred behind the projected hammers of their guns. Their ram-rods clanged loud with fury as their eager arms pounded the cartridges into the rifle-barrels. The front of the regiment was a smoke-wall penetrated by the flashing points of yellow and red.

Wallowing in the fight, they were in an astonishingly short time, re-smudged. They surpassed in stain and dirt all their previous appearances. Moving to and fro with strained exertion, jabbering the while, they were, with their swaying bodies, black faces and glowing eyes, like strange and ugly fiends jigging heavily in the smoke.

The lieutenant, returning from a tour after a bandage, produced from a hidden receptacle of his mind, new and portentous oaths suited to the emergency. Strings of expletives he swung lash-like over the backs of his men. And it was evident that his previous efforts had in no wise impaired his resources.

The youth, still the bearer of the colors, did not feel his idleness. He was deeply absorbed as a spectator. The crash and swing of the great drama made him lean forward, intent-eyed, his face working in small contortions. Sometimes, he prattled, words coming unconsciously from in him in grotesque exclamations. He did not know that he breathed; that the flag hung silently over him, so absorbed was he.

A formidable line of the enemy came within dangerous range. They could be seen plainly, tall, gaunt men with excited faces running with long strides toward a wandering fence.

At sight of this danger, the men suddenly ceased their cursing monotone. There was an instant of strained silence before they threw up their rifles and fired a plumping volley at the foes. There had been no order given; the men upon recognizing the menace, had immediately let drive their flock of bullets without waiting for word of command.

But the enemy were quick to gain the protection of the wandering line of fence. They slid down behind it with remarkable celerity and from this position, they began briskly to slice up the blue men.

These latter braced their energies for a great struggle. Often, white clenched teeth shone from the dusky faces. Many heads surged to and fro, floating upon a pale sea of smoke. Those behind the fence frequently shouted and yelped in taunts and gibe-like cries but the regiment maintained a stressed silence. Perhaps, at this new assault, the men re-called the fact that they had been named mud-diggers and it made their situation thrice bitter. They were breathlessly intent upon keeping the ground and thrusting away the rejoicing body of the enemy. They fought swiftly and with a despairing savageness denoted in their expressions.

The youth had resolved not to budge whatever should happen. Some arrows of scorn that had buried themselves in his heart, had generated strange and unspeakable hatreds. It was clear to him that his final and absolute revenge was to be achieved by his dead body lying, torn and guttering, upon the field. This was to be a poignant retaliation upon the officer who had said "mule-driver," and, later, "mud-digger." For, in all the wild graspings of his mind for a unit responsible for his sufferings and commotions, he always seized upon the man who had dubbed him wrongly. And it was his idea, vaguely formulated, that his corpse would be for those eyes a great and salt reproach.

The regiment bled extravagantly. Grunting bundles of blue began to drop. The orderly-serjeant of the youth's company was shot through the cheeks. Its supports being injured, his jaw hung afar down, disclosing in the wide cavern of his mouth, a pulsing mass of blood and teeth. And, with it all, he made attempts to cry out. In his endeavor there was a dreadful earnestness as if he conceived that one great shriek would make him well.

The youth saw him presently go rearward. His strength seemed in no wise impaired. He ran swiftly, casting wild glances for succor.

Others fell down about the feet of their companions. Some of the wounded crawled out and away, but many lay still, their bodies twisted into impossible shapes.

The youth looked once for his friend. He saw a vehement young man, powder-smeared and frowsled, whom he knew to be him. The lieutenant, also, was unscathed in his position at the rear. He had continued to curse but it was now with the air of a man who was using his last box of oaths.

For the fire of the regiment had begun to wane and drip. The robust voice that had come strangely from the thin ranks, was growing rapidly weak.

CHAPTER XXIII

THE colonel came running along back of the line. There were other officers following him. "We must charge 'm," they shouted. "We must charge 'm." They cried with resentful voices, as if anticipating a rebellion against this plan by the men.

The youth upon hearing the shouts, began to study the distance between him and the enemy. He made vague calculations. He saw that to be firm soldiers, they must go forward. It would be death to stay in the present place and, with all the circumstances, to go backward would exalt too many others. Their hope was to push the galling foes away from the fence.

He expected that his companions, weary and stiffened, would have to be driven to this assault but as he turned toward them, he perceived with a certain surprise that they were giving quick and unqualified expressions of assent. There was an ominous, clanging overture to the charge when the shafts of the bayonets rattled upon the rifle-barrels. At the yelled words of command, the soldiers sprang forward in eager leaps. There was new and unexpected force in the movement of the regiment. A knowledge of its faded and jaded condition made the charge appear like a paroxysm, a display of the strength that comes before a final feebleness. The men scampered in insane fever of haste, racing as if to achieve a sudden success before an exhilarating fluid should leave them. It was a blind and despairing rush by the collection of men in dusty and tattered blue, over a green sward and under a sapphire sky, toward a fence, dimly outlined in smoke, from behind which spluttered the fierce rifles of enemies.

The youth kept the bright colors to the front. He was waving his free arm in furious circles, the while shrieking mad calls and appeals, urging on those that did not need to be urged.

For, it seemed that the mob of blue men hurling themselves on the dangerous group of rifles were again grown suddenly wild with an enthusiasm of unselfishness. From the many firings starting toward them, it looked as if they would merely succeed in making a great sprinkling of corpses on the grass between their former position and the fence. But they were in a state of frenzy, perhaps because of forgotten vanities, and it made an exhibition of sublime recklessness. There was no obvious questionings, nor figurings, nor diagrams. There was, apparently, no considered loop-holes. It appeared that the swift wings of their desires would have shattered against the iron gates of the impossible.

He, himself, felt the daring spirit of a savage, religion-mad. He was capable of profound sacrifices, a tremendous death. He had no time for dissections but he knew that he thought of the bullets only as things that could prevent him from reaching the place of his endeavor. There were subtle flashings of joy within him, that thus should be his mind.

He strained all his strength. His eye-sight was shaken and dazzled by the tension of thought and muscle. He did not see anything excepting the mist of smoke gashed by the little knives of fire but he knew that in it lay the aged fence of a vanished farmer protecting the snuggled bodies of the grey men.

As he ran, a thought of the shock of contact gleamed in his mind. He expected a great concussion when the two bodies of troops crashed together. This became a part of his wild battle-madness. He could feel the onward swing of the regiment about him and he conceived of a thunderous, crushing blow that would prostrate the resistance and spread consternation and amazement for miles. The flying regiment was going to have a catapultian effect. This dream made him run faster among his comrades who were giving vent to hoarse and frantic cheers.

But presently he could see that many of the men in grey did not intend to abide the blow. The smoke, rolling, disclosed men who ran, their faces still turned. These grew to a crowd who retired stubbornly. Individuals wheeled frequently to send a bullet at the blue wave.

But at one part of the line there was a grim and obdurate

group that made no movement. They were settled firmly down behind posts and rails. A flag, ruffled and fierce, waved over them and their rifles dinned fiercely.

The blue whirl of men got very near until it semed that in truth there would be a close and frightful scuffle. There was an expressed disdain in the opposition of the little group, that changed the meaning of the cheers of the men in blue. They became yells of wrath, directed, personal. The cries of the two parties were now in sound an interchange of scathing insults.

They in blue showed their teeth; their eyes shone all white. They launched themselves as at the throats of those who stood resisting. The space between dwindled to an insignificant distance.

The youth had centred the gaze of his soul upon that other flag. Its possession would be high pride. It would express bloody minglings, near blows. He had a gigantic hatred for those who made great difficulties and complications. They caused it to be as a craved treasure of mythology, hung amid tasks and contrivances of danger.

He plunged like a mad horse at it. He was resolved it should not escape if wild blows and darings of blows could seize it. His own emblem, quivering and a-flare, was winging toward the other. It seemed there would shortly be an encounter of strange beaks and claws, as of eagles.

The swirling body of blue men came to a sudden halt at close and disastrous range and roared a swift volley. The group in grey was split and broken by this fire but its riddled body still fought. The men in blue yelled again and rushed in upon it.

The youth, in his leapings, saw as through a mist, a picture of four or five men stretched upon the ground or writhing upon their knees with bowed heads as if they had been stricken by bolts from the sky. Tottering among them was the rival color-bearer whom the youth saw had been bitten vitally by the bullets of the last formidable volley. He perceived this man fighting a last struggle, the struggle of one whose legs are grasped by demons. It was a ghastly battle. Over his face was the bleach of death but set upon it was the dark and hard lines of desperate purpose. With this terrible grin of resolution, he hugged his precious flag to him and was stumbling and staggering in his design to go the way that led to safety for it.

But his wounds always made it seem that his feet were retarded, held, and he fought a grim fight as with invisible ghouls, fastened greedily upon his limbs. Those in advance of the scampering blue men, howling cheers, leaped at the fence. The despair of the lost was in his eyes, as he glanced back at them.

The youth's friend went over the obstruction in a tumbling heap and sprang at the flag as a panther at prey. He pulled at it, and wrenching it free, swung up its red brilliancy with a mad cry of exultation even as the color-bearer, gasping, lurched over in a final throe and stiffening convulsively turned his dead face to the ground. There was much blood upon the grass-blades.

At the place of success there began more wild clamorings of cheers. The men gesticulated and bellowed in an ecstasy. When they spoke it was as if they considered their listener to be a mile away. What hats and caps were left to them, they often slung high in the air.

At one part of the line, four men had been swooped upon and they now sat as prisoners. Some blue men were about them in an eager and curious circle. The soldiers had trapped strange birds and there was an examination. A flurry of fast questions was in the air.

One of the prisoners was nursing a superficial wound in the foot. He cuddled it, baby-wise, but he looked up from it often to curse with an astonishing utter abandon straight at the noses of his captors. He consigned them to red regions; he called upon the pestilential wrath of strange gods. And, with it all, he was singularly free from recognition of the finer points of the conduct of prisoners-of-war. It was as if a clumsy clod had trod upon his toe and he conceived it to be his privilege, his duty, to use deep, resentful oaths.

Another, who was a boy in years, took his plight with great calmness and apparent good-nature. He conversed with the men in blue, studying their faces with his bright and keen eyes. They spoke of battles and conditions. There was an acute interest in all their faces during this exchange of view-points. It seemed a great satisfaction to hear voices from where all had been darkness and speculation.

The third captive sat with a morose countenance. He preserved a stoical and cold attitude. To all advances, he made one reply, without variation. "Ah, go t' hell."

The last of the four was always silent and, for the most part, kept his face turned in unmolested directions. From the views the youth received, he seemed to be in a state of absolute dejection. Shame was upon him and with it profound regret that he was perhaps no more to be counted in the ranks of his fellows. The youth could detect no expression that would allow him to believe that the other was giving a thought to his narrowed future, the pictured dungeons, perhaps, and starvations and brutalities, liable to the imagination. All to be seen was shame for captivity and regret for the right to antagonize.

After the men had celebrated sufficiently, they settled down behind the old rail fence, on the opposite side to the one from which their foes had been driven. A few shot perfunctorily at distant marks.

There was some long grass. The youth nestled in it and rested, making a convenient rail support the flag. His friend, jubilant and glorified, holding his treasure with vanity, came to him there. They sat side by side and congratulated each other.

CHAPTER XXIV

THE roarings that had stretched in a long line of sound across the face of the forest began to grow intermittent and weaker. The stentorian speeches of the artillery continued in some distant encounter but the crashes of the musketry had almost ceased. The youth and his friend, of a sudden, looked up, feeling a deadened form of distress at the waning of these noises which had become a part of life. They could see changes going on among the troops. There were marchings this way and that way. A battery wheeled leisurely. On the crest of a small hill was the thick gleam of many departing muskets.

The youth arose. "Well, what now, I wonder," he said. By his tone, he seemed to be preparing to resent some new monstrosity in the way of dins and smashes. He shaded his eyes with his grimy hand and gazed over the field.

His friend also arose and stared. "I bet we're goin' t' git along outa this an' back over th' river," said he.

"Well, I swan," said the youth.

They waited, watching. Within a little while, the regiment received orders to retrace its way. The men got up grunting from the grass, regretting the soft repose. They jerked their stiffened legs and stretched their arms over their heads. One man swore as he rubbed his eyes. They all groaned. "Oh, Lord." They had as many objections to this change as they would have had to a proposal for a new battle.

They tramped slowly back over the field across which they had run in a mad scamper.

The regiment marched until it had joined its fellows. The re-formed brigade, in column, aimed through a wood at the road. Directly they were in a mass of dust-covered troops and were trudging along in a way parallel to the enemy's lines, as these had been defined by the previous turmoil.

They passed within view of the stolid white house and saw in front of it, groups of their comrades lying in wait behind a neat breastwork. A row of guns were booming at a distant enemy. Shells thrown in reply were raising clouds of dust and splinters. Horsemen dashed along the line of entrenchments.

At this point of its march, the division curved away from the field and went winding off in the direction of the river. When the significance of this movement had impressed itself upon the youth, he turned his head and looked over his shoulder toward the trampled and debris-strewed ground. He breathed a breath of new satisfaction. He finally nudged his friend. "Well, it's all over," he said to him.

His friend gazed backward. "B'Gawd, it is," he assented. They mused.

For a time, the youth was obliged to reflect in a puzzled and uncertain way. His mind was under-going a subtle change. It took moments for it to cast off its battleful ways and resume its accustomed course of thought. Gradually his brain emerged from the clogged clouds and at last he was enabled to more closely comprehend himself and circumstance.

He understood then that the existence of shot and counter-shot was in the past. He had dwelt in a land of strange, squalling up-heavals and had come forth. He had been where there was red of blood and black of passion, and he was escaped. His first thoughts were given to rejoicings at this fact.

Later, he began to study his deeds—his failures and his achievements. Thus fresh from scenes where many of his usual machines of reflection had been idle, from where he had proceeded sheep-like, he struggled to marshal all his acts.

At last, they marched before him clearly. From this present view-point, he was enabled to look upon them in spectator fashion and to criticise them with some correctness, for his new condition had already defeated certain sympathies.

Regarding his procession of memory, he felt gleeful and unregretting, for, in it, his public deeds were paraded in great and shining prominence. Those performances which had been witnessed by his fellows marched now in wide purple and gold, hiding various deflections. They went gaily, with music. It was pleasure to watch these things. He spent delightful minutes viewing the gilded images of memory.

He saw that he was good. He re-called with a thrill of joy the respectful comments of his fellows upon his conduct.

Nevertheless, the ghost of his flight from the first engagement appeared to him and danced. There were small shoutings in his brain about these matters. For a moment, he blushed, and the light of his soul flickered with shame.

A spectre of reproach came to him. There loomed the dogging memory of the tattered soldier, he who gored by bullets and faint for blood, had fretted concerning an imagined wound in another, he who had loaned his last of strength and intellect for the tall soldier, he who blind with weariness and pain had been deserted in the field.

For an instant, a wretched chill of sweat was upon him at the thought that he might be detected in the thing. As it stood persistently before his vision, he gave vent to a cry of sharp irritation and agony.

His friend turned. "What's th' matter, Henry?" he demanded. The youth's reply was an outburst of crimson oaths.

As he marched along the little branch-hung road-way among his prattling companions, this vision of cruelty brooded over him. It clung near him always and darkened his view of the deeds in purple and gold. Whichever way his thoughts turned, they were followed by the sombre phantom of the desertion in the fields. He looked stealthily at his companions, feeling sure that they must discern in his face evidences of this pursuit. But they were plodding in ragged array, discussing with quick tongues, the accomplishments of the late battle.

"Oh, if a man should come up an' ask me, I'd say we got a dum good lickin'."

"Lickin'—in yer eye. We ain't licked, sonny. We're goin' down here aways, swing aroun', an' come in behint 'em."

"Oh, hush, with yer comin' in behint 'em. I've seen all 'a that I wanta. Don't tell me about comin' in behint——"

"Bill Smithers, he ses he'd rather been in ten hunderd battles than been in that heluva hospital. He ses they got shootin' in th' night-time an' shells dropped plum among 'em in th' hospital. He ses sech hollerin' he never see."

"Hasbrouck? He's th' best off'cer in this here reg'ment. He's a Whale."

"Didn't I tell yeh we'd come aroun' in behint 'em? Didn't I tell yeh so? We——"

"Oh, shet yer mouth."

For a time, this pursuing recollection of the tattered man took all elation from the youth's veins. He saw his vivid error and he was afraid that it would stand before him all of his life. He took no share in the chatter of his comrades, nor did he look at them or know them, save when he felt sudden suspicion that they were seeing his thoughts and scrutinizing each detail of the scene with the tattered soldier.

Yet gradually he mustered force to put the sin at a distance. And at last his eyes seemed to open to some new ways. He found that he could look back upon the brass and bombast of his earlier gospels and see them truly. He was gleeful when he discovered that he now despised them.

With this conviction came a store of assurance. He felt a quiet man-hood, non-assertive but of sturdy and strong blood. He knew that he would no more quail before his guides wherever they should point. He had been to touch the great death and found that, after all, it was but the great death. He was a man.

So it came to pass that as he trudged from the place of blood and wrath, his soul changed. He came from hot-plough-shares to prospects of clover tranquility and it was as if hot-ploughshares were not. Scars faded as flowers.

It rained. The procession of weary soldiers became a bedraggled train, despondent and muttering, marching with churning effort, in a trough of liquid brown mud under a low, wretched sky. Yet the youth smiled, for he saw that the world was a world for him though many discovered it to be made of oaths and walking-sticks. He had rid himself of the red sickness of battle. The sultry night-mare was in the past. He had been an animal blistered and sweating in the heat and pain of war. He turned now with a lover's thirst, to images of tranquil skies, fresh meadows, cool brooks; an existence of soft and eternal peace.

Over the river a golden ray of sun came through the hosts of leaden rain clouds.

THE FINAL MANUSCRIPT:
DISCARDED CHAPTER XII

FINAL MANUSCRIPT:
DISCARDED CHAPTER XII

IT WAS always clear to the youth that he was entirely different from other men; that his mind had been cast in a unique mold. Hence laws that might be just to the ordinary man, were, when applied to him, peculiar and galling outrages. Minds, he said, were not made all with one stamp and colored green. He was of no general pattern. It was not right to measure his acts by a world-wide standard. The laws of the world were wrong because through the vain spectacles of their makers, he appeared, with all men, as of a common size and of a green color. There was no justice on the earth when justice was meant. Men were too puny and prattling to know anything of it. If there was a justice, it must be in the hands of a God.

He regarded his sufferings as unprecedented. No man had ever achieved such misery. There was a melancholy grandeur in the isolation of his experiences. He saw that he was a speck raising his minute arms against all possible forces and fates which were swelling down upon him in black tempests. He could derive some consolation from viewing the sublimity of the odds.

As he went on, he began to feel that nature, for her part, would not blame him for his rebellion. He still distinctly felt that he was arrayed against the universe but he believed now that there was no malice in the vast breasts of his space-filling foes. It was merely law, not merciful to the individual; but just, to a system. Nature had provided the creations with various defenses and ways of escape that they might fight or flee, and she had limited dangers in powers of attack and pursuit that the things might resist or hide with a security proportionate to their strength and wisdom. It was | [*end* MS fol. 98] cruel but it was war. Nature fought for her system; individuals fought for liberty to breathe. The animals had the previlege of using their legs and their brains. It was all the same old philosophy. He could not omit a small grunt of satisfaction as he saw with what brilliancy he had reasoned it out.

He now said that, if, as he supposed, his life was being relentlessly pursued, it was not his duty to bow to the approaching death. Nature did not expect submission. On the contrary, it was his business to kick and bite and give blows as a stripling in the hands of a murderer. The law was that he should fight. He would be saved according to the importance of his strength.

His egotism made him feel safe, for a time, from the iron hands.

It being in his mind that he had solved these matters, he eagerly applied his findings to the incident of his flight from the battle. It was not a fault, a shameful thing; it was an act obedient to a law. It was——

But he was aware that when he had erected a vindicating structure of great principles, it was the calm toes of tradition that kicked it all down about his ears. He immediately antagonized then this devotion to the by-gone; this universal adoration of the past. From the bitter pinnacle of his wisdom he saw that mankind not only worshipped the gods of the ashes but that the gods of the ashes were worshipped because they were the gods of the ashes. He percieved with anger the present state of affairs in it's bearing upon his case. And he resolved to reform it all.

He had, presently, a feeling that he was the growing prophet of a world-reconstruction. Far down in the untouched depths of his being, among the hidden currents of his soul, he saw born a voice. He concieved a new world modelled by the pain of his life, and in which no old shadows fell blighting upon the temple of thought. And there were many personal advantages in it. |
[*end of* MS fol. 99; fol. 100 *wanting*]

[MS(d) fol. 86 *picks up after* 'advantages in it.' (¶)He thought for a time of piercing orations starting multitudes and of books wrung from his heart. In the gloom of his misery, his eyesight proclaimed that mankind were bowing to wrong and ridiculous idols. He said that if some all-powerful joker should take them away in the night, and leave only manufactured shadows falling upon the bended heads, mankind would go on counting the hollow beads of their progress until the shriveling of the fingers. He was a-blaze with desire to change. He saw himself, a sun-lit figure upon a peak, pointing with true and unchangeable gesture. "There!" And all men could see and no man would falter.

Gradually the idea grew upon him that the cattle which cluttered the earth, would, in their ignorance and calm faith in the next day, blunder stolidly on and he would be beating his fists against the brass of accepted things. A remarkable facility for abuse came to him then and in supreme disgust and rage, he railed. To him there was something terrible and awesome in these words spoken from his heart to his heart. He was very tragic. | (*end of* MS[d] fol. 86; fols. 87–89 *wanting*)]

[MS fol. 101]

He saw himself chasing a thought-phantom across the sky before the assembled eyes of mankind. He could say to them that it was an angel whose possession was existence perfected; they would declare it to be a greased pig. He had no desire to devote his life to proclaiming the angel, when he could plainly percieve that mankind would hold, from generation to generation, to the theory of the greased pig.

It would be pleasure to reform a docile race. But he saw that there were none and he did not intend to raise his voice against the hooting of continents.

Thus he abandoned the world to it's devices. He felt that many men must have so abandoned it, but he saw how they could be reconciled to it and agree to accept the stone idols and the greased pigs, when they contemplated the opportunities for plunder.

For himself, however, he saw no salve, no reconciling opportunities. He was entangled in the errors. He began to rage anew against circumstances which he did not name and against processes of which he knew only the name. He felt that he was being grinded beneath stone feet which he despised. The detached bits of truth which formed the knowledge of the world could not save him. There was a dreadful, unwritten martyrdom in his state.

He made a little search for some thing upon which to concentrate the hate of his despair; he fumbled in his mangled intellect to find the Great Responsibility.

He again hit upon nature. He again saw her grim dogs upon his trail. They were unswerving, merciless and would overtake him at the appointed time. His mind pictured the death of Jim Conklin and in the scene, he saw the shadows of his fate. Dread | [*end* MS fol. 101] words had been said from star to star. An event had been penned by the implacable forces.

He was of the unfit, then. He did not come into the scheme of further life. His tiny part had been done and he must go. There was no room for him. On all the vast lands there was not a foot-hold. He must be thrust out to make room for the more important.

Regarding himself as one of the unfit, he believed that nothing could accede for misery, a perception of this fact. He thought that he measured with his falling heart, tossed in like a pebble by his supreme and awful foe, the most profound depths of pain. It was a barbarous process with affection for the man and the oak, and no sympathy for the rabbit and the weed. He thought of his own capacity for pity and there was an infinite irony in it.

He desired to revenge himself upon the universe. Feeling in his body all spears of pain, he would have capsized, if possible, the world and made chaos. Much cruelty lay in the fact that he was a babe.

Admitting that he was powerless and at the will of law, he yet planned to escape; menaced by fatality he schemed to avoid it. He thought of various places in the world where he imagined that he would be safe. He remembered hiding once in an empty flour-barrel that sat in his mother's pantry. His playmates, hunting the bandit-chief, had thundered on the barrel with their fierce sticks but he had lain snug and undetected. They had searched the house. He now created in thought a secure spot where an all-powerful eye would fail to percieve him; where an all-powerful stick would fail to bruise his life.

There was in him a creed of freedom which no contemplation of inexorable law could destroy. He saw himself living in watchfulness, frustrating the plans of the unchangeable, making of fate a fool. He had ways, he thought, of working out his

EARLY DRAFT MANUSCRIPT

EARLY DRAFT MANUSCRIPT

[*Page* 2]
come aroun' in behint 'em.'"

To his attentive audience, he drew a loud and elaborate plan of a very brilliant campaign. When he had finished, the blue-clothed men scattered into small, arguing groups in the little lane between the rows of squat, brown huts. Here and there was a steel-glitter. Smoke drifted lazily from barrel-chimneys.

"It's a lie—that's all it is. A thunderin' lie," said young Wilson. His smooth face was flushed and his hands were thrust sulkily into his trouser's pockets. He took the matter as a personal affront. "I don't believe th' derned ol' army's ever goin' t' move. We're sot. I've got ready t' move eight times in th' last two weeks an' we aint moved yit."

Conklin felt called upon to defend the truth of a rumor he had introduced. He and young Wilson came near to fighting over it.

Simpson, a corporal, began to swear. He had just put a costly board-floor in his house, he said. He had refrained from adding extensively to the comfort of his environment during the spring because he had felt that the army might start on the march at any moment. Lately, however, he had been impressed that they were in a sort of eternal camp. So, he and his two mates had put in a board-floor! And now the army was going to move!

Many of the men engaged in a spirited |

[*Page* 4]
other end. A picture from an illustrated weekly was upon the log wall and three rifles were paralelled on pegs. Some tin dishes lay on a small pile of fire-wood. Equipments were hung on handy projections. The smoke from the fire at times neglected

the clay-chimney and wreathed into the room. A small window shot an oblique square of light upon the cluttered floor.

So, they were at last going to fight. On the morrow, perhaps, there would be a battle and he would be in it.

He could not convince himself of it. It was too strange. He could not believe with assurance that he was at last to mingle in one of those great affairs of the earth.

He had dreamed of battles all his life—of vague, bloody conflicts that had thrilled him with their sweep and fire. In visions, he had seen himself in many struggles. But, awake, he had regarded battles as crimson blotches on the pages of the past. He had put them, as things of the bygone, with his thought-images of heavy golden crowns and high dreary castles. There was a portion of the world's history which he had regarded as the time of war, but, that, he had thought, had gone over the horizon and disappeared forever.

From his home, his youthful eyes had looked at the war in his own country with distrust. | [Page 5] It must be a sort of a play affair. Greek-like struggles could be no more, he had said. Men were better. Secular and religious education had effaced the throat-grappling instinct.

He had burned several times to enlist. His mother had, however, discouraged him. She had affected to look with some contempt upon the quality of his patriotism. She could calmly seat herself and with no trouble at all, give him nearly a thousand reasons why he was of more importance on the farm than on the field of battle. And she had had certain ways of expression that told that her statements on the subject came from a deep conviction.

At last, he had rebelled against this yellow light thrown upon the color of his ambitions. The newspapers, the gossip of the village, his own picturings, had aroused him to an uncheckable degree. They were truly fighting down there. Almost every day, the country vibrated with the noise of a great and decisive victory.

One night as he lay in bed, the wind carried to him the clangoring of the church-bell as some enthusiast jerked the rope frantically to tell the twisted news of a battle. The voice calling in the night had made him shiver in a prolonged ecstacy of excitement. Later | [*Page* 6] he had gone down to his mother's room and had spoken thus: "Ma, I'm goin' t' enlist."

"Henry, don't you be a fool," his mother had replied. She had covered her head with the quilt and there was an end to the matter for that night.

Nevertheless, the next morning he had gone to a considerable town that was near his mother's farm and had enlisted in one of the companies that were forming there. When he had returned home, his mother was milking the brindle cow. Four others stood patiently waiting.

"Ma, I've enlisted," he had said to her, diffidently.

"The Lord's will be done, Henry," she had replied and had continued to milk the brindle cow.

When he had stood in the door with his soldier clothes on his back and a light of excitement and expectation in his eyes, he had seen two tears leave their burning trails on his mother's rough cheeks. Still she had disappointed him by saying nothing about returning with his shield or on it. To the contrary. She had doggedly peeled potatoes and addressed him as follows: "You watch out, Henry, in this here fightin' business—you watch out an' take good keer a' yerself. I've knit yeh eight pairs of socks an' I've put in all yer best shirts, b'cause I want my boy t' be jest as warm an' comf'table as | [*Page* 7] anybody in the army. Whenever, they git holes in 'em, I want yeh t' send 'em right-away back t' me, so's I kin darn 'em. An' allus be keerful, Henry, an' choose yer comp'ny. There's lots of bad men in th' army. Th' army makes 'em wild an' they like nothin' better than th' job of leadin' off a young fellah like you, as aint never been away from home much an' has allus had a mother; an' learnin' him t' drink an' swear. I don't want yeh t' ever do anything, Henry, that yeh would be ashamed t' let me know about an' if yeh keep right t' that, I guess yeh'll come out pretty straight. Young fellers in th' army git mighty keerless in their ways, bein' away from home, an' I'm afeard for yeh 'bout that Henry. Yeh mus' remember yer father, chil', an' remember he never drunk a drop a' licker in his life nor never swore a cross oath. I don't know what else t' tell yeh, Henry, exceptin' that yeh mustn't never do no shirkin', Henry, on my account. If so be a time comes when yeh have t' be kilt or do a mean thing, why,

Henry, don't think of anythin' excepts what's right, b'cause there's many a woman has t' bear up 'ginst sech things these times. Don't ferget t' send yer socks t' me th' minute they git holes in 'em, an' here's a little bible I want yeh t' take | [*Page* 8] along with yeh, Henry. I don't expect yeh'll be a-settin' readin' it all day long, child, ner nothin' like that. Many times yeh'll fergit yeh got it, I don't doubt. But there's many times, Henry, yeh'll be wantin' advice, Henry, an' all like that, an' there'll be nobody 'round, perhaps, t' show yeh. Then if yeh take it out, yeh'll find wisdom t' set yeh straight with little searchin', Henry. Don't fergit about th' socks, an' I've put some blackberry jam with yer things 'cause I know yeh like it above all. Good-bye, Henry, an' be a good boy."

He had born this speech with impatience. It was not quite what he had expected and it had made him feel sheepish. He had felt glad that no one of his friends had been there to listen to it.

From his home, he had gone to the seminary to bid adieu to many old schoolmates. There, a certain light-haired girl had made vivacious efforts to poke fun at his martial spirit. But there was another girl who, he thought, had become demure and sad at sight of his blue and brass. As he had walked down the aisle between the rows of oaks on the lawn, he had discovered her watching his departure from a window. As he had turned and |

[*Page* 10]
The only foes he had seen were the pickets on the river bank. They were a sun-tanned, philosophical lot who sometimes shot thoughtfully at the opposite pickets but usually seemed sorry for it afterwards. Fleming on guard duty one night had talked across the river with one. He was a slightly ragged man with a fund of sublime assurance. Fleming liked him personally.

Various veterans had told him tales. Some talked of grey, be-whiskered hordes who were advancing, cursing relentlessly and chewing tobacco with unspeakable valor; tremendous bodies of fierce soldiery who were sweeping along like the Huns. Others spoke of tattered and eternally hungry men who fired despondent rifles. From their stories, Fleming imagined the red bones sticking out through slits in the faded uniforms. Still, he could not put a whole faith in tales, for recruits were the veteran's prey. They talked much of smoke, fire and blood but he could not tell how much might be lies.

However, he percieved that it did not greatly matter what kind of soldiers he was going to fight. There was a more serious problem. He lay in his bunk debating the question. He tried to solve it mathematically. He was endeavoring to decide wether he would run from a fight or not.

It had suddenly come to his mind that perhaps in a battle he might run. He was | [*Page* 11] forced to admit that as far as war was concerned he knew nothing of himself. Before this, he had never been obliged to grapple too seriously with the question. He had taken certain things for granted, even as in thoughts about his life, he had never had doubts of the ultimate success of it and had bothered little about means and roads.

But he was now suddenly confronted. As his imagination went forward to a fight, he saw hideous possibilities. He contemplated the lurking menaces of the future and failed in an effort to see himself standing stoutly in the midst of them. He re-called his visions of broken-bladed glory but in the shadow of the impending tumult, he suspected them to be impossible pictures.

He sprang from his bunk and began to pace nervously up and down the floor. "Good Gawd, what's the matter with me," he cried to himself.

He felt that his laws of life were useless. Whatever he had learned of himself was now of no consequence. He was an unknown quantity. He would again be obliged to experiment, as he had in early youth, and get upon his guard, else those qualities of which he knew nothing might everlastingly disgrace him. "Good Gawd," he repeated. in dismay. | [*Page* 12]

After a time, Jim Conklin slid dexterously through the hole. Young Wilson followed. They were wrangling.

"That's all right," said Conklin waving his hand impressively as he entered. "Yeh kin b'lieve me er not—jest as yeh like. All yeh got t' do is t' sit down an' wait as quiet as yeh kin. Then pretty soon yeh'll find out I was right."

Young Wilson grumbled stubbornly. "Well, yeh don't know everything in th' world, do yeh?"

"Didn't say I knew everything in th' world," replied Conklin sharply. He dumped the contents of his knapsack out upon floor and then began to stow the things skilfully in again.

Fleming looked down at the busy figure. "Goin' t' be a battle sure, is there, Jim?" he asked.

"Of course," said Conklin. "Of course! Yeh jest wait 'til t'morrah an' yeh'll see th' bigges' battle ever was. Yeh jest wait."

"Thunder," said Fleming.

"Oh, yeh'll see fightin' this time, m' boy, what'ill be reg'lar fightin'," added Conklin with the air of a man who is about to exhibit a battle for the benefit of his friends.

"Huh," said Wilson from a corner.

"Well," remarked Fleming, "like as not this here story will turn out jest like them others did."

"Not much it won't," replied Conklin with exasperation. "Th' cavalry all started this morning, they say. They say there aint hardly no cavalry left in camp. Th' reg'ments got orders, too. I seen 'em go t' head-quarters. Besides, they're raisin' blazes all over camp—anybody kin see that." | [*Page* 13]

"Shucks," said Wilson.

Fleming was silent for a time. At last, he spoke to Conklin. "Jim!"

"What?"

"How d' yeh think th' regiment'll do?"

"Oh, they'll fight all right, I guess, after they once git inteh it," said Conklin with a fine use of the third person. "There's been more or less fun made of 'em, 'cause they're new, a' course, an' all that, but they'll fight good enough, I guess."

"Think any th' boys'ill run?" persisted Fleming.

"Oh, there may a few of 'em run but there's them kind in ev'ry reg'ment, 'specially when they first goes under fire," said Conklin in a tolerant way. "Of course, it might happen that th' hull kit an' boodle might start and run, an', then ag'in, they might stand and fight like fun. Yeh can't tell. Of course, they aint never been under fire yit an' it aint likely they'll lick th' hull rebel army all-t'-onct, but they'll fight better than some if worser than others. That's th' way I figger. Most of th' boys'll fight like sin after-they-onct-git-a-shootin'," he added with a mighty emphasis on the four last words.

"Oh, you think you know——" began Wilson with scorn.

Conklin turned wrathfully upon him. They called each other names.

Fleming interrupted them. "Did yeh ever think yeh might run yerself, Jim?," he asked. On concluding the sentence, he laughed as if he had meant to aim a joke. | [*Page* 14]

Conklin waved his hand. "Well," said he profoundly, "I've thought it might git too hot fer Jim Conklin in some of them scrimmages an' if a hull lot of boys started an' run, why, I s'pose I'd start an' run. But if e'rybody was a-standin' an' a-fightin, why, then, I'd stand an' fight. By jiminy, I would. I'll bet on it."

"Huh," said Wilson.

These words of Conklin, in a measure, re-assured Fleming. |

[*Page* 15]

II

Fleming was not at all relieved when he found that Jim Conklin had been the fast-flying messenger of a mistake. The tale had created in him a great concern for himself. He stood confronting the possibilities and with the new born question in his mind, he was compelled to sink back into his old place as part of a blue demonstration.

He kept up ceaseless calculations. They were wondrously unsatisfactory. He could establish nothing. He was anxious to prove beyond a doubt that he would not be afraid. He wished to go into the blaze and then figuratively to watch his legs to discover their merits and faults. So he fretted for an opportunity.

He was continually measuring himself by his comrades. Conklin, for one, re-assured him. The former's serene unconcern gave him some confidence because he had known him since childhood and from his intimate knowledge, he did not see how Conklin could be capable of anything that was beyond him, Fleming. Still, he thought Conklin might be mistaken about himself. Or, on the other hand, he might be a man heretofore doomed to obscurity in peace but in reality made for war.

He would have liked to have discovered another man who

suspected himself. A sympathetic comparison of mental notes would have been a great relief to him. He occasionally tried to fathom |

[*Page* 22]
sprightly, vigorous, and fiery in his desire for success. He looked into the future with clear proud eye.

"You're goin' t' do great things, I s'pose?" said Fleming.

Wilson blew a dignified cloud of smoke into the air. "Oh, I don't know," he remarked, thoughtfully, "I don't know. I s'pose I'll do as well as th' rest. I'm goin' t' try t', like thunder."

"How d'yeh know yeh won't run when th' time comes," asked Fleming.

" 'Run'?" said Wilson. " 'Run'? Of course not."

"Well," continued Fleming, "lots of good 'nough men have thought they was goin' t' do great things 'fore th' fight but when th' time come, they skedaddled."

"Oh, well, that's all true enough," said Wilson with great assurance, "but I'm not goin' t' skedaddle. Th' man that bets on my runnin' will lose his money that's all." He wagged his head with much self-confidence.

"Oh, shucks," said Fleming. "Yeh aint th' bravest man in th' world, are yeh?"

"No, I aint," replied Wilson, savagely, "An' I didn't say I was th' bravest man in th' world, neither. I said I was going t' do my share of fightin'—that's what I said. An' I am, too." He glared angrily at Fleming for a moment and then arose and strode away with an air of offended pride. | [*Page* 23]

Fleming felt alone in space when the injured Wilson retired. His confidence in the success of the army was as strong as any, but no one seemed to be wrestling with such a terrific personal problem. The valiant Wilson made him more miserable than before.

He went to his tent and stretched out on a blanket. He could hear serene voices. "I'll bid five." "Make it six." "Seven!" "Seven goes."

He saw visions of a thousand-tongued fear that would babble at his back and cause him to flee while others were going coolly about their country's business. He stared at the red, shivering reflection of a fire on the white wall of his tent until, exhausted and ill from viewing the pictures that thronged upon his mental vision, he fell asleep. |

[*Page* 28]
stupids. The enemy would presently encompass them and swallow the whole cammand. He glared about him as if hunted.

He thought that he must break from the ranks and harangue his comrades. They must not all be killed like pigs. And he was sure it would be so. And he was sure it would be so. The general were idiots to send them marching into a regular pen. He would step forth and make a speech. Shrill and passionate words were at his lips.

The line broken into moving fragments by the ground went calmly on through fields and woods. Fleming looked at the men nearest him and saw for the most part, expressions of deep interest as if they were investigating something that had fascinated them. Some stepped with an over-valiant air as if they were already plunged into war. Others went as upon thin ice. The greater part of the untested men appeared quiet and absorbed.

As he looked, Fleming gripped his out-cry at his throat. He saw that even if they were tottering with fear they would laugh at his oration. They would jeer him and, if practicable, pelt him with missiles. Admitting that he might be wrong, a frenzied declamation of the kind would turn him into a worm.

He assumed the demeanor of one who knows that he is doomed, alone, to unwritten responsibilities.

Presently, the brigade was halted in the cathedral-light of a forest. The busy skirmishers were still popping. Through the aisles of the wood could be seen the floating smoke from their rifles. | [*Page* 29]

Each front-rank man in the regiment began erecting a tiny hill in front of him. They used stones, earth and anything they thought would turn a bullet. Some built comparatively large ones while others seemed content with little ones. In a short time, there was quite a barricade along the regimental front. Directly, however, they recieved orders to withdraw from that place.

This astounded Fleming. He forgot his stewing over the advance movement. "Well, then, what did they march us out here fer?" he demanded of Jim Conklin. The latter with calm faith began a ponderous explanation. Fleming scoffed at him.

When the brigade was aligned in another position, each man's care for his safety caused another barricade to be created. They were moved from this one also. They ate their noon meal behind a third one. They were marched about from place to place with apparent aimlessness.

Fleming grew feverishly impatient. He considered that there was denoted a lack of purpose on the part of the generals. He began to complain to Jim Conklin. "I can't stand this much longer," he cried. "I don't see what good it does to make us jest wear out'r legs fer nothin'."

The philosophical Conklin measured a sandwhich of cracker and pork and engulfed in a nonchalant manner. "Oh, I s'pose we must go reconnoiterin' aroun' th' kentry jest t' keep 'em from gittin' too clost, or, t' develope 'em, or somethin'."

"Huh," said Wilson. |

[*Page* 36]
scattered the stragglers right and left.

A shell screaming like a storm-banshee went over the huddled heads of the reserves. It landed in the grove and, exploding redly, flung the brown earth. There was a little shower of pine-needles.

Bullets began to nip at the trees. The men of the reserved brigade crouched behind their various protections and peered toward the front. Some kept continually dodging and ducking their heads as if assailed by snow-balls.

An officer of Fleming's regiment was shot in the hand. He began to swear so wondrously that a nervous laugh went along the regimental line. The officer's profanity sounded conventional. It relieved the tightened senses of the new men. It was as if he had hit his fingers with a tack-hammer at home.

He held the wounded member away from his side so that the blood would not drip upon his trousers—while another bound it awkwardly with a handkerchief.

The battle-flag in the distance jerked about wrathfully. It seemed to be struggling to free itself from an agony. The billowing smoke was filled with horizontal flashes.

Men, running swiftly, emerged from it. They grew in numbers

until it was seen that the whole cammand was fleeing. The flag suddenly sank down as if dying. It's motion was like a gesture of despair. Wild yells came from behind the veil of smoke. A sketch in grey and red dissolved into a mob-like body of men who galloped like wild-horses.

The veteran regiments on the right and left of the 304th began to jeer. With the passionate song of the |

[*Page* 39]

V

There were moments of waiting. Fleming thought of the village street at home before the arrival of the circus parade. He remembered how he had stood a small thrillful boy, prepared to follow the band or the dingy lady upon the white horse. He saw the yellow road, the lines of expectant people, and the sober houses. He remembered an old fellow who used to sit upon a cracker-box in front of the store and fiegn to despise such exhibitions.

Some one cried: "Hear they come."

There was a rustling and muttering among the men. They displayed a feverish desire to have all their munitions ready to their hands. Cartridge-boxes were adjusted with great care. It was as if seven hundred new bonnets were being tried on. Gunlocks clicked.

Jim Conklin, having prepared himself, produced a red handkerchief. He was engaged in knotting it accurately about his throat when the cry was repeated up and down the line: "Here they come! Here they come!"

Across the smoke-infested fields came a brown bunch of running men who were giving shrill yells. They came on stooping and swinging their rifles at all angles. A flag, tilted forward, sped near the front.

As he caught sight of them, Fleming was suddenly smitten with the thought that perhaps his rifle was not loaded. | [*Page* 40]

A hatless general pulled his dripping horse to a stand near the colonel of the 304th. He shook his fist in the latter's face. "You've got t' hold 'em back," he shouted savagely. "You've got t' hold 'em back."

In his agitation, the colonel began to stammer. "A-all right, general, we-we'll d-do our b-best⟨."⟩ The general made a passionate gesture and galloped away. The colonel, perchance as a woman releaves her feelings with tears, began to swear sweepingly. Fleming, turning swiftly to make sure that the rear was unmolested, saw the cursing cammander regarding his regiment in a very resentful manner.

The man at Fleming's elbow was mumbling as if to himself: "Oh, we're in for it now. We're in for it now."

The captain of the campany had been pacing excitedly to and fro in the rear and had harangued like a school-mistress: "Reserve your fire, boys—don't shoot 'til I tell you—save your fire— wait 'til they git close up—don't be damned fools."

Perspiration streamed down Fleming's face which was soiled like that of a crying urchin. He frequently with a nervous movement wiped his eyes with his coat sleeve.

He got a swift glance at the foe-swarming field in front of him and, instantly, before he was quite ready to begin, before he had announced to himself that he was about to fight, he threw the obedient, well-balanced rifle into position and fired a first, wild shot. Directly, he |

[*Page* 42]

Following this came a red rage. He developed the acute exasperation of a pestered animal, a well-meaning cow worried by dogs. He had a furious feeling against his weapon that could only kill one man at a time. He wished to rush forward and strangle with his hands. He craved a power that would enable him to make a mad, world-sweeping gesture and brush all back. His impotency appeared to him and made his rage into that of a driven beast.

Buried in the smoke of many rifles, his anger was not directed so much against the men whom he knew were rushing toward him as against the swirling battle-phantoms who were choking him, stuffing their smoke-robes down his parched throat. He fought madly for respite, for air, as a babe, being smothered, attacks the deadly blankets.

There was a blare of heated rage, mingled with a certain expression of intentness, on all faces. Nearly every man was making a noise with his mouth. The cheers, snarls, imprecations, wailings, made a wild, barbaric song. The man at Fleming's elbow was babbling like an infant. Jim Conklin was swearing in a loud voice. From his lips came a black procession of curious oaths. Suddenly, another broke out in a querelous way like a man who has mislaid his hat: "Well, then, why don't they support us? Why don't they send supports? Do they think"—— |

[*Page* 45]
A small procession of wounded men was going drearily toward the rear. It was like a flow of blood from the torn body of the regiment.

To the right and left were the dark lines of other troops. Far in front, he could see lighter masses protruding in points from the woods. They were vaguely suggestive of untold thousands.

Once he saw a tiny battery go dashing along the line of the horizon. The tiny riders were beating the tiny horses.

From a sloping hill came the sound of cheering and clashes. Smoke welled steadily up. Batteries were speaking with thunderous oratorical effort. Here and there were flags, the red in the stripes dominating. They splashed bits of brilliant color upon the dark troops.

Fleming felt the old thrill at the sight of the emblems. They were like beautiful birds strangely undaunted in a storm.

As he listened to the din from the hill side, to a deep pulsating thunder that came from afar to the right and to the lesser clamors which came from many directions, it occurred to Fleming that they were fighting too over there and over there and over there. Heretofore he had supposed that the battle was directly under his nose.

As he gazed around him, Fleming felt a flash of astonishment at the blue, pure sky and the sun-gleamings on the trees and fields. It was surprising that nature had gone tranquilly with her golden processes in the midst of so much devilment. | [*Page* 46]

VI

Fleming awakened slowly. He came gradually back to a position from which he could regard himself. For moments, he had been scrutinizing his person in a dazed way as if he had never seen himself before. Then he picked up his cap from the ground. He wriggled in his jacket to make a more comfortable fit and kneeling down laced his shoe. He thoughtfully moped his reeking features.

So it was all over. He went into an ecstasy of self-satisfaction. He had the most delightful sensations of his life. Standing as if apart from himself, he viewed the late scene. He percieved that the man who had fought thus was magnificent.

He felt that he was a fine fellow. He saw himself even with those ideals which he had considered as being far beyond him. He smiled with deep gratification. He beamed good-will and tenderness on his fellows.

"Gee, aint it hot, eh?" he said affably to a man who was polishing his streaming face with his coat-sleeve.

"You bet," said the other grinning sociably. "I never seen sech dumb hotness." He sprawled out luxuriously on the ground. "I hope we don't have no more fightin' til—'til a week from Monday."

There were some hand-shakings and deep speeches with men whose features only were familar but with whom Fleming now felt the bonds of tied hearts. He helped a cursing comrade to bind up a wound of the shin. | [*Page* 47]

Of a sudden, cries of amazement broke out along the ranks of the new regiment. "Here they come ag'in! Here they come a'gin!"

Fleming turned quick eyes on the field. He saw forms begin to swell in masses out of a distant wood. He again saw the tilted flag, speeding forward.

Too, shells exploded in the grass and among the foliage. They were strange war-blossoms bursting into fierce bloom.

The men groaned. The slaves toiling in the temple of war felt a sudden rebellion. The lustre had faded from their eyes. Their smudged countenances expressed a profound dejection. They moved their stiffened bodies slowly and watched in sullen mood the frantic approach of the enemy.

Some began to fret and complain. "Oh, say, this is too much of a good thing. Why can't somebody send us supports?"

"We aint never goin' t' stand this second bangin'. I didn't come here t' fight th' hull damn rebel army."

There was one who raised a doleful cry. "I wish Bill Smithers had trod on my hand insteader me treddin' on his'n."

Fleming waited gingerly. It was as if he expected a cold plunge.

The firing began somewhere and ripped along the line in both directions. The level sheets of flame developed great clouds of smoke that tumbled and tossed near the ground for a moment and then rolled away toward the rear going through the ranks as through a grate.

The flag was often eaten and lost | [*Page* 48] in the great clouds that were tinged with an earthlike yellow in the sun-rays, and changed to a sorry blue in the shadows.

Fleming's eyes had a look in them that one can see in the orbs of a jaded horse. The muscles of his arms felt numb and bloodless. His hands, too, seemed large and awkward as if he were wearing invisible mittens. And there was a great uncertainty about his knee-joints.

The words that comrades had uttered previous to the firing began to appear to him. "Oh, say, this is too much of a good thing." "What do they take us fer—why don't they send us supports." "I didn't come here t' fight th' hull damn rebel army."

He began to exaggerate the endurance, the skill and the valor of those who were coming. They must be steel machines. Himself, reeling from nervous exhaustion, he could not understand such persistency.

He mechanically lifted his rifle and, catching a glimpse of the thick-spread field, he fired a shot at a cantering cluster. He stopped then and began to gaze as best he could through the smoke. He caught changing views of the ground covered with men who were all running and yelling like pursued imps.

To him, it was an onslaught of dragons. He became like the man who lost his legs at the approach of the red and green monster. He waited in a sort of a horrified, listening attitude. He seemed to shut his eyes and wait to be gobbled. | [*Page* 49]

A man near him who up to this time had been working feverishly at his rifle, suddenly dropped it and ran with howls. A lad whose face had born an expression of exalted courage, the majesty of he who dares give his life, was smitten abject. He blanched like one who has come to the edge of a cliff at midnight and is suddenly made aware. There was a revelation. He too threw down his gun and fled. There was no shame in his face. He ran like a rabbit.

Others began to scamper away through the smoke. Fleming turned his head, shaken from his trance by this movement as if the regiment was leaving him behind. He saw the few fleeting forms.

He yelled then with fright and swung about. For a moment, in the clamor, he was like a proverbial chicken. He lost the direction of safety. Destruction threatened him from all points.

Directly he began to speed toward the rear in great leaps. His rifle and cap were gone. The flap of his cartridge-box bobbed wildly. His canteen swung out behind him. On his face was a reflected horror of those things which he imagined.

He ran like a blind man. Two or three times, he fell down and once he knocked his shoulder so heavily against a tree that he went head-long. He felt that death was ever about to thrust him between the shoulder blades.

He ran on mingling with others. He vaguely saw men on his right and on his left, and he heard foot-steps behind him. He thought that all the regiment was running. Ominous noises were following. | [*Page* 50]

The sound of the footsteps behind him gave him a certain, meagre relief. The first clutchings of the dragons would be of the men who were following him. He displayed the zeal of a sprinter in his purpose to keep them in the rear. There was a race.

Shells were hurtling over his head. He imagined them to have rows of vindictively-grinning teeth turned toward him as they passed.

He experienced a thrill of amazement as he passed the battery in the field back of the grove. The artillerymen were going swiftly about their tasks. They were continually bending in coaxing postures over the guns. They seemed to be patting them on the back and encouraging them with words. The guns stolid and undaunted, spoke with dogged valor.

The precise gunners were cool save for their eyes which were lifted every chance toward a smoked-wreathed hillock from whence a hostile battery addressed them. Fleming pitied them as he ran. Methodical idiots! Machine-like fools! Staying to be eaten up! The face of a youthful rider who was jerking his frantic horse with the abandon of temper he might display in a placid barn-yard was impressed deep upon his mind. He knew he looked upon a man who would presently be dead.

He saw a brigade going to the relief of it's pestered fellows. He scrambled into some bushes and watched it, sweeping finely, keeping formation in difficult places. The blue of the line was crusted with steel-color and brilliant flags projected. Officers were shouting. | [*Page* 51]

This sight, also, filled him with wonder. The brigade was hurrying briskly to be gulped into the infernal mouth of the war-god. What kind of men were they, anyhow? Ah, it was some wondrous breed. Or else they didn't know—the fools.

Some furious order had caused commotion in the artillery. An officer on a bounding horse was making maniacal motions with his arms. The teams dashed up from the rear, the guns were whirled about, and the battery scampered away. The guns with their noses poked slantingly at the ground, grumbled and grunted like stout men unduly hurried.

Fleming ran on.

Later he came upon a general of division seated upon a horse that pricked it's ears in an interested way at the battle. There was a great gleaming of yellow and patent-leather about the saddle and bridle. The quiet man astride looked mouse-colored upon such a splendid charger.

A jingling staff was galloping hither and thither. Sometimes, the general was surrounded by horsemen and at other times he was quite alone. He looked much harassed. He had the appearance of a business man whose market is swinging up and down.

Fleming went slinking around the spot. He went as near as he dared, trying to over-hear words. Perhaps, too, the general, unable to comprehend chaos, might call upon him for information. And he | [*Page* 52] could tell him. He knew all about it. Of a surety, the force was in a fix and any fool could see that if they did not retreat while they had opportunity—why——

He felt that he would like to thrash the general—or at least approach him and tell him in plain words exactly what he thought him to be. It seemed criminal to stay calmly in one spot and make no effort to stay destruction.

As he went warily nearer, he heard the general call out irritably. "Tompkins, go over an' see Taylor an' tell him not to be in such a thunderin' sweat—tell him t' halt his brigade in the edge of th' woods. Tell him t' detach a reg'ment—tell him I think th' centre'ill break if we—tell him t' hurry up."

A moment later, Fleming saw the general bounce excitedly in his saddle.

"Yes—no—yes." His face was aflame with eagerness. "Yes—by Gawd—they've held 'im! They held 'im!"

He began to blithely roar at his staff.

"We'll wallop 'em, now! We'll wallop 'em now! We've got 'em!" Then he turned suddenly upon an aide. "Here—you—Jones—quick—ride after Tompkins—see Taylor—tell him t' go in—everlastingly go in—go in like eternal damnation."

His flurry of excitement made his horse plunge, and he merrily kicked and swore at it. He held a little carnival of joy on horseback. | [*Page* 53]

VII

Fleming cringed as if discovered at a crime. By heavens, they had won after all. That embecile line had remained and become victors. He could hear the cheering.

He lifted himself upon his toes and looked in the direction of the fight. A vast yellow cloud lay wallowing on the tree-tops. From beneath it came the clatter of musketry. The hoarse cheers told of an advance.

He turned away, sulky and angry. He felt that he had been wronged.

He had fled, he told himself, because annihilation was approaching. He had done his part in saving himself who was a little piece of the army. He had considered the time, he said, to be one in which it was the duty of every little piece to rescue itself if possible. Later, the officers could put the little pieces together again and make a battle-front. If no little pieces were wise enough to save themselves from the flurry of death at such a time, why, then, were would the army be? It was all very plain that he had proceeded according to very correct and commendable rules. His actions had been sagacious things. They were full of strategy.

He thought of his comrades. They had staid and won. It seemed that the blind ignorance and stupidity of those little pieces had betrayed him. He had been over-turned and crushed by their lack of sense in holding a position that a little thought would have convinced them to be impossible. He, the enlightened, had fled because of his superior knowledge. He felt a great anger against his comrades. |

[*Page* 55]
arms and turned their face-leaves toward him. He dreaded lest these voices and noisy motions would bring men to look at him.

He went far, seeking dark and intricate places. The musketry grew faint and the cannon boomed in the distance.

The sun, suddenly apparent, blazed among the trees. The insects were making rythmical noises. They seemed to be grinding their teeth in unison. A woodpecker stuck his insolent head around the side of a tree. A bird flew on light-hearted wing.

Off was the rumble of death. It seemed now that nature had no ears.

This landscape gave him assurance. It was the religion of peace. It would die if it's timid eyes were compelled to see blood. He concieved nature to be a woman with a deep aversion to tragedy.

He threw a pine-cone at a jovial and pot-valiant squirrel and it ran with chattering fear. There was the law, he thought. Nature had given him a sign.

He wended feeling that nature agreed with him. It reinforced his arguments with proofs that lived where the sun shone.

He found himself almost into a swamp once. He was obliged to walk on bog-tufts and watch his feet to keep from the oily mire. Pausing once to look about him, he saw, out on some black water, a small animal pounce in and emerge directly with a silver-gleaming fish. Presently, he was again in the deep thickets. The brushed branches made a noise that drowned | [*Page* 56] the sounds of cannon.

He went on, going from obscurity to promises of a greater obscurity.

At length, he reached a place where the high, arching boughs made a chapel. He softly pushed the green doors aside and entered. Pine-needles were a gentle brown carpet. There was a religious half-light.

Near the threshold, he stopped horror-stricken at the sight of a thing.

He was being looked at by a dead man who was seated with his back against a column-like tree. The corpse was dressed in a uniform that once had been blue but was now faded to a melancholy green. The eyes, staring at Fleming, had changed to the dull hue to be seen on the side of a dead fish. The mouth was opened. It's red had changed to an apalling yellow. Over the grey skin of the face ran little ants. One was trundling some sort of a bundle along the upper lip.

Fleming gave a shriek as he confronted the thing. He was for an instant turned to stone before it. He remained staring into the liquid-looking eyes. Then, he cautiously put one hand behind him and touched a tree. Leaning upon this he retreated step by step with his face still toward the thing. He feared that if he turned his back, the thing might spring up and stealthily pursue him.

The branches, pushing against him, threatened to throw him over upon it. His unguided feet, too, caught aggravatingly in brambles. And, withal, he recieved a subtle suggestion to touch the corpse. As he |

[*Page* 59]

VIII

The trees began softly to sing an evening hymn. The burnished sun sank until slanted bronze rays struck the tree-tops. There was a lull in the noise of insects as if they had bowed their beaks and were making a devotional pause. There was silence save for the chanted chorus of the trees.

Upon this stillness there suddenly broke a tremendous clangor of sounds. A crimson roar came from the distance.

Fleming paused. He was transfixed by this terrific medley of all noises. It was as if worlds were being rended. The ripping of musketry was mingled with the breaking crash of the cannon.

His mind flew in all directions. He concieved the two armies to be at each other panther-wise. He listened for a time. Then he began to run in the direction of the battle. He saw that it was an ironical thing for him to be running thus toward that which he had been at such pains to avoid. But he said, in substance, to himself that if the earth and moon were about to clash together, many would plan to get upon roofs to witness the collision.

As he ran, he was aware that the forest had stopped it's music as if at last becoming capable of hearing the foriegn sounds. The trees hushed and bended forward. Everything seemed to be listening to the crackle and clatter of the infantry firing and the ear-shaking thunder of the artillery. The chorus pealed over the still earth. | [*Page* 60]

It occurred to him that the fight he had been in, was, after all, but perfunctory popping. In the hearing of this present din, he was doubtful if he had seen real battle-scenes. Reflecting, he saw a sort of a humor in the point of view of he and his fellows during that encounter. They had taken themselves and the enemy very seriously and had imagined that they were deciding the war. Individuals might have supposed that they were cutting the letters of their names deep into everlasting tablets of brass or enshrining their reputations forever in the hearts of their countrymen, while, as to fact, the affair would appear in reports under a meek and immaterial title. But he saw that it was good, else, he said, in battle everyone would doubtless run save forlorn hope and their ilk.

He went rapidly on. He wanted to come to the edge of the forest and peer out.

As he hurried, there passed through his mind pictures of stupendous struggles. All his accumulations upon such subjects were used to form scenes. The uproar was as the voice of an eloquent being describing.

Sometimes, the brambles formed chains and held him back. Trees, confronting him stretched out their arms and forbade him to pass. He thought with a fine bitterness that nature could not be quite ready to kill him yet.

But he took roundabout ways. Presently he was in a place from which he could see long fringes of smoke where battle-lines lay. The voices of the cannon shook him. He stood for a moment and watched. His eyes had an awe-struck expression. His lower jaw hung down. | [*Page* 61a]

Presently, he continued his way. The battle was like the

grinding of an immense and terrible machine to him. It's complexities and powers, it's grim processes fascinated him. He must go close and see it produce corpses.

He came to some deserted rifle-pits and clambered over them. Within, the trench was littered with clothes and guns. A newspaper folded up lay in the dirt. A dead soldier was stretched with his face hidden in his arm, and further on there was a group of four or five bodies keeping mournful company. A hot sun had blazed upon the spot.

As he looked, Fleming felt like an invader and he hastened by. He came finally to a road from which he could see, in the distance, dark and agitated bodies of troops. In the lane, was a blood-stained crowd streaming to the rear. The wounded men were cursing, lamenting and groaning. In the air always, was a mighty swell of sound that it seemed could sway the earth. With the courageous words of the artillery and the spiteful sentences of the musketry was mingled red cheers. And from this place of noises came the steady current of the maimed.

One wounded man had a shoeful of blood. He was hopping like a school-boy in a game. He laughed hysterically.

One was marching with an air imitative of some sublime drum-major. Upon his features was an unholy mixture | [*Page* 61B] of merriment and agony. As he marched, he sang a bit of doggerel in a high and quavering voice.

"Sing a song of vict'ry"
"A pocketful a' bullets"
"Five an' twenty dead men"
"Baked in a—pie."

Parts of the procession limped and staggered to this tune.

Another had the grey seal of death already upon his face. His lips were curled in hard lines and his teeth were clenched. His hands were bloody from where he had pressed them upon his wound. He seemed to be awaiting the moment when he should pitch headlong. He stalked like the spectre of a soldier, his eyes burning with the power of a stare into the unknown.

There were some who proceeded sullenly, full of anger at their wounds and ready to turn upon anything as an obscure cause.

An officer was carried along by two privates. He was peevish. "Don't joggle so, Johnson, yeh fool," he cried. "Think m' leg is made of iron? If yeh can't carry me decent, leave me down an' let some one else do it."

He bellowed at the tottering crowd who blocked the quick march of his bearers. "Say, make way there, cant yeh? Make way, dickens take it all."

They sulkily parted and went to the roadsides. As he was carried past, they made pert remarks to him. When he raged in reply and threatened them, they told him to be damned.

The shoulder of one of the tramping bearers knocked heavily against the spectral soldier who was staring into the unknown. |

[*Page* 64]
yeh hit, ol' boy?" he asked in a brotherly way.

Fleming was startled by this question although at first it's full import was not born in upon him.

"What?" he asked.

"Where yeh hit?" repeated the tattered man.

"Why," began Fleming, "I—I—that is—why——"

He turned away suddenly and slid through the crowd.

The tattered man looked after him in astonishment. |

[*Page* 66]
wax-like face toward him, Fleming screamed.

"Gawd! Jim Conklin!"

Conklin made a little common-place smile. "Hello, Flem," he said.

Fleming swayed on his legs and glared wildly. He stuttered and stammered. "Oh, Jim—oh, Jim—oh, Jim"——

Conklin held out his gory hand. On it was a curious red and black combination of new blood and old blood. "Where yeh been, Flem?" he asked. He continued in a monotonous voice. "I thought mebbe yeh got keeled over. I was worryin' about it a good deal."

Fleming still lamented. "Oh, Jim—oh, Jim—oh, Jim"——

"Yeh know," said Conklin, "I was out there." He made a careful gesture. "An', Lord, what a circus. An', b'jiminy, I got shot—I got shot."

Fleming put forth anxious arms to assist his friend but the latter went firmly on as if propelled.

Suddenly, as they went, Conklin seemed to be overcome by a terror. His face turned to a semblance of grey paste. He clutched Flemings arm and began to talk to him in a shaking voice. "I'll tell yeh what I'm 'fraid of, Flem—I'll tell yeh what I'm 'fraid of. I'll fall down—an', then, yeh know—them damned artillery wagons—they like as not ull run over me—thats what I'm 'fraid of."

Fleming cried out to him hysterically. "I'll take keer of yeh, Jim. I'll take keer of yeh."

"Sure yeh will, Flem?" beseeched Conklin.

"Yes, yes, I'll take keer of yeh, Jim," protested Fleming. He could not speak accurately because of the great gulpings in his throat. | [*Page* 67]

Conklin still begged in a lowly way. His eyes rolled. He hung babe-like to Fleming. "I was allus a good friend of your'n, wasn't I, Flem? An' it aint much t' ask, is it, Flem? Jest t' drag me outa th' road. I'd do it fur you, wouldn't I, Flem?"

Fleming's anguish reached a heat where scorching sobs shook his chest, but, suddenly Conklin seemed to forget all those fears. He became again the grim stalking spectre of a soldier. He went stonily forward. Fleming wished his friend to lean upon him but the other always shook his head and strangely protested. "No—no—leave me be—leave me be."

His look again was fixed upon the unknown. He moved with mysterious purpose. And all of Fleming's offers he brushed aside. "No—no—leave me be—leave me be"——

Fleming had to follow after.

Presently, the latter heard a voice talking softly near his shoulder. Turning, he saw that it belonged to the tattered soldier. "Ye'd better tak 'im outa th' road, pardner. There's a bat'try comin' helitywhoop an' he'll git run over. He's goner anyhow in about five minutes—yeh kin see that. Ye'd better tak'im outa th' road. Where th' blazes does he git his stren'th from?"

"Lord knows," cried Fleming. He was shaking his hands helplessly.

He ran forward and grasped Conklin by the arm. "Jim—Jim," he coaxed, "come with me." | [*Page* 68] Conklin tried weakly to wrench away. "Huh?" he said vacantly. He stared at Fleming for a moment. At last, he spoke: "Oh, inteh th' fields? Oh!"

He went blindly through the grass. Fleming turning to look at the lashing riders and jouncing guns of the battery was startled from his view by a cry from the tattered soldier.

"Great Gawd, he's runnin'!"

Looking about swiftly, Fleming saw his friend running in a staggering and stumbling way toward a little clump of bushes. His heart almost wrenched itself from his body at the sight. He made a noise of infinite pain and started in pursuit.

There was a grotesque race.

When he overtook Conklin he began to beg him with all the words he could find. "Jim—Jim—what are yeh doin'—what makes yeh do this way—yeh'll hurt yerself."

The same mysterious purpose was in Conklin's face. He protested dully. "No—no—don't tech me—leave me be—leave me be"——

Fleming filled with wonder at the idea which seemed to absorb his friend, began quaveringly to question him. "Where yeh goin', Jim? What yeh thinkin' about? What yeh tryin' t' do? Where yeh goin?"

Conklin faced about as upon a relentless pursuer. In his eyes, there was an appeal. "Leave me be, won't yeh? Leave me be!" | [*Page* 69]

Fleming started back. "Why, Jim," he said in a dazed way.

Conklin turned and lurching dangerously, went on. Fleming and the tattered soldier followed, sneaking as if whipped, feeling unable to face the stricken man if he should again confront them.

At last they saw him stop and stand motionless. Hastening up, they percieved upon his face an expression as if he had at last found the spot for which he had struggled. His spare figure was erect. The bloody hands were quietly at his sides. He was waiting with patience for something that was coming.

There were years of silence. The chest of the doomed soldier heaved with a strained motion. Once as he turned his eyes, Fleming saw something in them that made him sink wailing to the ground. He raised his voice in a last, supreme call.

"Jim—Jim—Jim"——

His friend opened his lips and spoke, gratingly. He shook his head. "Leave me be! Leave me be!"

Suddenly, his form stiffened and straightened. Then it was shaken by a prolonged ague. He stared into space. It was seen that there was a curious and profound dignity in the firm lines of his awful face. | [*Page* 70]

Presently, he seemed invaded by a creeping ague that gradually enveloped him. For a moment, the tremor of his legs made him dance a sort of a hideous horn-pipe. His arms beat wildly about his head. His tall figure grew suddenly to unnatural proportions then it began to swing slowly forward like a falling tree. A last muscular contortion caused the left shoulder to first strike the ground.

The body seemed to bounce a little way from the earth. "Gawd," said the tattered soldier.

Fleming had watched, spell-bound, these rites of a departing life, this dance of death. His face had been twisted into every form of agony that he had imagined for his friend.

He now sprang to his feet and gazed at the paste-like face. The mouth was open and the teeth showed in a laugh.

As the flap of the blue jacket fell away from the body, he could see that the side looked as if it had been chewed by wolve's.

Fleming turned toward the battle ground. His hands were clenched and a rage was upon his face. He seemed about to deliver a phillipic.

"Hell"——

The red sun was pasted in the sky like a fierce wafer. | [*Page* 71]

XI

The tattered man stood musing.

"Well, he was a reg'lar jim-dandy fer nerve, w'a'nt he?" said he finally in a little, awe-struck voice. "A reg'lar jim-dandy, he was."

He thoughtfully pushed one of the dead hands with his toe. "I wonder where he got 'is stren'th from. I never seen a man do like that before. It was a curious thing. Well, he was a reg'lar jim-dandy."

Fleming desired to screech out his grief. He was stabbed. But his tongue lay dead in the tomb of his mouth. He threw himself upon the ground and began to brood.

The tattered man stood musing.

"Look-a-here, pardner," he said after a time. He regarded the corpse as he spoke. "He's up an' gone, aint, e' an' we might as well begin t' look out fer ol' number one. He's all right. Nobody won't bother 'im. An' I must say I aint enjoyin' any great health m'self these days."

Fleming, awakened by the tattered soldier's tone, looked quickly up. He saw that he saw swinging uncertainly on his legs and that his face had turned a blue shade.

"Good Lord," he cried. "You aint goin' t'—not you, too?"

The tattered soldier waved his hand. "Nary die," he said. "All I want is some pea-soup an' a good bed. Some pea-soup," he repeated dreamily. | [*Page* 72]

Fleming arose from the ground. "I wonder where he came from. I left him over there." He pointed. "An' now I find 'um here. An' he was a comin' from off yonder, too." He indicated a new direction.

They both turned toward the body as if to ask a question of it.

"Well," at length said the tattered man, wearily, "there haint no use in our stayin' here an' astin' im anything."

They gazed at the corpse for a moment.

Fleming murmured something.

"He was a jim-dandy, w'a'nt he," said the tattered man as if in response.

They turned their backs upon it and started away. It was still laughing there in the grass.

"I'm commencin' t' feel pretty bad," said the tattered man suddenly breaking one of his small silences.

Fleming groaned. "Oh, Lord!"

The other waved his hand again. "Oh, I'm not goin' t' die yit. There's too much dependin' on me fer me t' die yit. No, sir. Nary die. Ye'd oughta see th' swad of chil'ren I've got, an' all like that."

Fleming glancing at his companion could see by the shadow of a smile that he was making fun.

As they plodded on, the tattered man continued to talk. "Besides, if I died I wouldn't die th' way that feller did. I'd jest flop down, I s'pose. I never seen a feller die th' way that feller did. Yeh know, Tom Jamison, he lives next |

[*Page* 75]

Promptly, his old rebellious feelings returned. He thought the powers of fate had combined to heap misfortune upon him. He was a victim.

He rebelled against the source of things, according to his law that the most powerful should recieve the most blame.

War, he said bitterly to the sky, was a make-shift created because ordinary processes didn't furnish deaths enough. To seduce her victims, nature had to formulate a beautiful excuse. She made glory. This made the men willing, anxious, in haste, to come and be killed.

And, with heavy humor, he thought of how nature must smile when she the men come running. They regarding war-fire and courage as holy things and did not see that nature had placed them in hearts because virtuous indignation would not last through a black struggle. Men would grow tired of it. They would go home.

They must be inspired by some sentiment that they could call sacred and enshrine in their heart, something that would cause them to regard slaughter as fine and go at it cheerfully; something that could destroy all the bindings of loves and places that tie men's hearts. She made glory.

From his pinnacle of wisdom, he regarded the armies as large collection of dupes. Nature's dupes, who were killing each other to carry out | [*Page* 76] some great scheme of life. They were under the impression that they were fighting for principles and honor and homes and various things.

Well, to be sure; they were.

Nature was miraculously skilful in concocting excuses, he thought, with a heavy, theatrical contempt. It could deck a hideous creature in enticing apparel. When he saw how she, as a women beckons, had cozened him out of his home and hoodwinked him into wielding a rifle, he went into a rage.

He turned in tupenny fury upon the high, tranquil sky. He would have like to have splashed it with a derisive paint.

And he was bitter that among all men, he should be the only one sufficiently wise to understand these things. | [*Page* 77]

XI

He became aware that the furnace-roar of the battle was growing louder. Great brown clouds had floated to the still heights of air before him. The noise, too, was approaching. The woods filtered men and the fields became dotted.

As he rounded a hillock, he percieved that the road-way was now a crying mass of wagons, teams and men. From the heaving tangle issued exhortations, cammands and imprecations. Fear was sweeping it all along. The cracking whips bit, and horses plunged and tugged. The white-topped wagons strained and stumbled in their exertions like fat sheep.

Fleming felt in a measure comforted by the sight. They were all retreating. Perhaps, then, he was not so bad after all. He seated himself and watched the fleeing wagons. All the roarers and lashers served to help him to magnify the dangers and horrors of the engagement that he might try to prove to himself that the thing with which men could charge him, was, in truth, a symetrical act.

Presently, the calm head of a column of infantry appeared in the road. It came swiftly on. Avoiding the obstructions gave it the sinuous movement of a long serpent. The men at the head butted mules with their musket-stocks. They prodded teamsters, indifferent to all howls. The men forced their way through parts of the dense mass by strength. The blunt head of the column pushed. The wild teamsters swore many strange oaths.

The cammands to make way had the ring of a great importance in them. The men were going forward. They were to confront the eager rush of the | [*Page* 78] enemy. They felt the pride of their onward movement when the whole army seemed trying to dribble down this road. They tumbled teams about with a fine feeling that it was no matter so long as their column got to the front in time. This importance made their faces stern and quiet, and the backs of the officers were very rigid.

As he looked at them, Fleming knew all of his woe. He felt that he was regarding a procession of chosen beings. The separation was as great to him as if they had marched with weapons of flame and banners of sunlight. He could never be like them. He could have wept in his longings.

He searched about in his mind then for a proper malediction for the indefinite cause, that thing upon which men turn the words of final blame. It was responsible for him. There lay the fault.

The haste of the column to reach the battle-ground struck forlorn Fleming as being something much finer than stout fighting. Heroes he thought, could find excuses in that long, seething lane. They could retire with perfect self-respect and make explanations to the stars.

He wondered what those men had eaten that they could be so bitter to force their ways to chances of death. As he watched his envy grew until he wished to change lives with one of them. He would have like to have used a tremendous force, thrown off himself and became a better. Swift picture of himself apart yet in himself came to him—a blue desperate figure leading lurid charges with one knee forward and a broken blade high— a blue determined figure standing before a crimson and steel assault getting calmly killed on a high place before | [*Page* 79] everybody. He thought of the magnificent pathos of his dead body.

He was up-lifted. He felt the quiver of war-desire. In his ears, he heard the ring of victory and knew the frenzy of a rapid, successful charge. The music of the trampling feet, the sharp voices, and the clanking arms of the column made him soar on the red wings of war. For a few moments, he was sublime.

He thought that he was about to start fleetly for the front. Then the difficulties of the thing began to drag at him. He hesitated, balancing awkwardly on one foot.

He had no rifle; he could not fight with his hands. Well, rifles could be had for the picking.

Also, it would be miraculous if he found his regiment. Well, he could fight with any regiment.

He started forward slowly. He stepped as if he expected to tread upon an explosive thing. Doubts and he were struggling.

He would truly be a worm if any of them should see him returning thus, the marks of his flight upon him. He replied that the intent fighters did not care for what happened rear-ward saving that no hostile bayonets appeared there. In the battle-blur, his face would be as hidden as the face of a cowled man.

But, then, he said that his tireless fate would, when the strife lulled for an instant, bring forth a man to ask of him an explantion. And he saw the scrutinizing eyes of his comrades as he would painfully labor through some lies. | [*Page* 80]

Eventually, his courage expended itself upon his objections. The debates drained him of the fire.

Furthermore, various ailments had begun to cry out. In their presence, he could not persist in flying high with red wings of war. He tumbled head-long.

He discovered that he had a scorching thirst. His face was so dry and grimey that he thought he could feel his skin crackle. Each bone of his body had an ache in it and seemingly threatened to break. His feet were like two sores. His body, too, was calling for food. It was more powerful than a direct hunger. There was a dull, weight-like feeling in his stomach and when he moved, his head swayed and he tottered. He could not see with distinctness. Small patches of crimson mist floated before his vision.

While he had been tossed by many emotions, he had not been aware of ailments. Now they beset him and made clamor. As he was at last compelled to pay attention to them, his capacity for self-hate was multiplied. He groaned from his heart and staggered off through the fields. He was not like those others, he said, in despair. He now conceded it to be impossible that he should ever grow to be one of them. Those pictures of glory were piteous things.

A desire for news kept him in the vicinity of the battle-ground. He wished to know who was winning.

He told himself that in all his troubles he had never lost his greed for a victory, yet, he said in a half apologogetic manner, he could not but know that a defeat this | [*Page* 81] time might mean many things to him. The blows of the enemy would splinter regiments into fragments. Many men of courage, he thought, would be compelled to desert the colors and scurry like chickens. He would appear as one of them. They would all be sullen brothers in distress and he could then easily believe that he had not run any further or faster than others.

He said, as if in excuse, that, previously, the army had encountered great defeats and in a few months had shaken off all
blood and tradition of them emerging as bright and valiant as
a new one; thrusting out of sight the very traditions of disaster
and appearing with the valor and confidence of unconquered
legions. The shrilling voices of the people at home would pipe
dismally for a time but various generals would be compelled to
listen to the ditties.

In a defeat there would be a roundabout moral vindication of
himself. He thought that it would prove, in a way, that he had
fled early because of his superior powers of perception. This he
regarded as a very important thing. Without salve, he could not,
he said, wear the sore badge of his dishonor through life. With
his heart continually assuring him that he was despicable, he
could not exist without making it apparent to all men, imparting
the information through his actions.

But if the army had gone gloriously on, he would be indeed
lost. If the din meant that now his army's flags were tilted forward he was a condemned wretch. He would be compelled be
doom himself to isolation. If the men were advancing, their indifferent feet were trampling upon his chances for a successful
life. | [*Page* 82] As these thoughts went rapidly through his
mind, he suddenly turned upon them and tried to savagely thrust
them away. With woe upon his face, he denounced himself as a
villian. He was he said the most unutterably selfish man in
existence. His mind pictured the men who would place their defiant bodies before the spear of the yelling battle-fiend and as he
saw their weltering corpses on an imagined field, he said that
he was their murderer.

Again, he thought that he wished he was dead. He believed
that he envied the corpses. Too, he achieved a species of contempt for some of them as if they were guilty for thus becoming
lifeless. They might have been killed by lucky chances, he said,
before they had had opportunities to flee or before they had
been really tested. Yet they would recieve laurels from traditions.
He cried out bitterly that their crowns were stolen and their
robes of glorious memories were shams. However, he thought it
was a pity that he was not as they.

A defeat of the army had suggested itself to him as a means

of escape from the consequences of his fall. He considered how-
erer that it was useless to think of such a possibility. His education had been that success for that mighty, blue machine was
certain; that it would make victories as a contrivance turns out
buttons. He presently discarded all his speculations in the other
direction. He returned to the true creed of soldiers.

As he percieved again that it was not possible for the army to
be defeated, he began to bethink him of a fine tale which he
could take back to his regiment |

[Page 84]

XII

It was always clear to Fleming that he was entirely different
from other men, that he had been cast in a unique mold. Also,
he regarded his sufferings as peculiar and unprecedented. No
man had ever achieved such misery. There was a melancholy
grandeur in the isolation of his experiences. He saw that he
was a speck raising his minute arms against all possible forces
and fates which were swelling down upon him like storms. He
could derive some consolation from viewing the sublimity of
the odds.

But, as he went on, he began to feel that, after all, nature
would not blame him for his rebellion. He still distinctly felt
that he was arrayed against the universe but he began to believe that there was no malice agitating the vast breasts of his
space-filling foes. It was merely law.

Nature had provided her creations with various defenses and
ways to escape that they might fight or flee, and she had limited
dangers in powers of attack and pursuit, that the things might
resist or hide with a security proportionate to their strength and
wisdom. It was all the same old philosophy. He could not omit a
small grunt of satisfaction as he saw with what brilliancy he
had reasoned it all out.

He now said, that, if, as he supposed his life was | [Page 85]
being relentlessly pursued, it was not his duty to bow to the inevitable. On the contrary, it was his business to kick and scratch
and bite like a child in the hands of a parent. And he would be
saved according to the importance of his strength. His egotism
made him feel secure for a time from the iron hands.

It being in his mind that he had solved those matters, he eagerly applied his findings to the incident of his own flight from the battle. It was not a fault; it was a law. It was——

But he saw that when he had made a vindicating structure of great principles, it was the calm toes of tradition that kicked it all down about his ears. He immediately antagonized then this devotion to the by-gone; this universal adoration of the past. From the bitter pinnacle of his wisdom he saw that mankind not only worshipped the gods of the ashes but that the gods of the ashes were worshipped because they were the gods of the ashes.

He percieved with anger the present state of affairs in it's bearing upon his case.

And he resolved to reform it all. | [*Page* 86]

He had then a feeling that he was the growing prophet of a world-reconstruction. Far down in the pure depths of his being, among the hidden, untouched currents of his soul, he saw born a voice. He concieved a new world, modelled by the pain of his life, in which no old shadows fell darkening upon the temple of thought. And there were many personal advantages in it.

He thought for a time of piercing orations starting multitudes and of books wrung from his heart. In the gloom of his misery, his eyesight proclaimed that mankind were bowing to wrong and ridiculous idols. He said that if some all-powerful joker should take them away in the night, and leave only manufactured shadows falling upon the bended heads, mankind would go on counting the hollow beads of their progress until the shriveling of the fingers. He was a-blaze with desire to change. He saw himself, a sun-lit figure upon a peak, pointing with true and unchangeable gesture. "There"! And all men could see and no man would falter.

Gradually the idea grew upon him that the cattle which cluttered the earth, would, in their ignorance and calm faith in the next day, blunder stolidly on and he would be beating his fists against the brass of accepted things. A remarkable facility for abuse came to him then and in supreme disgust and rage, he railed. To him there was something terrible and awesome in these words spoken from his heart to his heart. He was very tragic. |

[*Page* 90]

XIII

The column that had butted stoutly at the obstacles in the roadway was barely out of Fleming's sight before he saw dark waves of men come sweeping out of the woods and down through the fields. He knew at once that the steel fibres had been washed from their hearts. They were bursting from their coats and their equipments as from entangling things. They charged down upon him like terrified buffalos.

Behind them, blue smoke curled and clouded, and, through the thickets, he could sometimes see a distant, pink glare. The voices of the cannon were clamoring in an interminable chorus.

Fleming was horror-stricken. He stared in pain and amazement. He forgot that nature had pointed him out as a victim. He again lost all concern for himself. He threw aside his mental pamphlets on the philosophy of the retreated and rules for the guidance of the doomed.

The fight was lost. The foe was coming storm-wise to flood the army.

Within him there was something that bade him cry out. He had the impulse to make a rallying speech, to sing a battle-hymn, but he could only get his tongue to call out into the air: "Why—why—what—what's th' matter?"

Soon he was in the midst of them. They were leaping and scampering all about him. Their blanched faces shone in the dusk. | [*Page* 91] He turned from one to another as they galloped along. His half-coherent questions were lost. He made insane appeals for information. The wild eyes seemed not to throw a glance in his direction.

Finally, he clutched a man by the arm. They swayed around face to face.

"Why—why——" stammered Fleming, struggling with his balking tongue.

The man screamed. "Let'go me! Let'go me!" His face was livid and his eyes rolled as if he had lost control of them. He was puffing and panting. He still clutched his rifle perhaps having forgotten to release his hold upon it. He tugged frantically and Fleming, being compelled to lean forward, was dragged several paces.

"Let'go me! Let'go me!"

"Why—why——" stuttered Fleming wildly.

"Well, then," bawled the man in a lurid rage. He adroitly and fiercely swung his rifle. It crushed upon Fleming's head. The man ran on.

Fleming's fingers had turned to paste upon the man's arm. He saw the burning wings of lightning flash before his eyes. There was a deafening rumble of thunder within his head.

Suddenly, his legs seemed to die. He fell writhing to the ground. He tried to get up. In his efforts against his pain he was like a man wrestling with a creature of the atmosphere. | [*Page 92*]

There was a sinister struggle. Sometimes, he would achieve a position half-erect, battle with the air for a moment, and then fall again. His face was of a clammy pallor. Deep groans were wrenched from him.

At last with a twisting movement he got upon his hands and knees and from thence, like a babe trying to walk, upon his feet. He went lurching over the grass.

And afterward, Fleming fought an intense fight with his body. His dulled senses wished him to swoon and he opposed them stubbornly, his mind picturing unknown dangers and mutilations if he fell upon the field. He went forward, Conklin-fashion. He thought of secluded spots where he could fall and be unmolested. To reach one, he strove against the tide of his pain.

He put his hand up to his head and timidly touched the wound under his hair. The scratching pain of the contact made him draw a long breath through his clenched teeth. His fingers were dabbled with blood. He regarded them with a fixed stare.

Around him, he could hear the grumble of jolting batteries as the scurrying horses were lashed toward the front. Once a young officer on a be-splashed charger near ran him down. He turned and watched the artilleryman controlling the mass of cannon, men, and horses by excited motions of his gauntleted hand. The guns followed the teams with a seeming air of unwillingness.

THE TEXT: HISTORY AND ANALYSIS

THE TEXT: HISTORY AND ANALYSIS

THE MANUSCRIPT

THE DRAFT

The complete final manuscript of *The Red Badge of Courage* consists of 176 leaves written throughout in black ink on legal-cap paper, roughly two-thirds of it on one side of unused sheets but with a scattering of pages inscribed on the versos of false starts of earlier leaves during the same inscription and a little less than one-third written on the versos of a draft that immediately preceded the present manuscript.[1]

The extant documents for the text of the *Red Badge* start with the fragments of this draft which have been preserved only because they were utilized to piece out Crane's supply of paper. In all, 57 leaves of the draft are known, starting with page 2 and ending with page 92, at its foot the last sentence of a paragraph corresponding to the sentence on page 107.4 of the final manuscript (71.18). If the MS, the last version, had expanded the draft in the same proportion for the remainder (and if the draft had been completed, a matter in some question), the whole of MS(d)—the draft—might have filled some 160 to 170 pages, as compared with the last page num-

---

[1] The earliest descriptions of this Barrett manuscript were made by John Winterich in his edition of the MS for the Folio Society (1950) and by Robert Stallman, *Stephen Crane: An Omnibus* (1952), both from photographs. The only previous description and analysis from consultation of the document itself is that of William L. Howarth, "*The Red Badge of Courage* Manuscript: New Evidence for a Critical Edition," *Studies in Bibliography*, XVIII (1965), 229–247. The present account is condensed from a more extended survey of the physical evidence of the draft and final manuscripts available in the Introduction to *The Red Badge of Courage: A Facsimile Edition of the Manuscript*, ed. Fredson Bowers, 2 vols. (NCR Microcard Editions, 1973). Reference to this study is made hereafter as *Facsimile*. The *Facsimile* analysis was much indebted to Professor Howarth's pioneering study, especially in the description of the paper stock, but it derived from a fresh examination of the manuscript, corrected a few details, and differed in parts of the interpretation of the evidence.

ber 193 of the revised final version.[2] The earliest MS page to be written on the verso of a draft leaf is 51; the last is 145. The pages of the discarded first draft must have been in some disarray and were used in no fixed order for the inscription of the final manuscript; nevertheless, some form of pattern is discernible.

We start, then, with this earliest known draft, of which 57 leaves have been preserved: pages 2, 4–8, 10–15, 22–23, 28–29, 36, 39–40, 42, 45–53, 55–56, 59–60, 61a, 61b, 64, 66–72, 75–82, 84–86, 90–92.[3]

Paper A: MS(d), the draft, was started with Paper A, of which nine leaves have been preserved for pages 2, 4–8, 10–12. On the evidence that MS(d) page 13 starts the second sequence with Paper B, it is clear that only twelve sheets of Paper A were originally used, pages 1–12. Paper A is wove unwatermarked legal-cap measuring 316 × 200 mm.[4] Extending from margin to margin are 29 blue horizontal rules at distances of 9.75 mm.; these rules start after a head space of 39–40 mm. and end with a tail space of 4 mm. (In general, head and tail space measurements will vary in relation to each other depending upon the cutting of the leaf.) At the left appears a vertical rule of three lines—pink, dark blue, pink—which is 42.5 mm. from the left margin.

Paper B: Pages 13 to 92, the last of the forty-eight leaves preserved in this sequence, were written on Paper B, a wove unwatermarked legal-cap differing in various respects from Paper A. The measurements are 317 × 205 mm.; each leaf has 28 blue horizontal rules extending from margin to margin 9.5 mm. apart with a head space of 43 mm. depth and a tail space of 8–10 mm. The vertical rule of two pink lines is 40 mm. from the left margin.

The draft manuscript is written in black ink that may well be the same as that used for the final manuscript. All corrections are made in this same ink. The majority of the alterations appear to have been written *currente calamo*, during the process of inscription; but some of the interlineations are just possibly changes made upon a review,

[2] The possibility exists that Crane abandoned writing out the draft (which was probably an expansion of some lost antecedent version) shortly after page 92 and proceeded directly to the fair-copy revised Barrett manuscript. The pages of the draft are only about two-thirds complete to page 92. Although in some irregular order, Crane inscribed the final MS leaves on the versos of MS(d) paper from sheets more or less currently discarded after copying. Yet the last series of sheets breaks this practice and returns to a pile of sheets long since set aside. Since the sheets are in some disarray it is odd that somehow a leaf from its latter third did not slip into the lots being used if the final part had been written. The matter is discussed in detail in *Facsimile*, pp. 25–31.

[3] The tables at the end of the Appendixes provide the list of MS(d) leaves and their use in MS.

[4] Because the manuscript is tightly bound, the width of the leaves of various paper, as described, cannot be guaranteed accurate within a millimeter and must be taken as the minimum width, not necessarily the maximum.

whether of the manuscript as a whole or chapter by chapter is not to be determined.

Most of the draft leaves have been deleted by heavy hill-and-dale pencil scribbles mostly with a thick pencil but a few perhaps with a finer pencil. Two leaves escaped deletion marks—page 14 used for MS 123 and page 85 used for MS 108. Five leaves were deleted exclusively in ink. Of these, three in sequence were ink-deleted with bold cross-hatching: page 4 used for MS 135, page 5 for 133, and page 12 for 134. Cross-hatched also in ink but with a different design is page 55 used for MS 79. Finally, page 77 for MS 116 was ink-deleted with a page-long cross. The left vertical half of page 40 used for MS page 52 was cross-hatched in ink, but the whole page was then deleted, also, by the usual pencil scribbles. Other leaves with vertical or slanting deleting strokes in ink but also scribbled over in pencil are 56 (for 80), 59 (for 78), 60 (for 77), and 61a (for 76). The general uniformity of the pencil deletion—especially the usual scribbles with the thick pencil—suggests a single operation, probably as part of the final preparation of the MS. Undeleted pages 14 (for 123) and 85 (for 108) were presumably overlooked. It would seem that the thorough ink cross-hatching was done currently with the inscription of MS on their backs and thus obviated the need for the later deletion in pencil, the more particularly because the combination of pencil and ink occurs only when the ink deletion was incomplete (as with the partial cross-hatching on page 40 or when there was deletion only by a few slanting ink strokes as on pages 56, 59, 60, and 61a). Evidence for the ink deletion of draft pages as current occurs in the offset on MS page 80 recto of cross-hatching on MS(d) page 55 used for MS page 79. It would seem that Crane inscribed page 79, then turned it over and deleted its draft verso, before going on to the short page 80, which thereupon absorbed some of the ink when laid on top of 79 verso.

This MS page 80 was inscribed below the deleted first five words of a false start of draft page 50 which had been turned over and used to inscribe draft page 56. With this exception, no false starts from the draft manuscript have been preserved.

It may be remarked, finally, that in the draft Chapter x was misnumbered xi on page 71 (back of MS 84) and never corrected.

THE FINAL MANUSCRIPT

The preserved final manuscript consists of 176 leaves, foliated [1] 2–40 45–65 67–85 90–97 104–125 127–165 167–193. During the last round of preparation Crane bridged the gaps in pagination by supplementary numbering. In lead pencil he wrote '41–' before paginal number 45 and '66–' before 67; in ink he added '–6' after 165; and in blue pencil '86–' before 90, '98–' before 104, and '126–' before 127. Other page numbers were altered currently in the inscription ink. Page 8 was written large after and partly over a smaller 8; in 27 the 7 is written over an ill-formed 7 but just possibly over an 8 instead; 123 was altered from 122, 161 from 167, 162 from 168, and 163 from 169; in later 169 the 6 is formed over the start of a 9; and 190 was paged after deleted 189. Page 15 was written by turning end for end a page which originally had 13 inscribed at its head. Owing to the removal of Chapter XII, in the final preparation Crane renumbered in blue pencil Chapters XIII–XVI as XII–XV but he failed to renumber XVII as XVI and so on to the end with original Chapter XXV which should have been renumbered XXIV.

More often than not when Crane came to write on a sheet he turned it so that the tail space was at the head and he wrote on its first ruled line, continuing one or two or even three lines down into the unruled head space at the foot. Or if he began with the head space, he was likely to write a line or two in the space above its first rule. A page beginning a chapter always uses the head space properly but seems to have been numbered only after the whole page had been written: some of the pagination is squeezed in above the chapter headings, and in the false starts of chapter-heading pages turned over and the blank versos used later, page numbers do not appear. Ordinarily after numbering a page Crane added a characteristic half circle beneath the number, but a few pages occur without this marking.

When Crane came to copy out and revise the final manuscript[5] from the preserved draft version, he began with a stock of paper different from the two varieties used for the draft, and indeed no unused sheets of Papers A and B appear in the MS. It is a curious fact that in the final MS the runs of the different stocks of paper all end on the last page of a chapter and a new stock always begins on the first page of the succeeding chapter, unless cancellation and substitution has taken place.

Paper C: The wove unwatermarked legal-cap Paper C measures 318 × 197 mm. and has 28 horizontal rules spaced 10 mm. apart with a head space of 48–50 mm. and a tail space of 4–6 mm. The vertical rule 35 mm. from the left margin consists of three lines—pink, blue, pink. The space between the left margin and the vertical rule is unlined, the only paper in which this feature occurs.

[5] 'Final' manuscript is a convenient and accurate term for the Barrett MS. Crane slightly revised a lost typescript made from the Barrett MS for the newspaper syndication, and he revised more thoroughly another copy of this same typescript later before it was sent to the printer of the book. No evidence exists, as has been suggested, that he ever copied out the text by hand after this present manuscript. Such a procedure would have been most unlikely; moreover, the nature of the variants from MS in the book do not encourage such a hypothesis.

On Paper C Crane wrote Chapters I–IV, pages 1–52, but only forty-six of these leaves are preserved: pages 41–44 ending Chapter IV have been removed to cut its original ending, and pages 51–52 ending Chapter V have been cancelled and replaced by a new ending (37.31–38.36) with correspondingly numbered pages written on the backs of MS(d) leaves 6 and 40, which had been Papers A and B. Well out of this sequence, MS page 139 (93.12–35) on C Paper which ends Chapter XVI (originally XVII) is a cancel leaf written on the back of a false start for page 33 to replace the original ending on Paper D. Thus forty-seven leaves of the established stock of Paper C have been preserved.

Two anomalous leaves exist. MS page 137 comes in a sequence of cancellations and substitutions just before the ending of Chapter XVI (originally XVII) on page 139 (93.12–35).[6] This page was written on the back of a leaf of what looks like C Paper, its recto consisting of page 3 of a story laid in Paris about Gustave and his wife Marie, the only preserved evidence for the existence of this piece.[7] The second anomaly is page 193, the final leaf of the manuscript (with blank verso) which continues the revision of the ending (135.34–37) begun on the original final page 192 of E Paper. It seems likely that these two leaves are of the same manufacture as the C Paper but of a different lot that came into Crane's possession at a later time. However, if for convenience these two leaves are included in the account, the total of preserved sheets of Paper C is raised to forty-nine.

Paper D: The laid legal-cap Paper D, watermarked 'HURLBUT | PAPER MFG. | CO.', measures 316 × 200 mm. (In some sheets the period after 'CO' is wanting.) Eleven vertical chainlines occur in each leaf spaced at intervals of 18.5 mm.; the horizontal wirelines are seven to each 10 mm. The paper is ruled off in 29 blue horizontal lines from margin to margin spaced 9.75 mm. apart with a head space of 38 mm. and a tail space of 3.5–4 mm. The vertical rule of three lines—pink, blue, pink—comes 40 mm. from the left margin.

Crane began Chapter VI on page 53 with this paper and continued it through page 66, the end of Chapter VII, page 59 within this sequence being written on the same paper but on the back of a false start of page 53. However, the last page of Chapter VI, page 60, a revision (44.27–37) written on the back of draft page 48 on Paper B, was substituted for the original page 60 on D Paper. In addition, the lower part of the text on page 65 was deleted and page 66, originally ending Chapter VII, presumably on Paper D, was removed. Beginning with Chapter VIII on page 67 the MS is written on the backs of MS(d)

---

[6] Page 139 is Paper C out of sequence because its verso was the false start of page 33; page 138 is Paper A on the back of page 7 of MS(d) and may not be a cancellans; pages 104–136 are all on the backs of MS(d).

[7] The text of the Gustave and Marie fragment is reproduced photographically in *Facsimile* and is reprinted in Volume X of *Works*.

leaves up to page 85, which cuts the ending of Chapter x by deleting the text of the lower part of the page and is followed by the removal of pages 86–89 originally ending the chapter. Chapter xi starts on page 90 once more with Paper D, and the sequence initially continued to the end of Chapter xii on page 103. However, the original Chapter xii running from page 98 to 103 was removed, a new ending to Chapter xi was written on page 97 (68.17–28) with MS(d) paper cancelling the D-Paper leaf 97, and the heading of Chapter xiii on page 104 was altered to read xii.

To summarize, the first section of Paper D beginning Chapter vi with page 53 and ending with the original conclusion of Chapter vii on page 66 constituted an unbroken run of fourteen leaves, of which twelve are now preserved, page 60 having been revised by the substitution of a page written on the back of an MS(d) leaf and page 66 removed. After an intervening sequence of MS(d) paper on pages 67 (Chapter viii) to 89 (86–89 having been withdrawn), Paper D is present again on page 90 and originally continued to page 103 for another group of fourteen leaves, of which seven are preserved in the manuscript after revision. Of the six removed leaves between 98 and 103, the deleted false start of original Chapter xii on page 98 is preserved at Harvard on the back of page 102 from the chapter; the revised substitute leaf 98 heading Chapter xii is preserved in the Berg Collection of the New York Public Library;[8] and pages 99 and 101 are in the Special Collections of the Columbia University Libraries.[9] The total is nineteen leaves of Paper D found in the MS of the twenty-eight originally used, to which may be added four of the removed leaves. Hence five leaves have been lost: two that were cancelled with substitution of MS(d) paper and three of the seven that were removed. The status of the two runs of MS(d) paper that interrupt Paper D and follow it after original page 103 to connect with Paper E is considered below in the analysis of the revision of the manuscript.

Paper E: The wove legal-cap Paper E measuring 319 × 200 mm.

[8] The Harvard leaf has a note in a strange hand identifying it as from the *Red Badge* manuscript. However, on the back of the Berg Collection leaf in Edith Richie's hand is written in ink, 'This page of the manuscript of "The Red Badge of Courage" belongs to Edith Richie. | 6.xii.00'. In another place a hand has inscribed in ink, 'Mrs. J. Howland Jones. 4 Aug. 53'. Written vertically in pencil in a bold hand, possibly that of Cora Crane, is 'Bit of the | Red Badge | of Courage | ms' in which 'age' of 'Courage' has been written over original 'ge'.

[9] Crane apparently preserved these leaves, as attested by the presence of pages 99 and 101 among the Crane papers at Columbia deriving from Cora, and by Cora's presentation of a leaf in 1900 to Edith Richie after Crane's death. Moreover, the lower blank half of the false start of Chapter xii on page 98 at Harvard contains what appears to be the scoring for some game, with two triple columns headed 'Cr Cora Camille' and 'Crane Cora Camille' in Cora's hand. This game would have been played in England; it could scarcely have been scored at the Hotel de Dream in Jacksonville, Florida.

is watermarked 'HURLBUT | PAPER | MFG. | CO.' (In some sheets the period after 'CO' is wanting.) It has 29 horizontal blue rules from margin to margin spaced 9.75 mm. with a head space of 39 mm. and a tail space varying from 6 mm. to 2.5 mm. since the last horizontal line runs at an angle. The vertical rule of three lines— pink, dark blue, pink—is placed 40 mm. from the left margin.

Crane started Chapter xvii (initially xviii) on page 140 with this paper and continued to the original ending on page 192. The end of Chapter xvii on page 145 is cancelled and a revised text written on MS(d) paper is substituted (98.3–16). Chapter xx (originally xxi) ends on page 164 and Chapter xxi begins on page 165, but since the next page is 167, Crane in the revising ink linked the two by adding a dash and a 6 to 165 to make it page 165-6. After writing 'The End' on page 192 Crane deleted it and in the general revision began a new ending which he finished on page 193, which is of the later lot of Paper C. In all, then, fifty-three leaves of Paper E were originally inscribed, of which one has been lost by substitution of cancellans leaf 145 on MS(d) paper, and another lost as part of a currently made revision that rewrote original pages 161–166 by the sequence 161–165 also on Paper E (112.21–115.6). Counting the cancelled leaves 161–165 with substituted matter, Crane used in all fifty-eight leaves of Paper E.

THE REVISION OF THE MANUSCRIPT

The first question about the Barrett final manuscript is whether it is a revised and expanded fair copy of the earlier draft preserved in part on the backs of various of the MS leaves. The case is not demonstrable, of course, but the preservation of the MS(d) leaves as a stock of paper for this MS and the sequence of their use strongly suggests a direct relationship between the two, this fortified by the lack of evidence for the existence of any intermediate copy.[10] Indeed, although the final revision is often important and thoroughgoing, a fair amount of its text is little more than a word-for-word transcript of the draft, and an intermediate manuscript is by no means required to account for the differences.

[10] Crane preserved one batch of paper from removed Chapter xii and had it in England, but no leaves from the preserved earlier draft have been found except for those used on the versos as paper for the final MS. If a manuscript later than this draft had been in existence, presumably the MS(d) leaves would have been discarded after it had been transcribed into the later version and the leaves of the intermediate manuscript would have supplied the stock for the inscription of the Barrett manuscript. The analysis of the order of the use of MS(d) leaves in inscribing MS found in the *Facsimile* comes close to demonstrating that in fact MS was written out from the MS(d) copy itself.

Once the final MS was inscribed, different sections were thereupon revised in different media. Previously, all parts had been altered during the act of writing out in a process of revision more extensive than anything that followed. These current alterations present no problem in assignment; ordinarily the original ink is not to be confused with the more intense revising ink. Subsequently pages 1–38 (3.1–28.37) were revised in a systematic manner first with the revising ink and then 1–39 (3.1–29.25) with pencil; pages 40–114 (29.26–77.8) once with ink; pages 115–137 (77.8–92.26) once with pencil; and pages 138–192 (92.27–135.34) once with ink. In the later part, scattered alterations during a final review were made with a blue pencil; in the earlier, in lead pencil and in ink.

Before these revisions are analyzed, one major problem must be settled that concerns the use of the versos of draft leaves to inscribe portions of the MS, chiefly within the area of Paper D. That some of these are cancellans leaves substituting for the blank paper originally used for the inscription can be demonstrated by their occurrence at the ends of chapters. By simple removal of original leaves, with or without deletion of material at the foot of the antecedent pages, Crane altered the end of Chapter IV on Paper C (pages 41–44 removed), Chapter VII on Paper D (page 66 removed), Chapter X on MS(d) paper (pages 86–89 removed), and Chapter XIV (originally XV) (page 126 removed). He also removed the whole of original Chapter XII on Paper D, pages 98–103.

In other cases he removed the original leaf and substituted a rewritten text of the chapter ending on one or more sheets of paper different from that used in the original sequence. The paper for the revised substitute was usually the versos of draft leaves, as in the replacement of pages 51–52 of Paper C by two leaves rewritten on MS(d) versos to end Chapter V, of page 60 of Paper D by a leaf of MS(d) to end Chapter VI, of page 97 of Paper D by a leaf of MS(d) to end Chapter XI, and of page 145 of Paper E by a leaf of MS(d) to end Chapter XVII (originally XVIII). However, other discarded sheets twice appear. The first is clear-cut in that a false start of page 33 on Paper C was put aside and its verso later used as the substitute page for cancelled page 139, the original of which seems to have been an MS(d) leaf. This is only part of a more extensive revision of the end of Chapter XVI (originally XVII) occurring on page 139. Page 137 marks the start of the revised ending by substitution of a page written on the verso of a leaf of Paper C (perhaps of a slightly different lot) containing on its original recto the text for page 3 of a Parisian story about Gustave and Marie. The intervening page 138 on MS(d) paper is just possibly original and not a rewritten substitute. Physical evidence therefore indicates alterations by cancellation or by cancellation and substitution of the endings of Chapters IV, V, VI, VII, X, XI, XIV (originally XV), XVI (originally XVII), and XVII (originally xviii). It is probable that the end of Chapter xx (originally xxi) and the first leaf of Chapter xxi (originally xxii) on pages 161–166 (112.21–116.1) were also revised by substituted leaves, although in this case since the same Paper E was used for the cancellans leaves as for the inscription of the original cancellanda the circumstances of revision differed, and it was either the first chapter ending so to be revised or else the cancellation and substitution was a current one.[11] The two runs of MS(d) paper within the area of Paper D do not appear to represent massive cancellation and substitution but instead paper used for the original inscription. All stocks of paper, including these two runs of draft leaves, terminate at the ends of chapters and hence so far as can be told not at the point of actual exhaustion of the supply. This arbitrary distinction suggests some arbitrary cause, such as periodic delays in recopying the draft, perhaps combined with some change in living accommodations or working arrangements. Crane shifted his quarters several times during 1893 and the first part of 1894. Hence it is possible that at two periods he was isolated from the supply of Paper D he had acquired and was thrust back for paper to the already copied discarded leaves of the draft in lieu of the unused paper he otherwise preferred to employ.

It is clear that the sheets of the draft had not been stacked in any regular numerical order after copying into the MS and were in considerable disarray. Nevertheless, the disorder was not total or random. Analysis suggests that the first run of MS(d) paper to appear in MS was relatively current in its use; that is, the copying of MS ran fairly close to the actual material being utilized from MS(d) and in some cases the sheets being reused were within two or three of those that were being copied from the MS(d) original. Within the second run of MS(d) leaves from pages 104–136 two major sequences develop. Of the thirty-two leaves in the second lot the first sixteen (with the exception of page 39 used for page 105) run from MS(d) pages 68 to 92 for MS pages 104–119. For the remaining MS pages 120–136, the MS(d) pages run from 2–36, with only two anomalous pages from the earlier half: page 82 used for MS page 125 and 53 for 132.

The distribution seems to point to some such conclusion as this. When Crane was copying the final manuscript from the draft version, he was accustomed to discard on the floor each draft leaf as he finished transferring it in revised form to MS. At the end of each stint he picked up the leaves wherever they had fallen and in the process of this unsystematic retrieval they were put together out of any

---

[11] For a technical discussion of these cancellations and a survey of other possible examples, see *Facsimile*, pp. 19–24. The conclusion is there drawn that the endings of the nine chapters cited above represent the only actual cancellation of leaves in the MS.

consecutive order. These carelessly assembled leaves (which at the time he thought were of no further use to him) were piled from day to day. When he had finished revised Chapter IV on MS page 44 he made a stack of draft leaves 1–39. For the start of Chapter V on MS page 45, continued on Paper C, he was copying out and revising something close to page 40 of the draft. At another interval, or a shift in the place where he was working, he changed paper to Paper D at MS page 53, Chapter VI, and continued to the end of MS Chapter VII on page 66, which corresponded with page 57 of MS(d). At this point, presumably after another shift, he started to use the backs of the draft leaves for his revision. Pages 1–39 earlier discarded from the draft seem not to have been available to him, but he had to hand a lot of MS(d) leaves starting with 40, 41, or 42 and ending with the most recently copied-out MS(d) page 57. These he used for paper, even to the point of starting page 75 on the verso of MS(d) 64 which he had just discarded. This is the closest that the pages of the draft used for copy for MS and the discarded MS(d) pages used as paper for current inscription ever come. The last preserved page in the sequence, MS 85, on the back of MS(d) 61b, copies from draft pages 74–75.

Within the second run of the use of MS(d) paper, the nature of the stock of MS(d) leaves available changes abruptly at MS page 120 from a run between MS(d) 68–92 to the original MS(d) lot between 1 and 39.[12] This shift from the use of relatively current discarded leaves to long-since revised MS(d) pages that takes place beginning with the inscription of MS page 120 on the verso of MS(d) 23 after the inscription of MS 119 on MS(d) 69 must have a significance. It is a not unreasonable conjecture that the cause for Crane's breaking his previously established pattern of writing on relatively current discarded MS(d) paper was that the supply after MS(d) pages 92–93 (more likely after the end of a chapter with page 97) had been exhausted, provided that it ever existed. A break in the continuity of revision, or a change of place, will not apply, for whenever he continued the revision he should have had available the leaves from the draft manuscript on which he had just worked. The most plausible reason for this change in circumstances is that the draft itself ended no earlier than the copying of draft page 92 on the upper part of MS 107 (the back of MS[d] 80), and probably no later than the end of draft Chapter XIII (renumbered XII by subsequent revision of MS) on MS page 111 that conjecturally revised draft page 97.

In short, the evidence suggests the possibility that Crane wrote the draft that we know no farther than page 97 before he stopped and went back to revise the beginning by inscribing the present MS ac-

---

[12] The relationship of the MS pages to all the MS(d) leaves on which they were copied is worked out in detail in *Fascimile*, pp. 19–31.

cording to his altered idea of what the novel should be, the result being the Barrett manuscript as we have it. If so, then beginning with MS Chapter XIII (originally XIV) on page 112 he was no longer revising the draft version of the novel that has been preserved. Whether he used an antecedent draft to it as the general basis for his revision cannot be known, for unfortunately he acquired a supply of the unused Paper E before he had exhausted his cache of the earliest leaves of the present draft, and thus he had no occasion to write the MS after page 139 (145 is a cancellans) on the backs of discarded leaves. What we can conjecture with some confidence is that at the very least the circumstances differed between the inscription of pages 1–111 of the Barrett manuscript and the inscription of pages 112–193.

It rests now to enquire into the evidence bearing on the state of the Barrett final manuscript in late April, 1894, when Crane took it to Hamlin Garland to read. This can best be isolated after a complete view of the whole set of alterations both early and late.

If we do not count the changes made currently during the course of inscription, we may say that the manuscript was given a preliminary revision in ink for at least the first three chapters before Garland saw it, and later, after he had criticized it, a final literary revision of the whole was made in lead pencil and in ink, starting once more with Chapter I. As a final preparation for the publication typescript Crane went over the earlier part of the manuscript in pencil and in ink, and from page 85 in blue pencil, to strengthen deletions and correct pagination and chapter headings as well as to delete the versos of MS leaves written on the backs of earlier draft sheets. In only two cases were verbal revisions made in this last looking-over, plus four changes in dialect forms. Following the preliminary revision in ink, which was broken off at the end of Chapter III on page 38 but may have extended to the end of Chapter IV on page 44,[13] Crane returned to page 1 and started in lead pencil the literary revision that was to continue to the end, this being the only text revision ever given the manuscript barring the broken-off preliminary attempt, a few casual final-ink changes in dialect, and the single blue-pencil intervention. The lead pencil runs from pages 1–39 but probably continued to original 44. From page 45–114 the revision was made in ink, from 115–137 again in pencil, and from 138 to the end on page 193 once more in ink. No reason exists not to believe that this was a generally continuous process despite the different media.

However, starting on page 14 and continuing to page 68, then

[13] Page 40 is neutral since it consists of nothing but completely untouched soldiers' dialogue. Pages 41–44 have been removed as a revision of the ending of Chapter IV. Page 39 did not contain names requiring ink revision.

after a gap resuming on page 147, and later, are some pencil markings in a hand that is not Crane's.

The nature of the revisions turns out to have a particular significance. In pages 1–38 during the preliminary or pre-Garland revision in ink Crane altered every name not in direct address. Fleming becomes *the youth*, Conklin first *the excited soldier* and then *the tall soldier*, Wilson first *the young private* as well as *the blatant young soldier* but later *the loud young soldier*. The revision is systematically devoted to the removal of names; only a limited number of minor stylistic changes and an addition or two are made in this ink, like the substitution of *separated* for *parted* on page 23.1 (17.6), or the addition of *Loud . . . defiance* on 23.31–34 (17.32–34) or simply of a phrase like *in his doubts* on 35.33 (26.33), or the insertion of a paragraph symbol at 27.25 (20.22), or the shortening to *view-points* from deleted *points of view* at 27.7–8 (20.8).

The pencil revision in pages 1–39 comes later since on occasion it alters changes made in the preliminary revising ink. In this pencil revision Crane had three objectives:

1. He rectified oversights in the removal of the names, and he changed his mind in a few particulars about the formulas he had substituted. All references to *young* in the ink-revised phrases for Wilson are removed lest he be confused with *the youth*, who is Fleming; moreover, Crane altered the ink-revision *blatant* to *loud* as applied to Wilson, and a few times altered *the excited soldier* to *the tall soldier*, that came to be applied uniformly to Conklin.

2. Some stylistic alterations were made in this pencil, as for example the deletion of a sentence *He had felt glad that none of his associates in the new company had been near to listen to it* (7.36), or the substitution of a few words like *calm* for *quiet* (8.7) and of *big* for *great* (29.9). Errors in the original inscription were touched up: *colums* is altered to *columns* (16.13) and *companion* to *companions* (16.21).

3. The most important change was a complete recasting of the use of dialect for Fleming, Conklin, and Wilson (as well as partially for Fleming's mother) and a return to relatively normal usage or at least to normal spelling. The pencil alterations in the dialect change *yeh* to *you*, *t'* to *to*, *th'* to *the*, restore final elided *d* and *g* as in *and* for *an'* and *searching* for *searchin'*. Dialect spellings like *jest, kin, inteh, onct,* and so on are normalized. These three characters, then, are set apart in their speech from the other soldiers and even from the officers.

The far-reaching decision to alter the speech of the central characters was made in response to queries marked in the manuscript by a strange hand using a light thin pencil. This hand has not previously been identified, but comparison with holograph letters of 1894–95 establishes it beyond question as Hamlin Garland's.

Garland's first mark in the manuscript occurs in the left margin of page 14 where he placed a question mark before lines 5 and 11 and underlined the dialect form *yeh* which occurs in both lines, first in Conklin's speech and then in Wilson's (10.27, 31). On page 15 opposite an underlined *yeh* in line 28 spoken by Conklin (11.35), Garland wrote 'Don't use this form | where it is accented', the last word being doubtful.[14] Other question marks appear in the margins at MS pages 25.20, 26.23, 29.3 + −.3 + 2, 39.22, 53.17,21–22, and 59.17. Those at 25.20 and 26.23 query *yeh* in Fleming's speech (19.1; 19.35) and at 29.3 + −.3 + 2 in Conklin's (21.28). Garland's dislike of Crane's insistent use of dialect extended itself from *yeh* to other forms, not always appropriately. At 39.22 in a soldier's speech he queried the use of *a'tall* (29.20+), at 53.17,21–22 various dialect forms in the speech of Fleming as well as a soldier (39.18,22–23), and finally at 59.17 in the speech of a general (44.14–15). It is interesting that Crane ignored the suggestions at 53.17,21–22 and at 59.17. Garland did not confine himself to these queries but on some occasions he himself altered the text. At 26.29 he underlined and then altered the *y*'s in *Napolyon Bonypart* to *e*'s and added a final *e* to altered *Bonepart* (20.1). It is possible that a light pencil stroke in *what'll* at 14.23 (11.4) is his suggested deletion, but if so Crane either overlooked it or disagreed, for no change was made.

Two markings that accidentally resulted in changes in the book text away from Crane's intentions were made on pages 22 and 29. At 22.1–3 (16.18–20) Garland drew a bold × through the top three lines of dialogue containing various dialect forms to which he objected. When Crane came to revise this in the pencil stage he accepted only part of the deletion. First he altered a *yeh* to *you* and then drew a series of pencil lines through one sentence; but he clearly intended "I told yeh so, didnt I?" to stand, for he transferred a closing quotation mark to follow it and strengthened the opening quote. In the third line he altered *blatant* in a preliminary-ink addition to pencil *loud*. The typist of the manuscript mistook Garland's × as deleting the three lines *in toto*, and they do not appear in the book. A similar accident occurred on page 29. Here Crane had added two sentences vertically in the left margin during the original inscription (21.27–28) and then had deleted *Wilson* and interlined *Conklin*. In the preliminary-ink revision he had altered *Conklin* to *the tall*

---

[14] Crane's pencil deletion of this notation obscures the final scrawled word. The first letter is very like Garland's initial *a*, and the final letter is clearly a *d*, probably preceded by an *e*. The letter before *e* could be an *l*, but Garland often formed a *t* in this manner either with an elementary cross stroke or one that was markedly detached. The actual word remains a real puzzle: *accented* is not likely to be right. One might have expected *underlined* or something of the sort, or *noted*, or *marked*, but the letters seemingly do not permit a firm reconstruction.

soldier and *Fleming* to *the youth.* Garland first put a question mark in the margin referring to the dialect forms in this addition but then he drew a large ✕ through the latter part of the three lines. When Crane came to this passage in the course of his alterations in pencil, he changed *Yeh kin* to *You can*, modified two more *yeh* forms to *you*, and completed the revision by changing *an'* to *and*, *d'* to *do*, and *wanta* to *want to.* But he made no deletion himself. The typist again misunderstood the Garland cross, which Crane had not erased (there is in fact only one erasure in the whole manuscript), and took it that only portions of sentences covered by the cross were intended for deletion. Thus it happens that the book prints unaffected *That's all yeh* (A1 reads 'you') *want to do* but in error omits *need. What d' yeh* and *—carry a hotel?* contrary to Crane's intention, as well as omitting *drink, sleep* in the preceding sentence. On page 23 Garland had drawn a large cross through the three lines 24–26 of soldiers' speech (17.27+). Whether Crane did not accept this suggested deletion at the time of his revision in pencil, or inadvertently overlooked the marking, cannot be known. But when in the very final look-through of the manuscript he made a few changes in ink, including attention to other of Garland's suggestions, he then deleted the lines heavily in ink.[15]

Garland also altered a few of the mechanical errors that caught his eye. In 25.13–14 (18.33–34) Crane wrote originally, *As he spoke his boyish face was voice was wreathed in a gleeful smile.* Garland not very intelligently interlined *and* with a guide-mark above partially deleted *was* following *face*; Crane deleted this *and* in pencil together with *voice* to correct the mistake. In 11.35 it was probably Garland who deleted the second of the dittographic *they | they* and in 27.12 crossed out the first *h* in Crane's *sandwhich.* Earlier, in 25.4 he probably deleted the error *to*, and in the next line it is certainly his hand that altered the error *coming* to *come* by the same sort of pencil Greek *e* he had used in 20.1. In this early section at 22.27 he deleted the awkward *head* and interlined *shoulder*; in the final preparation Crane traced over this emendation in ink to confirm it.[16] In 16.36 Garland deleted the superfluous *to his own* after *kindred emotions.* In the final survey Crane accepted the excision by strengthening the deletion in ink and adding a period after *emotions.* Somewhat later, at 37.1, Garland interlined *look* over deleted *air*, a change that Crane accepted by tracing it over in ink, in the final ink re-

---

[15] The deletion was so heavy that it offset on the verso of leaf 22. Similarly, the ink deletion in line 10 offset. However a deletion through the text in line 6 made as part of the preliminary revision had not fully covered the words at beginning and end, and this deletion was extended during the final preparation of the manuscript, only the touching-up offsetting of course. This similar offset helps to place the deletions in lines 10 and 24–26 as final.

[16] Crane seems to have intended the musket resting against Fleming's head as he carried it on his shoulder to have bounced 'from his head', but the intention is obscure and it was advisable for him to accept Garland's obvious emendation.

vision of this section. At 49.31 Garland corrected Crane's ungrammatical *he* by deletion and then he interlined *himself,* which Crane did not trouble to retrace in ink. Corrections, not revisions, appear in 37.20 where Garland put a vertical stroke through the final *e* of *silence,* presumably to indicate that it should be *silent,* but Crane overlooked the marking. In 44.18 he inserted *t* after *s* in Crane's *chesnut.*

After page 68.6 (49.31) a long interval occurs before Garland's hand again appears. Not until page 147.7 (100.6) does he reenter to interline *see,* then on 151.13 (104.13) to correct Crane's *where* to *were,* and to alter the spelling of Crane's *dieties* to *deities* at 155.17 (107.33) and *diety* to *deity* at 191.31 (135.17+); at 162.3 (113.13) he wrote in the margin (*sword?*) and Crane accepted the suggestion by deleting the underlined *cane* in the text and interlining *sword.*

This evidence of Garland's ministrations suggests the following reconstruction. The early part of the manuscript that Crane left with Garland comprised the first seven chapters and at least the start of the eighth on page 68 although it is probable that the bundle included all of Chapter VIII through page 73. In this area Garland made a number of suggestions as he read the manuscript that afternoon or night. When Crane returned the next day with the latter part of the manuscript, Garland was particularly hurried since he was on the point of leaving for Chicago. The evidence of his correction and revision shrinks markedly—only four changes are present in this latter part and they begin after a decided pause. Garland's chief effect on the revision of the novel was his partly successful attempt to persuade Crane to lighten and even to remove entirely much of the dialect in which the speech had originally been written. This was the main point of his queries and suggested deletions, and he presumably reenforced his opinions orally. Crane accepted the advice originally only in the matter of the three major characters Fleming, Conklin, and Wilson, but then included Fleming's mother. Garland's influence made itself felt, therefore, in the fundamental treatment of a considerable part of the dialogue early in the revision.

On the other hand, although at first Crane normalized the speech of the three soldiers to accord with Garland's suggestions, he subsequently changed his mind and retained the original dialect both for Conklin and for Wilson while altering only Fleming's speech. The retention of dialect on MS pages 75–77 (55–57.9) is not necessarily significant because Fleming's dialect is anomalously preserved. But an abrupt change takes place with the continuation of Fleming's speech at the head of MS page 78 (57.10). From this point on, Crane's revision (with a slip on page 113 [75.27–76.22]) gives Fleming relatively normal diction, but the original dialect of Conklin and (starting with page 112 of renumbered Chapter XIII [75.1–26]) that of Wilson is, in contrast, left untouched. Although neither in the MS nor in the typescript and printed versions made from it did Crane bother to return Conklin's and Wilson's earlier normalized speech to its original dialect, the evidence is incontrovertible that his final intention in the novel was to have Fleming speak correctly but Conklin and Wilson to speak in dialect as originally written. Without Garland, however, Fleming in the final version would not have differed from the others in his speech.

The evidence of the first thirty-eight pages points clearly to the hypothesis that when Crane brought the manuscript to Garland he had already begun a preliminary revision in ink that in the main concentrated on removing the names of the characters and substituting phrases like *the youth, the tall soldier,* and *the blatant soldier.* However this preliminary revision had progressed no farther, probably, than the end of Chapter IV on page 44. The case for this revision as a preliminary one is certain, for the physical evidence appears to admit no other interpretation. When Garland returned the manuscript Crane immediately set about a second round of revision, this time in pencil, which started back at the beginning and thus for a second time revised the pages that had previously been worked over in ink before being brought to Garland. This second revision in pencil was specifically triggered by Garland's criticism of the dialect and was aimed at meeting his suggestions in considerable part. As Crane went over the pages, however, he carried further the phrases that substituted for names, and thus in pencil he regularly removed *young* from Wilson and substituted *loud* for *blatant,* in this process sometimes revising an alteration made in the preliminary ink.

Having reached the end of Chapter IV in his revision in pencil, Crane then began to look over a part of the manuscript that had not been revised since its original inscription except, as will be shown below, by a certain amount of cancellation and substitution of leaves. Whether or not a break intervened, he began the revision of Chapter V on page 45 in an ink darker than that of the original inscription, probably from the same bottle as the ink he had used for the preliminary revision of the first four chapters. In this revision starting with Chapter V he combined the intent both of the preliminary and then of the revision in pencil made in the earlier pages. The names were removed as before, but Wilson is never *young* or *blatant* but instead only *loud.* Most importantly, he continued in ink the intent of the previous pencil revision by adjusting the dialect spellings and contractions of Fleming, Conklin, and Wilson to normal speech. Crane went ahead with these alterations, including a number of stylistic improvements and the deletion of superfluous words, phrases, and sentences until he reached page 111, the end of Chapter XII (originally XIII).[17]

By some oversight pages 112–114, the first three pages of Chapter

---

[17] The surviving pages of removed original Chapter XII also exhibit the same ink revision; hence this was continuous from Chapter V through original XII.

xiii (originally xiv), were not revised and thus the original names persist,[18] but systematic revision began again on page 115, this time shifting to pencil, and the names are removed as usual. The revision in pencil continued through page 137. On page 138 Crane continued the pencil revision by deleting *Fleming* in the very first line (92.27), but he then shifted to the darker ink and interlined *the youth* in this ink above the pencil-deleted *Fleming* and so continued in ink to the end of the novel, including the added conclusion written with the slightly thicker pen and the revising ink.

On the evidence of the several examples of darker ink tracing over Garland's pencil, at some point in the prepublication tidying-up of the manuscript Crane looked over matters that might trouble a typist and made a few adjustments in ink. It is possible that at this late point the final title was inscribed. The deletion of the early title in pencil could have occurred at any time: Garland recalled the manuscript as untitled, but his memory may be at fault since there is no sign of pencil deletion in the manuscript at the stage in which he saw it. In the latter part, from page 85 on, Crane used a blue pencil for this last going-over. Only eight changes were made in this blue pencil, most of them mechanical including the excision of text in blue for a chapter ending on page 125. While altering the chapter number on page 112, Crane noticed the uncorrected *Fleming* in the first line (75.1) and interlined *The youth* in blue, as remarked in footnote 18. This is the sole literary revision made in the blue pencil. Again as part of the final preparation of the manuscript Crane deleted all the versos of the leaves where he had used discarded draft pages for his paper, thus ensuring that the typist would not become confused. Two of these were missed, some versos that had been deleted in ink as part of the original inscription were ignored, but a few were strengthened or completed in pencil.[19] It is probable that at this time the pencil renumbering of the leaves to take account of removed pages was also accomplished.

The only remaining question of revision concerns the alteration of various chapter endings. These fall into two categories: (1) deletion of text without substitution, and (2) revision by rewritten text on the same number of cancellans leaves.

[18] In point of fact, at the very last moment when Crane was preparing the manuscript for typing and publication he corrected the chapter number xiv to xiii in blue pencil on page 112, and happening to notice that the first word of the chapter was *Fleming*, he altered it in blue pencil to *The youth* but did not bother to read further on the page, or in the next pages, to see if more changes were needed (as indeed they were).

[19] The preparation of the manuscript for publication by this pencil deletion of versos occasionally extended to the rectos, on the evidence of 74.17+ which strengthens in pencil the several deleting vertical strokes of the original inscription.

1. Fortuitously, the end of the text on page 40 coincided with the altered conclusion of Chapter IV that Crane at first proposed, although he was partly to restore the cut material for publication. Thus leaves 41–44 originally ending the chapter were abstracted and there was no need to delete or to alter any of the original inscription. The endings of Chapters VII, X, and XIV (originally XV) were also altered by simple deletion without substitution of text. The lower parts of the text on page 65 of VII and 85 of X are both deleted in lead pencil, the deletion on page 65 later being strengthened in pencil and that on page 85 in blue pencil. The third deletion of text, on page 125 of XIV, is anomalous because it was performed in blue pencil only. In this category should also be placed the total removal of original Chapter XII, pages 98–103. The preserved leaves had been revised before they were abstracted.

2. The other four chapter endings were altered by rewritten cancellans leaves in the original ink substituted for those removed. Cancellans pages 51–52 (37.31–38.36) closing Chapter V contain the normal revisions of names in the revising ink. No revisions appear on cancellans leaf 60 (44.27–37) ending Chapter VI and none was needed. In the cancellans leaves 137–139 (91.39–93.35)—possibly only 137 (91.39–92.26) and 139 (93.12–35)—concluding Chapter XVI (originally XVII), pages 137 and 138 show the normal revisions. Page 139 may contain conflicting evidence. At 139.8 (93.19–20) appears the anomalous phrase *Fleming's regiment* which ought to have been revised but was overlooked. On the other hand, it is not quite certain whether the revision of the last two sentences, 139.26–27 (93.34+), was made in the inscribing or in the revising ink. If in the latter, which seems more probable, then the original cancellans ending was touched up by a revision that improved its impact. The Chapter XVII (originally XVIII) cancellans page 145 (98.3–16) has only current revisions and required no later alteration.

From the simple fact that at least eight different chapter endings were changed in the manuscript,[20] one would expect that these alterations were of a piece and were performed substantially as part of one revisory operation. The evidence suggests the contrary, however, and a distinction in the kind of alteration apparently existed. That is, one group of revisions simply removed the text without substitution. On the three occasions when the ending of the antecedent page was deleted as an integral part of the cut, the material always concerns Fleming's reactions by means of a lengthy discourse on what was going on in his mind. These descriptions were ruthlessly weeded out. The material thus excised and not replaced was extensive, one page for Chapters VII and XIV but three for Chapter X.

---

[20] Nine were altered if one counts the perhaps current alteration in the ending of Chapter XX and the first page of XXI (originally XXI and XXII).

To these must necessarily be added the four-page cut in Chapter IV, pages 41–44, that produces a remarkably brief chapter, the shortest in the manuscript.

This excision of four leaves from the end of Chapter IV appears to have been made for other reasons, however. The removal of philosophizing was the reason for the other chapter-ending cuts, just as it was for the cancellation of the entire original Chapter XII. On the other hand, on the evidence of draft leaf 36, which corresponds with the added book text of 49.7–50.21 of the first edition (30.13–31.5), Chapter IV originally continued with an account of the preliminary fighting. Little room for any description of Fleming's internal reactions was left. The first edition cuts 182 words of soldiers' dialogue present in MS 40.14–32 and then continues with something short of 800 words of narrative. Thus if MS had been inscribed only partway down on original page 44, missing pages 41–44 would have contained about 1,000 words. If the account of the fighting was intermediate in the MS between the version in the preserved draft leaf 36 in this chapter and the book, the correlation of MS and of book text would have been close. The draft page 36 contains about 265 words covering an area to which about 310 words are devoted in the book. An expansion in the MS leaves from this draft to the book length would not have been unusual. In short, there is no discrepancy between the evidence of the draft leaf 36 and the book's corresponding text as to the contents of the deleted MS pages 41–44. They could not have consisted of descriptions of Fleming's feelings as had the other excised chapter endings, but instead they must have held some version of the fighting such as we know it in the draft leaf and the book text.

The question arises what in these pages of narrative could have caused the ruthless and ultimately unsatisfactory excision that had to be replaced. Probably the lengthy soldiers' dialogue had something to do with the cut. We know from Garland's queries that he disliked the extensive use of dialect; moreover, on three occasions he urged their complete removal by putting a large cross through dialect passages. Garland might well have conveyed to Crane in their discussion of his markings the warning that he was risking tedium for the reader by excessive speeches in dialect. In the later revision of the manuscript Crane rejected one of Garland's suggestions marked by the cross, partially accepted a second, and fully agreed with the removal of the third. Thereafter, the manuscript occasionally makes cuts in soldiers' speech. It is significant that the book removes a long passage of soldiers' dialect speech inscribed on MS 40.14–32, speech that was very likely continued on the next page 41 now lost.

However, the removal of dialect speech cannot have been the only or, indeed, the main reason for the excision of the four pages, for this material could scarcely have taken up much more of the text than represented on page 40. Simple deletion of text would have sufficed if the dialect alone had been in question. Instead, the best guess seems to be that at the moment Crane felt the two parts of the fight were repetitious and that the action had better be confined to the narration in Chapter v. On the evidence of the preservation of the removed leaves of original Chapter xii, Crane may have kept these four excised leaves from Chapter iv, or else he may have had to rely on the first typescript for which Garland had paid. At any rate, at some time following the final marking of the manuscript but before the preparation of copy for Bacheller (or even after that preparation but before presentation), Crane realized that the cut was too deep and he restored the text with some further revision but substantially in its post-Garland altered form.

Correspondingly, when rewritten material substitutes in cancellans leaves for the original endings of Chapters v, vi, xvi (originally xvii), and xvii (originally xviii), deep cuts could not have been effected because the substituted material takes up the same number of pages as the original inscription. It follows that the nature of the original matter for which these cancellans leaves substituted differed from that in which simple cuts were made. Something of a clue may be provided by the cancellans leaves 137–139 (91.39–93.35) which all concern dialogue and action but in which the original revised ending on the last of the three pages was apparently once more tinkered with to increase the sharpness of the last sentence. The natural inference is that in the cancellans leaves Crane was concerned not with removing extensive descriptions of Fleming's meditations but instead with better ordering the already existing original narrative, including the bold conclusion that he favored. It should be significant that whereas three of the four cuts required the deletion of antecedent text, in no case in the four examples of cancellation and substitution is a line of the immediately preceding page altered.

Physical evidence appears to settle the case for a further distinction. The substituted cancellans leaves 60 and 145 ending Chapters vi and xvii (originally xviii) are uninformative since only current alterations appear in them. But the normal stage of later revision in the darker ink occurs in cancellans leaves 51–52 and 137–139 of Chapters v and xvi (originally xvii). These revisions establish the fact that the text of the cancellans leaves had been rewritten and substituted for the original pages before Crane came to them in his revision of the manuscript. The contrary appears in the excised original Chapter xii, which had been revised and thus was removed at a time subsequent to the revision. The cancelled text on pages 85 and 125 of Chapters x and xiv (originally xv) is uninformative since it contains no revisions and needs none. On the other hand, the deleted text on page 65 ending Chapter vii does contain the standard revision of *Fleming* to *the youth* and thus agrees with original Chapter xii in the simple excision of material that can be dated as later than the systematic revision of the manuscript.

The time scheme, thus, joins with the nature of the alterations to indicate that the revision of chapter endings was made in two distinct operations, not in one. The cutting of Fleming's thoughts occurred after the revision of the entire manuscript had taken place; the rewriting to improve the narrative was not current like that in Chapter xx (originally xxi) or the insertion of page 189 (134.9–20) after page 190 was written but before 192, both on the same paper stock. Instead—on the evidence of the difference in the paper—the cancellations and substitutions were made at a point after the completion of the initial inscription but before the start of the preliminary revision of pages 1–38 present in the manuscript when brought to Garland.[21]

In 1914 (though not in 1900) Garland recalled that the "prodigious opening sentence which so impressed me on that memorable day disappeared entirely" from his copy and the printed book lacked many other of the most notable pages of the original manuscript.[22] Garland's persistent confusion about the opening sentence [23] has been remarked by Professor Levenson, but Garland was right about the missing pages not found in the book that he had read in manuscript. These were the removed pages in Chapters iv, vii, x, and xiv (xv when Garland saw the manuscript), together with the whole of Chapter xii. However, he did read the very earliest revisions represented by the cancellans leaves in Chapters v, vi, xvi (originally xvii), xvii (originally xviii), and xx (originally xxi), as well as the ink revisions in the text of the first four chapters.

This was the state of the manuscript in late April of 1894.

THE TYPESCRIPTS

On April 22, 1894, when Crane arrived in the rooms of Garland's brother with the first part of the manuscript of *The Red Badge of Courage*, he told Garland that a typist was holding the remaining manuscript (and presumably the typescript) until payment of $15

[21] If this is thought too early, at least the cancellans chapter endings must have been written out before the continuous revision of the preserved leaves that began with Crane returning to the beginning and—taking account of Garland's criticism—starting the systematic revision that is the only one subsequently present in the Barrett MS save for the cuts by removal of text and for the small amount of final preparation of the manuscript for publication.

[22] "Stephen Crane As I Knew Him," *Yale Review*, n.s., iii (1914), 505. Incidentally, his memory of the cuts suggests that his later reminiscences can provide authentic detail not present in 1900.

[23] One should note that Crane could not have cancelled the first page and substituted another after Garland saw the manuscript: the first page contains the preliminary ink revision that preceded Garland's reading of the novel. Moreover, it is unlikely that at that time Crane would have had a sheet of Paper A available.

was forthcoming. It would seem that he received the money from Garland's brother the night of April 23 and returned to Garland with the rest of the manuscript on April 24. The relative frequency of Garland's queries and revisions up to page 68 and then the hiatus until page 147, followed by only five markings between page 147 and the end, suggests that shortly after page 68 the manuscript available to him on April 22 was wanting. If the typist had released the manuscript at a chapter break, the nearest would have been the end of Chapter vIII on page 73. This is as good a guess as any about the amount of manuscript that Garland saw on the first day.

We have no information about the length of time that Crane had been in possession of pages 1–73 before he brought them to Garland. One may guess that the preliminary ink revision of pages 1–38 (probably of 1–44) had not been done before the manuscript was given to the typist, else Crane would have completed the revision of the whole in order to secure a clean typed copy. The odds favor the hypothesis that whatever interval existed between his recovery of the earlier portion of the manuscript and his showing it to Garland was occupied by the preliminary ink revision of Chapters I–IV. Indeed, it is possible that the incentive to persuade the typist to part with some of the manuscript was Crane's concern to interest Garland in the story before his departure and that on its receipt he undertook the preliminary revision in some haste for the express purpose of providing Garland with an adequate sample of his newly changed concepts of reference to the characters.

The revision of the manuscript that followed its return from Garland was so thoroughgoing as to leave the typescript bought for $15 substantially out of date without more marking up than would please a book printer. No further reference is ever made to this typescript and it was never submitted to a publisher so far as is known. (Some friends vaguely recall rejection of the story by one or two magazines; if these accounts are accurate it may have been the pre-draft short version that was earlier tried.)

Something of an ambiguity surrounds a second typescript. In an undated letter to his friend and fraternity brother John Henry Dick, Crane wrote: "Dear Dicon: Beg, borrow or steal fifteen dollars. —— like the Red Badge and want to make a contract for it. It is in pawn at the typewriter's for fifteen. Thine, Steve." [24] Stallman fills in the blank with *McClure's* within square brackets, but if McClure was indeed the concealed name that Crane did not wish to mention, the date of the letter cannot be late February of 1894 as is his conjecture, for Crane could not have submitted the novel to McClure before May after he had completed the revision found in the Barrett manuscript. Moreover, the letter cannot have been written before

[24] *Letters*, p. 30. The story of the loan and its aftermath for Dick with his employer *Godey's* is perhaps apocryphal.

May since it gives the title as the *Red Badge,* a form that does not seem to have been added to the manuscript until the last stage of its preparation after final revision. The request in the letter, then, cannot duplicate or be contemporaneous with the Garland loan in late April.[25]

In the accounts of his experience with McClure, Crane does not mention the nature of the copy that he gave the firm. The most circumstantial statement preserved comes in a letter to Garland on November 15, 1894: "McClure was a Beast about the war-novel and that has been the thing that put me in one of the ditches. He kept it for six months until I was near mad. Oh, yes, he was going to use it, but—— Finally I took it to Bacheller's. They use it in January in a shortened form" (*Letters,* p. 41). It is theoretically possible, but rather improbable, that during one of these periods of encouragement McClure asked for a typescript before going ahead with publication. The suggestion that McClure lost the typescript is a fantasy not supported by Crane's letter; but even so the carbon would have remained as a close copy of the Barrett manuscript. Yet when Crane took the copy to Bacheller, probably in October, Bacheller's memory is precise that it was a holograph manuscript.[26] Since the Barrett manuscript shows no signs of a printer's handling, a final typescript and carbon from it must have existed at some point. Only two possibilities are present. First, after revising the manuscript in May, 1894, Crane could have used the loan from Dick to pay for a typescript for McClure.[27] Second, after Bacheller accepted the novel in its manuscript form, Crane could have had a typescript made up as copy for the syndicate; with book publication in view he would not have wanted to sacrifice his manuscript.

Since the Barrett manuscript is the only one that could have been

[25] It is, of course, suspicious that both to Garland and to Dick, Crane asserted that the typist was holding the copy for $15 payment. One may guess, perhaps, that the Garland account is authentic and that Crane added this earlier experience to his letter to Dick as a fiction to authenticate the urgency of his need.

[26] "The manuscript was a bit soiled from much handling. It had not been typed. It was in the clearly legible and rather handsome script of the author" (Irving Bacheller, *Coming Up the Road* [1928], p. 278).

[27] An undated letter to Holmes Bassett has been associated with this occasion in its dating but must refer to Bacheller's acceptance, not to McClure: "I have just sold another book and my friends think it is pretty good and that some publisher ought to bring it out when it has been shown as a serial. It is a war-story and the syndicate people think that several papers could use it" (*Letters,* p. 29). If as seems quite certain 'sold another book' refers to the sale to the syndicate, this letter cannot be dated February 24, 1894, along with the letter to Dick, as Stallman conjectures, but very likely in October or early November, 1894, before Crane wrote Garland that Bacheller had the novel. Bacheller's form contract for the serialization of stories stated that service would start about October 29, 1894, and in the list of available authors he included Crane's name. Crane expected the serial to begin in January, 1895, but it actually started to appear in the first week of December, 1894.

in existence (the earlier draft—if it were ever complete—having been dissected as paper stock), no reason exists to doubt Bacheller's account. His statement that the manuscript was a bit soiled from much handling agrees with the evidence for revision, for Garland's reading, and doubtless for other readings before and afterward by Crane's friends. Some doubt has been expressed about the relation of this particular manuscript to Bacheller on the grounds that it is not particularly dirty, as he remarked. But the paper is by no means fresh, and most of the leaves are dog-eared. Moreover, the fact remains that unless we posit a further holograph transcript made from the Barrett manuscript before Bacheller saw it—and that is a near impossibility —this was the only manuscript that Bacheller could have read.[28] The Barrett manuscript seems best to fit the copy that reposed in McClure's office for five months [29] before being recovered and brought to Bacheller.

Bacheller does not report the copy that he gave to his printers but only the original brought to him by Crane: "I took it home with me that evening. My wife and I spent more than half the night reading it aloud to each other. We got far along in the story, thrilled by its power and vividness. In the morning I sent for Crane and made an arrangement with him to use about fifty thousand of his magic words as a serial." [30] The lack of marking on the pages indicates that Bacheller's staff did not cut the story for syndication from this manuscript but from some other copy.[31] On the evidence of the texts this copy was either the ribbon or the carbon of a fresh typescript made from the completely revised final Barrett manuscript,[32] perhaps to be

[28] After all, Crane did give this manuscript to Hawkins as the manuscript of the Red Badge, and he thought enough of it to preserve the leaves of abstracted original Chapter xii in England.

[29] This interval agrees sufficiently with Crane's submitting it in May and retrieving it to show Bacheller in October but certainly before the letter on November 15 to Garland. In an undated letter to the editor of Leslie's Weekly conjecturally written about November, 1895, Crane puts McClure's delay as eight months (Letters, p. 79), but this interval is clearly an impossibility.

[30] Coming Up the Road, p. 278. Here Bacheller's memory fails him, for the original is about fifty thousand words and the newspaper serialization is about eighteen thousand.

[31] The Elmo Watson statement that he was responsible for the syndicate cutting of the Red Badge has been shown to be sheer fantasy, or rather a confusion on his part, probably, with cutting some other and unknown book. See "An Editor's Recollection of 'The Red Badge of Courage,'" Stephen Crane Newsletter, ii, no. 3 (Spring, 1968), 3–6. Incidentally, it is this Watson account that gave Berryman the extraordinary notion that the Red Badge was syndicated in boiler plate in 750 newspapers. Search of forty-two prominent newspapers has disclosed only six reprintings, five of which were set in the respective newspaper offices from what must have been the common Bacheller proofs. The sixth appears to have used proofs of the first edition as supplementary copy.

[32] In theory agreement between A1 and $N versus MS should identify the readings of TMs, but in practice a small amount of fortuitous agreement is to

identified as the typescript paid for with Dick's money. If the typescript had been made up for McClure's consideration, it is odd that Crane showed Bacheller the original manuscript: even if he took the work to Bacheller before retrieving it from McClure he would have had the carbon copy.

The best guess that one can make is that on Bacheller's acceptance Crane had a new ribbon and carbon copy made, one set of which served the syndicate editor, the other set, eventually, being given to Appleton as printer's copy for the book. A typescript for the book made independently of the typescript for Bacheller, both stemming from the Barrett MS, is an impossible hypothesis: both the newspaper version and the book repeat common departures from the MS that can be identified as typist's errors. This typescript contained the revisions that were written in the MS during May after Garland saw the copy. It may have been made up in May for submission to McClure; but if the evidence that Crane showed Bacheller the Barrett manuscript has any bearing on the matter, then the likelihood is that October-November is the more probable date. If the typescript were commissioned as copy for Bacheller, at the time the novel was shown him the manuscript would have been the only document containing the revisions that Crane must have thought of as influencing the concept of the story in a crucial manner and thus it would have been the copy that he wanted read by any editor contemplating its acceptance. The typescript paid for by Garland was, in fact, out of date the moment it was finished.

As indicated by its text, the mate to the Bacheller typescript became the Appleton printer's copy. The delay in publication was imputed by Hitchcock to the proofreading that had had to be put off: "Owing to Mr. Crane's absence in the South and West, where he

---

be expected in A1 and $N. For example, it is not impossible that the Appleton and Bacheller editors or compositors would agree in the probable sophistication *see across it* (3.9) for MS *see, across,*; or in rejecting the MS sentence beginning with *And* at 15.5 and making it the second clause in a compound sentence; or in revising MS *others* (54.3) to *the others* or even MS *eye-sockets* (81.12) to *the eye sockets*. At a pinch MS *who befriended* (74.27) might have been altered independently in A1 and $N to *who had befriended*. Of course, such variants as MS *gota* but $N,A1 *got a* (61.1), or MS *Letgo . . . Letgo* but $N,A1 *Let go . . . Let go* (70.14, 19), or MS *strided* but $N,A1 *strode* (74.27) can scarcely be offered as evidence because of the strong possibility that they would be normalized independently. On the other hand, enough readings are left that are significant as evidence for common derivation of N and A1 from the same basic TMs. MS *processes* but $N,A1 *process* (38.35) is by no means an inevitable alteration, nor is the agreement *the* versus MS *th'* at 3.19. Particularly good evidence is $N,A1 *Also he* at 113.32 for MS *He*—just about a demonstrable case for copy. The variant sophistications at 48.19 *soughingly* in A1 and *slightly* in $N are also excellent evidence of some TMs error that each had to interpret without guidance.

acted as correspondent for a newspaper syndicate, there was delay in the proof reading, and the book was not issued until the autumn of 1895. It differed from the newspaper publication in containing much matter which had been cut out to meet journalistic requirements." [33]

The delay in publication was initially begun by a difficulty other than the late proofreading, however. Crane left New York abruptly for his Western trip in Bacheller's service, and in a letter from St. Louis conjecturally dated January 30, 1895, he wrote to Hitchcock: "I left New York so suddenly that I was unable to communicate with you." After giving addresses for the future in Lincoln, Nebraska, and in New Orleans, he continued: "Any news of the war story will be grateful to me. . . . I will be glad to hear from you at any time" (Letters, pp. 49–50). Hitchcock notified Crane immediately of its acceptance and elicited from Crane this response from Lincoln, dated February 12, 1895: "I've just recieved your letter. I would be glad to have Appleton and Co publish the story on those terms. I am going from here to New Orleans. The Mss could be corrected by me there in short order. I shall have to reflect upon the title. I shall not be back to New York for two months" (Letters, p. 51). On February 20 he addressed Hitchcock from New Orleans: "If the manuscript is sent here in care of Mr Baker of the Times-Democrat I shall be able to arrange it before I depart for Mexico. I will not leave here for ten days. [¶] I know it is a most inconvenient arrangement but as I am extremely anxious to have you bring out the book, I am hoping that the obstacle of the situation will not too much vex you. P.S. I shall only be in Mexico one week" (Letters, p. 53). On this letter Hitchcock penciled a note, "Ms. sent by express Feb. 25." Within a short interval Crane had corrected and revised the copy, as shown by a letter from Galveston, Texas, dated March 8: "I sent the Ms from New Orleans. I made a great number of small corrections. As to the name I am unable to see what to do with it unless the word 'Red' is cut out perhaps. That would shorten it" (Letters, p. 53). At this point information stops except for the contract, which was signed on June 17, 1895.[34] Copyright was applied for on September 27, 1895, and deposit made the same day. The book was published in October.

In the correspondence with Hitchcock one matter of particular importance appears that must have a direct bearing on the nature of the copy sent to the Appleton printers. It is clear that between Crane's mailing the newspaper clippings to Hitchcock and his departure from New York he had given Hitchcock the full copy for the book, and it was on the basis of this document—not of the newspaper

---

[33] Preface to *The Red Badge of Courage* (1900), pp. v–vi.
[34] The contract, deposited in the Lilly Library of Indiana University, is reproduced in facsimile with commentary in the *Stephen Crane Newsletter*, II, no. 4 (Summer, 1968), 5–9. Crane had returned to the United States by June 8 (see *Letters*, p. 58).

version—that the book was accepted in early February. In addition to outlining the terms of purchase the letter of acceptance apparently contained two additional points. First, Hitchcock raised the question of the title, which was still in discussion in Crane's letter of March 8 from Galveston. No satisfactory solution being arrived at, the book appeared under the title of the manuscript and included its full subtitle.

Second, since it is clear that Hitchcock insisted that Crane review and correct the typescript before setting, it may be that he was aware of typist errors overlooked but also of the various inconsistencies still present in the typescript such as the retention of names here and there instead of the descriptive phrases applied to the three soldiers. Although some signs of Appleton editing after the return of copy in early March may be detected in the book, it is probably to Crane's reading of the typescript in New Orleans that we may attribute most of the changes that in the book make uniform the substitution of *the youth* for *Fleming, the tall soldier* for *Conklin*, and so on, that had been only partially revised in the manuscript. On the evidence of the newspaper text, it was at this point that Crane also substituted *Henry* for *Flem* in dialogue (a feature absent in the typescript sent to Bacheller). Crane must have made a few stylistic and verbal revisions and deletions, and in New Orleans further altered the conclusion to its book form as against the manuscript.

The major addition in Chapter IV of the book version presents something of a problem. The cut in MS Chapter IV had been too drastic. In the newspaper version some expansion was made (although cut for syndication) of the narrative of the battle that on the evidence of the preserved draft leaf 36 had originally occupied most of removed pages 41–44 in the manuscript. The natural assumption is that these leaves had not been present in the manuscript given to the typist else they would have been included when the Barrett manuscript was later sent to Willis Brooks Hawkins on January 27, 1896. It follows that the decision to expand the ending of Chapter IV to something like its original form in the cancelled leaves was made just before copy was given to Bacheller. It is a plausible guess that Crane added to the new typescript—or to the copy for it— the appropriate leaves abstracted from the original typescript paid for by Garland, revising them for each occasion in a slightly different manner.[35] Some of this revision may have taken place in New Orleans, of course. Indeed, knowing Crane's carelessness we may easily guess that he had made few if any revisions in the typescript given to Hitchcock and that the majority of the changes in the book

[35] The book cuts some of the soldiers' lengthy dialogue present (probably by an oversight) on the lower half of page 40—one of the reasons perhaps for the original cut in MS—before carrying into the much revised narrative from the version found in MS(d) page 36.

that stem from authorial review were made in the typescript in New Orleans, not when it was initially submitted. At any rate, it is certain that Crane did not revise the ribbon and carbon copies of the new typescript simultaneously in any manner that can be detected. The alterations in the typescript that became the Appleton printer's copy were independently conceived and executed.

Hitchcock mentioned the delay in publication that resulted from Crane's absence from New York on his Western trip. Crane returned in early June, when proofs must have been ready for him. How many changes he made in this stage is problematical, for ordinarily he was a reluctant and careless proofreader. Printing and binding must have been completed by August or September for late September copyright and deposit, with publication in October.

On January 27, 1896, he expressed the manuscript to his friend Willis Brooks Hawkins.

THE EDITORIAL PROBLEM

When Bacheller accepted the *Red Badge* on the basis of his reading the manuscript, Crane had the option of trying to make use of the original typescript by collating it with his revised manuscript or of ordering a fresh one to be prepared. Although one or two small difficulties are present, the evidence overwhelmingly indicates that the Bacheller editor worked from a newly prepared typescript, not from the original brought into general conformity with the much altered manuscript. In the early pages of the newspaper version two particular anomalies appear when all newspapers ($N) follow original readings but ignore the later revision in MS of these readings. At 4.1 MS originally read dialect *sot*. In the general revision, which concerned itself in the early part with normalizing the dialect of all three soldiers, this *sot* spoken by Wilson was altered to *set*, which is the reading of the book (A1). However, $N print *sot* although observing all other normalizations in this particular speech. At 4.28 MS had originally read *Jim Conklin*, which in the preliminary revision was altered to interlined *the excited soldier*. This latter is the reading of $N, although A1 reads *the tall soldier* in agreement with the deletion of *excited* and the interlineation of *tall* in the general revision. One doubtful addition to these two anomalies may perhaps be made. At 10.25 MS read originally *Young Wilson*, which in the preliminary revision was changed first to *The young private* but in the general revision was once again altered to become *The loud private*. Here the Bacheller editor altered the text to take account of a cut and read *The loud young one*, just possibly picking up *young* from the preliminary revision. A less doubtful piece of similar evidence may be cited. At 16.18–19 the typist mistook a Garland cross for a Crane deletion of text and omitted (as in A1) the continuation of the passage *"I told yeh so, didnt I?"* [¶]*"Huh,"* said the loud soldier. Here N uses material that seems to have been present in its typescript when after *perception* it prints *"Didn't I tell you?"* If indeed this derives from a different reading in the two typescripts, its paraphrased form may perhaps be accounted for by the start of a $N cut in the next sentence. Just possibly, however, this N reading, or something like it, represents one of the few identifiable Crane revisions in the TMs behind the Bacheller text. On the other hand, the N readings are true anomalies, for these variants—even the first two—do not come in anything approaching a block of early readings; they are the only cases in which N reproduces the MS words earlier than the forms of the general revision; and—significantly—they occur within a range in which N as well as A1 follows words appearing only in the general revision, such as in the dialect changes that surround the curious artifact *sot*.[36]

On the positive side, in favor of N and A1 as set from a ribbon and a carbon copy of the same typescript comes a considerable array of evidence in two ranges. In the first range appears a group in which A1 and N agree against the MS in a series of relatively indifferent readings not to be assigned to Crane's revision. Some like the conventional *bent* for MS *bended* (15.22), *strode* for MS *strided* (74.27), *Let go* for MS *Letgo* (70.14, 19), or *exceeded* for MS *acceded* (23.22) could well have been independent editorial or compositorial alterations. Even the mutual correction *soldier* for MS *youth* (56.25) might not go beyond the possibility of separate editorial attention. Less likely as independent alterations would be such common indifferent changes as *process* for MS *processes* (38.35), *the others* for *others* (54.3), *the eye sockets* for *eye-sockets* (81.12), *took a* for *took* (105.25), or *impression* for *impressions* (105.25–26). These fall naturally into the classification of typist's variants. Quite impossible for independent editorial alteration, however, would be the addition of *Also* (113.32) where it is far from required. In the second range come dozens of readings in which the general-revision alterations are regularly followed in their final MS form by both N and A1. Except for the two or more anomalies described above, when N is not being separately altered by the Bacheller editor it agrees with A1 invariably

[36] No firm explanation can be given for these anomalies. If they represent a range of casual revision in TMs later than the general revision, the appearance of the final forms in A1 is inexplicable. Just possibly Crane did begin to bring the first few pages of the original typescript into conformity with his revised manuscript but gave it up shortly (particularly if the third example is fortuitous) and used these few pages for the Bacheller copy. It is apparently significant that these anomalous readings stop after MS page 3.23 (again considering the examples on MS pages 14.2 and 22.1–3 to be nonevidential) and that after this point no doubt can exist that N and A1 were set from the same TMs copy.

in the latest MS readings. The coincidences are too regular and sometimes too minute to support any hypothesis that Crane could have brought the early Garland typescript into conformity with the finally revised MS without slip-ups. On the evidence, then, the conclusion is inevitable that—with the possible exception of the first page or two—the typescript TMs* given to Bacheller was of the same manufacture as TMs^b which served as copy for the book, one the carbon and the other the ribbon pages.

It is an oddity, of course, that when the chance came to submit copy to Appleton, Crane sent Hitchcock clippings of the newspaper version instead of TMs^b. The reason is obscure and probably unrecoverable. However, it would be characteristic of Crane not to be able to lay his hands on TMs^b, wherever it was, and in his hurry to send the only readily available copy he had while he hunted up the typescript, either mislaid at Hartwood or at the moment in other hands, with a friend, or just possibly even with another publishing house. At any rate, Hitchcock received TMs^b before Crane left for the West.

It is of textual significance to inquire whether on receipt of what we may call the Dick typescript Crane looked it over and made any alterations in TMs* for Bacheller that he then transferred to the extra copy TMs^b. Comparison of the shared variants of N and A1 against MS provides no evidence that he did so. Various of the errors in MS such as the omission of *be* at 11.30 or of *had* at 61.24, the mistake *submitting* for *submitted* (76.36) and of *ground* for *the ground* (77.22), or the grammatical error *laying* for *lying* (78.14) might readily have been corrected by the typist or independently by each editor or compositor, and so with *His* for *He* (106.26) or *felt* for *fell* (110.20). In general the dialect conforms in the two versions although the compositors both of the Bacheller proof and of the book made occasional slips or—more frequently in N—normalizations. The half-a-dozen or so indifferent variants noted above—like *impression* for *impressions* (105.25–26) or *the others* for *others* (54.3)—do not encourage any hypothesis for a revisory reading-over with changes marked in each copy of the typescript. The conclusion is safe that in no case that can be identified except for the addition of the end of Chapter IV did Crane make changes in TMs* which he thereupon transferred to TMs^b. This conclusion is based not alone on the relatively few common variants in N and A1 against MS which—the changes in names overlooked in MS apart—total only about ten if one also excludes fortuitous dialect disagreements and the correction of MS slips and faulty grammar.

The nature of the variants themselves does not suggest revision. Indeed, only one probable case can be isolated, and it is subject to another explanation. This is the omission in N and A1 of the MS sentence *It was the soldier's bath* at 81.12+. As suggested in the

Textual Note to this crux, if we conjecture that the omission was not a unique typist's oversight, it is probable that in his independent revision of both typescripts Crane made the same alteration in TMs[b] at a later time from his memory of the deletion he had made in TMs[a] for Bacheller. The sentence is jejune and could easily stick in his memory as something that he wanted removed. Indeed, an interesting change at 90.5 suggests independent tinkering with a phrase that he questioned; in this case, at least, the alteration could not have been made simultaneously in the two copies. MS and presumably original TMs read *rumors again flew, like birds, but they were now for the most part, black and croaking creatures who flapped their wings drearily near to the ground and refused to rise on any wings of hope.* If the change in N is to be imputed to Crane and not to the Bacheller editor, he crossed out *black and* so that the passage read *croaking creatures*. When he came to revise TMs[b], he deleted, instead, *and croaking* so that A1 reads *black creatures*. If both alterations are authoritative, they show Crane to have worked over the phrase in two different ways at two different times. The only remaining possibly significant piece of evidence is the N,A1 agreement at 3.9 in *see across it* for MS *see, across,*. The original phrase was awkward and unidiomatic English and might well have been altered in the same manner by both editors, but the variant may also have been the typist's change. That it was Crane's is doubtful. The addition of *Also* at 113.32 must be assigned to the typist as well.

The working hypothesis for the present edition takes it, therefore, that correction and revision of the ribbon and carbon copies of a single TMs for Bacheller and for Appleton was performed in no case simultaneously but, instead, independently at two different times. That is, some evidence suggests that Crane did actually read over TMs[a] before he released it to Bacheller and wrote in various revisions of which he made no further note. Then when Hitchcock sent him TMs[b] in New Orleans, Crane read this over and made various cuts, alterations, and an addition or two, without reference to any other document.

The first consequence of this hypothesis is to remove from any question of authority all alterations (and even corrections) in which N and A1 agree against revised MS. With the probable exception of the excision of *It was the soldier's bath* at 81.12+, these shared agreements represent either the typist's departures from copy or else common editorial and compositorial emendation. The manuscript alone carries authority in these cases, and its readings are automatically adopted save for mechanical error or serious grammatical incorrectness that should be altered for a reading text.

Because of the singularly heavy editing given TMs[a] by the syndicate office in preparing the copy for newspaper distribution—editing that included not only severe cuts with new bridge passages but also condensation and considerable rewriting, this accompanied by careless typesetting into the Bacheller master proof—the nature and extent of Crane's own alterations in TMs^a cannot be determined with any precision. That they were many is doubtful, but that some revisions were made is indicated by the evidence for the treatment of the names that had been overlooked in the MS revision and hence presumably had been reproduced in TMs. In N, as in A1, no name appears except in dialogue, and formulas are invariably substituted. Whether Crane's usual carelessness would permit such rigor of alteration or whether he was assisted by the respective editors is scarcely to be determined. On the other hand, to assign all formulaic substitutions to the editors, particularly to the Bacheller editor, would be a bold procedure in view of the several places in the N text where Crane's revising hand seems to be present in other matters. On the occasions when Fleming's name had not been removed in MS, the invariable formula is *the youth.*[37] Variation appears in a patch of manuscript which Crane's general revision had skipped. Here in seven cases N and A1 agree only twice and differ five times in the formulas substituted for Wilson's name.[38] It would be asking too much of Crane's memory to take it that the two agreements of N and A1 in *the loud private* (76.29) and *his friend's* (76.34) necessarily identify authorial alteration; yet the whole lot perhaps represents Crane. On the other hand, later at 102.13–14 where A1 reads *The soldier* for MS *Wilson,* the reading of N^6, the only newspaper witness, *The youth* is an error, perhaps to be attributed to the Bacheller editor's misunderstanding of the situation, although Crane's own carelessness must not be automatically ruled out as a possible source. Since it is most probable that these formulaic revisions in N are chiefly authorial, their variation from A1 shows, of course, emendation of TMs^a and of TMs^b at different times.

One case of Crane's conjectured marking of TMs^a for Bacheller has been noticed at 81.12+ where it is plausible to take it that his dissatisfaction with the sentence *It was the soldier's bath* led him to excise it both in TMs^a and TMs^b. It is also plausible to conjecture that 90.5 represents an analogous case in which the MS,TMs phrase *black and croaking creatures* was independently revised in two different ways in each typescript. Other cases can rely less on the seeming literary appropriateness of N alterations than on examples

---

[37] At 47.20 N substitutes *He* for MS *The youth* written above deleted *Fleming* in the general revision, but this follows an N cut and is clearly editorial bridgework. Earlier, at 10.24–25 the N substitution of *private* for MS,A1 *soldier,* and then of *young one* for *private,* is also part of an editorial rearrangement consequent upon a cut.

[38] These are A1 *the loud soldier* (75.20–21) for N *his loud friend;* A1 *the other* (75.24) for N *the loud one; the loud soldier* (75.31) for *him; His friend* (76.6) for *The loud private;* and *his friend* (76.20) for *his loud friend.*

of Crane's characteristic idioms or syntax, for the Bacheller editor in the frequent verbal substitutions is not to be distinguished with any certainty. One of the more prominent of these conjectural alterations of TMs[a] by Crane has been mentioned above in the partial restoration in N of Garland's deleted passage, in which Crane's intended "*I told yeh so, didnt I?*" (16.18–19) omitted in A1 along with the rest seems to be reproduced in the N "*Didn't I tell you?*" This may perhaps be assigned to Crane's revision of TMs[a]. Another occurs at 5.4. In MS(d) this read: 'The smoke from the fire at times neglected the clay chimney and wreathed into the room. A small window shot an oblique square of light upon the cluttered floor.' In MS this became: 'A small window shot an oblique square of whiter light upon the cluttered floor. The smoke from the fire at times neglected the clay-chimney and wreathed into the room. This flimsy chimney of clay and sticks made endless threats to set a-blaze the whole establishment.' As a current alteration, however, the *T* of *This flimsy* was crossed through to reduce the capital to lower case, and *And* was interlined before it. In the later general revision a pencil stroke confirmed the alteration by strengthening the reduction of the capital. It may be remarked that Crane could have made an error in judgment in his alteration since the two statements about the chimney are only superficially so coordinate as to be linked by *And*. In fact, two discrete statements are made, as in the original declarative sentences: the chimney sent smoke out into the room; the chimney often threatened to set the shack afire. For the Bacheller editor to recognize the separateness of these two statements, too closely joined by *And*, and to contrive something to modify the effect of the *And* would not be surprising. What may be significant for authorial revision, instead, is the appearance in N of Crane's characteristic *too* beginning a clause: 'And, too, this flimsy chimney . . . made endless threats'. Examples are 'Too, he felt a pity for the guns' (43.12), 'Too, he remembered how he and his companions' (72.28–29), 'Too, it was important that he should have time for physical recuperation' (94.12–13), 'Too, the clothes seemed new' (113.35), 'The time, too, now that he reflected, he saw to have been short' (117.18–19). Another example occurs in MS(d) page 47 (158.26), 'Too, shells exploded in the grass and among the foliage.' The Bacheller editor could not have picked up this trick of Crane's as early as 5.4. Hence the addition of *too* here is so natural for Crane that it has been accepted in the present text as representing a genuine authorial second thought made in revising TMs[a].

Lesser possibilities might rest on Crane's characteristic language. At 102.39–103.1 MS,A1 read: 'The youth, turning, shot a quick, enquiring glance at his friend. The latter returned to him the same manner of look.' In N between the two sentences is inserted 'It was as if he had been stunned.' Although an editor might be tempted to make *a quick, enquiring look* more precise in view of the friend's return of *the same manner of look*, the Bacheller editor is not usually inclined to add to Crane's text such extra sentences [39] except as bridges between cuts, a condition not present here. Moreover, the syntax is characteristic in beginning *It was as if* and the word *stunned* appears elsewhere (see the Textual Note to the passage). The odds may doubtfully favor this sentence as an authorial addition in TMs^a, forgotten when TMs^b came to be revised, although it seems to vulgarize the situation and even to misconstrue it.

Typical of the indeterminate nature of many N variants is an example at 61.4 where MS,A1 read, 'But he continued his harangue' whereas N has 'But he continued to harangue vaguely'. The word *vague* appears at 5.13 but can scarcely be termed characteristic. Moreover, the N variant is to be rejected, for it seems to depend upon bridging the N cut just preceding at 61.2–4. Since there is no reason to suppose that Crane himself cut the text for Bacheller, an editorial change here—as so often after cuts to adjust the text—seems almost a certainty. Another possibility is the substitution of *Fate* for *These little battles* at 114.36. Possibly Crane added this portentousness; more likely, the Bacheller editor fancied the touching-up. Crane does not appeal to Fate elsewhere in the text (at 65.19 *fate* is not at all the same). Dozens of other possibilities could be cited, but uselessly, for there is nothing so distinctive in them as to suggest Crane's hand, and the extremely large number of substituted words and phrases in N indicates quite clearly that the Bacheller editor was active in altering the text.[40]

One curious anomaly is present among the N texts in the irregularity of N^6, the *San Francisco Examiner* version. This version is unusual in three respects: first, it was published on July 14, 21, 28, about six months later than the common syndication as found in N^{1-5}; second, although its cuts ordinarily follow those of N^{1-5} (representative of the state of the Bacheller proof), it contains passages from MS,A1 not present in N^{1-5}; and, third, although its text normally

---

[39] However, see 34.3+ where the sentence *He seemed greatly insulted* (N^6: *excited*) is added in N, whether by Crane or by the Bacheller editor. The two examples are somewhat analogous.

[40] The following are samples of possible alterations by Crane in TMs^a but, also, equally possible modifications of the text by the Bacheller editor: MS,A1 *He contemplated the lurking menaces of the future and failed* versus N . . . *close future, and his mind failed* (10.9–10); *onct-git-shootin'* versus *once get dead into it* (12.2); *"Huh," said the loud one* versus *"Shucks!" snorted the loud private scornfully* (12.19); *comrade* versus *tall comrade* (12.21); *Now, with the* versus *And now with this* (13.11); the addition in N (with an N^6 variant) of the sentence *He seemed greatly insulted* (34.3); MS,A1 *since the introduction of this topic* versus N *since the other had begun to speak of wounds* (61.13–14); *the noise of fighting* versus *the voices of fighting* (80.9–10); *among the treetops* versus *from the sky* (105.7). The N excision of the tattered soldier's delirious identification of the youth with Tom Jamison (61.32 *et seq.*) is probably exclusively editorial.

agrees with that of N^{1-5}, it does have a number of readings which concur, instead, with MS,A1 where N^{1-5} had been editorially altered. The three points of difference are related, of course. When N^6, as occasionally, either does not follow an N^{1-5} cut at all or, more commonly, when it cuts at the same places but less deeply, its text could not have derived from the Bacheller proofs. Correspondingly, the verbal agreements with MS,A1 against N^{1-5} are not all fortuitous and indicate the presence behind N^6 of another form of the text than that represented just by the Bacheller proofs. It is evident that in some manner the proofs of A1, which would have been available by July, were combined with the Bacheller proofs to produce a partially eclectic text. The exact nature of the N^6 copy can be subject only to speculation. The occasional practice of cutting at the same place as N^{1-5} but printing more of the text at beginning and end than is found in N^{1-5} does not suggest a division of copy between two or more compositors, one setting from the Bacheller and the other from the A1 proofs. And indeed the mixture of MS,A1 readings imbedded in the general texture of N^{1-5} editorial variants also prevents such a hypothesis.[41] It would not have been an impossibility for the N^6 compositors to have had both sets of proofs before them and while setting from the Bacheller lot to have made casual reference to the A1 proofs, but the evidence does not encourage such an odd procedure and it is questionable whether the San Francisco editor would have allowed his compositors complete discretion about following or not following the Bacheller cuts. Most likely for some reason the *Examiner* was sent a set of the A1 proofs as well as a set of the Bacheller proofs.[42] It would seem that the editor, rather oddly, chose to send to his composing room not the A1 proofs cut in rough conformity

[41] For instance, at 44.6 N^6 agrees with MS,A1 in the typical omission of the article in *while they had opportunity* for N^{1-5} *the opportunity* (almost an impossibility, seemingly, for independent N^6 editing), but the sentence then continues in N^6 as in N^{1-5} —*why—destruction*, whereas MS,A1 omit *destruction*. Thereupon N^{1-5} cut the next three paragraphs (44.7–21) but N^6 preserves the first of these paragraphs and joins N^{1-5} only in cutting 44.12–21. In the next line at 44.22 it agrees with N^{1-5} in reading *But a* for MS,A1 *A*, an editorial bridge necessitated by the cut. At 56.19 N^6 joins MS,A1 in the dialect *runned* versus N^{1-5} *run* but follows N^{1-5} at 56.32 in *bouncing* for MS,A1 *jouncing*. The list of these anomalies covers well over a dozen readings that could not be the work of chance. For instance, possibly the N^6 editor or compositor could have corrected N^{1-5} *craven* to MS,A1 *carven* (31.12), $N^{1,3-5}$ *bullet* to MS,A1 (and N^2) *bullets* (105.11); but chance was unlikely to have operated in the N^6 agreement with MS,A1 in *comrade* versus N^{1-5} *companion* (16.3) although following N^{1-5} a few lines below in *along* for *forward* (16.6); or in agreeing in *dreamfully* versus N^{1-5} *dreamily* (59.24), *sun-rays* versus *sun's rays* (80.4), *steadied* versus *steady* (106.13), *fixes* versus *fixed them* (113.18), or *noted* versus *noticed* (114.19).

[42] That the N^6 editor did not utilize a clipping from some other newspaper seems to be shown by the lack of agreement of N^6 with separate variants in the known five other newspaper versions, although the possibility of a clipping from an unobserved newspaper used as copy cannot be overlooked.

with the Bacheller model but instead the Bacheller proofs roughly compared with the A1 copy and annotated here and there with a few observed verbal differences and also with some paste-up additions to restore material cut by Bacheller. The procedure was an eccentric one at best, but the evidence is quite against the use of modified A1 proofs as the physical copy for the *Examiner*.[43]

Among the numerous unique N^6 variants a few might in theory represent early A1 readings altered before publication, provided the proofs utilized by the *Examiner* were early ones. However, when N^6 variants differ from MS as well as from A1 they are unidentifiable as possible early A1 proof readings and no doubt represent, instead, N^6 editorial as well as compositorial alterations. The best evidence for a connection between N^6 and uncorrected A1 proofs comes in the agreement of N^6 with MS at 36.11 in *feverishly* for A1 *furiously* and, shortly, at 36.13 in *flapped and bobbed* for A1 *bobbed*, N^{1-5} being absent for both. The latter case clearly requires correction, which was evidently given it in the A1 proofs at a later point than the state from which N^6 derived; the indifferent substitution in A1 of *furiously* for *feverishly* almost certainly may be identified as Crane's own alteration in proof. MS and N^6 agree in Crane's characteristic *bended* at 53.34 versus A1's normalization *bent*. This is as certain evidence as the little cluster at 36.11,13, since in each case N^{1-5} are missing and N^6 could have depended only on A1 proofs for its copy. This being so, we cannot take very seriously one small suggestion that N^6 could have utilized corrected A1 proof. In MS at 48.12 Crane had mistaken the word *bonds* and misspelled it as *bounds*, the form found in N^{1-5} and thus representing the TMs reading transferred to the Bacheller proofs. When N^6 follows A1 in the correct *bonds*, however, it is plausible to take it that this was an independent correction by N^6 of a fairly obvious mistake perpetuated in TMs instead of a case in which A1 had originally read *bounds*, been proof-corrected to *bonds*, and then influenced N^6 in the corrected reading.

The unique variants in A1, especially when N is present to agree with MS, show three forces operating to alter the MS copy.[44] First,

[43] The alternative would be the speculation that in July before the appearance of the novel Bacheller made another attempt at syndication and sent out different copy than before, copy that showed the effects of the A1 proofs. This is possible, but no July appearances in newspapers other than the *Examiner* have been observed. Another example would, of course, come close to confirming this procedure, particularly if it had the Bacheller copyright.

[44] The agreement of N with MS ordinarily establishes the readings of TMs. When N is absent, one can only guess what are typist's errors in TMs and what A1 compositorial, editorial, or even authorial variants. When N is wanting, whether ordinary errors like A1 *a* for MS *an* (47.2), *continued* for *continual* (89.4), or *friends* for *fiends* (124.26) could have originated with the typist or the A1 compositor is scarcely to be determined.

the A1 compositors demonstrably made various misprints not caught in proof. Since N confirms the TMs reading by agreeing with MS, such A1 variants as *bank* for *bunk* (4.33), *gate* for *grate* (40.29), *different* for *diffident* (52.28), *like* for *lick* (53.8), or *streaming* for *steaming* (81.38) can be isolated as A1 lapses not to be imputed to TMs except for possible Bacheller corrections. Small questions of usage such as the A1 preference for *farther* instead of MS *further* and what seems to be one A1 compositor's preference for *nowise* instead of MS *no wise*[45] may well be compositorial instead of editorial, but whether the A1 change to *bent* of characteristic MS *bended* was compositorial or editorial is difficult to determine, and so with A1 *strode* for MS *strided*.[46]

Second, the example of Crane's "Little Regiment" and other magazine stories collected in the Appleton book *The Little Regiment* shows that Ripley Hitchcock or some other editor felt the necessity to change on occasion Crane's idiosyncratic locutions or syntax.[47] The evidence of the *Red Badge* suggests that Hitchcock was in most circumstances prepared to pass Crane's syntax, however. No case occurs, for instance, in which a Crane split infinitive is corrected. Whether the dropping of MS *It was* and the joining of two sentences at 123.32 was compositorial or editorial is moot. Here Crane's own intervention is unlikely, but the change from MS *and laughing* to *with laughter* (123.12–13) was probably either editorial or authorial. Correspondingly, the normalization of Crane's grammar, unnecessarily with *deeply* for *deep* (43.10) but advisedly with *likely* for *like* (22.4), *were* for *was* (22.14), or *nearly* for *near* (36.22),[48] betrays editorial as much as typist or compositorial attention. Certain classes of variants are also perhaps of mixed editorial and compositorial origin. Crane's use of the plural where the collective singular would normally be expected—as in *Equipments hung on handy projections* (4.37)—is one of his stylistic characteristics although he was not systematic in his preference,[49] and indeed in the inscription of the

[45] A1 *nowise* appears in a cluster on A1 pages 210.12, 214.1, and 216.12. Earlier A1 had set *no wise* with MS.

[46] The concurrence of N with A1 *bent* as at 15.22 is not fully satisfactory evidence, for the Bacheller printer or editor may well have altered this form. However, if the evidence of 102.31 is valid, the typist may have been responsible for the change to *bent*: at 102.31 both N and A1 follow MS *bended*, demonstrating the TMs reading here and the willingness of the Bacheller and A1 compositor at this spot to set the word. N agrees with A1 in *strode* for MS *strided* (74.27), perhaps the TMs form although independent change by the Bacheller and Appleton editors or compositors is not impossible.

[47] See TALES OF WAR, *Works*, vi (1970), l, lvii, lxiii–lxvi, lxix, lxxvii, lxxix.

[48] But see *Letters*, p. 41, for Crane's use of *near*: 'He kept it until I was near mad.'

[49] For instance, in MS(d) he wrote, correctly, *A picture . . . was upon the log wall*, but in MS this becomes the literally impossible *walls* (4.36)—un-

MS he sometimes changed singular to plural and plural to singular in an arbitrary manner as part of its current revision. The later general revision was occupied with other matters, however, and thus this large category of A1 alterations seems to be almost entirely unauthoritative. Given Crane's customary usage, the reduction in A1 to *mood* of MS *moods* in 'He looked about to find men in the proper moods' (14.4) can only be editorial or compositorial sophistication. Change in the opposite direction seems equally unauthoritative, as in A1 *grumblings* for MS *grumbling* (21.20), *fronts* for *front* (26.11), and *traditions* for *tradition* (14.28–29). A1 sometimes supplied articles omitted by Crane as part of his conscious style, as in A1 *the roofs* for MS *roofs* (49.18) or *the others* for *others* (54.3). Occasionally awkwardnesses in Crane's style would be smoothed out in A1, as in *some moments* for *moments* (34.36) or *in* for *at* (45.1). Sometimes the A1 editor or compositor mistakenly thought that he was correcting Crane's carelessness as in the A1 change to *mule-drivers . . . mud-diggers* for MS singulars (125.30–31) and probably in altering MS *four last* to *last four* (12.3). Errors in MS were necessarily repaired, but without authority, as in the addition of *stopped* (41.20) for a word omitted in MS but recoverable from MS(d) as *dropped it*. A1 *soughingly* (48.19) may have altered MS *sighingly* because of some difficulty in TMs that had to be resolved by guesswork, on the evidence of N *slightly*. An alien system of usage was in part imposed on Crane, as in A1 *deprecating* for MS *deprecatory* (82.35), A1 *conciliating* for *conciliatory* (91.25), and probably A1 *recur* for MS *appear* (41.1), *use* for *used* (84.11), *continued* for *continual* (89.4), and *hurling* for *hurlying* (100.2). On the other hand, the egregious MS error of *illusions* for *allusions* (112.32–33) was repeated in A1, and the odd *gluttering* (125.29) remained unaltered.

In the nature of the case not only is it usually impossible to separate the editorial from the compositorial alteration of these small matters but it is completely conjectural, as well, to assign certain A1 variants to Crane instead of to the process of manufacture. Yet documentary evidence is available to show that Crane had been sent the TMs in New Orleans and that he returned it to New York after several days with a letter remarking that he had made a number of small changes. Hence his connection with a post-MS revision is established, and the different cuts of the analyses of the youth's state of mind that are made in A1 continue similar cuts Crane made in MS to prepare it for the typist. These cuts and a few additions may be automatically accepted as authorial. The major thrust of the revision, perhaps, was the application of formulas like *the youth*

---

consciously, one suspects, because of the tug the plural so frequently exercised on him.

when in MS (and presumably in TMs) the name had escaped the
changes made in the general revision. Very likely the editor assisted
in the process of normalization, for no oversights remain in A1. On
the other hand, Crane himself carried the treatment of the names
one step further in his revision of TMs by usually changing *Flem*
in dialogue to *Henry*, a form of address for which there had been
only one example in MS (18.25). The alteration in the names and
the cutting of the text, plus the correction of typist's literals, no
doubt, represent the major revisions that Crane made in TMs. Evidence exists, however, that he did look it over for stylistic matters
despite the fact that the most important work in this category had
been done during the course of inscribing and revising the manuscript. To Crane's hand may almost certainly be imputed the omission of *burnished* before *sun* at 49.1 and of *fierce* before *wafer* at
58.32 at chapter endings. The importance to Crane of colors identifies
the substitution of *green* for MS *crimson* at 66.1. For the rest, the
conjectured authorial changes may reduce adjectives, as in the omission of *considerable* (6.21), *hot* (6.32), *little* (54.11), *sad* (66.33),
or *tender* (130.33), or adverbs such as the omission of *fleetly* (64.37)
or *plentifully* (113.34). A few repetitions are ironed out (if this is
not editorial), such as the omission of *unceasing* (28.5) and of
flapped and (36.13). Some acceptable words are changed to Crane's
favorite language, such as *howled* substituted for *roared* (71.30),
contemplated for *looked at* (79.3), and probably *features* for *faces*
(80.14). A few changes sharpen the accuracy, as *forward* for *along*
(16.6), *circumstance* for *nature* in context (86.19–20), *desperate*
for *determined* (129.38), and presumably *the power of* for *human*
(62.21) and *little* for *bitter* (81.20) although this last is an odd
change. The stylistic attentions that may reasonably be assigned to
Crane are not especially thoroughgoing (although this is in general
also true for those made during the general revision), and they are
certainly less important ultimately than the cuts in the text and the
few additions, particularly that of the new ending; nevertheless, they
help to refine the style, and thus they contribute to the total effect of
the final form of the novel.

In two cases the first English edition published by Heinemann in
1896 (E1) agrees with MS against A1: at 81.38 it has *steaming*
for A1 *streaming*, and at 99.26 *into* for *onto*. Theoretically these
variants could have been reproduced in E1 if it had been set from an
early state of the A1 proof which had contained the original TMs
readings subsequently altered.[50] Practically speaking, however, there
should have been more evidence than these two readings if proofs

---

[50] The agreement of $N with MS in *steaming* indicates the TMs reading. N is
not present at 99.26 to act as a control.

had been used; also, neither variant—and especially a change from
into to *onto*—is beyond English correction. Moreover, in view of the
sending to England of American advance printed copies to establish
copyright,[51] the previous mailing of proofsheets cannot be demonstrated since the English edition was not set in such a hurry as to
require copy before the advance states of the book arrived. Hence E1
appears to have no authority as in any sense reproducing anything
but the known final state of the Appleton sheets, plus the English
compositorial or editorial variants.[52]

The authorities for the text remain the Barrett manuscript assisted
by the fragmentary draft MS(d) on some of its versos, the text of
the Bacheller proofs recovered from the multiple evidence of the
six observed newspapers, and the Appleton first edition. The Bacheller proofs when not editorially altered represent TMs[a] made from
MS and casually worked over by Crane, with especial reference to the
correction of the names but with a few stylistic alterations. The
Appleton edition when not editorially altered represents another copy
of the same TMs but lacking the changes—whatever these were in
addition to the attention to the names—that Crane had made in
TMs[a]. Thus TMs[b] as printer's copy for A1 contained a different and
more extensive set of authorial revisions from those in TMs[a], alterations made in New Orleans at a later time and without reference to
the previous changes in the copy of TMs sent to Bacheller.

The classic theory of copy-text accepted by this edition [53] separates
the authority of the accidentals in the MS (the spelling, punctuation,
word-division, capitalization, and italicization) from that of the
substantives, or the words themselves and their forms. The accidentals in MS are in Crane's holograph and in most cases represent,
therefore, what he intended to write according to his idiosyncratic
system that is worth preserving for its own interest and for the importance that it may have for indicating the rhythms and pauses that
he heard in his own ear as he wrote.

In this respect the authority of MS(d) in relation to that of MS
comes in question. Although Crane's system of punctuation and word-
division was relatively fixed and not random, he was not always consistent either within MS(d) or MS, or between them. As a general
proposition one may take it that in some cases of discrepancy be-

[51] See Bowers, "Crane's *Red Badge of Courage* and Other 'Advance Copies,'"
Studies in Bibliography, XXII (1969), 273–277.
[52] For a discussion of the penciled variants in the British Museum statutory
copy of the advance copy of A1, see under the description of the edition.
[53] W. W. Greg, "The Rationale of Copy-Text," *Studies in Bibliography*, III,
(1950–51), 19–36, reprinted in *W. W. Greg: Collected Papers*, ed. J. C. Maxwell
(1966), pp. 374–391. See also, Bowers, "Multiple Authority: New Problems
and Concepts of Copy-Text," *The Library*, 5th ser., XXVII (1972), 81–115.

tween the punctuation of MS(d) and MS in identical or substantially identical text, Crane's later form is an intentional change that must be respected. For instance, Crane often wrote a period where a question mark would ordinarily be expected in conventional styling. Occasional real errors appear, but on the whole the indication of his manuscripts is that though such sentences may be cast in the form of a query he did not intend the speaker's voice to be so inflected. Thus it seems to be a meaningful change of intention when he reduces such a question mark as that after *supports* at 40.14 present in MS(d) to a period in MS, especially since the same reduction is present in the repetition of the remark at 41.2–3.[54] Such changes must be respected. Another illustration comes at 44.7. In writing this novel Crane adopted a heavier punctuation, especially of parenthetical elements, than he had ordinarily used earlier and certainly than he came to use later when almost all such commas tend to disappear from his manuscripts. Hence it is clear that when at 44.7 he encloses the unpunctuated MS(d) phrase *at least* in commas when writing out MS, he was adding commas according to a system that he preferred at the time. That in other places this preference could be variable [55] does not alter the fact that, on the evidence, in the final MS he definitely preferred the heavy punctuation about the phrase in this particular place.[56]

It would be too much to assert that every difference in punctuation between MS(d) and MS is systematic. Certainly, in transcribing

[54] The A1 question marks in both places appear to represent editorial or compositorial interpretation, not a revision in TMs[b] or in proof by authorial marking to return to the original MS(d) inflection.

[55] For instance, MS 5.11–14 (5.26–29) reads: 'Men were better, or, more timid. Secular and religious education had effaced the throat-grappling instinct, or, else, firm finance held in check the passions.' The comma after or before *more timid* is syntactically dubious although such punctuation after *or* without parenthesis is found several times elsewhere in MS (see 86.23; 94.11; 114.2). The enclosure of *else* in commas in the second sentence is typical enough of the heavy punctuation often adopted in MS although it may have been affected by the preceding *or*. On the other hand, when this passage is repeated verbatim at MS 11.3–5 (8.35–37), the heavy commas do not appear: 'Men were better, or more timid. Secular and religious education had effaced the throat-grappling instinct or else firm finance held in check the passions.' Unfortunately, the syntax for the first quotation differs in MS(d) so that no parallel is present, and MS(d) is wanting for the second. What is illustrated, seemingly, is the difficulty Crane had in consistency when he tried to impose on this novel a system of heavy punctuation that was not entirely natural to him. The inconsistency may be internal in MS as is the above, or it may occur between MS(d) and MS. The imposition of almost automatic heavy punctuation in MS is illustrated at 55.5–6 when MS(d) read *a curious red and black combination of new blood and old blood* whereas in MS an improper comma separates *curious* from *red and black* according to Crane's general intention in MS to punctuate adjectives in a series before a noun.

[56] That A1 agrees with MS(d) in removing the comma has no more significance than its removal of the comma after *curious* at 55.5.

and rewriting MS(d) Crane was often careless and hasty, and variants cannot always be called conscious alterations. In some cases the present editor has called on MS(d) when MS appears to stray from Crane's usual punctuation habits by what appears to be an inadvertency in the copying. But ordinarily the MS variant has been accepted as chronologically the later and therefore the more likely to express Crane's final preferences, such as they were.

In word-division Crane's strong tendency to hyphenate compounds is slightly more prominent in MS than in MS(d), as compare MS(d) *sunlight* but MS *sun-light* (the invariable form elsewhere) at 64.9 and MS(d) *woodpecker* but MS *wood-pecker* at 46.30. In this respect, then, MS seems to represent a higher degree of consciousness about the requirements of publication and is thus more consistent and trustworthy than MS(d).

If in general the authority of MS is to be preferred to that of MS(d) in the accidentals, no case can be made for any authority in these respects in A1. Between MS and A1 intervenes TMs, with the changes in accidentals one would inevitably expect from a typist's normalizing of a system that in certain respects was unusual. To these TMs variants must then be added the relatively consistent housestyling applied to the TMs text by the A1 compositors. A1 adds a number of semicolons not present in MS, and not characteristic of Crane, to set off the major elements of sentences heavily punctuated with internal commas. Similarly, the A1 use of dashes as strong commas bears no relation to Crane's own style.[57] Question marks are regularly added at the slightest suggestion of a query—despite Crane's contrary preference—as well as a liberal addition of uncharacteristic exclamation marks. Crane used these exclamations sparingly, but the housestyling of the time ran contrary to his practice and demanded them. Crane frequently began sentences with *And*, a mannerism that the A1 compositors or the editor altered many times by making Crane's two declarative sentences into a single compound sentence. No authority for such changes can be claimed by A1.[58] The manuscript comes close to a system in seldom separating the clauses of a compound sentence with a comma before the conjunction and ordinarily by omitting the comma before the *and* in a series of three. (Both of these characteristics are strongly present in

---

[57] The compositor did not always understand Crane's limited use of the dash. At 133.27–28 he turned MS 'Later, he began to study his deeds—his failures and his achievements' into the series of three, 'Later he began to study his deeds, his failures, and his achievements', which offers quite a different meaning from Crane's.

[58] At 56.13, for instance, Crane revised a compound sentence in MS so that the second clause became an independent sentence beginning with *And* but the A1 compositor by his change returned fortuitously to the original version.

Crane's manuscripts of any period.) The book usually adds commas in a manner quite contrary to Crane's ordinary practice.

Since in this manuscript Crane was somewhat deliberately imposing a heavier system of parenthetical punctuation than was his usual custom, some inconsistencies develop. For instance, he may start a parenthetical unit with a comma but forget to close the parenthesis with another comma. In these cases A1 will sometimes remove the first comma to agree with the absence of the ending punctuation but sometimes it will add the second comma to close the intended parenthesis. The present edition consistently closes such parentheses with commas, regardless of the practice of A1, since the presence of the first comma is taken to represent Crane's intention for parenthetical pointing. The case is altered, it would seem, for the reverse situation, common in the manuscript and elsewhere, in which Crane omits what would normally be the first comma enclosing a parenthetical element but inscribes the second, or closing, comma. An example occurs at 15.24–25 where MS reads, 'Presently, a horseman with jangling equipment, drew rein before the colonel of the regiment.' In this sentence A1 removes the comma after *equipment* instead of adding a comma after *horseman*. In another example A1 removes the comma after *works* in MS 'He, in his thoughts, was careering off in other places, even as the carpenter who as he works, whistles and thinks of his friend or his enemy, his home or a saloon' (35.11–13). In these cases the present editor follows the MS system. Another one of Crane's punctuation habits led to consistent A1 restyling. Crane customarily did not punctuate between the two clauses of a compound sentence separated by *and* or *but* or *or*, but he usually set off with a comma a dependent clause inverted before an independent. When the complex structure occurs in the latter half of a compound sentence, something like the following usually appears in the MS: 'Once, a man fell down and as he reached for his rifle, a comrade, unseeing, trod upon his hand' (16.2–3). Here A1 added a comma after *down* and removed the comma after *rifle*. Another example appears at 22.22–25: MS reads, 'One grey dawn, however, he was kicked in the leg by the tall soldier and then before he was entirely awake, he found himself running down a wood-road in the midst of men who were panting from the first effects of speed.' Here the A1 compositor chose to add commas after *soldier* and *then* in order to distinguish the two clauses and set off parenthetical *before he was entirely awake*. By Crane's own standards the MS punctuation in these two sentences was not in error; hence, although unconventional, it has not been normalized in the present edition since it represents what may properly be called his individual system of pointing.

Crane does not ordinarily punctuate relative clauses beginning with *who* or *which* whether nonrestrictive or restrictive, although he does sometimes place a comma before *that*. He seldom punctuates before *for* in the sense of 'because' but he usually places a comma before a participial construction.

In the present edition Crane's idiosyncracies have been largely preserved, even when erratic in their appearances, except when omissions (chiefly) and some commissions appear to reflect inadvertent errors or careless mistakes by his own standards. When emendation of the punctuation in MS seems necessary, documentary authority is usually sought in MS(d) when it is available. N and A1 are called upon when MS(d) is wanting but only as a matter of historical record since neither has any authority in its accidentals. Word-division is normalized according to the predominant forms, again with appeal as much as possible to documentary authority. Crane's infrequent capitalizations for emphasis are retained, but the A1 personification of MS *nature* as *Nature* is rejected. A1 italics for foreign words like *débris* are ignored since not present in MS.

If the case is relatively simple for the accidentals based on the MS copy-text, the separate authority of the substantives is not so easily adjudicated.[59] Clearly, the duty of an editor is to substitute for the MS verbals what he takes to be the authorial revisions effected at a later time than its inscription. These revisions were made in the typescript and, possibly, in the proof for the book, A1. (We know that Ripley Hitchcock delayed printing until Crane could see the proofs after his return from Mexico in the summer of 1895.) However, the typescript existed in ribbon and in carbon-copy forms, and it is clear that Crane made alterations in TMs[a], the copy given to Bacheller, since the substitution of formulas for names in the narrative, overlooked in the revision of the MS, was doubtless not entirely editorial, even though some few may have been editorially substituted to repair Crane oversights. What other changes Crane may have made in this process of reading over TMs[a] are almost wholly unknown, for with only a few possible exceptions they are not to be distinguished from the heavy alteration and cutting given the text by the Bacheller editor before printing, to which must then be added various memorial lapses by the Bacheller compositors even though these may make sense, especially in indifferent context. Except for the sub-

[59] Although the authority of MS(d) is sometimes useful in confirming or correcting an MS accidental, its substantives can have no superior authority to MS except in case of positive MS error, for Crane himself wrote out MS by transcribing and revising MS(d) and must therefore be thought to have intended any variation that was not carelessly inadvertent. No doubt some small differences in idiom and phraseology are as unintentional as are some small variants in punctuation. Nevertheless, except in the case of palpable error an editor can scarcely determine what indifferent alterations were intentional and what unintentional, and thus he must follow the authority of MS as a revised holograph document.

stitution of phrases for names, therefore, the N text is of little help. This state of affairs is the more unfortunate because if Crane's revisions could be identified they would have equal technical authority with revisions subsequently made in TMs[b] several months later in New Orleans. Only very few cases occur in which A1 agrees with N against MS except in the correction of error. The paucity of this evidence suggests that when Crane came to the revision of TMs[b] he had little memory of changes he had made in TMs[a]. Thus failure to revise TMs[b] to bring it into conformity with altered TMs[a] could scarcely be interpreted as a rejection of the TMs[a] variants, and both would need to be considered on an equal basis.

The question is largely theoretical, however, because of the impossibility of assigning more than one or two N variants (the alteration of names excepted) to Crane's changes in TMs[a]. The variant phrases for names, in fact, constitute the major substantive problem that can be identified. When MS had already revised the names, the evidence of further variation in N suggests the hand of the Bacheller editor, ordinarily, not that of Crane. The reason is that this variation usually comes just before or after a cut in N when the Bacheller editor was adjusting the picked-up text to that before the cut. For instance, N cuts 10.15–22 (*aloud . . . repeated*), and then immediately following at 10.24 MS,A1 *soldier* becomes N *private* and at 10.25 *private* becomes *young one*. At 10.30 MS,A1 *comrade* becomes *companion* and a cut begins in N with the next sentence. At 11.32 MS,A1 *the other* becomes N *the tall soldier* and a cut begins with the next sentence. At 12.21 *comrade* is changed to *tall comrade*, but editorial alteration of the text had occurred immediately preceding at 12.19–20. The clustering of these variants about areas of Bacheller editing almost inevitably removes them from much possibility of authorial intention. The case differs in one patch of the MS in which Crane had skipped revision for several pages. Here alteration of names in N that differs from the forms adopted in A1 may very well be Crane's, even though the intervention of the Bacheller editor cannot be entirely discarded as a possibility. For instance, at 75.20–21 for MS *Wilson* N reads *his loud friend* but A1 *the loud soldier;* at 75.24 for MS *Wilson* N reads *the loud one* and A1 *the other*; at 75.31 for MS *Wilson* N reads *him* and A1 *the loud soldier*; and at 76.20 for MS *Wilson* N reads *his loud friend* and A1 *his friend*. Presumably by chance at 76.29 both N and A1 agree in *the loud private* and at 76.34 in *his friend's* where MS had retained *Wilson*. The possible question of the Bacheller editor's changes aside, both versions have equal authority and the choice of the A1 form by the present editor is a purely arbitrary one.

In other matters than the names and descriptive phrases the dangers, as remarked, of accepting plausible N variants from MS,A1 agreement are too acute to risk. As examples, one may cite at 12.10

the N substitution of *remarked the youth thoughtfully* for MS,A1 *he asked*. But since a cut begins in N at the very next sentence, a quite possible case of Crane's alteration of TMs[a] is cast under the same suspicion of editorial alteration in conjunction with cuts that was encountered with descriptive phrases for the characters. Even in such a case as 10.9–11 one may suspect Bacheller editing. MS,A1 read, 'He contemplated the lurking menaces of the future and failed in an effort to see himself standing stoutly in the midst of them.' Here N substitutes what could quite plausibly be an authorial change *and his mind failed* for *and failed*; but since with the next sentence at 10.11 an N cut begins, the odds strongly favor editorial not authorial tinkering. These examples are indicative of the constant barrage of other N alterations—few of which could be denied as Crane's on any concrete evidence—made in circumstances that are less suspiciously associated with cuts. They serve as an adequate warning that unique N variation is ordinarily quite untrustworthy. As a consequence, only one such reading from N has been admitted into the present text (the addition of *too* at 5.4) and even such a characteristically phrased addition as N's *It was as if he had been stunned*, inserted after *his friend* at 103.1, has been rejected although on mixed grounds (see the Textual Note). In short, there appears to be no possibility of quarrying the N text for Crane's own unique revisions of TMs[a] other than the alteration of names.

The N text has its uses in two respects, however. Agreement of N and A1 versus MS should indicate a typist's variant in TMs that can be disregarded as unauthorial save for such special cases, albeit shaky ones, in which when he came to revise TMs[b] Crane is conjectured to have recalled a variant he had marked in TMs[a]. Second, in one brief stretch where MS has been removed and N[1-5] substantially cut, the N[6] text provides the only check on that of A1, even though the value of this comparison is diminished by the hypothesis that N[6] derives from the A1 proof in areas where the Bacheller proof had been cut. Variants in this limited area, therefore, must be either N[6] departures from copy or else readings in the A1 proof in an earlier stage than that preserved in the final book form. The possibility of such early and variant proofs cannot be ignored, but their existence cannot be demonstrated as copy for N[6], and thus A1 must certainly hold the paramount authority. On the other hand, when in this particular area N[1-5] are also present, the authority of the recovered Bacheller proofs is equal to that of A1 for the accidentals and must be seriously considered for the substantives as well, for in the absence of MS only the features of TMs can be recovered in this area insofar as MS(d) is also wanting.

The prime difficulty in ordering the variants in A1 from MS is the determination of which were compositorial and editorial and which may be laid to Crane's working over TMs^b in New Orleans. In this process of selection between the two authorities, categories such as the frequent singular and plural variation are of assistance. The major stylistic revision of MS was certainly carried out during the course of its inscription, as a study of the list of current variants will indicate. In the general revision Crane was mainly concerned with his altered views about the use of names and the question of dialect revision, but he did occupy himself here and there with stylistic matters although scarcely in any systematic and thorough-going manner. Having already dealt once with his verbal expression in the general revision and approved these results in the very last working-over of the MS for errors, it is unlikely that in New Orleans Crane devoted himself in any major way to altering the minutiae of his style. It is clear that in New Orleans he did work over the names and invented formulaic phrases for Wilson without memory of what he had previously marked in TMs^a. Moreover, he did consistently alter all familiar uses of *Flem* in dialogue to *Henry*, a process representing a new departure from TMs^a in the treatment of names. The major thrust of his revision, however, was directed to his cutting the introspective examination of the youth's states of mind, thus sharpening and emphasizing the action by reducing materially the commentary. The final revision of TMs^b in this respect had an important effect on the shape of the latter part of the book by removing about 1,250 words that were basically unnecessary or else repetitious in their effect.

In the area of the stylistic variants between MS (joined to N when available) and A1, the present editor after a study of the categories has rejected all A1 changes between singulars and plurals and all minor alterations of indifferent idiom [60] as compositorial or editorial, in which category they join the clear-cut unauthoritative alterations of Crane's language like A1 *bent* for MS *bended* (which could have taken place in TMs) and also the different misreadings like *gate* for *grate* (40.29) or *different* for *diffident* (52.28) as well as the unnecessary grammatical changes like *deeply* for *deep* (43.10) and the several fairly certain editorial 'improvements' of Crane's language like *recur* for *appear* (41.1) or *listened* for *heard them* (42.27).

Sometimes useful in the difficult task of deciding between compositorial and other variants is Crane's occasional practice of skipping over pages without stylistic annotation and then clustering his revisions. Thus a series of A1 variants in close proximity can often be judged as a unit either as authorial as in the sequence between 61.17 and 61.24 or 61.25, or as editorial as in the sequence between 39.19 and 39.24, or between 40.29 and 42.29 or even 43.21. In such

---

[60] An example would be the rejection of A1 *all his life* for MS *all of his life* (5.13).

sequences the general identification of the nature of certain variants can be taken as applying to the more indifferent examples that might otherwise offer more difficulty in decision. Not all sequences are so easy to categorize as those mentioned above. For example, although to be conservative the present editor has accepted the A1 variants between 27.34 and 28.5, he is by no means certain that these may not represent editorial improvement rather than authorial. In any such general selection into authoritative and nonauthoritative as is required for the considerable number of substantive variants in an eclectic text of *The Red Badge of Courage*, full certainty is a complete impossibility and opinions may well differ here and there. In such cases it is basically a question of the editor's taste and judgment operating in such areas of evidence as the nature in MS of Crane's own revisions, of alterations in A1 that either seem to counter or agree with his stylistic characteristics, and of parallels in A1 with editorial attention given to Crane's work by Appleton's elsewhere. The bibliographical situation created by the agreement of readings in N and A1 as against MS can offer evidence of a more concrete order. In general, the present editor has chosen to be more cautious than not in his acceptance of A1 variation as Crane's when no good reason for its authority in revision could be avouched. A series of Textual Notes discusses the reasons behind many of the decisions.

A far-reaching editorial decision has been made that, in at least one important respect, shapes the present text. From the evidence contained in MS it is quite clear that Hamlin Garland objected to Crane's consistent use of dialect not only in his three central characters, specifically, but also as a general proposition, although less firmly for other persons. The evidence of Crane's general revision of the early manuscript pages already given a preliminary revision for names and occasional matters of style demonstrates that initially Crane was prepared to agree with Garland and that he proposed to normalize to ordinary correct speech the dialect of the youth, the tall soldier, the loud soldier, and to a lesser extent the youth's mother. With some consistency he set about this revision of the original dialect except that he retained this dialect—despite Garland's strictures—not only for his common soldiers but also for the officers.[61] The facts are these. On MS page 1 (3.18–20) and continuing on to page 2, the tall soldier's dialect is untouched although further down on page 2 the loud soldier's speech is revised (3.28–4.2). Again, on

---

[61] Occasional unsystematic variations occur. For instance, at 34.2–3 a general's speech has the contraction *t'* altered in the main later revision to *to* although his *'em* forms are untouched. But at 44.13–35 what seems to be the same general speaks in unrevised dialect.

page 3 (4.20,22–23) the tall soldier's dialect is not altered. The youth speaks first on page 6 (6.17), and in his speech has a dialect *t'* altered to *to* and a *goin'* altered to *going*. Thereafter, with only a few oversights, his speech is consistently normalized except for such words as *Gawd, ain't,* and *was.* Also beginning on page 6 (6.26) the mother's speech is partly adjusted. When the tall soldier next appears, on page 14 (10.26–29), his dialect is fully revised to normal speech, and consistently thereafter up to the point where Crane changed his mind. The loud soldier's first speech in dialect following that of the tall soldier on page 14 (10.31–32) is similarly altered. Thereafter all three speak in normalized forms through page 38, the end of Chapter III (28.24–34). No further speech from them occurs until the youth's repetition on page 55 (41.1–3) of what he had heard the soldiers of his regiment remark on page 54 (40.13–16), both of which have been normalized—the first anomalously.

None of the three soldiers speaks again until page 75 where—although Crane altered the names—he left the tall soldier's dialect untouched (55.7–13; 55.25 [. . . yeh what]). The lack of revision of the dialect at this point seems to have no significance, even though on the succeeding pages 76–77 Crane also altered the names and included these pages in his general revision but did not touch the original dialogue of the tall soldier or of the youth. The shift is then abrupt. At the foot of page 77 the youth inquires in dialect in MS 'Where yeh goin', Jim?' (57.9), but when the same speech is continued on page 78 his dialect is revised by the interlineation three times of *you* above deleted *yeh*. From this point on, the youth's original dialect is usually normalized. The tall soldier has no further words to say, and thus what Crane finally intended for him must be reconstructed by analogy.[62] Beginning with Chapter XI (63.1) narrative takes over until on page 112 at the start of renumbered Chapter XIII (75.1) the youth returns to camp and encounters the loud soldier on sentry duty. Pages 112–114 were skipped in Crane's general revision and not even the names were changed. On these three MS pages not only does the loud soldier speak in his original dialect, unrevised (75.24–26; 76.20–21; 76.30–33), but also the youth (75.31–76.5; 76.18). Since Crane never touched these pages after the original inscription, except to change the first word *Fleming* to *The youth* on page 112 in blue pencil on the final looking-over when he renumbered the chapter heading, the retention of the dialect has no significance for his final intentions.

Crane's revision starts again on page 115 (77.8–9 *made further investigation.*) when he again began to alter the names as part of the

[62] By an inadvertent confusion, it would seem, on page 79 (58.20) Crane altered the tattered soldier's *Gawd* to *God* although elsewhere he speaks only in dialect.

general revision. The first dialogue by the loud soldier comes on page 117 when Wilson's original dialect is undisturbed (78.25–26), and from this point on Crane did not regularize it. Inadvertently, on page 118 Crane missed correction of the youth's dialect (79.24–29), but when next he speaks in dialect, on page 121 (81.27–31), the speech is revised and the same on page 122 (82.26–28; 82.33–34). Again on page 123 the youth's first speech in dialect is untouched (83.3–6), but his next, immediately below, is revised (83.9–11), although the last time he speaks on this page (83.13) no changes in the dialect are made, nor is the dialect altered in his single speech on page 124 (84.8–9). This patch marks the last of Crane's inattentiveness, however, for beginning with renumbered Chapter xv (85.1) the youth's speech is normalized with almost complete consistency and Wilson's dialect is left unaltered for the rest of the novel.

From this evidence, mixed though it is, certain conclusions may be drawn. In the original concept as represented by MS(d) and by the inscription of MS, Crane intended all speech to be in dialect, the three soldiers as well as their comrades and even the officers. The queries that Garland placed in the manuscript opposite some of the dialect, his occasional alterations, and the several times he put a pencil cross through a dialect passage indicate that he disapproved of Crane's choice of reporting dialogue, especially in reference to the three soldiers but also, occasionally, elsewhere. After overlooking the tall soldier's dialect on the first three pages, Crane started on page 6 with 6.17 to revise the youth's dialect to ordinary speech; he partially altered the mother's dialect forms; and on page 14 with the return of the tall and loud soldiers at 10.26 he extended the revision to them. The most positive sign of a change in this revisory system comes early in renumbered Chapter xiv when on page 121 the youth's dialect is normalized (81.27–31) but Wilson's remains the same (81.23–24). With some slips in the youth's speech this is the differentiation maintained to the conclusion. It is evident, then, that at least as early as Chapter xiv Crane had changed his mind and altered his earlier intention to follow Garland's advice for the speech of the three soldiers and that he had arrived at his final system of retaining normal speech for the youth but dialect for Wilson.[63] In fact, however, the change in intention can be set before this, at least as early as Chapter ix. Pages 74–75 beginning Chapter ix contain no speech by the youth that offered the opportunity for dialect (54.1–55.25) but in contrast to the earlier revision of his speech the tall soldier's dialect is untouched. It may be that on page 76 the youth's one speech (55.29–30) not altered from its dialect form was overlooked in error, for on page 77 (57.2–3) and thereafter the youth's

[63] From the start he had rejected Garland's advice to remove dialect from the speech of every character—in short, from the novel as a whole—and had proposed to revise only the speech of the three soldiers and the mother.

dialect is normalized whereas the tall soldier's at 57.6–7 is not revised. Hence in Chapter IX there appears to be an overlap of unrevised speech for the tall soldier and revised for the youth similar
to that later established between the loud soldier and the youth in
Chapter XI. It is a legitimate conclusion, then, that somewhere between the revision in MS of Wilson's original dialect speech that
ends Chapter III (28.24–31)—accompanied by a revision of the
youth's dialect at 28.34—and the resumption of dialogue by the
three soldiers in Chapter IX and then XI, in which only the youth's
dialect is removed, Crane altered the method of his revision and
came to his final intention about the reproduction of dialect. This
was, quite simply, to revise the youth's speech to normality but to
leave all other dialogue, whether of the tall soldier, the loud soldier,
or the ranks and their officers, as he had written it in the original
dialect form. With only a few careless oversights, this is the system
from Chapter IX to the end in the revised MS.

It is an indication of Crane's frequent carelessness about detail
that having arrived at this system with the revision of Chapter IX
he did not ever in the MS or in the TMs made from it go back to
adjust Chapters I–III, nor did the Appleton editors discover the discrepancy. As a consequence, A1, derived from MS by way of TMs[b],
retains the irregularities of its source. For instance, it reproduces the
unaltered dialect of Conklin's first speeches (3.18–20; 4.20,22–23) [64]
despite the intervening revised speech of Wilson (3.28–4.2), but on
Conklin's next appearance both he and Wilson speak normal English
(10.26–12.19) as in the revised version of the MS. This normal
speech continues for Wilson at 18.28–20.1 in Chapter II and for
Conklin and then Wilson in Chapter III at 21.26–28, 26.36–27.11,
and 28.24–31. On Conklin's next introduction in Chapter IX and
Wilson's in Chapter XI they speak unrevised dialect. The youth's
speech also varies according to the uneven revision in the MS that
was not modified either in TMs or in A1.

It would be pedantic in the extreme to follow either the faulty MS
copy-text or the equally faulty revised A1 edition in these anomalies.
From the evidence of Chapters IX and XI we know beyond all question what Crane finally decided about the speech of his characters.
As a consequence, the present edition has made consistent everywhere in the text the distinction at which Crane arrived by Chapter
IX and thus has restored throughout from unrevised MS or from
MS(d), or in a few cases from independent emendation, the dialect
forms characteristic of the tall soldier and the loud soldier but has

[64] The newspapers normalize these passages to remove the dialect, certainly
an intervention by the Bacheller editor to make the opening consistent. That
it could not be Crane's marking of TMs[a] is suggested by the fact that normalizing Conklin's speech at this late date goes contrary to Crane's intention about
his dialect from Chapter IX on in the MS.

retained the revised substantially normal forms of the youth. All such alterations are recorded in the List of Emendations, of course. As a result, in the present text for the first time the dialogue conforms to Crane's full intentions which through his carelessness were only imperfectly realized in the authoritative documents.

The question of copy-text has already been discussed, but a statement in detail is needed. Whenever available, the revised form of the Barrett manuscript is accepted as the copy-text. The Bacheller newspaper proofs were set from one copy of a late typescript made from this MS, and A1 was set from the other copy. It is conjectured that Crane independently went over both typescripts but not at the same time. The substantive variants from A1 thought to represent, in general probability, Crane's marked revisions in TMs^b performed in New Orleans are inserted into the texture of the MS accidentals. The cuts in the A1 text, as well as its few additions, are taken to be authoritative. In the question of revised verbal readings of superior authority to those in the MS, no distinction is possible between Crane's revision of TMs^b and the corrections he may or may not have made in proof in the summer of 1895. The preserved parts of the earlier draft MS(d), being anterior to the MS, can have no superior verbal authority, but they are useful occasionally in confirming MS readings and in restoring desirably authoritative accidentals in which MS has lapsed. Because of the active editing given TMs^a in Bacheller's office, the general verbal revisions Crane may have made when he went through TMs^a to correct the names are unidentifiable. Of several possibilities, only one has actually been adopted in the present text. Neither N nor A1 is thought to have any authority in its accidentals superior to the MS; hence readings adopted from them in these matters are chosen for mere convenience as necessary corrections, not as authoritative revisions of the MS.

In the MS pages 41–44 ending Chapter IV were abstracted as part of a massive cut. It may be that the soldiers' dialogue that ends page 40 and is not present in any printed version was then intended to conclude the chapter, but it is probably sounder to believe that the cut in the MS text that begins after 30.8 and extends for nineteen more lines on page 40 was by an oversight not marked. At any rate, the continuation of the battle, present in pages 41–44 but now known chiefly from its version in A1 (partly reproduced also in N, with some text from MS[d] as well) offers something of a textual problem. That the material was present both in TMs^a and TMs^b is demonstrable from its presence in N (though severely cut by the editor) and presumably as a whole in A1 (less what may have been further dialogue on the top of page 41 continuing that cut from the foot of page 40).[65]

[65] The unprinted text of MS on page 40 is reproduced in the Historical Collation.

The copy for this text in TMs comes in question, however. If Crane had restored the missing pages in manuscript when TMs was made up, one would have expected the leaves to have been preserved with the rest of the manuscript. Moreover, one would have expected the cut to have been marked in the lower half of page 40. These leaves would have been abstracted before the typing of final TMs and thus as part of the general revision of the MS, which also reduced other chapter endings by omission or by cancellation of original leaves and substitution of rewritten text. In no other part of the novel is material printed in A1 that had been cut from the original in MS or altered in the general revision. The natural inference is that TMs was made up from the present MS and thus contained the text on the lower part of page 40 but not the text on pages 41–44. It would have followed, then, that when preparing TMs as printer's copy Crane crossed out the typed matter represented by the last nineteen lines of this leaf and added a substantial part of the text that had originally ended the chapter. Conjecturally, the copy for this restored material might well have been the pages with their carbons— no doubt independently revised for the purpose [66]—of the original lost typescript for which Hamlin Garland had paid, these sheets being inserted into the second typescript TMs^{a-b} to complete the chapter with a substantial amount of the full text.

In this area, A1 alone is complete, and since it would have been set directly from the added typescript it becomes the copy-text in the absence of MS and in the fragmentary status of MS(d). However, since N was also set from another copy of the same typescript, it is of equal authority for the accidentals, although both A1 and N must yield to MS(d) for the accidentals in the part where it is present. The newspapers reprint the text, with A1, between 30.9 and 30.26, presumably from the lost typescript. N$^{1-5}$ then omit 30.27–32, but N^6 alone divorces itself from this cut and reproduces the text from 30.27–28 and cuts only 30.29–32 along with N$^{1-5}$. All newspapers then resume with 30.33 until a further cut starts at 31.20, which in N^6 continues only to 31.29 but in N$^{1-5}$ extends itself to 31.32. Thereupon the newspapers resume, but all join in cutting 31.37–39 before returning to conclude the chapter at 32.8.

The history of the N^6 copy elsewhere suggests that in this sequence from 30.9 to 32.8 when N^6 prints text also found in N$^{1-5}$ it was being set from the common Bacheller proof; and this conclusion is reenforced by its agreement with N$^{1-5}$ in *tree trunks* for A1 *trees* at 30.19, in the spelling-out of the regimental numbers at 31.3 and 34.1, in the lack of a paragraph at 31.7, in the form *Saunders* for A1 *Saunders's* at 31.8, and so on. However, as is found elsewhere, N^6 variants from N$^{1-5}$ in which it agrees with A1 seem to have come from the

---

[66] The appearance of the phrase *the youth* for Fleming's name at 30.9,22; 31.8,11; 31.34; and 32.4 indicates the minimum revision, at least.

editorial marking of copy by some form of collation with the A1 proof-sheets. For instance, its reproduction with A1 and MS(d) of *new* at 30.25 omitted in N^{1-5} and of *carven* for N^{1-5} *craven* at 31.12 seem to be authoritative whereas its unique variants from the other newspapers and from A1—like *cheer* at 31.4 for N^{1-5}, A1 *jeer*, or *banshee* at 31.5 for *the banshee*—may be taken as N^6 errors of no authority. The N^6 text where N^{1-5} are wanting must have come directly from the A1 proofs and so is completely derived. This textual hypothesis has interesting consequences since it removes the possibility that in the area where N^{1-5} are cut, readings in N^6 variant from A1 can have any authority. Automatically, therefore, the present editor rejects N^6 *gibes* for A1 *jokes* (31.30) and also the N^6 *were apparently* for A1 *apparently were* (31.31). In theory *gibes* might have been the original reading of the proof from which N^6 was set, subsequently altered to *jokes* in a later stage of the proof; but a possibility is not a probability and an editor would not be justified on the present evidence in rejecting the general authority of A1 in such a circumstance.

The case is altered, however, for variants in which A1 differs from N, since when these are not possible Bacheller editorial or compositorial changes of the common kind, N could theoretically represent the original readings of the lost typescript (1) corrupted by the A1 compositor, (2) altered unauthoritatively by the A1 editor in the leaves inserted in TMsᵇ, or (3) authoritatively revised by Crane in TMsᵇ in New Orleans. At 30.24 the error *regimently* found in $N^{1,3-4}$ for *regimental* is quite clearly an error in the Bacheller syndicated proofs independently corrected by $N^{2,5}$, and possibly by N^6 with or without consultation of the A1 proofs, and so with N^{1-5} *craven* for correct A1 *carven*. Seven other substantive variants come in question in this area where MS provides no check. Of these, the present editor believes that the available evidence favors A1 authority and Bacheller editorial change in the N omission of *new* at 30.25 and of *for an instant* at 31.33. Whether TMs read *Saunders* with N or *Saunders's* with A1 at 31.8 is not demonstrable. (Unfortunately, the best parallel in A1 *Hannises'* at 29.22,24 occurs in an N cut.) At 30.19 N *tree trunks* might have sounded more like an original reading (see 100.17–18) and A1 *trees* as an alteration were it not for the evidence of *trees* in MS(d) which suggests the A1 reading as the original. Most interesting is N *bellowing* and A1 *following* at 31.15. The word *following* could readily be a misreading of MS *bellowing*, in which case one would need to conjecture that in looking over the added typescript leaves in TMsᵃ Crane caught and corrected the typist's error but missed it in his later revision of TMsᵇ. This is possible, of course, although—assuming *bellowing* to be correct—A1 *following* may be a compositorial error or editorial sophistication (see the Textual Note). At 32.2 the A1 plural *reserves* for N *reserve* could be another of the frequent A1 unauthoritative variants in singulars and plurals. In these circumstances MS has generally been almost demonstrably correct and A1 in error. However, in this case the parallel with 30.16 may encourage retention of the A1 form although technically the singular may be correct. The last variant turns on whether the color sergeant was *standing with his legs braced apart* as in N or simply *standing with his legs apart* (31.13–14). In view of Crane's use of *braced* in *he stood with braced and self-confident legs* (86.8), it may be possible with some tentativeness to assign authority to N and its omission in A1 to some unauthoritative factor or else to regard it as the original reading revised in TMs[a].

These questions of occasional substantive readings do not affect the choice of A1 as copy-text when MS is missing at 30.9–32.8. When $N are wanting at 30.29–32, 31.20–21, and 31.37–39, A1 is indeed the only preserved authority. When N^{1-5} are wanting but N^6 is present at 30.27–28 and 31.30–32, the derivation of N^6 from A1 copy elevates A1 to the position of sole authority except for whatever possibility may be remotely present that N^6 variants represent original readings in the A1 proof later altered before printing.

THE APPARATUS

In the transcript of the MS copy-text for the present reading edition certain conventions have been silently adopted. Crane's placement of punctuation marks like commas and periods in relation to end quotation marks was erratic and unsystematic—sometimes inside the quotes, sometimes outside, and sometimes directly beneath. These have been made regular within the quotation marks according to the American usage of A1. Crane usually placed quotation marks before instead of after a concluding dash, but in this edition the usual A1 practice of concluding with the quotes has been silently adopted.[67] The spacing of contractions is highly variable in MS and even occasionally in A1, but this spacing is normalized according to the generally prevalent custom of MS. All internal dashes are silently given a one-em length and all concluding dashes a two-em.

The MS(d) text is separately printed in a diplomatic transcript without emendation other than the normalization of dialect spacing. In order to decrease the length of the Historical Collation, the differences between MS and MS(d) are separately recorded with the exception of dialect alterations which have been accepted in the present edited text as emendations of the manuscript on the authority of the manuscript draft. In general it follows that the Virginia text and the

---

[67] On a few occasions when A1 misunderstands the intention and follows MS, some shade of meaning could be involved for a reader; hence such cases are recorded in the List of Emendations.

draft manuscript agree with MS(u) against MS(c) in such words as *th'* vs. *the*, *an'* vs. *and*, or *fer* vs. *for*. Thus a quick look at the emendations will show the reader the nature of these variants; moreover, the alterations in the final manuscript contain every alteration made so that a cross reference to this list will settle any doubt as to the relation of final and draft manuscript at a given point. A single dagger (†) has been used in this collation to show an agreement of MS(u) and MS(d). In the List of Emendations any alteration of the copytext drawn exclusively from MS(d) is of course noted. In addition, because of the interest in the draft readings as confirming either MS or A1 readings, whether adoptions or rejections, the MS(d) form is regularly provided in the List of Emendations. Absence of such notation signifies that MS(d) is wanting.

For convenience A1 is taken whenever possible as the primary and most immediate source for emendations, instead of N.[68] In the List of Emendations, if a text symbol does not appear it is to be understood that the missing text is cut at that point: a reference to the Historical Collation will indicate to the reader the exact extent of any such cut. E1 is completely derived from A1 and appears in the emendations only where a 'V' reading occurs (a V reading being one that the editor has made as a necessary correction, one that is not based on the authority of any of the texts utilized for this edition).

In the Historical Collation the symbol AE1 has been designated to show an agreement of the two first editions; where only E1 or A1 appears the other will agree with the lemma to the left of the bracket. The Historical Collation does not include variants in dialect that have been listed in the emendations (however, where there is an unemended variant in dialect from the printed text, this is recorded), nor does it include the differences of paragraphing in the N texts. The variant chapter arrangements of N are undoubtedly due to the Bacheller editor, but the facts about this division are provided in the Historical Collation.

The section on Alterations in the Manuscript contains all changes that Crane made in the Barrett manuscript whether by current (C) —at the time of inscription—or by subsequent revision. These stages have been discussed fully on pages 14–28 and concern:

1. (P) *Preliminary*: Made prior to Hamlin Garland's seeing the manuscript. This revision runs for the first 38 folios and is primarily concerned with the removal of surnames and the substitution of epithets for the central character and his companions.

2. (G) *General*: After the return of the manuscript from Hamlin

---

[68] The variant text of the six observed newspapers can be recovered, for substantives, from the Historical Collation. Readers wishing to consult a reading text of N are recommended to the facsimile of N¹, the *New York Press*, edited by Joseph Katz for the Scholars' Facsimiles and Reprint Series, Gainesville, Florida, 1967.

Garland, Crane went back over the first 38 pages and changed some of the preliminary epithets and altered much of the dialect to correct speech. After fol. 38 (28.27) the general revision in the same manner continues to remove most surnames and substitute the finally accepted epithets and to normalize the dialect. As the medium for this stage of revision is variously ink and pencil, there is occasionally an element of doubt as to whether an ink alteration is current (C) or general (G); in this case the alteration is listed as in the example: 'the] *interlined above deleted* "a" (C) *or* (G)'.

3. (F) *Final*: After completion of the general revision Crane went back over the entire manuscript, strengthening deletions of discarded material, adding bridging page numbers to accommodate pages removed, changing chapter headings after the removal of old chapter XII, and on fol. 38 altering some dialect that was missed in previous revisions (e.g., 28.24 and 28.27). Final revisions are variously in ink, pencil, and blue crayon.

Before Crane's general revision, Hamlin Garland (HG) had made certain notations throughout the manuscript. He queried Crane's use of dialect (a criticism that Crane honored well into the general revision before he finally evolved his own system), corrected several misspellings, and suggested a few word substitutions. Garland used a pencil for all his notations. When the editor is in doubt in the passages where the general revision is also in pencil, the alteration appears thus: 'the] *interlined above deleted* "a" (HG) *or* (G)'.

A cumulative list of alterations has been made, the appropriate symbol for each stage being given after the entry. In a multiple entry where Crane revised a certain word separately in the three stages, the symbol for each stage appears at the completion of the alteration in that particular stage. Where a word has been emended the entry reads 'dilapidated] MS "delapidated" *with first* "a" *over* "e" (C)', or in the case of some dialect changes *not* accepted in the Virginia edition, the entry reads 'an'] MS(c) "and" *with* "d" *over an apostrophe* (G)'. MS(c) as in the case of other volumes indicates the corrected manuscript and MS(u) the uncorrected.

WORD-COUNT COMPUTATIONS IN THE MANUSCRIPT

Crane's manuscripts show that he was often in the habit of noting the total words on each page on its verso, circled, and cumulating such a count either page by page or at the chapter's end. No such records appear in the draft manuscript of *The Red Badge of Courage*, however (perhaps an indication that he never seriously contemplated publication of this form of the novel), and the calculations that occur in the Barrett final manuscript are of a different pattern. No leaf has the characteristic circled individual word count. At intervals, the page counts of some chapters are noted in a column, usually by adding the first two or three paginal word counts and thereafter by cumulating each further page until the end of the chapter. These records do not cover all chapters. It is possible that a very few have been destroyed by the cancellation of chapter-ending leaves, but the evidence suggests that as a whole it is likely that most have been preserved. This conjecture is based on the fact that of the five verso pages containing cumulative word counts for chapters, four are on leaves of the first page of a chapter (fols. 67^v, 74^v, 179^v, 185^v) and only one is on the last leaf (fol. 145^v).[69] In this manuscript the endings of Chapters IV, VII, X, and XIV (originally XV) have been removed by cancellation without substitution, and all of Chapter XII. Moreover, the original last leaves of Chapters V, VI, XI, XVI (originally XVII), XVII (originally XVIII), and XXI (originally XXII) have been removed and cancellans leaves substituted. In this process of revision the only first leaf of a chapter to be affected appears to be fol. 166, the opening of Chapter XXI (originally XXII). Thus if the observed pattern of recording cumulative chapter totals on the verso of the first leaf of a chapter heading, and only rarely on the verso of a final leaf, had been maintained, some miscellaneous computations like those on fol. 73^v (and 110^v) may have been destroyed elsewhere but not many chapter word counts by the revision of chapter endings. Moreover, a sufficient number of uncancelled final leaves of chapters followed by uncancelled first leaves of the next chapters are preserved that contain no calculations; thus it seems clear that these calculations were not systematically entered in the manuscript chapter by chapter. The miscellaneous calculations (although they are difficult to evaluate) suggest that Crane did indeed make a detailed record of word counts but not always, it would seem, on pages of the manuscript. Moreover, from the paginal counts it is clear that he had performed his calculations before the complete revision of the manuscript, and certainly before the final stages of cancellation that altered various chapter endings.

At least at the start it would appear that Crane did not inscribe these figures currently with the completion of the chapters but instead that the computations were begun at some later time and were chiefly for the purpose of bringing him up to date either after the completion of the whole manuscript or possibly in its latter stages of composition. For example, the earliest page counts to appear are for fols. 45–52, but these are placed on fol. 74^v (*Facsimile*, ii, 222), the back of the first page of Chapter IX, along with other sets of figures. The addition of the page counts gives a total of 2,255 words,

[69] Other computations than those for chapters occur on the last leaf of Chapter VIII (fol. 73^v) and the penultimate leaf (fol. 110^v) of Chapter XII (originally XIII).

a count that can be identified as for Chapter V. On the preceding fol. 73^v, the last page of Chapter VIII (*Facsimile*, ii, 223), these 2,255 words are added to 11,145 for a total of 13,400 (corrected from 23,-400). The figure of 11,145 must be that for pages 1–44 (Chapters I–IV), the additions for which had been made elsewhere and not preserved. It is odd that the count of Chapter V should be placed so late in the manuscript; and indeed it appears on the same verso as the addition of the paginal word counts totaling 1,805 for pages 67–73, placed above it in the left margin also. Moreover, on this same fol. 74^v the total of 13,400 taken from fol. 73^v is added to 2,240, the word count from fol. 67^v for pages 53–60, to make a new total of 15,640, which would provide the cumulative total for pages 1–60. (The figure 2,240 is also repeated, circled, in the head space on fol. 53 recto, the first page of Chapter VI.) The size of the hand and probably the thickness of the pencil are the same both for the column of figures on fol. 74^v for Chapter V and for the addition of this total of 2,255 words to 11,145 found on fol. 73^v. The other calculations on fol. 74^v are larger in the size of their figures and thicker in the pencil and may have been made at the same time, although one cannot know why— if so—the total of 1,805 for Chapter VIII was not added to any fresh cumulation, the only total on the page being that of 15,640 for pages 1–60, Chapters I–VI.

The calculations for Chapter VII are wanting, but they may be recovered, for on fol. 145^v (*Facsimile*, ii, 243), the last page of Chapter XIX (originally XVIII), in the tail space are paginal word counts totaling 1,670 that represent pages 74–80, Chapter IX. This 1,670 is then added in a separate calculation to the figure 18,940 (which must represent the cumulated total for pages 1–73) for a new total of 20,610 words for pages 1–80, Chapters I–IX. If we take the total of 18,940 for pages 1–73 and subtract from this 1,805 (the total for pages 66–73), we derive 17,135 as the total for original pages 1–66. Subtracting from this the figure 15,640 (the total for pages 1–60), we are left with 1,495 as the word count for Chapter VII, pages 61–66, before fol. 66 was cancelled. The actual word total of pages 61–65 is difficult to establish because of the problems of hyphenated compounds and dialect contractions, but a rough count using as much as possible Crane's general system [70] gives about 1,325 words for the undeleted material, or about 1,415 words including the material crossed out on the lower part of fol. 65. This would leave a count of about 80 words which concluded the original chapter on cancelled fol. 66, a perfectly normal figure.

---

[70] In his word totals Crane did not count such contractions as *'ll* for *will*, and usually not *'em* for *them*, the latter of which he was inclined to hitch to the preceding word. He seems not ordinarily to have counted *t'* for *to* but to have associated it with the succeeding word; however, he did count each part of most hyphenated compounds.

The calculations for Chapter IX appearing on fol. 145ᵛ (the last page of new Chapter XIX) are preceded on fol. 97ᵛ (the final leaf of Chapter XI) by paginal word counts that refer to the pages of Chapter X. Chapter X begins on fol. 81 and, on the evidence of the paging of the first leaf of Chapter XI as 90, should have concluded on fol. 89; but the chapter has been drastically cut by the deletion of text at the foot of fol. 85 to form a new chapter ending and the removal of original fols. 86–89. The first five pages of Chapter X coincide with the first five cumulated counts on fol. 97ᵛ, the figures being 287, 293, 310, 290, and 265 (the last being the full count for fol. 85 before cutting). But whereas Chapter X should have continued to fol. 89, with four more pages, only two paginal word counts of 267 and 90 conclude the column to form a total of 1,802, the 90 obviously representing the last page of a chapter. Hence two pages are not found in the word count. The only conjecture that can explain this anomaly would require us to believe that at some early time before the general revision Crane had already revised this chapter ending, in the process removing two pages.

The paginal word counts after these for Chapter X are wanting until on fol. 179ᵛ (the first page of Chapter XXIII (originally XXIV) a column of figures is added cumulatively to form a total of 1,738 for pages 179–184, comprising Chapter XXIII. This 1,738 is then added to 46,440 (presumably the total for pages 1–178) to form a new total of 48,178. Finally, to the right 48,178 is added to 1,822 to total an even 50,000. This figure will be discussed below. The last paginal computation is found on fol. 185ᵛ, the back of the first page of Chapter XXIV (originally XXV). Here in a simple column of figures Crane adds, cumulating the totals after each page, 305, 289, 273, 332, 105, and 232 for a final total of 1,536 words. These represent fols. 185–190 of what is now the final chapter, but they include only the undeleted portion of fol. 190, omitting the three lines of dialogue that had been excised after MS 190.28, and they omit the continuation on fols. 191–192, including the revised ending that carries over onto new fol. 193.

No final explanation can be provided but some guesses can be made. On the evidence of short fol. 189 (105 words) it looks as if Crane may have intended to end a chapter with its last sentence, 'Fleming's reply was an outburst of crimson oaths' (134.20). Instead, it would seem, he decided to continue the chapter but—perhaps because he did not have the manuscript at hand—when he carried on he misnumbered the next page 189 (although correcting it to 190 before inscribing fol. 191) and started the continuation on this fresh page, leaving the lower two-thirds of fol. 189 blank, to be filled in later with a guideline. Still, the continuation on fol. 190 is contained in the column of figures, but no more. It seems somewhat improbable that Crane would have intended to end the chapter with the soldiers' dialogue at 135.5+, even though the totaling on fol. 185^v of pages 185–190 would suggest this possibility as the simplest explanation. At any rate, he carried on the chapter with the youth's reflections starting with 135.6 to complete approximately 319 words on fol. 191 and 216 words on fol. 192 up to the original ending. The last alteration, made in the general revision, extended the chapter by another 56 words for the new ending. These 535 words up to the old ending, or 591 to the new, are not cumulated, and on the evidence of fol. 179^v never were counted in as a whole. What seems to have happened on fol. 179^v is that Crane calculated he had written 48,178 words for Chapters I–XXIII, pages 1–184. Then when he added 48,178 to 1,822 to arrive at an even 50,000 words, the figure 1,822 evidently was quite arbitrary to indicate the minimum required in Chapter XXIV (originally XXV) to reach 50,000 words for the novel. One may speculate that when he had written the first extension of Chapter XXIV he counted the words only as far as his revised page 190 and when he reached 1,536, with only 286 words to go to complete 1,822 words for the chapter and 50,000 for the book, he simply stopped counting, for he had written, he knew, two further pages that in fact total over 500 words. Crane was not interested in the exact wordage of the novel, apparently, once he could claim that it was 50,000 words at a minimum. This reconstruction may seem to be more probable to the total evidence, especially to the arbitrary figures on preceding fol. 179^v, than the possibility that the word count for Chapter XXIV indicates an originally planned ending at the foot of fol. 190.

A few miscellaneous calculations occur, some of which can be interpreted and some not. For instance, on fol. 145^v along with the counts for pages 74–80 and the total words for the book up to page 80 occur three unidentifiable counts whereby 24 is added to 38 for a total of 62, and (independently) 32 is added to 17 for a total of 49 and 62 then added for a total of 111. On fol. 97^v, independent of the word count of 1,802 for pages 81–87, appear the following: first 17,747 is subtracted from 22,410 for a result of 4,663, and then to this is added 34,372 for a total of 39,035. The first figure 22,410 is identifiable as the total of pages 1–87 which may be arrived at by adding 1,802 (fol. 97^v) to the total of 20,610 for pages 1–82 (fol. 145^v) and rounding it off from 22,412. However, the source of the subtractor 17,747 is unknown as well as the purpose of the subtraction and also the derivation of the figure 34,372 which is thereupon added to 4,663. On fol. 110^v, the penultimate leaf of Chapter XII (originally XIII), more subtractions appear. First, 21,046 is subtracted from 26,410 for a result of 5,364. Separately, 34,372 (the figure used as an addition on fol. 97^v to secure a total of 39,035) is subtracted from 40,000 for a result of 5,628, and from this is then subtracted 5,364 for a remainder of 264. The round number 40,000 is suspicious and may be a substitute for the final total of 39,035 on fol. 97ᵛ, but the identification of the other figures is unknown. One may speculate that Crane may have been calculating in some manner how many more words he had to write at various stages, but how he reached his results cannot be recovered from the preserved word counts in the manuscript since they are missing between pages 88 and 177, a gap that by Crane's calculations (including the later withdrawn original Chapter XII) would have contained 24,028 words.

On fol. 179ᵛ above the present calculations is a deleted total 46,-654, the origin of which is unknown.

BIBLIOGRAPHICAL DESCRIPTIONS

Copyright for the first American edition of *The Red Badge of Courage* was applied for on September 27, 1895, and deposit was made the same day, not on September 28 as stated in the Williams and Starrett *Stephen Crane: A Bibliography* (1948). Announcement was made in the *Publishers' Weekly* on October 5. The price was one dollar.

The description is as follows:

The Red Badge | Of Courage | [red: plumed helmet orn.] | | An Episode of the American Civil War | [red: 5 plume orn.] | | By | [red: 4 plume orn.] | Stephen Crane | [red: 3 plume orn.] | | [Appleton device] | [red: 2 plume orn.] | | [red: 3 plume orn.] | | New York | D. Appleton and Company | 1895

Collation: [1]⁸(1₁ + x₁) 2–15⁸, pp. [i–iv] 1–233 [234–238]; leaf measures 7³⁄₁₆ × 4¹³⁄₁₆″, top edge trimmed and stained yellow, other edges rough-cut; text laid unwatermarked paper, horizontal chainlines 30 mm. apart, wove endpapers coated in light brown (57. l.Br) on pastedown and facing side of free conjugate, flyleaves front and back laid unwatermarked paper with vertical chainlines 30 mm. apart.

Contents: pp. i–ii: blank; p. iii: title-page; p. iv: 'COPYRIGHT, 1894, | BY STEPHEN CRANE. | COPYRIGHT, 1895, | BY D. APPLETON AND COMPANY.'; pp. 1–233: text headed 'THE RED BADGE OF COURAGE. | [short rule]', on p. 233 'THE END.' p. 234: blank; pp. 235–238: advertisements 'D. APPLETON & CO.'S PUBLICA-TIONS.' headed 'GILBERT PARKER'S BEST BOOKS.', first title *The Trail of the Sword*.

Binding: Light yellow brown (76. l.y Br) buckram. *Front*: '[red: floral orn.] | | [first letter of each word in red, rest in black; red initial 'T' 2 lines deep in gilt panel with pattern of black lozenges] T²HE RED BADGE | OF COURAGE | [black] BY | [red and black] STEPHEN CRANE | [red: small floral orn.].' *Spine*: '[red: orn.] |

[first letter of each word in red, rest in black] THE RED | BADGE OF | COURAGE | [red: orn.] | CRANE | [red: orn.] | APPLETONS'. *Back*: blank.

Dust Jacket: Tan (76. l.y Br) wove paper. *Front*: as the front cover except that the initial 'T' is in a pattern of black lozenges where gilt in binding. *Spine*: as binding. *Back*: blank. *Both flaps*: blank.

Copy Examined: University of Virginia–Barrett 551536.

Notes: (1) The title-leaf is an insert $1(x_1)$ on laid paper with vertical chainlines 30 mm. apart but of a different stock from that of the text since its chains are bolder and more translucent. (2) In this copy leaf 1_1 is present and is blank, the title-leaf being tipped in after it. The blank has been excised in some copies, but not in the four University of Virginia copies, giving the false effect of cancellation and substitution. (3) On p. 225 the word 'congratu-|lated' is perfect. (4) Except for the preserved blank leaf 1_1 this is the state of the Library of Congress deposit copy.

Variants: University of Virginia–Barrett copy 468450 text is on wove paper except for gathering 15 on laid with vertical chainlines. The inserted title-leaf is on wove paper as is the back flyleaf (1_1 missing). On p. 225 'congratu-|lated' is perfect. Parker advertisements on pp. 235–238. University of Virginia–Barrett copy 551538 wove text, front flyleaf laid paper with vertical chainlines, back flyleaf laid paper with horizontal chainlines, top edges gilt. Inserted title-leaf wove paper, leaf 1_1 wanting. Second line of 'congratu-|lated' is damaged. On p. 235 advertisements start with *The Red Badge of Courage* and continue with titles by A. Conan Doyle. The different advertisements (and the damaged word on p. 225) mark a later printing. Other copies are reported of this printing with laid paper but with vertical chainlines throughout. Copies are also reported of these later printings with the damaged type on p. 225 repaired and the 'd' of 'lated' out of perpendicular.

Advance Copies: Appleton prepared advance copies for Heinemann, who deposited the statutory copyright copy in the British Museum (012706.k.21) on September 27, 1895. The text of this copy is on laid paper with horizontal chainlines as in the University of Virginia–Barrett copy 551536 and the Library of Congress copy, but gathering 15 has been reimposed in 6's to remove the American advertisement leaves. Instead of the brown-coated endpapers the British Museum deposit copy has white wove endpapers conjugate with the flyleaves. Leaf 1_1 is wanting, and the inserted title-page is on slightly coated wove stock and reads (all in black): 'THE RED BADGE | OF COURAGE | An Episode of the American Civil War | BY | STEPHEN CRANE | [Appleton device] | NEW YORK | D. APPLETON AND COMPANY | 1895'. The verso contains the same copyright notice as the regular edition, in the same type-setting. On the recto, above the imprint, appears a purple rubber stamp reading 'LONDON &'. The binding is cream boards with the special title printed on the front, the back blank. The spine, without lettering, is of dark-brown cloth. On p. 225 the type is perfect. Another advance copy was deposited by Heinemann in the Bodleian Library of the University of Oxford (Fic. 2712 f.272) which received the date stamp '17.10.1895'. The copy is identical with that in the British Museum except that it is bound in cream-colored paper wrappers with the same title printed on the front.

The British Museum deposit copy contains a number of pencil markings evidently made in preparation for Heinemann's English edition. In the following list an asterisk signifies that the marked alteration was *not* made in the English edition; all unasterisked entries were followed in E1. The first reference is to the British Museum deposit copy (A1), the parenthetical reference is to the present edition.

*32.1 (21.1) *comma added after* 'came'
*34.20 (22.23) *semicolon formed from a comma following* 'soldier'
*56.11 (34.36) *'not' deleted*
*66.21 (40.23) *'to' deleted and inserted in line 22 before* 'stop'
*68.16 (41.22) *'he' deleted and 'him' substituted*
*77.4 (46.8) *comma added after* 'fate'
87.28 (52.15) *comma added after* 'blood'
*87.28 (52.16) *very lightly inscribed comma added after* 'stain'
109.19 (64.22) *comma added after* 'watched'
113.25 (66.36) *comma added after* 'afar'
113.27 (66.38) *semicolon added after* 'man' *but comma substituted in* E1
121.19 (71.2) *semicolon added after* 'swoon' *but comma substituted in* E1
*121.22 (71.4) *hyphen inserted between* 'tall soldier'
124.5 (72.14) *comma added after* 'it'
137.28 (79.35) *comma added after* 'arm'
139.15 (80.11) *'a' of 'began' deleted and 'u' substituted*
*140.10 (80.22) *semicolon formed from a comma following* 'dead'
193.28 (112.32–33) *'i' of 'illusions' deleted and 'a' substituted*
213.22(124.26) *'r' of A1 'friends' deleted*
*219.3 (128.9) *'s' of 'figurings' deleted*
*219.4 (128.9) *'s' of 'diagrams' deleted*
*219.5 (128.10) *'s' of 'loopholes' deleted*
219.23 (128.24) *comma added after* 'ran'
219.28 (128.28) *semicolon added after* 'him' *but comma substituted in* E1

220.16 (129.3) *semicolon added after 'them' but comma substituted in* E1

222.22 (130.12) *comma added after first 'it'*

222.24 (130.13) *semicolon added after 'exultation' but comma substituted in* E1

222.25 (130.14) *comma added after 'throe'*

*228.18 (133.20) *'to' transferred from before 'more' to follow 'closely'*

*228.22 (133.23) *comma after 'strange' moved to follow* AE1 *'upheavals'* 228.23 (133.24)

It seems probable, although strictly a conjecture, that the different title-page used as an insert in the advance copies sent to Heinemann was the original and that the more decorative title-page in red and black adopted for the American edition was a revised form. Some mystery attaches to the fact that gathering 1 begins with a blank and that the title-leaf (χ_1) is tipped in after it, whether the title of the advance copies or the red and black title of the American trade edition. We know from Crane's letter to Hitchcock of February 12 (?), 1895, from Lincoln, Nebraska, that Hitchcock must have raised a question about the title, for Crane wrote, 'I shall have to reflect upon the title' (*Letters*, p. 51), and again in a letter to Hitchcock dated March 8, 1895, from Galveston, Texas, he added, 'As to the name I am unable to see what to do with it unless the word "Red" is cut out perhaps. That would shorten it' (*Letters*, p. 53). No further evidence has been preserved about the question of the title, which Hitchcock obviously must have felt was too long. If the matter was unresolved when the first gathering was printed, the printer may have gone ahead with the first leaf, reserved for the title, blank, until a decision was made. The difficulty with associating the printing of the blank with Hitchcock's dislike of the title is that 'The Red Badge of Courage' was regularly printed as the head-title and in the running-heads, and to publish a book with a title-page that differed from these would be most unusual. It would seem, then, that the title had indeed been settled before printing of the book started and that the blank must be explained in some other fashion. Here the question of the two title-pages enters. One can only guess, but it is possible to speculate that it was not the book's title but the typography of the title-page that had not been settled and before the final form was decided the printer—whether or not because of some mixup—had machined the first gathering. The title-page of the advance copies is not nearly so attractive as the one in red and black for the trade edition. It may be that the titles found in the advance copies (oddly on wove paper, not on laid) were trials that were bound in and sent off before the final title-leaf was set up and printed. (The advance copy in the British Museum was deposited on the very day that Appleton deposited the Library of Congress copy and hence must have been mailed several weeks earlier.) Evidence is not available to settle the interesting question.

The two Barrett and the McGregor University of Virginia copies have been collated mechanically on the Hinman Collating Machine, and xeroxes both of the Library of Congress deposit copy and of the British Museum advance copy have been collated by hand against Barrett copy 551536. No textual variation in the plates appeared. In the 1900 printing the misprint 'bank' on 4.33 was corrected to 'bunk', but no other changes were made: in a printing as late as 1926, edited as a textbook for the Appleton Modern Literature Series by Max J. Herzberg, the original plates still showed no other textual correction than the change made in 1900 at page 4.33. Thus, on the evidence, the text of the American plates of *The Red Badge of Courage* can be established as invariant during Crane's lifetime and as undergoing no authoritative correction after his death.

According to the Heinemann records, the first English edition was published on November 26, 1895, but the British Museum deposit copy (012601.i.30/10) is stamped November 25.

The Red Badge | of Courage | An Episode of | The American Civil War | By | Stephen Crane | London | William Heinemann | 1896

Collation: π^2 A–I^8 K–M^8 N^6(–N6), pp. [i–iv] [1] 2–194 [195–202]; leaf measures 7⅟₁₆ × 4⅝″, edges rough-cut; laid paper with vertical chainlines, no watermark; wove glazed cream endpapers; following front endpaper is bound in the front wrapper from the paperbound edition (see below).

Contents: p. i: half-title, 'The Red Badge | of Courage'; p. ii: 'The Pioneer Series' (black-letter), followed by list of eleven titles starting with Annie E. Holdsworth, *Joanna Traill, Spinster*; p. iii: title-page; p. iv: '*All rights reserved*'; pp. 1–194: text, headed 'The | Red Badge of Courage', ending with colophon foot of p. 194 '*Printed by* BALLANTYNE, HANSON & Co. | *Edinburgh and London*'; pp. 195–202: advertisements for the Pioneer Series.

Binding: Dark olive green (128.d.gy.Ol G) smooth fine linen cloth. *Front*: '[stamped in white, in upper right corner within a rococo decorative oval frame] The | Red Badge | of | Courage | [short rule] | Stephen Crane'. *Spine*: '[stamped in white] The | Red Badge | of | Courage | [orn.] | Stephen | Crane | HEINEMANN'. *Back*: '[stamped in white, within an ornamental frame] The Pioneer Series'.

Copy Examined: University of Virginia–Barrett 551546.

Notes: During January and February 1896 five more printings were called for, a 6d. printing was published in July 1900, and a 3/6 printing in April 1925. For further information and identifications, see M. J. Bruccoli and J. Katz, "Scholarship and Mere Artifacts: The British and Empire Publications of Stephen Crane," *Studies in Bibliography*, XXII (1969), 278–279. The original price was 3/–. The text ends on sig. N1 followed by four unsigned leaves of advertisements. The paper of these advertisements is the same as that of the text. Thus it seems probable that the advertisement leaves should be associated with the single text leaf, that these were printed to be bound as N^6 with a final blank cancelled, and that the preliminary fold π^2 was imposed with these six leaves to form the usual sixteen pages for printing a sheet.

Cheap Binding: Selling at 2/6 a paper-bound state was published in the Pioneer Series. This has a pictorial front: '[green] THE PIONEER SERIES. | [short rule] | [black] The Red Badge | of Courage. | [printed in black, yellow, and green within a single black rule-frame, Japanese woodcut of four figures, two carrying standards and two blowing long horns, with the Japanese calligraphic signature of the artist Utamaro] | [green] London: WILLIAM HEINEMANN'. The verso of the front is blank. *Spine*: 'The | Red Badge | of | Courage. | THE | PIONEER | SERIES. | [double rule] | 2/6 net | HEINEMANN'. *Back*: Advertisements for Heinemann's International Library, edited by Edmund Gosse (recto blank).

Copies Examined: British Museum (012601.i.30/10) rebound; University of Virginia–Barrett 551546.

The same plates but repaged were used by Heinemann for another form of the text, published in July, 1898, as *Pictures of War* followed by the repaged plates for Heinemann's *The Little Regiment* in one volume selling at 6/–. For a description of this edition, see *Tales of War*, WORKS, VI (1970), xlii–xliii, and Bruccoli and Katz, "Scholarship and Mere Artifacts," p. 280.

Six newspaper printings have been observed:

N^1: *New York Press*, Sunday, December 9, 1894, PART VII, pp. 4–6, headlined across the two first left-hand columns 'THE RED BADGE OF COURAGE || AN EPISODE OF THE AMERICAN CIVIL WAR || BY STEPHEN CRANE. | (Copyright, 1894, by the Author.)' The sixteen chapters of the newspaper version span seven columns on pages 4 and 5 and two-and-a-quarter columns on page 6. There are twelve small illustrations and an illustrated initial 'T' at the start of Chapter 1 (the initial shows the youth with a bandaged head seated and holding a flag with another soldier firing in the background); the captions read 'HE SPRANG FROM HIS BUNK.', 'HERE THE YOUTH FORGOT MANY THINGS.', 'DIRECTLY HE WAS WORKING.', 'HE SPED TOWARD THE REAR.', 'HE STOPPED, HORROR

STRICKEN.', ' "GAWD! JIM CONKLIN!" ', 'HE COULD HEAR THE TATTERED MAN BLEATING.', 'IT CRUSHED UPON THE YOUTH'S HEAD.', ' "YEH'VE BEEN GRAZED BY A BALL." ', ' "CHARGE! CHARGE!" ', 'WRENCHED THE FLAG FROM THE DEAD MAN.', and 'SEVERAL MEN CAME.' The *Press* was the only newspaper to print the entire novelette on one day.

N²: *The Philadelphia Press*, December 3, p. 11; December 4, p. 9; December 5, p. 10; December 6, p. 13; December 7, p. 11; and December 8, p. 11, decorated title across first two left-hand columns: THE RED BADGE | of COURAGE | [to the left: circular portrait of Crane seated at his desk writing, joined to a rectangular vignette of a soldier holding a rifle, seated on a log in front of a fire] | [in a scroll under portrait] BY STEPHEN CRANE | COPYRIGHT, 1894, BACHEL-LER, JOHNSON & BACHELLER.' The decorated title is signed 'Kauffman' and appears each day. On December 3, page 11, Chapters I–III are printed in columns 1–3 with two illustrations, ' "He Sprang from His Bunk." ' and ' "The Youth Forgot Many Things." ' On December 4, page 9, Chapters IV–V appear in the 6th and 7th columns with two illustrations, ' "Directly He Was Working." ' and ' "He Sped Towards the Rear." ' On December 5, page 10, Chapters VI–IX are in columns 4–8 with two illustrations, 'He Stopped, Horror Stricken.' and ' "Gawd! Jim Conklin!" ' On December 6, page 13, Chapters IX (continued)–XI are in columns 3–5 with two illustrations, ' "The Fourth Climbed a Fence." ' and ' "It crushed upon the Youth's Head." ' On December 7, page 11, Chapters XII and XIII are in columns 1–3 with two illustrations, ' "Yeh've Been Grazed by a Ball." ' and ' "Charge! Charge!" ' On December 8, page 11, Chapters XIV–XVI are in columns 4–6 with two illustrations, 'Wrenched the Flag from the Dead Man's Hand.' and 'Several Men Came.' The illustrations are the same as those used in the *New York Press*, but are redrawn. ' "The Fourth Climbed a Fence." ' is the same illustration as 'HE COULD HEAR THE TATTERED MAN BLEATING.'

N³: *Nebraska State Journal*, December 4, p. 4; December 5, p. 5; December 6, p. 5; December 7, p. 5; December 8, p. 5; and December 9, part II, p. 9. The decorated title is as in N² but appears only for December 4 and 5. The copyright notice is at the end of each day's appearance and reads: 'Copyrighted 1894.' on December 4 and 'Copyright, 1894.' on the remaining days. The beginning ornamental initial used in N¹ is present on December 4–8. On December 4, page 4, Chapters I–III are in columns 1–3 with the first two illustrations, apparently the same cuts as N¹ including the full-cap captions. On December 5, page 5, Chapters IV–VI are in columns 1–4 with the 3rd and 4th illustrations described in N¹. On December 6, page 5, under a different title: 'The Red Badge of Courage | . . . . . By STEPHEN CRANE . . . . . | [orn. rule]', Chapters VII–IX are printed in columns 1–4 with the 5th and 6th illustrations as in N¹. On December

7, page 5 (title as December 6), Chapters IX (continued)–XI are in columns 1–4 with the 7th and 8th illustrations. On December 8, page 5 (title as December 6), Chapters XII and XIII are in columns 1–4 with the 9th and 10th illustrations. On December 9, part II, page 9 (title as December 6), Chapters XIV–XVI are in columns 1–5 with the 11th and 12th illustrations.

N^4: *Kansas City Star*, December 3, p. 5; December 4, p. 10; December 5, p. 8; December 6, p. 8; December 7, p. 9; and December 8, p. 7 unsigned. The copyright notice 'Copyright, 1894.' comes at the end of each day. On December 3, page 5, the decorated title as in N^{2-3} appears with the beginning initial 'T' as in $N^{1,3}$ and Chapters I–III are printed in columns 1–3 using the same first two cuts described in $N^{1,3}$. On December 4, page 10, under the heading 'THE RED BADGE OF COURAGE: | BY STEPHEN CRANE ||', Chapters IV–VI are in columns 1–3 with the 3rd and 4th cuts as in $N^{1,3}$. On December 5, page 8, Chapters VII–IX are in columns 1–2 with the 5th and 6th cuts as in $N^{1,3}$. On December 6, page 8, Chapter IX (continued)–XI are in columns 1–2 with the 7th and 8th cuts as in $N^{1,3}$. On December 7, page 9, Chapters XII–XIII are in columns 1–2 with the 9th and 10th cuts as in $N^{1,3}$. On December 8, page 7, Chapters XIV–XVI (Chapters XIV and XV are printed in reverse order) are in columns 1–3 with the final two cuts as in $N^{1,3}$. December 5–8 have the same heading as December 4.

N^5: *Minneapolis Tribune*, December 4, p. 4; December 5, p. 4; December 6, p. 4; December 7, p. 4; December 8, p. 6; and December 10, p. 4. The decorative title used in N^{2-4} is present each day, and the notation '(Copyright.)' appears before the opening chapter on December 4–6. The illustrations are those described in N^1 and present in N^{3-4}, but the captions have been reset to make the illustrations the width of the column; the 11th cut, 'WRENCHED THE FLAG FROM THE DEAD MAN.', has been dropped from the final installment. On December 4, page 4, Chapters I–III are in columns 4–6. On December 5, page 4, Chapters IV–VI are in columns 4–6. On December 6, page 4, Chapters VII–IX are in columns 4–6. On December 7, page 4, under the notice, '(Copyright, 1894, by the Auther.)', Chapters IX (continued)–XI are in columns 4–6. On December 8, page 6 (with no copyright notice), Chapters XII and XIII (misnumbered III) are in columns 5–7. On December 10, page 4, Chapters XIV–XVI are in columns 5–7 (the copyright notice has the period outside the parentheses).

N^6: *San Francisco Examiner*, July 14, 1895, p. 25; July 21, p. 23; July 28, p. 24. A decorative title appears on all three days, '[superimposed on a scene of men marching with an officer on horseback] THE RED BADGE OF COURAGE | [circular vignette (also imposed on marching scene) of soldiers sitting around a camp fire] | AN | EPISODE | OF THE | AMERICAN | CIVIL WAR | [asterisk] | BY |

STEPHEN CRANE [to the left of 'AN . . . CRANE' a standing soldier with right arm raised firing a pistol cutting into the circular vignette above]'. Copyright notice appears at the end of the July 14 installment only, '(Copyright, 1894, by the Author.)'. On July 14, page 25, Chapters I–VIII are in columns 1–7 with two three-column illustrations, 'The Men Dropped Here and There Like Bundles.' and ' "Leave Me Be fer a Minnit; Leave Me Be, Can't Yeh?" ' On July 21, page 23, Chapters VIII (continued)–XI are in columns 1–5 with no illustrations. On July 28, page 24, Chapters XII–XVI are in columns 1–7 with one illustration, 'He Made a Spring and Clutched the Pole.' The decorative title and the illustrations are signed 'H. Nap.'

Appendixes

THE RED BADGE OF COURAGE

TEXTUAL NOTES

3.9 see, across,] The agreement of $N and Aɪ in 'see across it' indicates only what the typescript behind both read; and since there is no firm evidence that it was read over and corrected by Crane in both copies, or that this is a reading he would alter independently, the odds favor the assumption that the 'it' is the typist's addition to mend what would be considered a clumsy phrase. If so, it is unauthoritative and has no business in the text. For a somewhat clearer example of this agreement of Aɪ and $N in the typist's sophistication, see MS,MS(d) 'processes' but Aɪ,$N 'process' at 38.35; also, see the Textual Note to 38.24.

3.9 gleam] This is the reading of MS and Aɪ, and thus of TMs[b]. The plural 'gleams' in $N is typical of Crane's use of the plural but is not necessarily an authoritative alteration in TMs[a]. The final 'm' of 'gleam' ends in MS with a distinct hook that might be misread by a typist as intended 'ms'; but if the plural were the typist's misreading, then one would be forced to account for the singular in Aɪ as an alteration in New Orleans or later in proof. The simpler hypothesis is certainly to take it that the N editor, or compositor, wanted the plural 'gleams' to go with the plural 'camp-fires' and thus sophisticated the text.

3.28–29 another private] This revision in MS begins an interesting change in Crane's intentions. The original reading in MS (as in MS[d]) was 'young Wilson', which in the preliminary revision was changed to 'another soldier' in order to remove the name, and then, immediately, to 'another private'. This is the first of a series of alterations, whether in the preliminary or the general revision, substituting a descriptive formula for Wilson's name but in the process removing 'young' as an adjective applied to him. For instance, at 4.4 'young Wilson' becomes 'the loud one' in the general revision. At 12.11 'Wilson' was altered in the preliminary revision to 'The blatant young soldier', but in the general working-over the 'young' was deleted, as at 21.20 where 'young' from the preliminary alteration of 'Wilson' to 'the loud young soldier' is deleted. This omission of 'young' continues with no exceptions at 26.39, 27.4, 28.23, and 28.27 until Wilson disappears from the narrative for some chapters after giving Fleming a packet of letters to keep for him. Later, starting at 111.8, but possibly as early as 30.22 (where the manuscript is missing), the original formula in MS for Hasbrouck, which had been 'the youthful lieutenant', is altered simply to 'the lieutenant' (see the Textual Note to 111.8). It is evident that the excision of 'youthful' before 'lieutenant' is of a piece with the earlier deletion of 'young' for Wilson and is a conscious effort to isolate Fleming as 'the youth' in a world that to his eyes is experienced and mature. Up to the time, then, that Fleming returns to his regiment after his flight, in the final manuscript text no one else is ever referred to as *young* or as *youthful* and certainly not as *a youth*. The only reference that Crane did not weed out of the text was the adjective 'girlish' applied to Wilson's lip at 28.25, which is bracketed, however, by the excision of 'young' before 'loud soldier' at 28.23 and 28.27. Since in the general revision the preliminary's 'loud young soldier' had invariably been altered to 'loud soldier', it does not seem to be Crane's forgetfulness or carelessness—but instead his design—when, following Fleming's return to his regiment, wounded, the revision of the narrative of Wilson's care of him alters 'Wilson' to 'the loud young soldier', thus introducing for the first time the word 'young' in connection with Wilson. The change is a subtle one, for it seems probable that it reflects Fleming's development during his flight and return so that he now sees Wilson as his equal: he is 'the youth' and Wilson is, to him, 'the loud young soldier'. How subjective this phrase is supposed to be is demonstrated at 81.35–36 and 82.3–7. In the first, the revised text reads, 'At the fire-side, the loud young soldier watched over his comrade's wants with tenderness and care.' But once Wilson had fed Fleming and partly revived him, 'The youth took note of a remarkable change in his comrade since those days of camp-life upon the river-bank. He seemed no more to be continually regarding the proportions of his personal prowess. He was not furious at small words that pricked his conceits. He was, no more, a loud young soldier.' From this point, with one exception, Wilson is never 'young' or 'loud' again: his formula changes in the general revision to 'the friend', 'his comrade', 'the other', and the like, as illustrated, for instance, by the revision at 85.9 of 'His friend' interlined above deleted 'The young soldier'. The exception is an artful one. At 85.4 the youth remembers the packet of letters 'which the loud young soldier with lugubrious words had entrusted to him.' In the general revision this 'loud young soldier' is interlined above original 'Wilson' and is not a slip but instead a conscious reference back to what Wilson had been when he had given Fleming the letters at 28.21–36. At that time Wilson had indeed been immature (as in his 'girlish lip' and his morbid premonition of death) whereas now, at the return, battle had hardened him so that he was 'no more, the loud young soldier'. It would seem to follow that Crane originally excised in his revision all references to Wilson's youth (as also the lieutenant's) in order to concentrate the effect of 'youth' exclusively on Fleming. However, when Fleming returned to his regiment and was welcomed and comforted by Wilson, the importance of the change in Wilson from 'loud' to his new maturity seemed to call also for a temporary revival of 'young' in order to emphasize the feeling of comradeship that Fleming now felt for him but also, and more important, to highlight the change when Fleming perceived that Wilson had altered in the interval and 'was, no more, the loud young soldier.' The change in Fleming's perception of Wilson's maturity is, of course, reflected in his own, as worked out from his early pettishness in being cared for to his ultimate assumption of responsibility. Fleming remains 'the youth' because, it would seem, he is in age actually the youngest, but Wilson has become 'his comrade', a responsible young man in control of himself and with a superior maturity than Fleming had wrongly attributed to him at the start of the novel.

5.4 And, too,] One of Crane's most persistent characteristics is his use of 'too' to begin a sentence or, rarely, to begin a new clause after a conjunction. The passage about the chimney was revised in MS from MS(d) in order to insert the remark about the danger from fire, and in MS the added sentence originally began 'This flimsy chimney . . .' but Crane then reduced the capital 'T' and interlined preceding 'And'. It would seem that the real lack of connection between the two sentences fostered by the change was recognized when Crane was reviewing TMs^a, and that he added 'too' at that time in order to repair the awkwardness. Since he did not thereupon transfer the alteration to TMs^b, this conjectural early revision was lost except in N. It seems authorial, however, and worth preserving. Failure to transfer it to TMs^b or to recall it in New Orleans cannot be taken as rejection of the alteration. For examples of Crane's use of 'too' see 43.12, 72.28, 94.12, and 113.35.

5.26–27 or$_\wedge$ more timid] Crane is inconsistent in his punctuation after 'or'; see 8.35 where the phrase is repeated and is without the comma in all texts.

5.28 or$_\wedge$ else$_\wedge$] As with 5.26–27 above, when Crane repeats this statement at 8.37, he does not use commas.

6.2 told] Crane here used 'told' in MS(d) and MS in the sense of *indicated*; the A1 added 'him' is superfluous, somewhat alters the sense, and would seem to proceed from typist or editorial interference. Because of their closeness, the two A1 variants here and at 6.4 where 'Moreover' is substituted for MS 'Besides' must doubtless stand or fall together. The A1 change to 'Moreover' is a clear case of removing a jingle—'Besides, on her side'. Possibly Crane recognized the awkwardness although he was usually concerned with other matters in TMs^b. On the other hand, that the substitution in A1 was very likely editorial is suggested by the absence of any other use of *moreover* in this text. Crane freely employed *too, presently, and, but, still, nevertheless*, and any number of similar words, but not *moreover*. 'Besides' (in the form 'Beside') appears at 86.32.

6.12 winds] Since MS(d) reads 'wind', the plural here may be something of an inadvertency, like MS 'walls' for MS(d) 'wall' at 4.36. But in this case insufficient evidence is present to emend MS.

7.7 knet] Although MS(d) reads 'knit', the 'e' in MS 'knet' is clearly formed and appears to be intentional. One may compare MS(d) 'darn' but MS,A1 'dern' at 7.11.

7.9 git] The A1 form 'get' is more likely to be a typist's error than a change by Crane himself since it is the only normalization in A1 of the dialect in the mother's speech except for 7.30, A1 'forgit' for MS 'fergit'. In the general revision of the MS Crane had altered some of the mother's dialectal forms, but not consistently or thoroughly. It is clear that in this revision he intended the youth to speak more correctly than the mother but did not want the mother to have too thick a dialect. At 7.16 A1's 'an'' is a TMs misreading of the squeezed-in MS alteration of 'an' to 'and'.

7.16 'im] A1 ' 'em' appears to be the typist's misreading of none-too-legible MS ' 'im'. MS(d) 'him' confirms the reading, although the form in MS is quite certain.

7.29 Lord'll] MS 'Lord 'ill' is the only time that MS employs such a form instead of the conventional '*ll*. However, MS(d) used the '*ill* form for MS 'what'll' (11.4), 'boys'll' (11.29), and 'centre'll' (44.16); and for 'not'll' (55.27) MS(d) read 'not ull'. In each case MS copies these variants in the normalized form. On this evidence it can be ascertained that 'Lord 'ill' in MS represents an inadvertent use of a form of dialect that Crane had abandoned. The A1 variant 'Lord'll' adopted here may or may not be authoritative, since typist, editor, or compositor could readily have normalized it. However one can take it that A1 here conforms more closely to Crane's ultimate intentions than does MS.

9.18 advancing_^] The A1 omission of MS comma was well-advised. MS repeated the comma in MS(d) which had a different construction—'advancing, cursing relentlessly, and chewing'.

9.22 powder] A1 'powders' for MS 'powder' forms an odd variant, the authority of which must remain uncertain. On the one hand, the curious use of such plurals is characteristic of Crane; on the other, his care in altering TMs^b in this specific matter cannot be established and it is the editor's opinion that, except in one or two cases of MS error, the A1 variants between singular and plural are editorial, typist, or compositorial smoothings, with a few possible misreadings included. The phrase 'despondent powder' may have provoked misunderstanding. Its meaning seems to be *gunpowder that was weak and unsuitable*; MS(d) reads 'eternally hungry men who fired despondent rifles', which should mean much the same thing, for it is unlikely that Crane intended the men to fire despondently. 'Despondent rifles' must signify rifles that did not have powerful enough charges to shoot far (see 'fierce rifles' [127.27]). Thus 'despondent powder' goes back to the central claim for the ineffectiveness of the fire. Whether the MS singular 'powder' in Crane's view required alteration in A1 to the plural is far from certain.

9.27 fire_^] Crane ordinarily did not place a comma before the *and* in a series. In this case MS read originally 'smoke, fire, blood', the comma not being removed when the 'and' was interlined.

11.23 regiment'll] When revising his dialect Crane ordinarily did not disturb the youth's use of *reg'ment*, just as he left it alone here and at 91.7,8. However, the odds favor these lapses more as oversights than as intentions. It is significant that at 11.16, 11.31, and 12.1 in the initial revision of the tall soldier's dialect (later abandoned) original 'reg'ment' in MS was changed to 'regiment'.

12.3 four last] A1's change to 'last four' of MS,MS(d) 'four last' is not the kind of logical syntactical alteration one expects from Crane, whereas it would be natural for a purist editor (or even a typist) to restore strict sense. MS is here retained as the authoritative reading.

14.4 moods] The A1 variant 'mood' is taken to be a sophistication. Crane was much more likely, as in MS here, to fit plural to plural; moreover, experience with this text suggests that there is no system in the A1 changes of MS singulars to plurals or plurals to singulars and that they are likely in most cases to be unauthoritative.

14.16 courage‸ unseen] The A1 removal of the MS comma is correct, although its transfer after 'unseen' is of uncertain authority. The MS comma was inadvertently retained when Crane deleted a period after 'unseen' and continued the sentence during inscription. It is not likely that 'unseen' should be enclosed in commas.

14.28–29 tradition] As a general rule the not always consistent system of singulars and plurals in MS is more trustworthy than the frequent A1 normalizings. In the present case MS is certainly ambiguous at first sight, since 'the gods of tradition' could mean, as readily, *the traditional gods*, whereas it is clear that Crane actually meant *the gods who guard tradition*. The best illustration comes at 23.10–11, 'And there were iron laws of tradition and law on four sides' but also 67.31–32 'Yet they would receive laurels from tradition'. It seems evident that the copy for A1 resolved the ambiguity but at the expense of Crane's intentional singular with its special meaning to him.

14.31 considered to be] The A1 omission of 'to be' is very likely an editorial or compositorial sophistication. Crane was fond of this construction, as in 'His head seemed swollen to a size that made him think his neck to be inadequate' (72.15–16), or 'His friend perceiving him to be awake' (81.16), or 'he looked to be an insane soldier' (104.21–22), or 'They caused it to be as a craved treasure of mythology' (129.17–18).

16.14 rearward] Crane had no fixed method of writing this word. Here and at 65.16 and 111.15 he hyphenates it in MS; at 36.18, 70.3, and 126.5 it is 'rearward', the form somewhat arbitrarily chosen here for emendation from A1.

16.18–20 "I . . . soldier.] In the MS, Garland put a large pencil cross through these lines. Crane accepted only part of the deletion and in the final round of revision in pencil he strengthened the double quotes before ' "I' and added quotes after 'didn't I?' as a consequence of his pencil deletion of 'We're going up the river, cut across, an' come around in behint 'em." ' The typist in error seems to have omitted all of this dialogue, restored for the first time in the present edition, although either Crane or the Bacheller editor seems to have sought to rectify the gap by paraphrasing ' "Didn't I tell you?" ' but omitting, of course, ' "Huh . . . soldier.'

16.30 ahead‸ often,] The A1 compositor inserted a comma after 'ahead'; that this represents the wrong modification is shown by MS which originally read 'often to' (which would have followed 'hear') but the 'to' was deleted and 'expecting' then inscribed. That is, 'often' is intended to modify 'ahead', not 'expecting'. Although characteristically the MS has no punctuation here, an editorial comma seems useful to straighten out the syntactical ambiguity.

17.2 behind] MS 'behint' may be correct here and A1 'behind' a sophistication if the phrase is to be understood as enclosed within quotation marks. But the quotation marks are not present in MS, and it is just as possible that 'behint' is a careless repetition influenced by the dialectal form in the dialogue.

17.10 loud] A1 'blatant' is readily explicable as the TMs reading of original MS 'blatant' not too clearly altered to 'loud'. Unfortunately, N is wanting here to confirm the TMs misreading, but there is no likelihood that having abandoned 'blatant' for 'loud' as the formula for Wilson, Crane would revert to it in revising TMs^b. See, for instance, the A1 alteration to 'loud' of MS uncorrected 'blatant' at 19.36.

18.10 himself] The A1 'himself' might possibly derive from TMs^b although in MS the original 'himself' has been altered by firm horizontal ink strokes through 'self'. The word 'self' although quite legible is not perhaps so likely to have been typed in by error despite the deleting strokes. On the other hand, it is just possible that in New Orleans, where he could not have referred to MS, Crane restored the 'self' by the same stylistic impulse that had led to his original choice of the word. It is unfortunate that MS(d), but particularly that N, is missing here, for the latter would have given us the TMs reading and thus have pinpointed the source of the alteration. As it is, the restoration in A1 seems more authoritative as a second thought than the deletion as a first thought in MS.

19.19 suppose] Crane's carelessness in restoring correct speech to the youth from the original dialect of MS produces a number of anomalies that require editorial intervention to complete what appear to be his actual intentions. The form 's'pose' is a part of all the soldiers' dialect and also of the youth's original speech. On the other hand, at 26.37 in the initial revision of the tall soldier's dialect Crane altered Conklin's 's'pose' to 'suppose' among other changes. Acting on this hint, the editor has emended the residual 's'pose' in MS and A1 to the full form in line with other normalizations of Fleming's speech.

20.17 could] A1 'would' might or might not be authoritative, but the odds are that it is a typist error or an editorial change, especially when one observes 28.7 in which MS 'could' is changed in A1 to 'would' but the context shows that the alteration is wrong.

21.20 grumbling] Like many of the shifts from singular to plural, and the reverse, between MS and A1, this A1 alteration of MS 'grumbling' to 'grumblings' is difficult to adjudicate. In general it seems to be the better editorial practice to retain MS (especially in the absence of MS[d]) and to hold that only in exceptional circumstances would Crane himself have made such alterations in TMs^b or in proof. An editor might well object to the lack of coherence in the MS phrase 'perspiration and grumbling'. Clear signs of Crane's revision are wanting in the immediate area, also.

21.26–28 drink, . . . hotel?"] The A1 omissions in this MS passage were caused by the typist's misunderstanding. Crane had written the tall soldier's dialogue vertically in the left margin as an addition. Garland had then put a pencil cross through it which Crane ignored. However, the typist omitted the words through which the arms of Garland's cross passed. They are reprinted for the first time in this edition from the MS.

24.20 this] Reference to 'this march' in 25.18–19 suggests that A1 'the march' at 24.20 is an editorial sophistication, as before at 22.4. Crane's editors were likely to alter his characteristic 'this' to the.

26.11 front] Again, there is a question of Crane's concern for minutiae in his revision. MS 'front' describes the hills of dirt and stones the regiment had constructed and seems to be correct since the paragraph mentions the division of opinion in the regiment about constructing this protection, followed by its general acceptance. On the other hand, since the brigade is involved in this action, and the veterans on the flanks have been entrenching themselves, the A1 'regimental fronts' would describe the appearance of the whole body of troops within the brigade, separated by regiments. But the focus of the paragraph being on the youth's regiment, the A1 plural seems to be a misunderstanding or sophistication.

27.8 yit an' yit] The A1 alteration to simple 'and yet' of MS(c) 'yet and yet' is suspiciously like a sophistication to remove the awkward repetition, especially in view of the MS(c) revision of the MS(u) dialect to normal discourse. The A1 reading ''ave' for MS(c) 'have' (MS[u] 'a) does not indicate that Crane was tinkering in TMs[b] with this dialogue, for the alteration in MS was made so lightly that ''ave' is almost certainly the typist's misreading of the copy. On the other hand, a patch of what may be Crane's alterations on A1's next page at 27.33,35 and 28.5 and, shortly, at 28.36 suggests the possibility that Crane could have interfered here. In this case, however, the general authority of A1 may well give way to a suspicious alteration in suspicious circumstances.

27.33 stupidity] This A1 reading for MS 'stupidity affair' may be suspect as an editorial excision. However, it is clearly to be attributed to the same agent who removed the awkward 'that' in MS 'thought that' of the second line down and who probably removed 'unceasing' before 'skirmish-fire' later on the same page (28.5) and the repetitive 'the' before 'gossip' later at 29.7. No evidence is available to be sure that this corrector and reviser was Crane, but it may have been and the alterations are suitable enough to be authorial, especially the removal of 'unceasing', unless one were to speculate idly that 'unceasing' was misread by the typist as 'increasing' (which it much resembles) and 'the increasing skirmish-fire increased' called for automatic editorial or compositorial attention. One cannot feel easy in joining A1 in removing 'affair', but there seems little choice.

31.15 bellowing] If as seems likely the 'wild yells' of 30.40 came from the men who were fleeing, and not from the pursuers, then the throng was 'bellowing' as in $N, and A1's 'following' is a compositorial misreading. Moreover, the A1 word makes less sense in context. The throng presumed to be 'following' would need to be some unmentioned group that came after the 'mob-like body of men who galloped like wild-horses' of 31.1–2. No evidence is present except this A1 reading (which is itself ambiguous) that Crane thought of the men as fleeing in two groups—an advance body and then a 'following throng'. At least, in subsequent references such as 31.25–26 and others to 'the running men', or 'the stampede' (31.40), no distinction seems to be made.

31.30 jokes] In this place N[6] reading 'gibes' is the only witness against A1's 'jokes'. Something is to be said for 'gibes' by analogy with 'gibe-like' at 125.18. However, the odds favor A1, for at this point N[6] could have been set up only from the A1 proof; hence to make 'gibes' authorial one would need to postulate that it was also the A1 reading but changed in a later proof-stage to 'jokes'. This is possible but no evidence exists in its favor. Moreover, this reading cannot be dissociated from the further variant in the next line, in which A1 reads 'apparently were' whereas N⁶ has 'were apparently'. Here neither reading has any intrinsic superiority; but in two such cases to put the known fallibility of N⁶ up against the comparative respectability of A1 for a choice of readings would be venturesome indeed without stronger cases for the authorial nature of the N⁶ variants. For example, with 'apparently were' one may compare 'plainly be' at 110.11 altered in N¹⁻⁵ to 'be plainly' but the A1 proof followed here by N⁶.

32.7 thought$_\Lambda$] The agreement of N⁴,⁶ with A1 in no comma here, versus the expectable parenthetic comma of N¹⁻³,⁵ practically demonstrates the lack of a comma in TMs.

34.36 moments] The reading 'For moments' in MS followed by $N indicates the TMs fidelity to MS. Thus the A1 'For some moments' is either an editorial or compositorial change, a part of Crane's revision of TMs^b, or else a late proof-change. This variant is part of a cluster in A1 comprising the addition of 'was' at 34.38, which is not entirely necessary, an unrequired change from Crane's plural 'thoughts' to 'thought' at 35.11, and one from 'who' to 'which' at 35.29, all of which have been rejected in the present edition in favor of MS readings. It is worth notice that the MS phrase *for moments* is also found at 47.39 without the qualifying 'some'. It may be that the same agent somewhat later made editorial improvements that are required from MS 'was' to 'were' at 36.21 and of Crane's idiomatic 'near' to 'nearly' at 36.22.

36.11 furiously] Agreement of N⁶, which in this place must have been set from A1 early proof, with MS in 'feverishly' versus A1 'furiously', establishes 'furiously' as a late alteration in proof, and so with the omission of 'flapped and' before 'bobbed' in A1 at 36.13. To know that these are proof-corrections is not to know whether they are Crane's or an editor's; but on Hitchcock's evidence we know that Crane did read proof in the summer of 1895, after his return from Mexico, and it is easy enough to accept these two variants as his.

38.24 emblems] Although in MS the final 's' is squeezed in at the right margin, probably as an addition, the reading of TMs with the plural is indicated by $N, even though by a compositorial slip N¹⁻⁵ omit the preceding 'the', which N⁶ picks up from A1. The A1 singular, thus, may be narrowed down to Crane's revision of TMs^b or to a compositorial fault, almost certainly the latter since the plural is required to agree with 'They' immediately following and with 'flags' at 38.22. In a similarly unauthoritative manner, below at 38.35 A1 changes MS,MS(d) 'processes' to 'process', but here the agreement of $N with A1 shows that the typist was to blame.

39.19 coat-sleeve] The A1 plural appears to be in error despite the lack of a nearby plural to serve as a contaminating source except for the distant 'fellows' of 39.17. One may compare 34.21–22, 'He frequently with a nervous movement wiped his eyes with his coat-sleeve.' At 117.28–29 the plural is correctly used in 'And they polished at their swollen and watery features with coat-sleeves and bunches of grass.'

39.25 only] The A1 omission of MS,MS(d) 'only' destroys the sense and appears to be an unauthoritative smoothing of Crane's rough writing. The contrast is between the youth's feeling *now* 'the bonds of tied hearts' with men whose names he did not know but with whom he was casually acquainted from seeing their faces. It is true that this editorial or compositorial intervention appears in A1 only a line above a necessary change from MS 'Fleming' to 'the youth'; but not all of these name changes can be attributed to Crane and some are very likely editorial since the absolute consistency of A1 in this respect is more than could be expected from Crane's survey of TMs[b] in New Orleans. If the omission of 'only' is non-authorial, then other small changes in this immediate area are called in question. One is the change from MS,MS(d) 'the' to A1 'that' at 39.12, perhaps intended to bridge the gap in reference between chapters. Another is the shift in A1 at 39.22 from the MS,MS(d) hesitation ''til—'til' to simple ''til'. These are also to be associated with the unauthoritative A1 shift at 39.19 from the singular 'coat-sleeve' to the plural, noticed in the Textual Note above.

40.34 back] The A1 'neck' is not an impossible alteration for Crane to have made in TMs[b] and it might be accepted instead of MS (and TMs) 'back' were it not for a clear-cut editorial or compositorial change only a few lines later whereby Crane's wholly characteristic use of 'appear' in MS and MS(d) seems to have troubled the editor or compositor—and indeed it is strained—who substituted 'recur'. It seems probable that the same agent made both changes; the unlikelihood of the second one being authorial infects the first.

42.7 headlong] The A1 form as emended here from MS 'head-long' is the more common, as in MS at 51.27, 65.31, and 105.24. Interestingly, although at 65.31 MS reads 'headlong', MS(d) has 'head-long' as an example of Crane's inconsistency.

42.27 heard them] Any isolated A1 variant like 'listened' for MS 'heard them' is subject to some suspicion, particularly when it modifies an awkwardness such as 'As he heard them, he imagined them'. Of course, authorial attention in TMs[b] is not impossible; but when this smoothing-out is associated with an even more suspiciously editorial smoothing of the MS repetition 'his way in his chosen direction', the odds begin to favor unauthoritative editing of the style. The variants in this general area, beginning at least as early as 'emblem' at 38.24 and carrying through the manifestly unauthoritative A1 'stopped' at 41.20, do not appear to come from Crane's alterations in TMs[b]. Indeed, true alterations do not certainly resume until the cut at 46.13. (Changes in the name at 43.3 are not necessarily authorial.)

43.10 deep] Proper grammar calls for the adverb 'deeply' here, which A1 naturally supplies, on the analogy of the more necessary grammatical changes of MS 'near' to A1 'nearly' (36.22) or MS 'like' to 'likely' (22.4). In contrast to these, however, the adjective 'deep' is idiomatically permissible and has been retained as characteristic of Crane's style if not of his sometimes uncertain grammar.

44.18 chesnut] This is an acceptable old-fashioned spelling that Crane preferred (or one that represents a mishearing or simple misspelling). In pencil Garland altered MS to 'chestnut', presumably followed by TMs and reproduced in A1.

44.26 'em . . . 'em] The pronouns in the general's speech are inconsistent. In line 26 MS, MS(d), and A1 read ' 'im' ($N variant with 'them'), but when in line 34 the same words are repeated, MS (MS[d] wanting) reads 'They've held 'em' with the 'e' of ' 'em' written currently over the 'i' of ' 'im'. Moreover, although the repeated MS 'wallop 'im' followed by A1 in lines 27–28 continues the ' 'im' pronoun, in MS(d) the first pronoun is 'em' and the second is 'em' altered from 'im'. An argument could be advanced that the general is speaking of his opposite number, the Confederate general, as ' 'im', or that the pronoun personifies the enemy. On the other hand, the later MS shift to ' 'em' in repeating the original words, combined with the inconsistency exhibited in MS(d) as to the intention, suggests that Crane's purpose was to use ' 'em' throughout but that his carelessness prevented the desirable uniformity developing from the confusion. $N agree with ' 'em' in the second series.

46.11 little] The A1 omission of MS 'little' appears to represent an editorial or compositorial misunderstanding. The whole context indicates that the youth did not think his guilt great, and the punishment equal to it, but instead that a great punishment awaited him for his little guilt. Otherwise, the 'words' (to protest his innocence) would not be required. This is an example of serious A1 sophistication that is by no means unique.

46.37 nature] Everywhere else in MS and MS(d) Crane wrote 'nature' although A1 regularly capitalized it as an editorial or compositorial alteration. In MS at this point the minuscule 'n' has been mended from a form that might have been misread as a majuscule. In view of this clear indication of intention, and of the usual practice elsewhere, MS is here transcribed as 'nature'.

47.35 opened] Despite the parallel 'The mouth was open' at 58.25 found in all authorities, in the present case the change from MS(d), MS, and $N(−N²) 'opened' to A1 'open' is an alteration of an original reading, one made either in TMs^b or unauthoritatively in the editing or printing. Especially in view of the N² sophistication of its copy to 'open', which shows the pull toward the conventional, the odds seem to favor A1 departure from MS authority. Little evidence appears that in New Orleans Crane occupied himself with such small matters.

48.19 sighingly] The chief argument for A1 'soughingly' instead of MS 'sighingly' is that it comes in the last paragraph of a chapter, where Crane was likely to pay particular attention to his language (as for example in his changes at 28.36 and 62.21). Against A1 is the fact that 'soughing' may not be used elsewhere in Crane (precise information is wanting). In itself this would be insufficient grounds for rejection; but in this case the fact that $N read 'slightly' suggests that its sophistication may have arisen from a typist's error which was also emended independently by A1 as 'soughingly'. This evidence for double error appears to maintain MS 'sighingly' as the only authoritative reading.

49.1 sun] Just so, in the last sentence of Chapter IX, Crane in TMs^b removed an adjective, changing MS,$N 'fierce wafer' to A1 'wafer'.

50.13 was] N^6—the only N witness here—sophisticated MS,A1 'thought' to 'thoughts' to agree with the plural verb 'were'. But the A1 correction is required. The plural 'were' in MS resulted from Crane's careless revision of MS(d) 'All his accumulations upon such subjects were used', not from a mistake in writing 'thought' for 'thoughts'.

51.7 was mingled] On the analogy of the $N change of MS,MS(d) 'was' to 'were', the A1 omission of the verb, thus changing 'mingled' from passive to active, appears to have been editorial in order to avoid a grammatical difficulty characteristic of Crane.

52.10 road-way] Crane was not consistent in his division of this word, found sometimes as 'roadway' in MS here and at 69.2 (this latter also in MS[d]). But the word is hyphenated in MS at 63.5, 71.21, 72.3, 100.12, and 134.21.

54.3 others] The agreement of $N with A1 in 'the others' appears to show the typist's alteration of MS 'others', part of an admittedly awkward phrase easily sophisticated.

55.19 their tragedies] The A1 insertion of 'own' is almost inevitable and is more likely to be editorial or compositorial than Crane's. Logically, of course, 'own' is not required, for the soldiers had not assisted in any physical manner the tall soldier's dragging his tragedy rearward.

55.38 pretty] A1's addition of 'a' before 'pretty' is a relatively clear indication of unauthoritative intervention. Conklin's language in his agony is like Pete's drunken speech in *Maggie*. With 'I've allus been pretty good feller, ain't I?' one may set up Pete's 'Yer damn goo f'ler', 'I'm damn goo' f'ler', 'I allus been goo' f'ler wi'yehs, ain't I, Nell?' and so on (WORKS, I, 72–73).

58.20 Gawd] The tattered soldier speaks in dialect throughout and there would be little point in normalizing him here. Apparently, Crane in error altered 'Gawd' in MS to 'God' as part of the general revision as if the exclamation came from the youth, whose dialect is normalized to regular speech.

60.28 infernal, tooty- . . . -too,] The A1 omission of this substitute for profanity looks like an editorial intervention, chiefly because of the inapposite exclamation point placed in A1 after 'infernal' with a following single quote, which makes little sense except as signs of a removal of material. It may be, of course, that Crane came to have second thoughts, especially since here and there in the text he himself reduced the swearing when writing MS from its MS(d) form. But whether he would have such second thoughts about 'tooty-tooty-tooty-too' is more problematic. It may seem likely that if he had himself removed the profanity here he might have substituted one or more dashes in the conventional manner. The omission of anything even mildly suggesting profanity combined with the oddly placed exclamation point (as if 'infernal' were a noun and not an adjective) appears to point to some outside agent, probably in TMs^b before typesetting. The omission of MS 'dumb' in A1 at 60.32 before 'skeared' may be another example, despite the earlier use of 'dumb' for this purpose, and its unexampled mildness.

61.25 hate] Despite the fact that this A1 variant of 'hatred' for MS 'hate' occurs in an area where Crane quite obviously had worked over TMs^b, it still appears to be more an editorial or compositorial variant of Crane's characteristic language than an authorial alteration. Crane used 'hate' as a noun frequently, as at 66.6, 95.29, 96.21, and 117.5. One can also find 'hatred', although somewhat clustered, at 124.17, 125.27, and 129.16.

62.9 fields] Like the variant above in A1 for 'hate', the A1 change of MS 'fields' to 'field' occurs in an area of authorial revision, but nevertheless appears to be an editorial or compositorial rationalization. Literally conceived, the tattered man might not have had time before the youth looked back to leave the specific field where the tragedy of the tall soldier had taken place. But the youth turned 'at a distance', and hence one cannot appeal to literalness in this reading. More to the point, at 71.25 precisely the same variant is found in A1 for MS,$N 'fields' in circumstances where no very good argument could be advanced for the specific use of the singular. Moreover, in almost every case of divergence between MS and A1 in these plurals and singulars, MS has proved to be the safer guide for an editor.

68.4 bethink] This A1 form of MS 'be-think' is doubtless not an authorial change, but the emendation brings the word into line with the MS(d) agreement here, with an unhyphenated form in MS at 107.3 and with MS 'bethought' at 75.2.

71.25 fields] As at 62.9, the A1 singular for MS plural appears to be in error. From the plural 'fields' in 72.3, for instance, it would appear that Crane is describing the coming of evening to the whole scene, not merely to one specific field in which the artillery was assembled.

72.1 blue_∧] The A1 omission of the MS comma is right. The comma in MS was written when the phrase was 'blue, sombre' and was not deleted when 'and' was inserted.

75.30 comrade] The A1 plural 'comrades' appears to be a sophistication, probably based on 75.2–5: 'As he reeled, he bethought him of the welcome his comrades would give him. He had a conviction that he would soon feel in his sore heart the barbed missiles of ridicule.' However, the MS singular 'comrade' is right in context. Only Wilson at this point knew of his return; hence his sleeping 'comrades' could scarcely have missiles 'already' at their lips. The remark can apply only to Wilson, who is properly described as 'redoubtable'.

76.1 Terrible] The youth's dialect on MS pages 113–114 was not corrected, and indeed the lack of alteration of the names *Fleming* and *Wilson* shows that in some manner Crane skipped the final revision of MS pages 112–114 (75.1–77.8 awkwardly |). The editor's duty is to restore the author's intention even when in A1, in part, the full series of necessary changes was not made in this area to bring the readings into conformity with Crane's changes before and after.

78.4 snoring$_\wedge$] The MS comma after 'snoring', removed correctly by A1, was written when the series read 'snoring, heaving, or lying' and by error was not removed when in the general revision 'and' was interlined.

78.21 companion] The expected word here would be 'companions', and the agreement of A1 with the MS singular may mean only agreement in a careless mistake in writing. (Unfortunately, MS[d] is not preserved here as a check.) Emendation is tempting, but the conservative position is to take it that Crane envisaged soldiers sleeping side by side with their particular friends so that 'the companion' here would be this comrade on whom the suddenly awaking soldier relied. For instance, one may compare Wilson's proposal to sleep next to the youth at 79.26–27. In general, MS is a relatively trustworthy guide to these vexed questions of singulars and plurals.

79.3 contemplated] The authority of this isolated variant in A1 for MS 'looked at' may be attested by such other examples as 'He sat down then and contemplated the youth's appetite with glee' (82.1–2).

81.12 eye-sockets.] The omission of $N and A1 of the succeeding sentence in MS 'It was the soldier's bath.' could have occurred only as a result of (1) the typist's omission; (2) Crane's catching the phrase in TMs^a when he altered 'Fleming' to 'The youth' at the start of the paragraph in the line below, and at the time making the same excision in TMs^b; (3) Crane's excising the phrase as in (2) above but then deleting it, independently, on his memory of the offending words when he was working over TMs^b in New Orleans. The omission in error in TMs is of course the simplest explanation but is undemonstrable. If it indeed occurred, it would have been the only example in the text of such a major omission during the typing. On the other hand, the analysis of the $N,A1 variants in the Textual History and Analysis suggests strongly that (2) is unlikely. The third possibility is far from demonstrable, but such a hypothesis fits the known facts, and the nature of the deletion suggests something more than a typist error. It is indeed a jejune sentence that Crane could have remembered for omission on a later occasion. The addition both in $N and A1 of 'the' before 'eye-sockets', characteristically wanting in MS, suggests here the typist's sophistication, not an authorial insertion at two different times consequent upon the deletion of the offending sentence. On the whole, then, although any explanation other than a typist's error has its complexities, the removal in this case of 'It was the soldier's bath.' seems to have been authoritative.

81.20 little] Were it not that this A1 variant from MS 'bitter' is within a series of pages containing a number of Crane's alterations in TMs^b, it might be seriously queried, for the reason for the change is obscure, and 'bitter' associates itself with other uses at 19.18, 90.32, 108.8, 117.23, and 125.21.

82.35 deprecatory] The A1 changes of MS 'deprecatory' and 'conciliatory' (91.25) to 'deprecating' and 'conciliating' are clear-cut editorial interventions. The case of 'conciliatory' is the more obvious, since although it is common enough in the United States, the O.E.D. lists only three appearances—in 1576, 1777, and 1855. It is evident that Hitchcock or some other Appleton editor was concerned with what he would have regarded as Crane's misuse of these two words. Actually, the line between *deprecatory* and *deprecating* in the present context is a thin one, but a purist might prefer 'deprecating'. It is interesting to see that 'deprecatory' later at 84.14 was missed by the editor and so appears in A1 in its MS form.

86.19–20 circumstance] The authority of this change as one made in TMs^b and reproduced in A1 is clear. The MS had read 'nature' in reference to 'The long tirades against nature' in a passage deleted from MS in TMs^b (see Historical Collation, 86.17). The excision of this reference caused Crane to alter 'nature' at 86.19–20 to 'circumstance', perhaps to agree with 'fortunes of yesterday' in 86.14.

89.1 spluttering] In this place MS reads 'sputtering', followed by $N and A1 so that there can be no doubt of the TMs reading as well. Moreover, a few lines down in the MS (89.3), Crane interlined 'thudding' above a second but deleted 'sputtering', an effective demonstration that it was, in fact, the word he had in mind at this point. Significantly, however, 'sputter' appears nowhere else in the text of MS and A1: both invariably read 'splutter' as in 'the protesting splutter of musketry became a steadied roar' (106.13); in 'with their faces toward the spluttering woods' (110.6), where 'spluttering' is interlined above deleted 'spattering'; in 'A spluttering sound had begun in the woods' (123.23); and 'from behind which spluttered the fierce rifles of the enemies' (127.27). These quotations indicate that Crane was attempting no fine distinction between 'splutter' and 'sputter' for the sound of rifle fire: 'splutter' was quite definitely what he wanted, on the evidence of every other use. The only variant is the single use of 'splatter' at 79.36, which is certainly intentional because it was interlined above deleted 'splutter'. Presumably, the 'spattering' revised to 'spluttering' at 110.6 is to 'splatter' as 'sputter' is to 'splutter'. (Unfortunately there is no draft manuscript at these two places.) Under the circumstances, the use of the 'sputter' form at 89.1 can only have been inadvertent, even though initially repeated, and should be emended to conform to his preference elsewhere. That 'splutter' is a relatively unusual word in its use here is suggested by the $N sophistication to 'sputter' at 106.13 and 110.6. The newspapers are not present for the final two uses.

90.1–2 uproar] The hyphenation in MS here is not paralleled by the form 'uproar' at 37.12 and 49.28. Crane was not consistent in his division of this word, but he may slightly have preferred the more conventional form, as emended here from A1.

90.5 black] MS here reads 'black and croaking', $N simple 'croaking', and A1 simple 'black'. It follows that TMs must have agreed with MS and that Crane independently altered the reading in TMs^a and then in TMs^b, later. If so, each variant, being independent, is of technically equal authority; however, it is convenient to take Crane's last version even though it is unlikely he remembered in New Orleans how he had altered the phrase for Bacheller.

90.7 omens] The agreement of N^6 with MS in 'many omens', although N^6 at this point must have been set from early proof of A1, indicates that the excision of 'many' in A1 was a late proof-revision. As such, it must be credited to Crane.

90.23 sentence] In view of Crane's use of the singular 'sentence' shortly before at 90.14 in the same context, the A1 plural appears to be an editorial attempt to help out the awkwardness of Crane's second construction.

91.15 generals'] The shift in A1 to the genitive singular from MS plural is probably unauthoritative, under the influence of the free use of the singular 'the commander of the forces' at 90.33–34, 'his fault' at 90.35, and, especially, below at 91.17–18 'some derned old lunkhead of a general'. However, in MS Crane first wrote 'general's' and then deleted the apostrophe to place it after the final 's', thus indicating what we must take as his final intention. In his manuscripts Crane often misplaces the apostrophe to make an apparent singular when he clearly intends a plural, but not *vice versa*. The youth is evidently expanding the fault back to the plural 'lunkheads' he had used at 90.25, and then narrowing it to their specific commander in the next sentence at 158.18.

91.22 Inward] A1 'Inwardly' is an obvious editorial attempt at correcting Crane's grammar. For Crane's frequent use of an adjective for an adverb, see the Textual Note to 43.10.

91.25 conciliatory] For the lack of authority in A1's change to 'conciliating', see the Textual Note to 82.35.

92.5 cleared] MS 'clearer' is almost certainly an error, for the comparative here has no previous reference. The troops have been 'sifting through the forest' (91.37). Very likely MS intended 'cleared space' as at 100.3, 104.23–24, and 122.13. The A1 'clear' appears to be a simple sophistication.

92.9 yelpings] The A1 variant 'yellings' may derive from a TMs misreading of MS. In MS 'yelpings' is interlined above deleted 'noise', and though scrutiny shows that the letter is indeed a 'p' and not an 'l', the smaller inscription and the loop on the 'p' could have made the word subject to mistranscription. For 'yelpings' see 125.17. Crane used 'yelling' at 67.23 and 90.21 and 'yelled' at 54.27, but these are all associated with human cries.

92.35 began] Original MS 'begin' was altered to 'began' as part of the general revision of the youth's dialect. A1 'begin' seems to derive from TMs, which must have misread the alteration since the dot over the 'i' had not been deleted and the 'a' was none too clear.

92.36;93.2 Me] The capitalization for emphasis is Crane's own in MS since he deleted original 'me' in order to interline 'Me' above it. That this was a current alteration is no doubt shown by original 'Me' in 93.2. Possibly Crane's intention was to have the printer set the words in small capitals, as ME.

93.5 There's] This emendation of MS,A1 'There' is drawn from the first English edition, which is without authority but was correcting what seemed to be an error. Such as it is, the evidence favors the view that MS was indeed in error here and passed on the mistake to A1, not that Crane was producing a special idiomatic effect. In similar context at 60.15 MS had had a similar error, passed on to A1 also, but that 'There' was mere carelessness is shown by correct 'There's' in MS(d).

94.10 uninitiated] The 'u' of the MS error 'unitiated' is clearly formed and has no dot, so that the A1 reading 'uninitiated' seems correct, not a sophistication of MS 'initiated'. Thus the contrast is not between the 'various scenes' and 'the processes of war', each discussed with experienced men; instead, the contrast lies in his description to inexperienced soldiers of the scenes he had observed whereas he would discuss tactics with other men who, like himself, had been fleshed.

94.30 hatefully] The slight possibility exists that A1 'hatefully' is the typist's misreading of MS 'balefully', but unfortunately the newspapers are not present here to confirm. The initial 'b' does indeed suggest an 'h' and the 'l' could have been mistaken for an uncrossed 't'. On the other hand, 'hatefully' is established as a word Crane could employ by the sentence in *The Third Violet*, Chapter XI (65.24–25 of A1), 'He glared hatefully at her and strode away.' The word 'balefully' itself may have displeased Crane. It is not likely that he objected to the alliteration 'burning balefully' in view of 'poor and puny' shortly after at 95.10, 'stormy spectre' (95.12), 'pitiful plights' (95.15), 'flashed in its front' (95.17), 'regiment roared' (95.18), 'settled slowly' (95.19), and 'slit and slashed' (95.20), all on the next page of A1.

95.17 others] The MS reading 'brothers' is by no means impossible, and thus there is always the chance that A1 'others' is a sophistication somewhere in the transmission. Yet the reading makes sense since it refers back to the initial statement about the single rifle, at 93.23–24: 'A single rifle flashed in a thicket before the regiment. In an instant, it was joined by many others.' It is also worthy of note that only a few lines below appears a fairly certain Crane alteration in A1, 'resembled' for 'were like' (95.21).

100.2 hurlying] Crane seems to have invented this word, as found in MS, from associations with *hurly-burly*. The A1 reading 'hurling' is almost certainly editorial and makes what would be good enough sense: *rushing impetuously or violently*, sometimes in association with *whirling*. However, it is unlikely that Crane confused 'hurlying' with 'hurling', and thus his nonce word should be preserved.

100.16 flip-flapping] In this case editor or compositor has corrected what appears to be the MS error 'flip-flopping', which had been copied in TMs on the evidence of $N. The latter would mean a somersault or turning end for end. Only a defective shell would *flip-flop* through the air; that shells were not flip-flopping when striking the ground before exploding is sufficiently indicated by the order in MS, 'flip-flopping and hooting'. Crane must have meant *flip-flapping* but confused the word. A1 correctly signifies *a repeated flapping sound*, which appropriately distinguishes itself from 'hooting'.

102.5 Fleming] Without consulting the manuscript, editors have customarily emended this passage by reversing the names and having Wilson (not Fleming) answer the direct accusation of lying in response to the soldiers' accusation of Wilson by name and then the youth backing him up (102.3–7). In fact, this 'correction' restores the original inscription of the manuscript before the general revision in which Crane not only interlined 'the youth' above deleted 'Wilson' but also altered to normal discourse three dialect forms in the speech reassigned to the youth while retaining the original dialect of the first inscription in Fleming's speech, now appropriate for Wilson. It seems impossible in view of the manuscript changes to argue that Crane mistook his men. Instead, he made a conscious revision which placed the youth in a position of leadership but which at any events maintained him as the primary character observing the incident with the general and, appropriately, reporting its conclusion. However, with typical carelessness this change in the characters was not brought into context by necessary alterations of the preceding action to take account of the switch. It seems incumbent on an editor not to take the easiest way out, which is to ignore Crane's expressed desire to revise the passage and to revert to the original that he wanted to change. Instead, the passage should be revised to conform to Crane's intention in a manner he would have done if he had not overlooked the need. This editorial revision (once Crane's change of 'Wilson' to 'the youth' and of 'Fleming' to 'his friend' [102.6 and 102.8] has been accepted) consists in assigning the news to Fleming, with appropriate speech, by altering MS ' "We're goin' t' charge—we're goin' t' charge," cried the youth's friend, hastening with his news' (101.37) to ' "We're going to charge—we're going to charge," cried the youth, hastening with his news.' Then at 102.5 the unrevised 'Wilson, you're lien' " ' is editorially altered to 'Fleming, you're lien' " ', after which Crane's own revision takes over in which he altered ' "I hope t' die," said Wilson. . . . "Sure as shootin' I tell yeh" ' to ' "I hope to die," said the youth. . . . "Sure as shooting, I tell you" ' and in the next paragraph also altered 'And Fleming spoke in reinforcement' to 'And his friend spoke in reinforcement.'

102.15 soldier] The A1 variant 'man' is not in any area of Crane's revision and appears to be an editorial attempt to avoid the possibly confusing repetition of 'soldier' in 102.13–14,15 for two different men, Wilson and someone in the ranks. However, the change to 'man' provokes an awkward clash, 'One man had a final objection . . . but the men, for a large part, nodded.'

102.39–103.1 his friend.] After this sentence, N adds, 'It was as if he had been stunned.' Variant readings from N are always to be viewed with caution, but the present case might perhaps represent an alteration in TMs* later forgotten. The distinctive locution starting a sentence 'It was as if' is highly characteristic of Crane, as in 'It was as if a thousand axes, wee and invisible, were being wielded' (30.19–20), 'It was as if he had hit his fingers with a tack-hammer at home' (30.25–26), 'It was as if seven hundred new bonnets were being tried on' (33.16–17), 'When they spoke it was as if they considered their listener to be a mile away' (130.17–19), and 'It was as if a clumsy clod had trod upon his toe' (130.32–33). At 110.27 'stunned' appears in 'The greater part of the men . . . acted as if stunned.' On the other hand, the inappositeness of the sentence suggests at least the possibility that the Bacheller editor was touching up a dramatic scene. A 'quick, enquiring glance' is not a description of the look of a stunned man. And the continuation, 'Still, they saw no hesitation in each other's faces' does not go with *stunned*, nor does their possession of 'an ironical secret'. One cannot be sure that Crane did not himself gild the lily here, but it would seem that at least as strong a presumption exists for the heavy hand of the Bacheller editor.

103.7 swallered] The A1 normalization 'swallowed' is either a typist's or printer's sophistication, perhaps to clarify the word intended. No reason is apparent why Crane would have altered TMs^b to normalize the dialect of a common soldier.

105.25 took mechanical] MS originally read 'took a mechanical but firm impression', but Crane then added a final 's' to make the plural 'impressions' without going back to delete the 'a' that had governed the singular. The typist, most probably, was influenced by the 'a' and ignored the added 's'; but there can be no doubt as to Crane's final intention.

110.3 coming] The 'going' found in $N at this point is no doubt the Bacheller editor's alteration. From the point of view of the youth and his friend, the regiment was indeed going back. From that of the main body not participating in the charge, it was 'coming', and this would also be true for those in the rear of the charge to whom it would appear that the forward men were 'coming' back. Actually, 'coming' is used very much in the sense of 'falling back' as in 110.20.

110.13 speeches] A1 'screeches' is very likely an editorial sophistication of what may have seemed an error or an inapposite word found in TMs deriving from MS and reproduced in $N. At 112.4 'screechings' is used for the noise of shells, and at 59.8 'The youth desired to screech out his grief'. These illustrate the improbability of 'screeches' here, whereas 'speeches' is found at 117.23 also in something of a strained sense. Of as much importance as the debatable idiomatic use of the A1 variant for Crane is the fact that this reading appears in a stretch where no other evidence exists for Crane's revisory hand.

111.8 lieutenant] This is the first of five places in which Crane failed to delete the prefixed adjective 'youthful' before 'lieutenant', the others being 113.25, 113.37, 117.10, and 121.7. The facts are as follows. When in the preliminary revision Crane began to change Fleming to 'the youth' he became aware of a duplication with the adjective 'young' often applied to Wilson, and he twice dropped it. Later, in the general revision, he systematically removed all references to Wilson as 'young' before Fleming's flight in order to emphasize Fleming's own feeling of youthfulness surrounded by a mature world (see Textual Note to 3.28–29). The lieutenant

makes his first entrance at 25.28 as 'the young lieutenant' and again at
29.26 by name only but thereafter in the original inscription he was
labeled 'the youthful lieutenant'. In the general revision, starting with
36.25, Crane deleted this adjective 'youthful' some seventeen times.
(Actually the figure could be nineteen, for it is 'the lieutenant' at 30.22
and 30.31 in A1 where MS is missing, and one should also add the
general-revision deletion of 'young' in 'the insane young lieutenant' at
MS 188.3 in a passage following 'upon his conduct.' [134.4] omitted in
A1. At first the deletion was systematic, eleven times between 36.25 and
110.9 with no exceptions. Then in what appears to be a relaxation in his
carefulness, although not in his intentions, he overlooked a 'youthful' on
MS 159.7 (111.8), which is thus preserved in TMs and thence transferred
to $N and A1. Continuing, at MS 160.7 (112.1) and MS 162.1 (113.12)
he crossed out 'youthful' but slipped lower on fol. 162 where the second
and third occurrences on the sheet are untouched (113.25,37). The same
situation holds in the next appearances, on MS fol. 167, where at 117.1
'youthful' is deleted but lower down is untouched at 117.10. Crane again
overlooked 'youthful' at 121.7 but then deleted its final two occurrences, at
124.28 and 126.13. Because of the run of eleven (perhaps thirteen) deletions at the start, the sporadic retentions toward the end of the novel
appear to have no significance. In the area where 'youthful' is unaltered,
no differences in its use or in the narrative situation exist from the con-
texts where it has been deleted. Given Crane's known carelessness, it seems
clear that in the MS he intended 'youthful' to be removed altogether but
overlooked five occurrences, none of which he spotted when he reviewed
TMs^b in New Orleans. The evidence is sufficiently clear to permit an editor
to fulfill Crane's manifest intentions by editorially striking out the five
cases of his oversight and retaining 'young' at 25.28 as a sufficient indication of age.

111.25 When] A capital 'S' deleted by two vertical strokes appears to have
been mistaken by the typist for a paragraph mark and thus a new paragraph starts here in A1 without Crane's intention.

113.32 He] Both A1 and $N read 'Also he', which must have originated in
the typescript. Perhaps the typist was confused by a certain amount of
revision in MS here. Crane first started the sentence with 'To', in error for
Too, followed by 'he noted'. Subsequently, he interlined 'perceived' above
deleted 'noted', deleted 'To' and capitalized 'He'.

119.22 he would have] Crane first wrote 'he'd a' and then in the general
revision of the youth's dialect he changed 'a' to 'would' but neglected to
alter 'he'd'. The typist evidently took the 'he'd' to be authoritative and
altered to 'he'd have' as found in A1.

123.12–13 and laughing] The isolated position of the A1 variant reading
'with laughter' and the conventionality of phrase that it represents suggests that this is an editorial change even though no very strong reason
for an alteration can be adduced, either for editor or for author. It may,
even, be compositorial. The case against this being one of Crane's revisions
may be strengthened slightly by the three editorial changes in the next
A1 page (123.19,32; 124.4) and the uncorrected compositorial mistake
shortly at 124.26, to which may be added the compositorial or editorial

change at 124.17 of Crane's characteristic 'bended' to 'bent'. The apparent lack of Crane's revisions extends through the A1 variants at 124.37, 125.27, 125.30–31, and 128.9 until in a new Chapter XXIII they seem to resume with 129.1 but at least with 129.38.

123.29 cups] A1 'up' seems to derive from a misreading by the typist. The 'c' of 'cups' is not well formed, and the 's' was squeezed in later.

123.32 men. It was] The removal of MS 'It was' to create a dependent phrase is suspicious as an editorial improvement of a typical but awkward Crane locution. The two other variants on the same A1 page are also suspect. The first at 123.19 is clearly a typist's sophistication (see the Textual Note), and the substitution of 'their' for 'these' at 124.4 is no better. Crane's specifications of *this* and *these*, as here, are typical.

124.37 in him] This 'in' in MS, omitted by A1, may be an anticipatory error but it may more readily be taken as meaning 'inside', in which case the phrase is correct though awkward. The A1 alteration comes in an area of general A1 corruption.

125.27 hatreds] The final 's' is squeezed in in MS, so that one cannot be sure whether its omission in A1 derives from a typist's error or from the printer's change of Crane's unusual plurals.

125.29 guttering] This is the usual emendation for MS,A1 'gluttering'. O.E.D. lists a rare and obsolete noun 'glutter' meaning *splutter*, but Crane could scarcely have been acquainted with this, nor does the sense recommend it. It may be that Crane's intention was too obscure to support emendation, but the idea that the youth would lose his life in spurts, like a dying or guttering candle alternately dimming and reviving before final extinction, seems to be almost inevitable. A candle image may possibly be present in 'the fire of the regiment had begun to wane and drip' (126.16).

125.30–31 mule-driver] That this MS singular is not inadvertent is demonstrated by the following singular 'mud-digger'. It is possible that Crane himself made the changes to the A1 plurals 'mule-drivers' and 'mud-diggers', but the change is more likely to have come from an editorial misunderstanding. In MS the youth is applying the hateful terms to himself, as if the officer had directly named him, this being the result of his now intense identification with the regiment. The conventional plurals (which in fact quote the officer) destroy this point. It would seem that 'dubbed him wrongly' in lines 33–34 below shows that the singulars are correct.

128.9 questionings] The final 's' in MS is faint and almost illegible against the edge of the paper but it is authentic, and the A1 singular probably results from the typist's misreading, especially in view of the succeeding plurals.

129.1 movement] The chief argument in favor of this A1 reading for MS 'movement to go' is that it occurs on page 129 of Chapter XXIII which, on pages 129 and 130 (129.38; 130.1,33), contains what appear to be authoritative revisions by Crane.

130.30 And, with it all,] Neither MS nor A1 has the parenthetical commas; but they appear surrounding this same phrase beginning a sentence at 48.9 and 126.1, and so have been added here for consistency.

132.20 repose] If this were an ordinary A1 change from MS plural to singular, the MS 'reposes' might well be given authority. But in this case Crane seems to have removed the succeeding phrase 'behind the rails' in TMs[b], and it is as possible that in the process he changed 'reposes' as that the alteration was the printer's or editor's. The circumstances suggest the advisability of following the A1 reading.

132.25 tramped] MS 'tramped' gives the right sense since it contrasts properly with 'run'. The alteration in A1 to 'trampled' could in theory be an unfortunate second thought and a partial misuse of the word (given in MS at 133.11 as 'trammeled'), for an authoritative cut starts at the end of the sentence in A1, and Crane could have altered the reading—even though under a misapprehension about its meaning—when his attention was fixed on the passage. On the other hand, his misuse of 'trammeled' for 'trampled' at 133.11 where 'trampled' is correct in A1 suggests that some accident may have occurred at 132.25. When one consults the MS one sees that the very open loop of the 'p' could readily be misread as an 'l' (see the Textual Note for 92.9 for another such possible misreading); thus the strong possibility exists that the typist misread MS 'tramped' as 'trampled'.

133.1 the stolid] A1 'a stolid' seems to represent editorial interference. The white house referred to here by MS 'the' had appeared in 123.2–4 in the youth's survey of the battle: 'In the rear of this row of guns stood a house, calm and white, amid bursting shells.'

133.11 trampled] The A1 'trampled' for MS 'trammeled' appears to be correct. An obsolete use of 'trammel' as *plaited* or *braided* is applied to women's hair exclusively and is not recorded in *O.E.D.* after the seventeenth century.

134.23–24 the deeds] A1 reads 'these deeds', probably as the result of the typist's misunderstanding of Crane's intentions in MS. In line 22 above he altered 'the vision' to 'this vision' and then in lines 23–24 seems to have wished to change, correspondingly, 'those deeds' to 'the deeds'. He wrote a large Greek 'e' over the 'os' with its long tail passing through the final 'e' of 'those'. The intention—and the context encourages this view—seems to have been to alter 'those' to 'the', but the result was misread as 'these'.

135.14 to open] MS 'to be opened' is much more characteristic of Crane's style than A1 'to open', but since in this immediate area Crane was cutting and reworking, the odds may favor the alteration as his and not the editor's, although some doubt may linger as to the authority of the change.

135.25 tranquility] MS 'tranquilly' followed by A1 appears to be an error. The sense—and the syntax—requires not that the youth came *tranquilly* from *hot-ploughshares* to *clover*, but instead that he came from the forgings of battle with its heat and din, expressed in *hot-ploughshares*, to the pastoral tranquility of fields of clover. See 135.35–36: 'He turned now with a lover's thirst, to images of tranquil skies, fresh meadows, cool brooks'.

EDITORIAL EMENDATIONS IN THE COPY-TEXT

[NOTE: Every editorial change from the manuscript copy-text is recorded here except for the few silent alterations of typographical detail as are remarked in "The Text of the Virginia Edition" prefixed to Volume I of this collected edition. The manuscript draft (MS[d]) is the first source for emendation of accidentals. The first American edition (A1) is the first source for other emendations followed by the six newspapers (N^{1-6}, or $N if they all agree in a reading). The absence of any of the above symbols in this order indicates that the text is lacking at that particular point. The first English edition (E1) is completely derived from A1 and is listed only in the case of a Virginia (V) emendation which replaces documentary authority. Asterisked entries are discussed in the preceding Textual Notes. The note *et seq.* signifies that all following occurences are identical in that particular text and thus that the same emendation has been made without further notice. It should be noted that the appearance of the lemma in capitalized or in lower-case form applies only to the first entry and that the same word will be variously upper and lower-case in subsequent appearances according to its position in the sentence. The wavy dash ($\sim$) represents the same word that appears before the bracket and is used exclusively in recording punctuation or other accidental variants. An inferior caret ($_\wedge$) indicates the absence of a punctuation mark; the dollar sign ($) is taken over from a convention of bibliographical description to signify *all* texts so identified. Occasionally a newspaper subsumed under the $ notation may be excluded from agreement by the use of the minus sign. Thus a notation such as $N(-N^4)$ would mean that $N^{1-3,5-6}$ agree in the reading but that N^4 is wanting or has a different reading which will be listed separately. When Crane was excising the names from the manuscript and substituting epithets he frequently removed the following punctuation or else inserted punctuation without deleting the original punctuation, situations that result in the total lack of necessary punctuation or in double punctuation. In order to avoid excessive listing of emendations these cases have been noted in the "Alterations to the Manuscript" in such forms as '*comma deleted in error*' or '*original comma not deleted in error*.']

3.5 *et seq.* its] A1,$N; it's MS
*3.9 see, across,] *stet* MS
*3.9 gleam] *stet* MS,A1
3.22–23 blue-clothed] MS(d),A1, $N^{3,6}$; $\sim _\wedge \sim$ MS,$N^{1-2,4-5}$

*3.28–29 another private] *stet* MS, A1
3.30 trousers'] A1; trouser's MS, MS(d)

3.31; 4.1 th'] MS(u),MS(d); the MS(c),A1,$N

3.31 ol'] MS(u),MS(d); old MS (c),A1,$N

3.31 goin'] MS(u),MS(d); going MS(c),A1,$N

4.1(*twice*) t'] MS(u),MS(d); to MS(c),A1,$N

4.1 sot] MS(u),MS(d),$N; set MS(c),A1

4.2 an'] MS(u), MS(d); and MS (c),A1,$N

4.2 *et seq.* ain't] A1,$N; aint MS, MS(d)

4.2 yit] MS(u),MS(d); yet MS (c),A1,$N

4.7 board-floor] MS(d); ~ ∧ ~ MS,A1

4.13 *et seq. all forms* commanding] A1(*except* 29.18: cammand),$N; cammanding MS

4.16 Meanwhile] A1; The while MS

4.23 hang."] A1; hang. I tell yeh what I know an' yeh kin take it er leave it. Suit yerselves. It dont make no difference t' me." MS

4.29 *et seq. all forms* receiving] A1,$N; recieving MS

4.30 attacks,] A1,N⁶; attack < > MS; attacks∧ N¹⁻⁵

4.31 to] A1,$N; t< > MS

4.33 across] A1,$N; acros< > MS

4.34 cracker-boxes] E1; ~ ∧ ~ MS,A1,$N

4.36 wall] MS(d); walls MS,A1

*5.4 And, too,] $N; And∧ MS; and∧ A1

5.21 but∧] A1; ~ , MS,MS(d)

*5.26–27 or∧ more timid] A1; ~ , ~ ~ MS

*5.28 or∧ else∧] A1; ~ , ~ , MS

6.2 ¹had∧] MS(d), A1; ~ , MS

*6.2 told] *stet* MS,MS(d); told him A1

6.4 ethical] A1; ethicical MS

*6.12 winds] *stet* MS,A1

6.21 town] A1; considerable town MS,MS(d)

6.24,28 brindle-cow] V; ~ ∧ ~ MS+

6.32 trails] A1; hot trails MS; burning trails MS(d)

7.2 a-thinkin'] A1; a-thinkin∧ MS

7.7 'I've] A1; ∧ ~ MS

*7.7 knet] *stet* MS,A1

*7.9 git] *stet* MS,MS(d)

7.10 so's] MS(d),A1; s'os MS

7.12 "An'] A1; ∧ ~ MS

*7.16 'im] *stet* MS

7.18 'shamed] A1; ∧ ~ MS; ashamed MS(d)

7.20–21 right. [¶] "Yeh] A1; right. [¶] ∧ Young . . . lasting. [¶] ∧ Yeh MS (*see* Historical Collation; *for* Draft *reading, see collation of* MS *vs.* MS [d])

7.24 ¶ "I] A1;¶ ∧ ~ MS; (*no* ¶) ∧ ~ MS(d)

*7.29 Lord'll] A1 (Lord 'll); Lord 'ill MS

7.29 care] V; keer MS,A1,E1

7.29 all.] A1; all. Don't . . . searching. MS (*see* Historical Collation)

7.30 ¶ "Don't] A1;(*no* ¶) ∧ ~ MS, MS(d)

7.30 fergit] MS(d); forgit MS,A1

7.36 borne] A1; bore MS(c); born MS(u)

8.8 privileges] A1; priveleges MS

8.16 *et seq. all forms* perceived] A1; percieved MS

8.19 in her movement] A1; *omit* MS

9.9 their] A1; *omit* MS

9.9,13 The youth] A1; Fleming MS,MS(d)

9.11 of them] A1; *omit* MS,MS(d)

9.17 him] MS(d),A1; Fleming MS

*9.18 advancing∧] A1; ~ , MS,MS (d)

*9.22 powder] *stet* MS

9.24 the youth] A1; Fleming MS, MS(d)

9.26 Still,] MS(d),A1; ~ ∧ MS

9.26 veterans'] A1; veteran's MS

*9.27 fire∧] MS(d); ~ , MS,A1

10.5 sufficient] A1; sufficent MS

10.12 but,] A1; *comma doubtful*
MS; ∼ ∧ MS(d)

10.15 the] MS(u),MS(d),$N; th'
MS(c),A1

10.27,28(*thrice*),29,31,32; 11.35
Yeh] MS(u),MS(d); You MS
(c),A1,$N

10.27,29; 11.18 kin] MS(u),MS
(d); can MS(c),A1,$N

10.27 b'lieve] MS(u),MS(d); believe MS(c),A1,$N

10.27 er] MS(u),MS(d); or MS
(c),A1,$N

10.27; 11.1,2 jest] MS(u),MS(d),
A1; just MS(c),$N

10.28(*twice*); 11.14,16,37; 12.16
t'] MS(u),MS(d); to MS(c),A1

10.28; 11.1,5,17,27,34(*twice*),36;
12.1,16(*twice*),17(*twice*),18
an'] MS(u),MS(d)(*except* MS
[d] ²and *at* 11.34); and MS(c),
A1,$N

10.32,33; 12.1 everythin'] MS(u);
everything MS(c),MS(d),A1,$N

10.32; 11.1,11,12,15,33,36,37,38
(*twice*); 12.1,16 th'] MS(u),
MS(d); the MS(c),A1,$N(*ex-
cept* N⁶ *omit at* 10.32)

10.33 th'] MS(d); the MS,A1

10.34–35 knapsack] MS(d),A1;
∼ - ∼ MS

11.1(*twice*) Yeh] MS(d); You
MS,A1

11.1 t'morrah] MS(u),MS(d); to
morrow MS(c); to-morrow A1

11.1 bigges'] MS(u),MS(d); biggest MS(c),A1

11.4,5,33 fightin'] MS(u),MS(d);
fighting MS(c),A1

11.4 m'] MS(u), MS(d); my MS
(c),A1

11.4 reg'lar] MS(u),MS(d); regular MS(c),A1

11.9 did."] MS(d),A1; ∼ . ∧ MS

11.10 *et seq.* won't] A1; wont MS,
MS(d)±

11.10 soldier,] A1; ∼ ∧ MS

11.11,13 mornin'] MS(u); morning MS(c),MS(d),A1

11.14 goin'] MS(u); going MS
(c),A1

11.16 Th'] MS(u),MS(d); The
MS(c),A1

11.16 reg'ment's] MS(u); regiment's MS(c),A1; reg'ments
MS(d)

11.17 raisin'] MS(u),MS(d); raising MS(c),A1

*11.23 regiment'll] MS(d); reg'-
ment'll MS,A1; regiment will
$N

11.24; 12.16 onct] MS(u); once
MS(c),MS(d),A1,$N

11.24; 12.14 git] MS(u),MS(d);
get MS(c),A1,$N

11.24 inteh] MS(u),MS(d); into
MS(c),A1,$N

11.26,32; 12.14 'a] MS(u); of
MS(c),MS(d),A1,$N

11.26 b'cause] MS(u); because
MS(c),A1,$N; 'cause MS(d)

11.27 'a] MS(u); of MS(c),A1,
$N; a' MS(d)

11.30 be] A1,$N; *omit* MS,MS(d)

11.31 reg'ment] MS(u),MS(d);
regiment MS(c),A1,$N

11.33 ¹an'] MS(u),MS(d); and
MS(c),A1

11.33 ²an'] MS(u); and MS(c),
MS(d),A1

11.34 come] MS(u); came MS
(c),A1

11.34 ag'in] MS(d); agin MS(u);
again MS(c),A1

11.35 *et seq.* can't] A1; cant MS,
MS(d)±

11.35 nothin'] MS(u); nothing
MS(c), A1

11.35 'A] V; Of MS(c),MS(d),
A1,$N,E1; A' MS(u)

11.36 yit] MS(u),MS(d); yet MS
(c),A1

11.38 worser] MS(u),MS(d);
worse MS(c),A1

12.1 reg'ment] MS(u),A1; regiment MS(c)

12.1 'a] V; of MS(c),MS(d),A1,
$N(−N²),E1; a' MS(u); to N²

12.2 an'] MS(u); and MS(c),A1,
$N

12.2 most 'a 'em'll] MS(u);

most of 'em'll MS(c),MS(d), A1; they'll $N

*12.3　four last] stet MS,MS(d)

12.14　fer] MS(u),MS(d); for MS (c),A1,$N

12.15　hull] MS(u),MS(d); whole MS(c),A1,$N

12.15　'a] V; of MS(c),MS(d),A1, $N(−N³),E1; a' MS(u); o N³

12.15　¹an'] MS(u),MS(d); and MS(c),A1,$N

12.15　²an'] MS(u),MS(d); and MS(c),A1; to $N(−N⁶); omit N⁶

12.17　a-standin'] MS(u),MS(d); a-standing MS(c),A1,$N

12.17　a-fightin'] MS(u),MS(d) (∼-∼ ∧); a-fighting MS(c), A1; ∧fighting N⁶

12.18　B'jiminy] MS(u); Bejiminy MS(c); Be jiminey A1; By jiminy MS(d); by jiminy $N

13.14　unsatisfactory] A1,MS(d), $N; unsatisfoctory MS

13.25　known] MS(d),A1,$N; know MS

*14.4　moods] stet MS

14.9　confidant] A1,$N; confidante MS

14.15 et seq. all forms conceive] A1; concieve MS,MS(d)

*14.16　courage∧ unseen,] A1; ∼ , ∼ ∧ MS

14.23　witness,] A1; ∼ ∧ MS

*14.28–29　tradition] stet MS

*14.31　considered to be] stet MS

14.32–33　river-bank] V; ∼ ∧ ∼ MS,A1,E1

15.10　The youth] A1,$N; Fleming MS

15.22　breathing] A1,$N; breatheing MS

16.6　forward] A1; along MS,$N

16.9　of] A1,$N; omit MS

*16.14　rearward] A1,$N; ∼-∼ MS

16.17　into praises] A1; out in praise MS,$N

*16.18–20　"I . . . soldier.] stet MS

16.18　yeh] MS(u); you MS(c), $N

16.19　didn't] $N (Didn't); didnt MS

16.26　youth∧] A1,$N; ∼ . MS

*16.30　ahead∧ often,] N²; ∼ ∧ ∼ ∧ MS,$N(−N²); ∼ , ∼ ∧ A1

*17.2　behind] A1; behint MS

17.4　-bank,] A1; ∼ ∧ MS

*17.10　loud] stet MS

17.18　followed∧] A1; ∼ , MS

17.18–20　The . . . statue.] A1; omit MS

17.39　intercourse] A1; intercouse MS

*18.10　himself] A1,MS(u); him MS(c)

18.23　head, discovered∧] A1; ∼ ∧ ∼ , MS

18.26,30　yeh] MS(u); you MS (c), A1

18.26　doin'] MS(u); doing MS (c),A1

18.28,29　Yeh're] V; You're MS,A1

18.29　gittin'] MS(u); gitting MS (c); getting A1

18.29　m'] MS(u); my MS(c), A1

18.29　lookin'] MS(u); looking MS(c),A1

18.29　thunderin'] MS(u); thundering MS(c),A1

18.29,35,37; 19.4,10,22,32,37 (twice) th'] MS(u),MS(d); the MS(c),A1

18.35　'em,] V; ∼ ∧ MS,A1,E1

18.36　lick 'em] A1; lickem MS (with apostrophe inserted)

18.37　soberly,] A1; ∼, | ,MS

18.38; 19.4,22,32,38　t'] MS(u), MS(d); to MS(c),A1

19.3–4　marchin'] MS(u); marching MS(c),A1

19.4,22,32　goin'] MS(u),MS(d); going MS(c),A1

19.4,38　fightin'] MS(u),MS(d); fighting MS(c),A1

19.5　gittin'] MS(u); getting MS (c),A1

19.5,6,10,36,38　an'] MS(u),MS (d); and MS(c),A1

19.5 comin'] MS(u); coming MS (c),A1
19.6 kin] MS(u); can MS(c),A1
19.6 exceptin'] MS(u); excepting MS(c),A1
19.6 damn'] MS(u); damned MS (c),A1
19.10 fer] V; for MS,A1,E1
*19.19 suppose] V; s'pose MS,MS (d),A1,E1
19.31 s'pose," . . . other;] A1; ~ ;" . . . ~ , MS
19.32 runnin'] MS(u),MS(d); running MS(c),A1
19.36 loud] A1; blatant MS
19.37 didn't] MS(d),A1; didnt MS
19.38 goin'] MS(u); going MS (c),MS(d),A1
19.39 [1,2]yeh] V; you MS,A1
19.39 [3]yeh] MS(u); you MS(c), A1
20.1 Napolyon Bonypart] MS(u); Napoleon Boneparte MS(c); Napoleon Bonaparte A1
20.4 you] A1; yeh MS
20.4 get] V; git MS,A1,E1
20.7 resemblance] A1; resemblace MS
*20.17 could] stet MS
20.19 thoughts,] A1; thought < > MS
21.7 solemnly] A1,$N; solomnly MS
21.12 its] stet MS
*21.20 grumbling] stet MS
21.25 clothing] A1; clotheing MS
21.26,28(twice) Yeh] MS(u); You MS(c),A1
21.26 kin] MS(u); can MS(c), A1
*21.26–28 drink, . . . hotel?"] stet MS
21.27 an'] MS(u); and MS(c), A1
21.28 d'] MS(u); do MS(c)
21.28 t'] MS(u); to MS(c),A1
21.29 ¶ There] A1; no ¶ MS
21.30 practice] A1; practise MS
22.4 likely] A1; like MS
22.7 Hey] A1; Hay MS

22.14 were] A1; was MS
22.26 rhythmically] A1,N[1-2,4-5]; rythmically MS,N[3,6]
22.29 men] A1; man MS
22.33 sech] MS(u); such MS(c); sich A1
22.33; 27.8 fer] MS(u); for MS (c),A1
22.39 tread] A1,N[6]; tred MS
23.7 et seq. all forms seized] A1; siezed MS
23.22 exceeded] A1,$N; acceded MS
23.32 receding] A1,$N; recedeing MS
24.5 solemn] A1,$N; solomn MS
*24.20 this] stet MS,$N
24.31 fields,] V; ~ ∧ MS,A1,N[6], E1
25.10 ground,] A1,$N; ~ ∧ MS, MS(d)
25.11 The youth] A1,$N; Fleming MS,MS(d)
25.28 young] A1; youthful MS
25.30 young man] A1; Fleming MS
26.10 time,] MS(d); ~ ∧ MS,A1
*26.11 front] stet MS
26.19 position,] MS(d); ~ ∧ MS, A1
26.24 became another] A1; became a another MS
26.30 nothing] V; nothin' MS,MS (d),A1,E1
26.35 sandwich] A1; sandwhich MS,MS(d)
26.37 s'pose] MS(u),MS(d); suppose MS(c),A1
26.37 reconnoiterin'] MS(u),MS (d); reconnoitering MS(c),A1
26.37 th'] MS(u),MS(d); the MS (c),A1
26.37 kentry] MS(u),MS(d); country MS(c),A1
26.37 jest] MS(u),MS(d),A1; just MS(c)
26.37,38 t'] MS(u),MS(d); to MS(c),A1
26.38 gittin'] MS(u),MS(d); getting MS(c),A1

26.38 clost] MS(u),MS(d); close MS(c),A1

26.38 develope 'em] MS(d); develope'm MS; develop 'em A1

26.38 somethin'] MS(d); something MS,A1

27.4,6(*twice*),7,8 yeh] MS(u); you MS(c),A1

27.7 an'] MS(u); and MS(c), A1

*27.8 yit an' yit] MS(u); yet and yet MS(c); and yet A1

27.9 do] A1; do a MS

27.9 fightin'] MS(u); fighting MS(c),A1

27.10 other;] MS(c) (*semicolon is slightly uncertain, may be a comma*); ~ . MS(u),A1

27.10(*twice*),11 t'] MS(u); to MS(c),A1

27.10 a'] V; have MS(c); 'a MS (u); 'ave A1,E1

27.11 th'] MS(u); the MS(c),A1

27.11 jest] MS(u),A1; just MS (c)

27.12 sandwich] A1; sandwhich MS

27.16 sandwiches] A1; sandwhiches MS

27.18 communing] A1; cummuning MS

27.28 familiar] A1; familar MS

*27.33 stupidity] A1; stupidity affair MS

27.35 thought] A1; thought that MS

28.5 skirmish-] A1; unceasing skirmish- MS

28.5 increased] A1; encreased MS

28.24,27 m'] MS(u); my MS(c), A1

28.24,27,30(*twice*) an'] MS(u); and MS(c),A1

28.24,27 ol'] MS(u); old MS(c), A1

28.28 Somethin'] MS(u); Something MS(c),A1

28.30 "I'm] A1; ——"I'm MS

28.30 yeh] MS(u); you MS(c), A1

28.30 t'] MS(u); to MS(c),A1

28.31 t'] V; 'to MS(c); 't MS(u); to A1,E1

28.36 and raised] A1; waved MS

29.7 in gossip] A1; in the gossip MS,$N

29.9 Perry] A1; Perrey MS

29.14,15,23,24 batt'ry] A1; bat'-try MS

29.22,24 Hannises'] A1; Hannises∧ MS

30.8 feller."] A1; feller." [¶] "Hear . . . lick'em." MS *text undeleted in error* (*see* Historical Collation)

30.9–32.8 The din . . . them.] A1,$N; *omit* MS; *for partial* MS(d) *see* 154.19–155.7

30.15 storm-banshee] MS(d),N⁶; ~ ∧ ~ A1,$N(–N⁶)

30.16 grove∧ and, . . . redly,] MS(d); ~ , ~ ∧ . . . ~ ∧ A1; ~ , ~ , . . . ~ , $N

30.17 pine-needles] MS(d); ~ ∧ ~ A1,$N

30.26 tack-hammer] MS(d); ~ ∧ ~ A1,$N

30.33 battle-flag] MS(d); ~ ∧ ~ A1,N⁴,⁶; battleflag N¹⁻³,⁵

30.36 Men, . . . swiftly,] MS(d); ~ ∧ . . . ~ ∧ A1,$N

31.1 grey] MS(d); gray A1,$N

31.1 mob-like] MS(d),$N; moblike A1

31.2 wild-horses] MS(d); ~ ∧ ~ A1,$N

31.5 cat-calls] N³,⁶; catcalls A1, N²; ~ -| ~ N¹,⁵; ~ ∧ ~ N⁴

31.7 Gawd,] $N; ~ ! A1

31.8 crushed,] $N; ~ ! A1

31.12 carven. And] $N(N¹⁻⁵: craven); ~ ; and A1

31.14 apart∧] $N; ~ , A1

*31.15 bellowing] $N; following A1

31.21 arms∧] V; ~ , A1,E1

*31.30 jokes] *stet* A1

31.31 veterans,] N⁶; ~ ; A1

31.40 flood-like] N¹⁻³,⁵; floodlike A1,N⁴; ~ -| ~ N⁶

32.7 it∧] $N(–N⁴); ~ , A1,N⁴

*32.7 thought∧] *stet* A1

33.8 feign] Aɪ; fiegn MS,MS(d)

33.8 despise] MS(d),Aɪ; dispise MS

34.7 colonel,] MS(d),Aɪ; ~ ∧ MS

34.15 school-] MS(d),Aɪ,$N; shool- MS

34.16–17 repetition] Aɪ,$N; repition MS

34.17 don't] MS(d),Aɪ,$N; dont MS

*34.36 moments] stet MS

36.3 querulous] Aɪ; querelous MS,MS(d)

*36.11 furiously] Aɪ; feverishly MS,N⁶

36.13 bobbed] Aɪ; flapped and bobbed MS,N⁶

36.17 magician's] Aɪ,N⁶; magacians' MS

36.21 were] Aɪ; was MS

36.22 nearly] Aɪ; near MS

37.20 silent] Aɪ; MS 'silence' partially corrected by Garland

37.23 grimy] Aɪ,$N; grimey MS

38.5 its] stet MS

38.5 formula] Aɪ; formulae MS

*38.24 emblems] stet MS,$N

38.33 blue,] MS(d),Aɪ,$N; ~ ∧ MS

39.7 mopped] Aɪ,$N; moped MS, MS(d)

*39.19 coat-sleeve] stet MS,MS(d)

*39.25 only] stet MS,MS(d)

39.25 familiar] Aɪ; familar MS, MS(d)

39.25 the youth] Aɪ; Fleming MS,MS(d)

39.29–30 ag'in . . . ag'in] Aɪ; a'gin . . . a'gin MS; ag'in . . . a'gin MS(d); again . . . again $N

40.9 countenances] MS(d),Aɪ, $N; coutenances MS

40.15,16 t'] MS(u),MS(d); to MS(c),Aɪ

40.15 bangin'] MS(u),MS(d); banging MS(c),Aɪ

40.16 th'] MS(u),MS(d); the MS (c),Aɪ

40.17 Smithers] MS(d),Aɪ; Smither's MS

40.30 shadow,] N⁶; ~ ∧ MS,Aɪ

*40.34 back] stet MS,$N

41.2 fer] MS(u),MS(d); for MS (c),Aɪ

41.3 t'] MS(d); to MS,Aɪ

41.3 th'] MS(u),MS(d); the MS (c),Aɪ

41.3 damn'] V; damned MS,Aɪ, Eɪ; damn∧ MS(d)

41.20 dropped it] MS(d); omit MS; stopped Aɪ

41.21 borne] Aɪ; born MS,MS (d)

41.22 instant,] Aɪ; ~ ∧ MS

41.28 trance∧] MS(d),Aɪ; ~ , MS

*42.7 headlong] Aɪ,$N; ~ - ~ MS; ~ - | ~ MS(d)

42.12 appalling] Aɪ; apalling MS

42.25 across] Aɪ,N⁶; a across MS

*42.27 heard them] stet MS

42.35 disputing] Aɪ; disputeing MS

43.3 The youth] Aɪ; Fleming MS, MS(d)

*43.10 deep] stet MS

43.22 didn't] MS(d),Aɪ; didnt MS

44.2 dared,] MS(d),$N(−N⁶); ~ ∧ MS,Aɪ,N⁶

44.3 chaos,] MS(d),Aɪ,$N; ~ ∧ MS

44.4 surety,] MS(d); ~ ∧ MS,Aɪ, $N

44.14 such an] Aɪ; such MS; such a MS(d)

*44.18 chesnut] stet MS

44.24,25,35 heavens] Aɪ,$N; Heavens MS

*44.26 'em! . . . 'em!] V; 'im. . . . 'im. MS; 'im! . . . 'im! MS(d), Aɪ,Eɪ; them. . . . them. $N

44.27–28 'em . . . 'em] MS(d); 'im . . . 'im MS,Aɪ

44.28 got 'em] MS(d),Aɪ; got'-| ∧em MS

44.34 paean] Aɪ,N³⁻⁴(Aɪ,N³: pæan); peaen MS; paeon N¹⁻²,⁵; peon N⁶

45.2 imbecile] A1,$N; embecile MS,MS(d)

45.24 over-turned] MS(d); overturned MS,A1

46.5–6 heaven's] A1; Heaven's MS

*46.11 little] stet MS

46.12 words.] A1; words; who, through his suffering, thinks that he peers into the core of things and see that the judgment of man is thistle-down in wind. MS

46.13 thick] A1,$N; thicks MS

46.15 shots$_\wedge$] A1,N^6; ~, MS (doubtful),N$^{1,3-5}$; shouts, N^2

46.29 rhythmical] A1; rythmical MS,MS(d)

*46.37 nature] stet MS,MS(d)

47.19 gleaming] A1; silver-gleaming MS,MS(d)

*47.35 opened] stet MS,MS(d)

47.35 appalling] A1,$N; apalling MS,MS(d)

48.5 feared$_\wedge$] MS(d),A1,$N; ~, MS

48.12 bonds] A1,N^6; bounds MS, $N(−N^6)

48.18 squawk] A1,$N; squwk MS

*48.19 sighingly] stet MS

*49.1 sun] A1; burnished sun MS, MS(d),$N

49.21 et seq. foreign] A1,N^6; foriegn MS,MS(d)

49.31 himself] A1; he MS,MS(d); Hamlin Garland deleted 'he' and wrote 'himself' above

*50.13 ¹was] A1; were MS,MS(d)

50.24 awe-struck] MS(d),N^6; ~ - | ~ MS; awestruck A1

50.39 swollen] A1; swollen and ghastly MS

51.1 see,] MS(d); ~$_\wedge$ MS,A1,$N

*51.7 was mingled] stet MS,MS(d)

51.11 school-boy] MS(d); ~$_\wedge$~ MS; schoolboy A1,N$^{1,4-6}$; ~ - | ~ N$^{2-3}$

51.18–21 "Sing . . . pie."] A1; MS and MS(d) have no end-of-line punctuation except for the final period, but both begin and end each line with double quotation marks

51.34,37; 53.10; 57.13 can't] stet MS

*52.10 road-way] V; roadway MS, A1,N$^{1,4-6}$,E1; ~ - | ~ N$^{2-3}$

52.14 officers] A1,$N; officiers MS

52.16 shoes,] A1,$N; ~$_\wedge$ MS

52.29 The] A1,$N; the MS

52.31 rag,] A1,$N; ~$_\wedge$ MS

52.34 sufficient] A1,$N; sufficent MS

52.35 et seq. (except when otherwise noted) wa'n't] A1; w'a'nt MS; wasn't $N

53.3 the youth] A1; Fleming MS

53.11 No,] A1,N^6; ~$_\wedge$ MS

53.14 but$_\wedge$] A1; ~, MS

53.18 ses, 'but] A1; ~$_{\wedge\wedge}$~ MS

53.21 Well (no ¶)] A1; ¶ MS

53.21 t'-day] V; t'day MS,A1,E1

53.26 boy?] MS(d),A1,$N; ~, MS

53.28 borne] A1,$N; born MS, MS(d)

*54.3 others] stet MS

54.6 sidelong] A1,$N(−N^6); ~ - ~ MS,N^6

54.11 red] A1; little red MS,$N

54.15 grey,] stet MS (comma appears semicolon due to fiber in paper)

54.15 appalling] A1,$N; apalling MS

54.29 the youth] A1,$N; Fleming MS,MS(d)

55.2,7,25,31 Henry] A1; Flem MS,MS(d),$N

55.5 curious$_\wedge$] MS(d),A1,$N; ~, MS

55.9 t'-day] A1; t'day MS; to-day N^{1,4,6}; to-|day N^2; today N^{3,5}

55.12 b'jiminy] MS(d),N^6; b'jiming MS; b'jiminey A1

55.16 soldier$_\wedge$] A1,N^6; soldier. MS; latter$_\wedge$ MS(d)

55.17 guardian] A1; gaurdian MS,N^6

*55.19 their tragedies] stet MS

55.29,30,32 care] A1,$N; keer MS,MS(d)

55.29,30,32(*twice*) you] V; yeh MS+

55.30 to] $N; t' MS,A1

55.37; 56.2 Henry] A1; Flem MS, MS(d)

*55.38 pretty] *stet* MS

56.5 loyalty] A1; loyality MS

56.16 Presently,] MS(d); ~ ∧ MS,A1,$N

56.17 Turning,] MS(d),$N; ~ ∧ MS,A1

56.19 batt'ry] A1,N⁴; bat'try MS, MS(d),N¹⁻³,⁶; battery N⁵

56.25 soldier] A1,$N; youth MS; Conklin MS(d)

56.27 Huh?] MS(d); ~ , MS,A1, $N

56.29 "Oh (*no* ¶)] MS(d),A1; ¶ MS,$N

57.3 yourself] $N; yerself MS, MS(d),A1

57.9 you going] V; yeh goin' MS,MS(d),A1,N⁶,E1

57.10; 59.16 won't] *stet* MS

57.20 solemn] A1,$N; solomn MS

57.24 ¹They] A1; They could not understand; they MS,$N

57.25 command∧] A1,$N; cammand, MS

57.35 increased] A1,$N; encreased MS

*58.20 Gawd] MS(u),MS(d); God MS(c),A1,$N

58.30 philippic] A1,N¹,³⁻⁵; phillipic MS,MS(d),N⁶; phillippic N²

58.32 wafer] A1; fierce wafer MS,MS(d),$N

59.2 wa'n't] A1; w'a'nt MS, MS (d); wan't $N

59.21 cried] MS(d),A1; cried, in fear MS,$N

59.21 going to] $N; goin' t' MS, MS(d),A1

59.26 ²him] V; 'im MS,A1,$N,E1; 'um MS(d)

59.31 stayin'] MS(d),A1,$N; ~ ∧ MS

60.12 He . . . was to be] A1; Was he to be MS,$N

60.13 encounter.] A1; ~ ? MS, $N

60.15 There's] MS(d); There MS, A1

60.16; 61.12 can't] *stet* MS (*not italicised at* 61.12)

60.16 'a] V; a' MS,A1,E1; of MS (d)

60.24 "Yeh] A1; ∧ ~ MS,MS(d)

60.27 -sudden∧] A1; ~ , MS

*60.28 infernal, tooty- . . . -too,'] *stet* MS

60.35 t'wa'n't] V; t'w'a'nt MS; t'was n't A1; 'twasn't E1

60.36 of 'em] A1; of' | 'em MS

61.2 Ye'd] A1; Yed MS (*unclear*)

61.5 ²a] V; 'a MS(*doubtful*),A1, E1

61.17–18 His . . . up-raising] A1; Was his companion ever to play such an intolerable part? Was he ever going to up-raise MS

61.18 up-raising] V; up-raise MS; upraising A1,E1

61.18 their] A1; his MS

61.19 curiosity.] MS(u),A1; ~ ? MS(c)

61.19 the tattered man] A1; him MS

61.19 one] A1; a man MS

61.22 other] A1; tattered man MS

61.23 'tend] $N(−N²); ∧tend MS, A1,N²

61.24 had] A1,$N; *omit* MS

*61.25 hate] *stet* MS

61.27 gaping] A1,$N; gapeing MS

61.28–29 The youth, looking] A1 (*no comma*); Fleming, looked MS; The youth looked $N

61.31–32 look—a—here] A1; *dashes might be hyphens* MS; look—here N¹⁻²,⁴⁻⁵; look | here N³; look ∧ here N⁶

61.32,33,37,38 won't] *stet* MS

61.35 look—a—here] A1; *dashes might be hyphens* MS; ~ - ~ - ~ $N(−N²) ~ ∧ ~ ∧ ~ N²

62.7 Look—a—here] A1; *dashes might be hyphens* MS; ~ - ~ - ~ $N

62.8 ¶ The] A1,$N; *no* ¶ MS

*62.9 fields] *stet* MS

62.21 the power of] A1; human MS

63.17 symmetrical] A1; symetrical MS,MS(d)

64.11 mind] A1; mind then MS,MS(d)

64.16 than] MS(d),A1; that MS

64.23 liked] A1; like MS,MS(d)

64.25 ²himself,] A1; ~ ∧ MS,MS(d)

64.37 start] A1; start fleetly MS,MS(d)

65.6 resentfully,] V; ~ ∧ MS,A1,E1

65.16 rearward] A1; rear-word MS; rear-ward MS(d)

65.19 forth,] *stet* MS (*comma appears semicolon due to fiber in the paper*)

65.21 explanation] A1; explantion MS,MS(d)

65.29 wings] A1; red wings MS,MS(d)

65.33 grimy] A1,$N; grimey MS,MS(d)

66.1 green] A1; crimson MS,MS(d),$N

66.33 ditties] MS(u),MS(d),A1; sad ditties MS(c)

66.33–34 compunctions] A1; cumpunctions MS

67.3,9 the youth] A1; Fleming MS

67.21 villain] A1; villian MS,MS(d)

*68.4 bethink] MS(d),A1; be-think MS

68.8 tale] A1; tale which MS

68.14 Henry] A1; *omit* MS

69.2 road-way] V; roadway MS,MS(d),A1,N⁶,E1

69.8–9 tree-tops∧] V; tree-top< > MS; treetops, A1,N³,⁶; tree tops, N¹⁻²,⁴⁻⁵; tree-tops, E1

69.15 damned.] A1; doomed. He

lost concern for himself. MS; doomed. MS(d)

69.21 -hymn,] MS(d),A1,$N; - ~∧ MS

69.23 the] N⁶; th' MS,MS(d),A1, N¹⁻⁵

69.26–27 The youth (*no* ¶)] A1; ~ ~ *doubtful* ¶ MS,MS(d)

69.31 ²-road?] $N; - ~. MS; - ~ ! A1

70.5 The youth] A1,$N; Fleming MS

70.22 the youth's] A1,$N; Fleming's MS,MS(d)

70.28 writhing] MS(d),A1; writheing MS; withering $N

71.5–6 search for] A1; reach MS,MS(d),$N

*71.25 fields] *stet* MS

71.30 howled] A1; roared MS,$N

*72.1 blue∧] A1; ~ , MS

72.3 lay∧] A1,$N; ~ , MS

72.37 whether] A1,$N; wether MS

73.9 lift] A1,$N; left MS

73.31 like that] A1; that color MS

73.37 -standin'] A1; - ~ ∧ MS

74.11 the youth] A1,$N; Fleming MS

74.15 The youth] A1,$N; Fleming MS

74.19 the youth] A1,$N; The youth MS

74.21 fire?] A1,$N; ~ ! MS

74.26 and∧] A1,$N; ~ , MS

75.20–21 the loud soldier] A1; Wilson MS; his loud friend $N

75.21 the youth's] A1,$N; Fleming's MS

75.22 Henry] A1; Flem MS,$N

75.24 ol'] A1; Flem, ol' MS,$N

75.24 the other] A1; Wilson MS; the loud one $N

75.27 The youth] A1,$N; Fleming MS

*75.30 comrade] *stet* MS

75.31 the loud soldier] A1; Wilson MS; him $N

76.1 the] N⁵; th' MS,A1,$N(−N⁵)

*76.1 Terrible] V; Ter'ble MS+

76.2,4 fighting] V; fightin' MS+
76.3 ¹the] E1; th' MS,A1,$N
76.3 regiment] N²; reg'ment MS, A1,$N(−N²)
76.3 ²the] $N(−N⁶); th' MS,A1, N⁶
76.3 ³the] V; th' MS+
76.4 saw] V; see MS+
76.4 such] N⁶; sech MS,A1,$N (−N⁶)
76.4 've] V; 'a MS,E1; a' A1
76.5 the regiment] V; th' reg'ment MS,A1,E1
76.6 His friend] A1; Wilson MS; The loud private $N
76.10 talkin'] A1,$N; ~ ∧ MS
76.12,28,39 Henry] A1; Flem MS,$N
76.18 ¹the] V; th' MS+
76.18 separated——"] N³·⁵; ~ "— MS,A1,N¹⁻²,⁴; ~ ," N⁶
76.18 the youth] A1,$N; Fleming MS
76.20 his friend] A1; Wilson MS; his loud friend $N
76.23,27 the youth's] A1,$N; Fleming's MS
76.25 The youth] A1,N⁶; Fleming MS
76.27; 77.1 the corporal] A1,$N; Simpson MS
76.29 the loud private] A1,$N; Wilson MS
76.30 a] A1,$N; 'a MS
76.34 The youth's] A1,$N; Fleming's MS
76.34 his friend's] A1,$N; Wilson's MS
76.35–36 the corporal's] A1,$N; Simpson's MS
76.36 submitted] A1,$N; submitting MS
76.39 The corporal] A1,$N; Simpson MS
77.1 The youth] A1,$N; Fleming MS
77.1 aside] A1; down MS,$N
77.2 rifle,] A1,$N; ~ ∧ MS
77.6 with] A1,$N; omit MS
77.22 the ground] A1,$N; ground MS

*78.4 snoring∧] A1; ~ , MS
78.4 lying] A1; lieing MS
78.14 lying] A1,$N; laying MS
*78.21 companion] stet MS,A1
78.24 soldier,] $N; soldi< > MS; soldier∧ A1
78.25 Henry] A1; Fleming MS,$N
78.27 amateur] A1,$N; ameteur MS
78.38 tying] A1,$N; tieing MS
*79.3 contemplated] A1; looked at MS,$N
79.4 aching] A1,$N; acheing MS
79.4 cloth] A1,$N; clothe MS
79.8 Henry] A1; Flem MS
79.9 a'] A1; 'a MS
79.14 rest."] A1,$N(−N²); ~ . ∧ MS,N²
79.16 lying] A1,$N; lieing MS
79.24,28 Hold] V; Hol' MS,A1,E1
79.24,28 minute] V; minnit MS, A1,E1
79.25,29 going to] V; goin' t' MS,A1,E1
79.28 you] V; yeh MS,A1,E1
80.11 begun] $N; began MS,A1
80.14 features] A1; faces MS,$N
80.18 up∧] A1; ~ , MS (comma doubtful)
80.20 pallid∧] V; palli< > MS; pallid, A1,E1
80.23 squawking] A1; sqawking MS
80.28 his friend] A1; Wilson MS; the loud soldier $N
*81.12 eye-sockets.] A1,$N(A1, N¹⁻⁵: ∧ ~.); -sockets. It was the soldier's bath. MS
81.13 The youth] A1,$N; Fleming MS
81.17 Henry] A1; Flem MS,$N
*81.20 little] A1; bitter MS,$N
81.23 ye'd] A1; yed MS
81.25 until] A1; until suddenly MS
81.27 hangdest] A1; hangest MS
81.29 can't] stet MS
81.30 ¹and] V; an MS; an' A1,E1
81.30 ²and] V; an' MS,A1,E1
82.7 conceits] A1; conciets MS

82.19   peak] A1; peek MS
82.24,36   Henry] A1; Flem MS
82.26   -before-] V; -b'fore-
 MS,A1,E1
82.28   -and-] V; -an'- MS,A1
*82.35   deprecatory] stet MS
83.3   saw] V; seen MS,A1,E1
83.4(twice)   the] V; th' MS,
 A1,E1
83.5   getting] V; gittin' MS;
 gettin' A1,E1
83.5   pounding] V; poundin'
 MS,A1,E1
83.6   yesterday] V; yestirday
 MS,A1,E1
83.13   Yes] A1; Yep MS
83.13   the] V; th' MS,A1,E1
83.23   them,] A1; ~ ∧ MS
83.27   red-faced] A1; ~ ∧ ~ MS
84.5   He] A1; He's MS
84.8   You've] V; Yer MS,A1,E1
84.8   You] V; Yeh MS,A1,E1
84.9   ¹you] V; yeh MS,A1,E1
84.9   and] V; an' MS,A1,E1
84.9   fellow] V; feller MS,A1,E1
84.10   He] A1; he MS
84.15   Henry] A1; Fleming MS
84.19   kep'] A1; kep∧ MS; keep
 $N
84.20   didn't] A1,$N; didnt MS
84.21   fightin'] A1,$N; ~ ∧ MS
86.15   distance∧] A1; distance
 < > MS
86.17   sight.] A1; sight. The long
 . . . perhaps. MS (see Historical Collation)
*86.19–20   circumstance] A1; na-
 ture MS
86.24   marbles.] A1; marbles. [¶]
 Since . . . deserved it. MS
 (see Historical Collation)
86.27; 87.22   had] A1; omit MS
86.32   Besides] A1; Beside MS
88.1   gaping] gapeing MS
89.0   XVI] A1; XVII MS
*89.1   spluttering] V; sputtering
 MS+
89.31   Rappahannock] A1; Rappahanock MS
*90.1–2   uproar] A1; ~ - ~ MS
90.3   at] A1; At MS

90.3   among] A1; Among MS,$N
*90.5   black] A1; black and croak-
 ing MS; croaking $N
*90.7   omens] A1; many omems
 MS; many omens N⁶
90.10   borne] A1,N⁶; born MS
90.10   into] A1,N⁶; in to MS
*90.23   sentence] stet MS
90.24   of] V; 'a MS,A1,E1
90.25   a] A1; a' MS
91.7,8   regiment] V; reg'ment
 MS,A1,E1
91.7   yesterday] V; yestirday
 MS,A1,E1
91.7   didn't] A1; didnt MS
91.9; 94.26   can't] stet MS
91.9   the] E1; th' MS,A1
91.10   ¶ In] A1; ¶ doubtful MS
91.14   and] V; an' MS,A1,E1
*91.15   generals'] stet MS
91.17   losing] A1; lossing MS
91.18   a] A1; 'a MS
*91.22   Inward] stet MS
*91.25   conciliatory] stet MS
91.34   person] A1; man MS
91.38   the youth's] A1; Fleming's
 MS
*92.5   cleared] V; clearer MS;
 clear, A1,E1
*92.9   yelpings] stet MS
92.10   hounds,] A1; ~ ∧ MS
92.10   increased] A1; encreased
 MS
92.13   crackle] A1; crackl< >
 MS
92.20   lying] A1; lieing MS
92.31   makes] A1; make MS
*92.35   began] stet MS
*92.36; 93.2   Me] stet MS
93.2   Don't] A1; Dont MS
*93.5   There's] E1; There MS,A1
93.6   wastin'] A1; ~ ∧ MS
93.8   t' fight] V; to fight MS,A1,E1
93.12   his] A1; his | his MS
93.19   the youth's] A1; Fleming's
 MS
93.31   was] A1; omit MS
94.0   XVII] A1; XVIII MS
*94.10   uninitiated] A1; unitiated
 MS

*94.30　hatefully] A1; balefully MS

95.4　throat] A1; neck MS

*95.17　others] A1; brothers MS

95.21　resembled] A1; were like MS

95.23　his] A1; *omit* MS

96.10　borne] A1; born MS

97.15　Henry] A1; Flem MS

97.34　down,] A1; ~ ₄ MS

98.4　tree,₄] A1; ~ ,' MS

98.5　₄Th'] A1; '~ MS

98.5　be.] V; ~ , MS; ~ ! A1,E1

98.6　That's] A1; *indented* MS

98.7　an] E1; an' MS,A1

98.9　an] V; an' MS,A1,E1

99.0　XVIII] A1; XIX MS

99.1　its] *stet* MS

99.20　shrieked] A1; shreiked MS

*100.2　hurlying] *stet* MS

100.6　deep₄] A1; ~ , MS

*100.16　flip-flapping] A1; flip-flopping MS,$N (*except* N³: *unclear*)

100.20　the youth] A1,$N; Fleming MS

100.27　sliding] MS(u),A1,N⁶; slideing MS(c)

100.28　breathing] A1,N⁶; breatheing MS

101.12　a] A1,$N; 'a MS

101.23　companion₄] A1,$N; ~ , MS

101.35　t'] $N; *omit* MS; to A1

101.37(*twice*) going to] V; goin' t' MS+

101.38　the youth] V; the youth's friend MS+

*102.5　Fleming] V; Wilson MS+

102.5　lyin'] A1,$N; liein' MS

102.9　lyin'] A1,N⁶; liein' MS

102.9　talkin'] A1,N⁶; ~ ₄ MS

102.13–14　The soldier] A1; Wilson MS; The youth N⁶

*102.15　soldier] *stet* MS

102.27　shepherds] A1; sheperds MS

102.33　grimy] A1,$N; grimey MS

*102.39–103.1　his friend] *stet* MS,A1

*103.7　swallered] *stet* MS

104.0　XIX] A1; XX MS

104.14　goal] A1,$N; gaol MS

104.14　throughout,] V; ~ ₄ MS,A1,$N,E1

105.3　-footed,] A1,$N; ~ ₄ MS

*105.25　took mechanical] V; took a mechanical MS,A1,N⁶,E1

105.36　the youth] A1; Fleming MS

106.26　He] A1,$N; His MS

107.36　on'y] A1; o'ny MS; only N⁶

107.36　then——"] N⁶; ~"— MS,A1

107.38　" 'Cross] V; "₄ ~ MS,A1, N⁶,E1

108.8　yourself] V; yerself MS,A1,N⁶,E1

108.16　dilapidated] A1,$N; delapidated MS

108.21　valueless] A1,N⁶; valuless MS

109.2　back,] A1,$N; ~ ₄ MS

109.3　ludicrous] A1,$N; ludicruos MS

109.3　ways,] A1; ~ ₄ MS,$N

110.0　XX] A1; XXI MS

*110.3　coming] *stet* MS,A1

110.11,12　into] A1,$N; in to MS

*110.13　speeches] *stet* MS

110.20　fell] A1,$N; felt MS

110.22　again,] A1,$N; ~ ₄ MS

110.23　time₄] A1,$N; ~ , MS

*111.8; 113.25,37; 117.10; 121.7　lieutenant] V; youthful lieutenant MS+

111.15　rearward] A1,N¹⁻³; ~ - ~ MS; ~ - | ~ N⁴⁻⁶

111.15　rage] A1,$N; *obliterated by ink blot* MS

111.16　the] A1,$N; *obliterated by ink blot* MS

111.17　his] A1; as his MS; to his $N

*111.25　When (*no* ¶)] *stet* MS

112.32–33　allusions] $N; illusions MS,A1

*112.35　buffed] *stet* MS,A1

112.39　preceding] A1,$N; precedeing MS

113.4　Henry] A1; Flem MS,$N

113.22   it] A1; them MS,N⁶
*113.32   He] stet MS
113.34   accented] A1; prentifully
accented MS; plentifully accented $N
114.13   The youth] A1,$N; Flem-
ing MS
116.0   XXI] A1; XXII MS
116.10   who] A1; who | who MS
116.11   grimmest] A1,N²; grimest
MS,$N(−N²)
117.18   incredibly] A1,$N;
incrediby MS
117.26   perspiration] A1;
perpiration MS
117.37   mule-drivers] E1; ~ ∧ ~
MS,A1
118.4   -breathing] A1; -breatheing
MS
118.37   whether] A1; wether MS
119.11   The youth] A1; Fleming
MS
119.18,20,31   didn't] A1; didnt
MS
119.21   yesterday] V; yestirday
MS,A1,E1
*119.22   he] V; he'd MS,A1,E1
119.33   stoutly.] A1; ~ , MS
120.6   him] V; 'im MS,A1,E1
120.14   damn'dest] V; damndest
MS; damnedest A1,E1; durndest $N(−N⁶); derndest N⁶
120.24   kep'] A1,$N; kep∧ MS
120.25   ²th'] A1,N⁶; th∧ MS; the
N¹⁻⁵
120.26   ²th'] A1,$N; th∧ MS
120.30   hey] $N; hay MS,A1
120.36   -generals.' "] $N; - ~ .'
MS,A1
120.37   lyin'] A1,$N(−N³); liein'
MS; lyin∧ N³
122.0   XXII] A1; XXIII MS
122.21   most∧] A1; ~ , MS
123.11   dark-blue] A1; ~ , ~ MS
123.12; 124.11   The youth] A1;
Fleming MS
*123.12–13   and laughing] stet MS
123.16   solemn] A1; solomn MS
123.18   quiet,] A1; ~ ∧ MS
123.21   new] A1; MS reads 'nw'
or 'nev'

123.29   The youth's] A1; Fleming's MS
*123.29   cups] stet MS
*123.32   men. It was] stet MS
123.38   the youth] A1; Fleming
MS
124.36   small∧] A1; ~ , MS
(comma not deleted, in error)
*124.37   in him] stet MS
125.4   ceased their] A1; their
ceased MS ('ceased' interlined
with a caret in error after
'their')
125.5   an] A1; omit MS
*125.27   hatreds] stet MS
125.29   lying] A1; lieing MS
*125.29   guttering] V; gluttering
MS,A1,E1
*125.30–31   mule-driver] stet MS
125.37   the youth's] A1; Fleming's MS
126.6   swiftly,] A1; ~ ∧ MS
127.0   XXIII] A1; XXIV MS
*128.9   questionings] stet MS
128.13   himself,] V; ~ ∧ MS,A1,
E1
*129.1   movement] A1; movement
to go MS
129.9   were] A1; was MS
129.22   a-flare,] A1; ~ ∧ MS
129.31   writhing] A1; writheing
MS
129.38   desperate] A1; determined
MS
130.1   terrible] A1; omit MS
130.6   Those (no ¶)] A1; ¶ MS
*130.30   And, with it all,] V;
~ ∧ ~ ~ ~ ∧ MS,A1,E1
130.33   toe] A1; tender toe MS
130.33   privilege] A1; privelege
MS
131.8   be] A1; omit MS
131.11; 132.5   The youth] A1;
Fleming MS
131.16   sufficiently] A1;
sufficenty MS
132.0   XXIV] A1; XXV MS
132.5   sudden,] V; ~ ∧ MS,A1,E1
132.14   grimy] A1; grimey MS
*132.20   repose.] A1; reposes be-
hind the rails. MS

*132.25 tramped] *stet* MS
132.26 scamper.] A1; scamper. The fence . . . away. MS (*see* Historical Collation)
132.30 parallel] A1; paralell MS
*133.1 the stolid] *stet* MS
133.2 lying] A1; lieing MS
133.5–6 entrenchments.] A1; entrenchments. [¶] As . . . over. MS (*see* Historical Collation)
*133.11 trampled] A1; trammeled MS
133.14 They (*no* ¶)] A1; ¶ MS
133.18 it] A1; his mind MS
133.34 sympathies.] A1; sympathies. [¶] His friend . . . swore. MS (*see* Historical Collation)
133.35 Regarding] A1; But the youth, regarding MS
133.35 he] A1; *omit* MS
134.4 conduct.] A1; conduct. He . . . coronation. MS (*see* Historical Collation)
134.6 danced.] A1; danced. Echoes of his terrible combat with the arrayed forces of the universe came to his ears. MS
134.8 shame.] A1; shame. [¶] However . . . worship. MS (*see* Historical Collation)
134.9 A] A1; As Fleming was

thus fraternizing again with nature, a MS
134.10 he∧] A1; ~ , MS
134.13 the tall soldier] A1; Conklin MS
134.15 him] A1; Fleming MS
134.19 Henry] A1; Flem MS
134.20 The (*no* ¶)] A1; ¶ MS
*134.23–24 the deeds] *stet* MS
134.26 companions,] A1; ~ ∧ MS
134.29 accomplishments] A1; accomplishment MS
134.33 behint 'em] A1; ~ ' | ∧ ~ MS
135.5 mouth."] A1; mouth." [¶] "You make me sick." [¶] "G' home, yeh fool. MS
135.13 distance.] A1; distance. And . . . contented. MS (*see* Historical Collation)
135.14 And at last his (*no* ¶)] A1; ¶ His MS
*135.14 to open] A1; to be opened MS
135.17 them.] A1; them. [¶] He . . . lost. MS (*see* Historical Collation)
135.22 death.] A1; death and was for others. MS
*135.25 tranquility] V; tranquilly MS,A1,E1
135.38–39 Over . . . clouds.] A1; *omit* MS

WORD-DIVISION

1. *End-of-the-Line Hyphenation in the Virginia Edition*

[NOTE: No hyphenation of a possible compound at the end of a line in the Virginia text is present in the copy-texts except for the following readings, which are hyphenated within the line in the manuscript. Except for these readings, all end-of-the-line hyphenation in the Virginia text may be ignored except for hyphenated compounds in which both elements are capitalized.]

3.22	blue-|clothed	75.25	sure-|enough
7.39	up-|raised	78.1	brass-|mounted
8.34	Greek-|like	78.4	death-|like
9.17	be-|whiskered	90.1	up-|roar
11.4	out-|an'	90.3	rifle-|pits
11.16	head-|quarters	90.17	sun-|rays
12.22	re-|assured	97.8	awe-|struck
17.15	door-|yard	100.6	murder-|red
22.15	color-|bearer	100.17	tree-|trunks
33.2	circus-|parade	100.33	over-|hear
41.9	thick-|spread	104.29	wedge-|shaped
43.9	barn-|yard	108.23	foot-|ball
49.27	battle-|scenes	111.32	mule-|drivers
50.21	battle-|lines	112.14	pre-|arranged
51.14	drum-|major	113.4	good-|bye
54.28	wax-|like	122.1	dark-|hued
58.29	battle-|field	122.2	self-|confidence
59.3	jim-|dandy	122.21	awe-|inspiring
62.13	knife-|thrusts	123.10	lighter-|hued
66.15	half-|apologetic	127.26	out-|lined
67.23	battle-|fiend	128.26	battle-|madness
68.27	slang-|phrase	129.33	color-|bearer
69.8	tree-|tops	135.25	hot-|ploughshares
75.18	rifle-|barrel		

2. *End-of-the-Line Hyphenations in the Manuscript*

[NOTE: The following compounds, or possible compounds, are hyphenated at the end of the line in the manuscript. The form in which they have been transcribed in the Virginia text, listed below, represents the practice of the manuscript as ascertained by other appearances or parallels, or—

failing that—by the known characteristics of Crane as seen in his other manuscripts.]

9.6	sun-tanned	72.6	war-machines
9.22	hell's-fire	73.25	t'-night
10.12	broken-bladed	73.28	a-draggin'
12.17	a-fightin'	87.4	terror-struck
13.11	new-born	95.20	knife-like
17.37	Camp-fires	104.5	a-horseback
18.29	peek-ed	111.24	mule-driver
21.12	camping-place	113.19	under-lip
23.28	sun-struck	130.13	color-bearer
43.21	war-god	130.32	prisoners-of-war
51.2	smoke-fringed	135.19	man-hood
61.30	animal-like	135.24	hot-ploughshares

3. *Special Cases*

[NOTE: In the following list the compound is hyphenated at the end of the line in the manuscript and in the Virginia edition.]

6.7 news-|papers (i.e. newspapers)

18.6 tree-|top (i.e. tree-top)

73.21 sure-|'nough (i.e. sure-'nough)

81.28 good-|thunderation (i.e. good-thunderation)

93.28 battle-|roar (i.e. battle-roar)

107.34 lunk-|head (i.e. lunkhead)

120.19 jim-|hickey (i.e. jim-hickey)

125.30 "mule-|driver," (i.e. "mule-driver,")

133.22 counter-|shot (i.e. counter-shot)

HISTORICAL COLLATION

[NOTE: All substantive variants from the Virginia text are listed here excepting those variants of dialect from the manuscript which have been adopted from other sources and thus appear in the List of Emendations. A text not mentioned to the right of the bracket will either agree with the lemma before the bracket or will be lacking at that point. All cuts in the various texts are listed here. The symbol AE1 is used to designate an agreement of A1 and E1; where either appears alone it is understood that the other agrees with the lemma before the bracket. Where alterations are incorporated into an entry, they will be followed by one of these symbols: C, P, HG, G, or F, these refer to the stage at which the alteration occurred, C = Current, i.e. at the time of inscription; P = Preliminary, prior to Hamlin Garland seeing the manuscript, this stage only applies to the first 38 folios and is primarily concerned with the removal of surnames and the substitution of epithets; Hamlin Garland's notations; G = General, a stage of revision concerned with changing some of the Preliminary epithets and with the normalization of dialect; F = notations made during the Final preparation of the manuscript for the printer.]

3.5 cast] casts N²
3.5 et seq. its] it's MS
3.7 shadow] shadows N⁵
3.9 see, across,] see across it₍
AE1,$N
3.9 gleam] gleams $N
3.12 a brook] the brook $N
3.13 was swelled with] had heard $N
3.13–17 he had . . . gold] omit $N
3.18 goin' t' move t'morrah] going to move tomorrow $N (N¹⁻²,⁴: to-morrow)
3.18 pompously] promptly $N
3.19 goin'] going $N
3.19 th'] the $N,AE1
3.20 an'] and $N
3.20 behint 'em] behind them $N
3.21 attentive] omit N⁶
3.24–26 A . . . down.] omit $N
3.28–29 "It's . . . loudly.] "It's a

thundering lie!" said a loud young private. $N
3.29–31 His . . . him.] omit $N
3.30 trousers'] trouser's MS
4.6–11 A . . . camp.] omit $N
4.12 in a] in the $N
4.14 advocated] contended $N
4.16–26 Meanwhile . . . it.] omit $N
4.16 Meanwhile] The while MS
4.23 hang."] hang. I tell yeh what I know an' yeh kin take it er leave it. Suit yerselves. It dont make no difference [preceded by deleted 'dif'f'(C)] t' me." MS
4.28 tall] excited $N
4.30 attacks] attack< > MS
4.33 on] upon N⁵
4.33 bunk] bank AE1
4.34 end] side $N

4.35–37 A . . . pegs.] *omit* $N
4.36 wall] walls MS,AE1
4.38–5.2 and some . . . floor] *omit* $N
5.3 from] of $N
5.4 And, too,] And MS; and AE1
5.5 a-blaze] afire $N
5.8 would] was going to $N
5.13 all of] all AE1
5.13–14 vague and] vague, $N
5.14–15 that . . . fire] *omit* $N
5.15 struggles.] struggles that had thrilled him with their sweep and fire. $N
5.15–10.2 He . . . run.] But monotonous weeks of camp life had made him finally regard himself as merely a part of a vast blue demonstration [N³: the vast; N⁴: *omit* vast]. He had come prepared to devastate the enemy; instead, he was made to sit still in one place and try to keep warm during the winter. He decided then that war was a legend. [¶] However, he was now told that he was going to fight. He was mutely astonished, and lay in his bunk trying to prove mathematically that he would not run. Here was a great problem. $N (*accidentals from* N¹)
6.2 told] told him AE1
6.4 Besides] Moreover AE1
6.21 town] considerable town MS
6.25 ¶ "Ma] *no* ¶ AE1
6.26 ¶ There] *no* ¶ AE1
6.32 trails] hot trails MS
7.9 git] get AE1
7.16 and a-learning] an' a-learning AE1
7.16 'im] 'em AE1
7.20 right.] right. [¶] Young fellers in the ['e' *over apostrophe* (G)] army get ['e' *over* 'i' (G)] awful careless [*interlined above deleted* 'keerless' (G)] in their ways, Henry. They're away f'm home and ['d' *added*

(G)] they don't have nobody to ['o' *over apostrophe* (G)] look after [*interlined above deleted* 'atter' (G)] 'em [' 'e' *over* ' 'i' (G)]. I'm 'feard fer yeh about ['a' *over apostrophe* (G)] that. Yeh aint never been used to ['o' *over apostrophe* (G)] doing ['g' *over apostrophe* (G)] fer yerself. So yeh must keep writing ['g' *over apostrophe* (G)] to ['o' *over apostrophe* (G)] me how yer clothes are lasting ['g' *over apostrophe* (G)]. MS
7.29 all.] Don't fergit to ['o' *over apostrophe* (G)] send yer socks to ['o' *over apostrophe* (G)] me the ['e' *over apostrophe* (G)] minute they git holes in 'em and ['d' *over apostrophe* (G)] here's a little bible I want yeh to ['o' *over apostrophe* (G)] take along with yeh, Henry. I dont presume yeh'll be a-setting reading [*both* 'g's *over apostrophes* (G)] it all day long, [*comma inserted after deleted period* (C)] child, ner nothin' like that. Many a time, yeh'll fergit yeh got it, I don't doubt. But there'll be many a time, too, Henry, when yeh'll be wanting ['g' *over apostrophe* (G)] advice, boy, and ['d' *over apostrophe* (G)] all like that, and ['d' *over apostrophe* (G)] there'll be nobody round, perhaps ['e' *over apostrophe* (G)], to ['o' *over apostrophe* (G)] tell yeh things. Then if yeh take it out, boy, yeh'll find wisdom in it—wisdom in it, Henry—with little or no searching ['g' *over apostrophe* (G)]. MS
8.19 in her movement] *omit* MS
9.8 afterwards] afterward A1
9.9 their] *omit* MS
9.9,13 The youth] Fleming MS
9.11 of them] *omit* MS

9.17 him] Fleming MS
9.22 powder] powders AE1
9.24 the youth] Fleming MS
9.26 veterans'] veteran's MS
10.5–7 A . . . it.] *omit* $N
10.9 a] this $N
10.9 fight] flight N²
10.9 saw] saw the N³
10.10 future and failed] close future, and his mind failed $N
10.11–13 He . . . pictures.] *omit* $N
10.14 the] his $N
10.15–22 aloud . . . repeated] *omit* $N
10.24 soldier] private $N
10.25 private] young one $N
10.26 said . . . soldier] the tall soldier was saying $N
10.26–27 He . . . expressively.] *omit* $N
10.28–29 All . . . right.] *omit* $N
10.28 All yeh] All you've E1
10.30 comrade] companion $N
10.30–31 For . . . he] and $N
10.32 th'] *omit* N⁶
10.33–35 "Didn't . . . knapsack.] *omit* $N
10.36–37 looked . . . figure.] interrupted their quarrel. $N
10.37 he asked] *omit* $N
10.38 replied] said $N
10.38–11.22 "Of . . . What?"] Presently the youth asked: $N
11.9 just] jest AE1
11.24 I guess,] *omit* $N
11.25–26 He . . . person.] *omit* $N
11.26 'em] them $N
11.27 they're] they are $N
11.27 'a . . . that,] *omit* $N
11.29 boys'll] boys will N⁶
11.30 be] *omit* MS
11.30 'em] them N¹⁻⁵
11.31 'specially] especially $N
11.32 other] tall soldier $N
11.32–12.1 "'A . . . but] *omit* $N
11.34 come] came MS(c),AE1

11.37; 12.2 -onct] -oncet AE1 (*no hyphen at* 12.2)
11.38 worser] worse MS(c), A1
12.1 an'] and AE1
12.1 come 'a] come to N²
12.2 most 'a 'em'll] they'll $N
12.2 like sin] all right $N
12.2 -onct-git-shootin'] once get dead into it $N
12.3–9 he . . . them] *omit* $N
12.3 four last] last four AE1
12.10 he asked.] remarked the youth thoughtfully. $N
12.10–12 On . . . giggled.] *omit* $N
12.13 tall] *omit* N³
12.14 I've] I N³
12.15 'a boys] of boys MS,AE1; of the boys $N(N³: o the boys)
12.15 an' run] to run N¹⁻⁵; run N⁶
12.16–17 An' . . . mistake.] *omit* $N
12.17 a-fightin'] fighting N⁶
12.18 why,] why then $N
12.18 I would . . . it.] *omit* $N
12.19 "Huh . . . one.] "Shucks!" snorted the loud private scornfully. $N
12.20 ¶ The . . . gratitude] (*no* ¶) But the youth felt grateful $N
12.21 comrade] tall comrade $N
12.21 possessed] felt $N
12.22 now was] was now $N
13.1 The . . . youth] Fleming discovered the next mornin MS (*false start*)
13.1 his] the N²
13.3–7 There . . . severely.] *omit* $N
13.8 ¶ The youth] (*no* ¶) He $N
13.8 no wise] nowise N¹⁻⁴
13.11 Now, with the] And now with this $N
13.12 part] a part N³
13.15 He finally] Finally he $N
13.16 to watch] watch N¹⁻⁵
13.17–21 He . . . opportunity.] *omit* $N
13.25 known] know MS

13.25   since] from $N
13.26   ²he] this man $N
13.27–30 the youth . . . war.]
    omit $N
14.2   joy] great joy $N
14.4–7   He looked . . . himself.]
    omit $N
14.4   moods] mood AE1
14.8   concern] condition $N
14.8   he dreaded to] it might $N
14.9   confidant] confidante MS
14.11–37 In . . . veteran.] omit
    $N
14.28–29   tradition] traditions
    AE1
14.31   to be] omit AE1
15.2   the day] day $N
15.4   a yellow] a a yellow N²
15.5   sun. And] ~ ; and AE1; ~ ,
    and $N
15.7   trampling] tramping N³
15.10   The youth] Fleming MS
15.11–12   were to be kept] would
    be kept N¹⁻³,⁵; would be kept in
    N⁴
15.13–19   As . . . moustache.]
    omit $N
15.15   be] he E1
15.22   bended] bent AE1,$N
15.24   jangling] a jangling N⁶
15.26   ranks] rank N⁴
15.28–31   As . . . war.] omit
    N¹⁻⁵
15.33   of] omit N⁶
15.38   creakings] crackings N¹⁻⁵;
    cracklings N⁶
16.2   as] omit N¹⁻²
16.3   comrade] companion N¹⁻⁵
16.6   forward] along MS,$N
16.9   of] omit MS
16.11   sun-rays] sun's rays N²
16.11–12   mellowingly]
    mellowing N⁴
16.14   a hill] the hill $N
16.17   into praises] out in praise
    MS, $N
16.18–20   "I . . . soldier.] omit
    A1; "Didn't I tell you?" $N
16.21–25   Some . . . discus-
    sion.] omit $N

16.30   ahead∧ often,] ~ ∧ ~ ∧ MS,
    $N(−N²)
16.30   rattle] rattling N⁴
16.32–20.24   But . . . asleep.]
    omit $N
17.2   behind] behint MS
17.10   loud] blatant AE1 (unclear
    alteration in MS)
17.18–20   The . . . statue.] omit
    MS
18.10   himself] him MS
19.9   fer] for AE1
19.36   loud] blatant MS
20.1   yeh was] you was AE1
20.17   could] would AE1
21.8–22.16   After . . . pole.]
    omit $N
21.18   fingers. And] ~ , and AE1
21.20   grumbling] grumblings
    AE1
21.26–27   drink, sleep] omit AE1
21.28   need . . . hotel?"] want
    to do." AE1
22.4   this] the AE1
22.4   likely] like MS
22.14   ¶ And] no ¶ AE1
22.14   were] was MS
22.17   down] dawn N⁶
22.29–33   He . . . fer?"]
    omit $N
22.29   men] man MS
22.34   The youth] He $N
22.37–23.2   He . . . mob.] omit
    N¹⁻⁵
23.7–15   He . . . slaughtered!]
    omit $N
23.17–18   The mournful . . .
    men.] omit N¹⁻⁵
23.19   on the] of the N⁵
23.19,33   further] farther AE1,N⁶
23.22   exceeded] acceded MS
23.23   battle-] little N³
23.25   in] omit N⁴
23.37   trees] tree N³
24.1   startling] starting $N(−N³)
24.3   advance] front N²
24.4   thickets] the thickets N³
24.6–19   Once . . . Question.]
    omit $N
24.20   this] the AE1

24.20 the youth] Fleming MS
(*false start*)

24.21 when . . . field] in his
scramble up the bank MS(*false
start*)

24.24 nature] Nature AE1

24.29 ²that] *omit* N⁵

24.30 no] not N⁵

24.31–25.2 A house . . . death.]
omit N¹⁻⁵

24.31 to him] *omit* N⁶

25.4 all] *omit* N²

25.11 fields] the fields N²

25.11 The youth] Fleming MS

25.13–14 fascinated] interested
N³

25.15 into] in N¹⁻⁵

25.16 untested] interested N⁵

25.20 his throat] the throat N⁶

25.28–28.37 He . . . away.]
omit $N

25.28 young] youthful MS

25.30 young man] Fleming MS

26.11 front] fronts AE1

26.24 another] a another MS

27.3 just] jest AE1

27.8 ¹yit] *omit* AE1

27.9 do] do a MS

27.33 stupidity] stupidity affair
MS

27.35 thought] thought that MS

28.5 skirmish-] unceasing
skirmish- MS

28.7 could] would AE1

28.36 and raised] waved MS

29.4 this] the N³

29.7 gossip] the gossip MS,$N

29.8 the unknown] an unknown
N²

29.9–30.8 "They . . . feller."]
omit $N

29.9 Perry] Perrey MS

29.18 command] cammand MS,
A1

29.22,24 Hannises'] Hannises∧
MS

30.6 So] Se A1

30.8 feller."] feller." [¶] "Hear
that what th' ol' colonel ses ['e'
over 'a' (C)], boys. He ses he'll
shoot th' first man what'll turn

an' run." [¶] "He'd better try it.
I'd like t' see him shoot at *me*."
[¶] "He wants t' look fer his
ownself. He don't wanta go
'round talkin' big." [¶] "They
say Perrey's division's a-givin'-
em thunder." [¶] "Ed Williams
over in Company A, he ses th'
rebs'll all drop their guns an'
run an' holler if we onct giv'em
['e' *over* 'i' (C)] one good
lickin'.'." [¶] "Oh, thunder, Ed
Williams, what does he know?
[*question mark over period*
(C)] Ever since he got shot at
on picket, he's been runnin' th'
war." [¶] "Well, [*comma over
possible beginning of a dash*
(C)] he——" [¶] "Hear th'
news, boys? [*question mark
over period* (C)] Corkright's
crushed th' hull rebel right an'
captured two hull divisions.
We'll be back in winter quarters by a short cut t'-morrah."
[¶] "I tell yeh I've been all over
that there kentry where th'
rebel right is an it's th' nastiest
part th' rebel line. It's all
mussed up with hills an' little
damn creeks. I'll bet m' shirt
Corkright never harmed 'em
down there." [¶] "Well he's a
fighter an' if they could be
licked, he'd lick 'em." MS (*end
of page 40; pages 41–44 wanting*)

30.9–32.8 The din . . . them.]
omit MS

30.13 fields] field N³

30.16 the grove] a grove N³

30.19 trees] tree trunks $N

30.20 wielded] welded N⁵

30.24 regimental] regimently
N¹,³⁻⁴

30.25 new] *omit* N¹⁻⁵

30.27–32 He . . . done.] *omit*
N¹⁻⁵

30.29–32 The . . . done.] *omit*
N⁶

30.40–31.1 in grey] of gray N³

31.3; 34.1 304th] Three Hundred and Fourth $N

31.4 jeer] cheer N[6]

31.5 the banshee] banshee N[6]

31.5 shells] the shells N[5]

31.8 Saunders's] Saunders$_\wedge$ $N

31.11 blue] *omit* N[3]

31.12 carven] craven N[1-5]

31.12 afterward] afterwards N[6]

31.14 apart] braced apart $N

31.15 bellowing] following AE1

31.16 along] *omit* N[4]

31.20-29 A . . . directions.] *omit* N[6]

31.20-32 A . . . audience.] *omit* N[1-5]

31.30 jokes] jibes N[6]

31.31 apparently were] were apparently N[6]

31.33 for an instant] *omit* $N

31.35 heaven] Heaven N[1-2,4-5]

31.35 been able to have] *omit* N[3]

31.37-39 There . . . desire.] *omit* $N

32.2 reserves] reserve $N

32.7 thought$_\wedge$] ~ , N[1-3,5]

33.0 CHAPTER V] *omit* $N

33.1-11 The youth . . . prominence.] *omit* $N

33.12 ¶ Some one] (*no* ¶) Then someone $N (N[1-2,5-6]: some one)

33.15 The] Their $N

33.16 seven hundred] 700 N[1-5]

33.18-20 The . . . cry] At last a cry $N

33.19 knotting] knitting AE1

33.22 "Here (*no* ¶)] ¶ AE1

33.25 all] right N[6]

33.27-30 As . . . not.] *omit* $N

33.31 A hatless] CHAPTER V. | A hatless $N

34.1 fist] hat N[3]

34.3 back."] back." He seemed greatly insulted. N[1-5]; back." He seemed greatly excited. N[6]

34.4 A-all r-right] A-all-right $N (−N[3]); A all right N[3]

34.5-6 —we-we'll . . . general."] best." $N

34.7-11 The colonel . . . them.] *omit* $N

34.17-18 'til . . . 'til] till . . . till AE1; until . . . until $N

34.18 get] are N[6]

34.25 piece] peace N[2]

34.36 moments] some moments AE1

34.37 a hand] the hand N[5]

34.38 about] was about AE1

35.3 vitality] fatality N[2]

35.3 fades] dies N[3]

35.3 a] *omit* $N

35.8 and] an N[3]

35.9-15 He . . . shapes.] *omit* $N

35.11 thoughts] thought AE1

35.29 who] which AE1

35.33-36.7 There . . . hears.] *omit* N[6]

35.33-36.35 There . . . him.] *omit* N[1-5]

36.11 furiously] feverishly MS, N[6]

36.13 bobbed] flapped and bobbed MS,N[6]

36.16 which] *omit* N[6]

36.16 had] which had N[6]

36.18-35 The . . . him.] *omit* N[6]

36.21 were] was MS

36.22 nearly] near MS

36.38 out] *omit* $N

37.6 was] was a N[2]

37.7-11 Further . . . tree.] *omit* $N

37.7 Further] Farther AE1

37.13 firing] fire N[2]

37.13 last] *omit* $N

37.14 eddied] ebbed N[2]

37.15 were] was N[6]

37.16-17 straddle the rail] *omit* $N

37.20 silent] silence MS (*partially corrected by* Hamlin Garland; *see alterations*)

37.21 that] *omit* $N

37.25 warmed] warm $N

37.27(*twice*) helt] held $N

37.27 derned] darned N[3-4]

37.28 The] Then N[1-4]

37.32   in which] *omit* $N
37.33   ghastly] ghastily N[1]
37.34   bended] bent AE1
37.39–38.9   From . . . thither.]
  omit N[1-5]
38.1–6   The . . . confusion.]
  omit N[6]
38.5   formula] formulae MS
38.10   were] was N[5]
38.11   toward] to $N
38.14   lighter] other N[3]
38.21   effort] effect N[6]
38.23   troops] the troops $N
38.24   the emblems] the emblem
  AE1; emblems N[1-5]
38.28   clamors] clamor N[3]
38.34   nature] Nature AE1
38.35   processes] process AE1,$N
39.1   The youth] Fleming MS
  (*false start*)
39.1   came] came came MS (*false start*)
39.7   mopped] moped MS
39.10–27   [1]He . . . shin.] *omit* $N
39.12   [1]the] that AE1
39.19   -sleeve] ∧sleeves AE1
39.22   'til—'til] till AE1
39.25   only] *omit* AE1
39.25   the youth] Fleming MS
39.29,30   ag'in] a'gin MS; again $N
39.30–31   The . . . Gosh!"]
  omit $N
40.2   begin to swell] swelling $N
40.10–12   They . . . tasks.]
  omit N[6]
40.10–32   They . . . resplendent.] *omit* N[1-5]
40.13–18   "Oh . . . his'n."]
  omit N[6]
40.17   Smithers] Smither's MS
40.22–23   He . . . bowing.] *omit* N[6]
40.29   grate] gate AE1
40.30   [1]the] *omit* N[6]
40.34   back] neck AE1
40.36   was] were $N
40.39–41.3   The . . . army."]
  omit $N
41.1   appear] recur AE1

41.2–3   thing." "What . . . supports?" "I] ~ · ∧ ∧ ~ · · ·
  ~ · ∧ ∧ ~ AE1
41.7–8   It . . . sun-down.] *omit* $N
41.14   dragons] dragoons N[4]
41.16   of a] of $N
41.19–26   A . . . rabbit.] *omit* $N
41.20   dropped it] *omit* MS; stopped AE1
41.21; 53.28; 90.10; 96.10   borne] born MS
41.27   Others] Men $N
41.28   this] his $N
41.29   was] were $N
41.31–33   For . . . points.]
  omit N[1-5]
41.36   bobbed] bobbled $N
  (−N[4])
41.36   wildly] widely N[5]
41.39–42.4   The . . . occasion.]
  omit N[1-5]
42.6   shoulder] shoulders $N
42.11–14   When . . . crushed.]
  omit $N
42.15   [1]on] *omit* N[2]
42.15   others] the others N[2]
42.15   men] the men N[6]
42.17   these] those N[3]
42.19–24   In . . . race.] *omit* N[6]
42.19–43.30   In . . . noises.]
  omit N[1-5]
42.25   leading] *omit* N[6]
42.25   across] a across MS
42.26   a region] the region N[6]
42.26   hurtled] hurled N[6]
42.27   heard them,] listened AE1
42.29   his way] the way AE1
42.32–43.28   He . . . hurry.]
  omit N[6]
43.3   The youth] Fleming MS
43.10   deep] deeply AE1
43.20   mouth] mouths AE1
43.29   went on, moderating] moderated N[6]
43.29   since] when N[6]
43.30   of noises.] and noises behind. N[6]
43.31   division] the division N[2]; a division N[3]

43.34   saddle and] *omit* N⁶
44.3   chaos] the chaos N³ˑ⁶
44.5   and] *omit* N²
44.6   opportunity] the opportunity N¹⁻⁵
44.6   why——] why—destruction. $N
44.7–21   He . . . dust.] *omit* N¹⁻⁵
44.10   destruction] tempestuous defeat N⁶
44.12–21   As . . . dust.] *omit* N⁶
44.13   an' tell] and tell E1
44.14   an] *omit* MS
44.15   ²th'] the E1
44.22   ¶ A] (*no* ¶) But a $N
44.26   'em . . . 'em] 'im . . . 'im MS,AE1; them . . . them $N
44.26   They've held 'em!] *omit* N³
44.27–33   "We'll . . . general] He $N
44.34   paean] peon N⁶
45.1   at] in AE1
45.2   ¹had] have N⁵
45.5   fog] flag N⁵
45.6   clatter] clattering $N
45.10–46.12   He . . . words.] *omit* $N
45.29   proven] proved AE1
46.11   little] *omit* AE1
46.12   words.] words; who, through his suffering, thinks that he peers into the core of things and see that the judgment of man ['a' *over* 'e' (C)] is thistle-down in wind. MS
46.13   fields] field $N
46.13   thick] thicks MS
46.13   woods] wood N²,E1
46.14   crackling] cracking N¹ˑ³⁻⁴
46.15   shots] shouts N²
46.16–26   The . . . him.] *omit* $N
46.26   So] *omit* $N
46.29–30   The insects . . . unison.] *omit* $N
46.31   around] round N⁴
46.32   wing] wings N¹⁻⁵
46.33,37; 47.12   nature] Nature AE1

46.35–47.19   This . . . fish.] *omit* $N
47.2   an] a A1
47.6   a] *omit* AE1
47.12   ¶ The youth] *no* ¶ AE1
47.13   arguments] argument AE1
47.19   gleaming] silver-gleaming MS
47.20   The youth] He $N
47.21   sounds] sound N³
47.21   cannon] the cannon N³; cannons N⁶
47.22   a] *omit* N³ˑ⁶
47.25   a chapel] chapel N⁶
47.29   a thing] the thing N⁵
47.31   column-like] *omit* N²
47.35   opened] open AE1,N²
47.37   along] across N⁵
48.1   living man] living N¹⁻⁵
48.5   his back] back N¹⁻⁵
48.8   upon] *omit* $N
48.8–9   in brambles] at branches N¹⁻⁵
48.12   bonds] bounds MS,N¹⁻⁵
48.15   horribly] *omit* $N
48.19   sighingly] soughingly AE1; slightly $N
49.1   sun] burnished sun MS,$N
49.7   clangor] clange N⁵
49.8   this] the N²
49.8   terrific] *omit* N³
49.10   ripping] rippling $N
49.10   breaking] creaking $N (−N⁵); cracking N⁵
49.17   the moon] moon $N(−N⁴)
49.18   roofs] the roofs AE1; the roof N³
49.20–50.39   As . . . begone.] *omit* N¹⁻⁵
49.30–50.8   Reflecting . . . ilk.] *omit* N⁶
49.31   himself] he MS (*see alterations for* Hamlin Garland *correction*)
50.8   everyone] every one AE1
50.12   thought] thoughts N⁶
50.13   ¹was] were MS,N⁶
50.15–20   Sometimes . . . ways and] *omit* N⁶
50.19   nature] Nature AE1
50.22   voices] voice N⁶

50.30–39   He . . . begone.] *omit* N[6]
50.33   Further] Farther AE[1]
50.39   swollen] swollen and ghastly MS
51.1   could] cold N[6]
51.7   was] *omit* AE[1]; were $N
51.13–22   One . . . tune.] *omit* $N
51.24   lips were] lips was N[5]
51.24   clenched] clinched AE[1],N[5]
51.28   with] *omit* N[2]
51.32–52.5   An . . . unknown.] *omit* $N
52.6   this] the $N
52.16   -stain] -stains N[6]
52.17–26   He . . . abashed.] *omit* N[1-5]
52.22   a-gape] a-gap N[6]
52.24   keerful] careful N[6]
52.25   a-ketchin'] catching N[6]
52.28   diffident] different AE[1]
52.28   try] tried $N
52.29   pleading] pleasing N[2]
52.35,38; 53.5   wa'n't] wasn't $N
52.36   its] his N[5]
53.1–4   There . . . fellow.] *omit* $N
53.3   the youth] Fleming MS
53.5   Was] Was a N[4]
53.5   began] persisted $N
53.7–11   I . . . be.] *omit* N[1-5]
53.7,10   knowed] knew N[6]
53.7–8   th' boys'd] the boys would N[6]
53.8   lick] like AE[1]
53.8   onct] once N[6]
53.8   Th'] The N[6]
53.9   chanct up t'] chance up to N[6]
53.10   it'd] it would N[6]
53.10   Yeh] You N[6]
53.12   breath] sigh N[5]
53.12–22   2He . . . fit."] *omit* $N
53.19   t'um] t' 'um AE[1]
53.25   Where yeh] Were you N[1-5]; Where you N[6]
53.25   ol'] old $N
53.27   this] the N[1-5]
53.29–30   "What . . . man.] *omit* N[1-5]

53.30   yeh] you N[6]
53.32–35   His . . . problem.] *omit* N[1-5]
53.34   bended] bent AE[1]
54.3   others] the others AE[1],$N
54.10   peculiarly] particularly N[4]
54.11   red] little red MS,$N
54.20   great] *omit* N[6]
54.23   passions] passion AE[1]
54.28   latter] later N[2,4]
54.29   the youth] Fleming MS
55.2,7,25,31,37; 56.2   Henry] Flem MS,$N
55.7–8   in . . . voice] monotonously N[4]
55.8   mebbe yeh] maybe you $N
55.9   t' pay t'-day] to pay to-day $N(N[2-3,5]: today)
55.9   worryin'] worrying $N
55.9   it] you N[6]
55.11–19   "Yeh . . . rear.] *omit* N[1-5]
55.12   2An'] And N[6]
55.19   tragedies] own tragedies AE[1]
55.21   a terror] terror N[3]
55.23   about] around N[1-5]
55.26   them] then N[2]
55.32   I] I'll N[6]
55.33   gulpings] gulping $N
55.35–56.6   But . . . gestures.] *omit* $N
55.38   pretty] a pretty AE[1]
56.7   those] his N[5]
56.11   2no—] *omit* $N
56.12–14   His . . . be——"] *omit* N[1-2]
56.12   fixed again] again fixed N[5]
56.17   shoulder] shoulders A[1]
56.19   batt'ry] battery N[5]
56.19   helitywhoop] helitywoop N[3]
56.19   runned] run N[1-5]
56.20   about] *omit* N[6]
56.20   yeh] ye N[4]
56.22   stren'th] strength $N
56.25   soldier] youth MS
56.32   jouncing] bouncing $N
56.32   this] his $N
56.37–38   His . . . pain.] *omit* $N

56.39   a pursuit] pursuit N[2]
57.5   dulled] dull N[5-6]
57.5   place] face N[5]
57.6   leave me be—] *omit* N[2]
57.8–14   The . . . minnit."] *omit* N[1-5]
57.22–24   And . . . -crushing.] *omit* $N
57.24   [1]They] They could not understand; they MS,$N
57.28   [2]had] *omit* N[1-3,5]
57.30   sides] side AE[1]
57.38   of gradual strangulation] *omit* $N
57.39–58.1   and . . . ground] *omit* $N
58.8   by] with N[4]
58.9   in the] of the N[4]
58.12–14   For . . . enthusiasm.] *omit* $N
58.15–16   There . . . sound.] *omit* N[6]
58.21–23   The . . . friend.] *omit* N[1-5]
58.24   He] The youth N[1-5]
58.32   wafer] fierce wafer MS,$N
59.0   CHAPTER X] *continuation of* Chapter IX N[1-5]; Chapter IX *heading repeated in* N[6]
59.2   was] was a N[4]
59.2   fer] for $N
59.5   wonner] wonder N[1-5]
59.12   Look-a-here] ~ ∧ ~ - ~ $N
59.13   an' we] and' we N[2]
59.14   t'] to N[5]
59.14–17   This . . . days.] *omit* $N
59.16   enjoyin'] enjoying AE[1]
59.20   to] *omit* N[1-5]
59.21   cried] cried, in fear MS,$N
59.24   dreamfully] dreamily N[1-5]
59.28–29   ask . . . question] interrogate it $N
60.3–8   The . . . grass.] *omit* N[1]
60.11   damn'] damn∧ N[1-5]; d— N[6]
60.12   He . . . was] Was he MS, $N
60.13   tortured] *omit* $N
60.13   grim] *omit* $N
60.15   There's] There MS,AE[1]

60.15–19   There's . . . fun.] *omit* $N
60.21   th' way] the way N[6]
60.22   jest] just N[5]
60.22   seen] see N[5]
60.24–35   "Yeh . . . Jamison."] *omit* $N
60.28   infernal, tooty- . . . -too,] infernal! AE[1]
60.32   dumb] *omit* AE[1]
60.35   t'wa'n't] t'was n't A[1]; 'twasn't E[1]
60.36   There's] Ther's N[1-5]
60.37   t'] to $N
60.38   b'lieve] believe $N
60.39   went] walked N[2]
60.39   peek-ed] peeked $N
61.1   gota] got a AE[1],$N
61.2–4   Ye'd . . . thunder.] *omit* $N
61.4   his harangue] to harangue vaguely $N
61.5–12   "I . . . located?"] *omit* $N
61.7   t'] to AE[1]
61.13   been] begun N[5]
61.13–14   introduction . . . topic.] other had begun to speak of wounds. $N
61.15–19   He . . . bay.] *omit* $N
61.17–18   His . . . up-raising] Was his companion ever to play such an intolerable part? Was he ever going to up-raise MS
61.18   their] his MS
61.19   the tattered man] him MS
61.19   one] a man MS
61.20   desperate] a desperate N[5]
61.21   wanta] want a N[4]
61.22   other] tattered man MS,$N
61.23   gota] got a N[4]
61.24   had] *omit* MS
61.25   hate] hatred AE[1]
61.27   tattered] battered N[5]
61.28–29   The youth] Fleming MS
61.29   looking] looked MS,$N
61.29   that other] the other $N
61.32   a—] *omit* $N
61.32,37,39;62.1,7   Tom Jamison] *omit* $N

61.34   pointed] replied N[5]
61.38   It . . . devil.] *omit* $N
62.2–3   —fer . . . [4]ain't] *omit* $N
62.9   fields] field AE[1]
62.10–21   He . . . vigilance.] *omit* $N
62.21   the power of] human MS
63.0   CHAPTER XI] ~ X. $N
63.5–65.31   As . . . headlong.] *omit* N[1-5]
63.11–19   The . . . vindication.] *omit* N[6]
63.28–64.5   The . . . rigid.] *omit* N[6]
64.6   them] the regiments N[6]
64.11–65.31   He . . . headlong.] *omit* N[6]
64.11   mind] mind then MS
64.16   than] that MS
64.23   liked] like MS
64.37   start] start fleetly MS
65.29   wings] red wings MS
65.35   movement] moment $N
65.35   sores] scores N[2]
66.1   green] crimson MS,$N
66.3   [1]had] had not N[3]
66.3   not] *omit* N[3]
66.4–10   As . . . off.] *omit* $N
66.12   battle] battles $N
66.14–68.28   He . . . -phrase.] *omit* N[6]
66.14–69.2   He . . . saw] He saw N[1-5]
66.23   further] farther AE[1]
66.33   ditties] sad ditties MS
67.3,9   the youth] Fleming MS
68.8   tale] tale which MS
68.14   Henry] *omit* MS
69.0   CHAPTER XII] *omit* N[6]
69.7   buffaloes] buffalo N[3]
69.13–15   He . . . damned.] *omit* $N
69.15   damned.] doomed. He lost concern for himself. MS
69.16   dragons] dragoons N[1-5]
69.20   him, something bade] something bade him N[1-5]
69.22   what—] *omit* N[3]
69.26   They . . . men.] *omit* $N
70.1   dismay] misery N[5]

70.5   The youth] Fleming MS
70.6   gotten] got AE[1]
70.7   the fleeing] fleeing N[5]
70.12   his] a N[2]
70.13   balking] balky $N
70.14,19   Letgo . . . Letgo]   Let go . . . Let go AE[1],$N
70.16   his rifle] the rifle N[6]
70.22   the youth's] Fleming's MS
70.25   The] Then N[5]
70.26   wings of] *omit* N[5]
70.28   writhing] withering $N
70.30   like] a like N[2]
70.34   grass] air N[5]
70.34   a] *omit* N[3]
70.35.1   *omit*] CHAPTER XI. $N
71.4   went] went in $N(−N[3]); went on N[3]
71.5–6   search for] reach MS,$N
71.8   scratching] scorching N[6]
71.9   clenched] clinched A[1],N[1-5]
71.11   grumble] rumble N[2,5-6]
71.21   in] of N[6]
71.25   fields] field AE[1]
71.30   howled] roared MS,$N
71.33   illumine] illume N[4]
71.38   place] places $N
72.1   blue and] *omit* $N
72.3   forest] forests $N
72.3   The (*no* ¶)] ¶ AE[1]
72.20   that] *omit* $N
72.23–36   Amidst . . . ground.] *omit* $N
72.23   Amidst] Amid AE[1]
73.4   be in] bein N[6]
73.7   of] with N[5]
73.8   your] yeh N[4]
73.8–9   Th' . . . way.] *omit* N[4]
73.9   your] yeh N[1-3,5]
73.9   lift] left MS
73.12   the replies] replies N[6]
73.12   the mind] the replies N[5]
73.13–74.9   Sometimes . . . it."] *omit* $N
73.31   like that] that color MS
74.10–11   the man . . . youth] he seemed $N
74.11   the youth] Fleming MS
74.11   a magic] magic N[6]
74.12   forest] forests $N
74.13   displayed] betrayed N[5]

74.15 became of] became N^4
74.15 The youth] Fleming MS
74.16 by] near $N
74.19 cheery] cherry N^3
74.21 there] ther $N($N^2$ possi-bly: ther')
74.23 reg'ment] regiment N^5
74.25 and] omit N^6
74.27 strided] strode AE1,$N
74.27 who] who had AE1,$N
75.0 CHAPTER XIII] omit $N
75.1 The youth] He $N
75.7 made] made some N^4
75.15 black] dark $N
75.19.1 omit] CHAPTER XII $N
75.20–21 the loud soldier] Wilson MS; his loud friend $N
75.21 the youth's] Fleming's MS
75.22 Henry] Flem MS,$N
75.23 it's—] omit $N
75.24 ol'] Flem, ol' MS,$N
75.24 the other] Wilson MS; the loud one $N
75.25 fer] for $N^{2,5}$
75.25 ³yeh] you E1
75.26 voice.] voice. | dead sure enough." There was husky emo-|tion in his voice. N^1
75.27 The youth] Fleming MS
75.30 comrade] comrades AE1
75.31 the loud soldier] Wilson MS; him $N
76.1 on] there to N^5
76.4 saw] see MS,AE1,$N
76.4–5 Awful . . . too.] omit $N
76.4 could've] could 'a MS,E1; could a' A1
76.6 His friend] Wilson MS; The loud private $N
76.7 first] at first $N
76.7–8 we . . . Simpson] omit $N
76.10 that it] it $N
76.12 Yer] Yeh AE1; You're $N
76.12 th'] the $N
76.12 derndest] durndest $N^{1,3-5}$; darndest N^2
76.12,28,39 Henry] Flem MS,$N
76.14–17 We . . . yeh?] omit $N
76.18 the youth] Fleming MS

76.20 his friend] Wilson MS; his loud friend $N
76.20 had] omit $N
76.21 th'] the $N
76.21 t'] to $N
76.22 and] and put $N
76.23,27 the youth's] Fleming's MS
76.24–26 "Gee . . . voice.] omit N^{1-5}
76.25; 77.1 The youth] Fleming MS
76.27; 77.1 the corporal] Simpson MS
76.28 'a] a' $N(-N^{3,5})$; o' $N^{3,5}$
76.29 the loud private] Wilson MS
76.30 t'] to $N(-N^1)$
76.30 my] the N^3
76.30 hol'] hold $N
76.31 'a] of $N
76.31–33 Look . . . him.] omit $N
76.34 The youth's] Fleming's MS
76.34 his friend's] Wilson's MS
76.35–36 the corporal's] Simpson's MS
76.36 submitted] submitting MS
76.38 wobbled] wabbled $N^{1-2,4-5}$
76.39 The corporal] Simpson MS
76.40 look] a look $N^{3,5}$
77.1 down] omit $N
77.1 aside] down MS,$N
77.2 in] into N^4
77.5 drew] draw AE1
77.6 with] omit MS
77.10–18 It's . . . yeh.] omit $N
77.16 an'] and E1
77.22 form] from N^2
77.22 the ground] ground MS
77.24 posture] fashion N^2
77.24 into] in $N
77.27 tired] tried N^4
77.29 a scene] the scene N^{1-5},E1
77.31–78.9 On . . . brambles.] omit $N
78.11 with] which N^2
78.14 lying] laying MS
78.16–22 Occasionally . . . content.] omit $N
78.24 canteens] light canteens N^2

78.25 Henry] Fleming MS,$N
78.25 ol'] old N⁴
78.26 jest] just $N
78.28 around] about N⁵
78.28 brilliant] greater N⁵
78.31 afar] far N³
78.32 caressingly] caressing N⁵
78.34 comrade] companion N⁵
79.1 his deed] the deed $N
79.2 th'] the $N,E1
79.3 contemplated] looked at MS, $N
79.4 cold] cool $N
79.4 cloth] clothe MS
79.6–12 "Yeh . . . jacket.] *omit* $N
79.8 Henry] Flem MS
79.9 a'] 'a MS; 'a' E1
79.14 t'] to N²
79.14 git] get $N
79.17 stooped] stopped $N(–N⁵); stoped N⁵
79.18 rubber one] rubber N¹⁻⁵
79.24–32 But . . . more.] *omit* $N
79.32 this] the AE1
79.33 had] *omit* $N
79.35 weighted] weighed N²
79.35–36 softly down] down softly $N
79.37 sometimes] ever $N
80.0 CHAPTER XIV] ~ XIII. $N (–N⁵); ~ III. N⁵ (*in error*)
80.4 sun-] sun's N¹⁻⁵
80.6 arousing] rousing N⁵
80.7 further] farther AE1
80.7 a while] awhile $N(–N³)
80.9 noise] voices $N
80.11 begun] began MS,A1
80.14 the awakening] awakening $N
80.14 features] faces MS,$N
80.15 dusty] dusky N¹⁻⁵
80.17–26 The . . . prophecy.] *omit* $N
80.27 then] *omit* $N
80.28 his friend] Wilson MS; the loud soldier $N
81.8 the] *omit* N⁴
81.10 movement] movements N²

81.12 eye-sockets] the eye sockets AE1,$N(N⁶: ~ ~ - ~)
81.12 -sockets.] sockets. It was the soldier's bath. MS
81.13 The youth] Fleming MS
81.17; 82.24,36 Henry] Flem MS, $N
81.20 little] bitter MS, $N
81.23–34 "Thunder . . . better."] *omit* $N
81.25 until] until suddenly MS
81.27 hangdest] hangest MS
81.38 steaming] streaming A1
82.3–84.16 The . . . pause.] *omit* $N
82.19 peak] peek MS
82.27 would've] would 'a' AE1
82.35 deprecatory] deprecating AE1
82.39 off'cers] officers AE1
83.3 saw] seen MS,AE1
83.13 Yes] Yep MS
83.25 'a] *omit* AE1
84.5 He] He's MS
84.11 used] use AE1
84.15 Henry] Fleming MS
84.17 reg'ment] regiment N¹⁻⁵
84.17 yestirday] yesterday $N
84.17–18 remarked the friend] he remarked $N
84.18 'a] of N³
84.18 was] were N³,⁵
84.19 kep'] keep $N
84.21 th'] the $N
84.22 everything] everythinₐ N⁶
84.22 Jest] Just N¹⁻⁵
84.23–88.6 "So . . . destroyed.] *omit* $N
86.17 sight.] sight. The long tirades against nature he now believed to be foolish [*preceded by deleted* 'silly' (C)] compositions born of his condition. He did not altogether repudiate them because he did not remember all that he had said. [*period inserted before independently deleted* 'and' *and* 'He was inclined to regard his fevered self with an indulgent smile.' *of which* 'his' *preceded*

by deleted 'the' (C)] He was inclined to regard his past rebellions with an indulgent smile. They were all right in their hour, perhaps. MS

86.19–20 circumstance] nature MS

86.24 marbles.] marbles. [¶] Since he was comfortable and contented, he had no desire to set things straight. Indeed, he no more contended that they were not straight. How could they be crooked when he was restored to a requisite amount of happiness. There was a slowly developeing conviction that in all his red speeches he had been ridiculously mistaken. Nature was a fine thing moving with a magnificent justice. The world was fair and wide and glorious. The sky was kind, and smiled tenderly, full of encouragement, upon him. [¶] Some poets now recieved his scorn. Yesterday, in his misery, he had thought of certain persons who had written. Their remembered words, broken and detached, had come piece-meal to him ['h' *over possible* 'm' *with* 'i' *formed from one minim* (C)]. For these people he ['e' *over* 'a' (C)] had then [*inserted* (C)] felt a glowing, [*followed by deleted* 'an (*and beginning of* 'd')' (C)] brotherly regard. They had wandered in paths of pain and they had made pictures of the black landscape that others might enjoy it with them. He had, at that time, been sure that their wise, contemplating spirits had been in sympathy with him, had shed tears from the clouds. He had walked alone, but there had been pity, made before a [*interlined above deleted* 'the' (C)] reason

for it. [¶] But he was now, in a measure, a successful man and he could no longer tolerate in himself a spirit of fellowship for poets. He abandoned them. Their songs about black landscapes were of no importance to him since his new ['n' *over* 'e' (C)] eyes said that his [*interlined above deleted* 'his' (C)] landscape was not black. People who called ['who called' *interlined above deleted* 'were idiots to call' (C)] landscapes [*final* 's' *added* (C)] black were [*beginning stroke of* 'w' *deletes with intent a period following* 'black' (C)] idiots. [¶] He achieved a mighty scorn for such a snivelling race. [¶] He felt that he was the child of the powers. Through [*preceded by deleted* 'Throug' (C)] the peace of his heart, he saw the earth to be a garden in which grew no weeds of agony. Or, perhaps, if there [*preceded by deleted* 'they' (C)] did grow a few, it was in obscure corners [*first* 'r' *over beginning of* 'n' (C)] where no one was obliged to encounter them unless [*preceded by deleted* 'ul' (C)] a ridiculous search was made. And ['d' *over* 't' (C)], at any rate, they were tiny ones ['s' *added* (C)]. [¶] He returned to his old belief in the ultimate, astonishing success of his life. He, as usual, did not trouble about processes. It was ordained, because he was a fine creation. He saw plainly that he was the chosen of some gods. By fearful and wonderful roads he was to be led to a crown. He was, of course, satisfied that he deserved it. MS

86.27 had] *omit* MS

86.32 Besides] Beside MS

89.0 CHAPTER XVI] *omit* $N

89.1   spluttering] sputtering MS+
89.3–5   The . . . existence.]
    omit $N
89.4   continual] continued AE1
89.8   been] *omit* N²
89.11   beyond] from beyond N⁵
89.15   turn] return N³
89.16–17   The . . . sleep.] *omit*
    $N
89.24–90.3   Always . . . stopped
    and] *omit* N¹⁻⁵
89.28–29   impossible] almost im-
    possible N⁶
89.30–90.3   The . . . stopped
    and] *omit* N⁶
90.3   ¶ But] *no* ¶ AE1
90.4   but] However $N
90.4   now] *omit* N³
90.5   black] black and croaking
    MS; croaking $N
90.5–6   near to] near N⁶
90.6–16   The . . . defeat.] *omit*
    N¹⁻⁵
90.7   omens] many omens MS
    (omems),N⁶
90.10   into] in to MS
90.11   genie] genii N⁶
90.13–16   The . . . defeat.] *omit*
    N⁶
90.17   sun-] sun's N⁶
90.19   carefully] gracefully N²
90.22–99.20   At . . . sentences.]
    omit $N
90.23   sentence] sentences AE1
91.15   generals'] general's AE1
91.22   Inward] Inwardly AE1
91.25   conciliatory] conciliating
    AE1
91.34   person] man MS
91.38   the youth's] Fleming's MS
92.5   cleared] clearer MS; clear
    AE1
92.9   yelpings] yellings AE1
92.31   makes] make MS
92.35   began] begin AE1
92.36; 93.2   Me] me AE1
93.5   There's] There MS,A1
93.6   wastin'] wasting E1
93.7   an' th'] and th' E1
93.8,9,14   an'] and E1
93.10   fer] for AE1

93.12   his] his | his MS
93.19   the youth's] Fleming's MS
93.31   was] *omit* MS
94.1–2   This . . . a ruthless] As
    Fleming had watched this ap-
    proach of the enemy which
    had seemed to him like a r MS
    (*false start*)
94.12   proven] proved AE1
94.30   hatefully] balefully MS
95.4   throat] neck MS
95.17   others] brothers MS
95.21   resembled] were like MS
95.23   his] *omit* MS
96.38   has] had AE1
97.15   Henry] Flem MS
97.29   degree] degrees AE1
99.4   rushings] rushing AE1
99.21   friend] friends N⁴
99.24   ladened] laden E1
99.25–100.8   feeling . . . sky]
    omit $N
99.26   into] onto A1
100.2   hurlying] hurling AE1
100.9   ¶ Looking over] (*no* ¶)
    Upon their return they looked
    over $N
100.9   they] and $N
100.11   To] It was N⁶
100.11   a glimpse of] *omit* N³
100.13   arose] rose N⁶
100.16   flip-flapping] flip-flopping
    MS,$N(−N³); flip fl pping N³
100.17   Occasional] Occasionally
    N²
100.17   in] into N³
100.18   stragglers] travellers N³
100.20   the youth] Fleming MS
100.22–28   The . . . gently.]
    omit N¹⁻⁵
100.29   moment] month N³
100.33   near] *omit* $N
100.34   Perhaps, they thought,]
    ~ ∧ ~ ~ ∧ $N
100.36   whom] who N⁶
100.36   their] the $N
100.37   other] *omit* $N
100.38   Th'] The $N
100.38   formin'] forming N²
100.39   Whiterside] Winterside
    $N

101.1 I fear] I'm afraid $N
101.2,16 t'] to $N
101.3–6 The . . . general.] *omit* $N
101.6 to talk] talking N²
101.10 for] *omit* N³·⁵
101.11 ¹th'] the $N
101.11 12th . . . 76th] Twelfth . . . Seventy-sixth $N(−N⁵)
101.12 any.] any. Troops are scarce with me. $N
101.12 th'] the $N
101.12 304th] Three Hundred and Fourth N⁶
101.13 'a] of $N
101.13 best] the best N⁵
101.16 an'] and $N
101.18 fingers] finger N¹⁻⁵
101.25–32 These . . . strange.] *omit* $N
101.25 occupied] occupied but MS(*false start*)
101.33 As . . . lieutenant] As they approached the young lieutenant who commanded the company $N
101.35 t'] *omit* MS; to AE1
101.35 been——] been to. AE1; been? $N
101.37 ¹t'] to $N
101.37 —we're goin' t' charge] *omit* $N
101.38 his] the N²·⁵⁻⁶
101.39–102.1 Now . . . fightin'.] *omit* $N
102.1 soiled] *omit* $N
102.4 -'nough] enough N¹⁻⁵
102.6–22 "I . . . trousers.] *omit* N¹⁻⁵
102.13–14 The soldier] Wilson MS; The youth N⁶
102.15–17 One . . . truth.] *omit* N⁶
102.15 soldier] man AE1
102.18 They] The men N⁶
102.18 into] then, in N⁶
102.24 a better] better N¹⁻⁵
102.26 attitudes] attitude N⁵
102.27–28 They . . . sheep.] *omit* $N
102.31 sprinters] springers $N

102.33 toward] towards N⁵
102.34 calculations] calculation $N
102.37 small] smaller N⁶
103.1 friend.] friend. It was as if he had been stunned. $N
103.1 returned] turned N³
103.1 same] *omit* N²
103.3 hell t' pay—] *omit* $N
103.7 swallered] swallowed AE1
104.0 CHAPTER XIX] ~ XIV. $N
104.1–109.9 The . . . shoulder.] N⁴ *prints in error as* Chapter XIV *following* 110.1–113.35, Chapter XV
104.1 foliages] foliage $N
104.3 orders] the orders N²
104.4 corners] corner N⁵
104.5 a-horseback] on horseback N²
104.12 eye] eyes N¹⁻⁵
104.14 goal] gaol MS
104.16 a] *omit* N⁵
104.23 into a] into the N⁵
104.25 toward] towards N⁵
105.6 rifles] rifle N⁵
105.7 among the tree-tops] from the sky $N
105.9 instant's] instant N²
105.11 bullets] bullet N¹·³⁻⁵
105.13 ¶ They] *no* ¶ E1
105.18–27 It . . . there.] *omit* N¹⁻⁵
105.19 that] *omit* N⁶
105.21 sheets] the sheets N⁶
105.25 took] took a MS,AE1,N⁶
105.25–26 impressions] impression AE1,N⁶
105.28 this] his $N
105.29 cheerings] cheering N²
105.31 the stoic] stoic N¹⁻⁵
105.33 the delirium] a delirium N³
105.34–37 It . . . there.] *omit* $N
105.36 the youth] Fleming MS
105.38 ate] eat N²
106.2 seeming] seemingly N⁶
106.3 stolid] solid N²
106.4 men] man N²
106.6 to] *omit* N⁶

106.7–8   They . . . again.] *omit*
$N
106.13   splutter] sputter $N
106.13   steadied] steady N¹⁻⁵
106.21   This] The N¹⁻⁵
106.22   over-come] to overcome
$N
106.24   It . . . silence.] *omit* $N
106.26   He] His MS
106.28   bellowed] hollowed N⁴
106.29   more] no more N⁴
106.32–108.13   The . . . savages.] *omit* N¹⁻⁵
106.32–33   blank and] blank N⁶
106.39   suddenly] *omit* N⁶
107.6   involved in] in N⁶
107.13–17   The . . . side.] *omit*
N⁶
107.17   further] farther AE1
107.21–22   as if] *omit* N⁶
107.23–28   The . . . them.] *omit*
N⁶
107.32   ²were] *omit* N⁶
107.36   on'y] o'ny MS; only N⁶
108.1   Cer'ly] Certainly AE1
108.5   on] *omit* N⁶
108.10   friend] friends N⁶
108.18–21   Over . . . valueless.]
omit N⁵
108.20   blue] the blue $N
108.23   low] *omit* N⁶
108.27   this] his N¹⁻⁵
108.33   went] went up N²
108.37   He] Then he $N
108.37   a clutch] clutch N⁶
110.0   CHAPTER XX] ~ XV. $N
110.3   coming] going $N
110.6   spluttering] sputtering $N
110.11   plainly be] be plainly N¹⁻⁵
110.11,12   into] in to MS
110.12   Gawd damn] Curse $N
110.12   their] thir N⁴
110.13   speeches] screeches AE1
110.20   fell] felt MS
110.24   again] *omit* N³
110.25   about] around N⁵
110.28   was of] was to N⁴
110.29   of no] no N⁴
111.8;   113.25,37;   117.10;   121.7
lieutenant]   young   lieutenant
MS+

111.11   would] *omit* N³
111.16   a] *omit* N²
111.17   his] as his MS; to his $N
111.22–31   A . . . answer.] *omit*
N¹⁻⁵
111.25   When (*no* ¶)] ¶ AE1
112.1   losing] loosing E1
112.3   manner] manners N²
112.11   a cloud] the cloud N³
112.18   to depend again] again to
depend N²
112.24   pushing] rushing N³
112.27   lines] troops $N
112.27–28   At . . . troops.] *omit*
$N
112.32–33   allusions] illusions
MS,A1
113.4   friend] friends N²
113.4   Henry] Flem MS,$N
113.4   this] it N³
113.10   depressions] depression
N²
113.18   fixes] fixes them N¹⁻⁵
113.21   The men, hiding] hiding
the men N²
113.22–23   waited . . . regi-
ment] *omit* N¹⁻⁵
113.22   it] them MS,N⁶
113.26   a roar] the roar N⁵
113.32   He] Also he AE1,$N
113.34   accented] prentifully accented MS; plentifully accented
$N
113.35   Too] Also N²
113.36–115.5   These . . .
hands.] N⁴ *transfers to follow*
109.9 *as part of its misplaced*
Chapter XIV
114.3   youth's] youths' N²
114.13   The youth] Fleming MS
114.19   noted] noticed N¹⁻⁵
114.21   broom] groom N⁵
114.23   antagonist] antagonists
N³
114.23   more] *omit* N⁶
114.28   a ground] the ground N²
114.36   impotent] important N²
114.36   These little battles] Fate
$N
114.37   the men] he men N¹
114.38   submission] surrender N²

114.39 showed] shown N³
115.5 weapons] weapon N¹⁻⁵
115.5–6 And . . . men.] omit $N
116.0 CHAPTER XXI] ~ XVI. $N
116.3 lines] line N²
116.3 of their friends] omit N³
116.9 journey] the journey N⁶
116.13 times] time $N
116.14 deaths] death E1
116.17–117.11 As . . . curses.] omit $N
116.26 sojers] sodgers E1
117.4 these] those E1
117.14 this] his N¹⁻⁵
117.19 number] numbers N²
117.23–26 It . . . dishevelled.] omit $N
117.27 They] The men $N
117.28 mite] might N¹⁻²; migte N³
117.30 a] omit N⁴
117.31 had had] had N²
117.33 there was now] now there was N⁴
117.33 quietly] quickly N⁶
117.36–120.6 As . . . what——"] omit $N
118.14 further] farther AE1
119.11 The youth] Fleming MS
119.22 he] he'd MS,AE1
119.22 would] omit AE1
119.33 'A] Of AE1
119.35 fer] for AE1
119.35 heared] heard AE1
119.36 argyment] argument AE1
120.7 He . . . come] Several men came $N
120.11 Yeh] Ye E1
120.11 and] as $N
120.12 his] the N⁶
120.14 damn'dest] damndest MS; damnedest AE1; the durndest N¹⁻⁵; th' derndest N⁶
120.14 ahem,' he ses] ses he $N
120.15 what] that N⁶
120.16–17 There . . . ses,] omit N¹⁻⁵
120.16 Flemin'] Flem N⁶
120.16 d'] do N⁶
120.16 'a] o' N⁶
120.17 th' lad] the lad N⁶

120.17 an' th'] an' the N⁶
120.18–22 right . . . shet] omit N⁶
120.19–23 he ses . . . jim-hickey,'] omit N¹⁻⁵
120.23 an' th'] and the N¹⁻²,⁴⁻⁵; and th' N³
120.23 Ahem, ahem,] Ahem, $N
120.24–25 man . . . good] repeated in N¹
120.24 ahem] omit $N
120.24 th' front] the front $N
120.25(twice),30,33,34,35 th'] the N¹⁻⁵
120.26 'a] o' N⁶
120.27 like] lik N¹,³⁻⁴; lik' N²
120.27 th' time] the time N⁶
120.27–28 'Head . . . ²ses.] omit N¹⁻⁵
120.30 An' th'] An' the N⁶
120.32 'At . . . ¹ses.] omit N⁵
120.32 ¹,²th'] the N⁶
120.32 'a] o' $N
120.32 reg'ment] regiment N⁴
120.32 ³th'] the N¹⁻⁵
120.33,34,35 th'] the N⁶
120.34 ²ses] says E1
120.35 t'] blank space N¹; to N²,⁴⁻⁵
120.37 had] omit $N
120.37–38 Thompson] Thomson N²
120.38 t'] to $N
120.38 sed] said $N
121.1 flushing] flushed N¹⁻⁵
121.1 from] with N⁶
121.2 joy] pleasure N³
121.5 very] omit N⁵
121.5–135.39 ²and . . . clouds] omit $N
122.25; 124.32; 126.6 no wise] nowise AE1
123.12; 124.11 The youth] Fleming MS
123.12–13 and laughing] with laughter AE1
123.29 The youth's] Fleming's MS
123.29 cups] up AE1
123.32 men. It was] men‸ AE1
123.38 the youth] Fleming MS

124.4   these] their AE1
124.17   bended] bent AE1
124.26   fiends] friends A1
124.37   in him] him AE1
125.4   ceased their] their ceased MS
125.5   an] *omit* MS
125.15   clenched] clinched AE1
125.27   hatreds] hatred AE1
125.29   guttering] gluttering MS, AE1
125.31   -driver . . . -digger] -drivers . . . -diggers AE1
125.37   the youth's] Fleming's MS
128.9   questionings] questioning AE1
129.1   movement] movement to go MS
129.9   were] was MS
129.38   desperate] determined MS
130.1   terrible] *omit* MS
130.33   toe] tender toe MS
131.8   be] *omit* MS
131.11; 132.5   The youth] Fleming MS
132.16   outa] out of AE1
132.20   repose.] reposes behind the rails. MS
132.25   tramped] trampled AE1
132.26   scamper.] scamper. The fence, deserted, resumed with its careening posts and disjointed bars, an air of quiet rural depravity. Beyond it, there lay spread a few corpses. Conspicuous, was the contorted body of the color-bearer in grey whose flag the youth's friend ['the youth's friend' *interlined with a caret above deleted* 'Wilson' (G)] was now bearing (*followed by deleted* 'jovially' (C)) away. MS
133.1   the stolid] a stolid AE1
133.5–6 entrenchments.] entrenchments. [¶] As they passed near other cammands [*first* 'a' *altered from* 'o' (C)], men of the delapidated regiment pro-

cured the captured flag from Wilson and, tossing it high into the air cheered tumultuously as it turned, with apparent reluctance, slowly over and over. MS
133.11   trampled] trammeled MS
133.18   it] his mind MS
133.34   sympathies.] sympathies. [¶] His friend ['His friend' *interlined with a caret above deleted* 'Wilson' (G)], too, seemed engaged with some retrospection for [*preceded by deleted* 'o' (C)] he suddenly gestured and said: "Good Lord!" [¶] "What?" asked the youth. ['the youth.' *interlined above deleted* 'Fleming.' (G)] [¶] "Good Lord!" repeated his friend ['his friend' *interlined above deleted* 'Wilson.' *of which the period deleted in error* (G)] "Yeh know Jimmie Rogers? Well, he—gosh, when he was hurt I started t' git some water fer 'im ['i' *over* 'e' (C)] an', thunder, I aint seen 'im from that time 'til this. I clean forgot what I—say, has anybody seen Jimmie Rogers?" [¶] "Seen 'im? No! He's dead," they told him. [¶] His friend ['His friend' *interlined with a caret above deleted* 'Wilson' (G)] swore. MS
133.35   Regarding] But the youth ['the youth' *interlined above deleted* 'Fleming' (G)], regarding MS
133.35   he] *omit* MS
133.39   hiding] having AE1
134.4   conduct.] conduct. He said to himself again the sentence of the insane lieutenant [*preceded by deleted* 'young' (G)]: "If I had ten thousand wildcats like you, I could tear th' stomach outa this war in less'n a week." It was a little coronation. MS
134.6   danced.] danced. Echoes of

his terrible [*preceded by deleted* 'terrific' (C)] combat with the arrayed forces of the [*interlined above deleted* 'nature' (C)] universe came to his ears. MS

134.8 shame.] shame. [¶] However, he presently procured [*beginning stroke of* 'procured' *deletes with intent comma after* 'presently' (C)] an explanation and an apology [*first* 'o' *over* 'a' (C)]. He said that those tempestuous moments were of the wild mistakes and ravings of a novice who did not comprehend. He had been a mere man railing at a condition but now he was out of it and could [*preceded by deleted* 'he' (C)] see that it had been very proper and just. It had been necessary for him to swallow swords that he might have a better throat for grapes. Fate had, in truth, been [*interlined with a caret* (C)] kind to him; she had stabbed him with benign purpose and diligently cudgeled him for his own sake. In his rebellion, he had been very portentious, no doubt, and ['doubt, | and' *with a second comma inserted in error preceding* 'and' (C)] sincere, and anxious for humanity [*preceded by deleted* 'the' (C)], but now that he stood safe, with no lack of blood, it was suddenly clear to him that he had been wrong not to kiss the knife and bow to the cudgel. He had foolishly squirmed. [¶] But the sky would forget. It was true, he admitted, that in the world it was the habit to cry devil at persons who refused to trust what they could not trust, but he thought that perhaps the stars dealt differently. The imperturbable sun

shines on insult and worship. MS

134.9 A] As Fleming was thus fraternizing again with nature, a MS

134.13 the tall soldier] Conklin MS

134.15 him] Fleming MS

134.16 it] he AE1

134.19 th'] the AE1

134.19 Henry] Flem MS

134.23 the] these AE1

134.29 accomplishments] accomplishment MS

134.34 yer] your AE1

134.36 hunderd] hundred AE1

135.2 Whale] whale AE1

135.5 yer] yeh AE1

135.5 mouth.''] mouth.'' [¶] ''You make me sick.'' [¶] ''G' home, yeh fool. [*followed by deleted* '(¶) ''Wasn't you that sed it, anyhow. What yeh talkin' about? (*question mark altered from a period*)'' (¶) ''It's a de-e-rn good pla-a-an if th' other fellow's a go-o-at but it a-a-aint no use if he's a mu-u-ule.'' ' (C)] MS

135.8 of] *omit* AE1

135.13 distance.] distance. And then he regarded it with what he thought to be great calmness. At last, he concluded that he saw in it quaint uses. He exclaimed that [*preceded by deleted* 'that's' (C)] it's importance in the aftertime would be great to him if it even succeeded in hindering the workings of his egotism. It would make a sobering balance. It would become [*followed by deleted* 'assimu' (C)] a good part of him. He would have upon him often the consciousness of a great mistake. And he would be taught to deal gently and with care. He would be a man. [¶] This plan for the utilization of a sin did not give

him complete joy but it was
the best [*followed by deleted*
'he could do' (C)] sentiment
he could formulate under the
circumstances and when it was
combined with his successes,
or public deeds, he knew that
he was quite contented. MS

135.14 And at last his (*no* ¶)]
¶ His MS

135.14 to open] to be opened MS

135.17 them.] them. [¶] He was
emerged from his struggles,
with a large sympathy for the
machinery of the universe.
With ['W' *over beginning of*
possible 'H' (C)] his new eyes,
he could see that the secret
[*followed by deleted* 'blo(*and*
beginning of a 'w')' (C)] and
open blows which were being
dealt about the world with
such heavenly lavishness were

in truth blessings [*final* 's'
added (C)]. It was a [*inter-*
lined above deleted 'chasten-
ing' (C)] deity ['ei' *over* 'ie'
(HG)] laying about him with
the bludgeon of correction. [¶]
His loud mouth against these
things had been lost as the
storm ceased. He would no
more stand upon places high
and false, and denounce the
distant planets. He beheld that
he was tiny but not inconse-
quent to the sun. In the space-
wide whirl of events no grain
like him would be lost. MS

135.22 death.] death and was for
others. MS

135.25 tranquility] tranquilly
MS,AE1

135.38–39 Over . . . clouds.]
omit MS

ALTERATIONS IN THE MANUSCRIPT

[NOTE: Each entry is followed by a symbol denoting the stage at which the alteration occurred. These symbols are as follows: C—Current, *i.e.* at the time of inscription; P—Preliminary, prior to Hamlin Garland seeing the manuscript; HG—notations made by Hamlin Garland; G—General Revision; and F—Final preparation of the manuscript for the printer.]

3.0 omit] *false start (verso of* p. 2): 'Private Fleming. | His various' *and beginning of probable* 'b' (C); *on* MS f. 1 *original* 'Private Fleming | His various battles. | By Stephen Crane.' *deleted in pencil* (G) *or* (F); *above is added in ink* 'The Red Badge of Courage. | An Episode of* ['o' *over* 'a' *or possible* 'o' (F)] *the American Civil War. | By Stephen Crane.'* (F)

3.2 revealed] *interlined with a caret* (C)

3.6 long] *followed by deleted* 'red th' (C)

3.11 a certain tall soldier] 'a certain soldier' *interlined with a caret above deleted* 'Jim Conklin' (P); 'tall' *interlined with a caret* (G)

3.14 it] *mended* (C)

3.14 truthful] *preceded by deleted* 'reliable' (C)

3.16 He] *interlined above deleted* 'Conklin' (G)

3.25 a] *preceded by deleted* 'the' (C)

3.28–29 another private loudly.] 'another private.' *interlined above deleted* 'Young Wilson.' *with* 'private.' *interlined above deleted* 'soldier' *and a period*

not deleted in error (P); 'loudly.' *interlined with a caret which deletes the period following* 'private' (G)

3.31; 4.1 th'] MS(c) 'the' *with* 'e' *over an apostrophe* (G)

3.31 ol'] MS(c) 'old' *with* 'd' *over an apostrophe* (G)

3.31–4.1 goin' t'] MS(c) 'going to' *with final* 'g' *and final* 'o' *over apostrophes* (G)

4.1 sot] MS(c) 'set' *with* 'e' *over* 'o' (G)

4.1 t'] MS(c) 'to' *with* 'o' *over an apostrophe* (G)

4.2 an'] MS(c) 'and' *with* 'd' *over an apostrophe* (G)

4.2 yit] MS(c) 'yet' *with* 'e' *over* 'i' (G)

4.3 The tall soldier] 'A' *interlined above deleted* 'Conklin' *then deleted and followed by* 'The first' *which was deleted and* 'The excited soldier' *interlined above with* 'excited' *interlined with a caret* (P); 'The tall soldier' *interlined with a caret after deleted* 'The excited soldier' (G)

4.4 the loud one] *interlined above deleted* 'young Wilson' (G)

4.6 A] *over* 'a' *and preceded by deleted* 'Simpson,' (P)

4.6 corporal] *followed by a deleted comma* (P)

4.9 environment] *followed by deleted* 'during the spring' (C)

4.10 moment] *ends short line of* MS f. 2, *after which is drawn a run-on line to indicate no paragraph but to continue with* 'Of' *at top of* f. 3 (C)

4.14 general] *interlined with a caret* (C)

4.14 advocated] MS 'advo-|' *followed by deleted* 'cated other plans of campaign.' (C)

4.16–17 the . . . rumor] *interlined with a caret above deleted* 'Jim Conklin' (P)

4.27 There . . . who] *interlined above deleted* 'Fleming, a certain youthful private,' (P)

4.28 the tall soldier] 'the excited soldier' *interlined above deleted* 'Jim Conklin' (P); 'tall' *interlined above deleted* 'excited' (G)

4.31 as] *interlined* (P)

4.32 thoughts] 's' *added later* (C)

4.32 come] *interlined above deleted* 'just' (C)

4.34 made] *interlined with a caret* (C)

4.36 weekly] *preceded by deleted* 'weakl' (C)

4.38 and some] 'and' *interlined above deleted period;* 'S' *reduced to lower case by vertical stroke* (C); *stroke strengthened leaning to right* (G)

5.4 room. And, too, this] MS 'room. And this' *with* 'And' *interlined and* 'T' *reduced to lower case by vertical stroke* (C); *stroke strengthened leaning to right, period deleted in error* (G)

5.7 The youth] *interlined with a caret above deleted* 'Fleming' (P)

5.13 vague] *followed by deleted comma* (C)

5.16 peoples] 's' *added later* (C)

5.17 blotches] 'l' *over* 'o'; *preceded by deleted* 'blothches' (C)

5.21 wars] 's' *added later* (C)

5.21 it,] *followed by deleted* 't[and beginning of an upstroke]' (C)

5.25 had] *interlined with a caret* (C)

5.25 witnessing] *preceded by deleted* 'ever' (C)

5.32 glory] *followed by deleted period* (C)

5.32 had] *interlined* (C)

5.34 had drawn] 'had' *interlined;* 'drawn' *originally* 'drew' *with* 'a' *over* 'e' *and* 'n' *added* (C)

5.36 discouraged] *followed by deleted period* (C)

5.37 upon] *followed by deleted* 'the color of pa' (C)

5.39 reasons] *final* 's' *added later* (C)

5.39 he] *preceded by deleted* 'his' (C)

6.2 ²had] *interlined* (C)

6.4 ethical] MS 'ethicical' *with second* 'i' *over* 's' (C)

6.17 going to] *final* 'g' *and final* 'o' *over apostrophes* (G)

6.23 home,] *comma squeezed in before deleted period; followed by deleted* 'Hi' (C)

6.24 brindle] *a final* 'd' *added* (C); 'd' *deleted* (P)

6.26 The] 'e' *over an apostrophe* (G)

6.26 done,] *followed by deleted closing double quotes* (C)

6.28 brindle] *a final* 'd' *deleted* (P)

6.30 on his back] *interlined with a caret* (P)

6.30 with] *preceded by deleted* 'the' (C)

6.30 ²and] *preceded by deleted* 'o[and beginning of 'f']' (C)

6.30 expectancy] *followed by deleted* 'almost defeating' (C)

6.34 Still, she] 'Still,' *squeezed in at beginning of line;* 'S' *of*

'She' *reduced to lower case by a slash leaning to right* (C)

7.1,2 care] *interlined above deleted* 'keer' (G)

7.1 fighting] *final* 'g' *over an apostrophe* (G)

7.2 a-thinkin'] MS 'a-thinkin₍ₐ₎' *with hyphen inserted* (C)

7.2–3 you can] *interlined above deleted* 'yeh kin' (G)

7.3(*twice*) the] 'e' *over an apostrophe* (G)

7.3,8 because] *first* 'e' *over an apostrophe* (G)

7.4 amongst] 'a' *over an apostrophe* (G)

7.4 of] *over* ''a' (G)

7.4 and] 'd' *over an apostrophe* (G)

7.5,8,10(*twice*) to] 'o' *over an apostrophe* (G)

7.7 of] 'o' *mended from* 'a''; 'f' *added* (G)

7.7,8,13 and] 'd' *over an apostrophe* (G)

7.9,13,14 the] 'e' *over an apostrophe* (G)

7.10 so's] MS 's'os' *followed by deleted* ''at' (C)

7.12 careful] *interlined above deleted* 'keerful' (G)

7.12 of] *original* 'of' *deleted and* ''a' *interlined* (C); 'of' *over* ''a' (G)

7.13 The] 'e' *over an apostrophe* (G)

7.14 nothing] 'g' *over an apostrophe* (G)

7.14 leading] 'g' *over an apostrophe* (G)

7.14 feller] 'er' *over* 'ah' (G)

7.15,16(*twice*),22,28 and] 'd' *over an apostrophe* (G)

7.15 has] *followed by deleted* 'ha' (C); *preceded by deleted* 'as' (G)

7.16 -learning] 'g' *over an apostrophe* (G)

7.16 'im] *apostrophe added* (G)

7.16,17,18,24,26 to] 'o' *over an apostrophe* (G)

7.17 of] *over* ''a' (G)

7.17 anything] 'g' *over an apostrophe* (G)

7.19 ²yeh] 'y' *over* 'h' (C)

7.22 drunk] 'u' *over* 'a' (P)

7.22 of] *over* ''a'' (G)

7.24–25 excepting . . . shirking] 'g's' *over apostrophes* (G)

7.25 child] *preceded by deleted* 'Hen' (C)

7.27 anything] 'g' *over an apostrophe* (G)

7.27,31 because] *first* 'e' *over an apostrophe* (G)

7.28,30(*twice*) the] 'e' *over an apostrophe* (G)

7.29 all.] *period inserted before deleted* 'I b'lieve.' (G)

7.30(*twice*),32 and] 'd' *over an apostrophe* (G)

7.36 borne] MS 'born' *with* 'e' *over* 'n' (C)

7.36 irritation.] *followed by deleted* 'He had felt glad that none of his associates in the new company had been near to listen [preceded by deleted* 'over-hear' (C)] *to it.'* (G)

7.38 his] *preceded by deleted* 'his' *with* 'is' *over* 'er' (C)

8.5 schoolmates] *preceded by deleted* 'old' (C)

8.5 him] *interlined* (C)

8.7 calm] *interlined with a caret above deleted* 'quiet' (G)

8.14 had] *interlined* (C)

8.16 at] *preceded by deleted* 'wat' (C)

8.16 perceived] MS 'percieved' *preceded by deleted* 'had had' (C)

8.17 begun] *preceded by deleted* 'turned his head' (C)

8.18 had] 'h' *over* 's' (C)

8.21 spirit] *a final* 's' *deleted* (C)

8.22–23 the youth] *interlined above deleted* 'Fleming' (P)

8.23 believed] *interlined above deleted* 'felt' (C)

8.23 that] *followed by deleted* 'me' (C)

8.31 meals but since] 'but' interlined with a caret above deleted period; 's' of 'since' over 'S' (P)

8.32 done] interlined above deleted 'performed' (C)

8.32 sit] final 'ting' deleted (C)

8.32 try] final 'ing' deleted (C)

8.35 -like] followed by deleted 'like' (C)

8.38 had] interlined with a caret (HG)

9.1 comfort] end of line hyphen strengthened after 'com' possibly not by Crane (G) or (HG)

9.3 he was] 'he' followed by deleted 'could be' (C); 'was' interlined (P)

9.4 reviewed,] followed by deleted 'and | reviewed' (C)

9.9 had] interlined with a caret (C)

9.12 a great] interlined with a caret above deleted 'a' (C)

9.15–16 This . . . war.] squeezed in later; 'him . . . war.' falling below the line, 'had' interlined above deleted 'md' (P)

9.17 Various] preceded by deleted 'But' (C)

9.22 hell's-fire] MS 'hell's-|-fire' with second hyphen inserted (C)

9.27 and] interlined (C)

9.31 However] preceded on the line above at indent point by 'H' which Crane then deleted realizing he had completed a paragraph at the far right of the same line (C)

9.32 kind] followed by independently deleted 'of' and 'and con' (C)

10.5 have] interlined with a caret (C)

10.12 visions] final 's' added (C)

10.15 the] MS(c) 'th' ' with apostrophe over 'e' (C)

10.24 the tall soldier] 'the soldier who had f' interlined with a

caret above deleted 'Jim Conklin'; 'who had f' deleted and 'whom they called "Jim," ' interlined above (P); 'tall' interlined with a caret above, and 'whom they called "Jim," ' deleted (G)

10.25 The loud private] 'A young private' interlined with a caret above deleted 'Young Wilson' (P); 'The' over 'A' and 'loud' interlined above deleted 'young' (G)

10.26 the tall soldier] 'tall soldier' interlined above deleted 'Conklin' (P); 'the' interlined with a caret (G)

10.27 expressively.] 'ex' over 'im'; period altered from a comma (C)

10.27 Yeh kin] MS(c) 'You can' interlined above deleted 'Yeh kin' which had originally been underlined by HG whose pencil question mark appears in the left margin (G)

10.27 b'lieve] MS(c) 'believe' with first 'e' over an apostrophe (G)

10.27 er] MS(c) 'or' with 'o' over 'e' (G)

10.27 jest] MS(c) 'just' with 'u' over 'e' (G)

10.28(thrice),31 yeh] MS(c) 'you' interlined above deleted 'yeh' (G); 'yeh' underlined by HG at 10.31 with his pencil question mark in the left margin

10.28(twice) t'] MS(c) 'to' with 'o' over an apostrophe (G)

10.28; 11.1,5 an'] MS(c) 'and' with 'd' over an apostrophe (G)

10.29 kin] MS(c) 'can." ' interlined above deleted 'kin' and a period not deleted in error; double quotes in error (G)

10.29 yeh'll] MS(c) 'you'll' interlined above deleted 'yeh'll' (G)

10.30 His comrade] *interlined with a caret above deleted* 'Young Wilson' (P)

10.31 said] *interlined above deleted* 'asked' (C)

10.32,33 everythin'] MS(c) 'everything' *with* 'g' *over an apostrophe* (G)

10.32; 11.1 th'] MS(c) 'the' *with* 'e' *over an apostrophe* (G)

10.32 yeh?"] MS(c) 'you?"' *interlined above deleted* 'yeh' *and a question mark and closing double quotes not deleted in error* (G)

10.33 the other] *interlined above deleted* 'Conklin' (P)

10.36 The youth] 'The youth of this tale,' *interlined with a caret above deleted* 'Fleming' *and a comma not deleted in error* (P); 'of this tale' *deleted* (G)

10.36 pausing] 'ing' *over* 'ed' (C)

10.37 Going] *final* 'g' *over an apostrophe* (G)

10.37 to] 'o' *over an apostrophe* (G)

10.38 the tall soldier] *interlined with a caret above deleted* 'Conklin' *and a period deleted in error* (P)

11.1 jest] MS(c) 'just' *with* 'u' *over an apostrophe* (G)

11.1 t'morrah] MS(c) 'tomorrow' *with first* 'o' *over an apostrophe and* 'ow' *over* 'ah' (G)

11.1 bigges'] MS(c) 'biggest' *with* 't' *over an apostrophe* (G)

11.2 jest] MS(c) 'just' *with* 'ju' *over* 'je' (G)

11.2 was.] *followed by deleted closing double quotes* (C)

11.3 the youth.] *interlined above deleted* 'Fleming.' (P); *deletion reinforced* (G)

11.4 fightin'] MS(c) 'fighting' *with final* 'g' *over an apostrophe* (G)

11.4 m'] MS(c) 'my' *with* 'y' *over an apostrophe* (G)

11.4 reg'lar] MS(c) 'regular' *with* 'u' *over an apostrophe* (G)

11.5 the tall soldier] *interlined with a caret above deleted* 'Conklin' (P)

11.7 the loud one] 'the other youth,' *interlined above deleted* 'Wilson'; 'youth,' *then deleted and* 'soldier' *interlined above* (P); 'loud one' *interlined with two carets after deleted* 'other soldier'; 'loud' *connected to preceding* 'the' *by a line* (G)

11.8 the youth] *interlined above deleted* 'Fleming' (P)

11.8 this] *followed by deleted* 'here' (G)

11.9 just] 'u' *over* 'e' (G)

11.10 the tall soldier] *interlined with a caret above deleted* 'Conklin' (P)

11.11,15,33,36,37 th'] MS(c) 'the' *with* 'e' *over an apostrophe* (G)

11.11,13 mornin'] MS(c) 'morning' *with* 'g' *over an apostrophe* (G)

11.12,16 Th'] MS(c) 'The' *with* 'e' *over an apostrophe* (G)

11.14 goin'] MS(c) 'going' *with final* 'g' *over an apostrophe* (G)

11.14 t'] *apostrophe added* (P); 'o' *over an apostrophe* (G)

11.16 reg'ment's] *preceded by deleted* 're' *with* 'r' *over illegible letter* (C); 'i' *over first apostrophe and second apostrophe added* (G)

11.16,37 t'] MS(c) 'to' *with* 'o' *over an apostrophe* (G)

11.17 An'] MS(c) 'And' *with* 'd' *over an apostrophe* (G)

11.17 raisin'] MS(c) 'raising' *with* 'g' *over an apostrophe* (G)

11.18 camp—] *dash inserted* (C)

11.18 kin] MS(c) 'can' *interlined*

with a caret above deleted 'kin'
(G)

11.19   the loud one.] *original* 'Wilson.' *deleted* (P); 'the loud
one.' *interlined* (G)

11.20   The youth] *interlined
above deleted* 'Fleming' (P)

11.20–21   the tall soldier.] *interlined above deleted* 'Conklin.'
(P)

11.21   "Jim!"] *preceded by deleted*
' "What' (C)

11.23   do you] *first* 'o' *over an
apostrophe;* 'you' *interlined
above deleted* 'yeh' (G)

11.23,29   the] 'e' *over an apostrophe* (G)

11.24   onct git inteh] MS(c) 'once
get into' *with first* 'e' *over* 't',
second 'e' *over* 'i', *and final* 'o'
over 'eh' (G)

11.25   the other] *interlined above
deleted* 'Conklin' (P)

11.25   cold] *interlined above deleted* 'fine' (C)

11.26   'a] *interlined above deleted*
'of' (C); MS(c) 'of' *written
over* ' 'a' (G)

11.26   b'cause] MS(c) 'because'
with first 'e' *over an apostrophe* (G)

11.27   'a] MS(c) 'of' *over* ' 'a' (G)

11.27,33(*twice*),34(*twice*),36
an'] MS(c) 'and' *with* 'd' *over
an apostrophe* (G)

11.29   of] *over* ' 'a' (G)

11.29   the youth] *interlined above
deleted* 'Fleming' *and a period
deleted in error* (P)

11.31   reg'ment,] *followed by deleted double quotes* (C); 'i'
over apostrophe (G)

11.32   " 'A] *preceded by deleted*
' "Of' (C); MS(c) 'Of' *over*
' 'A' (G)

11.33   fightin'] MS(c) 'fighting'
with final 'g' *over an apostrophe* (G)

11.34   come] 'o' *over* 'a' (C)

11.34   ag'in] MS(c) 'again,' *with*
'ain,' *over* 'in,' (G)

11.35   yeh] MS(c) 'you' *interlined
above deleted* 'yeh' (G) *which
HG had previously underlined
opposite his marginal note, see*
p. 195.

11.35   nothin'] MS(c) 'nothing'
with 'g' *over an apostrophe*
(G)

11.35   'A] MS(c) 'Of' *over* 'A' '
(G)

11.35   they] *followed by deleted*
'they' (HG) *or* (G)

11.36   yit] MS(c) 'yet' *with* 'e'
over 'i' (G)

11.37   fight] *interlined with a
caret* (C)

11.38   worser] MS(c) *final* 'r' *deleted* (G)

11.38   ¹th] MS(c) 'the' *with* 'e'
over an apostrophe (G)

11.38   They] 'e' *written below deleted apostrophe* (C)

11.38   ²th] *final* 'ey' *deleted and
apostrophe inserted* (C); 'e'
over apostrophe (G)

12.1   reg'ment] MS(c) 'regiment'
with 'i' *over an apostrophe* (G)

12.1,2,15(*twice*),16,17(*twice*),18
an'] MS(c) 'and' *with* 'd' *over
an apostrophe* (G)

12.1   everythin'] MS(c) 'everything' *with* 'g' *over an apostrophe* (G)

12.1,16   th] MS(c) 'the' *with* 'e'
over an apostrophe (G)

12.1   'a] MS(c) 'of' *over* 'a' ' (G)

12.2   'a 'em'll] MS(c) 'of 'em'll'
with 'of' *over* ' 'a' *and first
apostrophe strengthened* (G)

12.2   -git-] 'git-' *interlined with a
caret; preceding hyphen
strengthened* (P)

12.4   the loud soldier] 'the blatant
soldier' *interlined above deleted* 'Wilson' (P); 'loud' *interlined with a caret above
deleted* 'blatant' (G)

12.6   The other] *interlined above
deleted* 'Conklin' (P)

12.9   The youth] *interlined above
deleted* 'Fleming' (P)

12.9(*twice*) you] *interlined above deleted* 'yeh' (G)

12.10 yourself] 'your' *interlined above deleted* 'yer' (G)

12.10 Jim?] *question mark altered from a comma* (C)

12.11 The loud soldier] 'The blatant young soldier' *interlined with a caret above deleted* 'Wilson' (P); 'loud' *interlined above deleted* 'blatant young' (G)

12.13 The tall private] *interlined above deleted* 'Conklin' (P)

12.14 git] MS(c) 'get' *with* 'e' *over* 'i' (G)

12.14 fer] MS(c) 'for' *with* 'o' *over* 'e' (G)

12.14 'a] *interlined above deleted* 'of' (C); MS(c) 'of' *over* ' 'a' (G)

12.15 hull] MS(c) 'whole' *over* 'hull' (G)

12.15 'a] MS(c) 'of' *over* 'a' ' (G)

12.16 An'] MS(c) 'And' *with* 'd' *over an apostrophe* (G)

12.16 onct] MS(c) 'once' *with* 'e' *over* 't' (G)

12.16 t'] MS(c) 'to' *with* 'o' *inserted with a caret over an apostrophe* (G)

12.17 -standin' . . . -fightin'] MS(c) '-standing . . . -fighting' *with final* 'g's' *over apostrophes* (G)

12.18 B'jiminy] MS(c) 'Bejiminy' *with* 'e' *over an apostrophe* (G)

12.19 the loud one.] 'the blatant one.' *interlined above deleted* 'Wilson.' (P); 'loud' *interlined above deleted* 'blatant' (G)

12.20 The youth of this tale] *interlined with a caret above deleted* 'Fleming' (P)

12.20–21 his comrade] *interlined above deleted* 'Conklin' *and a period deleted in error* (P)

12.21 all] *preceded by deleted* 'every o' (C)

12.21 possessed] *original* 'had'

interlined above deleted 'felt' (C); 'possessed' *interlined with a caret before deleted* 'had' (P)

12.22 was,] *interlined above deleted* 'felt' (C)

13.1 The . . . discovered] *false start* (*verso of MS 22*); 'II. | Fleming discovered the next mornin' (C)

13.1 the youth] *interlined above deleted* 'Fleming'; *a final* 'ful' *deleted* (P)

13.1–2 his tall comrade] *interlined with a caret above deleted* 'Conklin' *with an independently deleted* 'the' *immediately above* 'Conklin' (P)

13.3 was] *preceded by deleted* 'were' (C)

13.4 , even,] *interlined with a caret* (C)

13.5 men] *preceded by deleted* 'the' (G)

13.5 had] 'h' *over* 'w' (C)

13.5–6 The tall one] *interlined with a caret above deleted* 'Conklin' (P)

13.6 Corners] 'C' *over* 'c' (C)

13.8 The youth] *interlined above deleted* 'Fleming' (P)

13.9 on the contrary, an] *interlined above deleted* 'a mere' (C)

13.13 calculations,] *comma squeezed in before deleted period* (C)

13.15 to prove himself] 'to firmly prove himself' *interlined with two carets above deleted* 'establish the fact' (C); 'firmly' *deleted and large caret inserted* (P); *line drawn to connect* 'to' *and* 'prove'; 'himself' *followed by line which continues to the end of the written line* (G)

13.17 discover] *interlined with a caret* (C)

13.17 faults] 's' *added* (C)

13.19 an] 'n' *added* (C)

13.19 blaze,] *preceded by deleted* 'blood,' (C)

13.20 even] *interlined with a caret* (C)

13.20 requires] *preceded by deleted* 'retorts' (C)

13.23 The tall soldier] *interlined above deleted* 'Conklin' (P)

13.23 some] *preceded by deleted* 'since boy' (C)

13.24 This man's] *interlined above deleted* 'His friend's' (P)

13.24 dealt] *interlined above deleted* 'gave' (C)

13.25 childhood] *preceded by deleted* 'boyhood' (C)

13.27 the youth. Still] 'the youth.' *interlined above deleted* 'Fleming.' (P); *line written beneath* 'the youth.' *curving up to above* 'Still', *indicating a paragraph?* (G)

13.27–28 that his comrade] *interlined with a caret above deleted* 'Conklin' (P)

13.31 The youth] *interlined above deleted* 'Fleming' (P)

13.31 another] *followed by deleted* 'man' (P)

14.4 looked] *followed by deleted* 'like' (C)

14.4 moods.] 's' *inserted* (C)

14.6 any] 'ny' *added later* (C)

14.6 like] *followed by deleted* 'those' (C)

14.8 concern] *interlined above deleted* 'doubts' (C)

14.10 could] 'c' *over* 'w' (C)

14.11 companions] 's' *added* (C)

14.12 opinions] 's' *added* (C)

14.12 [1]to] *preceded by deleted* 'two' (C)

14.12 mood.] *preceded by deleted* 'mind.' (C)

14.13 In fact he] *original* 'He' *followed by independently deleted* 'had all' *and* 'a' (C); 'In fact he' *interlined above deleted* 'He' (P)

14.13 , in secret,] *preceded by deleted* 'secretly' (C)

14.14 qualities] 'ies' *interlined above deleted* 'y' (C)

14.14 He] *preceded by deleted* 'And ev' (C)

14.16 load] *preceded by deleted* 'm' (C)

14.16 unseen] *followed by a deleted period* (C)

14.16 had] *interlined* (C)

14.18 had] *preceded by deleted* 'wa' (C)

14.18 in] *interlined above deleted* 'at' (C)

14.22 drama] *interlined above deleted* 'battle' (C)

14.24 faces.] *followed by deleted* 'If' (C)

14.26 thoughts] *followed by deleted comma* (C)

14.28 crimes] 'r' *mended* (C)

14.30 great] *interlined with a caret* (C)

14.32 to] *followed by deleted* 'sit tr' (C)

14.34 not] *interlined with a caret* (C)

14.36 stage] *interlined with a caret* (C)

14.38 One] *preceded by deleted* 'At last,' (C)

15.1 before] *followed by deleted* 'dawn' (C)

15.2 From] *preceded by deleted* 'Across' *with* 'A' *over the start of an illegible letter* (C)

15.4 was] *preceded by deleted* 'were' (C)

15.5 , black and pattern-like,] *interlined above deleted* 'like a black pattern,' (C)

15.7–8 The youth] *interlined with a caret* (P)

15.8 dark] *interlined above deleted* 'black' (P)

15.14 any] *inserted* (C)

15.14 ominous] *preceded by deleted* 'sombre' *which is preceded by deleted* 'fl' (C)

15.15 might] *followed by deleted* 'light'

15.15 the] *interlined* (C); *caret supplied* (G)

15.16 Staring] 'S' *over* 'F' (C)

15.16 at the] *preceded by deleted* 'he'; 'the' *interlined with a caret* (C)

15.22 orders.] *period inserted before deleted* 'and' (C)

15.22 bended] *interlined above deleted* 'bened' (C)

15.25 two] *followed by deleted probable* 'o' (C)

15.30 The youth] *interlined with a caret above deleted* 'Fleming'; 'he' *of* 'The' *mended; a line drawn under caret* (P)

15.32 the regiment] *interlined with a caret* (C)

15.33 moving] *preceded by deleted* 'other' (C)

15.34 The] *preceded by deleted* 'A mass' (C)

15.35 silk.] *followed by deleted* 'There was an' (C)

15.36 the] 't' *over beginning of illegible letter* (C)

16.3 a] *preceded by deleted* 'a[*and beginning of* 'n']' (C)

16.3 trod] 'o' *altered from* 'e' (C)

16.3 He] *preceded by deleted* 'He swore aloud' *and the beginning of another letter* (C)

16.10 The] *preceded by partially erased line which connected* 'The' *to the end of the preceding paragraph* (G)

16.10 developing day] 'ing' *interlined above deleted* 'ement of the' (C)

16.11 backs.] *period inserted; followed by deleted* 'and grain' (C)

16.12 earth] 'h' *mended* (C)

16.12 the youth] *interlined above deleted* 'Fleming' (G)

16.12 landscape] *interlined above deleted* 'earth' (C)

16.13 columns] 'ns' *over* 's' (G)

16.17 The tall soldier] *interlined above deleted* 'Jim Conklin' (P)

16.17 into praises] MS 'out in praise' *with* 'praise' *preceded by deleted* 'what' (C)

16.18–20 "I . . . I?" . . . soldier.] *first double quotes strengthened, second quotes inserted;* MS(c) 'you' *interlined above deleted* 'yeh'; 'I?" ' *followed by deleted* 'We're going [*final* 'g' *over apostrophe* (G)] up [*followed by deleted comma* (C)] the [*'e' over apostrophe* (G)] river, cut across, an' come around in behint 'em." ' (G); 'the blatant soldier.' *inserted after deleted* 'Wilson.' (P); 'loud' *interlined above deleted* 'blatant' (G); *the whole deleted with a large* × *by* HG

16.21 the . . . companions] 'the tall one's' *interlined with a caret above deleted* 'Conklin's'; 's' *of* 'companions' *added* (G)

16.23–24 the tall one's] *interlined above deleted* 'Conklin's'; *a final* 's' *deleted from* 'tall' (P)

16.26 The youth] MS 'The youth.' *with the period in error interlined above deleted* 'Fleming' (P)

16.30 often] *followed by deleted* 'to' (C)

16.35 The youth] *interlined with a caret above deleted* 'Fleming' (P)

16.36 emotions.] *followed by deleted* 'to his own.' (HG); *period after* 'emotions' *inserted and* HG *pencil deletion strengthened in ink* (F)

16.37 ²the] *final* 'm' *deleted* (C)

17.1 the tall soldier] *interlined above deleted* 'Conklin' (P)

17.3 commiseration] *preceded by deleted* 'sorrow' (C)

17.3 army] *followed by deleted* 'for' (C)

17.6 The youth] *interlined above deleted* 'Fleming' (P)

17.6 separated] *interlined above deleted* 'parted' (P)

17.7　blithe and] *the beginning stroke of the 'a' deletes with intent a comma following* 'blithe' (C)

17.10　The loud soldier] *'The blatant soldier' interlined above deleted* 'Young Wilson' (P)*; 'loud' interlined below deleted* 'blatant' (G)

17.11　the tall one.] *interlined above deleted* 'Jim Conklin.' (P)*; deletion strengthened in ink* (F)

17.15　soldier] *followed by* 'of Fleming's company' *interlined with a caret* (C)*; then deleted in ink* (F)

17.16　planned] *interlined above deleted* 'wished' (P)

17.16　knapsack] *followed by deleted period* (C)

17.21　observant] *interlined with a caret* (P)

17.21　at] *preceded by deleted* 'upon' (C)

17.23　The men] *a final* 'y' *deleted from* 'They' *and* 'men' *inserted* (P)

17.24　entirely ceased] 'ent' *inserted after* 'ceased' *and then deleted and* 'entirely' *interlined with a caret* (C)

17.25　attention] *a final* 's' *deleted* (C)

17.27　girl.] *followed by* '[¶] "Gin' it to 'em ['e' over 'i' (C)], Mary, 'gin' it to 'em ['e' over 'i' (C)]." [¶] "Don't let 'em steal yer horse." [¶] "Gin' him thunder." ' *deleted by HG with large* ×*; deletion strengthened in ink* (F)

17.28　To] *preceded by deleted opening double quotes and the beginning of a probable* 'H' (C)

17.31–32　downfall] *followed by deleted period and* 'and' (P)

17.32–34　Loud . . . defiance.] *added* (P)

17.32　Loud] 'L' *over* 'l' (P)*; pre-*

ceding period not inserted in error

17.33　who] *preceded by deleted* 'standin' (P)

17.33　the troops] *a final* 'm' *deleted from* 'them' *and* 'troops' *interlined* (P)

17.35　pieces] *preceded by deleted* 'fragments' (C)

17.36　fields] 's' *added later* (C)

17.39　The youth] *interlined above deleted* 'Fleming' (P)

18.2　few paces] *interlined above deleted* 'little way' (C)

18.3　black] *inserted* (C)

18.4　made . . . effects.] *interlined above deleted* 'was a weird scene.' (C)

18.5　blades] *preceded by deleted* 'soft' (C)

18.6　moon] *followed by deleted* 'was' (C)

18.6　lighted] 'ed' *added* (C)

18.7　, enveloping him,] *interlined with a caret* (C)

18.7　²him] *interlined above deleted* 'Fleming' (P)

18.8　winds] *preceded by deleted* 'night' (C)

18.10　sympathy] *interlined with a caret above deleted* 'pity' (C)

18.10　himself] MS(c) 'him' *with* 'self' *deleted* (C)

18.15　had] *interlined with a caret* (C)

18.15　milking-] 'ing' *added later beneath hyphen* (C)

18.16　there] *followed by deleted* 'were halo' (C)

18.17　have] *interlined with a caret* (C)

18.18　them] 't' *added and* 'e' *over* 'i' (C)

18.20　himself] 'e' *followed by possible* 'a' (C)

18.21　-like,] *followed by deleted* 'before' (C)

18.23　the loud soldier.] 'the blatant soldier.' *interlined above deleted* 'young Wilson.' (P)*;*

'loud' *interlined above deleted* 'blatant' (G)

18.25 Henry,] *interlined above deleted* 'Flem,' (P)

18.26,30 yeh] MS(c) 'you' *above deleted* 'yeh' (G)

18.26 doin'] MS(c) 'doing' *with* 'g' *over an apostrophe* (G)

18.26 here?] *question mark added after period which was not deleted in error* (G)

18.27 thinking] 'g' *over an apostrophe* (G)

18.27,31 the youth.] *interlined above deleted* 'Fleming.' (*no period in error after* 'youth' *at* 18.31) (P)

18.28 The other] *interlined above deleted* 'Wilson' (P)

18.29 gittin' . . . lookin' thunderin'] MS(c) 'getting . . . looking thundering' *with final* 'g's' *over apostrophes* (G)

18.29 m'] MS(c) 'my' *with* 'y' *over an apostrophe* (G)

18.29 peek-ed] MS 'peek-|-ed' *with second hyphen inserted* (P)

18.29 th'] MS(c) 'the' *with* 'e' *over an apostrophe* (G)

18.31 nothing] 'g' *over an apostrophe* (G)

18.32 The loud soldier] 'The blatant soldier' *interlined above deleted* 'Wilson' (P); 'loud' *interlined above deleted* 'blatant' (G)

18.34 face was] MS(u) 'face was voice was'; HG *inserted pencil comma after* 'face', *deleted first* 'was' *and interlined* 'and' *above;* Crane *deleted* 'and voice' *but did not delete the comma in error* (G)

18.34 his] *preceded by deleted* 'vo' (C)

18.35 "We've] *preceded by deleted* ' "At' (C)

18.35,37; 19.4,10 th'] MS(c) 'the' *with* 'e' *over an apostrophe* (G)

18.36 lick 'em] *preceded by de-*

leted 'li [*and the beginning of a* 'k'] ' (C)

18.37 soberly] *preceded by deleted* 'seriously' *with* 'i' *over* 'e' (C)

18.38; 19.4 t'] MS(c) 'to' *with* 'o' *over an apostrophe* (G)

18.39 'em] 'e' *over* 'i' (G)

19.1 you] *interlined above deleted* 'yeh' (G); *to the left, in the margin, is a pencil* HG *question mark*

19.1 objecting] 'g' *over an apostrophe* (G)

19.1 to] 'o' *over an apostrophe* (G)

19.2 the youth] *interlined above deleted* 'Fleming' (P)

19.3–4 marchin' . . . goin'] MS(c) 'marching . . . going' *with final* 'g's' *over apostrophes* (G)

19.4 fightin'] MS(c) 'fighting' *final* 'g' *added* (G)

19.5 gittin'] MS(c) 'getting' *with* 'e' *over* 'i' *and final* 'g' *over an apostrophe* (G)

19.5,6,10 an'] MS(c) 'and' *with* 'd' *over an apostrophe* (G)

19.5 comin'] MS(c) 'coming' *with* 'g' *over an apostrophe* (G)

19.6 kin] MS(c) 'can' *interlined above deleted* 'kin' (G)

19.6 exceptin'] MS(c) 'excepting' *with* 'g' *over an apostrophe* (G)

19.6 damn'] MS(c) 'damned' *with* 'ed' *added beneath deleted apostrophe* (G)

19.7 get] 'e' *over* 'i' (G)

19.7 fighting] *final* 'g' *over an apostrophe* (G)

19.9 fer] 'e' *over* 'o' (C)

19.11 we] *preceded by deleted* 'we' ' (C)

19.12 arose] *preceded by deleted* 'g' (C)

19.17 The youth] *interlined above deleted* 'Fleming' (P)

19.17 him] *interlined* (C)

19.18 finally] *inserted* (C)

19.18–19.29 going to] *final* 'g' *and final* 'o' *over apostrophes* (G)

19.20 The loud soldier] *original* 'Wilson' *preceded by deleted opening double quotes* (C); 'The blatant soldier' *interlined with a caret above deleted* 'Wilson' (P); 'loud' *interlined above deleted* 'blatant' (G)

19.21 dignity] 'g' *over an upstroke* (C)

19.22,37(*twice*) th'] MS(c) 'the' *with* 'e' *over an apostrophe* (G)

19.22,32,38 goin' t'] MS(c) 'going to' *with final* 'g' *and final* 'o' *over apostrophes* (G)

19.25 do] 'o' *over an apostrophe* (G)

19.25(*twice*),35 you] *interlined above deleted* 'yeh' (G)

19.25,29,30,34,35 the] 'e' *over an apostrophe* (G)

19.26 the youth.] *interlined above deleted* 'Fleming.' (P)

19.27 the loud one.] 'the blatant one.' *interlined with a caret above deleted* 'Wilson' *and a period not deleted in error* (P); 'loud' *interlined above deleted* 'blatant' (G)

19.28 the youth,] *original* 'Fleming,' *with comma preceded by deleted period* (C); 'the youth' *interlined above deleted* 'Fleming' (P)

19.28 a'-nough] 'a' *over* 'i' (G)

19.29 things] *followed by deleted* 'but' (C)

19.31 replied] 'r' *over* 's' (C)

19.31 the other] *interlined above deleted* 'Wilson' (P)

19.32 Th'] MS(c) 'The' *with* 'e' *over an apostrophe* (G)

19.32 runnin'] MS(c) 'running' *with* 'g' *over an apostrophe* (G)

19.33 confidently] *preceded by deleted* 'self-' (C)

19.34 the youth.] *interlined above deleted* 'Fleming' *and a period not deleted in error* (P)

19.34 You] *interlined above deleted* 'Yeh' *which had been underlined by* HG *whose question mark appears in the left margin* (G)

19.36 the loud soldier] MS 'the blatant soldier' *interlined above deleted* 'Wilson' (P)

19.36 indignantly] *first* 'i' *over beginning of illegible letter* (C)

19.36 An'] MS(c) 'And' *with* 'd' *over an apostrophe* (G)

19.38 fightin'] MS(c) 'fighting' *with final* 'g' *over an apostrophe* (G)

19.38 I] *followed by deleted* 'am to' (C)

19.39 Who] *inserted and preceded on line above by deleted* 'You' (C)

19.39 anyhow?] *question mark altered from a period* (C)

19.39 ²yeh] MS(c) 'you' *interlined above deleted* 'yeh' (G)

20.1 Napolyon Bonypart] HG *inserted* 'e's' *over the* 'y's' *and added a final* 'e' *to* 'Bonypart'

20.1 the youth] *interlined above deleted* 'Fleming' (P)

20.3 The youth] *original* 'Fleming' *first word of MS f. 27 of which* '7' *over* '1' (C); 'The youth' *interlined above deleted* 'Fleming' (P)

20.6 his] *interlined above deleted* 'the' (P)

20.6 comrade] *interlined with a caret above deleted* 'Wilson' *and preceded by interlined* 'and' *deleted* (P)

20.8 view-points] *interlined above deleted* 'points of view' (P)

20.11 slowly to] *interlined with a caret above deleted* 'to' (P)

20.11 a] *preceded by deleted* 'the' (C)

20.12 tall soldier.] *interlined above deleted* 'Conklin.' (P)

20.17 voices,] *preceded by de-*

leted 'ap'; *comma added after deleted period* (C)

20.19 the] *interlined* (C)

20.20 low,] *interlined* (C)

20.20 sentences.] *interlined above deleted* 'voices.' (P)

20.22 He] *preceded by paragraph symbol* (P)

21.2 pontoon] *final* 's' *deleted* (C)

21.7 insect-] *interlined* (C)

21.8 the youth] *interlined with a caret above deleted* 'Fleming' (P)

21.12 But] *preceded by vertical stroke at left margin* (C)

21.12 -place] MS 'camping-|-place' *with second hyphen inserted* (C)

21.13 slept] 'l' *over* 'e' (C)

21.14 hustled] *followed by deleted* 'mile after mile' (C)

21.14 a] *preceded by deleted* 'a road' (C)

21.16 rapid] *interlined with a caret* (C)

21.20 the loud soldier.] 'the loud, young soldier.' *interlined above deleted* 'Wilson.' (P); 'young' *deleted* (G), *but the preceding comma not deleted in error*

21.25 blankets] *preceded by deleted* 'two' (C)

21.25 haversacks] *final* 's' *added later* (C)

21.26 canteens,] *interlined above a comma not deleted in error* (C)

21.26-28 "Yeh . . . hotel?"] *written in left margin with a line joining it to the written line and with a caret following* 'ammunition.' (C); *deleted by* HG *with a large* ×; *an* HG *pencil question mark appears in the margin*

21.26 Yeh kin] MS(c) 'You can' *interlined above deleted* 'Yeh kin' (G)

21.27 an'] MS(c) 'and' *with* 'd' *over an apostrophe* (G)

21.27 [1]the . . . youth.] 'Conklin' *interlined above deleted* 'Wilson' (C); 'the . . . youth.' *interlined above deleted* 'Conklin to Fleming' *and a period not deleted in error* (P)

21.28(*twice*) yeh] MS(c) 'you' *interlined above deleted* 'yeh' (G)

21.28 d'] MS(c) 'do' *with* 'o' *over an apostrophe* (G)

21.28 want] *a final* 'a' *deleted* (G)

21.28 t'] MS(c) 'to' *interlined* (G)

22.1 much] *preceded by deleted* 'a' (C)

22.3 regiment] *final* 's' *deleted* (C)

22.3 yet] *followed by* 'by any means' *interlined with a caret* (C); *then deleted* (P)

22.3 appearance] *final* 's' *deleted* (C)

22.4 to] *preceded by deleted* 'tw' (C)

22.5 the command] MS 'cammand' *with final* 'y' *deleted from* 'the' *and* 'cammand' *interlined with a caret* (C)

22.6 noting] *preceded by deleted* 'seein' ' (C)

22.7 their] 'ir' *added* (C)

22.11 [1]hats.] *interlined above deleted* 'head-gear.' (C)

22.17 the army] *interlined with a caret above deleted* 'Fleming had' *and preceded by deleted* 'the youth' *also interlined* (P)

22.17 odor] *preceded by deleted* 'resinous' (C)

22.18 pines] *preceded by deleted* 'od' (C)

22.19 rang through the forest] *interlined above deleted* 'was in the air' (C)

22.20 old] *preceded by deleted* 'sleepy' (P)

22.20 The youth] *interlined with a caret above deleted* 'He' (P)

22.22   dawn] 'd' *over possible* 'h' (C)

22.22–23   the tall soldier] *interlined above deleted* 'Jim Conklin' (P)

22.27   shoulder] *interlined in pencil above deleted* 'head' (HG); *traced over in ink* (F)

22.30   skedaddlin'] *preceded by deleted* 'skedd' (C)

22.31–32   the loud soldier's] 'the loud young soldier's' *interlined with a caret above deleted* 'Wilson's' (P); 'young' *deleted* (G)

22.33   sech] 'e' *over* 'i' (C); MS (c) 'u' *over* 'e' (G)

22.33   fer] MS(c) 'for' *with* 'o' *over* 'e' (G)

22.34; 23.4   The youth] *interlined above deleted* 'Fleming' (P)

22.34   moved] 'v' *over illegible letter* (C)

22.36   firing.] *followed by deleted* 'One' *and the beginning of an upstroke* (C)

23.2   mob] 'o' *over upstroke* (C)

23.5   the] *inserted* (C)

23.6   his] *interlined above deleted* 'the' (C)

23.11   sides.] *originally begun with* 'si' *at far right of page then deleted* (C)

23.11   moving] *preceded by deleted* 'sort' (C)

23.12   it] *preceded by deleted* 'that' (C)

23.18   some] *inserted* (C)

23.20   the youth] *interlined above deleted* 'Fleming' (P)

23.21   curiosity] 'sity' *added with* 'si' *over* 'us' (C)

23.36;24.15   The youth] *interlined above deleted* 'Fleming' (P)

23.37   constantly] *preceded by deleted* 'knocking' (C)

24.1   red] *interlined above deleted* 'strange' (C)

24.1   of] *followed by deleted* 'gree' (C)

24.2   [1]a] *preceded by deleted* 'the' (C)

24.8   The youth] *interlined with a caret above deleted* 'Fleming' (G)

24.10   And] *preceded by deleted* 'Fleming felt a flush of' (C)

24.12–13   concealed from] *originally* 'concealed even from' *with* 'even' *interlined with a caret* (C); *then* 'concealed from' *deleted and* 'concealed from' *interlined with a caret and written over* 'even' (P)

24.14–15   invulnerable] *interlined above deleted* 'impregnable' (C)

24.17   He] *interlined above deleted* 'Fleming' (P)

24.20–22   During . . . easily] *false start* [*verso of* MS f. 139]: 'During this march, the ardor which Fleming had acquired in his scramble up the bank [*followed by deleted comma*] rapidly faded to nothing. His curiosity was quite easily' (C); *the whole deleted in pencil* (F)

24.20   the youth] *interlined above deleted* 'Fleming' (P)

24.27   Absurd] *originally* 'A' *with* 'bsurd' *added* (C)

24.27   thought] *preceded by deleted* 'that' (C)

24.33   there] *first* 'e' *over* 'r' (C)

24.37–38   generals] *preceded by deleted* 'camm' (C)

24.38   swallow] *preceded by deleted* 'encompass and' (P)

25.4   be] *preceded by pencil deleted* 'to' (HG) *or* (G)

25.5   come] 'e' *over* 'ing' (HG)

25.5   they] *preceded by deleted* 'some one' (C)

25.6   The] *a final* 'se' *deleted* (C)

25.7   pen] *preceded by deleted* 'trap' (C)

25.13   had] *interlined above deleted* 'was' (C)

25.15   as] *interlined* (C)

25.18 blood-] *preceded by deleted* 'blood' (C)

25.18 were] *followed by deleted* 'curious.' (C)

25.20 the youth] *interlined above deleted* 'Fleming' (P)

25.20 at] *strengthened* (C)

25.20 throat.] *interlined above deleted* 'lips.' (C)

25.21 if] 'f' *over beginning of upstroke* (C)

25.25 he] *interlined with a caret* (C)

25.28 He] *preceded by paragraph symbol* (P)

25.28 was] *interlined with a caret* (C)

25.29 began heartily to] *interlined with a caret above deleted* 'began to' *with* 'heartily' *preceded by independently deleted* 'to' (C)

25.29 him] *followed by deleted* 'heartily' (C)

25.29 a] *interlined above deleted* 'his' (P)

25.29 calling] *interlined above deleted* 'and called' (C)

25.31 skulking'll] *apostrophe inserted above deleted* 'wi' (P)

25.31 He . . . pace] *inserted before* 'P' *deleted at paragraph point* (C)

25.31 with] *followed by deleted* 'the alcrity' (C)

25.32–33 And . . . brute.] *added later and* 'the . . . brute.' *written between two ruled lines* (C)

25.33 minds.] *interlined above deleted* 'things' *and a period not deleted in error* (C)

25.37 white] *preceded by deleted* 'roun' (C)

25.38 During] 'D' *over* 'E' (C)

25.38 many] *preceded by deleted* 'each' (C)

26.1 sticks,] *inserted* (C)

26.2 bullet] *preceded by deleted* 'battl' (C)

26.6 it] *interlined* (C)

26.7 be] *preceded by deleted* 'look' (C)

26.8 ³the] *the beginning of a* 'y' *has been deleted by the continuance of the upstroke ending* 'e' (C)

26.9 who] *followed by deleted* 'no s' (C)

26.10 terriers.] *followed by deleted* 'Also, they indicated a venerable fence the rails of which were vanishing' *with independently deleted* 'a venerab moss-grown' *and beginning of another letter following* 'indicated'; 'venerab' *inserted* (C)

26.13 the youth.] *interlined above deleted* 'Fleming.' (P)

26.15,30 for] 'o' *over* 'e' (G)

26.15 the tall soldier.] *interlined above deleted* 'Jim Conklin.' (P)

26.17 dirt] *followed by deleted* 'which' (C)

26.18 had] *interlined with a caret* (C)

26.20 line] *preceded by deleted* 'b[and beginning of another letter]' (C)

26.20–21 intrenchments] 's' *added* (C)

26.24 The youth] *interlined above deleted* 'Fleming' (P)

26.25 saw] *preceded by deleted* 'was' (C)

26.25 his salvation] *interlined with a caret* (C)

26.25 change.] *period inserted before deleted* 'his only salvation.' (C)

26.28 generals.] 's' *squeezed in* (C)

26.28 the tall soldier.] *original* 'Jim Conklin.' *followed by deleted* ' "Oh, I s'pose' (C); 'the tall soldier' *interlined above deleted* 'Jim Conklin.' (P)

26.30 ¹to] *original* 't ' *preceded by deleted* 'to' (C); 'o' *over apostrophe* (G)

26.30 our] *interlined with a caret above deleted* ''r' (G)

26.31 return] *preceded by deleted* 'go ba' (C)

26.32 else] *first* 'e' *over* 's' (C)

26.32 ²a] *interlined with a caret* (P)

26.32 in his doubts] *interlined with a caret* (P)

26.35 tall soldier] *interlined above deleted* 'Conklin' (P)

26.36 a] *preceded by deleted* 'an' (C)

26.37 s'pose] MS(c) 'suppose' *interlined above deleted* 's'pose' (G)

26.37 reconnoiterin'] 'er' *over* 're' (C); MS(c) 'reconnoitering' *with* 'g' *over an apostrophe* (G)

26.37; 27.11 th'] MS(c) 'the' *with* 'e' *over an apostrophe* (G)

26.37 kentry] MS(c) 'country' *interlined with a caret above deleted* 'kentry' (G)

26.37; 27.11 jest] MS(c) 'just' *with* 'u' *over* 'e' (G)

26.37,38; 27.10(*twice*),11 t'] MS(c) 'to' *with* 'o' *over an apostrophe* (G)

26.38 gittin'] MS(c) 'getting' *with* 'e' *over* 'i' *and final* 'g' *over an apostrophe* (G)

26.38 clost] MS(c) 'close' *with* 'e' *over* 't' (G)

26.39 the loud soldier.] 'the loud young soldier.' *interlined above deleted* 'Wilson.' (P); 'young' *deleted* (G)

27.1 the youth] *interlined above deleted* 'Fleming' (P)

27.1 still] *preceded by deleted* 'ir [*and the beginning of an* 'r']' (C)

27.1 fidgeting] *interlined above deleted* 'fretting' (C) *or* (P)

27.1–2 anything . . . tramping] *final* 'g's' *over apostrophes* (G)

27.2 the country] 'e' *over an apostrophe;* 'country' *interlined with a caret above deleted* 'kentry' (G)

27.2 doing] 'g' *over an apostrophe* (G)

27.3 to] 'o' *over an apostrophe* (G)

27.3 and] 'd' *over an apostrophe* (G)

27.3 just] 'u' *over* 'e' (G)

27.3 tiring] 'g' *over an apostrophe* (G)

27.4 the loud soldier] 'the loud young soldier' *interlined with a caret above deleted* 'Wilson' *and a period deleted in error* (P); 'young' *deleted* (G)

27.4,8 yeh] MS(c) 'you' *interlined above deleted* 'yeh' (*with a caret at* 27.8) (G)

27.6 the tall private] *interlined above deleted* 'Conklin' *and a period deleted in error* (P)

27.6(*twice*),7 Yeh] MS(c) 'You' *interlined above deleted* 'Yeh' *which had been underlined by HG twice at* 27.6 (G)

27.7 damn'-cuss] *original* 'damn'-fool-cuss' *with first hyphen strengthened and second hyphen inserted* (P); '-fool' *deleted* (G)

27.7,8 an'] MS(c) 'and' *with* 'd' *over an apostrophe* (G)

27.8 fer] MS(c) 'for' *with* 'o' *over* 'e' (G)

27.8(*twice*) yit] MS(c) 'yet' *with* 'e' *over* 'i' (G)

27.9 some] *interlined above deleted* 'little' (C)

27.9 fightin'] MS(c) 'fighting' *with final* 'g' *over an apostrophe* (G)

27.9–10 the other;] *interlined above deleted* 'Wilson.' (P)

27.10 a'] MS(c) 'have' *written over* ''a' (G)

27.12 The tall one] *interlined above deleted* 'Conklin' (P)

27.12 sandwich] 'h' *following* 'w' *struck through* (HG)

27.14 gradually,] *followed by deleted* 'his face became' (C)

27.16 sandwiches] 'h' *following* 'w' *struck through* (HG)

27.16] air] *preceded by deleted* 'ex' (C)

27.18 then] *interlined with a caret* (P)

27.19 new] *preceded by deleted* 'all' (C)

27.19 circumstance] *a final* 's' *deleted* (C)

27.20 coolness] *preceded by deleted* 'calmness,' (C)

27.21 went] *interlined above deleted* 'strode' (C)

27.21 stride] *preceded by deleted* 'gait' (C)

27.21 a] *interlined with a caret* (C)

27.24 earth] *preceded by deleted* 'dirt each and stone' (C)

27.24 had been] *interlined above deleted* 'was' (C)

27.27 landscape] *followed by deleted* 'then' (C)

27.28 the youth.] *interlined above deleted* 'Fleming' *and a period not deleted in error* (P)

27.28 and] 'a' *over beginning of an upstroke* (C)

27.32 them] *inserted with a caret over* 'it' (P)

27.33 his] *interlined with a caret* (C)

27.37 nothing] *followed by deleted* 'die' (C)

27.38 momentary] *interlined above deleted* 'mom' *of which* 'om' *over* 'ore' (C)

27.39 extraordinary] *first* 'a' *over* 'o' (C)

27.39 mere] *interlined with a caret* (C)

28.1 getting] *preceded by deleted* 'merely' (C)

28.3 senses] *final* 's' *added* (C)

28.7 the youth] *interlined above deleted* 'Fleming' (P)

28.14 it] *preceded by deleted* 'he' (C)

28.14 exploded] *second* 'e' *over beginning of another letter* (C)

28.18 The youth] *interlined above deleted* 'Fleming' (P)

28.23 the loud soldier.] 'the loud young soldier.' *preceded by deleted* 'young Wilson.' (P); 'young' *deleted* (G)

28.24,27 m'] MS(c) 'my' *with ink* 'y' *over an apostrophe* (F)

28.24,27 an'] MS(c) 'and' *with ink* 'd' *over an apostrophe* (F)

28.24,27 ol'] MS(c) 'old' *with ink* 'd' *over an apostrophe* (F)

28.26,32,34 the youth] *interlined above deleted* 'Fleming' (P)

28.27 the loud soldier.] *original* 'Wilson.' *preceded by deleted* 'Fl' (C); 'the loud young soldier.' *interlined above deleted* 'Wilson' *and a period not deleted in error* (P); 'young' *deleted* (G)

28.28 Somethin'] MS(c) 'Something' *with ink* 'g' *over an apostrophe* (F)

28.30(*twice*) an'] MS(c) 'and' *with* 'd' *over an apostrophe* (G)

28.30 yeh] MS(c) 'you' *interlined above deleted* 'yeh' (G)

28.30 t'] MS(c) 'to' *with* 'o' *over an apostrophe* (G)

28.31 t'] MS(c) ' 'to' *with* 'o' *added* (G)

28.32 done] 'd' *over* 'i' (C)

28.34 ¹the] 'e' *over an apostrophe* (G)

28.35 the other] *interlined above deleted* 'Wilson' (P)

[28.35 represents the last alteration made in the preliminary revision of the manuscript before it was shown to Hamlin Garland and is on MS f. 38.]

28.36 limp] *interlined with a caret* (C)

29.6 of the new regiment] *interlined with a caret* (C)

29.6–7 eagerly while] *the beginning stroke of* 'w' *deletes with* intent a comma following 'eagerly' (C)

29.9 Perry] MS 'Perrey' *interlined above deleted* 'Perrett' (C)

29.9 big] *interlined above deleted* 'great' (G)

29.10 t'] *interlined above deleted* 'to' (C)

29.10,15 th'] *final* 'e' *deleted and apostrophe inserted* (C)

29.11 'G' Company] *closing single quote over double;* 'C' *over* 'c' (C)

29.12–13 They allus] *interlined with a caret above deleted* 'He a' (C)

29.13 a——"] *followed by deleted* ' "Dern this bein' in reserve, anyhow. I didnt come here to be in reserve. I"——' (G)

29.20 done."] *followed by deleted* '[¶] "Th' boys of th' 47th, they took a hull string of rifle-pits." [¶] "It wasn't th' 47th [*followed by a deleted comma* (G)] at all [MS(u) 'a't'all' *preceded by deleted* 'a'tall' (C); MS(c) 'at all' *with* 't' *inserted over an apostrophe and* 't' *of* 't'all' *deleted* (G)]. It was th' 99th Vermont." [¶] "There haint nobody took no rifle-pits. Th' 47th driv 'a lot 'a Johnnies from behint [*followed by deleted* ' 'em." ' (C)] a fence." [¶] "Well——" ' (G); *deletion with HG question mark to the left*

[The above deletion after 29.20 represents the last pencil alteration in the general revision until 77.19 where Crane switches from ink back to pencil. This alteration (29.20) occurs on folio 39, folio 40 contains only current alterations, and folios 41–44 are wanting; it is therefore not demonstrable exactly where Crane switched from pencil to ink. The first ink alteration in the general revision occurs at 33.1.]

29.26 Hasbrouck,] *comma inserted after deleted period* (C)

29.26 He] 'H' *over* 'h' (C)

29.28 Maine] 'M' *over* 'm' (C)

30.4 be] 'b' *over possible* 'd' (C)

33.0 33] MS f. 45 *with* '41–' *added in pencil* (F)

33.1 The youth] *interlined above deleted* 'Fleming' (G)

33.10 The] *followed by deleted* 'form of the' (G)

33.18 The tall soldier] *interlined above deleted* 'Gun-locks clicked. Jim Conklin' (G)

33.18 his rifle, produced a red] *interlined above deleted* 'himself was a silk' (C)

33.19 of] 'o' *over period* (C)

33.19 in knotting] *interlined with a caret* (G)

33.21 the line . . . sound.] *interlined above deleted* 'the line.' (G)

33.22 Gun-locks clicked.] *squeezed in at the end of the line with* 'clicked.' *interlined with a caret* (G)

33.24 running] *preceded by deleted* 'men,' (C)

33.27 the youth] *interlined above deleted* 'Fleming' (G)

33.29 so] *preceded by deleted* 'and' (C)

34.2,3 to] 'o' *over an apostrophe* (G)

34.7 colonel] *interlined above deleted* 'general' (C)

34.8 The youth] *interlined above deleted* 'Fleming' (G)

34.10 regarding] '-ing' *interlined above deleted* 'ed' (C)

34.12 the youth's] *interlined above deleted* 'Fleming's' (G)

34.13 ²Oh] *preceded by deleted* 'It' (C)

34.14 of] 'o' *mended* (C)

34.15 coaxed] *preceded by deleted* 'like' (C)

34.15–16 congregation] *interlined above deleted* 'lot' (C)

34.16 His] 'is' *over* 'e' (C)

34.16–17 repetition.] MS 'repition.' *with a final 's' squeezed in and then deleted* (C)

34.17 boys—] *dash over comma* (C)

34.20 the youth's] ' 's' *added to original* 'Fleming' (C); 'the youth's' *interlined above deleted* 'Fleming's' (G)

34.21 nervous] 'n' *over beginning of an illegible letter* (C)

34.24 field] *a final 's' deleted* (C)

34.25 him] *preceded by deleted* 'them' (C)

34.26 Before] *preceded by deleted* 'He threw' (C)

34.26 begin] *preceded by deleted* 'being' (C)

34.28 fired] *preceded by deleted* 'first' (C)

34.29 weapon] *interlined above deleted* 'rifle' (C)

34.31 lost] 'o' *over illegible letter* (C)

34.37 ¹a] *preceded by deleted* 'an' (C)

34.37 ²a] *interlined above deleted* 'the' (G)

35.5 There] 'T' *over* 't' *and preceded by deleted* 'Too,' (C)

35.7 even] *preceded by deleted* 't[*and the beginning of an* 'h']' (C)

35.9 ¹was] *preceded by deleted* 'wat' (C)

35.9 carpenter] *followed by deleted comma and* 'whose' (C)

35.11 movements.] *preceded by deleted* 'haste.' *and followed by deleted* 'He' *of which* 'e' *is over* 'is' (C)

35.11 He, in his] *inserted* (C)

35.11 was] *interlined above deleted* 'were' (C)

35.11 off] *followed by deleted* 'across' (C)

35.12 other] 'o' *over illegible letter* (C)

35.12 even] *first* 'e' *over possible* 'v' (C)

35.13 ³his] *immediately preceded by a possible upstroke* (C)

35.13 saloon.] *period over comma* (C)

35.14 jolted] 'j' *over* 'g' (C)

35.21 mad] *interlined above deleted* 'furious' (C)

35.25 rage] *preceded by deleted* 'rg' (C)

35.28 so] 's' *over beginning of* 'a' (C)

35.28 were] *preceded by deleted* 'where' (C)

35.31 respite] *preceded by deleted* 'air' (C)

35.32 blankets.] *squeezed in at end of line* (C)

35.33 rage] *preceded by deleted* 'anger' (C)

35.34 intentness] *preceded by deleted* 'the' (C)

35.34 men] *followed by deleted* 'wh' (C)

35.36 wild] *preceded by deleted* 'will' (C)

35.38 ¹the] *interlined* (C)

35.38–39 the youth's] *interlined above deleted* 'Fleming's' (G)

36.1 The tall soldier] *interlined with a caret above deleted* 'Jim Conklin' (G)

36.4 why] *interlined with a caret* (C)

36.6 The youth] *interlined with a caret above deleted* 'Fleming' (G)

36.15 aim] *followed by a caret interlining deleted:* 'into the smoke, or,'; *followed on the line by deleted* 'at the blurred and shifting' (C)

36.16 which] *preceded by deleted* 'that' (C)

36.18 at] *over* 'in' (C)

36.25 lieutenant] *preceded by deleted* 'youthful' (G)

36.25,37 the youth's] *interlined above deleted* 'Fleming's' (G)

36.25 company] *followed by deleted* 'was' (C)

36.26　soldier] 'i' *over* 'e' (C)

36.27　Behind] *preceded by deleted* 'He blubbe' (C)

36.27　two] *followed by deleted comma* (C)

36.29　lieutenant] *second* 'n' *over an upstroke* (C)

36.29　collar] *interlined above deleted* 'color' (C)

36.29　was] *inserted* (C)

36.30　him.] *period inserted before deleted* 'as if he had insulted his wife.' (*although the ink deletion is dark, it does not appear to be the later general revision ink*) (C)

36.30　with many blows.] *interlined with a caret which deletes a period following* 'ranks' (C)

36.32　expressed] *first* 'e' *over* 'i' (C)

36.34　re-load] 're-' *inserted later* (C)

36.37　killed] *interlined above deleted* 'shot' (C)

36.39　resting,] *comma inserted before deleted period* (C)

37.1　look] *interlined above deleted* 'air' (HG); *traced over in ink* (F)

37.11　withdraw] *preceded by deleted* 'leave loo' (C)

37.14,21　the youth] *interlined above deleted* 'Fleming' (G)

37.20　silent] MS 'silence' *with an HG vertical stroke over the final* 'e' *in a possible attempt to correct to* 'silent'

37.21　fever] *preceded by deleted* 'river' (C)

37.28　it] *followed by deleted* 'with' (C)

37.30　The youth] *interlined above deleted* 'Fleming' (G)

37.30　²and] *inserted with a caret* (C)

37.33　few] *interlined with a caret* (C)

37.34　in] *preceded by deleted* 'into' (C)

37.36　have] *interlined* (C)

37.37　to be] *interlined above deleted* 'thrown,' (C)

38.1　it. The flash] *interlined above deleted* 'their heads' (C)

38.1　the youth] *interlined above deleted* 'Fleming' (G)

38.4　worked] *preceded by deleted* 'hastened' (C)

38.9　thither.] *preceded by deleted* 'there.' (C)

38.10　drearily] *inserted* (C)

38.11　torn] *interlined above deleted* 'wounded' (C)

38.13　and] *followed by deleted* 'left' *and the beginning of a* 'w' (C)

38.14　thought] *preceded by deleted* 'coul' (C)

38.18　riders] *interlined above an ink blot under which can be seen the original* 'riders' (C)

38.19　cheerings] 's' *added* (C)

38.22　red] *followed by deleted* 'an [*and the beginning of* 'd']' (C)

38.24　The youth] *interlined above deleted* 'Fleming' (G)

38.24　emblems.] 's' *squeezed in* (C)

38.26–27　side, . . . left,] *commas mended* (C)

38.32　the youth] *interlined above deleted* 'Fleming' (G)

38.35　her] 'h' *over beginning of* 'g' (C)

39.1　The youth . . . gradually] *false start* (*verso of* p. 59): 'Fleming awakened slowly. He came came [*inkblot under which is discernible the descender of a* 'g']' (C)

39.1　The youth] *interlined above deleted* 'Fleming' (G)

39.3　person] *interlined above deleted* 'position' (C)

39.6　re-laced] 're-' *interlined;* 'up' *after* 'laced' *deleted* (C)

39.9　formidable] 'le' *over* 'e' (C)

39.16　in] *interlined above deleted* 'with' (G)

39.16 gratification] *a final 's' deleted* (C)

39.17 Upon] *preceded by deleted* 'He' (C)

39.17 ¶ Upon] *to the left of this paragraph, in the margin, appears an HG pencil question mark*

39.17 Gee,] *final 'e' and comma mended* (G)

39.19 face] *preceded by deleted* 'f' (C)

39.20 ¶"You] *to the left of this paragraph, in the margin, appears an HG pencil question mark*

39.21 sprawled] *preceded by deleted* 'sprawed' (C)

39.29 regiment] *preceded by deleted* 'men' (C)

39.31 "Gosh!"] *closing quotes and exclamation point added before deleted* '—all—hemlocks." ' (G)

40.1 The youth] *interlined above deleted* 'Fleming' (G)

40.1 discerned] *interlined above deleted* 'saw' (G)

40.4 the regiment] *a final 'm' deleted from* 'the' *and* 'regiment' *interlined* (G)

40.6 They] *preceded by deleted* 'On the sward' *of which* 'O' *over* 'I' (C)

40.6 flowers] *interlined above deleted* 'blossoms' (C)

40.8 faded] *preceded by deleted* 'had' (C)

40.9 expressed] *interlined above deleted* 'expre' *with remainder covered by an ink blot* (C)

40.11 of] 'o' *altered from a period* (C)

40.13 They] 'T' *over* 'F' (C)

40.15,16 t'] MS(c) 'to' *with* 'o' *over an apostrophe* (G)

40.15 this] *followed by deleted* 'here' (G)

40.15 bangin'] MS(c) 'banging' *with final 'g' over an apostrophe* (G)

40.16 here] *final 'e' mended* (G)

40.16 th'] MS(c) 'the' *with* 'e' *over an apostrophe* (G)

40.18–20 The . . . repulse.] *squeezed in between two ruled lines* (C)

40.21 The youth] *interlined with a caret above deleted* 'Fleming' (G)

40.29 ranks] *preceded by deleted* 'g' (C)

40.32 more often] *interlined above deleted* 'usually' (C) *or* (G)

40.32 projected,] *followed by deleted* 'brilliant with resplenden' (C)

40.33 the youth's] *interlined above deleted* 'Fleming's' (G)

40.34 orbs] *interlined above deleted* 'eyes' (C)

40.35 muscles] *preceded by an ink blot which obscures several letters* (C)

40.36 awkward] *followed by a deleted period* (C)

40.36–37 as . . . mittens.] *interlined with a caret* (C)

40.37 And] 'A' *over the beginning of* 'T' (C)

41.2 fer] MS(c) 'for' *with* 'o' *over* 'e' (G)

41.3 th'] MS(c) 'the' *with* 'e' *over an apostrophe* (G)

41.4 and] 'a' *over* 't' (C)

41.5 Himself] *preceded by deleted* 'They' (C)

41.6 was] *preceded by deleted* 'could not' (C)

41.7 gloomy] *second 'o' over beginning of an 'm'* (C)

41.7 struggling] *preceded by deleted* 'fighting such' (C)

41.13 yelling.] *followed by deleted* 'It seemed that this swift-swarming crowd, crying savagely, would surely break the brittle line of new men in blue.' (C)

41.14 the youth] *interlined with a caret above deleted* 'Fleming,'; *the caret deletes the* comma following 'Fleming' *and therefore one is added on the line after the caret* (G)

41.14 redoubtable] *preceded by deleted* 'dragon' (C)

41.20 rifle,] *comma inserted after deleted period* (C)

41.27 The youth] *interlined above deleted* 'Fleming' (G)

41.28 shaken] *interlined above deleted* 'moved' (C)

41.31 yelled] *interlined above deleted* 'tell' (C) *or* (G)

41.35 ²His] 'i' *over illegible letter* (C)

41.35 in] *preceded by deleted* 'out' (C)

41.37 cord] *preceded by deleted* 'ch' (C)

41.37 On] 'O' *over* 'A' (C)

41.38 all] *interlined with a caret* (C)

41.39 lieutenant] *preceded by deleted* 'youthful' (G)

41.39 The youth] *original* 'Fleming' *followed by deleted* 'was conscious of his' (C); 'The youth' *interlined above deleted* 'Fleming' (G)

42.2 that] *interlined with a caret* (C)

42.3 a] *interlined with a caret* (C)

42.3 creature] *interlined above deleted* 'being' (C)

42.9 Death] *followed by* 'was' *interlined with a caret and then deleted* (G)

42.12 better to] *preceded by deleted* 'far' *and followed by deleted* 'be in si' (C)

42.14 believed] *interlined above deleted* 'concieved' (C)

42.17 that] *interlined with a caret* (C)

42.17 pursued] *interlined above deleted* 'followed' (C)

42.17 by these] *interlined above deleted* 'by these' (C)

42.19 flight] *interlined above deleted* 'retreat' (C)

42.19 these] 'es' *over* 'i[and the beginning of 's']' (C)

42.20 must] *interlined above deleted* 'was' (C)

42.21 men] *preceded by deleted* 'victims' (C)

42.21 nearest;] *semicolon inserted before deleted* 'to him;' (C)

42.21 initial] *a final* 's' *deleted* (C)

42.22 those] 'ose' *added with* 'o' *over* 'e' (C)

42.22 him.] *comma inserted before the period and followed by* 'Fleming' *interlined* (C); 'Fleming' *deleted but the comma not deleted in error* (G)

42.25 field] *a final* 's' *deleted* (C)

42.25 found] 'f' *over a vertical stroke* (C)

42.26 They] *followed by deleted* 'went hurtlin[and the beginning of a 'g']' (C)

42.28 grinned] *followed by deleted period* (C)

42.28 Once] *preceded by deleted* 'He cou' (C)

42.29–30 his chosen] *interlined with a caret above deleted* 'one' (C)

42.34 altogether] *preceded by deleted* 'and' *and followed by* 'unaware' *interlined with a caret* (C)

42.35 disputing] MS 'disputeing' *with* 'in' *over* 'n' (C)

42.35 antagonist] *preceded by deleted* 'foe' (C)

42.36 were] *interlined* (C)

43.2 from] *preceded by deleted* 'who' (C)

43.12 he] *preceded by deleted* 'fe' (C)

43.13 a] *interlined above deleted* 'their' (C)

43.17–18 Officers] *an apostrophe preceding* 's' *deleted* (C)

43.21 manner] *interlined above deleted* 'kind' (C)

43.22 wondrous] 's' *over* 's' (C)

43.23 order] *interlined with a caret* (C)

43.29 The youth] *interlined above deleted* 'Fleming' (G)

43.33 a] *preceded by deleted* 'g' (C)

43.33 yellow] *preceded by deleted* 'silve' (C)

44.1 The youth] *interlined above deleted* 'Fleming' (G)

44.2 unable] *followed by deleted* 'too' (C)

44.5 not] *interlined above deleted* 'n't have' (C)

44.9 It] 'I' *over* 'H' (C)

44.9 calmly] *interlined above deleted* 'commo' (C)

44.12 ¶ As] *to the left of this paragraph, in the margin, appears an* HG *pencil question mark*

44.13 t'] *preceded by deleted* 'to' (C)

44.18 chesnut] 't' *inserted following* 's' (HG)

44.18 swift] *interlined* (C)

44.20 a] *interlined with a caret* (C)

44.22 the youth] *interlined above deleted* 'Fleming' (C)

44.24 by] 'y' *added beneath deleted apostrophe* (C)

44.25 a-flame] *hyphen inserted into one word* (C)

44.25 excitement] *preceded by deleted* 'eag' (C)

44.30–31 anything."] *followed by deleted* '[¶] He turned wi[*and the beginning of an upstroke*]' (C)

44.32 horse] 's' *altered from* 'e' (C)

44.32 messenger] *preceded by deleted* 'genera' (C)

44.34 paean.] MS 'peaen.' *preceded by deleted* 'pae' *and* 'paen'; *period inserted before deleted* 'and bi' (C)

44.34 'em] 'e' *over* 'i' (C)

44.36 and] *followed by deleted* 'rear' (C)

45.1 The youth] *interlined with a caret above deleted* 'Fleming' (G)

45.1 discovered] *preceded by deleted* 'sudd' (C)

45.2 remained] *second* 'e' *interlined* (C)

45.3 and] 'd' *over the third minim of an* 'm' *of which the remainder forms the* 'n' (C)

45.6 musketry] 'r' *over beginning of possible* 'y' (C)

45.6 cries] *interlined above deleted* 'cheers' (C)

45.10 approached] 'e' *over illegible letter* (C)

45.11 piece] *interlined above deleted* 'part' (C)

45.14 Later,] *comma added after deleted comma and* 'then' (C)

45.16–17 at such a time] *interlined with a caret* (C)

45.21 line] *interlined with a caret* (C)

45.22 blows] *interlined above deleted* 'shocks' (C)

45.25 the] 'th' *over* 'a' (C)

45.25 when] *interlined above deleted* 'that' (C)

45.26 would] *preceded by deleted* 'w[*and the beginning of an* 'h']' (C)

45.28 perceptions] 's' *added* (C)

46.2 sharper] *interlined above deleted* 'finer and deeper' (C)

46.7 war] *followed by a deleted comma* (C)

46.9 bowed] *interlined with a caret* (C)

46.22 his] *interlined above deleted* 'it's' (C)

46.22 was] *interlined above deleted* 'seemed' (C)

46.24 -leaves] *followed by deleted* 'toward him.' *at far right of the line below and the end of the page* (C)

46.25 men] 'n' *added* (C)

46.26 dark] *a final* 'er' *deleted*

and followed by deleted 'and more' (C)

46.26 places.] *preceded by deleted period and* 'Af' (C)

46.27 After] *preceded by inserted paragraph symbol* (C) *or* (G)

46.31 impudent] *preceded by deleted* 'ins' (C)

46.35 assurance.] *followed by deleted* 'In it was the religion of peace.' (C)

46.36 if] 'f' *over illegible letter* (C)

46.37 nature] 'n' *over beginning of possible* 'N' (C)

46.38 tragedy] *preceded by deleted* 'trade' (C)

46.39 ¹a] *interlined above deleted* 'a' *and below independently deleted* 'a pebble at' (C)

46.39; 47.1 he] *interlined above deleted* 'it' (C)

47.1 his] *interlined above independently deleted* 'hi' *and* 'it's' (C)

47.2 from behind] *interlined above deleted* 'around' (C)

47.2 branch] 'b' *over possible* 't' (C)

47.2 down] *interlined above deleted* 'back' (C)

47.4 The youth] *interlined with a caret above deleted* 'Fleming' (G)

47.5 sign. The squirrel] *originally the paragraph ended with* 'sign.' *and a new paragraph was begun:* 'He wended, feeling that nature'; *this was deleted and* 'The' *added after* 'sign.'; 'squirrel' *follows deleted* 'nature' (C)

47.6 had taken] *interlined above deleted* 'took' (C)

47.8–9 heavens] *preceded by deleted* 'H' (C)

47.10 too;] *interlined with a caret above a semicolon not deleted in error* (C)

47.10 doubtless,] *interlined above deleted* 'doubtless' (C)

47.11 race.] *original* 'race.' *with period deleted, a comma added, and followed by* 'else he would have been [*squeezed in at end of line*] likely to have [*'likely to have' interlined above deleted* 'doubtless'] defied their traditions instead of obeying them with rare promptitude.' (C); 'else . . . promptitude.' *deleted and period inserted* (G)

47.12,20,38 The youth] *interlined with a caret above deleted* 'Fleming' (*no caret at* 47.20) (G)

47.15 Once he] 'Once' *inserted and preceded by paragraph symbol;* 'O' *over* 'A'; 'h' *over* 'H' (C)

47.15 swamp.] *period inserted before deleted* 'on' (C)

47.17 out] *followed by deleted* 'near some' (C)

47.18 directly] *interlined with a caret* (C)

47.24 boughs] *interlined above deleted* 'bows' (C)

47.30 dead] 'a' *over* 'e' (C)

47.33; 48.2 the youth] *interlined above deleted* 'Fleming' (G)

47.37 trundling] *preceded by deleted* 'trud[*and the beginning of an* 'l']' (C)

48.3 brought] *preceded by deleted* 'touched' (C)

48.5 the] *preceded by deleted* 'the' (C)

48.7 ¹him,] *interlined above deleted comma and* 'th' (C)

48.8 unguided] 'n' *over beginning of illegible letter* (C)

48.14 black] *a final* 's' *deleted* (C)

48.14 greedily] *interlined with a caret* (C)

48.18 squawk] MS 'squwk' *with* 'u' *over* 'a' (G)

48.18 in] *interlined with a caret* (G)

48.19 The trees] *indented to para-*

graph point and preceded by deleted 'The trees' *flush with the margin* (C)

48.20 edifice.] *followed by* '[¶] Again the youth ['the youth' *interlined above deleted* 'Fleming' (G)] was in despair. Nature no longer condoled with him. There was nothing, then, after all, in that demonstration she gave—the frightened squirrel fleeing (*preceded by deleted* 'al' *over which is written an* 'f' (C)] aloft from the missile. [¶] He thought as he remembered the small animal [*followed by deleted comma* (C)] capturing the fish and the greedy ants feeding upon the face of the dead soldier, that there was given another law which far-over-topped it—all life existing upon death, eating ravenously, stuffing itself with the hopes of the dead. [¶] And nature's processes were obliged to hurry (*end of* MS folio 65, folio 66 *wanting*)' (C); *deleted in pencil* (F)

49.0 49] MS f. 67 *with* '66–' *added in pencil* (F)

49.6 stillness] *preceded by deleted* 'silence' (C)

49.8 The youth] *interlined with a caret above deleted* 'Fleming' (G)

49.8 this] 'i' *over* 'e' *and a final* 'e' *deleted* (C)

49.9 It] *preceded by deleted* 'A' (C)

49.9 if worlds] 'if' *interlined;* 's' *added* (C)

49.15 an] *interlined with a caret* (C) *or* (G)

49.16 avoid. But] *period over comma and* 'B' *over* 'b' (C) *or* (G)

49.17 earth] 'e' *over beginning of an* 'm' (C)

49.22 sounds] *final* 's' *added* (C)

49.22 Everything] *preceded by deleted* 'Everybody' (C)

49.23 be] *interlined* (C)

49.25 the youth] *interlined above deleted* 'Fleming' (G)

49.27 present din,] *beginning stroke of* 'd' *deletes with intent a comma following* 'present' (C)

49.27–28 battle-scenes.] *preceded by deleted* 'war.' (C)

49.28 uproar] *followed by deleted* 'set the' (C)

49.31 himself] *interlined above deleted* 'he' (HG)

50.11 hastened] *interlined above deleted* 'hurried' (C)

50.12 His] 'H' *over* 'h'; *preceded by deleted* 'All' (C)

50.12 such] *squeezed in* (C)

50.17 After] 'A' *over beginning of a* 'T'; *preceded by deleted* 'This resistance' (C)

50.17 previous] *followed by independently deleted* 'resistance,' *and* 'this' (C)

50.23 played] 'a' *over beginning of* 'y' (C)

50.25 He . . . fight.] *interlined above deleted* 'His lower jaw hung down.'; 'fight' *preceded by deleted* 'battle' (C)

50.28 powers,] *comma inserted followed by deleted* 'fascinated him.' (C)

50.33 off] 'ff' *over* 'n' (C)

50.33 or] *preceded by deleted* 'o[*and beginning of an* 'f']' (C)

50.36 the youth] *interlined above deleted* 'Fleming' (G)

50.36 felt] *interlined* (C)

50.38 and] *followed by deleted comma* (C)

50.38 ¹the] *followed by deleted* 'the' (C)

50.38 vague] 'gu' *over illegible letter* (C)

51.3 lane] 'a' *over* 'i' (C)

51.4 cursing,] *followed by deleted* 'wailing' (C)

51.12 was swearing] *interlined*

above deleted 'swore by the sun,' (G)

51.12 had] *preceded by deleted* 'been' (C)

51.12–13 arm . . . of] *interlined above deleted* 'arm because the cam[*and the beginning of* 'm'] (C)

51.16 ¹a] *over* 'in' (G)

51.27 the] *followed by deleted* 'grim' (C)

51.28 burning] *interlined above deleted* 'buring' (C)

51.29 proceeded] *third* 'e' *over* 'i' (C)

51.34 an'] *preceded by deleted* 'and' (C)

51.35 let] *followed by deleted* 'someonelse' *with* 'lse' *added* (C)

51.37–38 "Say . . . all."] *squeezed in and* 'take it all." ' *interlined* (C)

51.38 way] 'a' *mended* (C)

52.1 roadsides] *final* 's' *added* (C)

52.2 past,] *interlined above deleted comma and* 'th' (C)

52.2 pert] 'e' *over illegible letter* (C)

52.5 spectral soldier] *interlined above deleted* 'spectral shoulder' (C)

52.6 The youth] *interlined above deleted* 'Fleming' (G)

52.16–17 the youth's] *interlined above deleted* 'Fleming's' (G)

52.21 sugar-] *preceded by deleted* 's[*and beginning of an upstroke*]' (C)

52.24 sardonic] 'do' *over* 'ca' (C)

52.26 The] *preceded by deleted* 'At this,' (C)

52.27 the youth] *interlined above deleted* 'Fleming' (G)

52.29 The youth] MS 'the youth' *interlined above deleted* 'Fleming' (G)

52.33 together] *preceded by deleted* 'along' (C)

52.35 The youth] *interlined above deleted* 'Fleming' (G)

52.39; 53.13 the youth] *interlined above deleted* 'Fleming' (G)

53.3 to] *interlined with a caret* (C)

53.3 time] *preceded by deleted* 'little' (C)

53.6 then] *followed by deleted* 'to' (C)

53.16 Georgie] 'r' *mended* (C)

53.18 don't] ''t' *over* 'e' (C)

53.19 it,' I ses, 'an'] *single quotes deleted and then reinserted* (C)

53.19 t'um] 'u' *altered from* 'i' (C)

53.20 ses.] *followed by deleted double quotes* (C)

53.21 larfed.] *followed by deleted double quotes and* 'Well they' (C)

53.21 Well,] *preceded by deleted* 'The man' *at paragraph point* (C)

53.25 the youth.] *interlined above deleted* 'Fleming' *and a period not deleted in error* (G)

53.27 The youth] *interlined above deleted* 'Fleming' (G)

53.31 the youth] *interlined above deleted* 'Fleming' (G)

53.34 bended] 'ded' *added with first* 'd' *over* 't' (C)

54.1 The youth] *interlined with a caret above deleted* 'Fleming' (G)

54.1 tattered] *followed by deleted* 'man' (C)

54.10 persons] *interlined above deleted* 'men' (C)

54.11 red] *preceded by deleted* 'woun' (C)

54.14 man's] 'a' *over* 'e' (C)

54.19 alone.] *followed by deleted* 'There could be seen a certain stiffness in the' (C)

54.23 wounds.] *followed by deleted* 'And as' (C)

54.26 away] *preceded by deleted* 'aside' (C)

54.26 the youth] *interlined above deleted* 'Fleming' (G)

54.30 Jim] *followed by deleted* 'Willikin' (C)

55.1,5 The tall soldier] *interlined with a caret above deleted* 'Conklin' (*no caret at* 55.5) (G)

55.1 "Hello] *double quotes over beginning of possible* 'H' (C)

55.3,10,15 The youth] *interlined above deleted* 'Fleming' (G)

55.7 Henry?] MS 'Flem' *preceded by deleted* 'P'; *question mark altered from a comma* (C)

55.10 Jim——"] MS 'Jim"——' *with dash over a period* (C)

55.11,20 the tall soldier] *interlined with a caret above deleted* 'Conklin' (*no caret at* 55.20) (G)

55.13 ²shot.] *followed by deleted double quotes* (C)

55.13 reiterated] 'a' *over* 'e' (C)

55.15–16 the tall soldier] *interlined with a period above deleted* 'Conklin'; *period in error* (G)

55.16 propelled.] *followed by deleted* 'The other wounded men' *of which* 'other' *is interlined* (C)

55.16 Since] *preceded by deleted* 'Since Fleming [*final* ' 's' *deleted*] had appeared to' (C)

55.16,22 the youth's] *interlined above deleted* 'Fleming's' (G)

55.17 guardian] MS 'gaurdian' *preceded by deleted* 'help and' (C)

55.19 in] 'i' *over beginning of illegible letter* (C)

55.20 friends] *an apostrophe before* 's' *deleted* (C)

55.23 dreading] *interlined above deleted* 'fearing' (C)

55.29; 56.4,15 The youth] *interlined with a caret above deleted* 'Fleming' (*no caret at* 56.15) (G)

55.31,35; 56.7 the tall soldier]

interlined with a caret above deleted 'Conklin' (*no caret at* 55.35) (G)

55.32 care] MS(c) 'keer' *preceded by deleted* 'care' (C)

55.32 protested] *a following period deleted by a caret interlining* 'Fleming.' (C); 'Fleming' *deleted, but the period not deleted in error and* 'the youth.' *interlined* (G)

55.36; 56.13 the youth's] *interlined above deleted* 'Fleming's' (G)

56.8 soldier] 'i' *over* 'e' (C)

56.9 The youth] *original* 'Fleming' *with* 'F' *over* 'B' (C); 'Fleming' *deleted and* 'The youth' *interlined* (G)

56.13 purpose. And] *period inserted;* 'A' *over* 'a' *and followed by deleted* 'to' (C)

56.15 follow.] *period inserted before deleted* 'after.' (G)

56.23,28,35 the youth.] *interlined above deleted* 'Fleming.' (*no periods at* 56.28,35) (G)

56.25 He] *preceded by deleted* 'Pres' (C)

56.25 the tall soldier] MS 'the tall youth' *interlined above deleted* 'Conklin' (G)

56.26 Jim! Jim!] *exclamation points inserted before deleted dashes* (C)

56.27 The tall soldier] *interlined with a caret above deleted* 'Conklin' (G)

56.28 vacantly] *an* 'n' *following first* 'a' *deleted* (C) *or* (G)

56.29 comprehending] *second* 'e' *over beginning of an upstroke* (C)

56.31;57.8 The youth] *interlined above deleted* 'Fleming' (G)

56.39 singular] *interlined above deleted* 'grotesque' (C)

57.1,8 the tall soldier] *interlined above deleted* 'Conklin' (G)

57.1–2 all the] 'all' *inserted;* 'the' *interlined with a caret* (G)

57.2,3 you] *interlined above deleted* 'yeh' (G)

57.2 doing] 'g' *over an apostrophe* (G)

57.3 you'll] *interlined above deleted* 'yeh'll' (G)

57.4 purpose] *preceded by deleted* 'mysterious' (G)

57.4 the tall soldier's] *interlined above deleted* 'Conklin's' (G)

57.10(*thrice*),16 you] *interlined above deleted* 'yeh' (G)

57.10 thinking] 'g' *below deleted apostrophe* (G)

57.10 going] *final* 'g' *over apostrophe* (G)

57.12,17 The tall soldier] *interlined with a caret above deleted* 'Conklin' (*no caret at* 57.17) (G)

57.13 a] *preceded by deleted* 'an a' (C)

57.13 can't] *preceded by deleted* 'can't' *and beginning of* 'y' (C)

57.15 The youth recoiled.] *interlined above deleted* 'Fleming recoiled' *and a period not deleted in error* (G)

57.16 the] 'e' *over an apostrophe* (G)

57.18 The youth] *interlined above deleted* 'Fleming' (G)

57.18 the] *interlined with a caret* (C)

57.19 whipped,] 'ped,' *added with* 'pe' *over* 's,' (C)

57.19 he] *interlined with a caret* (C)

57.20 They] 'y' *over* 'n' (C)

57.21 these] *first* 'e' *over* 'i'; *second* 'e' *added* (C)

57.22 soldier. And] *period follows deleted period;* 'A' *over* 'a' (C)

57.22 there] 't' *inserted later* (C)

57.22 to] *preceded by deleted* 'a' (C)

57.23 devotee] *interlined above deleted* 'priest' (C)

57.23 a] *interlined above deleted* 'some' (C)

57.27 wore] *followed by deleted* 'a look' (C)

57.28 struggled.] *interlined above deleted* 'sought.' (C)

57.30 sides] *final* 's' *added later* (C)

57.30–31 that . . . at] *interlined above deleted* 'that was coming. They paused' (C)

57.31 the rendezvous. They paused] *interlined with a caret above* 'There was' *which began at paragraph point and is deleted with a line extending to the left margin* (C)

57.35–36 as if an animal] *interlined above deleted* 'was an ani' (C)

57.36 ¹was] *interlined above deleted* 'were' (C)

57.36 ²was] *interlined* (C)

57.38 This] *preceded by deleted* 'This gradual strangulat' (C)

57.38 of] *followed by deleted* 'a' (G)

57.38 the youth] *interlined above deleted* 'Fleming' (G)

57.38 writhe] *followed by deleted period and* 'Once as' (C)

58.4 The tall soldier] *interlined with a caret above deleted* 'Conklin' (G)

58.4 lips and] 'a' *formed from a period* (C)

58.6 waited.] *period inserted before deleted comma and* 'panting.' (C)

58.14 in expression of] *interlined with a caret above deleted* 'in' (C)

58.16 it] *interlined above deleted* 'he' (C)

58.20 "Gawd,"] MS(c) ' "God," ' *interlined above incompletely deleted* ' "Gawd," ' (G)

58.21,29 The youth] *interlined above deleted* 'Fleming' (G)

58.21–22 this . . . meeting.] *interlined above deleted* 'these rites, this dance.' (C)

58.27 from] *first word f.* 80 MS;
'80' *added below original* '50'
and before start of f. 50 *of*
MS(d): '[¶] The footsteps that
he heard' (C)

58.29 turned] 't' *over* 's' (C)

59.2 wa'n't] MS 'w'a'nt' *with* 'w'
over the beginning of possible
'n' (C)

59.3 said] *preceded by deleted*
'he' (C)

59.4 He] *beginning stroke of* 'H'
*deletes the beginning of open-
ing double quotes* (C)

59.5 foot.] *interlined above deleted* 'hands.' (C) *or* (G)

59.8 The youth] *interlined with
a caret above deleted* 'Fleming'
(G)

59.8 grief.] *period altered from
comma* (C)

59.14 out] *interlined with a caret*
(C)

59.15 He's] *followed by deleted*
'a' (C)

59.16 'im. An'] *period inserted;*
'A' *over* 'a' (C)

59.16 enjoyin'] *apostrophe inserted before deleted final* 'g'
(C)

59.18,25 The youth] *interlined
above deleted* 'Fleming' (G)

59.20 and] *preceded by deleted
period* (C)

59.21 too."] *closing quotes added
and a line drawn beneath to
indicate continuity* (G)

59.23 a] *interlined with a caret*
(C)

59.23 bed.] *following quotes deleted* (C)

59.26,27 And] 'd' *over an apostrophe* (G)

59.27 coming] 'g' *over an apostrophe* (G)

59.30 man, "there] *comma added
after deleted period;* 't' *over* 'T'
(C)

60.1,3,12,18 The youth] *interlined above deleted* 'Fleming'
(*with a caret at* 60.3) (G)

60.7 laughing] 'l' *over* 's' (C)

60.14 hand] *followed by deleted
period* (C)

60.16 oughta] *preceded by deleted* 'out' *with beginning of* 'g'
over uncrossed 't' (C)

60.16 'a] MS 'a'' *with* 'a' *over
possible* 'o' (C)

60.20 talk] 't' *over* 'w' (C)

60.22 funniest] *second* 'n' *over* 'i'
(C)

60.28 infernal] *preceded by deleted* 'ifner' (C)

60.30 looked] 'ed' *added* (C)

60.34 an_∧] *preceded by deleted*
'an'' (C)

61.2 don't] *preceded by deleted*
't'wont' (C)

61.4 located?"] 'd' *added and
question mark squeezed in
above a period* (C)

61.7 'Hurt] *single quote altered
from double* (C)

61.7 hurt much?'] *interlined
above deleted* 'much hurt?''
(G)

61.9 didn't] *interlined above deleted* 'neednt' (C)

61.11 kind 'a] ''a' *interlined
above deleted* 'a' *of* 'kinda' (C)

61.13 The youth] *interlined with
a caret above deleted* 'Fleming'
(G)

61.14–15 a . . . hand.] 'a' *inserted in line and* 'motion . . .
hand.' *interlined with a caret
above deleted* 'gesture.' (C)

61.16 the] *interlined above deleted* 'that' (C)

61.19 curiosity.] MS(c) 'curiosity?' *with question mark altered from period* (C)

61.20 repeated] *interlined above
deleted* 'said' (C)

61.24,34 The youth] *interlined
above deleted* 'Fleming' (G)

61.34 pointed] *followed by deleted period and* ' "O' (C)

61.35 here—] *dash over comma*
(C)

61.37 slurred] 'l' *over* 'u' (C)

62.3 right—] *dash over comma* (C)

62.4 the youth] *interlined above deleted* 'Fleming' (G)

62.4 a] *interlined above deleted* 'the' (C)

62.8 The youth] *interlined above deleted* 'Fleming' (G)

62.10 believed] *second* 'e' *over* 'v' (C)

62.11 bodies] 'e' *either inserted or mended* (C)

62.12 fallen] *interlined above deleted* 'dead' (C)

62.14 asserted] *interlined above deleted* 'proclaimed' (C)

62.14 at] *preceded by independently deleted* 'at' *and* 'until' (C)

62.20 admitted] *interlined above deleted* 'saw' (C)

62.21 vigilance.] *followed by* '[¶] Promptly, then, his old rebellious feelings returned. He thought the powers of fate had combined to heap misfortune upon him. He was an innocent victim. [¶] He rebelled against the source of things, according to a law, perchance, that the most powerful shall recieve the most blame. [¶] War, he said bitterly to the sky, was a make-|shift created because ordinary processes could not furnish deaths enough. Man had [followed by deleted 'grown' (C)] been born [followed by deleted 'of the drea' (C)] wary of the grey skeleton and had expended much of his intellect in erecting whatever safeguards were possible, so that he had long been ['he . . . been' interlined above deleted 'now he was' (C)] rather strongly intrenched behind the mass of his inventions. He kept an ['n' added and followed by deleted 'calm' (C)] eye on his bath-tub, his fire-*

engine, his life-boat, and compelled' (*end of MS f. 85, ff. 86–89 wanting*); *the whole deleted in pencil and the deletion strengthened in blue crayon* (F)

63.0 63] MS f. 90 *with* '86—' *added in blue crayon* (F)

63.11 The youth] *interlined with a caret above deleted* 'Fleming' (G)

63.12 retreating] *preceded by deleted* 'fleeing' (C)

63.15 dangers and horrors] 'dangers' *interlined above deleted* 'hor-|' *and* 'and hor' *inserted before* 'rors' *on the line below* (C)

63.15 ²the] *interlined above deleted* 'an' (C)

63.17 could] *preceded by deleted* 'charge' (C)

63.20 forward-going] *interlined with a caret* (C)

63.31 remainder] *preceded by deleted* 'whole army' *with* 'l' *over* 'r' (C)

64.2 it] 't' *altered from* 's' (C)

64.6 As the youth] *original* 'Fleming' *interlined above deleted* 'he' (C); 'As the youth' *inserted before deleted* 'As Fleming' (G)

64.12 thing] *final* 's' *deleted* (C)

64.15 ³the] 't' *over beginning of* 'f' (C)

64.23 used] *followed by deleted comma and* 'he sa' (C)

64.24 throw off himself] 'off' *interlined with a caret above deleted final* 'n' *of* 'thrown'; 'himself' *followed by deleted* 'off' (C)

64.24 become] 'o' *over* 'a' (C)

64.28 steel] *preceded by deleted* 'stel[*and upstroke of second* 'l']' (C)

64.29 all.] *interlined above deleted* 'everybody' *which is followed by period not deleted in* error *and of which first* 'y' *inserted* (C)

64.31 him.] *followed by deleted* 'In his ears, he heard the ring of' (C)

64.32 victory.] *period inserted before deleted* 'an' (C)

64.38 himself] *preceded by deleted* 'his fl' *and followed by deleted* 'flying' (C)

64.38 flying] *interlined* (C)

65.4 balancing] '-ing' *interlined above deleted* 'ed' (C)

65.6 the] *interlined with a caret* (C)

65.8 if] 'i' *over* 'o' (C)

65.9 fight] *interlined with a caret* (C)

65.14 ¹him] *inserted* (C)

65.15 intent] *preceded by deleted* 'deny' (C)

65.17 would,] *followed by deleted* 'be'; *comma inserted;* 'I' *strengthened* (C)

65.19 would] *followed by deleted comma and* 'when the' (C)

65.23 these] 'se' *added* (C)

65.26 ¹the] *interlined with a caret* (C)

65.28 Furthermore] *preceded by deleted* 'Further, various ailments' (C)

65.32 thirst] *an* 'r' *after* 'h' *deleted* (C)

65.34–35 threatened] 'th' *over beginning of illegible letter* (C)

65.35 break] *followed by deleted period* (C)

65.38 ¹and] *followed by deleted* 'his head' (C)

66.4 clamor.] *followed by deleted* 'The dogs of pain' (C)

66.8 loon.] *interlined above deleted* 'look.' (C)

66.11 ²him] *interlined with a caret* (C)

66.12 ²to] *possibly inserted* (C)

66.14 that, despite] *comma inserted before deleted* 'with all'

of which 'with' *interlined with a caret;* 'despite' *interlined with a caret* (C)

66.19 he] *followed by deleted* 'could' (C)

66.20 be] *followed by deleted* 'compelled to' (C)

66.23 they.] *interlined above deleted* 'others' *and a period not deleted in error* (C)

66.26 in] 'i' *over* 'a' (C)

66.26 this] 'i' *over* 'e' (C)

66.26 hope,] *preceded by independently deleted* 'p' *and* 'unshaped' *interlined above deleted* 'unrecognized' (C)

66.28 off] *second* 'f' *added* (C)

66.28 tradition] *preceded by deleted* 'memor[and beginning of probable* 'y']' (C)

66.28 them] *preceded by deleted* 'it' (C)

66.28 ²and] *altered from* 'as' (C)

66.29 valiant] 'v' *below beginning of a letter* (C)

66.33 ditties] MS 'sad ditties' *preceded by deleted* 'ditties' (C)

66.33 felt] 'l' *over* 't' (C)

66.34 sacrifice.] *period altered from a comma, preceded by a deleted period* (C)

66.35 who] *followed by deleted* 'he' (C)

66.35 chosen] *followed by deleted* 'audience' *interlined above deleted* 'for the bar' (C)

66.35 barbs] 's' *added* (C)

66.36 and] *interlined with a caret* (C)

66.38 who] *followed by deleted* 'hav' (C)

66.38 had] *interlined* (C)

67.1 writing replies] 'w' *over* 'r'; 'r' *of* 'replies' *over* 'R' (C)

67.1 songs] *final* 's' *added* (C)

67.1 alleged] *interlined with a caret* (C)

67.4 there] *followed by deleted* 'lay a moral' (C)

67.4 vindication] *preceded by deleted* 'mo' (C)

67.5 prove] *preceded by deleted* 'proceed' (C)

67.6 because] *followed by deleted* 'because' (C)

67.6 his] *interlined with a caret* (C)

67.6 serious] *interlined above deleted* 'serious' (C)

67.9 A moral] *inserted before deleted* 'A' *interlined above deleted* 'This' (C)

67.14 be] *followed by deleted* 'indeed' (C)

67.16 a] *interlined with a caret* (C)

67.16 would] 'w' *over* 'c' (C)

67.24 fiend] *preceded by deleted* 'field' (C)

67.26 He] 'H' *over beginning of another letter, possibly an* 'A' (C)

67.27 ¹he] *interlined with a caret* (C)

67.27 ¹a] *interlined above deleted* 'the' (C)

67.27 corpse] *a final* 's' *deleted* (C)

67.36 considered,] *comma inserted before deleted comma and* 'however,' (C)

67.38 been] *followed by deleted* 'for th' (C)

68.8 ¹he] *interlined with a caret* (C)

68.11 was] *preceded by deleted* 'much' (C)

68.17 and] *followed by independently deleted* 'laugh at his stammering hesitation.' *and* 'try to keep watch of him to discover his merits and faults'; 'hesitation.' *interlined with a caret* (C)

68.20 would] 'w' *over* 'c' (C)

68.21 himself] *preceded by deleted* 'p' (C)

68.26 humorous] *second* 'o' *over beginning of* 'u' (C)

68.27 cackled.] *first* 'c' *strengthened* (C)

69.0 XII] *added in blue crayon below deleted* 'XIII.' *and* '98–104' *written in blue crayon over* '104.' (F) (*MS ff.* 98–103 *represented the discarded* Chapter XII; *for alterations made in the extant pages of this chapter see pp.* 385–386)

69.1 obstacles] *interlined above deleted* 'obsta' *of which* 'a' *over possible* 'c' (C)

69.2 the youth's] *interlined with a caret above deleted* 'Fleming's' (G)

69.8 above] 'a' *over possible* 'n' (C)

69.12 The youth] *interlined above deleted* 'Fleming' (G)

69.12 -stricken] 'n' *mended* (C)

69.15 damned.] MS 'doomed. [*interlined above deleted* 'damned'] He lost concern ['r' *over beginning of* 'n'] for himself.' (C)

69.16 invincible] *followed by deleted period* (C)

69.17 thickets,] *followed by deleted* 'was going to be swallowed.' (C)

69.24 them. They] *period altered from comma and* 'T' *over* 't' (C)

69.26–27 The youth] *original* 'Fleming' *preceded by deleted* 'They' (C); 'The youth' *interlined with a caret above deleted* 'Fleming' (G)

69.27 of them] *interlined with a caret* (C)

69.29 appeals. They] *period inserted;* 'They' *interlined above deleted* 'and' (C)

69.30 They] *preceded by an inserted paragraph symbol* (G)

70.1 It] *preceded by deleted* 'It' (C)

70.1 He] 'H' *over possible* 't' (C)

70.5 the gathered gloom.] *interlined with a caret above de-*

leted 'the darkness.' *of which the period is deleted by the caret* (C)

70.7 perceive] MS 'percieve' *interlined above deleted* 'see' (C)

70.7 From the mouths of] *interlined with a caret above deleted* 'Among' (C)

70.8 answers.] *preceded by deleted* 'replies' (C)

70.9 The youth] *original* 'Fleming' *preceded by independently deleted* 'Finally,' *and* 'he' (C); 'The youth' *interlined with a caret above deleted* 'Fleming' (G)

70.10 heedless] 'h' *over possible* 'i' (C)

70.10 clutched] *first* 'c' *over possible* 'a' (C)

70.12,17 the youth] *interlined above deleted* 'Fleming' (G)

70.14 ¹Letgo] 't' *inserted over deleted apostrophe* (C)

70.19 ²Letgo] 't' *and* 'g' *joined later; preceded by deleted* 'Legl' (C)

70.20 the youth.] *interlined above deleted* 'Fleming crazily.' (G)

70.22 crushed] *interlined above deleted* 'smashed' (C)

70.24 The youth's] *interlined above deleted* 'Fleming's' (G)

70.27 within] 'with' *inserted* (C)

70.27 head.] *preceded by deleted* 'ears.' (C)

70.33 again,] *followed by deleted* 'his weak fingers' *of which* 'weak' *was interlined with a caret* (C)

70.38 ¹his] *interlined above deleted* 'both' *of which a final* 's' *was deleted* (C)

70.38 temples] *interlined above deleted* 'head' (C)

71.3 he] *preceded by deleted* 'sh' (C)

71.4 tall soldier-] *original* 'Conklin-' *preceded by deleted* 'for-

ward,' (C); 'tall soldier-' *interlined above deleted* 'Conklin' *and a hyphen not deleted in error* (G)

71.5 search] MS 'reach' *with* 'r' *over* 's' (C)

71.6 pain.] *followed by independently deleted* '[¶] He put his hand to the' [*with* 'put' *followed by deleted* 'u(and beginning of probable* 'p')'] *and* 'Once he timidly touched' (C)

71.11 jolted] 'ed' *over* 'ing' (C)

71.11 cannon] *followed by deleted* 'batteries' (C)

71.15 sweeping] *followed by deleted* 'through' (C)

71.17–18 unwillingness— . . . heels.] *dash over a period;* 'of . . . heels.' *added* (G)

71.20 Their] 'ir' *over* 're' (C)

71.21 jumble] *interlined with a caret* (C)

71.24 The] 'T' *over beginning of* 'A' (C)

71.28 the youth] *interlined above deleted* 'Fleming' (G)

71.38 place] 'p' *over illegible letter* (C)

72.1 and] *inserted* (C)

72.2 munitions] 's' *added* (C)

72.3 lay] MS 'lay,' *with comma inserted after deleted* 'like a' *of which* 'like' *was interlined* (C)

72.4 lifeless.] *period inserted; followed by deleted* 'torrent.' (C)

72.5 torrent was] *beginning stroke of* 'w' *deletes with intent a comma following* 'torrent' (C)

72.6 horses] *followed by deleted period* (C)

72.6 splintered] *preceded by deleted* 'the' (C)

72.16 made] *followed by deleted* 'his neck' (C)

72.35 head] *preceded by deleted* 'hea' *of which* 'ea' *over* 'un' (C)

72.37 He held] *interlined above deleted* 'It caused' *which followed deleted* 'He argued w' (C)

72.37 as to] *interlined with a caret altered from a comma* (C)

72.38 until] *followed by deleted* 'until' (C)

73.5 The youth] *interlined with a caret above deleted* 'Fleming' (G)

73.8 with] *crosshatch to the left, above, deleting quote marks* (C)

73.11 the youth] *interlined above deleted* 'Fleming' (G)

73.12 ²the] *preceded by deleted* 'a' (C)

73.15 I] *over illegible letter* (C)

73.21 ²was] *interlined with a caret* (C)

73.24 It'll] 'I' *over illegible letter* (C)

73.27 an off'cer,] *preceded by deleted* 'an [*followed by deleted* 'orf'] officer' *of which* 'i' *is deleted later* (C)

73.28 won't] *followed by deleted* 'go' (C)

73.30 My] 'y' *over an apostrophe* (C)

73.33 boy] *preceded by deleted* 'fel' (C)

73.34 Jack] *preceded by deleted* 'His nam' (C)

73.35 thunder] 'under' *added after deleted apostrophe* (C)

73.35 We] *preceded by deleted* 'Yeh t'' (C)

73.36 spell] *preceded by deleted* 'still' (C)

73.38 big] *followed by deleted* 'feller' (C)

73.38 elbow] *preceded by deleted* 'eb' (C)

73.39 ses:] *colon over comma* (C)

73.39 where's] *apostrophe and* 's' *added* (C)

74.3 all th' time] *interlined with a caret* (C)

74.6 river.'] *single quote possibly altered from double* (C)

74.6 then] *followed by deleted* 'I' (C)

74.8 Thunder] *preceded by deleted* 'Oh, Lo' (C)

74.9 It's] 'I' *over* 'T' (C)

74.9 huntin'.] *interlined above deleted* 'searchin'.' (C)

74.15 him] *interlined with a caret* (C)

74.15 became] *followed by deleted* 'helps.' (C)

74.16 companion] *a final* 's' *deleted* (C)

74.17 things.] *followed by deleted* '[¶] The forest seemed a vast hive of men buzzing [*followed by deleted upstroke* (C)] about in frantic circles. The enemy was still beating away fitfully and, ['away fitfully' *inserted with a connecting line to* 'and,' *which is preceded by deleted* 'away fitfully an' *of which* 'fitfully' *interlined* (C)] in the darkness, [*followed by deleted* 'intelligent defense seemed impossible' *of which* 'intelligent' *interlined above deleted* 'way of' (C)] it seemed to Fleming that no intelligent defense [*followed by deleted* 'would be made.' *of which* 'w' *over* 'c' (C)] *original current deletion strengthened in pencil* (F)

74.18 vast] *interlined above deleted* 'hive' (C)

74.19 circles] *preceded by deleted* 'cir[*and beginning of* 'c']'; *followed by deleted period* (C)

74.19 the youth] MS 'The youth' *interlined with a caret above deleted* 'Fleming' (G)

74.19–20 mistakes] *preceded by* 'great' *which was interlined with a caret and then deleted* (G)

74.22 The youth] *interlined with a caret above deleted* 'Fleming' (G)

74.25 the youth's] *interlined above deleted* 'Fleming's' (G)

74.26 ¹and] *preceded by deleted* 'later' (C)

74.26 then] 't' *over* 'a' (C)

74.28 his] *interlined with a caret* (C)

74.28–29 to the youth] 'to' *and original* 'Fleming' *interlined with a caret* (C); 'the youth' *interlined above deleted* 'Fleming' (G)

74.29 his] *interlined above deleted* 'the other's' (G)

[74.29 represents the last ink alteration in the general revision stage for 27 MS folios. Pencil alterations recommence at 77.19]

75.0 XIII] *blue crayon* 'III' *over* 'IV.' (F)

75.1 The youth] *interlined with a caret in blue crayon above deleted* 'Fleming' (F)

75.2 him] *interlined with a caret* (C)

75.6 target.] *followed by deleted* 'He made vague' (C)

75.13 it] *preceded by deleted* 'he' (C)

75.15 monstrous] *interlined above deleted* 'nervous' (C)

75.15 figure.] *followed by deleted* 'The glints' *with* 't' *over illegible letter* (C)

75.20 **rifle**] *followed by deleted* 'b' (C)

75.21 peered] *preceded by deleted* 'tried to' (C)

75.23 me.] *period altered from an exclamation point* (C)

75.25 a goner] *preceded by deleted* 'dead' (C)

75.26 was] *followed by deleted* 'emo[and upstroke of* 't']' (C)

75.26 **voice**] *preceded by deleted* 'dea' (C)

75.28 forces. He] *period over deleted period followed by inde-* pendently deleted 'but' *and* 'He' *with* 'H' *over* 'h'; 'He' *inserted* (C)

75.29 tale] *preceded by deleted* 'prote' (C)

75.29 missiles] *preceded by deleted* 'impending' (C)

76.6 had] *interlined* (C)

76.6 Got] *upward stroke of* 'G' *deletes beginning of possible* 'g' (C)

76.8 am] 'a' *altered from* 'I' (C)

76.11 to?] *question mark mended* (C)

76.12 here?] *question mark over a period* (C)

76.15 forty-] 'r' *over* 'u[and beginning of* 'r']' (C)

76.16 all] *preceded by deleted* 'back' (C)

76.16 mornin'] *followed by deleted period and* 'Wh' (C)

76.22 rested] *preceded by deleted* 'put' (C)

76.24 "Gee,] *followed by deleted double quotes* (C)

76.25 his] *preceded by deleted* 'him.' *which is followed by deleted open quotes* (C)

76.28 'a] *interlined above deleted* 'of' (C)

76.29 As] *preceded by deleted* 'Wilson calle' (C)

76.31 canteen] *preceded by deleted* 'cat' (C)

76.33 t' him] 'h' *inserted* (C)

76.37 upon] 'up' *inserted* (C)

76.38 breast.] *preceded by deleted* 'chest' (C)

77.4 He] *preceded by deleted* 'He pu' (C)

77.11 a] *interlined with a caret* (C)

77.13 number-] *preceded by deleted* 'nu' (C)

77.14 be] *preceded by deleted* 'all' (C)

77.14 burnt] *interlined above deleted* 'burned' (C)

77.15 mornin'.] *period inserted*

before deleted comma and 'but'
(C)

77.16 It's] ' 's' *added* (C)

77.18 Then] *possibly inserted*
(C)

77.19 The corporal] *interlined
above deleted* 'Simpson' (G)

77.19 away.] *interlined above deleted* 'on' (C)

77.19 The youth] *interlined
above deleted* 'Fleming' (G)

77.20 with] *followed by independently deleted* 'stupid e'
and 'vacant' (C)

77.21 things] *preceded by deleted* 'obj' (C)

77.22 in] *preceded by deleted*
'about' (C)

77.25 visages] *interlined above
deleted* 'faces' (C)

77.27 lines] 'li' *over* 'n'; *preceded
by deleted* 'lines' (C)

77.27 They] *interlined above deleted* 'It' (C)

77.28 like] *tail of* 'e' *mended* (C)

77.29 have] *preceded by deleted*
'ha' *over possible* 'o[*and upstroke of another letter, possibly an* 'f']' (C)

77.29 to] *interlined* (C)

77.29 a] *interlined with a caret
above deleted* 'the' (C)

77.31 the youth] *interlined above
deleted* 'Fleming' (G)

77.32 seated] *followed by deleted*
'with his back' (C)

77.32 with] *interlined with a
caret* (C)

77.32 his back] *inserted* (C)

77.33 Badgered] *preceded by deleted* 'He s' (C)

77.33–34 dreams, perhaps,] *commas strengthened* (C)

77.34 little] *preceded by deleted*
'like' (C)

77.34–35 an old, toddy-stricken]
interlined above deleted 'a
tired, old' *of which* 'a' *interlined with a caret* (C)

77.36 jaw] *preceded by deleted*
'l' (C)

78.2 parts] *interlined above deleted* 'burning sticks' (C)

78.3 gleam] *preceded by deleted*
'rose-gleam' (C)

78.3 light] *interlined with a caret*
(C)

78.4 and] *interlined* (C)

78.5 slumber. A . . . legs] 'slumber.' *followed by independently
deleted* 'Legs struck straight'
and 'Legs' *of which* 's' *of*
'struck' *over an upstroke;*
'A . . . legs' *interlined* (C)

78.6 shoes] 'es' *over possible beginning of* 'w' (C)

78.6 or] *interlined above deleted*
'and' (C)

78.11 leaves] *preceded by deleted*
'foli' (C)

78.13–14 a window in the forest]
*interlined above independently
deleted* 'a' *and* 'window-like
opening' *of which* 'a' *preceded
by interlined* 'an', *also deleted*
(C)

78.14 seen] *interlined above deleted* 'seen the stars' (C)

78.14 like] 'l' *over possible beginning of* 'g' (C)

78.16 Occasionally,] *followed by
independently deleted* 'a' *and*
'in the bivouac' (C)

78.16 low-arched] *hyphen deletes
a comma with intent* (C)

78.17 sleep] *preceded by deleted*
'l' (C)

78.19 under] *preceded by deleted*
'ud' (C)

78.20 posture,] *comma inserted
before deleted period* (C)

78.20 throw] 'o' *altered from* 'e'
(C)

78.23; 79.3 The youth] *interlined
above deleted* 'Fleming' (G)

78.23–24 his . . . soldier] *interlined with a caret above deleted* 'Wilson' (G)

78.24 by] *interlined above deleted* 'ca' (C)

78.27 fussed] *preceded by de-*

leted 'fusse' *with* 'se' *possibly over* 'e' (C)

78.28 sticks] *followed by deleted* 'to greater exert' (C)

78.29 patient] *preceded by deleted* 'canteen' (C)

78.30 the youth] *interlined above deleted* 'Fleming' (G)

78.30 draught] 'd' *over upstroke* (C)

78.30 He] *inserted at end of paragraph with new paragraph beginning* 'The d' *deleted on the following line; deletion line extends to left margin* (C)

78.31 afar back and] *interlined with a caret above deleted* 'and' (C)

78.31 the canteen] *interlined above independently deleted* 'the' *and* 'it' (C)

78.31 cool] *interlined above deleted* 'cold' (C)

78.34 The . . . soldier] *interlined with a caret above deleted* 'Wilson' (G)

78.34 his comrade] *interlined with a caret above deleted* 'him' (C); *second caret added over deleted* 'him' (G)

78.37 middle] 'l' *over* 'e' (C)

78.38 the youth's] *interlined above deleted* 'Fleming's' (G)

79.1 deed,] *followed by deleted closing quotes* (C)

79.3 contemplated] MS 'looked' *interlined with a caret* (C)

79.3 Upon] *preceded by deleted* 'Th' (C)

79.4 a] *interlined above deleted* 'the' (C)

79.6 his friend] *interlined above deleted* 'Wilson' (G)

79.6–7 approvingly] *preceded by deleted* 'approval' (C)

79.7 'a] *preceded by deleted* 'of' (C)

79.11 The youth] *interlined above deleted* 'Fleming' (G)

79.12 jacket.] *followed by deleted* 'W' (C)

79.13 his friend] *interlined above deleted* 'Wilson' (G)

79.13 on.] *period altered from a comma* (C)

79.15 The] *preceded by deleted* 'Flemin' (C)

79.15 the . . . soldier] *interlined with a caret above deleted* 'Wilson' (G)

79.17 blankets.] *interlined above deleted* 'over-co' *and followed in the line by independently deleted* 'from the ground.'; *the period following* 'blankets' *added after the second deletion made* (C)

79.17 spread] *preceded by deleted* 'p'; *followed by deleted* 'out' (C)

79.19 the youth's] *interlined above deleted* 'Fleming's'; 't' *of* 'the' *over* 'T' (G)

79.19 shoulders.] *final* 's' *inserted* (C)

79.21 The youth] *original* 'Fleming' *followed by deleted comma and* 'lay down,' (C); 'The youth' *interlined above deleted* 'Fleming' (G)

79.21–22 obedience got . . . stooping.] 'obedience' *followed by deleted period*; 'got . . . stooping.' *added below the line with* 'down' *preceded by deleted comma and* 'd' (C)

79.23 relief] *followed by deleted period* (C)

79.23 the] *interlined with a caret* (C)

79.26 His friend] *interlined above deleted* 'Wilson' (G)

79.28 the youth] *interlined with a caret over deleted* 'Fleming' (G)

79.29 your] *preceded by deleted* 'you'r' (C)

79.30 The . . . soldier] *interlined with a caret above deleted* 'Wilson' (G)

79.30 on] 'o' *over* 'a' (C)

79.32 the youth] *interlined above deleted* 'Fleming' (G)

79.34 him] *followed by deleted period* (C)

79.36 eyes.] *interlined above deleted* 'li' (C)

79.36 splatter] *interlined above deleted* 'splutter' (C)

80.0 Chapter] *inserted in pencil* (F)

80.0 XIV] *blue crayon* 'XIV' *over* 'XV' (F)

80.1 the youth] *interlined with a caret above deleted* 'Fleming' (G)

80.3 Grey] *preceded by deleted* 'The'; 'G' *over* 'g' (C)

80.4 mists] *followed by deleted* 'of' (C)

80.7 further] *interlined with a caret* (C)

80.8 day.] *followed by deleted* 'He heard the noise of a fire [*followed by deleted comma* (C)] crackling briskly in the cold air, and turning his head listlessly he saw Wilson [*followed by deleted* 'and' (C)] busily pottering about a small blaze. Many other figures' (C)

80.9 The] *although indented, preceded by paragraph symbol* (C)

80.9 distance] *interlined above deleted* 'distant' (C)

80.9 was] *interlined with a caret and followed by deleted* 'in a state of' *all above deleted* 'was' (C)

80.9 blaring] *followed by deleted comma* (C)

80.10 fighting.] *period inserted before deleted* 'with a deadly persistency.' (C)

80.10 in] *followed by deleted* 'it' (C)

80.11 had] *preceded by deleted* 'were not to cease' (C)

80.12 About him] *preceded by deleted* 'Near him' (C)

80.13 previous night.] *interlined above deleted* 'night before' (C)

80.13 a] *inserted* (C)

80.14 awakening] *preceded by deleted* 'qu' (C)

80.14 gaunt] *preceded by deleted* 'gamt' (C)

80.16 ²the] *interlined with a caret* (C)

80.17 appear] *interlined above deleted* 'seem' (C)

80.17 dead.] *followed by deleted* 'The scene seemed' [*all interlined above deleted* 'It seemed'] to be a dreary prophecy.' (C)

80.17–18 The youth] *interlined above deleted* 'Fleming' (G)

80.18 little] *interlined above deleted* 'strange' (C)

80.19 motionless] 'mot' *squeezed in at end of line and* 'ionless' *inserted on next line* (C)

80.21 the hall] *preceded by deleted* 'this h' (C)

80.21 place. He] *period inserted before deleted* 'and'; 'H' *over* 'h' (C)

80.22 the house] 'house' *interlined above deleted* 'land', 'the land' *having been interlined above deleted* 'a sp' (C)

80.22 did] *interlined above deleted* 'dared' (C)

80.23 squalling] 'i' *mended* (C)

80.24 however] 'v' *mended* (C)

80.26 mere] *interlined with a caret* (C)

80.27 He heard then] 'He' *followed by interlined deleted comma and* 'then,'; 'then' *interlined with a caret* (C)

80.28 head,] *followed by deleted* 'listlessly' (C)

80.29 and] *followed by deleted comma and* 'from off,' (C)

80.31 hollow] *preceded by deleted* 'dull' (C)

81.1 Similar] *interlined above deleted* 'These' (C)

81.1 came] 'c' *over possible beginning of* 'w'; *preceded by deleted* 'went' (C)

81.3   brazen] 'zen' *added with* 'ze' *over* 'ss' (C)

81.3   the] *interlined* (C)

81.7   Strange] *preceded by deleted* 'An officer's' (C)

81.11   unravelled. The] *period inserted before deleted* 'and'; 'T' *over* 't' (C)

81.11   behind] 'e' *over* 'i' (C)

81.12   eye-] *preceded by deleted* 'the' (C)

81.14   then] *inserted* (C)

81.15   the] 't' *over probable* 'h' (C)

81.16   His friend,] *interlined above deleted* 'Wilson' *and a comma not deleted in error* (G)

81.16   him] *followed by deleted comma* (C)

81.16   to be] *interlined with a caret* (G)

81.17   do] 'o' *added* (C)

81.19; 82.3   The youth] *interlined above deleted* 'Fleming' (G)

81.19   mouth] *followed by independently deleted* 'into a' (*with* 'a' *interlined above deleted* 'an'), 'to a p' (*with* 'p' *deleted*), *and* 'to a pucke' (C)

81.20   head] 'he' *over* 'tru' *with* 't' *uncrossed* (C)

81.23   the other] *interlined above deleted* 'Wilson' (G)

81.23   ye'd] MS 'yed' *interlined above deleted* 'yeh'd' (C)

81.25–26   the youth] *interlined above deleted* 'Fleming' (G)

81.27   sharp] 's' *over* 'ir' (C)

81.27   the] *original* 'th'' *followed by deleted possible* 'cha' (C); 'e' *over apostrophe* (G)

81.28   saw] 'aw' *over* 'ee' (G)

81.28   your] 'our' *over* 'er' (G)

81.28   in] 'i' *altered from beginning of* 'I' (C)

81.29   you] *interlined above deleted* 'yeh' (G)

81.29   you'd] *interlined above deleted* 'yed' (G)

81.30   you] *interlined with a caret above deleted* 'yeh' (G)

81.31   nailing] 'g' *over an apostrophe* (G)

81.32   his friend] *interlined above deleted* 'Wilson' (G)

81.32   latter] *first* 't' *inserted* (C)

81.33   answered] *interlined above deleted* 'spoke' (G)

81.35   ²the . . . soldier] *interlined with a caret above deleted* 'Wilson's' (G)

81.35   over] 'o' *falls below the beginning downstroke of possible* 'h' (C)

81.37   marshalling] *second* 'l' *inserted* (C)

81.37   vagabonds of] 's' *added;* 'of' *interlined with a caret* (C)

81.38   them] *followed by deleted comma* (C)

81.38   small] *preceded by deleted* 'sooty' (C)

82.1   then] *interlined above deleted* 'and' (C)

82.1–2   the youth's] *interlined above deleted* 'Fleming's' (G)

82.2   appetite] *first* 'e' *over* 'i'; *preceded by deleted* 'appitite' (C)

82.4   of . . . upon] *interlined above deleted* 'upon the river' (C)

82.4   He] *preceded by deleted* 'There' (C)

82.6   furious at] *interlined above deleted* 'jealous of' (C)

82.7   was,] *comma added* (G)

82.7   no . . . soldier] *interlined with a caret above deleted* 'not a youth' *and a period deleted in error* (G)

82.8   showed] *preceded by deleted* 'shoul' (C)

82.9   confidence] *interlined above deleted* 'assurance' (C)

82.12   The youth reflected.] *interlined above deleted* 'Fleming thought' *and a period not deleted in error* (G)

82.12 used] *interlined above deleted* 'accustomed' (C)

82.12 regarding] 'ing' *added* (C)

82.12–13 his comrade] *inserted with a caret; preceded by deleted* 'Wilson' (G)

82.15 courage] *preceded by deleted* 'babe' (C)

82.16 The youth] *interlined with a caret above deleted* 'Fleming' (G)

82.17 eyes;] *semicolon preceded by deleted period* (C)

82.19 Apparently] *preceded by deleted* 'He' (C)

82.19 the other] *interlined above deleted* 'Wilson' (G)

82.20–21 the youth] *interlined above deleted* 'Fleming' (G)

82.21 it would] *interlined above deleted* 'his friend would' (C)

82.21 in] *preceded by deleted* 'in' (C)

82.23 His comrade] *original* 'Wilson' *preceded by deleted* 'Af' (C); 'His comrade' *interlined with a caret above deleted* 'Wilson'; 'His' *preceded by* 'His' *which was interlined then deleted* (G)

82.24 ²think] *followed by deleted* 'th' chances' (C)

82.25 'em] 'e' *over* 'i' (C)

82.26,32 The youth] *interlined above deleted* 'Fleming' (G)

82.26 -yesterday] *second* 'e' *over* 'i' (G)

82.27,33 you] *interlined above deleted* 'yeh' (G)

82.27 would've] ' 've' *over* ' 'a' (G)

82.27 you'd] *original* 'yed' *preceded by deleted* 'yeh'd lick' (C); 'you'd' *interlined above deleted* 'yed' (G)

82.27 the] 'e' *over an apostrophe* (G)

82.28 yourself."] *interlined above deleted* 'yerself." ' (G)

82.29 His friend] *interlined with*

a caret above deleted 'Wilson' (G)

82.35 deprecatory] *second* 'e' *over possible* 'i' (C)

82.38 There] *first word* MS f. 123 *numbering of which has* '3' *over* '2' (C)

82.39 off'cers] *apostrophe over deleted* 'i' (C)

82.39 rebs] *interlined above deleted* 'rebels' (C)

83.1 the friend] *interlined above deleted* 'Wilson' (G)

83.2 seem] 'm' *altered from* 'n' (C)

83.3,9 the youth] *interlined above deleted* 'Fleming' (G)

83.7 the friend] *interlined with a caret above deleted* 'Wilson' (G)

83.7 handled] *preceded by deleted* 'han' (C)

83.9 you] *interlined above deleted* 'yeh' (G)

83.10 nothing] 'g' *over an apostrophe* (G)

83.10 of] *over* ' 'a' (G)

83.10 the] 'e' *over an apostrophe* (G)

83.12 His friend] *inserted before deleted* 'Wilson' *above which is* 'The youth' *interlined and deleted* (G)

83.13 The youth] *interlined with a caret above deleted* 'Fleming' (G)

83.14 Conklin?] *question mark over period* (C)

83.15 All] *preceded by deleted* 'Mea' (C)

83.15 small] *interlined above deleted* 'little' (C)

83.19 coffee] *preceded by deleted* 'his' (C)

83.20 had] *preceded by deleted* 'swor' (C)

83.23 The friend] *interlined above deleted* 'Wilson' (G)

83.24 use?] *question mark altered from exclamation point* (C)

83.25 an] *interlined above deleted* 'an' ' (C)

83.27 soldiers] *preceded by deleted* 'sl' (C)

83.32 the friend] 'the youth's friend' *interlined with a caret above deleted* 'Wilson' *then* 'youth's' *deleted* (G)

83.34–35 with . . . -fingers.] *sentence originally ended:* 'with | injured airs.', '*injured airs.*' *being inscribed at the far right of the page; it was then deleted and* 'accusative [*preceded by deleted* 'an'] *forefingers.*' *was inscribed at the left of the same line* (C)

83.37 Well—] *dash over comma* (C)

84.2 the friend] *interlined with a caret above deleted* 'Wilson' (G)

84.2 returned] *preceded by independently deleted* 'ret' *and* 'with' (C)

84.2 seat.] *period inserted before deleted* 'and' (C)

84.5 the friend] *interlined above deleted* 'Wilson' (G)

84.5 ses] *preceded by deleted* 'h [*and beginning of* 'e'] (C)

84.6 boys] *preceded by deleted* 'fellers f' (C)

84.8 The youth] *interlined above deleted* 'Fleming' (G)

84.11 t'] *preceded by deleted* 'to' (C)

84.11 his friend] *interlined above deleted* 'Wilson' (G)

84.13 the youth.] *interlined above deleted* 'Fleming' *and a period not deleted in error* (G)

84.14 The friend] *original* 'Wilson' *preceded by deleted double quotes* (C); 'The friend' *interlined with a caret above deleted* 'Wilson' (G)

84.15 Henry] MS(u) 'Flem' *with* 'ing' *added* (G)

84.17 remarked] *interlined above deleted* 'began' (C)

84.17–18 the friend,] *original* 'Wilson,' *with comma over beginning of* Crane's *circled period* (C); 'the friend' *interlined above deleted* 'Wilson' (G)

84.20 we] *preceded by deleted* 'would mean' (C)

84.21 an'] *preceded by deleted* 'and' (C)

84.23 the youth] *interlined above deleted* 'Fleming' *with* 'yo' *over* 'fro' (G)

84.23 youth.] *followed by* '[¶] He went into a brown mood. He thought with deep contempt of all his grapplings and tuggings with fate [*followed by deleted period* (C)] and the universe. It now was evident that a large proportion [*final* 's' *deleted* (C)] of the men of the regiment had been ['had been' *interlined above deleted* 'were' (C)], if they chose, [*a second* 'o' *deleted* (C)] capable of ['capable of' *interlined above deleted* 'open to' (C)] the same quantity of condemnation of the world and could as righteously have taken arms against everything. He laughed. [¶] He now rejoiced in a view of what he took to be the universal resemblance. He decided that he was not, as he had supposed, a unique man. There [*preceded by deleted* 'He' (C)] were many in ['i' *over* 'o' (C)] his type. And he had believed that he was suffering new agonies and feeling new wrongs. On the contrary, they were [*interlined above deleted* 'had been' (C)] old, all of them, they were born—perhaps with the first life. [¶] These thoughts took the element of [*interlined with a caret* (C)] grandeur from his experiences. Since many had had them there could be nothing fine about them. They were now ridiculous. [¶] However, he [*followed by deleted* 'considered' (C)] yet considered himself to be ['to be' *interlined with a caret* (C)] below the standard of traditional man-hood. He felt abashed when [*interlined above deleted* 'in the' (C)] confronting ['c' *over beginning of* 'p'; *followed by deleted* 'the' (C)] memories of some men he had seen. [*followed by independently deleted* 'These | Th' [¶] These thoughts did not appear in his attitude. He now considered the fact of his having fled, as being buried. He was returned to his comrades and unimpeached. So despite the [*followed by deleted* 'lit' (C)] little shadow of his sin upon his mind, he felt his self-respect growing strong within him. His pride had almost recovered [*followed by deleted* 'hi' (C)] it's balance and was about' (*end of* MS f. 125, f. 126 *wanting*); *the whole deleted in blue crayon* (F)

85.0 MS f. 127 *with* '126–' *added in blue crayon to* '127' *and* 'V' *over* 'VI.' *for the chapter number, also in blue crayon* (F)

85.2 command] MS 'cammand' *interlined above deleted* 'order' (C)

85.3 the youth] *interlined above deleted* 'Fleming' (G)

85.4 the . . . soldier] *interlined with a caret above deleted* 'Wilson' (G)

85.8 "What?"] *question mark and closing quotes inserted before deleted* 'Fleming?"' *of which* 'ing?"' *is added over deleted original question mark and closing quotes* (G)

85.9 His friend] *interlined above deleted* 'The young soldier' (G)

85.11 moment] *preceded by deleted* 'very' (C)

85.11 The youth] *interlined above deleted* 'Fleming' (G)

85.12 nothing,] 'g' *over apostrophe* (G)

85.14 His friend] *interlined above deleted* 'Wilson' (G)

85.14 turned his] *interlined above deleted* 'look aroun' (C)

85.16 nothing,] 'g' *over apostrophe and, in error, over comma* (G)

85.16 the youth] *interlined above deleted* 'Fleming' *and a period deleted in error* (G)

85.18–19,24 his friend] *interlined above deleted* 'Wilson' (G)

85.19 on] 'o' *over* 'w' (C)

85.19 ²the] *interlined with a caret* (C)

85.22 altered] *interlined above deleted* 'changed' (C)

85.22 comrade] *interlined above deleted* 'Wilson' (G)

85.23 tantalize] 'i' *inserted* (C)

85.25 relate] *preceded by deleted* 're [and upstroke]'; *followed by deleted* 'all' (C)

85.28 It] 'I' *over beginning of possible* 'H' *or* 'F' (C)

85.30 The friend] *interlined above deleted* 'Wilson' (G)

85.30 own] *interlined above deleted* 'orat' (C)

86.1 funeral] *preceded by deleted* 'death' (C)

86.1 had] *interlined with a caret* (C)

86.1 in] *preceded by deleted* 'presented' (C)

86.2 relatives.] 'r' *altered from vertical stroke; preceded by deleted* 'friends' *and a period not deleted in error* (C)

86.3 the youth.] *interlined above deleted* 'his friend.' (G)

86.4 The latter] *original* 'Fleming' *interlined above deleted*

'He' (C); 'the latter' *inserted before deleted* 'Fleming' (G)

86.4 his friend] *original* 'Wilson' *followed by deleted period* (C); 'his friend' *interlined above deleted* 'Wilson' (G)

86.6 patronizing] *first* 'i' *over beginning of* 'z' (C)

86.7 In] *preceded by deleted* 'It' *of which* 'I' *over beginning of* 'H' (C)

86.7 its] MS 'it's' *with apostrophe and* 's' *added* (C)

86.8 flourishing] 'f' *over beginning of* 'w' (C)

86.9 could now be] *interlined above deleted* 'had been' (C)

86.10 no] *followed by deleted* 'mite of self-con' (C)

86.14 when] *preceded by deleted* 'as' *and upstroke* (C)

86.14 he] *followed by deleted* 'tho' (C)

86.14 his] *followed by deleted* 'wea' (C)

86.14 yesterday] 'd' *altered from* 'a' (C)

86.16 license] 'ce' *over* 'nc' (C)

86.17 His] *preceded by deleted* 'All'; 'H' *over* 'h' (C)

86.18 he] 'h' *over possible* 't' (C)

86.18 only] 'n' *over upstroke* (C)

86.19 roared] 'o' *over* 'a' (C)

86.20 Few] *followed by deleted* 'eve [*and beginning of* 'r']' (C)

86.20 ever] *preceded by deleted* 'eved' (C)

86.21 business to] *interlined above independently deleted* 'rig' *and* 'right to' (C)

86.22 that] *followed by two deleted illegible letters* (C)

86.22 he] *inserted* (C)

86.22 think to be] *interlined above deleted* 'be thought' (G)

86.22 in] *interlined above deleted* 'with' (G)

86.24 rail;] *semicolon over comma* (C)

86.26 should] *interlined with a caret* (C)

87.1 how] *preceded by deleted* 'why' (C)

87.2 doomed] *second* 'o' *over* 'm' (C)

87.3 ²the] *preceded by deleted* 'their' (C)

87.8 his friend] *interlined above deleted* 'Wilson' (G)

87.11 Fleming!] 'ing!' *added over possible exclamation point* (G)

87.13 The friend] *interlined above deleted* 'Wilson' (G)

87.17 cheeks] *preceded by deleted* 'face.' *and followed by possible beginning of a period* (C)

87.18 Wilson] 'W' *over closing quotes* (C)

87.18 the youth.] *interlined above deleted* 'Fleming.' (G)

87.18 He] *followed by deleted* 'unloosed' (C)

87.19 packet] 'a' *altered from* 'o' (C)

87.20 his friend] *interlined above deleted* 'Wilson' (G)

87.22 remarkable] *preceded by deleted* 'so' (C)

87.23 could] *interlined with a caret* (C)

87.23 sufficient] *second* 'i' *inserted* (C)

87.24 his friend] *interlined with a caret above deleted* 'Wilson' (G)

87.27 His friend] *interlined above deleted* 'Wilson' (G)

87.28 the youth] *interlined with a caret above deleted* 'Fleming' (G)

87.30 acts;] *semicolon preceded by deleted period* (C)

87.31 ¹bad!] *exclamation point over a comma* (C)

87.32 The] 'e' *over an apostrophe* (G)

87.33 pictures] *interlined above deleted* 'scenes' (C)

87.34 return] *interlined with a caret above deleted* 'go' (C)

87.35 stories] *interlined above deleted* 'tales' (C)

87.37 district] *followed by inserted deleted* 'and | at a time,' (C)

88.3 ejaculations] 's' *added* (C)

88.5 beloved] *preceded by deleted* 'I' (C)

89.1 was] *interlined with a caret* (G)

89.1 to be heard] *interlined above deleted* 'was in the air' *and a period deleted in error* (C)

89.2 cannon] *followed by deleted* 'the' (C)

89.3 thudding] *interlined above deleted* 'sputtering' (C)

89.3 The] *preceded by deleted* 'This' (C)

89.6 The youth's] *interlined with a caret above deleted* 'Fleming's' *and followed by deleted* 're[*and the beginning of a* 'g']' (G)

89.8 had] *interlined with a caret* (C)

89.10 stretch] 's' *over illegible letter* (C)

89.10 From] *preceded by deleted* 'Off' (C)

89.13 fracas.] *preceded by deleted* 'racket.' (C)

89.14 behind] *preceded by deleted* 'down' (C)

89.16 The youth's] *interlined above deleted* 'Wilson' (G)

89.16 friend] *inserted* (G)

89.16 in] *interlined above deleted* 'a [*and beginning of* 'n']' (C)

89.17 almost] *a final* 'ly' *deleted* (C)

89.18 The youth] *interlined above deleted* 'Fleming' (G)

89.19 woods] *followed by deleted period* (C)

89.21 were perched] *preceded by deleted* 'per' (C)

89.22 dirt-] 'i' *mended* (C)

89.24 Always] *preceded by deleted* 'Amon[*and beginning of probable* 'g']' (C)

89.25 ²and] *followed by deleted* 'from' (C)

89.27 cannon] *second* 'n' *over* 'o' (C)

89.29 a sentence] *preceded by independently deleted* 'a qu' *and* 'wo' (C)

89.30 The youth] *original* 'Fleming' *preceded by inserted paragraph symbol* (C); 'The youth' *interlined with a caret above deleted* 'Fleming' (G)

89.30 launch] *interlined above deleted* 'make' (C); *pencil caret over deleted* 'make' (G)

89.30–31 — . . . newspapers.] *interlined above deleted period* (C); *pencil caret over original period* (G)

89.31 Rappahannock] MS 'Rappahanock' *followed by deleted period* (C)

90.2 successfully . . . sentence.] *interlined above deleted* 'successfully concluded the sentence for, when they ceased, he had forgotten it.'; *of which a deleted period after* 'sentence', 'when' *preceded by deleted* 'by' *and* 'he . . . it.' *written below the line* (C)

90.3 But . . . among] 'At . . . and' *inserted before* 'Among' *of which* 'A' *not reduced in error; then* 'But' *inserted before* 'At' *and again* 'A' *not reduced in error* (C)

90.4 again] *preceded by deleted* 'had' (C)

90.4 flew] *interlined with a caret above deleted* 'flowed' *of which* 'ed' *added later* (C)

90.4 birds,] *comma inserted before deleted period* (C)

90.8 place] *followed by deleted comma* (C)

90.10 din of musketry] *inserted before deleted* 'din' (C)

90.11   a released] *interlined with a caret* (C)

90.12   and] *inserted* (C)

90.15   it] *interlined with a caret* (C)

90.16   the] *interlined with a caret* (C)

90.17   totally] *second* 't' *altered from* 'l' (C)

90.17   obliterated] 'a' *over* 'e' (C)

90.18   spread] *interlined above deleted* 'line' (C)

90.18   column] *inserted* (C)

90.20   seen] *followed by deleted period* (C)

90.22   the youth] *original* 'Fleming' *preceded by deleted* 'w' (C); 'the youth' *interlined with a caret above deleted* 'Fleming' (G)

90.25   has] 'h' *over* 's' (C)

90.25   a] *interlined with a caret* (C)

90.26   His friend,] *original* 'Wilson,' *followed by deleted* 'w' (C); 'His friend' *interlined with a caret above deleted* 'Wilson' (G)

90.26   drowsy.] *interlined above deleted* 'sleepy.' (C)

90.30   The youth] *interlined above deleted* 'Fleming' (G)

90.30   it] *preceded by deleted* 'w' (C)

90.31   freely] *interlined with a caret* (C)

90.31   men.] *period preceded by deleted period* (C)

90.36   his friend] *interlined above deleted* 'Wilson' (G)

90.38   caned] *preceded by deleted* 'ki' (C)

90.39; 91.7   the] 'e' *over an apostrophe* (G)

90.40   can] *interlined with a caret above deleted* 'kin' (G)

90.40   the youth] *interlined above deleted* 'Fleming' (G)

91.1   sentiment] 'i' *inserted* (C)

91.6   The] 'e' *over an apostrophe* (G)

91.6   said] *interlined above deleted* 'sed' (G)

91.7   saw] *interlined above deleted* 'saw' *of which* 'aw' *over* 'ee' (G)

91.7   fought] *interlined above deleted* 'fit' (G)

91.8   And] 'd' *over an apostrophe* (G)

91.8   do] *interlined above deleted* 'no' (G)

91.9   ¹you] *interlined above deleted* 'yeh' (G)

91.9   the] MS 'th' ' *interlined with a caret* (C)

91.9   can] *interlined above deleted* 'kin' (G)

91.9   you?"] *inserted before deleted* 'yeh?" ' (G)

91.10   the friend's] *interlined above deleted* 'Wilson's' (G)

91.11   said.] *period altered from a comma* (C)

91.12   hell-roosters] *preceded by deleted* 'devil' (C)

91.14,26   the] 'e' *over an apostrophe* (G)

91.14   whip] *preceded by deleted* 'ha' (C)

91.15   ¹the] 'e' *over an apostrophe* (G)

91.15   generals'] *final apostrophe added and an apostrophe following* 'l' *deleted* (C)

91.15   the youth] *interlined above deleted* 'Fleming' (G)

91.16   And] 'd' *over an apostrophe* (G)

91.16   any] *interlined above deleted* 'no' (G)

91.16(*twice*),17   fighting] *final* 'g' *over an apostrophe* (G)

91.16(*twice*)   and] 'd' *over an apostrophe* (G)

91.17   yet always] *interlined above deleted* 'yit allus' (G)

91.17   losing] MS(c) 'lossing' *with* 'g' *over an apostrophe* (G)

91.17   old] 'd' *over an apostrophe* (G)

91.19 the youth's] *interlined above deleted* 'Fleming's' (G)

91.21 Fleming] *'g' over an apostrophe* (G)

91.22 speech] *preceded by deleted* 'barb' (C)

91.22 the youth.] *interlined above deleted* 'Fleming.' (G)

91.22 Inward] *preceded by deleted* 'He was reduced to' (C)

91.22–23 an abject] *preceded by deleted* 'abjectness' (C)

91.26 fought] *interlined with a caret above deleted* 'fit' (G)

91.26 whole] *interlined with a caret above deleted* 'hull' (G)

91.26 yesterday] *second 'e' over* 'i' (G)

91.28 information . . . habit.] *period after* 'information' *deleted in error in the independent deletion of following* ' "Oh," ' *and* 'he merely said, as if relieved, "I thought mebbe yeh did." ' *of which* 'merely' *interlined with a caret;* 'It . . . habit.' *interlined* (C)

91.28 "Oh,"] *inserted* (C)

91.29 replied] *preceded by deleted* 'merely' (C)

91.30 The youth] *interlined above deleted* 'Fleming' (G)

91.32–33 loud moods] *interlined above deleted* 'moods' (C)

91.33 would] *interlined above deleted* 'might' (C)

91.35 low-toned] *followed by deleted* 'and' (C)

91.35 officers] *'e' over* 'ie' (C)

92.2 way] *followed by deleted* 'off' (C)

92.3 cursed,] *followed by deleted* 'a' (C)

92.9 yelpings] *interlined above deleted* 'noise' (C)

92.11 went] *preceded by deleted* 'stro' (C)

92.11 sky,] *followed by deleted* 'it became prolonged' (C)

92.14 Everybody] *'E' over* 'T' (C)

92.17 lieutenant who] *upstroke*

of 'w' *deletes with intent period following* 'lieutenant' (C); 'youthful' *preceding* 'lieutenant' *deleted* (G)

92.17–18 the youth's] *interlined above deleted* 'Fleming's' (G)

[92.17–18 represents the last pencil alteration in the general revision. On 92.27 there is a mixed ink and pencil alteration marking the bridge back to ink for the remainder of the manuscript.]

92.20 men] *preceded by deleted* 'company.' (C)

92.20 had] *interlined with a caret* (C)

92.20 and] *'an' over* 'w[and beginning of 'a']* (C)

92.25 them] *interlined* (C)

92.25 be] *interlined with a caret before independently deleted* 'light' *and* 'lit by the slashing lines of' (C)

92.26 growling] *interlined above deleted* 'grumbling' (C)

92.27 the youth] *an ink general revision alteration interlined with a caret above a pencil general revision deleted* 'Fleming' (G)

92.27; 93.1 always] *interlined above deleted* 'allus' (G)

92.27 being] *'g' over an apostrophe* (G)

92.28,29,32,33,35 to] *'o' over an apostrophe* (G)

92.29 or] *interlined above deleted* 'ner' (G)

92.29,34 We] 'W' *over beginning of an* 'H' (C)

92.29 just] *'u' over* 'e' (G)

92.29,30(*twice*) get] *'e' over* 'i' (G)

92.29 pillar] *interlined above deleted* 'piller' (G)

92.30(*thrice*),34,35,36 and] 'd' *over an apostrophe* (G)

92.31 for] *'o' over* 'e' (G)

92.31 damn' kitten] *preceded by deleted* 'ki[and beginning of a 't']* (C)

92.32,33,36; 93.1   the] 'e' over an apostrophe (G)

92.33   into] interlined above deleted 'inteh' (G)

92.33   these] followed by deleted 'here' (G)

92.33   for, anyhow,] original 'fer,' with 'anyhow,' interlined with a caret inserted before the comma; a second comma then inserted preceding the caret but the original comma not deleted in error (C); 'o' of 'for' over 'e' (G)

92.34   regular] 'u' inserted below deleted apostrophe (G)

92.35   cussed] preceded by deleted 'here' (G)

92.35   began] 'a' over 'i' (G)

92.36   Me] interlined above deleted 'me' underlined (C)

92.36   just] 'j' possibly over 'g'; interlined above deleted 'jest' (G)

92.37   old] 'd' over an apostrophe (G)

92.38   The friend] interlined with a caret above deleted 'Wilson' (G)

93.1   a dog-] preceded by deleted 'dod-' (C)

93.3   an] followed by deleted upstroke and beginning of another letter (C)

93.3   savage-minded] '|-age-minded' inserted before deleted '|age young' (G)

93.11   paused,] followed by deleted 'for a moment' (C)

93.11   who] followed by deleted 'had the' (C)

93.12   resumed] interlined above deleted 'continued' (G)

93.17   white] preceded by deleted 'until' (C)

93.17   his] preceded by deleted 'its' (C)

93.18   upon the] followed by deleted 'earth.' (C)

93.19   that] 'at' added with 'a' over 'e' (C)

93.21   was] followed by independently deleted 'a' and 'a moment's pause' and 'a wait.' and 'It was' (C)

93.21   passed] 'pa' over 'w' (C)

93.21–22   intense] interlined above deleted 'intent' (C)

93.24   ²was] followed by deleted 'sweep' (C)

93.26   guns] preceded by deleted 'batte' with 't's' uncrossed (C)

93.27   suddenly] preceded by deleted 'inv' (C)

93.31   regiment] preceded by deleted 'Fleming's' (G)

93.33   rolled] 'r' over 't' (C)

93.33   eyes] followed by deleted 'strangely' (C)

93.34–35   shock . . . stakes.] 'shock.' followed by deleted 'Many seemed tied to stakes.'; 'Some . . . stakes.' added later (C) or (G)

94.1–2   This . . . hunting.] false start (verso of p. 141): 'XVIII. | As Fleming had watched this approach of the enemy which had seemed to him like a r[and beginning of 'u']' (C)

94.1   advance] preceded by deleted 'ap' (C)

94.1   the youth] interlined with a caret above deleted 'Fleming' (G)

94.2   ruthless hunting.] interlined above deleted 'pitiless hunting.' of which 'ing' over a period (C)

94.3   beat] interlined above deleted 'stamped' (C)

94.3   upon the ground] interlined with a caret (C)

94.4   approaching] 'i' altered from an upstroke (C)

94.5   flood. There . . . maddening] paragraph originally ended with 'flood.'; 'There . . . maddening' inserted before deleted beginning of original new paragraph 'There' (C)

94.8 had been] *interlined above deleted* 'many' (C)

94.9 opportunities] *first* 'o' *over* 'r' (C)

94.10 listeners] *preceded by deleted* 'spe' (C)

94.11 or,] *followed by deleted* 'd' (C)

94.13 have] *interlined with a caret* (C)

94.14 received] MS 'recieved' *interlined above deleted* 'had' (C)

94.15 he] 'h' *over* 'w' (C)

94.17–18 relentless] *preceded by deleted* 'rl' (C)

94.21 by] *interlined with a caret* (C)

94.24 leaned,] *followed by deleted* 'over'; *comma possibly inserted* (C)

94.24 his friend's] *original* 'Wilson's' *with* 'W' *over* 'F' (C); 'his friend's' *interlined with a caret above deleted* 'Wilson's' (G)

94.25 chasing] 'g' *over an apostrophe; preceded by deleted* 'a-' (G)

94.26 they'd] ' 'd' *added* (G)

94.26 better] *interlined above deleted* 'want' *of which a final* 'a' *deleted* (G)

94.27 The friend] *interlined with a caret above deleted* 'Wilson' (G)

94.29 The youth] *interlined above deleted* 'Fleming' (G)

94.30 little] *preceded by deleted* 'tree' (C)

94.30 eyes] *interlined with a caret* (C)

95.2 and] *followed by deleted* 'hung' (C)

95.3 cloth] *a final* 'e' *deleted* (C)

95.7 His fingers] *preceded by deleted* 'The f' (C)

95.9 companions] 's' *added* (C)

95.9–10 convictions that . . . puny.] *period following* 'convictions' *deleted and* 'that . . . puny.' *written below the line* (C)

95.12 ¹him] *followed by deleted period* (C)

95.18 valiant] *interlined above deleted* 'valorous' (C)

95.19 was] *followed by deleted possible* 'wo' (C)

95.21 the youth] *interlined with a caret above deleted* 'Fleming' (G)

95.22 There] *preceded by deleted* 'It seeme' (C)

95.23–24 onslaughts] *interlined above deleted* 'attac[*and beginning of* 'k']' (C)

95.24 creatures] *preceded by deleted* 'intan' (C)

95.26 them] *preceded by deleted* 'thes' (C)

95.28 , in a dream, it] *interlined above deleted* 'it dreamfully' (C)

95.28 the youth] *interlined with a caret above deleted* 'Fleming' (G)

95.30 the] *interlined above deleted* 'that' (C)

95.31 upon] *interlined above deleted* 'was' (C)

95.31 enemies.] *followed by deleted* 'A' (C)

95.33 swung] *followed by deleted* 'h' (C)

95.34 rage.] *interlined above deleted* 'hate' (C)

95.35 The youth] *interlined above deleted* 'Fleming' (G)

95.38 chaos] 'c' *over upstroke* (C)

96.1 flew away] *interlined above deleted* 'did not' (C)

96.1 at] 'a' *over* 't' (C)

96.1 think] *preceded by deleted* 'care to debate' (C)

96.3 behind] *interlined above deleted* 'with' *and beginning of another letter* (C)

96.3 with] *preceded by deleted* 't [*and upstroke*]' (C)

96.12   pounding] *preceded by deleted* 'stuffing' (C)

96.12   If] *preceded by deleted* 'It was only' (C)

96.13   through] *interlined above deleted* 'in' (C)

96.14   ²with] *followed by deleted* 'each muscle' (C)

96.16   him] 'im' *over* 'e' (C) *or* (G)

96.18   upon] 'up' *inserted* (C)

96.21   ¹was] *preceded by deleted* 'he' (C)

96.30   seemed] *preceded by deleted* 'we' (C)

97.3   lieutenant] *preceded by deleted* 'young' (G)

97.3   seemed] *inserted following deleted* 'called out to' (C)

97.4   the youth.] *interlined above deleted* 'Fleming' *and a period not deleted in error* (G)

97.8   the youth] *original* 'Fleming' *with a final apostrophe and* 's' *deleted* (C); 'the youth' *interlined above deleted* 'Fleming' (G)

97.13   The friend] *interlined above deleted* 'Wilson' (G)

97.14   Fleming?] 'ing' *added, partially over question mark* (G)

97.17   No] 'N' *over possible* 'W' (C)

97.17   the youth] *interlined with a caret above deleted* 'Fleming' (G)

97.19   the youth] *interlined above deleted* 'Fleming' (G)

97.19   It] *over* 'He' (C)

97.20   ³a] *interlined with a caret* (C)

97.21   Regarding] *preceded by deleted* 'It' *with* 'I' *over beginning of possible* 'H'; *followed by deleted* 'o' (C)

97.26   process. He] *period altered from comma;* 'H' *over* 'h' (C)

97.26   slept and,] *interlined above deleted* 'gone to' (C)

97.28   the occasional stares of] 'stares of' *interlined above de-* leted 'smiles of'; *then* 'the occasional' *interlined with a caret above deleted* 'the'; *large caret inserted for entire entry* (C)

97.31   their] *preceded by deleted* 'bre' (C)

97.33   ²Hot] 'H' *over beginning of* 'G' (C)

97.33   lieutenant] *preceded by deleted* 'young' (G)

97.38   the youth.] *interlined with a caret above deleted* 'Fleming.' (G)

98.4   dog] *interlined above deleted* 'man' (C)

98.5   more] 'm' *mended* (C)

98.7   men,] *comma preceded by deleted period* (C)

98.8   woods] *preceded by deleted possible* 't[and beginning of 'r']' (C)

98.9   ¹she'll] *preceded by deleted* 'we' (C)

98.11   forest] 'f' *over* 'w' (C)

98.14   smouldering] *preceded by deleted* 'a' (C)

98.14   ruins] 's' *added* (C)

98.14   toward] *preceded by deleted* 'to' (C)

99.1   minutes] *followed by independently deleted comma and* 'the'; *period possibly over the comma* (C)

99.1   its] *interlined above deleted* 'their' (C)

99.3   trees] *interlined above deleted* 'earth' (C)

99.6   men] *followed by deleted* 'cra' (C)

99.9   when came] *interlined above deleted* 'during' (C)

99.10   during] *interlined above deleted* 'during' (C)

99.11   him.] *followed by deleted* 'His soldier fellows hearing' *with* 'The men' *interlined above independently deleted* 'His soldier fellows' (C)

99.14   ¹Rogers.] *period altered from an exclamation point* (C)

99.15 eyes] *followed by deleted comma and* 'turning,' (C)

99.15 him] *interlined with a caret* (C)

99.16 near.] *period inserted before deleted* 'to him.' (C)

99.16 in] 'i' *over* 'o' (C)

99.17 grass] *interlined above deleted* 'ground.' (C)

99.18 screaming] '-ing' *interlined above deleted* 'ed' (C)

99.19 tremendous,] *comma inserted; followed by deleted* 'and' (C)

99.20 shrieked] MS 'shreiked' *preceded by deleted* 'high,' (C)

99.21 The youth's friend] 'The youth' *interlined above deleted* 'Wilson', *and then deleted and* 'The youth's friend' *inserted; close-up line drawn below deletion* (G)

99.21 had] *followed by deleted* 'an illusion' (C)

99.23 "Fill] *preceded by deleted* ' "W' (C)

99.25 The youth] *interlined above deleted* 'Fleming' (G)

99.27 for the] *followed by* 'stream but di' *deleted with a line continuing to the right margin* (C)

99.28 here] *preceded by deleted comma; upstroke of* 'h' *deletes closing double quotes* (C)

99.28 the youth] *interlined above deleted* 'Fleming' (G)

99.30–31 place of the] *interlined above deleted* 'battle line' (C)

100.1 , of course,] *interlined with a caret* (C)

100.1 battle] *preceded by deleted* 'f' (C)

100.3 a] *interlined with a caret* (G)

100.6 see] *interlined* (HG)

100.7 squarely] *interlined with a caret* (G)

100.9 Looking] *preceded by inserted paragraph symbol* (G)

100.9 slowly] 'l' *over* 'in'; 'y' *altered from* 'g' (C)

100.10 made] 'm' *over beginning of possible* 't' (C)

100.11 To] *preceded by deleted* 'On' (C)

100.11 a distant] *interlined with a caret above deleted* 'a' (C)

100.15 a blaring.] *interlined above deleted* 'the' (C)

100.25 man. The latter] *period inserted;* 'The latter' *interlined above deleted* 'who' (C)

100.27 sliding] MS(c) 'slideing' *with* 'e' *inserted* (C)

100.28 lay] *interlined above deleted* 'still' (C)

100.28 breathing] MS 'breatheing' *with second* 'e' *over* 'r' (C)

100.34 inner] *interlined above deleted* 'inme' (C)

100.37 and spoke, coolly,] *preceded by deleted* 'coolly'; *comma and* 'coolly,' *interlined with a caret* (C)

101.3 other] *followed by deleted* 'off' (C)

101.6 presume] *preceded by deleted* 'thin[*and beginning of* 'k']' (C)

101.7 a] *over* 'as' (C)

101.10 who] *interlined above deleted* 'on the' (C)

101.12 But] *a final apostrophe and* 's' *deleted* (C)

101.14 The . . . friend] *interlined with a caret above deleted* 'Fleming and Wilson' (G)

101.15 sharply.] *interlined above deleted* 'abruptly.' (C)

101.18 and,] *comma inserted before deleted* 'started away' (C)

101.19 away,] *followed by deleted* 'the general wheeled his horse and started away,' (C)

101.23 the youth] *interlined above deleted* 'Fleming' (G)

101.25 These . . . time] *false start (verso of p. 163):* 'These happenings had occupied but an incredibly short time' (C)

101.26 the youth] *interlined above deleted* 'Fleming' (G)

101.26 felt] *over* 'saw' (C) *or* (G)

101.29 he] *interlined with a caret* (C)

101.31 properly] *interlined with a caret* (C)

101.33 boys] *interlined above deleted* 'men' (C)

101.33,39 lieutenant] *preceded by deleted* 'young' (G)

101.36 their eyes] 'ir' *interlined with a caret and* 'eyes' *followed by deleted* 'of Wilson' (G)

101.36 large] *interlined above deleted* 'swelled' (C)

101.37 great tales.] *preceded by deleted* 'a'; 's' *inserted* (G)

101.38 the youth] MS 'the youth's friend' *interlined above deleted* 'the private' (G)

102.4 derned] 'rn' *over possible* 'ar' (C)

102.4 at] 'a' *written below the deleted beginning of a question mark* (C)

102.6 ¹to] 'o' *over an apostrophe* (G)

102.6 the youth] *interlined above deleted* 'Wilson' (G)

102.7 shooting] 'g' *over an apostrophe* (G)

102.7 you] *interlined above deleted* 'yeh' (G)

102.8 his friend] *interlined above deleted* 'Fleming' (G)

102.14 them,] *followed by deleted* 'with' (C)

102.15 soldier] *interlined above deleted* 'man' (C)

102.16 men] 'e' *over* 'a' (C)

102.19 hundred] *preceded by deleted* 'th' (C)

102.20 expression] *a final* 's' *added then deleted* (C)

102.20 an] 'n' *added; followed by deleted* 'interesting' (C)

102.20 thing] 'g' *over* 'k' (C)

102.24 compact] *second* 'c' *over upstroke, probably a* 't' (C)

102.25 that] *interlined with a caret* (C)

102.25 few] *inserted* (C)

102.26 seemed to show] *interlined above deleted* 'did' (C)

102.33 curtains] 's' *added* (C)

102.36 between] *interlined with a caret above deleted* 'of' *which was interlined above an original* 'between' (C)

102.39 The youth] *interlined above deleted* 'Fleming' (G)

102.39–103.1 his friend] *original* 'Wilson' *preceded by deleted* 'Fl' (C); 'his friend' *interlined above deleted* 'Wilson' (G)

104.1,9 The youth] *interlined with a caret above deleted* 'Fleming' (*no caret at* 104.9 (G)

104.1 land] *preceded by deleted* 'foliage' (C)

104.5 a-horseback] 'back' *added* (C)

104.8 cheer,] *comma preceded by deleted period* (C)

104.11 ahead] *interlined above deleted* 'forward' (C)

104.13 were] *an* 'h' *after* 'w' *is deleted* (HG)

104.13 met,] *followed by deleted* 'with' (C)

104.15,16 a] *interlined with a caret* (C)

104.18 eyes] *interlined with a caret* (C)

104.19 soiled] 'so' *over* 're' (C)

104.25 leaped] *preceded by deleted* 'sl' (C)

104.25 many] *preceded by deleted* 'eve' (C)

105.2 it] *interlined with a caret* (C)

105.3 The youth] *interlined above deleted* 'Fleming' (G)

105.5 enemy] *interlined above deleted* 'eme' (C)

105.9 it,] *interlined with a caret* (C)

105.10 up] *interlined with a caret* (C)

105.15 them] *followed by deleted period* (C)

105.18 the youth] *interlined above deleted* 'Fleming' (G)

105.18 saw] *interlined above deleted* 'was' (C)

105.20 aware] *first* 'a' *over probable beginning of* 'w' (C)

105.21 sheets.] *period inserted before deleted period and* 'just be[*and beginning of an upstroke*]' (C)

105.21 of the trees] *interlined above deleted* 'reve[*and beginning of* 'a']' (C)

105.22 And] *preceded by deleted* 'H' (C)

105.25–26 impressions] *final* 's' *added later* (C)

105.28 furious rush.] *interlined above deleted* 'insane an' (C)

105.30 tuned] *interlined above deleted* 'pitched' (C)

105.31 it] *interlined* (C)

105.32 checking] *preceded by deleted* 'of halting at granite' (C)

105.33 that] *followed by deleted* 'heedlessly' (C)

105.34 It] *preceded by deleted* 'There' (C)

105.34 a temporary but] *interlined with a caret above deleted* 'a' (C)

105.38 Presently] *preceded by deleted* 'But'; 'P' *over* 'p' (C)

106.2 a] *followed by deleted* 'windlike' (C)

106.3 effect.] *period inserted before deleted* 'against them.' (C) *or* (G)

106.5 distant] *preceded by deleted* 'wa' (C)

106.5–6 disclose] *a final* 'd' *deleted* (C)

106.6 strength] *preceded by deleted* 'bo'; *followed by deleted comma* (C)

106.9 The youth] *interlined above deleted* 'Fleming' (G)

106.11 land.] *squeezed in at end of line* (C)

106.22 paralyze] *preceded by independently deleted* 'para-|' *and* 'paralaz' (C)

106.24 ²a] *inserted* (C)

106.26 lieutenant] *preceded by deleted* 'youthful' (G)

106.28 bellowed. "Come] *period altered from comma;* 'C' *over* 'c' (C)

106.31 with] *preceded by deleted* 'lo' (C)

106.34–35 delivered] *an* 'e' *after* 'i' *deleted* (C)

106.36 and force] *interlined with a caret* (C)

106.39 The . . . youth] *interlined with a caret above deleted* 'Wilson' (G)

107.2 woods.] *period altered from a comma* (C)

107.4 weapons] *followed by deleted period* (C)

107.5 regiment] *interlined above deleted* 'cart' (C)

107.6 muddle] 'l' *over beginning of* 'e' (C)

107.7 , now,] *interlined above deleted* 'every' (C)

107.7 few] 'w' *mended* (C)

107.7 fire] *preceded by deleted* 'load' (C)

107.8 load] 'l' *over beginning of another letter* (C)

107.14 was in] *interlined above deleted* 'made' (G)

107.14 confusing] 's' *mended* (C)

107.14 made] *preceded by deleted* 'magn' (C)

107.16 curling] 'c' *mended* (C)

107.16 the youth] *original* 'Fleming' *followed by independently deleted* 'felt poignant' *and* 'would'; 'would' *deletion being probably a* general *revision alteration* (C); 'the youth' *interlined with a caret above deleted* 'Fleming' (G)

107.16 wondered] 'ed' *added* (C)

107.18 The] *preceded by an inserted paragraph symbol* (G)

107.20 trees] 's' *added* (C)

107.24 showed a lack] *interlined above deleted* 'could be seen' (C)

107.26 supreme] *preceded by deleted* 'critical' (C)

107.29 lieutenant] *preceded by deleted* 'youthful' (G)

107.31 about] *interlined with a caret* (C)

107.33 deities] 'ei' *over* 'ie' (HG)

107.34 Once] 'O' *deletes opening double quotes* (C)

107.34; 108.2,4 the youth] *interlined above deleted* 'Fleming' (G)

107.34 on] 'o' *over* 'a' (C)

107.38 The youth] *interlined with a caret above deleted* 'Fleming' (G)

108.2 He] *preceded by deleted* 'In his frenzy,'; 'H' *over* 'h' (C)

108.3 on!] *exclamation point altered from a period* (C)

108.10 The friend] 'The' *interlined above deleted* 'Wilson'; 'friend' *inserted* (G)

108.12 danced] *second* 'd' *over* 's' (C)

108.16 dilapidated] MS 'delapidated' *with first* 'a' *over* 'i' (C)

108.18 scurrying] *interlined above deleted* 'lungeing' (G)

108.18 handful] 'l' *mended* (C)

108.19 splattered] *interlined above deleted* 'spattered' (G)

108.20 vast] *interlined with a caret* (C)

108.22 The youth] *interlined above deleted* 'Fleming' (G)

108.23 could] *interlined with a caret* (C)

108.23 He] 'e' *over* 'i' (C)

108.24 player.] *period probably inserted before deleted* 'a[and beginning of 'n']' (C)

108.27 this] 'i' *over* 'e' (C)

108.29 form] 'f' *over* 'p' (C)

108.30 loving,] 'ing' *over* 'e'; *comma inserted* (C)

108.31 the] *interlined with a caret* (C)

108.31 Because] *preceded by deleted* upstroke (C)

108.33 lives] *preceded by deleted* 'life' (C)

108.37 pole. At] *period inserted;* 'A' *over* 'a' (C)

108.38 his friend] *interlined above deleted* 'Wilson' (G)

109.3 obstinately] *preceded by deleted* 'p' (C)

109.3 ludicrous] MS 'ludicruos' *with final* 's' *over* 'us' *of which* 's' *deleted; preceded by deleted* 'a' (C)

109.3 ways] *preceded by independently deleted* 'postu' *and* 'attitude, fo' (C)

109.8 the friend's] *interlined above deleted* 'Wilson's' (G)

110.2 regiment had] *interlined above deleted* 'remainder' (C)

110.6 spluttering] *interlined above deleted* 'spattering' (G)

110.9 lieutenant] 'u' *over an upstroke; preceded by deleted* 'youthful' (G)

110.12 Gawd] *interlined with a caret* (G)

110.13 ordered] MS 'or-|dered' *with* 'or' *under an ink blot* (C)

110.15 The . . . friend] *interlined with a caret above deleted* 'Fleming and Wilson' (G)

110.18–19 The youth] *interlined above deleted* 'Fleming' (G)

110.22 Presently it] 'Presently' *interlined with a caret;* 'i' *over* 'I' (C)

110.24 again] *interlined with a caret* (C)

110.24 reached] *followed by deleted* 'agai[and beginning of 'n']' (C)

110.26 The . . . the] *interlined above deleted* 'The' (C)

110.28 bowed] *preceded by deleted* 'bound a' (C)

110.29 walls.] *period altered from comma* (C)

111.1 ^{1}to] *preceded by deleted* 'the' (C)

111.1 ²to] *interlined* (C)

111.6 who] *interlined with a caret* (C)

111.7 seemed] *interlined above deleted* 'were' (C)

111.8 The] *preceded by deleted* 'He was still' (C)

111.10 hung] *followed by deleted comma* (C)

111.13 incredible] 'a' *deleted after second* 'i' (C)

111.14 The youth] *original* 'Fleming' *followed by* 'had' *interlined with a caret and then deleted; caret also deleted* (C); 'The youth' *interlined above deleted* 'Fleming' (G)

111.15 and rage] 'and' *is followed by* 'rage' *under an ink blot* (C)

111.16 had] *preceded by deleted* 't[*and beginning of* 'h']' (C)

111.16 upon the] 't[*and part of* 'h']' *under an ink blot* (C)

111.17 his] *interlined with a caret* (C)

111.22 A] *over beginning of possible* 'H' (C)

111.22 face] *preceded by deleted* 'g' (C)

111.25 When] *preceded by deleted* 'S' (C)

111.26 the little] *interlined with a caret above deleted* 'the' (C)

111.27 the youth] *interlined above deleted* 'Fleming' (G)

111.28 This] 'T' *over beginning of* 'H' (C)

111.29 epithets] *preceded by deleted* 'his' (C)

111.29 unconcernedly] *interlined above deleted* 'coldly' (C)

111.29 finer] 'r' *added* (C)

111.30 ¹he] *interlined above deleted* 'Fleming' (G)

111.31 truly in] 'truly' *followed by deleted period;* 'in' *followed by deleted* 'return.' (C)

111.32 curious] *preceded by deleted* 'a' (C)

111.35 He] *preceded by deleted* 'So'; 'H' *over* 'h'; *at far left, in the margin, is inserted* 'He made' *which was then deleted* (C)

111.35 presently] *interlined with a caret* (C)

111.35 ¹his] *interlined above deleted* 'in the' (C)

111.37 those] 'o' *over* 'e' (C)

112.1 lieutenant] *preceded by deleted* 'youthful' (G)

112.3 protests.] *period inserted before deleted* 'but the' (C)

112.5 The] *preceded by deleted* 'Woun[*and beginning of probable* 'd']' (C)

112.7 speed] *inserted (original ink despite appearance)* (C)

112.9 skins.] *preceded by deleted* 'life.' (C)

112.9 black] *interlined above deleted* 'sombre' (C)

112.10,18 The youth] *interlined above deleted* 'Fleming' (G)

112.19 and buzzing] *interlined with a caret* (C)

112.21 The] *first word of MS f. 161 of which second* 'I' *over* '7' (C)

112.25 fired] *interlined with a caret* (C)

112.28 troops.] *interlined above deleted* 'regiment' (C)

112.28 ambitious to make] *interlined above deleted* 'one of the foremost' (C)

112.34 roads] *preceded by deleted* 'way' (C)

112.36 The youth] *interlined with a caret above deleted* 'Fleming' (G)

112.37 expected] *followed by deleted* 'to be pushed over,' *and beginning of possible* 'a' (C)

112.38 assumed] *interlined above deleted* 'assuming' (C)

113.1 did] *interlined above deleted* 'would' (C)

113.4 His friend] *interlined above deleted* 'Wilson' (G)

113.6 shut] 'u' *over* 'e' (G)

113.6 you] *interlined above deleted* 'yeh' (G)

113.6 damned] 'ed' *added* (G)

113.6 the youth] *interlined above deleted* 'Fleming' (G)

113.8 officers labored] 'labored' *preceded by deleted* 'w' *the beginning stroke of which deleted with intent a comma following* 'officers' (C)

113.10 curled] *preceded by deleted* 'curl' *with a mended* 'u' (C)

113.12 The] *first word of MS f.* 162 *of which* '2' *over* '8' (C)

113.12,14 The youth] *interlined above deleted* 'Fleming' (G)

113.12 lieutenant] *preceded by deleted* 'youthful' (G)

113.13 far] 'a' *over* 'o' (C)

113.13 sword] *interlined above deleted* 'cane' (G) *which had been underlined in pencil by* HG *with, to the left, his notation* '(sword?)'; *this in turn was deleted by the* general revision ink

113.14 cane.] *interlined above deleted* 'walking-stick.' (G)

113.15 cursed.] *interlined with a caret* (C)

113.17 which] *interlined above deleted* 'who' (C)

113.17 wept] *a final* 's' *deleted; followed by independently deleted possible* 't' *and* 'it's fill' *and a comma not deleted in error;* 'it's' *interlined with a caret above deleted* 'his' (C)

113.17 its] MS 'it's' *preceded by beginning stroke of possible* 'f' (C)

113.19 quivered] *preceded by deleted* 'tr' (C)

113.22 disclose] *followed by deleted* 'to them their' (C)

113.26 b'] 'b' *over upstroke* (C)

113.26 further] 'u' *mended* (C)

113.28 The youth's] *interlined above deleted* 'Fleming's' (G)

113.32 at] *preceded by deleted* 't [*and upstroke of possible* 'h']' (C)

113.32 He perceived] *preceded by deleted* 'To'; 'H' *over* 'h'; MS 'percieved' *interlined above deleted* 'noted' (C)

113.34 accented] *interlined above deleted* 'trimmed' (C)

113.35 new.] *period inserted before deleted* 'and' (C)

113.36 going] *interlined above deleted* 'moving' (C)

113.38 movement] *interlined above deleted* 'movement' (C)

113.39 From] *interlined above deleted* 'In' (C)

113.39 moment's] *interlined above deleted* 'instant's' (C)

114.1 unaware] *interlined above deleted* 'unconscious' (C)

114.1 ²of] *interlined and deleted above is* 're' (C)

114.2 foes,] *comma inserted before deleted period* (C)

114.2 direction] *preceded by deleted* 'cor[*and beginning of* 'r']' (C)

114.2 Almost] *first word of MS f.* 163 *of which* '3' *over* '9' (C)

114.2–3 instantly,] *interlined above deleted* 'instantly' (C)

114.3 the youth's] *interlined above deleted* 'Fleming's' (G)

114.8 fast,] *interlined with a caret* (C)

114.8 back] 'b' *mended* (C)

114.11 ¹Their] *preceded by deleted* 'Their belchings swelled loud and valiant' *of which* 'belchings' *interlined above interlined, deleted* 'rifle' *which was interlined above deleted* 'voices' (C)

114.14 achieved] *preceded by deleted* 'got' (C)

114.14 ²a] *followed by deleted* 'view' (C)

114.15 appeared to be] *interlined above deleted* 'seemed' (C)

114.16   seemed] *followed by deleted* 'to be' (C)

114.16   toward] *preceded by deleted* 'f' (C)

114.21   have] *preceded by deleted* 'console' (C)

114.23   antagonist] *followed by deleted* 'grew weak' (C)

114.25   dark] *preceded by deleted* 'a' (C)

114.29   thrown] 't' *over beginning of* 'a'; *preceded by deleted* 'twisted' (C)

114.31   from] *followed by deleted* 'their' (C)

114.33   broke] *interlined with a caret* (C)

114.36   evidently] *preceded by deleted* 'app' (C)

114.38   ²the] *interlined above deleted* 'a' (G)

114.39   had] *followed by deleted* 'been a measure to them,' (G)

114.39   showed] 'ed' *over* 'ing'; *tail of* 'g' *deleted* (G)

114.39   impossible,] *comma preceded by deleted period* (C)

115.4   about] *preceded by deleted* 'upon' (C)

116.0   116] MS f. 165 *with* '–6' *added in ink* (F)

116.1   knew] *preceded by deleted* 'percieved' (C)

116.4   many] *followed by deleted* 'crashes and' (C)

116.7   into] *preceded by deleted* 'in' *over an upstroke of possible* 't' (C)

116.8   trip.] *followed by deleted* 'An' (C)

116.11   could] *preceded by deleted* 'denoted an' *and the beginning of another letter* (C)

116.12   an] 'n' *added* (C)

116.12   anxiety] *interlined above deleted* 'haste' (C)

116.12   It] *preceded by deleted* 'They hastened [*followed by deleted comma*] with backward [*final* 's' *deleted*] looks of perturbation.' (C)

116.13   insignificant] *preceded by deleted* 'an' (C)

116.14   they thought it] *interlined with a caret above deleted* 'it' (C)

116.25   One] *preceded by deleted opening double quotes* (C)

116.25   taunting] 'i' *altered from* 'e' *and* 'n' *over* 'i' (C)

116.28   man   made] *beginning stroke of* 'made' *deletes with intent a comma following* 'man' (C)

116.30   tall] 't' *over* 'c' (C)

117.1   lieutenant] *preceded by deleted* 'youthful' (G)

117.4   The   youth's] *interlined above deleted* 'Fleming's' (G)

117.6   many] *followed by deleted* 'hung thei[*and beginning of* 'r']' (C)

117.8   that] *followed by deleted* 'many of' (C)

117.8   trudged] *preceded by deleted* 'trug'; *followed by deleted* 'heavily' (C)

117.9   bended] *first* 'd' *inserted* (C)

117.14   The youth] *original* 'Fleming' *preceded by deleted* 'To' (C); 'The youth' *interlined above deleted* 'Fleming' (G)

117.17   where] *interlined above deleted* 'were' (C)

117.17   had] *preceded by deleted* 'had t[*and beginning of possible* 'a']' (C)

117.20   little] *interlined above deleted* 'short' (C)

117.20   Elfin] *preceded by deleted* 'Little'; 'E' *over* 'e' (C)

117.23   speeches] *interlined above deleted* 'remarks' (C)

117.27   They] *preceded by inserted paragraph symbol* (C)

117.30   However, to the youth] *original* 'To Fleming' *preceded by inserted* 'However,' *and* 'T' *of* 'To' *reduced to lower case with a vertical stroke;* 'Flem-

ing' *followed by deleted comma
and* 'however,' (C); 'to the
youth' *interlined above deleted*
'to Fleming' (G)

117.30 in] *followed by deleted* 'a'
(C)

117.32 previously] *preceded by
deleted* 'in' (C)

117.32 so] *preceded by independently deleted* 'an' *and* 'but he'
(C)

117.33 of] *followed by deleted*
'them.' (C)

117.34 had] *preceded by deleted*
'that' (C)

117.35 senses] *second* 'e' *mended*
(C)

117.36 exertions] 'x' *uncrossed
in error* (C)

118.1 dark] *interlined above deleted* 'black' (C)

118.1 wrath.] *interlined above
deleted* 'rage.' (C)

118.3 and] 'd' *mended* (C)

118.3 wrenched savagely] *beginning stroke of* 's' *deletes with
intent a comma following*
'wrenched' (C)

118.3 ²his] *interlined* (C)

118.4 -breathing] MS '-breatheing'
with second 'e' *over* 'i' (C)

118.4 with a furious pull] *interlined with a caret* (C)

118.5 exploded] '-ed' *interlined
above deleted* 'd' (C)

118.9 you made] *interlined with
a caret* (C)

118.10 attempted] *preceded by
deleted* 'tried' (C)

118.11 certain] 'c' *mended; preceded by deleted* 'the' (C)

118.17 listening] 'l' *altered from
beginning of possible* 't' (C)

118.20 The] *preceded by deleted*
'He s' (C)

118.22 deacon] *preceded by deleted* 'deco[*and beginning of*
'n']' (C)

118.22 of] *first word MS f.* 169
of which '6' *over beginning of*
'9' (C)

118.24–25 changed . . . Frenchman.] 'changed' *followed by a
deleted period and* 'He'; 'from
. . . Frenchman.' *added below
the line* (C)

118.25 He] *inserted* (C)

118.28 a] *interlined with a caret*
(C)

118.33 hear] *interlined above deleted* 'listen to' (C) *or* (G)

118.34 damnations.] 's' *inserted*
(C)

118.35 lieutenant] *preceded by
deleted* 'youthful'; *followed by
interlined, deleted* 'of the' (G)

118.36 interview] *interlined
above deleted* 'rage' (C)

119.4 an] *interlined with a caret*
(C)

119.11 see this] *strengthened* (C)

119.13 cuffed] *preceded by deleted* 'beaten' (C)

119.13 animals] 'n' *over* 'in' (C)

119.14 The friend] *interlined
above deleted* 'Wilson' (G)

119.14 the youth.] *interlined
above deleted* 'Fleming.' (G)

119.17 The youth] *interlined
above deleted* 'Fleming' (G)

119.19 nothing] 'g' *over an apostrophe* (G)

119.19(*twice*),22 and] 'd' *over
an apostrophe* (G)

119.20 were] *interlined above
deleted* 'was' (G)

119.20 of] 'o' *over* ' 'a' (G)

119.20 just] 'u' *over* 'e' (G)

119.20 because] *first* 'e' *over an
apostrophe* (G)

119.20 he] 'h' *over* 'w' (C)

119.21 old] 'd' *over an apostrophe* (G)

119.22 would . . . that] *interlined with a caret above deleted* 'a knowed' (G)

119.22 did] 'i' *altered from* 'o';
second 'd' *over* 'ne' (G)

119.22 fought] *interlined above
deleted* 'fit' (G)

119.23 just] *interlined above deleted* 'jest' (G)

119.24,33 the friend] *interlined above deleted* 'Wilson' (G)

119.24 He] 'e' *over* 'is' (C)

119.24 seemed] *interlined above deleted* 'sense' (C)

119.27 no] *followed by deleted dash* (C)

119.27 behind] 'e' *over apostrophe* (C)

119.30; 120.4 The youth] *interlined above deleted* 'Fleming' (G)

119.30 comrade.] *interlined above deleted* 'friend' *and a period not deleted in error* (G)

119.31 did] *interlined above deleted* 'done' (G)

119.31 to] 'o' *over an apostrophe* (G)

119.31 the] 'e' *over an apostrophe* (G)

119.33 'A] *over* 'Of' (G)

119.34 feller's] 'f' *over* 'm' (C)

119.34 he] 'h' *over beginning of probable* 'w' (C)

119.34,37 a] *interlined with a caret* (C)

119.37 had] *preceded by deleted* 'hat' (C)

119.37 t'] *preceded by deleted apostrophe* (C)

119.37 seen] *interlined above deleted* 'never' (C)

119.38 ¹th'] 't' *mended* (C)

120.2 stand] *preceded by deleted* 'unnerstan' (C)

120.6 him] MS ' 'im' *with* 'i' *over* 'e'; *followed by deleted* 'up' (C)

120.7 had] *interlined with a caret* (C)

120.7 come] 'o' *over* 'a' (C)

120.9 cried] *interlined above deleted* 'said' (C)

120.10 "Heard what?"] *inserted before deleted* ' "What?" ' (C)

120.10 the youth.] *interlined above deleted* 'Fleming' *and a period not deleted in error* (G)

120.12 tell] *followed by deleted* 'with' (C)

120.17 what] 'a' *over* 'o' (C)

120.17–18 flag?' . . . 'That's] *single quotes over double* (C)

120.19 hickey] *interlined above deleted* 'dandy' (C)

120.22 Th'] *preceded by deleted* 'An' ' (C)

120.24 He] 'H' *over beginning of* 'W' (C)

120.25 'You] *direction of quotation mark made more clear* (C)

120.31 ahem.] 'a' *over deleted beginning of* 'A'; *period altered from a comma* (C)

120.31–32 ses. 'At] *period altered from a comma;* 'A' *over beginning of another letter* (C)

120.32 reg'ment?] *question mark over a comma* (C)

120.34 babies?] *question mark altered from exclamation point* (C)

120.34 were!] *exclamation altered from a question mark* (C)

120.35 -generals] 's' *added* (C)

120.37 The . . . friend] *interlined with a caret above deleted* 'Fleming and Wilson' (G)

120.37 had] 'h' *over* 's' (C)

120.37 Yer] 'er' *over* 'ou' (C)

121.1 from] *interlined above deleted* 'in a' (C)

121.2 thrills] 's' *added later* (C)

121.4 pictures] *preceded by deleted* 'eternal' (C)

122.2 the youth] *interlined above deleted* 'Fleming' (G)

122.4 duck] 'k' *mended* (C)

122.7 His] *preceded by deleted* 'Unmole' (C)

122.8 the] *interlined with a caret* (C)

122.9 parts] *preceded by deleted* 'some very' (C)

122.9 hard] *preceded by deleted* 'great' (C)

122.9 relief] *interlined above deleted* 'revelation' (C)

122.10 some] 's' *mended* (C)

122.10 which] *preceded by de-*

leted 'to'; *followed by deleted* 'he' (C)

122.12 short way,] *interlined above deleted* 'little way' *and a comma not deleted in error* (C)

122.13 battle] *interlined* (C)

122.22 the] *interlined above deleted* 'that' (C)

122.22 The] *preceded by deleted* 'They passed in' (C)

122.23 this] 'is' *added with* 'i' *over* 'e' (C)

122.24 prodigious,] *comma inserted and followed by deleted* 'uproar' *and a comma not deleted in error* (C)

122.25,26 its] MS 'it's' *interlined above deleted* 'their' (C)

122.26 were] 'er' *over* 'as'; *followed by deleted* 'absolutely' (C)

123.2 groups] *preceded by deleted* 'the' (C)

123.3 white] *interlined above deleted* 'wide' (C)

123.7 detached] *preceded by deleted* 'se[and beginning of possible 'p']' (C)

123.11 faltered] *preceded by deleted* 'dr' (C)

123.15 changed] *interlined above deleted* 'settled' (C)

123.17 -like,] *comma preceded by deleted period* (C)

123.19 unimpressed] *preceded by deleted* 'an' *of which* 'n' *added* (C)

123.19 boys.] *inserted;* 's' *over a period; second period added below* (C)

123.19–20 The . . . would] *interlined with a caret above independently deleted* 'boy.' *and* 'It would' (C)

123.20 their] 'ir' *added* (C)

123.20 ears] *followed by deleted* 'of the men' (C)

123.21 new] *interlined with a caret;* Crane *actually wrote* 'nw' *or* 'nev' (C)

123.25 splitting] *interlined above deleted* 'clattering' (C)

123.26 developed.] *first* 'd' *over illegible letter; period inserted before deleted* 'w[and beginning of 'h']' (C)

123.29 cups.] 's' *inserted* (C)

123.31 On] *preceded by deleted* 'And on' (C)

123.31 saw] *preceded by deleted* 'saw' (C)

123.32 It] *preceded by deleted* 'It' (C)

123.32–33 backward . . . forward] *final* 's' *deleted from each* (C)

123.33 These] *preceded by deleted* 'Here one side' *of which* 'e' *of* 'one' *added* (C)

123.33 the] *interlined* (C)

123.34 long] *followed by deleted comma and* 'controlled' (C)

123.34 madly] 'm' *over* 'o' (C)

123.36 decisive] 'c' *over* 's' (C)

123.36–37 a moment] *preceded by deleted* 'in' (C)

123.37 all] 'a' *over beginning of* 'y' (C)

123.39 waving] *preceded by deleted* 'ro' (C)

123.39–124.1 There . . . presently] *interlined with a caret above deleted* 'And' (C)

124.2 saw] *followed by deleted* 'h [and beginning of 'e']' (C)

124.2 with] *interlined with a caret above deleted* 'so thunderously' (C)

124.4 always,] *followed by deleted* 'the men were yelling' (C)

124.5 rushes] *inserted* (C)

124.7 fence] *a final* 's' *deleted* (C)

124.7 positions] *final* 's' *added later* (C)

124.8 over,] *followed by deleted* 'by t' (C)

124.10 bandied] *followed by independently deleted* 'to and fro' *and* 'between like toys' *with deletion line continuing to right margin* (C)

124.12 flying] *interlined above deleted* 'shooting' (C)

124.12 crimson foam] *interlined above deleted* 'stars' (C)

124.13 directions] 's' *added* (C)

124.13 color] *preceded by deleted* 's' (C)

124.13 cloth] *a final* 'e' *deleted* (C)

124.13 was] 'as' *over* 'ere' (C)

124.15 fierceness] 'r' *over* 'c' (C)

124.15 again by] *interlined with a caret above deleted* 'by' (C)

124.16 a barbaric] *preceded by deleted* 'b' (C)

124.16 They] 'y' *added* (C)

124.18 hammers] *interlined with a caret above deleted* 'triggers' (C)

124.19 arms] *preceded by deleted* 'han' (C)

124.20 The] *preceded by deleted* 'They bended' (C)

124.20 penetrated] *preceded by deleted* 'pente' (C)

124.21 red.] *interlined at end of line* (C)

124.24 exertion,] *followed by deleted* 'they' (C)

124.28 lieutenant] *preceded by deleted* 'youthful' (G)

124.30 emergency] *preceded by deleted* 'occasion' (C)

124.33 The youth] *interlined above deleted* 'Fleming' (G)

124.35 forward,] *comma added after deleted comma and* 'i' (C)

124.36 face] 'ace' *added with* 'ac' *over* 'or' (C)

124.36 small] MS 'small,' *of which the comma not deleted in error when following* 'and grotesque' *deleted* (C)

124.36 contortions] 's' *added later* (C)

124.37 words] *preceded on line above by deleted* 'exclama-' (C)

124.38 the] *inserted* (C)

124.39 silently] *preceded by deleted* 'still' (C)

125.1 range] 'g' *mended* (C)

125.4 At . . . danger, the] 'At . . . danger,' *inserted before* 'The' *of which* 'T' *reduced with a vertical stroke* (C)

125.4 ceased] *interlined with a caret* (C)

125.5 monotone] 'e' *added* (C)

125.5 strained] *preceded by deleted* 'deep' (C)

125.11–12 with remarkable celerity] *interlined with a caret* (C)

125.13 men.] *preceded by deleted* 'regiment.' (C)

125.17 frequently] 'f' *over possible* 's' (C)

125.19 at] *preceded by deleted* 'the' (C)

125.23 denoted] *preceded by deleted* 'upon their' (C)

125.25 The youth] *interlined with a caret above deleted* 'Fleming' (G)

125.25 not] *interlined with a caret* (C)

125.26 themselves] *preceded by deleted* 'itself' (C)

125.27 hatreds.] 's' *inserted* (C)

125.27 It was] *preceded by independently deleted* 'And, he' *and* 'And'; 'I' *over* 'i' (C)

125.32 unit] *preceded by deleted* 'responsible ut' (C)

125.34 was] *followed by deleted* 'for those eyes that it was' *with* 'eyes' *interlined above deleted* 'ideas' (C)

125.35 corpse] 'o' *mended; preceded by deleted* 'd' (C)

125.36 extravagantly.] *followed by deleted* 'The orderly serjeant' (C)

125.38 Its] MS 'It's' *preceded by deleted* 'I' *over* 'F' (C)

126.5,11 The youth] *interlined above deleted* 'Fleming' (G)

126.8 about] 'a' *over beginning of possible* 'n'; *followed by de-*

leted 'their compa[*and begin-ning of* 'n']' (C)

126.11 his friend.] *interlined above deleted* 'Wilson' *and a period not deleted in error* (G)

126.12 knew] *followed by deleted* 'it' (C)

126.13 him.] *interlined above deleted* 'his friend' *and a period not deleted in error* (G)

126.13 The] *preceded by deleted* 'Also' (C)

126.13 lieutenant] *preceded by deleted* 'youthful' (G)

126.13 also,] 'a' *over beginning of possible* 'w' (C)

126.16 The] *interlined above deleted* 'It's' (C)

127.3 We] 'W' *over* 'w' (C)

127.6 The youth] *interlined with a caret above deleted* 'Fleming'; *the caret deletes with intent a possible comma following* 'Fleming' (G)

127.6 shouts,] *followed by independently deleted* 'thought' *and* 'turned' (C)

127.11 galling] 'g' *over* 'e' (C)

127.14 with a certain surprise] *interlined with a caret* (C)

127.14 they] *interlined with a caret* (C)

127.17 rifle-] *preceded by deleted* 'rattle' (C)

127.18 leaps.] *period altered from comma and followed by deleted* 'racing for success.' (C)

127.29 The youth] *interlined above deleted* 'Fleming' (G)

128.1 the] *interlined with a caret* (C)

128.3 wild] *preceded by deleted* 'with' (C)

128.8–9 was no obvious] *interlined above deleted* 'was no' (C)

128.9 questionings] 'ings' *added later* (C)

128.9(*twice*) ,nor] *interlined above deleted* 'and' (*comma not*

interlined with second 'nor') (C)

128.13 He,] *original* 'Fleming' *followed by deleted* 'fe' (C); 'He,' *interlined above deleted* 'Fleming' (G)

128.14 was] *preceded by deleted* 'k' (C)

128.17 place] *interlined above deleted* 'gaol' (C)

128.17 within] *interlined above deleted* 'in' (C)

128.21 excepting] *interlined with a caret above deleted* 'but' (C)

128.22 it] *interlined with a caret* (C)

128.24 contact] *preceded by deleted* 'can[*and beginning of* 't']' (C)

128.26 his] *interlined with a caret* (C)

128.26 wild] *followed by deleted* 'enthusiasm,' (C)

128.28 and] *preceded by deleted* 'and' (C)

128.30 flying] *interlined above deleted* 'impelled' (C)

128.33 many of the] *interlined above deleted* 'the' (C)

128.35 who ran] *interlined above deleted* 'running' (C)

128.36 frequently] *preceded by deleted* 'to send' (C)

128.37 wave.] *inscribed at left margin;* 'wave.' *deleted at right margin* (C)

129.5 scuffle] *preceded by deleted* 'struggle' (C)

129.6 opposition] *preceded by deleted* 'little' (C)

129.8 cries] *interlined above deleted* 'shouts' (C)

129.10 eyes] *interlined above deleted* 'teeth' (C)

129.11 at] *interlined with a caret* (C)

129.11 throats] 's' *added* (C)

129.11–12 stood resisting.] *interlined above deleted* 'held the fence.' (C)

129.12 an] 'n' *added* (C)

129.14 The youth] *interlined with a caret above deleted* 'Fleming' (G)

129.14 other] *inserted* (C)

129.17 great] *followed by deleted* 'possibilities.' (C)

129.18 a craved treasure] 'a craved' *written below deleted* 'a'; 'treasure' *interlined above deleted* 'apple' (C)

129.20 plunged] *followed by deleted* 'tow[*and beginning of another letter*]' (C)

129.20 at] *interlined above deleted* 'toward' (C)

129.22 a-flare] *hyphen inserted* (C)

129.22 toward] *preceded by deleted* 'at' (C)

129.25 swirling] *preceded by deleted* 'sw' (C)

129.30 The youth] *original* 'Fleming' *with a final* 's' *deleted* (C); 'The youth' *interlined above deleted* 'Fleming' (G)

129.30 ²a] *preceded by deleted* 'saw' (C)

129.32 they had been] *interlined with a caret* (C)

129.33 Tottering] *preceded by deleted* 'A[*and the beginning of* 'm']' (C)

129.34 the youth] *interlined above deleted* 'Fleming' (G)

129.37 Over] *interlined above deleted* 'Upon' (C)

129.37 was the] *interlined with a caret above deleted* 'in' (C)

130.2 in] 'i' *over* 'o' (C)

130.2 his] *preceded by deleted* 'the way which' (C)

130.3 led to] *interlined above deleted* 'would be' (C)

130.4–5 retarded] *preceded by deleted* 'hel' (C)

130.5 held,] *followed by deleted* 'by invisible ghouls fastened' (C)

130.10 The youth's friend] *interlined above deleted* 'Wilson' (G)

130.12 swung] *preceded by deleted* 'an' (C)

130.17 The] *a final* 'y' *deleted* (C)

130.24 birds] *followed by a deleted period* (C)

130.27 from] *followed by deleted* 'h' (C)

130.29 called] *followed by deleted* 'down' (C)

130.31 recognition] 'r' *over probable* 'a' (C)

130.32 had] 'd' *mended* (C)

130.32 trod] *preceded by deleted* 'tread' (C)

131.5 "Ah] 'A' *over* 'O' (C)

131.8 the youth] *interlined with a caret above deleted* 'Fleming' (G)

131.10 was] *preceded by deleted* 'pe' (C)

131.11 The youth] MS 'Fleming' *preceded by deleted* 'There was no ex' (C)

131.12 ¹to] *followed by deleted* 'think' (C)

131.12 his] *preceded by deleted* 'the' (C)

131.15 shame] *preceded by deleted* 're' (C)

131.15 antagonize] 'i' *inserted* (C)

131.16 had] *followed by deleted* 'settled do' (C)

131.17 side] *inserted* (C)

131.18 A few] *interlined above deleted* 'Some' (C)

131.20 There] *preceded by paragraph symbol* (C) *or* (G)

131.20 grass.] *period inserted before deleted* 'and' (C)

131.20 The youth] *interlined above deleted* 'Fleming' (G)

131.21 His friend] *interlined with a caret above deleted* 'Wilson' (G)

132.4 crashes] *preceded by deleted* 'cry' (C)

132.6 looked] 'ed' *over* 'ing' *with tail of* 'g' *deleted* (C)

132.11 The youth] *interlined above deleted* 'Fleming' (G)

132.11 By] *over* 'In' (C)

132.15 His friend] *interlined with a caret above deleted* 'Wilson' (G)

132.17 swan] 'n' *mended* (C)

132.17 the youth] *interlined above deleted* 'Fleming' *and a period deleted in error* (G)

132.20 repose] MS 'reposes' *followed by deleted* 'in the grass' *which was interlined with a caret* (C)

133.2 lying] MS 'lieing' *followed by deleted* 'down' (C)

133.5–6 entrenchments] *initial* 'e' *over* 'i'

133.9–10 the youth] *interlined above deleted* 'Fleming' (G)

133.10 toward] *preceded by deleted* 'a[*and beginning of* 't']' (C)

133.11 -strewed] *first* 'e' *over* 'u' (C)

133.12 He] *beginning stroke of* 'H' *deletes with intent opening double quotes* (C)

133.12 his friend.] *interlined above deleted* 'Wilson.' (G)

133.14 His friend] *interlined above deleted* 'Wilson' (G)

133.16 the youth] *interlined above deleted* 'Fleming' (G)

133.17 under-] 'u' *over illegible letter* (C)

133.20 clouds] *followed by independently deleted* 'of his s' *and* 'the' (C)

133.20 more] *preceded by deleted* 'cl' (C)

133.21 closely comprehend] 'closely' *inserted;* 'comprehend' *interlined above deleted* 'understand' (C)

133.25 escaped] 'es' *over* 'ec' (C)

133.25 His] *preceded by deleted* 'There was joy in this thought.' (C)

133.36 ²in] *interlined above deleted* 'with' (C)

134.1 pleasure] *preceded by deleted* 'a' (C)

134.6 shoutings] *preceded by deleted* 'spectacles' (C)

134.9–20 A . . . oaths.] MS 'As Fleming was thus fraternizing again with nature, a . . . oaths.' *added after* f. 190 *was begun* (C)

134.9 spectre] *preceded by deleted beginning of* 'p' (C)

134.10 soldier] *a final* 's' *deleted* (C)

134.13 he who] *beginning stroke of* 'w' *deletes with intent comma following* 'he' (C)

134.19 His friend] *interlined above deleted* 'Wilson' (G)

134.20 The youth's] *interlined above deleted* 'Fleming's' (G)

134.20 oaths.] *following is a close-up line to link this folio,* 189, *with* f. 190 (C)

134.21 As] *first word* MS f. 190 *which is written to right of deleted* '189' (C)

134.21 among] 'a' *over beginning of illegible letter* (C)

134.22 prattling] *preceded by deleted* 'careless' (C)

134.22 this] 'is' *over* 'e' (C)

134.23 the] 'e' *over* 'ose' (C)

134.26 feeling] *second* 'e' *over an upstroke* (C)

134.28 plodding] 'ing' *interlined below deleted* 'ed' (C)

134.31 dum] *a final* 'n' *deleted* (C)

134.33 'em."] *at far right, preceded at far left by deleted* 'em' (C)

134.34 yer] *followed by deleted possible double quotes* (C)

134.34 'a] *interlined* (C)

134.36 ten] *preceded by deleted* 'a' (C)

135.1 off'cer] *preceded by deleted* 'orfcer' (C)

135.3 Didn't] *preceded by deleted* 'We' (C)

135.7 the youth's] *interlined above deleted* 'Fleming's' (G)

135.8 He] *preceded by deleted* 'He, protested' (C)

135.10 felt] *interlined above deleted* 'would feel' (C)

135.11 were] *interlined with a caret* (C)

135.11 detail] *preceded by deleted* 'deal' (C)

135.14 his] MS 'His' *with* 'is' *over* 'e' (C)

135.17 despised] *preceded by deleted* 'he' (C)

135.18 With] *preceded by inserted paragraph symbol* (C)

135.21 should] *preceded by deleted* 'd' (C)

135.21 and] *followed by vertical stroke not touching line* (C)

135.22 found] *preceded by deleted* 'that' (C)

135.23 as] *interlined with a caret* (C)

135.26 -ploughshares] *followed by deleted* 'tran[*and beginning of* 'q']' (C)

135.27–28 bedraggled] 'b' *over* 'd' *over* 't' (C)

135.28 muttering,] *comma preceded by deleted period* (C)

135.28 marching] *followed by deleted* 'in a trough of' (C)

135.29 effort] 'or' *mended over* 'ec' (C)

135.29 under] *preceded by deleted* 'ud' (C)

135.30 youth] *interlined above deleted* 'man' (G)

135.32–37 and . . . peace.] 'and' *followed by independently deleted* 'walking-sticks.' *and* 'The End.'; 'walking-sticks. . . . peace.' *added* (G)

135.33 battle.] *interlined above deleted* 'war.' *of which period over a comma and followed by deleted* 'for he could now' *with* 'f' *over beginning of a* 'w' (G)

135.35 images] *preceded by deleted* 'fair, imagined ima[*and beginning of a* 'g']' (G)

135.36 brooks;] *semicolon inserted before deleted period and* 'The hideous' (G)

DISCARDED CHAPTER XII

FULL COLLATION OF THE FINAL MANUSCRIPT AND THE EARLY DRAFT

[NOTE: All variants between the final manuscript and the early draft are listed here except those variants in dialect which have been adopted from the draft as emendations to the final manuscript and thus appear in the Emendations to the Copy-Text. The reading to the left of the bracket is that of the final manuscript unless otherwise stated. A dagger indicates the complete agreement of the early draft (MS[d]) with the uncorrected manuscript (MS[u]). The symbol MS(f) denotes the false start of MS f. 98 of the final manuscript.]

139.2   men;] ~ , MS(d), MS(f)
139.2   his mind] he MS(d),MS(f)
139.3–12   Hence . . . God.] omit MS(d)
139.3   Hence₍₎] ~ , MS(f)
139.4   outrages] out-rages MS(f)
139.6   general] omit MS(f)
139.6   right] just MS(f)
139.7   world-wide] universal MS(f)
139.8–10   because . . . color] omit MS(f)
139.10   on the earth] under the sky MS(f)
139.12   justice,] ~ ₍₎ MS(f)
139.12   God.] last word MS(f)
139.13   ¶ He] (no ¶) Also, he MS(d)
†139.13   unprecedented] peculiar and unprecedented MS(d)
139.17   in black tempests] like storms MS(d)
139.20   As] But, as MS(d[c]); As MS(d[u])
139.20   that . . . part,] that, after all, nature MS(d)
139.20   would] would MS(d[u and final c]); could MS(d[first c])

†139.22   believed now] began to believe MS(d)
139.23   in] agitating MS(d)
139.24–25   not . . . system] omit MS(d)
139.25   Nature (no ¶)] ¶ MS(d)
139.25   the] her MS(d)
139.26   of] to MS(d)
139.27   pursuit₍₎] ~ , MS(d)
139.29–140.1   It was . . . brains.] omit MS(d)
140.3   out] all out MS(d)
140.4   now₍₎ said₍₎] ~ , ~ , MS(d)
140.4   supposed,] ~ ₍₎ MS(d)
140.5–6   approaching death] inevitable MS(d)
140.6   Nature . . . submission.] omit MS(d)
140.7–8   bite . . . murderer.] scratch and bite like a child in the hands of a parent. MS(d)
140.8–9   The law . . . He] And he MS(d)
140.11   ¶ His] no ¶ MS(d)
140.11   safe,] secure₍₎ MS(d[c]); safe₍₎ MS(d[u])
140.11   time,] ~ ₍₎ MS(d)
140.13   these] those MS(d)
140.14   flight] own flight MS(d)

140.15–16 fault, . . . law.]
fault; it was a law. MS(d)

140.17 was . . . erected] saw
that when he had made MS(d)

140.24 He (no ¶)] ¶ MS(d)

140.25 And (no ¶)] ¶ MS(d)

140.27 had,] ~ ∧ MS(d)

†140.27 presently,] then∧ MS(d);
then, MS(u)

140.28 untouched] pure MS(d)

140.29 hidden currents] hidden,
untouched MS(d)

†140.31 and] *omit* MS(d)

140.31 blighting] darkening
MS(d)

140.32 it] *end of* MS fol. 98 (ff.
99–100 *wanting*) *and line 8 of*
MS(d) fol. 86; MS(d) fol. 86
continues for another 24 lines;
MS(d) fol. 87–89 *wanting*

139.1–12   It . . . God.] *false start (verso of p. 102)*: '[¶] It was always clear to Fleming that he was entirely different from other men, that he had been cast in a unique mold. Hence, laws that might be just to the ordinary man, were, when applied to him, peculiar and galling out-rages. Minds, he said, were not ['all' *deleted*] made all ['all' *interlined with a caret*] with one stamp and colored green. [*period over a comma followed by deleted* 'there was variety.' *with* 'was' *followed by independently deleted* 'an' *and* 'sl'] He was of no pattern. It was not just to measure his acts by a universal standard. The laws of the world were ['were' *interlined above deleted* 'are'] wrong. There was no justice under the sky when justice was meant. Men were too puny and prattling to know anything of it. If there was a [*followed by deleted* 'univers'] justice it must be in the ['the' *interlined*] hands of a God ['G' *over* 'g'] (C)

139.1   the youth] *interlined above deleted* 'Fleming' (G)

139.4   man] *interlined above deleted* 'specta' (C)

139.4   peculiar] 'i' *possibly altered from* 'c' (C)

139.7   ²world] *interlined above deleted* 'wron[*and beginning of* 'g']' (C)

139.9   , with all men,] *interlined with a caret following a comma not deleted in error* (C)

139.9   ¹a] *interlined above deleted* 'the' (C)

139.13   unprecedented] *preceded by deleted* 'peculiar and' (C)

139.15   experiences] 's' *added later* (C)

139.18   sublimity] 'sub' *inserted after* 'sub-|' *deleted on line above* (C)

139.22   believed now] *interlined above deleted* 'began to believe' (C)

139.28   hide] *preceded by deleted* 'flee' (C)

139.28   security] *interlined above deleted* 'strength' (C)

139.29   wisdom.] *preceded by deleted* 'wids' (C)

139.31   their] 'ir' *over* 're'(C)

140.7   business] *interlined above deleted* 'duty' (C)

140.8–9   The law . . . fight.] *interlined with a caret* (C)

140.10   strength.] *followed by deleted* 'His' (C)

140.14   incident] *interlined above deleted* 'findings' (C)

140.15   an] *interlined above deleted* 'not' (C)

140.16   obedient] *interlined above deleted* 'according' (C)

140.17   aware] *interlined with a caret* (C)

140.17   vindicating] *followed by a deleted* 's' (C)

140.27   presently] *interlined above deleted* 'then' (C)

140.29 ¹his] *interlined with a caret* (C)

140.31 and] *interlined with a caret* (C)

[For alterations in Draft p. 86 see pp. 419–420 (178.1–178.37).]

141.18 they] 'e' *mended* (C)

141.22 be] *interlined above deleted* 'a' (C)

141.22 reform] *followed by deleted* 'to' (C)

141.27 stone] *preceded by deleted* 'cla' (C)

141.34 grinded] *interlined above deleted* 'dragged' (C)

141.34 despised.] *interlined above deleted* 'was' (C)

141.36 him.] *followed by deleted* 'Misinterpreted, they often combated [*interlined above deleted* 'foiled' (C)] each other and made mangles of intellect. There was a dreadful, unwritten martyrdom in his state.' (C)

141.38 search] 's' *over* 'a' (C)

142.3 ²He . . . grim] *added before deleted* 'He' *which had been at the paragraph point with* 'her grim' *preceded by deleted* 'the grim' (C)

142.6 scene] *followed by an inserted question mark* (C)

142.9 scheme] 'c' *inserted* (C)

142.10 further] *interlined with a caret* (C)

142.10 life.] *period inserted before deleted* 'n' (C)

142.12 more] *interlined with a caret* (C)

142.15 misery] *interlined above deleted* 'suffering' (C)

142.15 this] 'is' *added with* 'i' *over* 'e' (C)

142.16 thought] *preceded by deleted* 'believed' (C)

142.18 process] *interlined above deleted* 'affair w' (C)

142.19 man] *interlined above deleted* 'giant' *which was interlined above deleted* 'rose' (C)

142.19 the oak, and] *interlined with a caret above deleted* 'the giant' (C)

142.19 rabbit] *interlined above deleted* 'weed.' (C)

142.21 an] *inserted* (C)

142.25 a babe.] *interlined above deleted* 'without power.' (C)

142.29 hiding] *preceded by deleted* 'once' (C)

142.30 sat] *preceded by deleted* 'had' (C)

142.30 playmates] 'e' *over illegible letter* (C)

142.31 ¹the] *interlined above deleted* 'p' (C)

EARLY DRAFT MANUSCRIPT

WORD DIVISION

1. *End-of-the-Line Hyphenation in the Virginia Edition*

[NOTE: No hyphenation of a possible compound at the end of a line in the Virginia text is present in the manuscript except for the following readings, which are hyphenated within the line in the manuscript. Hyphenated compounds in which both elements are capitalized are excluded.

145.3	blue-|clothed	175.1	battle-|blur
151.12	a-|fightin'	179.19	battle-|hymn

2. *End-of-the-Line Hyphenation in the Early Draft*

[NOTE: The following compounds, or possible compounds, are hyphenated at the end of the line in the manuscript. The form in which they have been transcribed in the Virginia text, listed below, represents the practice of the manuscript as ascertained by other appearances or parallels, or—failing that—by the known characteristics of Crane as seen in his other manuscripts.]

151.1	onct-git	156.23	well-meaning
152.19	self-confidence	160.16	head-long
153.26	cathedral-light		

3. *Special Cases*

[NOTE: In the following list the compound is hyphenated at the end of the line in both the manuscript and in the Virginia edition.]

154.21	pine-|needles (i.e.	155.20	Gun-|locks (i.e.
	pine-needles)		Gunlocks)

FULL COLLATION OF FINAL MANUSCRIPT
AND EARLY DRAFT

[Note: The word to the left of the bracket is the Virginia text reading and will agree with the manuscript except in cases where MS has been emended. If the word has been emended to a MS(d) reading, then the MS reading will be to the right of the bracket; if an emendation has been made on the authority of any of the other texts utilized for this edition, then both the MS and MS(d) readings will appear, each with its appropriate symbol. All variants have been recorded between the two texts, excepting those of dialect which constituted emendations, and where the concurrence of the uncorrected manuscript (MS[u]) and MS(d) was preferred over the corrected manuscript (MS[c]). A dagger preceding an entry indicates a complete agreement of MS(u) and MS(d); MS(u) is listed only when it disagrees with both MS(c) and MS(d). The capitalization or lack of it for *et seq.* and multiple readings refers only to the first line reference, and will be variously upper and lower case in subsequent places. First and last words for each MS(d) page are recorded so that the reader may have the most accurate information in the cases where a page of draft is wanting. In the draft there are instances where a sentence begins at the head of a page and it is not clear whether Crane intended a paragraph; these sentences have been transcribed as part of the preceding paragraph despite the fact that in the final manuscript the parallel sentences form new paragraphs. See entries at 9.5, 38.10, 56.27, 67.19, and 69.26.]

[*Page 1* MS(d) *wanting*]

3.20 come] *first word page 2* MS(d)
3.20 around] aroun' MS(d)
3.21 audience‸] ~ , MS(d)
3.22–23 blue-clothed] ~ ‸ ~ MS
3.23 between] in the little lane between MS(d)
3.24 squat‸] ~ , MS(d)
3.24–26 huts. . . . down.] huts. Here and there was a steelglitter. MS(d)
3.27 a . . . chimneys] barrel-chimneys MS(d)

†3.28–29 another private loudly] young Wilson MS(d)
3.31 an . . . him.] a personal affront. MS(d)
†4.3 *et seq. (except as noted in other entries)* The tall soldier] Conklin (*except* 10.24; 26.15,28; 33.18; 36.1 Jim Conklin) MS(d)
4.4 himself] *omit* MS(d)
†4.4 *et seq.* the loud one] young Wilson (*except* 11.7; 12.19 Wilson) MS(d)

†4.6   A corporal] Simpson, a corporal, MS(d)
4.6   before the assemblage] *omit*
MS(d)
4.7–8   During . . . spring] *omit*
MS(d)
†4.9   environment] environment
during the spring MS(d)
4.10   Of late] Lately MS(d)
4.11   camp.] camp. So, he and
his two mates had put in a
board-floor! And now the army
was going to move! MS(d)
4.12   spirited] *last word page 2*
MS(d)

[*Page* 3 MS(d) *wanting*]

4.34–35   other end, . . . fire-
place.] other end. MS(d); *first*
words page 4 MS(d)
4.36   wall] walls MS
4.37–38   Equipments . . . fire-
wood.] Some tin dishes lay on
a small pile of fire-wood.
Equipments were hung on
handy projections. MS(d)
4.38–5.1   A . . . shade.] *omit*
MS(d)
5.1–4   A . . . room.] The
smoke from the fire at times
neglected the clay-chimney
and wreathed into the room.
A small window shot an
oblique square of light upon
the cluttered floor. MS(d)
5.4–6   And . . . establishment.]
omit MS(d)
5.7   The . . . astonishment.]
omit MS(d)
5.7   So_∧] ~ , MS(d)
5.8   ∧ perhaps_∧] , ~ , MS(d)
5.9–10   For . . . believe. (*no* ¶)]
¶ He could not convince himself of it. It was too strange.
MS(d)
5.10   accept] believe MS(d)
5.11   an omen] *omit* MS(d)
5.11   about] at last MS(d)
5.13   of course] *omit* MS(d)
5.13   all of] all MS(d)

†5.13–14   vague and] vague,
MS(d)
5.15–17   He . . . prowess.] *omit*
MS(d)
5.17   ∧ awake_∧] , ~ , MS(d)
5.18   ∧ as . . . bygone_∧] , ~ ,
MS(d)
5.19   crowns] golden crowns
MS(d)
5.19   castles] dreary castles
MS(d)
†5.21   wars] war MS(d)
5.21   but_∧ it,] but, it, MS; but,
that, MS(d)
5.21   thought] had thought
MS(d)
5.21   been long] *omit* MS(d)
5.22   had] *omit* MS(d)
5.23   home_∧] ~ , MS(d)
5.23   upon] at MS(d)
5.24   some] a MS(d)
5.25–26   He . . . would] Greek-
like struggles could MS(d)
5.26–27   better, . . . timid.] better. MS(d)
5.28–29   instinct, . . . passions.]
instinct. MS(d)
5.30–35   Tales . . . deeds.] *omit*
MS(d)
5.36   ¶ But his] (*no* ¶) His MS(d)
5.36   ¹had] had, however, MS(d)
5.37–38   war-ardor and] *omit*
MS(d)
5.38–39   apparent difficulty] trouble at all, MS(d)
5.39   many hundreds of] nearly a
thousand MS(d)
6.1   vastly] *omit* MS(d)
6.2   She] And she MS(d)
6.2   ¹had_∧] ~ , MS
6.4–5   Besides . . . impregnable.]
omit MS(d)
6.6   however,] *omit* MS(d)
6.6   made firm rebellion] rebelled
MS(d)
6.9   in truth] truly MS(d)
6.9   finely] *omit* MS(d)
6.10   newspapers printed ac-
counts] country vibrated with
the noise MS(d)

6.11 decisive] great and decisive MS(d)
6.12 night,] ~ ∧ MS(d)
6.12 winds had] wind MS(d)
6.14 great] *omit* MS(d)
6.14–15 This . . . rejoicing] The voice calling MS(d)
6.15 night,] ~ ∧ MS(d)
6.16 Later,] ~ ∧ MS(d)
†6.17 going to] goin' t' MS(d)
6.19 then] *omit* MS(d)
6.19 face] head MS(d)
6.19 quilt. There] quilt and there MS(d)
6.21 morning,] ~ ∧ MS(d)
6.22 a company] one of the companies MS(d)
6.23 was] were MS(d)
6.24 waiting] patiently waiting MS(d)
6.25 her∧] ~ , MS(d)
6.26 There . . . silence.] *omit* MS(d)
6.27 finally] *omit* MS(d)
6.27 then] *omit* MS(d)
6.29 door-way] door MS(d)
6.29 soldier's] soldier MS(d)
6.30 with the] a MS(d)
6.30 expectancy] expectation MS(d)
6.31 eyes . . . bonds,] eyes, MS(d)
6.32 leaving] leave MS(d)
6.32 trails] hot trails MS; burning trails MS(d)
6.32 scarred] rough MS(d)
6.34 ¶ Still,] (*no* ¶) ~ ∧ MS(d)
6.34 whatever] *omit* MS(d)
6.35–38 He . . . plans.] To the contrary. MS(d)
6.39–7.7 Henry, an' . . . Henry. [¶] "I've] Henry, in this here fightin' business—you watch out an' take good keer a' yerself. I've MS(d)
7.7 knet] knit MS(d)
7.7 pair] pairs MS(d)
7.7 socks, Henry, and] socks an' MS(d); MS(u) *read* 'an' '
†7.8,27 because] b'cause MS(d)
†7.8 to] t' MS(d)

†7.8,13,15,16(*twice*) and] an' MS(d)
7.9 comf'able] comf'table MS(d)
7.9 Whenever∧] ~ , MS(d)
†7.10(*twice*) to] t' MS(d)
7.11 dern] darn MS(d)
7.12 ¶ An'] *no* ¶ MS(d)
7.12 careful] keerful, Henry, MS(d); MS(u) *read* 'keerful'
†7.13,14 the] th' MS(d)
7.13 army, Henry.] army. MS(d)
†7.13 The] Th' MS(d)
†7.14 nothing] nothin' MS(d)
†7.14 leading] leadin' MS(d)
†7.14 feller] fellah MS(d)
7.15 you—] ~ , MS(d)
7.16 mother—] ~ ; MS(d)
7.16 and a-learning 'im to] an' learnin' him t' MS(d); an' a-learnin' ∧im t' MS(u)
7.16–17 Keep . . . Henry.] *omit* MS(d)
†7.17 to ever] t' ever MS(d)
7.18 'shamed to] ∧shamed to MS; ashamed t' MS(d); ∧shamed t' MS(u)
7.18–19 about. . . . If] about an' if MS(d)
7.19–20 that . . . allus] right t' that MS(d)
7.20 about right.] pretty straight. MS(d)
7.20.1 [*Omit* Va.—cf. p. 296] Young fellers in the army get awful careless in their ways, Henry. They're away f'm home and they don't have nobody to look after 'em. I'm 'feard fer yeh about that. Yeh aint never been used to doing fer yerself. So yeh must keep writing to me how yer clothes are lasting.] Young fellers in th' [†] army git [†] mighty keerless [†] in their ways, bein' away from home, an' I'm afeard for yeh 'bout [†] that Henry.
7.21 ¶ "Yeh must allus] (*no* ¶) Yeh mus' MS(d)

7.21   too, child] chil' MS(d)

†7.22   of] a' MS(d)

7.22   and seldom] nor never MS(d)

7.24   ¶ 'I] no ¶ MS(d)

†7.24,26   to] t' MS(d)

†7.24   excepting] exceptin' MS(d)

7.25   must] mustn't MS(d)

†7.25   shirking] shirkin' MS(d)

7.25   child] Henry MS(d); MS has 'Hen' deleted before 'child'

†7.27   anything] anythin' MS(d)

7.27   'cept] excepts MS(d)

7.28–29   and . . . all] omit MS(d)

7.29.1   [Omit Va.—cf. p. 296] Don't fergit to send yer socks to me the minute they git holes in 'em and here's a little bible I want yeh to take along with yeh, Henry. I dont presume yeh'll be a-setting reading it all day long, child, ner nothin' like that. Many a time, yeh'll fergit yeh got it, I don't doubt. But there'll be many a time, too, Henry, when yeh'll be wanting advice, boy, and all like that, and there'll be nobody round, perhaps, to tell yeh things. Then if yeh take it out, boy, yeh'll find wisdom in it—wisdom in it, Henry—with little or no searching.] Don't ferget t' [†] send yer socks t' [†] me th' [†] minute they git holes in 'em, an' [†] here's a little bible I want yeh t' [†] take along with yeh, Henry. I don't expect yeh'll be a-settin' [†] readin' [†] it all day long, child, ner nothin' like that. Many times yeh'll fergit yeh got it, I don't doubt. But there's many times, Henry, yeh'll be wantin' [†] advice, Henry, an' [†] all like that, an' [†] there'll be nobody 'round, perhaps, t' [†] show yeh. Then if yeh take it out, yeh'll find wisdom t' set yeh

straight with little searchin' [†], Henry. MS(d)

7.30   the socks . . . child,] th' socks, MS(d); MS(u) read 'th' socks'

†7.30   ²and] an' MS(d)

7.31   a cup of] some MS(d)

7.31   bundle] things MS(d)

7.31   because] 'cause MS(d); b'cause MS(u)

7.32   things] omit MS(d)

7.32   Henry. . . . and] Henry, an' MS(d); MS(u) read 'an' '

7.34–35   ¹of . . . speech.] born this speech with impatience. MS(d)

7.35   had not been] was not MS(d)

7.35   expected] had expected, MS(d[c])

7.35–8.3   ²he . . . purposes.] it had made him feel sheepish. He had felt glad that no one of his friends had been there to listen to it. MS(d); MS has the following deleted passage: '. . . irritation. He had felt glad that none of his associates in the new company had been near to over-hear [deleted] listen to it. He . . .'

†8.5   schoolmates] old schoolmates MS(d)

8.5–10   They . . . strutted.] omit MS(d)

8.11   ¶ A] (no ¶) There, a MS(d)

8.11   fun] efforts to poke fun MS(d)

8.12   martial-spirit but] martial spirit. But MS(d)

8.12–13   and darker . . . grew] girl who, he thought, had become MS(d)

8.15   path] aisle MS(d)

8.15   oaks,] oaks on the lawn, MS(d)

8.15–16   turned . . . window] discovered her MS(d)

8.16   departure] departure from a window MS(d)

8.16   perceived] had turned and

MS(d); *last words page* 8
MS(d)

[*Page* 9 MS(d) *wanting*]

9.5   ¶ The] ¶ (*doubtful*) The
MS(d); *first word page* 10
MS(d)

9.5   some] the MS(d)

9.5   along] on MS(d)

9.7   reflectively] thoughtfully
MS(d)

9.7   blue] opposite MS(d)

9.7–9   pickets.   When . . . permission.] pickets but usually
seemed sorry for it afterwards.
MS(d)

9.10   night,] ~ ∧ MS(d)

9.10   conversed] had talked
MS(d)

9.10   stream] river MS(d)

9.11–13   who . . . assurance.]
with a fund of sublime assurance. MS(d)

9.14–16   "Yank . . . war.]   *omit*
MS(d)

9.17   him] Fleming MS

9.18   with relentless curses] cursing relentlessly MS(d)

9.21   eternally-hungry] ~ ∧ ~
MS(d)

9.22   powder] rifles MS(d)

9.22–24   "They'll . . . told.]
omit MS(d)

9.24   ¹the] their MS(d)

9.24   red, live] red MS(d)

9.26   ¶ Still,] ¶ ~ ∧ MS; (*no* ¶)
~ , MS(d)

9.26   veterans'] veteran's MS;
omit MS(d)

9.27   their] the veteran's MS(d)

9.27   fire∧] ~ , MS

9.28–30   They . . . trusted.]
omit MS(d)

9.31   now] *omit* MS(d)

9.32–33   fight, . . . disputed.]
fight. MS(d)

9.34   pondering upon it.] debating
the question. MS(d)

9.34–35   mathematically . . .
battle.] solve it mathematically. He was endeavoring to

decide wether he would run
from a fight or not. MS(d)

9.36   Previously,] It had suddenly
come to his mind that perhaps
in a battle he might run. He
was forced to admit that as
far as war was concerned he
knew nothing of himself. Before this, MS(d), *see* 10.1–4

9.36   felt] been MS(d)

9.36   wrestle] grapple MS(d)

9.37   this] the MS(d)

9.37   In his life, he] He MS(d)

9.38   never . . . in] even as in
thoughts about his life, he had
never had doubts of the MS(d)

9.38   success] success of it MS(d)

9.39   bothering] had bothered
MS(d)

9.39   But here he (*no* ¶)] ¶ But
he MS(d)

9.39–10.1   confronted . . . moment.] now suddenly con-
fronted. MS(d)

10.1–4   It . . . himself.]   MS(d)
sets at 9.36

10.1–2   appeared to him] come to
his mind MS(d)

10.5–8   A . . . mind.]   *omit*
MS(d)

10.12   but,] ~ ∧ MS(d)

10.14   the] his MS(d)

10.14–15   to and fro.] up and
down the floor. MS(d)

10.15,22   Lord] Gawd MS(d)

10.15   said aloud.] cried to himself. MS(d)

10.16   in this crisis] *omit* MS(d)

10.17   here of no avail.] now of
no consequence. MS(d)

10.18   He saw that he] He MS(d)

10.19   experiment∧] ~ , MS(d)

10.19–21   youth. . . . close]
youth, and get MS(d)

10.21   guard∧ lest] guard, else
MS(d)

10.22   should] might MS(d)

†10.25 *et seq.*   The loud private]
Young Wilson MS(d)

10.26   the tall soldier] Conklin

waving his hand impressively
MS(d)

10.26–27 He . . . expressively.]
omit MS(d)

10.30 His . . . grunted] Young
Wilson grumbled MS(d);
MS(u) *read* 'Young Wilson'

10.30–31 For . . . said:] *omit*
MS(d)

10.33 retorted the other] replied
Conklin MS(d); MS(u) *read*
'Conklin'

10.34–35 He . . . knapsack.]
~ . . . knap-sack. MS; He
dumped the contents of his
knapsack out upon floor and
then began to stow the things
skilfully in again. MS(d)

10.36 The youth, . . . walk,]
Fleming MS(d)

†10.37 Going to] Goin' t' MS(d)

10.38 there is] *omit* MS(d)

10.38 replied] said MS(d)

10.38–11.1 course there is.]
course! MS(d)

11.1,2 Yeh] You MS

11.1,4 yeh'll] you'll MS

11.1 one of] *omit* MS(d)

11.2 battles] battle MS(d)

†11.3 *et seq.* (*except as noted in
other entries*) the youth]
Fleming MS(d)

11.4 what'll] what'ill MS(d)

11.4–5 out-an'-out] *omit* MS(d)

11.8 this story'll] this here story
will MS(d)

†11.9 just] jest MS(d)

11.10 exasperated.] with exasperation. MS(d)

11.10–11 Not . . . th'] ~ . . .
the MS; Th' MS(d)

11.11 start] started MS(d)

11.11–13 mornin'? . . . continued.] morning? . . . ~ MS;
morning, they say. MS(d)

11.13 "They] ₐ~ MS(d)

11.14 any] no MS(d)

11.14–15 They're . . . that.]
omit MS(d)

11.16 A feller what] I MS(d)

11.17 told . . . ago] *omit*
MS(d)

11.17 An'ₐ] Andₐ MS; Besides,
MS(d)

11.20 remained] was MS(d)

11.20 lastₐ] ~, MS(d)

†11.23 do you] d' yeh MS(d)

†11.23 the] th' MS(d)

†11.24 onct] once MS(d)

†11.25,32; 12.6 the other] Conklin
MS(d)

11.25 cold . . . made] *omit*
MS(d)

11.26 heaps 'a] ~ of MS; more
or less MS(d)

11.26 poked at] made of MS(d)

11.26 'emₐ] ~ , MS(d)

11.27 all right] good enough
MS(d)

11.29 of the boys'll] th' boys'll
MS(d)

11.31 every] ev'ry MS(d)

11.33 kit-an'-boodle] ~ -and- ~
MS; kitₐan'ₐboodle MS(d)

11.33–34 if . . . -off,] *omit*
MS(d)

11.34 stay] stand MS(d)

11.35 But . . . nothin'.] ~ . . .
nothing. MS; Yeh can't tell.
MS(d)

11.35 courseₐ] ~ , MS(d)

11.37 th' first time] the ~ ~ MS;
omit MS(d)

11.37 I think] *omit* MS(d)

11.37 some,] ~ ₐ MS(d)

†11.38 worser] worse MS

11.38–12.2 They . . . 'a 'em'll]
~ . . . of ~ MS; Most of th'
boys'll MS(d)

12.2 -shootin'] -a-shootin' MS(d)

†12.4 *et seq.* the loud soldier]
Wilson MS(d)

12.6 savagely] wrathfully MS(d)

12.6–8 had . . . epithets.] called
each other names. MS(d)

12.9 at last] *omit* MS(d)

†12.9(*twice*) you] yeh MS(d)

†12.10 yourself] yerself MS(d)

12.10 sentenceₐ] ~, MS(d)

12.11–12 The . . . giggled.]
omit MS(d)

†12.13 The tall private] Conklin MS(d)

12.16–17 An' . . . mistake.] And . . . ~ MS; *omit* MS(d)

12.17 everybody] e'rybody MS(d)

12.18 why,] why, then, MS(d)

12.18 B'jiminy] Bejiminy MS; By jiminy MS(d)

12.20–22 The . . . confidence.] *omit* MS(d)

12.22–23 He . . . re-assured.] These words of Conklin in a measure re-assured Fleming. MS(d)

13.1 The . . . discovered] Fleming was not at all relieved when he found MS(d)

13.1–2 his tall comrade] Jim Conklin MS(d); Conklin MS(u)

13.3–10 There . . . prolongation] *omit* MS(d)

13.10–11 himself. Now,] himself. He stood confronting the possibilities and MS(d)

13.11 new-born] ~ ∧ ~ MS(d)

13.11 mind∧] ~ , MS(d)

13.13 For . . . made] He kept up MS(d)

13.13 calculations, but they] calculations. They MS(d)

13.13 all] *omit* MS(d)

13.14 found that he] *omit* MS(d)

13.15–16 He . . . was] He was anxious to prove beyond a doubt that he would not be afraid. He wished MS(d)

13.17–20 He . . . other.] *omit* MS(d)

13.20 So,] ~ ∧ MS(d)

13.22 Meanwhile, . . . measure] He was continually measuring MS(d)

13.23 gave . . . assurance] re-assured him MS(d)

13.24 This man's] The former's MS(d)

†13.24 dealt] gave MS(d)

13.24 a measure of] some MS(d)

13.25 for] because MS(d)

13.26 knowledge∧] ~ , MS(d)

13.26 ²he] Conklin MS(d)

†13.27–28 that his comrade] Conklin MS(d)

13.29 peace and obscurity] obscurity in peace MS(d)

13.29–30 but, in reality,] ~ ∧ ~ ~ ∧ MS(d)

13.31 The youth] He MS(d); MS(u) *read* 'Fleming'

†13.31 another] another man MS (d)

14.2 joy] great relief MS(d)

14.3 fathom] *last word page* 15 MS(d)

[*Pages* 16–21 MS(d) *wanting*]

19.14 sprightly,] *first word page* 22 MS(d)

19.14 fiery] and fiery MS(d)

19.14 belief in] desire for MS(d)

19.15 clear,] ~ ∧ MS(d)

19.15–18 And . . . dregs.] *omit* MS(d)

19.18 Oh, you're] You're MS(d)

†19.18–19,29 going to] goin' t' MS(d)

19.19 suppose."] s'pose." MS; s'pose?" said Fleming. MS(d)

19.20 thoughtful] dignified MS (d)

19.20–21 from his pipe] into the air MS(d)

19.21 remarked with dignity.] remarked, thoughtfully, MS(d)

19.22 try∧] try t', MS(d)

19.23–24 He . . . statement.] *omit* MS(d)

†19.25 do you] d'yeh MS(d)

†19.25 you] yeh MS(d)

†19.25,29 the] th' MS(d)

19.25 comes?] ~ , MS(d)

19.27(*twice*) "Run?] " '~'? MS(d)

19.27 He laughed.] *omit* MS(d)

19.28 a-'nough] 'nough MS(d)

19.29 before the] 'fore th' MS(d); MS(u) *read* 'th' '

19.31 Oh, . . . s'pose] Oh, well, that's all true enough MS(d)

19.31 replied the other] said Wilson with great assurance MS(d)

19.33 money,] ~ ∧ MS(d)

19.33 nodded confidently.] wagged his head with much self-confidence. MS(d)

†19.34,35 You] Yeh MS(d)

†19.34 ²the] th' MS(d)

†19.35 the] th' MS(d)

19.36 exclaimed the loud soldier indignantly.] ~ ~ blatant ~ ~. MS; replied Wilson, savagely, MS(d); MS(u) *read* 'Wilson'

19.39–20.1 Who . . . Bonypart.] ~ . . . Boneparte. MS; *omit* MS(d)

20.1 glared] glared angrily MS(d)

20.2 then strode away.] then arose and strode away with an air of offended pride. MS(d)

20.3–5 The . . . reply.] *omit* MS(d)

20.6 He] Fleming MS(d)

†20.6 his injured comrade] the injured Wilson MS(d)

20.6–7 had disappeared] retired MS(d)

20.7–8 His . . . before. No] His confidence in the success of the army was as strong as any, but no MS(d)

20.10 He . . . out-cast.] The valiant Wilson made him more miserable than before.

†20.11 slowly to] to MS(d)

20.11 himself] out MS(d)

20.11–12 blanket. . . . he] blanket. He could hear serene voices [†]. "I'll bid five." "Make it six." "Seven!" "Seven goes." [¶] He MS(d), *see* 31.5–6

20.15–19 He . . . thoughts,] *omit* MS(d)

20.19–21 he . . . goes."] MS(d) *sets at* 30.22–23

†20.22 ¶ He] (*no* ¶) He MS(d)

20.23 until∧] ~ , MS(d)

20.23–24 the . . . suffering] viewing the pictures that thronged upon his mental vision MS(d)

20.24 asleep.] *last word page* 23 MS(d)

[*Pages* 24–27 MS(d) *wanting*]

24.38 stupids.] *first word page* 28 MS(d)

24.38 swallow] encompass them and swallow MS(d); encompass and swallow MS(u)

25.1–2 him, . . . death.] him∧ as if hunted. MS(d)

25.5–6 come . . . dangers.] be so. And he was sure it would be so. MS(d)

25.6 generals] general MS(d)

25.7 There . . . corps.] *omit* MS(d)

25.9 came to] were at MS(d)

25.10 line,] ~ ∧ MS(d)

25.10 ground,] ~ ∧ MS(d)

25.12 saw,] ~ ∧ MS(d)

25.14 One or two] Some MS(d)

25.14 over-valiant airs] an over-valiant air MS(d)

25.15 walked] went MS(d)

25.17–19 They . . . march.] *omit* MS(d)

25.21 the men] they MS(d)

25.21 fear,] ~ ∧ MS(d)

25.22 warning.] oration. MS(d)

25.22 and∧ if practicable∧] ~ , ~ ~ , MS(d)

25.25 assumed, then,] assumed MS(d)

25.26–33 He . . . brute.] *omit* MS(d)

25.34 After a time] Presently MS(d)

25.37 Sometimes . . . compact.] *omit* MS(d)

25.38–26.1 During . . . them.] Each front-rank man began erecting a tiny hill in front of him. MS(d)

†26.1 sticks,] *omit* MS(d)

26.2 might] would MS(d)

26.5–10 This . . . terriers.] *omit* MS(d)

26.10 time,] ~ ∧ MS

26.11–12 Directly∧ however∧] ~ , ~ , MS(d)

26.12　were ordered] received orders MS(d)

†26.15　for] fer MS(d)

26.16　heavy] ponderous MS(d)

26.16–18　explanation . . . skill.] explanation. Fleming scoffed at him. MS(d)

26.19　regiment] brigade MS(d)

26.19　position,] ∼ ∧ MS

26.20　regard] care MS(d)

26.20–22　line . . . also.] barricade to be created. They were moved from this one also. They ate their noon meal behind a third one MS(d)

26.22　marched] marched about MS(d)

26.24–26　The . . . him.] *omit* MS(d)

26.26　He . . . impatience.] Fleming grew feverishly impatient. MS(d)

26.30　wear] jest wear MS(d)

†26.30　out . . . for] out'r legs fer MS(d)

26.30–34　He . . . intolerable.] *omit* MS(d)

26.36　swallowed it] engulfed MS(d)

26.37　around] aroun' MS(d)

26.38　¹or∧] ∼ , MS(d)

†26.39　the loud soldier.] 'Wilson.' (*last word page* 29)MS(d)

[Pages 30–35 MS(d) *wanting. MS pages* 41–44 *wanting. Reading to left of bracket is* A1, *except where emended to* MS(d), *through* 31.3–4.]

30.13–14　scattered] *first word page* 36 MS(d)

30.15　storm-banshee] ∼ ∧ ∼ A1

30.16　grove∧ and, exploding redly,] ∼ , ∼ ∧ ∼ ∼ ∧ A1

30.17　pine-needles] ∼∧∼ A1

30.18　whistle . . . and] *omit* MS(d)

30.19–21　Twigs . . . dodging] The men of the reserved brigade crouched behind their various protections and peered toward the front. Some kept continually dodging MS(d)

30.21　heads.] heads as if assailed by snow-balls. MS(d)

30.22　The lieutenant . . . company] An officer of Fleming's regiment MS(d)

30.26　tack-hammer] ∼ ∧ ∼ A1

30.27　carefully] *omit* MS(d)

30.28–32　trousers. . . .done.] trousers, while another bound it awkwardly with a handkerchief. MS(d)

30.33　battle-flag] ∼ ∧ ∼ A1

30.33　madly] wrathfully MS(d)

30.36　Men, running swiftly,] ∼ ∧ ∼ ∼ ∧ A1

30.37　command] cammand MS(d)

30.38　Its] It's MS(d)

30.38　²as . . . was] was like MS(d)

30.40　¶ Wild] *no* ¶ MS(d)

30.40　walls] veil MS(d)

31.1　grey] gray A1

31.1　mob-like] moblike A1

31.2　wild-horses] ∼ ∧ ∼ A1

31.3–4　immediately] *omit* MS(d)

31.4　of the] *last words page* 36 MS(d)

[*Pages* 37–38 MS(d) *wanting*]

33.1　There] *first word page* 39 MS(d)

33.2–3　circus-parade] ∼ ∧ ∼ MS(d)

33.3　on . . . spring] *omit* MS(d)

33.4　stood,] ∼ ∧ MS(d)

33.4–5　dingy . . . chariot.] band or the dingy lady upon the white horse. MS(d)

33.7　particularly] *omit* MS(d)

33.8　despise] dispise MS

33.9–11　A . . . prominence.] *omit* MS(d)

33.12　come!"] ∼ ." MS(d)

33.13　rustling] a rustling MS(d)

33.14　every possible cartridge] all their munitions MS(d)

33.15 The boxes] Cartridge-boxes MS(d)
33.15–16 pulled . . . and] *omit* MS(d)
33.17 on.] on. Gun-locks clicked. MS(d); on. [¶] Gun-locks clicked. MS(u)
33.18 soldier₍] Conklin, MS(d)
†33.18 his rifle] himself MS(d)
33.19 of some kind] *omit* MS(d)
33.19 it] it accurately MS(d)
33.20 throat, . . . position,] throat₍ MS(d)
33.21 line . . . sound.] line: MS(d); line. MS(u)
†33.22 Gun-locks clicked.] MS(d) *sets at* 33.17
33.23 swarm] bunch MS(d)
33.25 flag₍ . . . forward₍] ~ , . . . ~ , MS(d)
33.27–28 momentarily . . . a] suddenly smitten with the MS(d)
33.28 gun] rifle MS(d)
33.28–30 He . . . not.] *omit* MS(d)
34.1 other's] latter's MS(d)
†34.2,3 to] t' MS(d)
34.4 r-right] right MS(d)
34.5 all . . . Gawd. We-] we- MS(d)
34.5–6 d-d-do—do] d-do MS(d)
34.6 best, general."] our b-best." MS(d)
34.7 colonel,] ~ ₍ MS
34.7–8 to . . . parrot.] as a woman releaves her feelings with tears, began to swear sweepingly. MS(d)
34.8 The youth₍] Fleming, MS(d) ; Flem₍ MS(u)
34.9 commander] cammander MS; cursing cammander MS(d)
34.10 men] regiment MS(d)
34.10 highly] very MS(d)
34.10–11 as . . . them] *omit* MS(d)
34.13 it,] ~ ₍ MS(d)
34.13 ²Oh, we're] We're MS(d)
34.14 company] campany MS(d)

34.15–17 rear. . . . repetition.] rear and had harangued like a school-mistress: MS(d)
34.17 don't] dont MS
34.18 get] git MS(d)
34.19 fools——"] fools." MS(d)
34.21 weeping] crying MS(d)
34.22 coat-sleeve] ~ ₍ ~ MS(d)
34.22–23 His . . . open.] *omit* MS(d)
34.24 the one] a swift MS(d)
34.25–26 and₍ instantly₍ . . . Before] and, instantly, before MS(d)
34.26 ready] quite ready MS(d)
34.28 first₍ wild] ~ , ~ MS(d)
34.29 he] *last word page* 40 MS(d)

[*Page* 41 MS(d) *wanting*]

35.19 Following] *first word page* 42 MS(d)
†35.21 mad] furious MS(d)
35.21 rifle which] weapon that MS(d)
35.22 be . . . life] kill one man MS(d)
35.23 fingers] hands MS(d)
35.24 world-sweeping] mad, world-sweeping MS(d)
35.27 directed not] not directed MS(d)
35.29 him,] ~ ₍ MS(d)
35.31 frantically] madly MS(d)
35.31 for his senses] *omit* MS(d)
35.34 intentness₍] ~ , MS(d)
35.34–35 Many . . . subdued] Nearly every man was making a noise with his mouth. The MS(d)
35.36 prayers] wailings MS(d)
35.37–38 that . . . -march] *omit* MS(d)
35.39–36.1 babbling. . . . babe.] babbling like an infant. MS(d)
36.3 Of a sudden₍] Suddenly, MS(d)
36.4 hat. "Well,] hat: "Well, then, MS(d)

36.5 think——"] *last word page*
42 MS(d)

[*Pages* 43–44 MS(d) *wanting*]

38.10 ¶ A] ¶ *doubtful* MS(d);
first word page 45 MS(d)
38.10 were] was MS(d)
38.11 was a] was like a MS(d)
38.12 brigade] regiment MS(d)
†38.13 to the left] left MS(d)
†38.14 he thought] *omit* MS(d)
38.15 forest] woods MS(d)
38.15 suggestive of unnumbered]
vaguely suggestive of untold
MS(d)
†38.19 cheerings] cheering MS(d)
38.20 slowly . . . leaves]
steadily up MS(d)
38.21 ¶ Batteries] *no* ¶ MS(d)
38.23 warm] brilliant MS(d)
38.23 lines of] *omit* MS(d)
38.26 deep,] ∼ ∧ MS(d)
38.27 left,] right∧ MS(d)
38.28 him] Fleming MS(d)
38.29 too,] ∼ ∧ MS(d)
38.30 Heretofore,] ∼ ∧ MS(d)
38.30 all] *omit* MS(d)
38.33 blue,] ∼ ∧ MS
38.35 on] *omit* MS(d)
39.4 before seen himself] seen
himself before MS(d)
39.6 and, kneeling, re-laced] and
kneeling down laced MS(d);
∼ , ∼ , laced up MS(u)
39.8–10 over at . . . vanquished. [¶] He] over. He
MS(d)
39.12 last] late MS(d)
39.15 far] being far MS(d)
†39.16 in] with MS(d)
39.17 ¶ Upon . . . good-will.
"Gee] (*no* ¶) He beamed good-
will and tenderness on his fellows. [¶] "Gee MS(d)
39.18 hey] eh MS(d)
39.20 other,] ∼ ∧ MS(d)
39.22 Gee, yes! An'] *omit* MS(d)
39.28 But, of] Of MS(d)
39.30–31 The . . . Gosh!"] *omit*
MS(d)
40.1 upon] on MS(d)

†40.1 discerned] saw MS(d)
40.4–6 The shells, . . . be] Too,
shells exploded in the grass
and among the foliage. They
were MS(d)
†40.6 war-flowers] war-blossoms
MS(d)
40.8 groaned. The] groaned. The
slaves toiling in the temple of
war felt a sudden rebellion.
The MS(d)
†40.8 faded] had faded MS(d)
40.9 now] *omit* MS(d)
40.11–12 The . . . tasks.] *omit*
MS(d), *see* 40.8
40.13 They . . . each.] Some began to fret and complain.
MS(d)
40.14 can't] cant MS
40.14 supports.] ∼? MS(d)
40.16 damn'] ∼ ∧ MS(d)
40.18–22 The . . . happen.]
omit MS(d)
40.22 He] Fleming MS(d)
40.22–24 as . . . mistake.]
gingerly. It was as if he expected a cold plunge. MS(d)
40.25 But the] The MS(d)
40.25 on . . . line] *omit* MS(d)
40.26 along] along the line
MS(d)
40.27–28 in . . . wind] *omit*
MS(d)
40.28 rolled] rolled away toward
the rear going MS(d)
40.29–32 The . . . resplendent.]
The flag was often eaten and
lost in the great clouds that
were tinged with an earthlike
yellow in the sun-rays, and
changed to a sorry blue in the
shadows. MS(d)
40.33 Into . . . look] Fleming's
eyes had a look in them MS(d)
40.34–35 His . . . the] The
MS(d)
40.36 was] were MS(d)
41.3 damn'] damned MS ; damn∧
MS(d)
41.4 skill,] ∼ ∧ MS(d)
41.5–7 Himself∧ . . . steel.]

They must be steel machines. Himself, reeling from nervous exhaustion, he could not understand such persistency. MS(d)

41.7–8 It . . . sun-down.] *omit* MS(d)

41.9 slowly] mechanically MS(d)

41.9 and$_\wedge$] ~ , MS(d)

41.10 field$_\wedge$] ~ , MS(d)

41.10 blazed] fired a shot MS(d)

41.11 peer] gaze MS(d)

41.13 like . . . yelling.] and yelling like pursued imps. MS(d)

41.14 the youth] him MS(d)

†41.14 redoubtable] *omit* MS(d)

41.20 dropped it] *omit* MS

41.22 was, at an instant,] was MS(d)

41.32 great] *omit* MS(d)

41.35–36 ^{2}His . . . wind.] *omit* MS(d[c]); MS(d[u]) *read* 'His unbuttoned coat streamed out.'

41.36 wildly and his] wildly. His MS(d)

41.37 canteen, . . . behind.] canteen swung out behind him. MS(d)

41.38 all the] a reflected MS(d)

41.39–42.4 ^{1}The . . . occasion.] *omit* MS(d)

42.5 times$_\wedge$] ~ , MS(d)

42.5–6 down. Once] down and once MS(d)

42.8–9 ¶ Since . . . Death] (*no* ¶) He felt that death was ever MS(d)

42.10–15 shoulder-blades . . . [¶] As he] shoulder blades. [¶] He MS(d)

42.15 on, he mingled] on mingling MS(d)

42.15 dimly] vaguely MS(d)

42.16 footsteps] foot-steps MS(d)

42.17–18 fleeing, . . . crashes.] running. Ominous noises were following. MS(d)

42.19 In . . . the] The MS(d)

42.19 these . . . footsteps] the footsteps behind him MS(d)

42.20 his one] a certain MS(d)

42.20–22 He . . . for] The first clutchings of MS(d)

42.22 be, then, those] be of the men MS(d)

42.23 So he] He MS(d)

42.23 an insane] a MS(d)

42.25–26 As . . . hurtled] Shells were hurtling MS(d)

42.26–27 head . . . ^{2}he] head. He MS(d)

42.28 cruel] vindictively grinning MS(d)

42.28–31 teeth . . . bushes.] teeth turned toward him as they passed. MS(d)

42.32–33 when . . . action.] as he passed the battery in the field back of the grove. MS(d)

42.33–36 The . . . shooting.] The artillerymen were going swiftly about their tasks. MS(d)

43.1–2 coolly . . . eyes] cool save for their eyes which were lifted MS(d)

43.2 to the] toward a MS(d)

43.3 the] a MS(d)

43.4–8 The . . . [¶] The face] Staying to be eaten up! The face MS(d)

43.9 an] the MS(d)

43.10 that] *omit* MS(d)

43.12–13 Too . . . row.] *omit* MS(d)

43.15 upon . . . hill] into some bushes MS(d)

43.15 it$_\wedge$] ~ , MS(d)

43.17 the] *omit* MS(d)

†43.21 manner] kind MS(d)

43.21 anyhow.] ~ ? MS(d)

43.22 didn't] didnt MS

43.22 comprehend] know MS(d)

43.23 A] Some MS(d)

43.23 caused] had caused MS(d)

43.24 made] was making MS(d)

43.25 went swinging] dashed MS(d)

43.26 cannon] guns MS(d)

43.27–28 ground∧ . . . grum-
bled] ground, grumbled and
grunted MS(d)

43.28 men, . . . hurry.] men
unduly hurried. MS(d)

43.29–30 The . . . noises.]
Fleming ran on. MS(d)

43.31 Later,] ∼ ∧ MS(d)

43.34 man, astride,] ∼ ∧ ∼ ∧
MS(d)

43.36 Sometimes∧] ∼ , MS(d)

43.38 to be] *omit* MS(d)

44.1 this] the MS(d)

44.2 dared,] ∼ ∧ MS

44.2 Perhaps∧] Perhaps, too,
MS(d)

44.3 chaos,] ∼ ∧ MS

44.4 concerning] about MS(d)

44.4 surety,] ∼ ∧ MS

44.7 general, or, at least,] ∼ ∧
∼ ∧ ∼ ∼ ∧ MS(d)

44.8 approach] approach him
MS(d)

44.9 was] seemed MS(d)

44.10–11 He . . . him.] *omit*
MS(d)

44.12 warily moved about] went
warily nearer MS(d)

†44.13 t'] to MS(d)

44.14 an . . . hurry] a thunderin' sweat MS(d)

44.14 th'] the MS(d)

44.15 woods—tell] woods. Tell
MS(d)

44.15 say] tell him MS(d)

44.16 centre'll] centre'ill MS(d)

44.16 don't . . . some] *omit*
MS(d)

44.18–21 A . . . dust.] *omit*
MS(d)

44.24 "Yes . . . forward.] "Yes
—no—yes." MS(d)

†44.25 a-flame] aflame MS(d)

44.25 excitement] eagerness
MS(d); MS(u) *read* 'eag'

44.25 Yes, by heavens,] ∼ , ∼
Heavens, MS; Yes—by Gawd—
MS(d)

44.26 They've] They MS(d)

44.26 'em!] 'im. MS; 'im! MS(d)

44.27 "We'll (*no*¶)] ¶ MS(d)

44.27 'em∧] 'im∧ MS; 'em, MS(d)

44.27,28 now.] ∼ ! MS(d)

44.28 ¹'em] 'im MS

44.28 'em sure."] 'em!" MS(d)

44.28 He] Then he MS(d)

44.30–31 everlastingly . . . anything."] everlastingly go in—go
in like eternal damnation."
MS(d)

44.32–35 As . . . heavens."] ∼
. . . Heavens." MS; *omit*
MS(d)

44.36 excitement] flurry of excitement MS(d)

44.36 plunge∧] ∼ , MS(d)

45.2 The] That MS(d)

45.3 cheering] the cheering
MS(d)

45.5 yellow fog] vast yellow
cloud MS(d)

45.6 Hoarse cries] The hoarse
cheers MS(d); MS(u) *read*
'cheers'

45.8 amazed] sulky MS(d)

45.10 approached] was approaching MS(d)

45.11 a good] his MS(d)

45.14 fit] put MS(d)

45.15 none of the] no MS(d)

45.17 where] were MS(d)

45.17 be the army?] the army
be? MS(d)

45.17 plain] very plain MS(d)

45.19–20 had been] were MS(d)

45.20 They . . . legs.] *omit*
MS(d)

45.21 Thoughts] He thought
MS(d)

45.21 came to him] *omit* MS(d)

45.21–22 The . . . won.] They
had staid and won. MS(d)

45.22 He . . . it.] *omit* MS(d)

45.24 over-turned] overturned
MS

45.25–26 the . . . deliberation]
a position that a little thought
MS(d); MS(u) *read* 'a position, that'

45.26 that it was] to be MS(d)

45.27 man . . . dark] *omit*
MS(d)

45.28 perceptions and] *omit* MS(d)

45.29 comrades.] *last word page* 53 MS(d)

[*Page* 54 MS(d) *wanting*]

46.24 arms] *first word page* 55 MS(d)

46.25 noisy . . . should] voices and noisy motions would MS(d)

46.26 So, he (*no* ¶)] ¶ He MS(d)

46.27 ¶ After . . . of] (*no* ¶) The MS(d)

46.28 The (*no* ¶)] ¶ MS(d)

46.30 wood-pecker] woodpecker MS(d)

46.31 impudent] insolent MS(d)

46.33 Off,] ~ ∧ MS(d)

46.35 A . . . life.] *omit* MS(d)

46.39 jovial] jovial and pot-valiant MS(d)

†46.39 he] it MS(d)

47.1–4 High . . . exhibition.] *omit* MS(d)

47.5 said] thought MS(d)

47.5–11 The . . . race.] *omit* MS(d)

47.12 The youth] He MS(d)

47.12 wended,] ~ ∧ MS(d)

47.12 was . . . She] agreed with him. It MS(d)

†47.15 Once he] He MS(d)

47.15 swamp.] swamp once. MS(d); MS(u) *read* 'swamp on [*unfinished*]'

47.16 upon] on MS(d)

47.17 at one time] once MS(d)

47.17 ²at] on MS(d)

47.19 gleaming] silver-gleaming MS(d)

47.20 ¶ The . . . into] (*no* ¶) Presently, he was again in MS(d)

47.21–22 He walked (*no* ¶)] ¶ He went MS(d)

47.22 into] to MS(d)

47.33 shade of] *omit* MS(d)

47.38–39 was, for moments,] was for an instant MS(d)

48.1–2 The . . . look.] *omit* MS(d)

48.2 the youth] he MS(d)

†48.3 brought it against] touched MS(d)

48.3–4 this, he retreated,] ~ ∧ ~ ~ ∧ MS(d)

48.4 step,] ~ ∧ MS(d)

48.5 feared,∧] ~ , MS

48.5 body] thing MS(d)

48.9 with it all] withal MS(d)

48.10 ¹he] *last word page* 56 MS(d)

[*Pages* 57–58 MS(d) *wanting*]

49.1 The trees] *first words page* 59 MS(d)

49.1 a hymn of twilight] an evening hymn MS(d)

49.1 sun] burnished sun MS(d)

49.2 forest] tree-tops MS(d)

49.3 noises] noise MS(d)

49.6 Then, . . . stillness,] Upon this stillness∧ MS(d)

49.8 stopped] paused MS(d)

49.9–10 There . . . sound] The ripping MS(d)

49.10 and] was mingled with MS(d)

49.11 artillery] cannon MS(d[c]); MS(d[u]) *read* 'artillery'

49.13 -fashion] -wise MS(d)

49.17 the moon] moon MS(d)

49.17 clash] clash together MS(d)

49.18 persons would doubtless] many would MS(d)

49.20 became] was MS(d)

49.21 music,] ~ ∧ MS(d)

49.22 stood motionless] bended forward MS(d)

49.23–24 clatter . . . thunder.] clatter of the infantry firing and the ear-shaking thunder of the artillery. MS(d)

49.25 It . . . the youth] It occurred to him MS(d); ~ . . . Fleming MS(u)

49.25–26 in . . . been] he had been in MS(d)

49.28–29 This . . . air.] *omit* MS(d)

†49.31 himself] he MS(d)

49.31 the late] that MS(d)

50.2 must] might MS(d)

50.6 printed] *omit* MS(d)

50.8 surely] doubtless MS(d)

50.8 hopes] hope MS(d)

50.9 wished] wanted MS(d)

50.10 that he might] and MS(d)

†50.11 hastened] hurried MS(d)

50.12 conflicts] struggles MS(d)

50.12 His . . . thought] All his accumulations MS(d); MS(u) *read* 'All his'

50.13 noise] uproar MS(d)

50.14 being,] ∼ ∧ MS(d)

50.15 tried to hold] held MS(d)

50.16 him,] ∼ ∧ MS(d)

50.17–18 After . . . him] He thought MS(d)

50.18 bitterness. It seemed] bitterness MS(d)

50.19 him] him yet MS(d)

50.20 obstinately] *omit* MS(d)

50.20 ways and presently] ways. Presently MS(d)

50.21 ¹where] in a place from which MS(d)

50.21 grey . . . where] fringes of smoke where MS(d)

50.21–22 lay battle-lines] battle-lines lay MS(d)

50.22 cannon] the cannon MS(d)

50.22–23 The . . . ears.] *omit* MS(d)

50.24 stood, . . . moment.] stood for a moment and watched. MS(d)

†50.25 He . . . fight.] His lower jaw hung down. MS(d)

50.26 proceeded . . . way] continued his way MS(d)

50.28 processes,] ∼ ∧ MS(d)

50.30 a fence] some deserted rifle-pits MS(d)

50.30 it] them MS(d)

50.30–31 On . . . ground] Within, the trench MS(d)

50.31–32 newspaper, folded up,] ∼ ∧ ∼ ∼ ∧ MS(d)

50.33 arm. Further off,] arm, and further on∧ MS(d); MS(u) *read* 'on'

50.34 corpses,] bodies∧ MS(d)

50.36–39 In . . . begone.] As he looked, Fleming felt like an invader and he hastened by. MS(d)

51.1 ¶ He] no ¶ MS(d)

51.1 see,] ∼ ∧ MS

51.2 troops, smoke-fringed] troops MS(d)

51.4 groaning and wailing] lamenting and groaning MS(d)

51.4 air,] ∼ ∧ MS(d)

51.8 region] place MS(d)

51.10 ¹of . . . men] wounded man MS(d)

51.10 hopped] was hopping MS(d)

51.11 was laughing] laughed MS(d)

51.12–13 One . . . army.] *omit* MS(d)

51.16 marched∧] ∼ , MS(d)

51.18 'a vic'try] of vict'ry MS(d)

51.19 'a] a' MS(d)

51.34 put] leave MS(d)

52.5 unknown.] *last word page 61B* MS(d)

[*Pages 62–63 MS(d) wanting*]

53.25 yeh] *first word page 64* MS(d)

53.26 boy?] ∼ , MS

53.26 tone] way MS(d)

53.27 felt . . . ¹at] was startled by MS(d)

53.31 I——] *omit* MS(d)

53.32–35 His . . . problem.] *omit* MS(d)

53.36 astonishment.] *last word page 64* MS(d)

[*Page 65 MS(d) wanting*]

54.28–29 wax-like features] wax-like face (*first words page 66*) MS(d)

55.3 strangely] wildly MS(d)

55.5　There] On it MS(d)
55.6　upon it] *omit* MS(d)
55.8–9　There's . . . t'-day.]
　~ . . . t'day. MS; *omit* MS(d)
55.12　b'jiminy] b'jiming MS
55.13–14　Yes . . . about.] *omit*
　MS(d)
55.15　him] his friend MS(d)
55.15–16　tall soldier] latter
　MS(d)
55.16–19　Since . . . rear.] *omit*
　MS(d)
55.20　¹the . . . on] they went
　MS(d)
55.21　over-come] overcome
　MS(d)
55.22–24　looked . . . speak] be-
　gan to talk to him MS(d)
55.24　whisper] voice MS(d)
55.25　"I] "I'll MS(d)
55.26　I'm 'fraid I'll] I'll MS(d)
55.26　an'ₐ thenₐ] ~ , ~ , MS(d)
55.27　not'll] not ull MS(d)
55.27　me. That's] me—that's
　MS(d)
55.28　of——"] ~ ." MS(d)
55.30　Jim!] ~ . MS(d)
55.30　you! . . . will."] yeh! . . .
　~ MS; yeh." MS(d)
55.31　Sure—will yeh] Sure yeh
　will MS(d)
55.31　the . . . beseeched]
　beseeched Conklin MS(d)
55.32　Yes— . . . you—] ~—
　. . . yeh—MS; Yes, yes,
　MS(d)
55.33　gulpings] great gulpings
　MS(d)
55.35　But . . . beg] Conklin still
　begged MS(d)
55.35–37　He now . . . terror.]
　His eyes rolled. He hung babe-
　like to Fleming. MS(d)
55.37　t' . . . wa'n't] of your'n,
　wasn't MS(d)
55.38　I've . . . I?] *omit* MS(d)
56.1　it?] it, Flem? MS(d)
56.1　pull . . . outer] drag me
　outa MS(d)
56.1　road?] ~ . MS(d)
56.1　fer] fur MS(d)

56.3　He . . . reply.] *omit* MS(d)
56.4–7　The . . . [¶] However,]
　Fleming's anguish reached a
　heat where scorching sobs
　shook his chest, but, suddenly
　MS(d)
56.7　seemed suddenly] seemed
　MS(d)
56.8　grim,] ~ ₐ MS(d)
56.11　²no—] *omit* MS(d)
56.11　be——"] ~ ." MS(d)
56.12　was fixed again] again was
　fixed MS(d)
†56.15　follow] follow after MS(d)
56.16　Presently,ₐ] ~ , MS(d)
56.18　take 'im] tak 'im MS(d)
56.19　down th' road] *omit* MS(d)
56.19　runned] run MS(d)
56.20　a] *omit* MS(d)
56.21　take 'im] tak'im MS(d)
56.25　forward, presently,] for-
　ward MS(d)
56.26　Jim! Jim!] ~ — ~ , MS(d)
56.27　¶ The] ¶ *doubtful* MS(d)
56.27　weakly tried] tried weakly
　MS(d)
56.27　himself free] away MS(d)
56.27　Huh?"] ~ , MS
56.28　lastₐ] ~ , MS(d)
56.29　spoke . . . comprehend-
　ing.] spoke: MS(d)
56.29　"Oh (*no* ¶)] ¶ MS
56.30　started] went MS(d)
56.31　¶ The . . . once] (*no* ¶)
　Fleming turning MS(d)
56.32　battery. He was] battery
　was MS(d)
56.32　this] his MS(d)
56.33　shrill out-cry] cry MS(d)
56.33　man] soldier MS(d)
56.34　"Gawd! He's runnin'!"]
　"Great Gawd, he's runnin'!"
　MS(d)
56.35　Turning his head] Looking
　about MS(d)
56.37　seemed . . . free] almost
　wrenched itself MS(d)
56.38　this] the MS(d)
56.38–39　pain. . . . began a] in-
　finite pain and started in
　MS(d)

56.39 There (*no* ¶)] ¶ MS(d)

†56.39 singular] grotesque MS(d)

57.1 over-took] overtook MS(d)

57.1 soldier,] Conklin‸ MS(d)

57.1 plead] beg him MS(d)

†57.2,3 you] yeh MS(d)

†57.2 doing] doin' MS(d)

†57.3 you'll] yeh'll MS(d)

†57.4 purpose] mysterious purpose MS(d)

57.5–6 in . . . intentions] dully MS(d)

57.8 youth, aghast and] Fleming‸ MS(d)

57.8 tall soldier] idea which seemed to absorb his friend MS(d)

†57.10 ¹you] yeh MS(d)

†57.10 thinking] thinkin' MS(d)

57.10–11 Where . . . Jim?] What yeh tryin' t' do? Where yeh goin'? MS(d)

57.12 relentless pursuers] a relentless pursuer MS(d)

57.13 a great] an MS(d)

57.13 can't] won't MS(d)

57.14 be . . . minnit."] be!" MS(d)

57.15 recoiled] started back MS(d)

57.15–16 way, . . . you?"] way. MS(d)

57.17 and,] ∼ ‸ MS(d)

57.20–25 They . . . weapon.] *omit* MS(d)

57.26 last,] ∼ ‸ MS(d)

57.27 perceived that] percieved ∼ MS; percieved upon MS(d)

57.27 wore] *omit* MS(d)

57.27 telling that] as if MS(d)

57.28 place] spot MS(d)

57.29 erect; his] erect. The MS(d)

†57.30–31 that . . . meet] that was coming MS(d)

57.31–32 He . . . expectant.] *omit* MS(d)

57.33 was a silence] were years of silence MS(d)

57.34 ¶ Finally, the] (*no* ¶) The MS(d)

57.34 began to heave] heaved MS(d)

57.35–39 It . . . he saw] Once as he turned his eyes, Fleming saw MS(d)

58.4 The tall soldier] His friend MS(d); Conklin MS(u)

58.4 spoke. . . . gesture.] spoke, gratingly. He shook his head MS(d)

58.5 be . . . be———"] be! Leave me be!" MS(d)

58.6 There . . . waited.] *omit* MS(d)

58.8–9 To . . . watchers,] It was seen that MS(d)

58.11 He was] Presently, he seemed MS(d)

58.11 strangeness that slowly] ague that gradually MS(d)

58.12–13 caused him to] made him MS(d)

58.13 hideous] a hideous MS(d)

58.14 in . . . enthusiasm.] *omit* MS(d)

58.15 ¶ His] *no* ¶ MS(d)

58.15–16 stretched . . . Then] grew suddenly to unnatural proportions then MS(d)

58.16–17 forward . . . of] slowly forward like MS(d)

58.17 swift] last MS(d)

58.18 made] caused MS(d)

58.18 strike . . . first] to first strike the ground MS(d)

†58.20 Gawd] God MS

58.21–22 this . . . meeting.] these rites of a departing life, this dance of death. MS(d); these rites, this dance. MS(u)

58.22–23 an . . . agony] every form of agony that MS(d)

58.24 , going closer,] *omit* MS(d)

58.24 upon] at MS(d)

58.29–30 turned, . . . battlefield] turned toward the battle ground MS(d)

58.30 ¹He . . . fist.] His hands were clenched and a rage was upon his face. MS(d)

59.2 he,] ∼ ? MS(d)

59.3   little₍ₐ₎] ~ , MS(d)
59.3-4   jim-dandy." He] jim-
dandy, he was." [¶] He MS(d)
59.4   poked] pushed MS(d)
59.4   docile] dead MS(d)
59.5   foot] toe MS(d)
59.5   wonner] wonder MS(d)
59.5   from?] ~ . MS(d)
59.6   funny] curious MS(d)
59.10   again] omit MS(d)
59.12   said,] ~ ₍ₐ₎ MS(d)
59.14-15   This . . . 'e?] omit
MS(d)
59.15   An' he's] He's MS(d)
59.15   here] omit MS(d)
59.19   was] saw MS(d)
59.20   to . . . blue] a blue shade
MS(d)
59.21   cried, "you] ~ , in fear, "~
MS; ~ . "You MS(d)
59.21   too.] ~ ? MS(d)
59.22   man] soldier MS(d)
59.24   dreamfully] dreamily
MS(d)
†59.26,27   And] An' MS(d)
59.26   ²him] 'im MS; 'um MS(d)
59.27   coming] a comin' MS(d);
comin' MS(u)
59.27   over there] off yonder
MS(d)
59.28   They (no ¶)] ¶ MS(d)
59.29   of it a question] a question
of it MS(d)
59.30   spoke . . . man] said the
tattered man wearily MS(d)
59.30   ain't] aint MS; haint
MS(d)
59.31   stayin'] ~ ₍ₐ₎ MS
59.31   tryin' t' ask him] astin' im
MS(d)
60.1   The . . . wearily.] omit
MS(d)
60.1-2   They . . . corpse.] They
gazed at the corpse for a
moment. MS(d)
60.4   Well, he] He MS(d)
60.4   'e?] he, MS(d)
60.6-7   For . . . toes.] omit
MS(d)
60.7   remained] was still MS(d)
60.9   man,] ~ ₍ₐ₎ MS(d)

60.10   little] small MS(d)
60.10-11   "I'm . . . bad."] omit
MS(d)
60.12-13   He . . . encounter.]
Was he . . . encounter? MS;
omit MS(d)
60.14   But his companion] The
other MS(d)
60.14   re-assuringly] again
MS(d)
60.16   sir!] ~ . MS(d)
60.16   die! I can't!] die. MS(d)
60.16   'a] a' MS; of MS(d)
60.19   some kind of] omit MS(d)
60.20   soldier] man MS(d)
60.21-22   That . . . thing.] omit
MS(d)
60.22   would] s'pose MS(d)
60.24   next] last word page 72
MS(d)

[Pages 73-74 MS(d) wanting.
MS(d) pages 75-76 represent the
draft ending of Chapter X which
was rejected by Crane in the final
manuscript. After 62.21 'vigilance.'
on MS 85 appears half a page of
deleted material that corresponds
to MS(d) page 75 (draft 172.4-10).
Page 86 of MS is wanting, refer to
draft 172.11-173.2 for the text
which presumably stood behind this
lacking page MS 86. This portion of
the collation is keyed to the draft
and the word to the left of the
bracket is the draft lemma.]

172.4   his] the MS
172.6   a victim] an innocent victim MS
172.7   his law] a law, perchance,
MS
172.8   should] shall MS
172.10   didn't] could not MS
172.10   enough. To] enough. Man
had been born wary of the grey
skeleton and had expended
much of his intellect in erecting whatever safe-guards were
possible, so that he had long
been rather strongly intrenched
behind the mass of his inven-

tions. He kept an eye on his bath-tub, his fire-engine, his life-boat, and compelled (*end MS page 85*) *see* 172.11–173.2

63.1 He] *first word* MS(d) *page 77*

63.7 commands,] cammands, MS; cammands and MS(d)

63.8 bit$_\wedge$] $\sim$, MS(d)

63.11 comforted in a measure] in a measure comforted MS(d)

63.11 this] the MS(d)

63.13 terror-stricken] fleeing MS(d)

63.13–14 They . . . animals.] *omit* MS(d)

63.17 him$_\wedge$ was$_\wedge$ in truth$_\wedge$] $\sim$, $\sim$, $\sim \sim$, MS(d)

63.18–19 There . . . vindication.] *omit* MS(d)

†63.20 forward-going] *omit* MS(d)

63.22 serpent] long serpent MS(d)

63.26 raving] wild MS(d)

63.29–30 to . . . din] *omit* MS(d)

†63.31–64.1 the remainder . . . army] the whole army MS(d)

64.4 grave . . . And] stern and quiet, and MS(d)

†64.6 the youth] he MS(d)

64.6–7 ²the . . . him] Fleming knew all of his woe MS(d)

64.9 sun-light] sunlight MS(d)

64.11 an adequate] a proper MS(d)

64.12 the thing] that thing MS(d)

64.13 —whatever it was—] *omit* MS(d)

64.14 him, he said] him MS(d)

64.15–16 battle . . . be] battle-ground struck forlorn Fleming as being MS(d)

64.17 Heroes,] $\sim$ $_\wedge$ MS(d)

64.17 long$_\wedge$] $\sim$, MS(d)

64.19 excuses] explanations MS(d)

64.20–21 in such haste] so bitter MS(d)

64.21 way] ways MS(d)

64.21 grim] *omit* MS(d)

64.22 he thought that] *omit* MS(d)

64.24 he said,] *omit* MS(d)

†64.24 throw] thrown MS(d)

†64.24 become] became MS(d)

64.25 ¹himself, apart,] $\sim$ $_\wedge$ $\sim$ $_\wedge$ MS(d)

64.27 blue,] $\sim$ $_\wedge$ MS(d)

64.28 assault,] $\sim$ $_\wedge$ MS(d)

64.29 ¹the . . . all] everybody MS(d)

64.31 These . . . him.] He was up-lifted. MS(d)

64.32 victory. He] victory and MS(d); MS(u) *read* 'an [*unfinished*]'

64.33 rapid$_\wedge$] $\sim$, MS(d)

64.34 voices, the] voices, and the MS(d)

64.34 near him] *omit* MS(d)

64.37 start] start fleetly MS(d)

64.37–65.2 Indeed . . . calamity.] *omit* MS(d)

65.3 ¶ Then] *no* ¶ MS(d)

65.5–6 hands, . . . plan] hands MS(d)

65.7 They . . . profuse.] *omit* MS(d)

65.8 he continued,] *omit* MS(d)

65.8 a miracle] miraculous MS(d)

65.11 some] an MS(d[c]); some MS(d[u])

65.13 his comrades] them MS(d)

65.14–15 There . . . reply] He replied MS(d)

65.16 rearward] rear-word MS, MS(d[u]); rear-ward MS(d[c])

65.17 -blur$_\wedge$]- $\sim$, MS(d)

65.17 would, . . . like] would be as hidden as MS(d)

65.19 But then, he said,] $\sim$, $\sim$, $\sim \sim$ $_\wedge$ MS(d)

†65.19–20 would . . . when the] would, when the MS(d)

65.20 a moment, a] an instant bring forth a MS(d)

65.21 In . . . scrutiny] And he saw the scrutinizing eyes MS(d)

65.21–22   companions] comrades MS(d)

65.22   painfully labored] would painfully labor MS(d[c]); painfully labored MS(d[u])

65.23   these] his MS(d); MS(u) *read* 'the'

65.24   his] the MS(d)

65.25–27   He . . . formidable.] *omit* MS(d)

65.29   the] *omit* MS(d)

65.30–31   war; . . . light.] war. MS(d)

65.31   headlong] head-long MS(d)

†65.35   with each movement] *omit* MS(d)

65.36   Also, his body] His body, too, MS(d)

65.38   tried to walk] moved MS(d)

66.6–10   In . . . off.] He groaned from his heart and staggered off through the fields. He was not like those others, he said, in despair. He now conceded it to be impossible that he should ever grow to be one of them. Those pictures of glory were piteous things. MS(d)

66.11   A . . . him] A desire for news MS(d)

66.12   battle] battle-ground MS(d)

66.12   He . . . news.] *omit* MS(d)

66.14   that, . . . suffering,] that in all his troubles MS(d)

66.15   said,] ~ ₄ MS(d)

66.16   to his conscience] *omit* MS(d)

66.17   for the army] *omit* MS(d)

66.17   favorable] *omit* MS(d)

66.18   for] to MS(d)

66.19   Thus, many] Many MS(d)

66.19–20   considered] thought MS(d)

†66.20   obliged to] compelled to MS(d)

66.21   would] would all MS(d)

66.22   believe] believe that MS(d)

†66.23   they] others MS(d)

66.23–25   And . . . others.] *omit* MS(d)

66.26   excuse₄ . . . previously] excuse, that, previously, MS(d)

66.28   them,] ~ ₄ MS(d)

66.29   memory] very traditions MS(d)

66.32   were usually] would be MS(d)

66.33   these] these sad MS; the MS(d)

66.33–67.3   He . . . youth.] ~ . . . Fleming. MS; *omit* MS(d)

67.4   vindication] moral vindication MS(d); MS(u) *read* 'mo [*unfinished*]'

67.5   thought] thought that MS(d)

67.5   manner] way MS(d)

67.6–8   A . . . seer.] *omit* MS(d)

67.9   A . . . was] This he MS(d)

67.9   by the youth] ~ Fleming MS; *omit* MS(d)

67.10   thought] said MS(d)

67.13   , through his actions,] *omit* MS(d)

67.13   men.] men, imparting the information through his actions. MS(d)

67.14   ¹If] But if MS(d)

†67.14   lost] indeed lost MS(d)

67.16   ¹to] be MS(d)

67.19   ¶ As] ¶ *doubtful* MS(d)

67.19   turned] suddenly turned MS(d)

67.20   thrust] savagely thrust MS(d)

67.20   He] With woe upon his face, he MS(d)

67.21   He . . . was] He was he said MS(d)

67.22   soldiers] men MS(d)

67.24   dripping] weltering MS(d)

67.26   Again₄] ~ , MS(d)

†67.27   a corpse] the corpses MS(d)

67.27   Thinking . . . slain,] Too, MS(d)

67.28   great] species of MS(d)

67.32   tradition] traditions MS(d)

67.33–34   still said that] thought MS(d)

67.34 great] *omit* MS(d)

67.34 he] that he MS(d)

†67.36–37 considered, now, however,] considered however MS(d) (MS[u]: ~ , ~ ,)

67.38 mighty_∧] ~ , MS(d)

68.2 creed] true creed MS(d)

68.3 When] As MS(d)

68.4 tried to] began to MS(d)

68.4 bethink] be-think MS

68.5 regiment] *last word page 82* MS(d)

[*Page* 83 MS(d) *wanting. Pages* 84–89 MS(d) *represent the draft of* Chapter XII *discarded by* Crane *in the final manuscript* (MS 98–103). *Extant are 3 pages of* MS(d), 84–86 *and 4 pages of* MS, 98–99 *and* 101–102, *plus a false start of* MS 98. *See pp.* 383–384 *for collation.*]

†69.0 XII] XIII MS(d)

69.6 entanglements] entangling things MS(d)

69.7 buffaloes] buffalos MS(d)

69.8–9 clouded_∧ . . . and_∧] clouded, and, MS(d)

69.9 thickets_∧] ~ , MS(d)

69.9 distant_∧] ~ , MS(d)

69.10–11 interminable] an interminable MS(d)

69.12 agony] pain MS(d)

69.13 he . . . universe.] nature had pointed him out as a victim. He again lost all concern for himself. MS(d), *see* 69.15 *below*

69.15 damned.] doomed. He lost concern for himself. MS; doomed. MS(d)

69.16–19 ²The . . . fill.] The foe was coming storm-wise to flood the army. MS(d)

69.20 him,] him there was MS(d)

69.20 bade to] that bade him MS(d)

69.22 call] call out MS(d)

69.26 They . . . men.] *omit* MS(d)

69.26–27 The youth] ¶ (*doubtful*) He MS(d); Fleming MS(u)

†69.27 of them] *omit* MS(d)

69.28 incoherent] half-coherent MS(d)

69.28–29 They . . . him.] He made insane appeals for information. The wild eyes seemed not to throw a glance in his direction. MS(d)

69.30–70.10 They . . . infantry,] *omit* MS(d)

70.10 finally] ¶ Finally he MS(d)

70.11 swung] swayed MS(d)

70.12 the youth_∧] Fleming, MS(d)

70.14(*twice*),19(*twice*) Letgo] Let'go MS(d)

70.15 were . . . uncontrolled] rolled as if he had lost control of them MS(d)

70.15 heaving] puffing MS(d)

70.16 grasped] clutched MS(d)

70.16 rifle,] ~ _∧ MS(d)

70.17–18 the youth_∧ . . . forward_∧] Fleming, . . . ~ , MS(d)

70.20 the youth] Fleming wildly MS(d); Fleming crazily MS(u)

70.21 then——"] ~ ," MS(d)

70.24 other's] man's MS(d)

70.25 The . . . muscles.] *omit* MS(d)

70.25 flaming] burning MS(d)

70.26 vision] eyes MS(d)

70.28 Suddenly_∧] ~ , MS(d)

70.28 sank] fell MS(d)

70.28 writhing] writheing MS

70.29 arise] get up MS(d)

70.29 the numbing] his MS(d)

70.30 the air] the atmosphere MS(d[c]); air MS(d[u])

70.32 ¶ Sometimes] *no* ¶ MS(d)

70.33–34 again, . . . grass.] again. MS(d)

70.36 last, . . . movement,] ~ _∧ . . . ~ _∧ MS(d)

70.37 ²to] upon MS(d)

70.38 Pressing . . . temples] *omit* MS(d)

71.1 He] And afterward, Fleming MS(d)

71.1 battle] fight MS(d)

71.3 portraying] picturing MS(d)

71.3–4 should fall] fell MS(d)

†71.4 went] went forward MS(d)

†71.4 tall soldier-fashion] Conklin-fashion MS(d)

71.4 imagined] thought of MS(d)

71.5–6 search for] reach MS(d)

71.7 Once, he] He MS(d)

71.7 to . . . of] up to MS(d)

71.8 wound] wound under his hair MS(d)

71.11 jolted cannon] jolting bat-teries MS(d); jolting cannon batteries MS(u)

71.12 Once,] ~ ∧ MS(d)

71.13 nearly] near MS(d)

71.14 mass of guns] artilleryman controlling the mass of can-non MS(d)

71.15–16 sweeping . . . making] by MS(d)

71.16 with a] of his MS(d)

71.17 an] a seeming MS(d[c]); an MS(d[u])

71.17–18 unwillingness . . . heels.] unwillingness. MS(d); *last word page* 92 MS(d) *which is the last preserved draft page*

ALTERATIONS IN THE EARLY
DRAFT MANUSCRIPT

[NOTE: All alterations are in the inscribing ink and are *currente calamo*.]

145.3   brilliant] *preceded by deleted* 'successful'

145.5   there] 'er' *over* 'r'

145.14   young] *preceded by deleted beginning of possible* 'F'

145.18   his] 'h' *mended*

145.19   might] *followed by deleted* 'move'

145.22   move!] *exclamation point over a period*

145.25   paralelled] *first* 'e' *over an* 'l'; *second* 'l' *interlined above undeleted* 'e'

146.11   had] *interlined*

146.11   ¹the] 'th' *over beginning of another letter*

146.12   the bygone,] *interlined above deleted* 'history,'

146.13   castles.] *period over comma*

146.23   had] *possibly inserted*

146.27   ²had] *interlined with a caret*

146.34   vibrated] *preceded by deleted* 'had'

147.3   ²had] *interlined with a caret*

147.6   gone] *followed by deleted* 'over'

147.7   one] 'o' *over* 'a'

147.8   of] *over* 't[*and the beginning of an* 'h']'

147.8   had] *interlined above deleted* 'had'

147.11   had] *interlined with a caret*

147.11   said] *followed by deleted period*

147.17   him] *preceded by deleted* 'by'

147.19   had] *interlined*

147.21   out] *followed by deleted period*

147.25   so's] *followed by deleted* 'thet'

147.33–34   their ways,] *interlined above deleted* 'th' army,' *of which the comma not deleted in error*

147.36   ²never] *interlined with a caret*

148.2   there's] 'r' *over illegible letter*

148.5   yeh] 'e' *over possible* 'o'

148.5   it] *interlined with a caret*

148.6   times] *followed by deleted comma*

148.8   there'll] *second* 'l' *mended*

148.12   all.] *period inserted before deleted* 'things.' *of which period altered from a comma*

148.15   ¹had] *interlined with a caret possibly not in Crane's hand*

148.19   had] *preceded by deleted* 'm[*and beginning of an* 'a']'

148.21   thought] *preceded by deleted* 'had'

148.21   demure] *preceded by deleted* 'v[*and the beginning of an* 'e']'

148.22   As] 'A' *over beginning of another letter*

148.33   advancing,] *followed by deleted* 'chewing tobacco'

149.1 Fleming] *interlined above independently deleted* 'one' *and* 'could'

149.1 imagined] 'd' *added*

149.2 slits] *preceded by deleted* 'the'

149.3 put] *followed by deleted* 'faith'

149.13 this,] *interlined with a caret which deleted a comma*

149.16 ²had] *interlined with a caret*

149.17 had] 'ha' *over* 'w'

149.18 imagination] 'in' *strengthened*

149.22 visions] *preceded by deleted* 'sha'

149.23 them] *followed by deleted period*

149.23 impossible] *followed by deleted* 'impossible'

149.28 an] *inserted*

149.32 repeated in dismay.] 'in dismay.' *added after an undeleted period*

150.1 know] *interlined with a caret*

150.4 the contents of] *interlined above deleted* 'everything from'

150.17 Th'] *apostrophe over deleted* 'e'

150.19 cavalry] *preceded by deleted* 'cala'

150.35 run,] *comma preceded by deleted period*

150.38 fight] *followed by deleted* 'like sin after they once'

151.7 On] 'O' *over* 'o'; *preceded by deleted* 'He laughed,'

151.9 Conklin] 'n' *over upstroke*

151.12 run.] *followed by deleted closing double quotes*

151.13 would.] *period altered from comma*

151.19 He] *followed by deleted* 'now'

151.20 possibilities] *followed by deleted period*

152.5 proud] 'u' *mended*

152.12 ¹'Run'?] *question mark over a comma*

152.18 runnin'] *second* 'n' *mended*

152.24 said.] *followed by deleted closing double quotes*

152.24 too] *originally inscribed at far right of line then deleted and* 'too.". . . Fleming' *inserted at the left*

152.27 when] *followed by deleted* 'Wilson'

152.29 seemed] *preceded by deleted* ', but he,'

152.37 the] *interlined with a caret*

153.2 vision,] *comma inserted before deleted period and* 'He'

153.10 lips.] 's' *possibly inserted*

153.17 appeared] *interlined above deleted* 'seemed'

153.17–18 absorbed] 'd' *possibly over the beginning of another letter*

153.23 kind] *followed by deleted period*

153.24 who] *followed by deleted* 'is doomed, a-|'

153.30 man] *interlined with a caret*

154.4 created] *preceded by deleted* 'erected'

154.5 noon] *interlined above deleted* 'none'

154.19–20 huddled] *preceded by deleted* 'heads of'

154.23 reserved] 'd' *added*

154.25–26 Some . . . -balls.] *added with* '|ually . . .-balls.' *below the line*

154.27 officer] *preceded by deleted* 'officiers'

154.27 Fleming's] ' 's' *added*

154.29 regimental] *preceded by deleted* 'rebel line'

154.33 trousers—] *preceded by deleted* 'clothes.'; *dash over deleted period and undeleted comma*

154.34 handkerchief.] *written partially below the line*

154.36 be] *followed by deleted* 'in an'

155.7   ²the] *interlined*

155.10   had] *interlined*

155.10   boy,] *comma added after deleted period*

155.11   horse] 'h' *over beginning of possible* 'c'

155.18   all their munitions] *interlined above deleted* 'everything'

155.20   tried] 't' *over beginning of possible* 'c'

155.31   thought] *preceded by deleted* 'chanc[*and the beginning of an* 'e']'

155.31   was not] *preceded by deleted* 'wasn[*and the beginning of a* 't']'

155.35   ¹You've] 'Y' *over beginning of another letter*

156.15   like] *followed by deleted* 'a crying urchins'

156.23   animal] *preceded by deleted* 'cow'

156.30   rifles,] *followed by independently deleted* 'as in a sea', *of which the comma not deleted in error, and* 'he'

156.33   him,] *followed by deleted* 'with'

156.33   his parched] *interlined above independently deleted* 'at' *and* 'his'

156.36   rage,] *preceded by deleted* 'anger,'

157.11   woods] *preceded by deleted* 'one'

157.12   thousands] 's' *added*

157.16   Smoke] *final* 's' *deleted*

157.17   there] *followed by deleted comma*

157.18   dominating] 'd' *over upstroke*

157.19   the] *interlined*

157.22   hill] *interlined above deleted* 'hillside' *with a hyphen possibly inserted*

157.22   side,] *followed by deleted* 'and'

157.25   too] *followed by deleted comma*

157.28   he] *interlined*

157.34   his] 'is' *over* 'e'

158.5   scene] *a final* 's' *deleted*

158.7   even] *first e' mended*

158.9   gratification.] *period inserted before deleted* 'on his fellows'

158.12   ¹his] *followed by deleted* 'fac[*and the beginning of an* 'e']'

158.14   dumb] *final* 'ness' *deleted*

158.14   sprawled] *preceded by deleted* 'sp'

158.24   wood] *interlined with a caret*

158.24   the] *interlined with a caret*

158.25   flag] *final* 's' *deleted*

158.28   of war] *interlined with a caret*

158.29   their] 'ir' *added*

158.29   eyes.] *period inserted before deleted* 'of the men.'

158.34   somebody] 'e' *over an upstroke*

158.34   us] *interlined with a caret*

158.37   Smithers] *an apostrophe before* 's' *deleted*

158.38   insteader] 'er' *over* 'a'

159.1   gingerly. It] *period inserted;* 'I' *over* 'i'

159.4   developed] *interlined above deleted* 'made'

159.7   grate.] *followed by deleted* 'The fl[*and the beginning of an* 'a']'

159.9   that were] *interlined with a caret*

159.12   horse] *final* 's' *deleted*

159.12   felt] *interlined above deleted* 'left'

159.24   of] *followed by deleted* 'a cantering cluster'

159.25   cantering] *final* 'ly' *deleted*

159.30   man] 'a' *over* 'e'

159.33–34   feverishly] *interlined with a caret*

159.34   it] *followed by deleted* 'r[*and the beginning of an* 'a']'

160.1   fled.] *interlined above deleted* 'ran.'

160.11   gone.] *followed by deleted*

'His unbuttoned coat streamed out.'

160.11 -box] *followed by deleted* 'and his'

160.12 swung] *followed by deleted* 'on a cord'

160.12 On . . . a] *inserted before deleted* '[¶] On'

160.18 He] *followed by deleted* 'saw men'

160.23 meagre] *interlined with a* caret

160.23 of] *interlined above deleted* 'upon'

160.24 who] *preceded by deleted* 'f' *over* 'w'

160.25 rear.] *period inserted before deleted* 'of him.'

160.28 him] *interlined with a* caret

160.33 They] 'y' *added*

160.37 a] *preceded by possible beginning of another letter*

161.5 fellows] 'f' *over illegible letter*

161.12 anyhow] *preceded by deleted* 'unho'

161.13 Or] *followed by deleted* comma

161.14 artillery] *interlined above deleted* 'battery' *and a period deleted in error*

161.16 teams] *followed by deleted* 'from the'

161.17 scampered] *preceded by deleted* 'w'

161.23 a great] *interlined above deleted* 'much'

161.27 horsemen] *second* 'e' *over* 'a'

161.35 had] *interlined with a* caret

161.35 opportunity—] *dash over deleted period*

161.36 general—] *dash over deleted period*

161.37 approach] *preceded by deleted* 'go'

161.37 and] *preceded by deleted* 'in'

161.39 make] *interlined above deleted* 'may'

162.1 warily] *preceded by deleted* 'nea'

162.4 Tell] *preceded by deleted* 'An' send'

162.6 A] *preceded by deleted* 'Flemin [and the beginning of a* 'g']'

162.7 saddle.] *followed by deleted* '[¶] "No—yes'

162.9 ¹'im!] *exclamation point over a period*

162.11 ²wallop 'em] 'e' *over* 'i'

162.12 he] *preceded by deleted* 'his eyes suddenly'

162.12–13 Here—. . . Taylor—] *all dashes over commas*

162.12 Jones] *preceded by deleted* 'quic'

162.19 and] *interlined with a* caret

162.23 it] *preceded by deleted* 'cam'

162.23 hoarse cheers] *preceded by deleted* 'cheers'

162.32 If] *preceded by deleted* 'J'

162.33 save] *preceded by deleted* 'rescue'

163.8 arms] *inserted*

163.8 him.] *period inserted before deleted* 'with reproach.'

163.9 would] *preceded by deleted* 'brought'

163.25 It] *preceded by deleted* 'It reenforced' *with* 're' *inserted*

163.30 pounce] *preceded by deleted* 'dive'

163.37 He] 'H' *over* 'S'

164.6 column-] *preceded by deleted* 'tree'

164.7 was] *preceded by deleted* 'it'

164.15 liquid-] *preceded by deleted* 'dulled,'

164.20 throw] *interlined above deleted* 'push'

164.22 withal, he] *interlined above deleted* 'he'

164.33–34 cannon.] *preceded by deleted* 'artillery.'

165.2   said,] *comma inserted after deleted* 'to himself'
165.9   clatter] *preceded by deleted* 'clamo'
165.12   was, | after] *a second comma inserted in error preceding* 'after' *at beginning of the line*
165.13   popping.] *interlined with a caret which deletes a period*
165.14   real] *followed by deleted* 'war'
165.15   sort of a] 'sort' *followed by* 'of a' *which has been blotted out by the off-print of an alteration on p.* 78 *recto*
165.22   meek] *interlined above deleted* 'curious'
165.22   immaterial] *interlined above deleted* 'meek'
165.25   on.] *preceded by deleted period and* 'on' *of which the period was inserted*
165.25   ¹to] *interlined*
165.29   the] 't' *over possible* 'a'
165.33   He thought] *preceded by deleted* 'It seemed to him that'
165.38   eyes] *preceded by deleted* 'I'
165.40   Presently] *first word f.* 61a *of which* 'a' *over a period*
165.40   the] 't' *over possible* 'a'
166.3   close] *followed by deleted* 'up'
166.4   He] *preceded by deleted* 'It'
166.5–6 newspaper] 'w' *altered from* 'v'
166.12   dark] *preceded by deleted* 'the'
166.14   were] *interlined with a caret*
166.16   words] *interlined above deleted* 'voices'
166.18   ¹the] *interlined above deleted* 'a'
166.20   game] 'g' *mended*
166.21   imitative] *preceded by deleted* 'imia'
166.22   Upon] *preceded by deleted* 'His'

166.23   ¹of] *first word of f.* 61B *of which* 'B' *added*
166.29   Parts of the] 'Parts of' *inserted;* 'T' *of* 'The' *reduced with a slash*
166.29   limped] *preceded by deleted* 'seeme'
167.6   roadsides.] *final* 's' *inserted*
167.7   raged] 'a' *over* 'e'
167.9   the] *followed by deleted* 'bearers'
167.19   wax-like] *inserted before deleted* 'waxlike'
167.25   gory] *preceded by deleted* 'bloody'
167.26   new] *interlined above deleted* 'old'
167.26   been,] *comma added after deleted question mark*
167.27   Flem?] *question mark over a comma*
167.27   He] *followed by deleted* 'went'
167.28   keeled] *preceded by deleted* 'kelle'
167.30   ²Jim—] *dash over a comma*
168.4   'fraid] *an initial* 'a' *deleted and apostrophe added*
168.10   Flem] *tail of* 'm' *extended to delete* 'i' *beneath it*
168.12   speak] *followed by deleted* 'be'
168.16   ¹Flem] *final* 'ing' *deleted; dot of* 'i' *separately deleted*
168.17   Flem?] *followed by deleted* 'And kee[and the beginning of probable* 'p']'
168.18   a] *interlined above deleted* 'the'
168.18   where] *followed by deleted* 'the'
168.21   wished] *preceded by deleted comma and* 'striding'
168.23   "No . . . be."] *possibly added later*
168.24   look] *preceded by deleted* 'eyes'
168.24   again] *followed by deleted* 'became'

168.25 mysterious] 'ous' *added with 'ou' over 'os'*

168.28 Presently] *preceded by deleted 'At last'*

168.28 a] *interlined with a caret*

168.29 soldier.] *preceded by deleted 'man.'*

168.33 road. Where] *period inserted; 'W' over 'w'*

168.36 Jim—] *dash over a comma*

169.12 yeh'll] 'eh' *over* 'ou'

169.17 friend,] *comma added after deleted period*

169.18 ¹What] *followed by deleted 'are'*

169.24 lurching dangerously,] 'ing dangerously,' *interlined above deleted 'ed dangero'*

169.25 the] *interlined*

169.26 he] 'h' *over* 's'

169.28 At] *preceded by deleted 'They'*

169.28 stop] *followed by deleted 'as if he had at last found the spot for which he had been' of which first 'he' interlined*

169.28 and] 'a' *mended*

169.28 stand] 'd' *mended*

169.29 percieved] *interlined above deleted 'saw'*

169.29 an] 'n' *added; following is the beginning of a possible 'e'*

169.30 had] *interlined with a caret*

169.30 struggled.] *period altered from a comma and followed by a deleted 'a'*

169.31 sides.] *preceded by deleted 'hand'*

169.32 that] *interlined above deleted 'which'*

169.35 in them] *interlined with a caret*

169.38 opened] *second 'e' over 'a'*

169.38 spoke,] *followed by deleted 'in a'*

169.38 gratingly.] *period inserted before deleted 'and monotonous voice.'*

170.5 Presently,] *interlined above deleted 'Finally'*

170.8 suddenly to] 'suddenly' *interlined with a caret and 'to' followed by deleted 'sudden,'*

170.10 first] *interlined with a caret*

170.11 ground.] *period inserted before deleted 'fir'*

170.12 The] *apparent deletion is a blot from an ink alteration on p. 146 recto*

170.14 rites] *preceded by deleted 'str'*

170.17 feet] *first 'e' over 'o'*

170.23 clenched] *followed by deleted period*

170.26 red] *interlined above deleted 'fierce'*

170.27.1 XI.] *added later; this is incorrect and should be 'X'*

170.28 he?"] *followed by deleted 'he'*

170.31 his] 's' *mended*

171.5 aint 'e,] *a comma inserted in error preceding ' 'e'*

171.7 bother | 'im] *apostrophe after 'bother' not deleted in error when ' 'im' written on following line*

171.20 They] *preceded by deleted opening double quotes*

171.22 anything."] *interlined above deleted 'ay[and the beginning of a 't']'*

171.25 jim-dandy] *a circle covering 'm . . . n' with a vertical line through it (the line drawn through the space between the words); a pie-shaped mark has been made on the right side of the circle*

171.27 still] 's' *over an upstroke*

171.29 commencin' t'] *a circle as in 171.25 covers 'n't' '*

171.32 Oh] 'O' *over beginning of 'I'*

171.34 die.] *a circle as in 171.25 (except without the vertical line) covers this word*

172.2 a] *over possible beginning of* 'I'

172.9 said] *followed by deleted* comma

172.12 men] *followed by deleted* 'a'

172.14 humor] *interlined above deleted* 'satire'

172.15 regarding] *followed by independently deleted* 'ador' *and* 'ardor,'

172.20 some] *final* 'thing' *deleted*

172.20 that] *followed by deleted* 'would enable'

172.21 cause] *interlined above deleted* 'make'

172.22 cheerfully;] *semicolon preceded by deleted period*

172.23 destroy all the bindings of] *interlined above deleted* 'out-shadow all the'

172.30 sure;] *semicolon possibly altered from a comma*

172.31 was] 'wa' *inserted with* 'a' *over* 'i'

172.32–33 It . . . apparel.] *added between lines with* 'It could deck a' *written below deleted* 'And it was'; 'creature' *followed by deleted* 'decked'

172.33 she] *preceded by deleted* 'they'; *followed by deleted* 'had cozened him out of his home,'

172.36 fury] *preceded by deleted* 'furr[*and the beginning of a* 'y']'

173.10 The] *followed by deleted* 'biting'

173.17 the] *interlined above deleted* 'an'

173.18 could] *interlined above deleted* 'might'

173.33 faces] *preceded by deleted* 'column'

174.4 upon] *interlined above deleted* 'to'

174.8 much finer] *interlined above deleted* 'more'

174.8–9 fighting] 'f' *over* 's[*and the beginning of a* 't']'

174.10 lane] 'a' *over* 'i'

174.12 had eaten] *interlined with a caret*

174.12 they] 'th' *over* 'co'

174.20 calmly] 'c' *over beginning of an upstroke*

174.23 of] *followed by deleted* 'a rapid' *and a comma not deleted in error*

174.23–24 In his ears, he] *interlined above deleted* 'He'

174.27 a few] *interlined above deleted* 'a'

174.27 moments] 's' *added*

174.36 an] *interlined above deleted* 'some'

174.39 -ward] 'a' *altered from* 'o'

175.2 be] *interlined*

175.3 strife] *a final* 'd' (*possibly added later*) *deleted*

175.6 would] *inserted*

175.6 labor] *final* 'ed' *deleted*

175.10 flying] *preceded by deleted* 'remaining'

175.14 Each] *preceded by deleted* 'His feet we'

175.14 of] *over* 'in'

175.25 He . . . others,] *inserted before deleted* '[¶] A desire for news kept him in the vicinity of the battle-ground'

175.32 ²a] *interlined*

175.32 apologogetic manner,] *originally* 'apology,' *with hyphen interlined above deleted* 'y' *and* 'ogetic' *inserted in line below to create* 'apologogetic' *in error;* 'manner,' *interlined with a caret*

175.36 like] 'l' *over beginning of illegible letter*

176.1 as] 's' *over an upstroke*

176.1–2 encountered] *preceded by deleted* 's[*and the beginning of a possible* 'h']'

176.3 them] *interlined above deleted* 'it'

176.4 one;] *semicolon preceded by deleted illegible punctuation*

176.4 the] *interlined*

176.6 would] *interlined*

176.6 pipe] *final* 'd' *deleted*

176.7 generals] 'a' *mended*

176.7 would] *preceded by deleted* 'were'

176.8 to] *preceded by deleted* 'to'

176.18 flags] 's' *added*

176.21 for] *preceded by deleted* 'of'

176.28 weltering] 'l' *over* 't'

176.30 ¶ Again, he] '¶ Again,' *inserted before* '[¶] He' *of which* 'H' *reduced to lower case by a slash*

176.32 they] *followed by deleted* 'had done a wrong action' *of which* 'a' *preceded by independently deleted* 'a' *and* 'an'

176.33 lifeless.] *period mended*

176.37 However,] *interlined above deleted* 'Yet'

177.2 useless] *preceded by deleted* 'very'

177.3 blue] *followed by deleted* 'and steel'

177.11 had] *interlined*

177.13 ever] *final* 'y' *deleted*

177.15 minute] *interlined above deleted* 'tiny'

177.16 which] *preceded by deleted* 't[and the beginning of an* 'h']'

177.17 the] *interlined above deleted* 'his'

177.19 But, as he] 'But,' *inserted and* 'he' *interlined;* 'A' *not reduced in error*

177.19 all,] *followed by comma deleted in error and deleted* 'his rebellion, nature perhaps had not concentrated herself against him, or, at least, that' *of which* 'him' *interlined*

177.20 would] 'w' *over* 'c' *which was over original* 'w'

177.20 still] *interlined with a caret*

177.22 the . . . his] *interlined with a caret above deleted* 'his'

177.23 It] *preceded by deleted* 'He w'

177.26 things] 's' *added*

177.31 said,] *interlined above a comma not deleted in error*

177.32 ²to] *interlined with a caret*

177.36 secure] *interlined above deleted* 'safe'

178.1 had] *interlined*

178.2 findings] *interlined above deleted* 'laws'

178.4 had] 'h' *over beginning of* 'm'

178.7 adoration] *interlined above deleted* 'worship'

178.8 that] *the apparent deletion is an ink blot from an alteration on p.* 109 *recto*

178.11 ashes.] *followed by deleted* '[¶] He had a feeling that he was the coming prophet of a social reconstruction. Far down in his being, [final* 's' *deleted]* in the hidden, untouched currents of his soul, [followed by deleted* 'there was born'] he saw born a voice.

178.12 with anger] *preceded by deleted* 'with bitterness'

178.12 affairs] *preceded by deleted* 'his'

178.12 it's] *altered from* 'his' *which was interlined above deleted* 'his'

178.15 had] *interlined*

178.17 among] 'a' *over* 'in'

178.21 piercing] *preceded by deleted beginning of a* 'p'

178.23–24 wrong and ridiculous] *interlined with a caret above deleted* 'the wrong'

178.25 should] *followed by deleted* 'chan'

178.25 in] *preceded by deleted* 'upon'

178.25 night,] *followed by deleted* 'mankind would'

178.25 only] *followed by deleted* 'a'

178.26 shadows] 's' *added*

178.28 was] *followed by deleted* 'h[and the beginning of an* 'a']'

178.30 "There"!] *quotation*

marks and exclamation point strengthened or added

178.34 stolidly] *preceded by deleted* 'tr'

178.35 remarkable] *final* 'e' *added after deleted* 'y'

178.37 he] *preceded by deleted* 'spok'

179.1 column] 'co' *over* 's[*and an upstroke*]'

179.7 upon] 'n' *mended*

179.9 see] *interlined with a caret*

179.10 voices] *preceded by deleted* 'cannons'' *with apostrophe added and an apostrophe before the* 's' *deleted*

179.19 rallying] *followed by deleted* 'or [*and possible beginning of an* 'a']'

179.25 along. His] *period inserted;* 'H' *over* 'h'

179.26 information.] *period inserted before deleted* 'in'

179.32 face] *interlined with a caret*

179.34 having] *interlined with a caret*

179.35 release] *preceded by deleted* 'lelax'

179.35 and] *followed by deleted comma*

179.36 being] *interlined above deleted* 'was'

180.4 head.] *followed by deleted* 'The latter's fingers'

180.10 ^{2}his] *preceded by deleted* 'the'

180.11 a man] *interlined above deleted* 'a'

180.11 wrestling . . . atmosphere.] 'wrestling' *followed by deleted* 'with a phantom.' *written at the far right of the page;* 'with . . . atmosphere.' *written at the left of the page with* 'the' *preceded by deleted* 'air.'

180.13 achieve] *preceded by deleted* 'ac'

180.18 knees] *followed by deleted period and* 'From'

180.18 babe trying] *interlined above deleted* 'child learning'

180.25 To] 'T' *mended*

180.25 one,] *interlined above deleted* 'them,'

180.30 him] 'i' *mended*

180.31 scurrying] *interlined above independently deleted* 'I' *and* 'running' *of which* 'I' *over* 'r'

180.34 by] 'b' *over* 'w'

180.35 a seeming] *interlined with a caret above deleted* 'an'

180.35 air of] *followed by deleted* 'being'

TABLES

MANUSCRIPT LEAVES WITH INSCRIBED VERSOS

MS RECTO	MS VERSO	MS RECTO	MS VERSO
2	false start MS[1]	111	MS(d) 92
22	false start MS [17]	112	MS(d) 86
51	MS(d) 6	113	MS(d) 84
52	MS(d) 40	114	MS(d) 91
59	false start MS [53]	115	MS(d) 81
60	MS(d) 48	116	MS(d) 77
67	MS(d) 49	117	MS(d) 78
68	MS(d) 51	118	MS(d) 75
69	MS(d) 50	119	MS(d) 69
70	MS(d) 47	120	MS(d) 23
71	MS(d) 52	121	MS(d) 22
72	MS(d) 46	122	MS(d) 15
73	MS(d) 45	123	MS(d) 14
74	MS(d) 42	124	MS(d) 13
75	MS(d) 64	125	MS(d) 82
76	MS(d) 61a	127	MS(d) 36
77	MS(d) 60	128	MS(d) 28
78	MS(d) 59	129	MS(d) 11
79	MS(d) 55	130	MS(d) 8
80	MS(d) 56	131	MS(d) 10
81	MS(d) 29	132	MS(d) 53
82	MS(d) 67	133	MS(d) 5
83	MS(d) 66	134	MS(d) 12
84	MS(d) 71	135	MS(d) 4
85	MS(d) 61b	136	MS(d) 2
97	MS(d) 76	137	Gustave & Marie, p. 3
102	false start MS 98	138	MS(d) 7
104	MS(d) 68	139	false start MS 33
105	MS(d) 39	141	false start MS [140]
106	MS(d) 72	145	MS(d) 70
107	MS(d) 80	163	false start MS 149
108	MS(d) 85	179	calculations
109	MS(d) 79	185	calculations
110	MS(d) 90		

DRAFT LEAVES WITH MANUSCRIPT VERSOS

DRAFT RECTO	DRAFT VERSO	DRAFT RECTO	DRAFT VERSO
2	MS 136	55	MS 79
4	MS 135	56	MS 80 and false
5	MS 133		start of MS(d) 50
6	MS 51	59	MS 78
7	MS 138	60	MS 77
8	MS 130	61a	MS 76
10	MS 131	61b	MS 85
11	MS 129	64	MS 75
12	MS 134	66	MS 83
13	MS 124	67	MS 82
14	MS 123	68	MS 104
15	MS 122	69	MS 119
22	MS 121	70	MS 145
23	MS 120	71	MS 84
28	MS 128	72	MS 106
29	MS 81	75	MS 118
36	MS 127	76	MS 97
39	MS 105	77	MS 116
40	MS 52	78	MS 117
42	MS 74	79	MS 109
45	MS 73	80	MS 107
46	MS 72	81	MS 115
47	MS 70	82	MS 125
48	MS 60	84	MS 113
49	MS 67	85	MS 108
50	MS 69	86	MS 112
51	MS 68	90	MS 110
52	MS 71	91	MS 114
53	MS 132	92	MS 111